DISNEY MASTERS

MICKEY MOUSE: NEW ADVENTURES OF THE PHANTOM BLOT

by Paul Murry

Publisher: GARY GROTH
Senior Editor: J. MICHAEL CATRON
Editor: DAVID GERSTEIN
Design: KEELI McCARTHY and DAVID GERSTEIN
Production: PAUL BARESH and CHRISTINA HWANG
Associate Publisher: ERIC REYNOLDS

Mickey Mouse: New Adventures of the Phantom Blot is copyright © 2021 Disney Enterprises, Inc. All contents copyright © 2021 Disney Enterprises, Inc. unless otherwise noted. "Paul Murry" copyright © 2021 Germund von Wowern. "What the Blot Wrought" © 2021 Joe Torcivia. Photo on page 237 copyright © 2021 Richard Huemer. All rights reserved.

Disney Masters showcases the work of internationally acclaimed Disney artists. Many of the stories presented in the *Disney Masters* series appear in English for the first time. This is *Disney Masters* Volume 15. Permission to quote or reproduce material for reviews must be obtained from the publisher.

Fantagraphics Books, Inc. | 7563 Lake City Way NE | Seattle WA 98115 | (800) 657-1100

Visit us at fantagraphics.com. Follow us on Twitter at @fantagraphics and on Facebook at facebook.com/fantagraphics.

Cover art by Paul Murry, color by Paul Baresh. Title page art by William Van Horn, color by Gary Leach and David Gerstein.

Thanks to Joakim Gunnarsson, Thomas Jensen, Ken Shue, Joe Torcivia, and Germund Von Wowern.

First printing: February 2021 | ISBN 978-1-68396-411-7
Printed in China
Library of Congress Control Number: 2017956971

The stories in this volume were originally published in English in the United States:

"The Phantom Blot Meets the Mysterious Mr. X" in *The Phantom Blot* #1, October 1964 (W PB 1-02). "The Phantom Blot Meets Super Goof" and "Oh, What a Tangled Rope We Wield" in *The Phantom Blot* #2, April 1965 (W PB 2-01 and W PB 2-02). "Culprits, Inc." and "Safe Surprise" in *The Phantom Blot* #3, July 1965 (W PB 3-02 and W PB 3-03). "The Phantom Blot Meets Madam Mim," "Me and My Shadow-Boxing," and "Hi-Yo, Beagle! Away!" in *The Phantom Blot* #4, October 1965 (W PB 4-02, W PB 4-01, and W PB 4-03). "The Crown of Tasbah," "Tough Old Bird," and "Dogged Pursuit" in *The Phantom Blot* #5, April 1966 (W PB 5-02, W PB 5-01, and W PB 5-03). "Secret Sea Raider," "Blotless Blot," and "Blotsa Laughs" in *The Phantom Blot* #6, July 1966 (W PB 6-02, W PB 6-01, and W PB 6-03). "The Case of the Disappearing Diamonds," "By a Waterfall," and "Stairway to Seeing-Stars" in *The Phantom Blot* #7, November 1966 (W PB 6-02, W PB 6-01, and W PB 6-03).

TITLES IN THIS SERIES
Mickey Mouse: The Delta Dimension (Romano Scarpa) (*Disney Masters* Vol. 1)
Donald Duck: Uncle Scrooge's Money Rocket (Luciano Bottaro) (*Disney Masters* Vol. 2)
Mickey Mouse: The Case of the Vanishing Bandit (Paul Murry) (*Disney Masters* Vol. 3)
Donald Duck: The Great Survival Test (Daan Jippes and Freddy Milton) (*Disney Masters* Vol. 4)
Mickey Mouse: The Phantom Blot's Double Mystery (Romano Scarpa) (*Disney Masters* Vol. 5)
Uncle Scrooge: King of the Golden River (Giovan Battista Carpi) (*Disney Masters* Vol. 6)
Mickey Mouse: The Pirates of Tabasco Bay (Paul Murry) (*Disney Masters* Vol. 7)
Donald Duck: Duck Avenger Strikes Again (Romano Scarpa with Carl Barks) (*Disney Masters* Vol. 8)
Mickey Mouse: The Ice Sword Saga Book 1 (Massimo De Vita) (*Disney Masters* Vol. 9)
Donald Duck: Scandal on the Epoch Express (Mau and Bas Heymans) (*Disney Masters* Vol. 10)
Mickey Mouse: The Ice Sword Saga Book 2 (Massimo De Vita) (*Disney Masters* Vol. 11)
Donald Duck: The Forgetful Hero (Giorgio Cavazzano) (*Disney Masters* Vol. 12)
Mickey Mouse: The Sunken City (Paul Murry) (*Disney Masters* Vol. 13)
Donald Duck: Follow the Fearless Leader (Dick Kinney and Al Hubbard) (*Disney Masters* Vol. 14)

COMING SOON
Donald Duck: Jumpin' Jupiter! (Luciano Bottaro) (*Disney Masters* Vol. 16)

ALSO AVAILABLE
Wa lt Disney's Uncle Scrooge: "The Twenty-four Carat Moon" (Carl Barks)
The Complete Life and Times of Scrooge McDuck Volumes 1 and 2 (Don Rosa)
Mickey Mouse: The Greatest Adventures (Floyd Gottfredson)

Walt Disney
Mickey Mouse

New Adventures of
The Phantom Blot

CONTENTS

The Phantom Blot Meets the Mysterious Mr. X 1
Art and Lettering by Paul Murry • Color by Digikore Studios

The Phantom Blot Meets Super Goof 33
Story by Del Connell • Art and Lettering by Paul Murry • Color by Digikore Studios

Oh, What a Tangled Rope We Wield! 65
Art and Lettering by Paul Murry • Color by Susan Daigle-Leach

Cover to *The Phantom Blot* #3 66
Art by Paul Murry • Color by David Gerstein

Culprits, Inc. 67
Art by Paul Murry • Lettering by Rome Simeon Color by Digikore Studios

Safe Surprise. 99
Art and Lettering by Paul Murry • Color by Susan Daigle-Leach

Cover to *The Phantom Blot* #4 . . . 100
Art by Paul Murry • Color by David Gerstein

The Phantom Blot Meets Mad Madam Mim. 101
Story by Bob Ogle • Art by Paul Murry Lettering by Rome Simeon • Color by Digikore Studios

Me and My Shadow-Boxing 133
Art and Lettering by Paul Murry • Color by Susan Daigle-Leach

Hi-Yo, Beagle! Away! 134
Art and Lettering by Paul Murry • Color by Digikore Studios

The Crown of Tasbah 135
Art by Paul Murry • Lettering by Rome Simeon Color by Digikore Studios

Tough Old Bird 167
Art and Lettering by Paul Murry • Color by Digikore Studios

Dogged Pursuit. 168
Art and Lettering by Paul Murry • Color by Digikore Studios

Secret Sea Raider 169
Story by Bob Ogle • Art by Paul Murry Lettering by Rome Simeon • Color by Digikore Studios

Blotless Blot 201
Art and Lettering by Paul Murry • Color by Digikore Studios

Blotsa Laughs 202
Art and Lettering by Paul Murry • Color by Digikore Studios

The Case of the Disappearing Diamonds 203
Art by Paul Murry • Lettering by Rome Simeon Color by Amy Noetzel and Darrin Brege

By a Waterfall 235
Art by Tony Strobl • Lettering by Rome Simeon Color by Digikore Studios

Stairway to Seeing-Stars. 236
Art by Tony Strobl • Lettering by Rome Simeon Color by Digikore Studios

Paul Murry 237
Germund Von Wowern

Covers to *The Phantom Blot* #1, 2, 5, and 6 . . . .238, 240, 242, 244
Art by Paul Murry • Color by Paul Baresh and David Gerstein

What the Blot Wrought. 245
Joe Torcivia

Cover to *The Phantom Blot* #7 . . .246
Art by Paul Murry • Color by Paul Baresh

The stories in this volume were first created in 1964–1966.

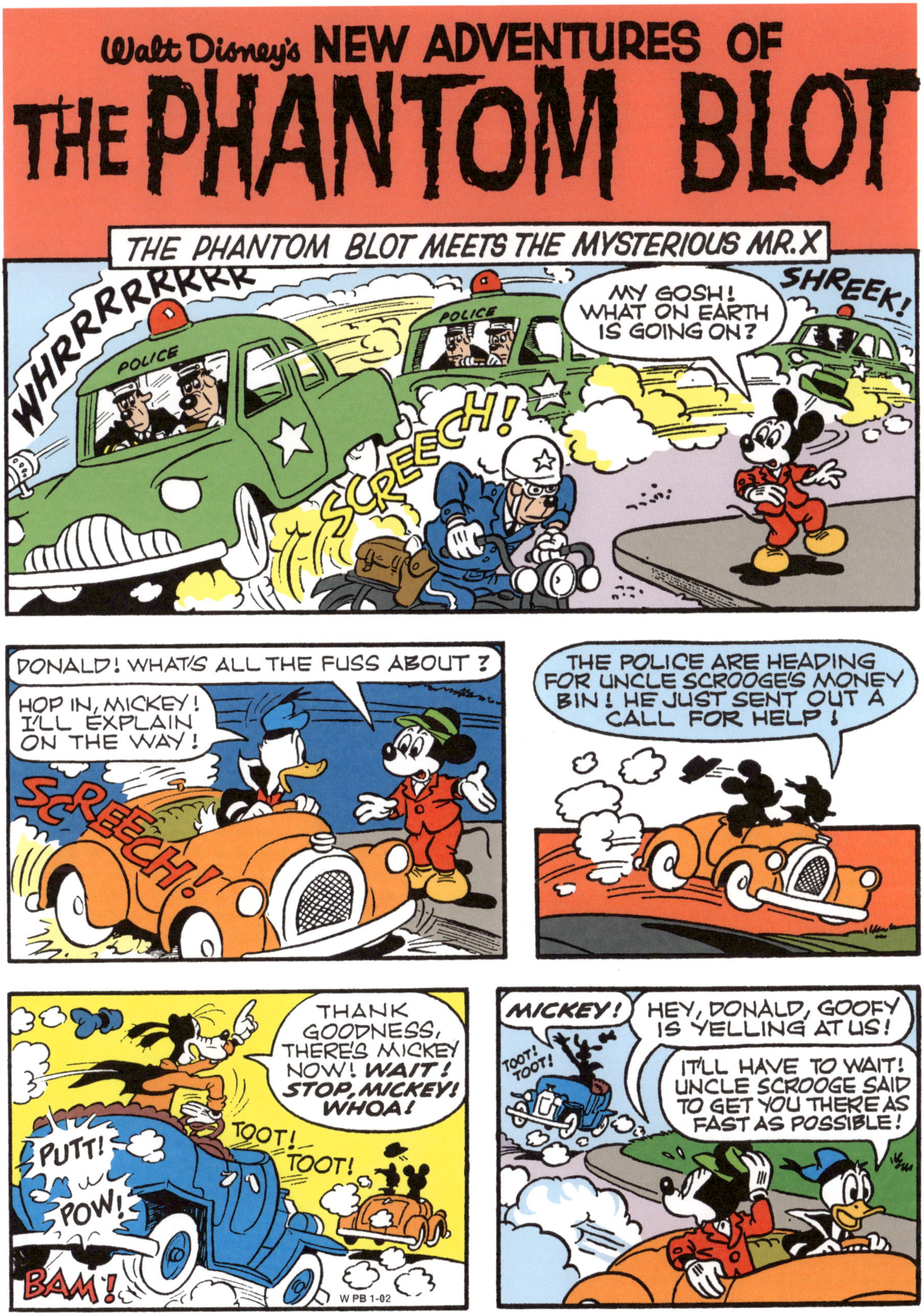
Walt Disney's NEW ADVENTURES OF
THE PHANTOM BLOT
THE PHANTOM BLOT MEETS THE MYSTERIOUS MR. X
WHRRRRRRRR
POLICE
SCREECH!
MY GOSH! WHAT ON EARTH IS GOING ON?
SHREEK!
DONALD! WHAT'S ALL THE FUSS ABOUT?
HOP IN, MICKEY! I'LL EXPLAIN ON THE WAY!
SCREECH!
THE POLICE ARE HEADING FOR UNCLE SCROOGE'S MONEY BIN! HE JUST SENT OUT A CALL FOR HELP!
THANK GOODNESS, THERE'S MICKEY NOW! WAIT! STOP, MICKEY! WHOA!
TOOT! TOOT!
PUTT!
POW!
BAM!
W PB 1-02
MICKEY!
TOOT! TOOT!
HEY, DONALD, GOOFY IS YELLING AT US!
IT'LL HAVE TO WAIT! UNCLE SCROOGE SAID TO GET YOU THERE AS FAST AS POSSIBLE!

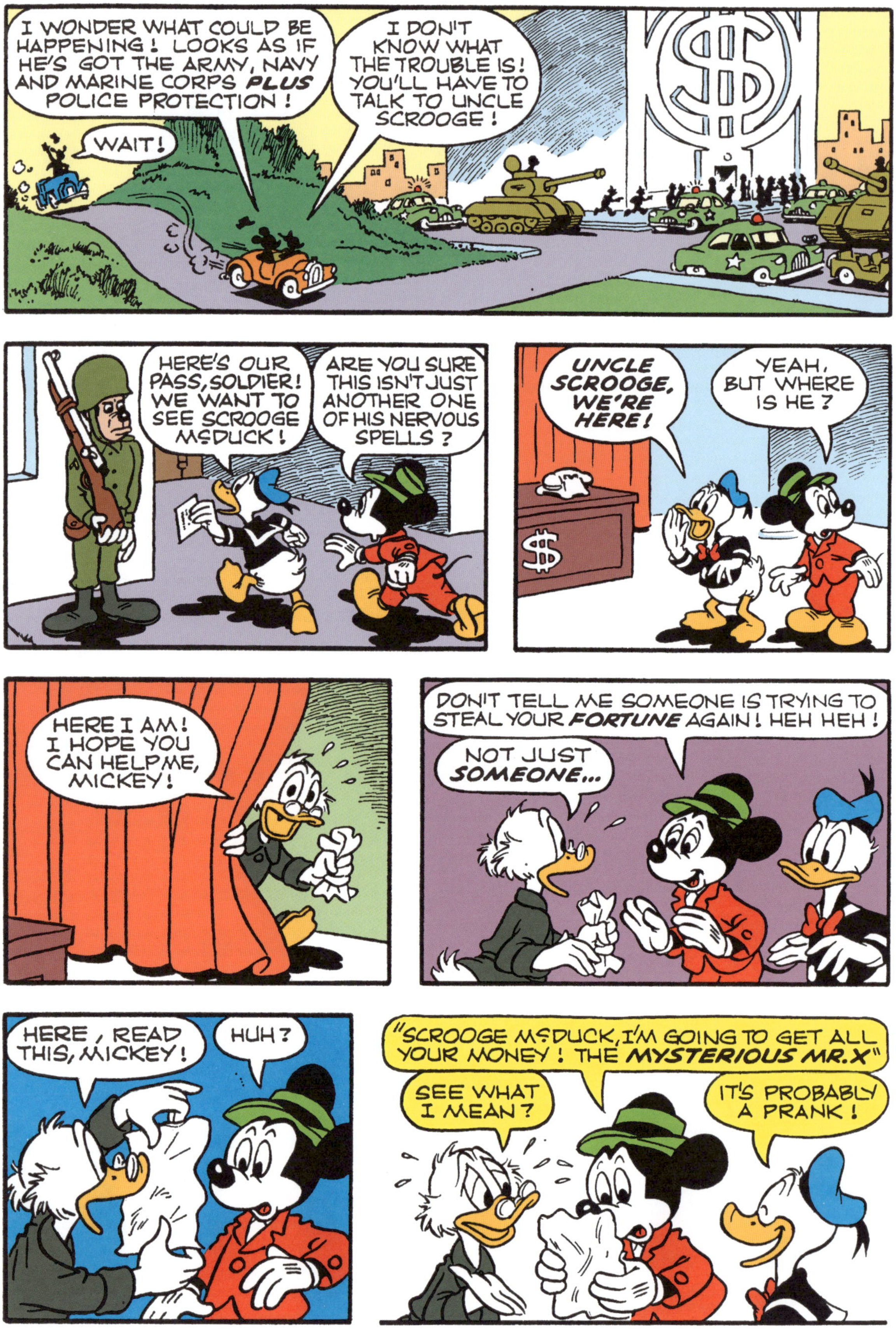
I WONDER WHAT COULD BE HAPPENING! LOOKS AS IF HE'S GOT THE ARMY, NAVY AND MARINE CORPS PLUS POLICE PROTECTION!
I DON'T KNOW WHAT THE TROUBLE IS! YOU'LL HAVE TO TALK TO UNCLE SCROOGE!
WAIT!
HERE'S OUR PASS, SOLDIER! WE WANT TO SEE SCROOGE McDUCK!
ARE YOU SURE THIS ISN'T JUST ANOTHER ONE OF HIS NERVOUS SPELLS?
UNCLE SCROOGE, WE'RE HERE!
YEAH, BUT WHERE IS HE?
HERE I AM! I HOPE YOU CAN HELP ME, MICKEY!
DON'T TELL ME SOMEONE IS TRYING TO STEAL YOUR FORTUNE AGAIN! HEH HEH!
NOT JUST SOMEONE...
HERE, READ THIS, MICKEY!
HUH?
"SCROOGE McDUCK, I'M GOING TO GET ALL YOUR MONEY! THE MYSTERIOUS MR. X"
SEE WHAT I MEAN?
IT'S PROBABLY A PRANK!

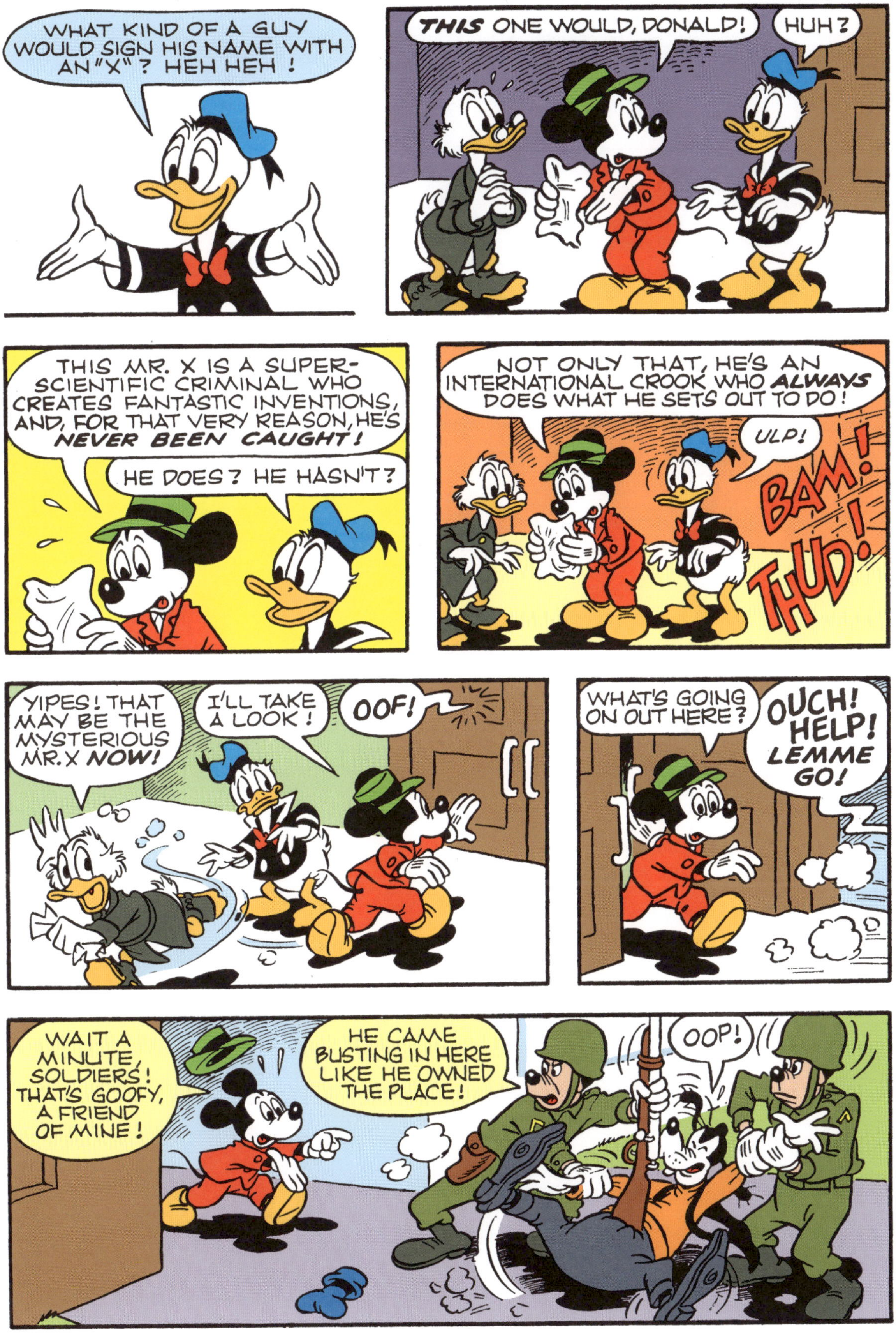
WHAT KIND OF A GUY WOULD SIGN HIS NAME WITH AN "X"? HEH HEH!
THIS ONE WOULD, DONALD!
HUH?
THIS MR. X IS A SUPER-SCIENTIFIC CRIMINAL WHO CREATES FANTASTIC INVENTIONS, AND, FOR THAT VERY REASON, HE'S NEVER BEEN CAUGHT!
HE DOES? HE HASN'T?
NOT ONLY THAT, HE'S AN INTERNATIONAL CROOK WHO ALWAYS DOES WHAT HE SETS OUT TO DO!
ULP!
BAM!
THUD!
YIPES! THAT MAY BE THE MYSTERIOUS MR. X NOW!
I'LL TAKE A LOOK!
OOF!
WHAT'S GOING ON OUT HERE?
OUCH! HELP! LEMME GO!
WAIT A MINUTE, SOLDIERS! THAT'S GOOFY, A FRIEND OF MINE!
HE CAME BUSTING IN HERE LIKE HE OWNED THE PLACE!
OOP!

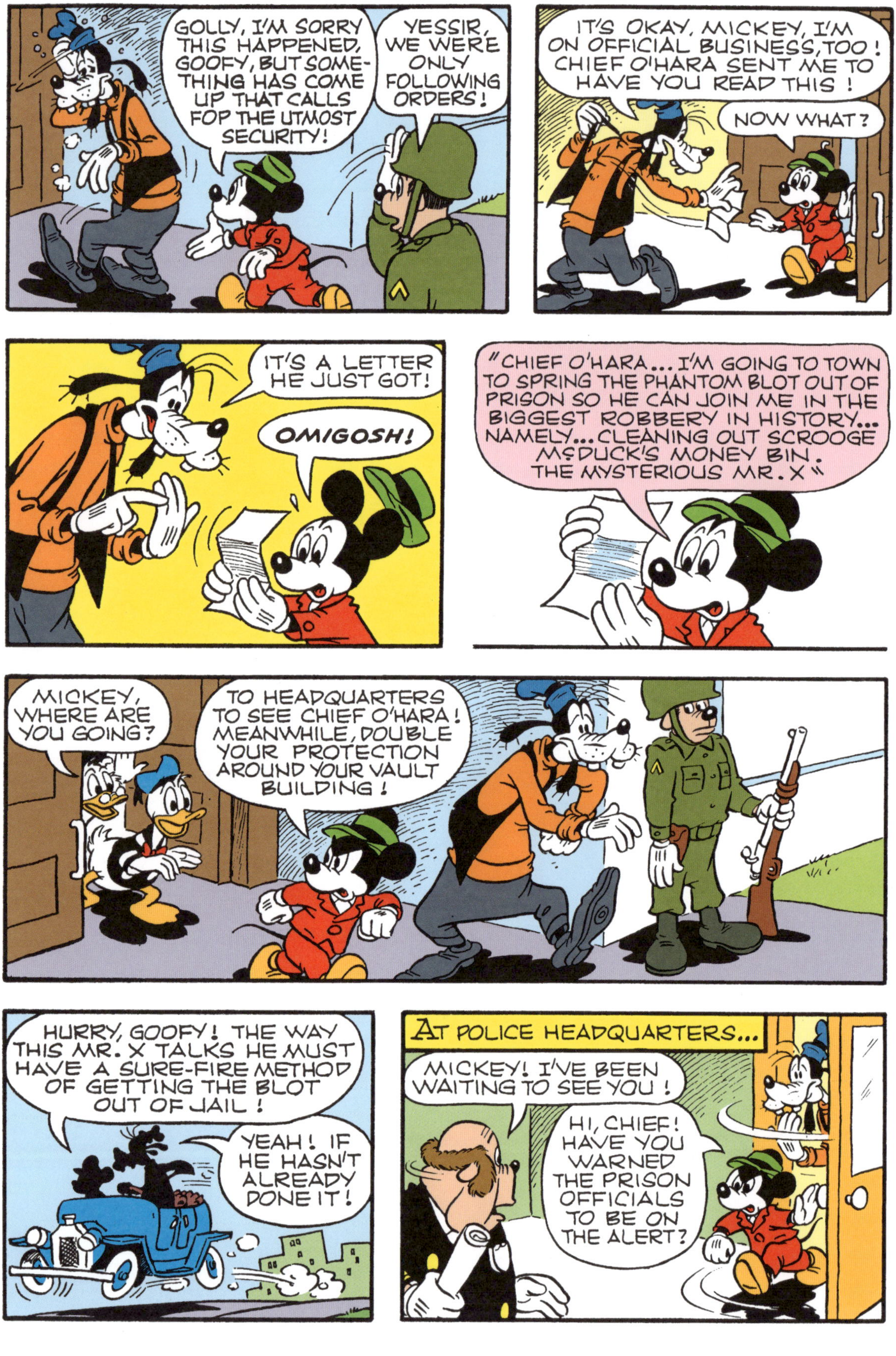
GOLLY, I'M SORRY THIS HAPPENED, GOOFY, BUT SOMETHING HAS COME UP THAT CALLS FOR THE UTMOST SECURITY!
YESSIR, WE WERE ONLY FOLLOWING ORDERS!
IT'S OKAY, MICKEY, I'M ON OFFICIAL BUSINESS, TOO! CHIEF O'HARA SENT ME TO HAVE YOU READ THIS!
NOW WHAT?
IT'S A LETTER HE JUST GOT!
OMIGOSH!
"CHIEF O'HARA... I'M GOING TO TOWN TO SPRING THE PHANTOM BLOT OUT OF PRISON SO HE CAN JOIN ME IN THE BIGGEST ROBBERY IN HISTORY... NAMELY... CLEANING OUT SCROOGE McDUCK'S MONEY BIN. THE MYSTERIOUS MR. X"
MICKEY, WHERE ARE YOU GOING?
TO HEADQUARTERS TO SEE CHIEF O'HARA! MEANWHILE, DOUBLE YOUR PROTECTION AROUND YOUR VAULT BUILDING!
HURRY, GOOFY! THE WAY THIS MR. X TALKS HE MUST HAVE A SURE-FIRE METHOD OF GETTING THE BLOT OUT OF JAIL!
YEAH! IF HE HASN'T ALREADY DONE IT!
AT POLICE HEADQUARTERS...
MICKEY! I'VE BEEN WAITING TO SEE YOU!
HI, CHIEF! HAVE YOU WARNED THE PRISON OFFICIALS TO BE ON THE ALERT?

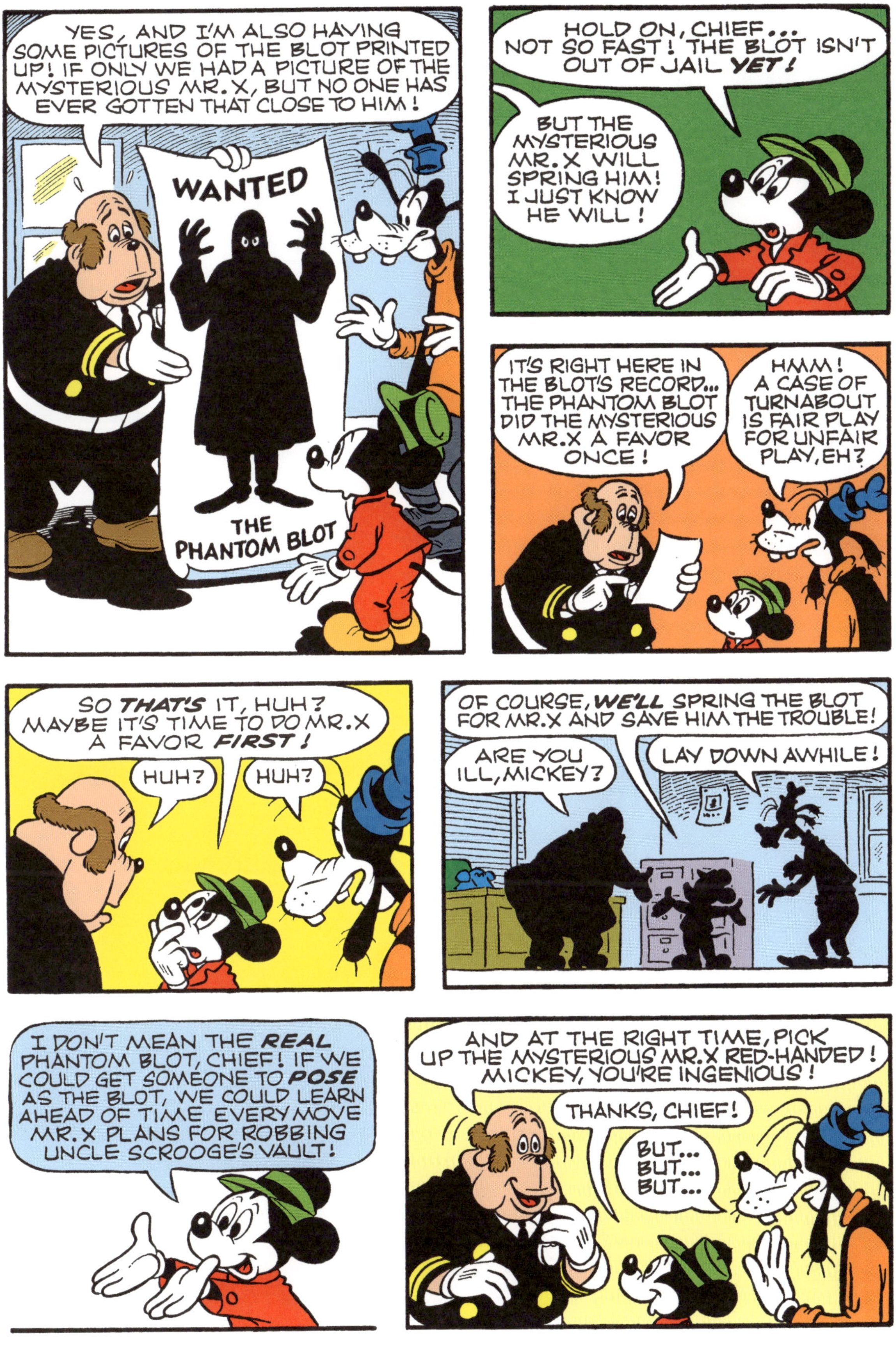
YES, AND I'M ALSO HAVING SOME PICTURES OF THE BLOT PRINTED UP! IF ONLY WE HAD A PICTURE OF THE MYSTERIOUS MR. X, BUT NO ONE HAS EVER GOTTEN THAT CLOSE TO HIM!
WANTED
THE PHANTOM BLOT
HOLD ON, CHIEF... NOT SO FAST! THE BLOT ISN'T OUT OF JAIL YET!
BUT THE MYSTERIOUS MR. X WILL SPRING HIM! I JUST KNOW HE WILL!
IT'S RIGHT HERE IN THE BLOT'S RECORD... THE PHANTOM BLOT DID THE MYSTERIOUS MR. X A FAVOR ONCE!
HMM! A CASE OF TURNABOUT IS FAIR PLAY FOR UNFAIR PLAY, EH?
SO THAT'S IT, HUH? MAYBE IT'S TIME TO DO MR. X A FAVOR FIRST!
HUH?
HUH?
OF COURSE, WE'LL SPRING THE BLOT FOR MR. X AND SAVE HIM THE TROUBLE!
ARE YOU ILL, MICKEY?
LAY DOWN AWHILE!
I DON'T MEAN THE REAL PHANTOM BLOT, CHIEF! IF WE COULD GET SOMEONE TO POSE AS THE BLOT, WE COULD LEARN AHEAD OF TIME EVERY MOVE MR. X PLANS FOR ROBBING UNCLE SCROOGE'S VAULT!
AND AT THE RIGHT TIME, PICK UP THE MYSTERIOUS MR. X RED-HANDED! MICKEY, YOU'RE INGENIOUS!
THANKS, CHIEF!
BUT... BUT... BUT...

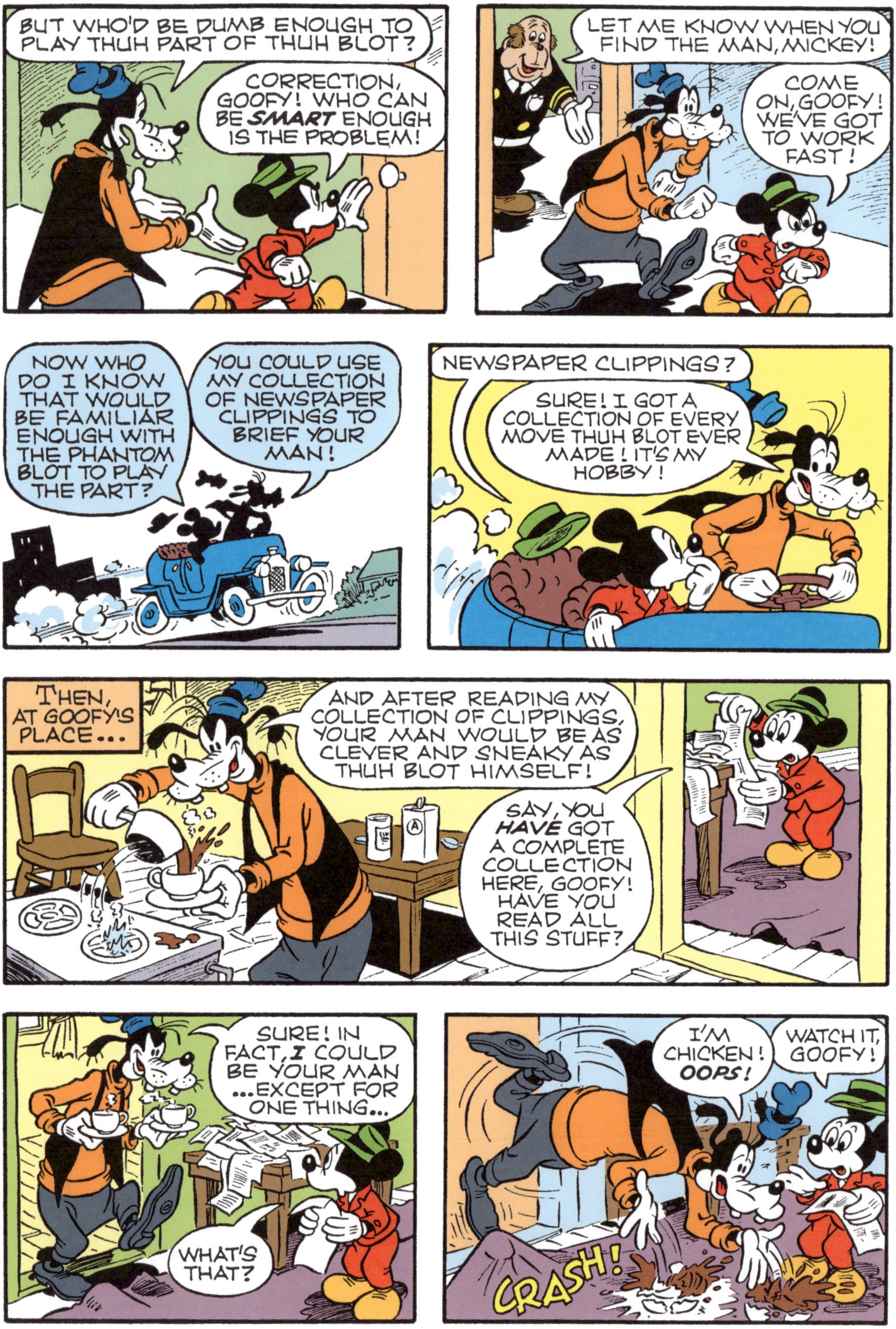
BUT WHO'D BE DUMB ENOUGH TO PLAY THUH PART OF THUH BLOT?
CORRECTION, GOOFY! WHO CAN BE SMART ENOUGH IS THE PROBLEM!
LET ME KNOW WHEN YOU FIND THE MAN, MICKEY!
COME ON, GOOFY! WE'VE GOT TO WORK FAST!
NOW WHO DO I KNOW THAT WOULD BE FAMILIAR ENOUGH WITH THE PHANTOM BLOT TO PLAY THE PART?
YOU COULD USE MY COLLECTION OF NEWSPAPER CLIPPINGS TO BRIEF YOUR MAN!
NEWSPAPER CLIPPINGS?
SURE! I GOT A COLLECTION OF EVERY MOVE THUH BLOT EVER MADE! IT'S MY HOBBY!
THEN, AT GOOFY'S PLACE...
AND AFTER READING MY COLLECTION OF CLIPPINGS, YOUR MAN WOULD BE AS CLEVER AND SNEAKY AS THUH BLOT HIMSELF!
SAY, YOU HAVE GOT A COMPLETE COLLECTION HERE, GOOFY! HAVE YOU READ ALL THIS STUFF?
SURE! IN FACT, I COULD BE YOUR MAN ...EXCEPT FOR ONE THING...
WHAT'S THAT?
I'M CHICKEN! OOPS!
WATCH IT, GOOFY!
CRASH!

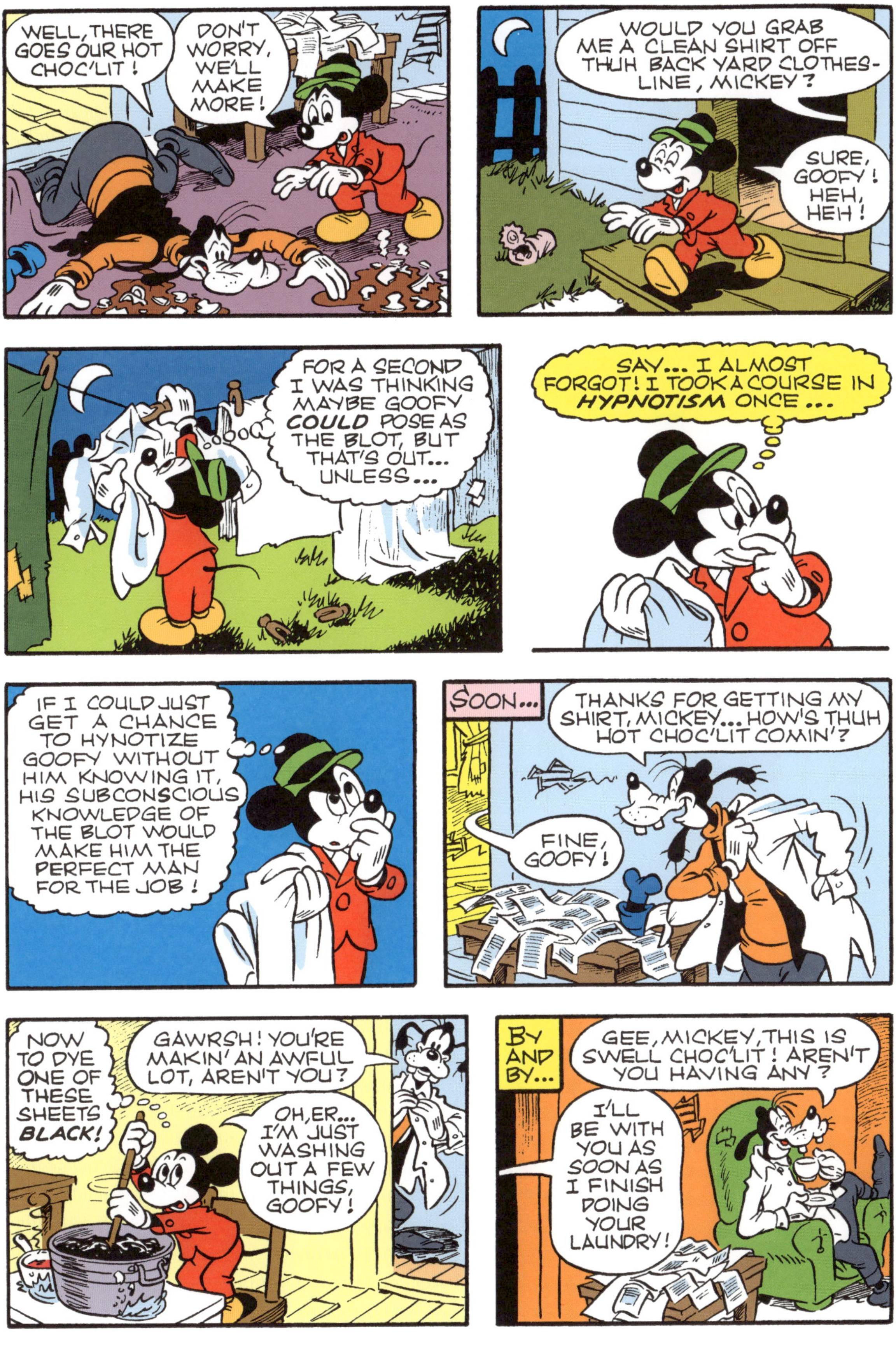

WELL, THERE GOES OUR HOT CHOC'LIT!
DON'T WORRY, WE'LL MAKE MORE!
WOULD YOU GRAB ME A CLEAN SHIRT OFF THUH BACK YARD CLOTHES-LINE, MICKEY?
SURE, GOOFY! HEH, HEH!
FOR A SECOND I WAS THINKING MAYBE GOOFY COULD POSE AS THE BLOT, BUT THAT'S OUT... UNLESS...
SAY... I ALMOST FORGOT! I TOOK A COURSE IN HYPNOTISM ONCE...
IF I COULD JUST GET A CHANCE TO HYNOTIZE GOOFY WITHOUT HIM KNOWING IT, HIS SUBCONSCIOUS KNOWLEDGE OF THE BLOT WOULD MAKE HIM THE PERFECT MAN FOR THE JOB!
SOON...
THANKS FOR GETTING MY SHIRT, MICKEY... HOW'S THUH HOT CHOC'LIT COMIN'?
FINE, GOOFY!
NOW TO DYE ONE OF THESE SHEETS BLACK!
GAWRSH! YOU'RE MAKIN' AN AWFUL LOT, AREN'T YOU?
OH, ER... I'M JUST WASHING OUT A FEW THINGS, GOOFY!
BY AND BY...
GEE, MICKEY, THIS IS SWELL CHOC'LIT! AREN'T YOU HAVING ANY?
I'LL BE WITH YOU AS SOON AS I FINISH DOING YOUR LAUNDRY!

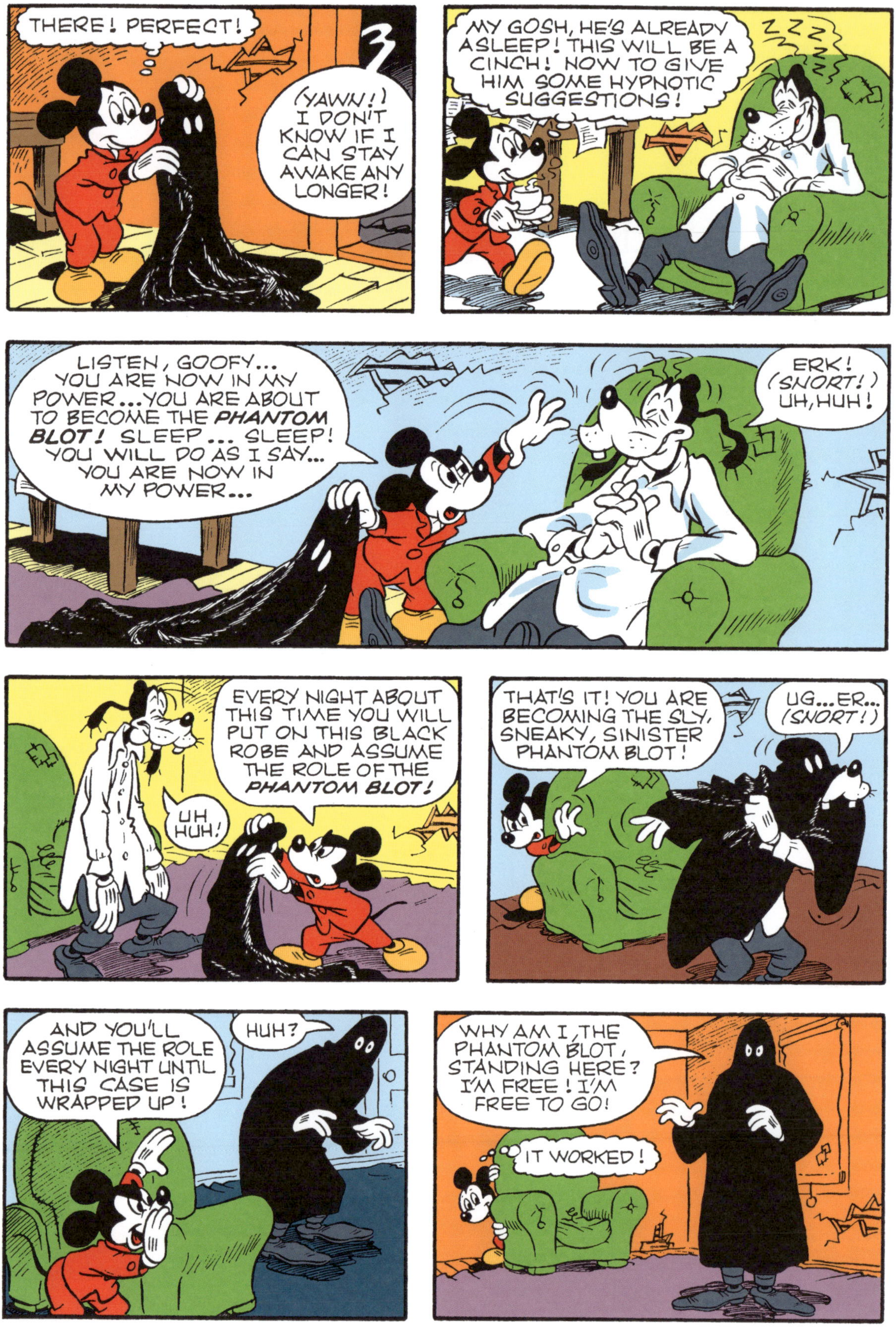
THERE! PERFECT!
(YAWN!) I DON'T KNOW IF I CAN STAY AWAKE ANY LONGER!
MY GOSH, HE'S ALREADY ASLEEP! THIS WILL BE A CINCH! NOW TO GIVE HIM SOME HYPNOTIC SUGGESTIONS!
Z Z Z
LISTEN, GOOFY... YOU ARE NOW IN MY POWER...YOU ARE ABOUT TO BECOME THE PHANTOM BLOT! SLEEP... SLEEP! YOU WILL DO AS I SAY... YOU ARE NOW IN MY POWER...
ERK! (SNORT!) UH, HUH!
EVERY NIGHT ABOUT THIS TIME YOU WILL PUT ON THIS BLACK ROBE AND ASSUME THE ROLE OF THE PHANTOM BLOT!
UH HUH!
THAT'S IT! YOU ARE BECOMING THE SLY, SNEAKY, SINISTER PHANTOM BLOT!
UG...ER... (SNORT!)
AND YOU'LL ASSUME THE ROLE EVERY NIGHT UNTIL THIS CASE IS WRAPPED UP!
HUH?
WHY AM I, THE PHANTOM BLOT, STANDING HERE? I'M FREE! I'M FREE TO GO!
IT WORKED!

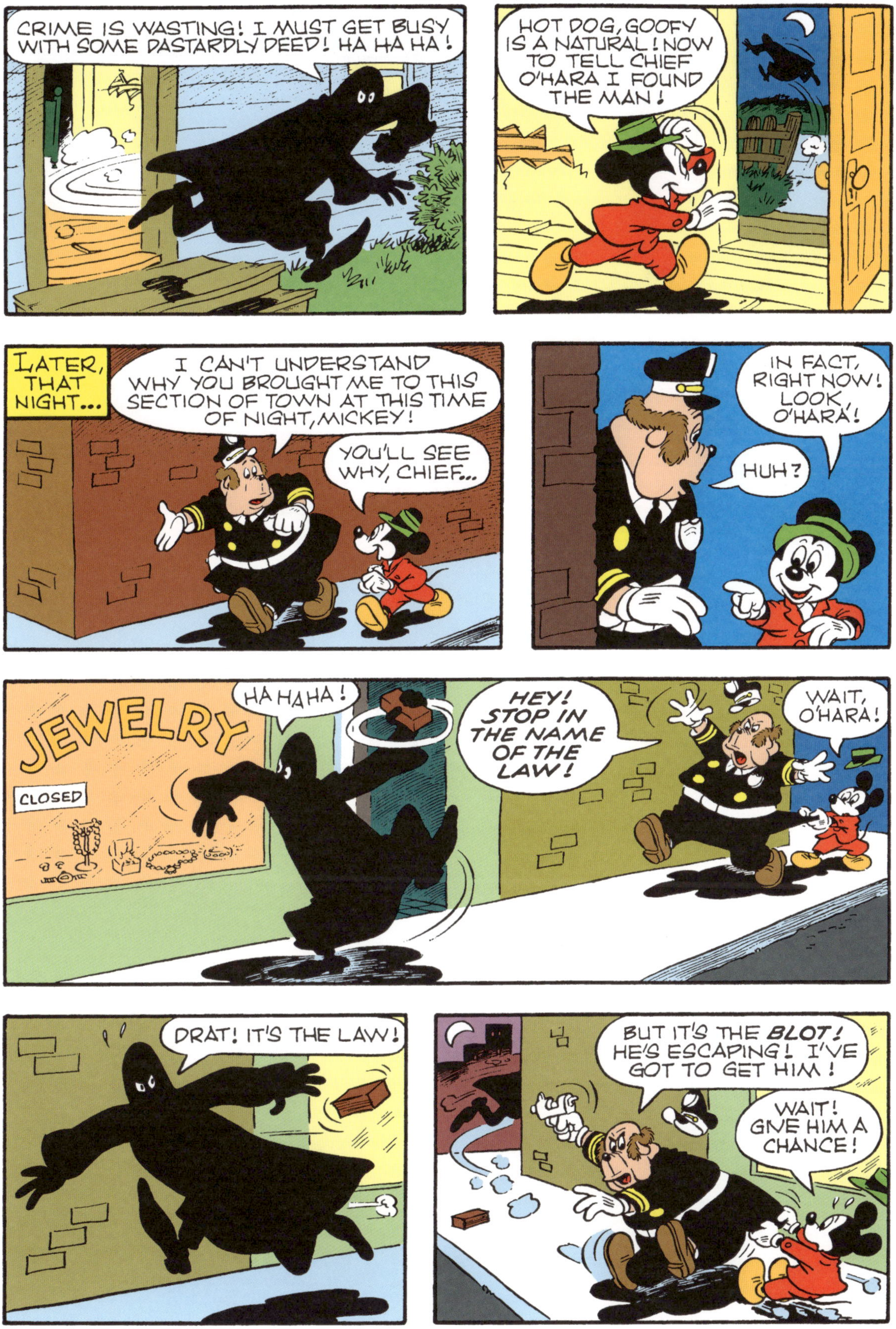
CRIME IS WASTING! I MUST GET BUSY WITH SOME DASTARDLY DEED! HA HA HA!
HOT DOG, GOOFY IS A NATURAL! NOW TO TELL CHIEF O'HARA I FOUND THE MAN!
LATER, THAT NIGHT...
I CAN'T UNDERSTAND WHY YOU BROUGHT ME TO THIS SECTION OF TOWN AT THIS TIME OF NIGHT, MICKEY!
YOU'LL SEE WHY, CHIEF...
IN FACT, RIGHT NOW! LOOK, O'HARA!
HUH?
JEWELRY
CLOSED
HA HA HA!
HEY! STOP IN THE NAME OF THE LAW!
WAIT, O'HARA!
DRAT! IT'S THE LAW!
BUT IT'S THE BLOT! HE'S ESCAPING! I'VE GOT TO GET HIM!
WAIT! GIVE HIM A CHANCE!

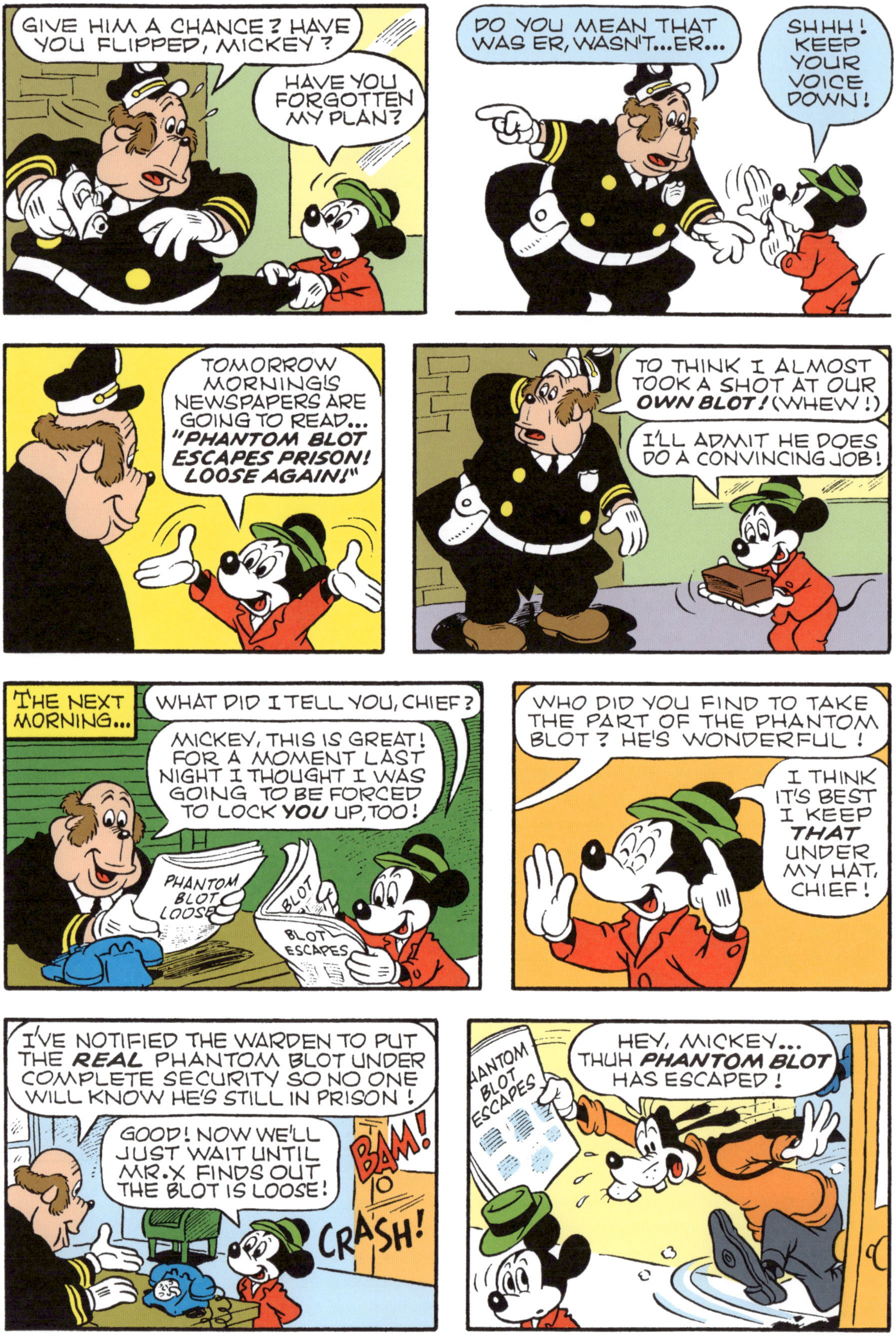
GIVE HIM A CHANCE? HAVE YOU FLIPPED, MICKEY?
HAVE YOU FORGOTTEN MY PLAN?
DO YOU MEAN THAT WAS ER, WASN'T...ER...
SHHH! KEEP YOUR VOICE DOWN!
TOMORROW MORNING'S NEWSPAPERS ARE GOING TO READ... "PHANTOM BLOT ESCAPES PRISON! LOOSE AGAIN!"
TO THINK I ALMOST TOOK A SHOT AT OUR OWN BLOT! (WHEW!)
I'LL ADMIT HE DOES DO A CONVINCING JOB!
THE NEXT MORNING...
WHAT DID I TELL YOU, CHIEF?
MICKEY, THIS IS GREAT! FOR A MOMENT LAST NIGHT I THOUGHT I WAS GOING TO BE FORCED TO LOCK YOU UP, TOO!
PHANTOM BLOT LOOSE
BLOT
BLOT ESCAPES
WHO DID YOU FIND TO TAKE THE PART OF THE PHANTOM BLOT? HE'S WONDERFUL!
I THINK IT'S BEST I KEEP THAT UNDER MY HAT, CHIEF!
I'VE NOTIFIED THE WARDEN TO PUT THE REAL PHANTOM BLOT UNDER COMPLETE SECURITY SO NO ONE WILL KNOW HE'S STILL IN PRISON!
GOOD! NOW WE'LL JUST WAIT UNTIL MR. X FINDS OUT THE BLOT IS LOOSE!
BAM!
CRASH!
HEY, MICKEY... THUH PHANTOM BLOT HAS ESCAPED!
PHANTOM BLOT ESCAPES

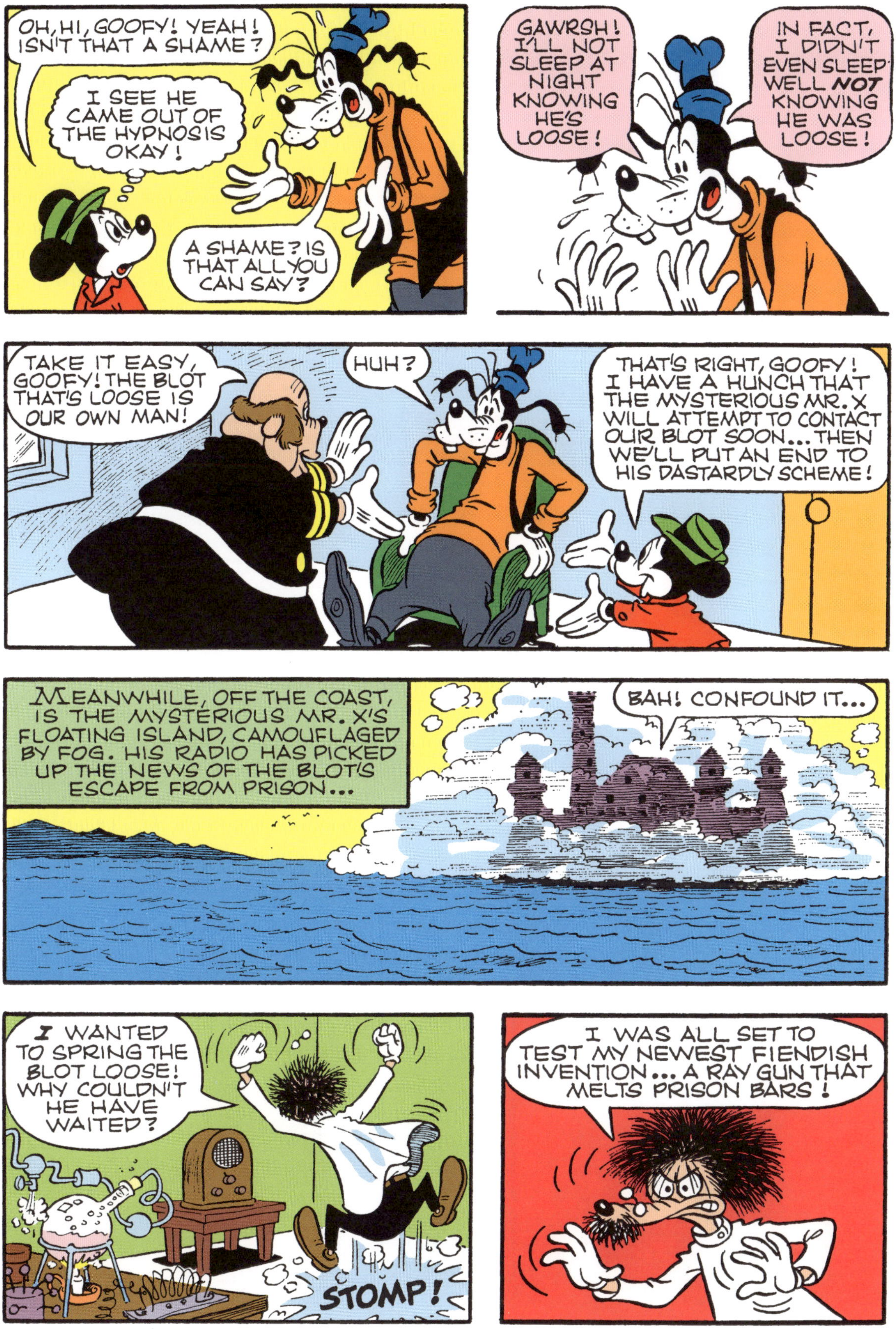

OH, HI, GOOFY! YEAH! ISN'T THAT A SHAME?
I SEE HE CAME OUT OF THE HYPNOSIS OKAY!
A SHAME? IS THAT ALL YOU CAN SAY?
GAWRSH! I'LL NOT SLEEP AT NIGHT KNOWING HE'S LOOSE!
IN FACT, I DIDN'T EVEN SLEEP WELL **NOT** KNOWING HE WAS LOOSE!
TAKE IT EASY, GOOFY! THE BLOT THAT'S LOOSE IS OUR OWN MAN!
HUH?
THAT'S RIGHT, GOOFY! I HAVE A HUNCH THAT THE MYSTERIOUS MR. X WILL ATTEMPT TO CONTACT OUR BLOT SOON... THEN WE'LL PUT AN END TO HIS DASTARDLY SCHEME!
MEANWHILE, OFF THE COAST, IS THE MYSTERIOUS MR. X'S FLOATING ISLAND, CAMOUFLAGED BY FOG. HIS RADIO HAS PICKED UP THE NEWS OF THE BLOT'S ESCAPE FROM PRISON...
BAH! CONFOUND IT...
I WANTED TO SPRING THE BLOT LOOSE! WHY COULDN'T HE HAVE WAITED?
STOMP!
I WAS ALL SET TO TEST MY NEWEST FIENDISH INVENTION... A RAY GUN THAT MELTS PRISON BARS!

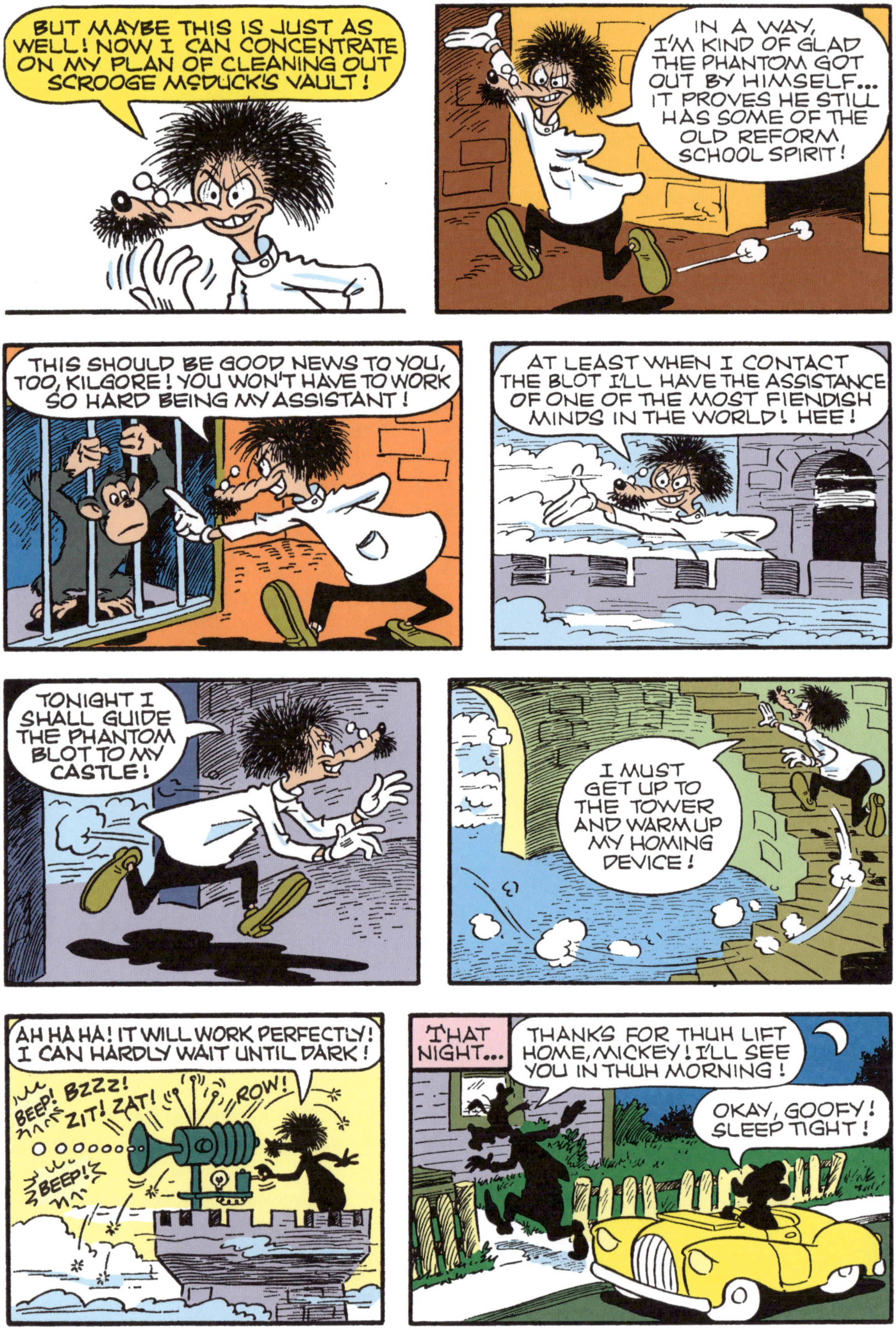
BUT MAYBE THIS IS JUST AS WELL! NOW I CAN CONCENTRATE ON MY PLAN OF CLEANING OUT SCROOGE McDUCK'S VAULT!
IN A WAY, I'M KIND OF GLAD THE PHANTOM GOT OUT BY HIMSELF... IT PROVES HE STILL HAS SOME OF THE OLD REFORM SCHOOL SPIRIT!
THIS SHOULD BE GOOD NEWS TO YOU, TOO, KILGORE! YOU WON'T HAVE TO WORK SO HARD BEING MY ASSISTANT!
AT LEAST WHEN I CONTACT THE BLOT I'LL HAVE THE ASSISTANCE OF ONE OF THE MOST FIENDISH MINDS IN THE WORLD! HEE!
TONIGHT I SHALL GUIDE THE PHANTOM BLOT TO MY CASTLE!
I MUST GET UP TO THE TOWER AND WARM UP MY HOMING DEVICE!
AH HA HA! IT WILL WORK PERFECTLY! I CAN HARDLY WAIT UNTIL DARK!
BEEP! BZZZ! ZIT! ZAT! ROW!
BEEP!
THAT NIGHT...
THANKS FOR THUH LIFT HOME, MICKEY! I'LL SEE YOU IN THUH MORNING!
OKAY, GOOFY! SLEEP TIGHT!

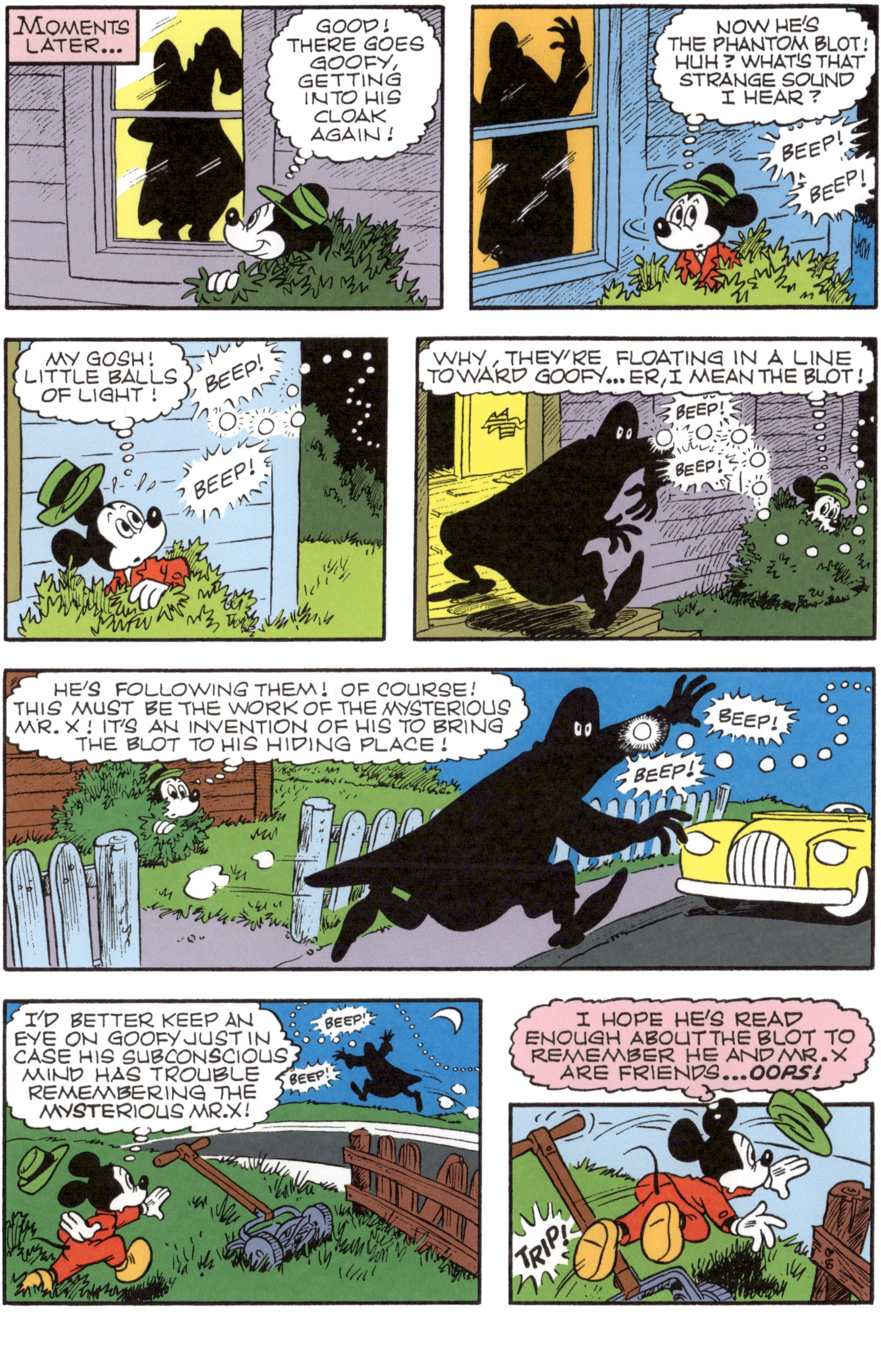
MOMENTS LATER...
GOOD! THERE GOES GOOFY, GETTING INTO HIS CLOAK AGAIN!
NOW HE'S THE PHANTOM BLOT! HUH? WHAT'S THAT STRANGE SOUND I HEAR?
BEEP!
BEEP!
MY GOSH! LITTLE BALLS OF LIGHT!
BEEP!
BEEP!
WHY, THEY'RE FLOATING IN A LINE TOWARD GOOFY... ER, I MEAN THE BLOT!
BEEP!
BEEP!
HE'S FOLLOWING THEM! OF COURSE! THIS MUST BE THE WORK OF THE MYSTERIOUS MR. X! IT'S AN INVENTION OF HIS TO BRING THE BLOT TO HIS HIDING PLACE!
BEEP!
BEEP!
I'D BETTER KEEP AN EYE ON GOOFY JUST IN CASE HIS SUBCONSCIOUS MIND HAS TROUBLE REMEMBERING THE MYSTERIOUS MR. X!
BEEP!
BEEP!
I HOPE HE'S READ ENOUGH ABOUT THE BLOT TO REMEMBER HE AND MR. X ARE FRIENDS... OOPS!
TRIP!

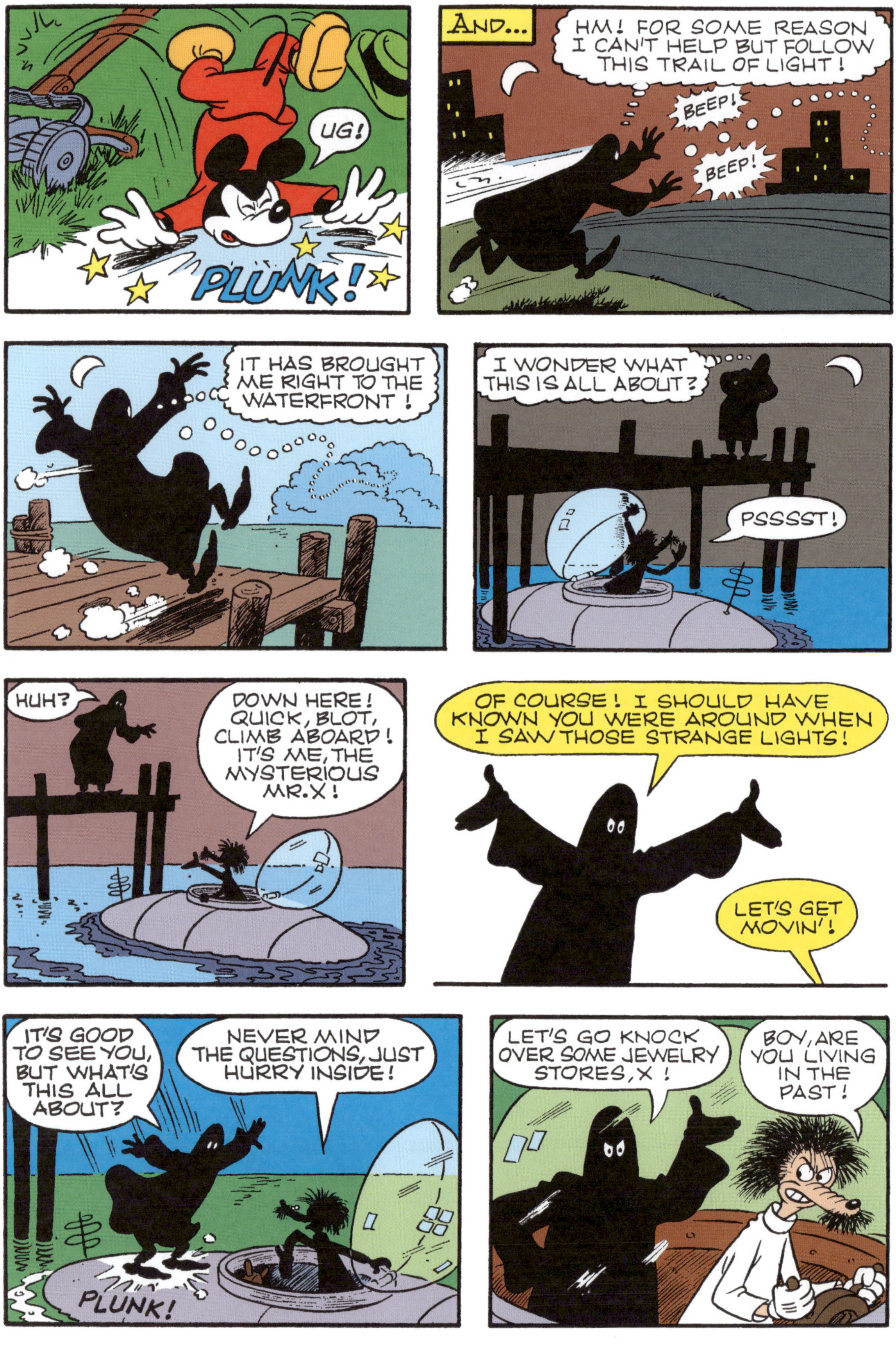
UG!
PLUNK!
AND...
HM! FOR SOME REASON I CAN'T HELP BUT FOLLOW THIS TRAIL OF LIGHT!
BEEP!
BEEP!
IT HAS BROUGHT ME RIGHT TO THE WATERFRONT!
I WONDER WHAT THIS IS ALL ABOUT?
PSSSST!
HUH?
DOWN HERE! QUICK, BLOT, CLIMB ABOARD! IT'S ME, THE MYSTERIOUS MR. X!
OF COURSE! I SHOULD HAVE KNOWN YOU WERE AROUND WHEN I SAW THOSE STRANGE LIGHTS!
LET'S GET MOVIN'!
IT'S GOOD TO SEE YOU, BUT WHAT'S THIS ALL ABOUT?
NEVER MIND THE QUESTIONS, JUST HURRY INSIDE!
PLUNK!
LET'S GO KNOCK OVER SOME JEWELRY STORES, X!
BOY, ARE YOU LIVING IN THE PAST!

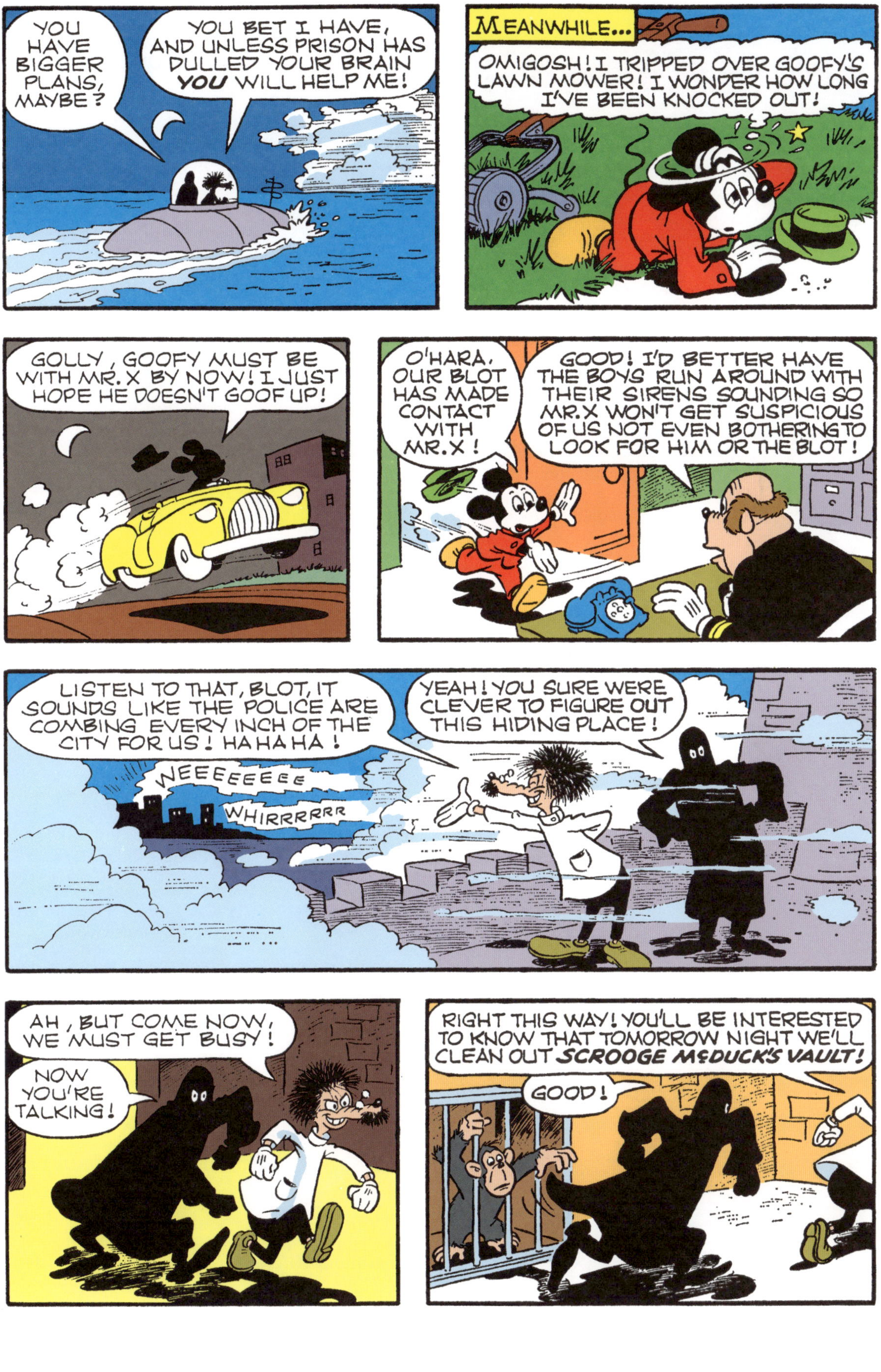
YOU HAVE BIGGER PLANS, MAYBE?
YOU BET I HAVE, AND UNLESS PRISON HAS DULLED YOUR BRAIN **YOU** WILL HELP ME!
MEANWHILE...
OMIGOSH! I TRIPPED OVER GOOFY'S LAWN MOWER! I WONDER HOW LONG I'VE BEEN KNOCKED OUT!
GOLLY, GOOFY MUST BE WITH MR. X BY NOW! I JUST HOPE HE DOESN'T GOOF UP!
O'HARA, OUR BLOT HAS MADE CONTACT WITH MR. X!
GOOD! I'D BETTER HAVE THE BOYS RUN AROUND WITH THEIR SIRENS SOUNDING SO MR. X WON'T GET SUSPICIOUS OF US NOT EVEN BOTHERING TO LOOK FOR HIM OR THE BLOT!
LISTEN TO THAT, BLOT, IT SOUNDS LIKE THE POLICE ARE COMBING EVERY INCH OF THE CITY FOR US! HA HA HA!
YEAH! YOU SURE WERE CLEVER TO FIGURE OUT THIS HIDING PLACE!
WEEEEEEEEE
WHIRRRRRR
AH, BUT COME NOW, WE MUST GET BUSY!
NOW YOU'RE TALKING!
RIGHT THIS WAY! YOU'LL BE INTERESTED TO KNOW THAT TOMORROW NIGHT WE'LL CLEAN OUT **SCROOGE McDUCK'S VAULT!**
GOOD!

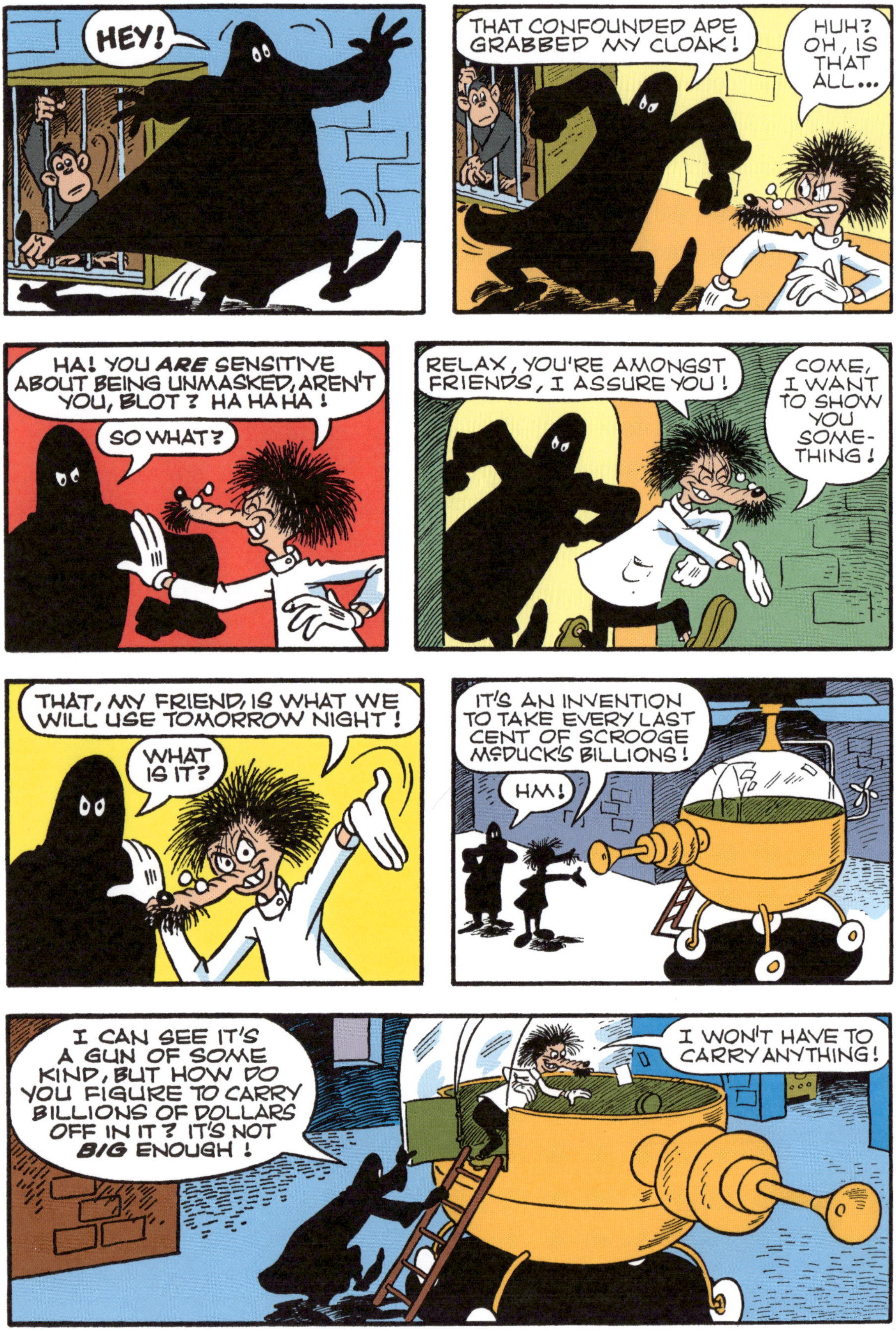
HEY!
THAT CONFOUNDED APE GRABBED MY CLOAK!
HUH? OH, IS THAT ALL...
HA! YOU ARE SENSITIVE ABOUT BEING UNMASKED, AREN'T YOU, BLOT? HA HA HA!
SO WHAT?
RELAX, YOU'RE AMONGST FRIENDS, I ASSURE YOU!
COME, I WANT TO SHOW YOU SOME-THING!
THAT, MY FRIEND, IS WHAT WE WILL USE TOMORROW NIGHT!
WHAT IS IT?
IT'S AN INVENTION TO TAKE EVERY LAST CENT OF SCROOGE McDUCK'S BILLIONS!
HM!
I CAN SEE IT'S A GUN OF SOME KIND, BUT HOW DO YOU FIGURE TO CARRY BILLIONS OF DOLLARS OFF IN IT? IT'S NOT BIG ENOUGH!
I WON'T HAVE TO CARRY ANYTHING!

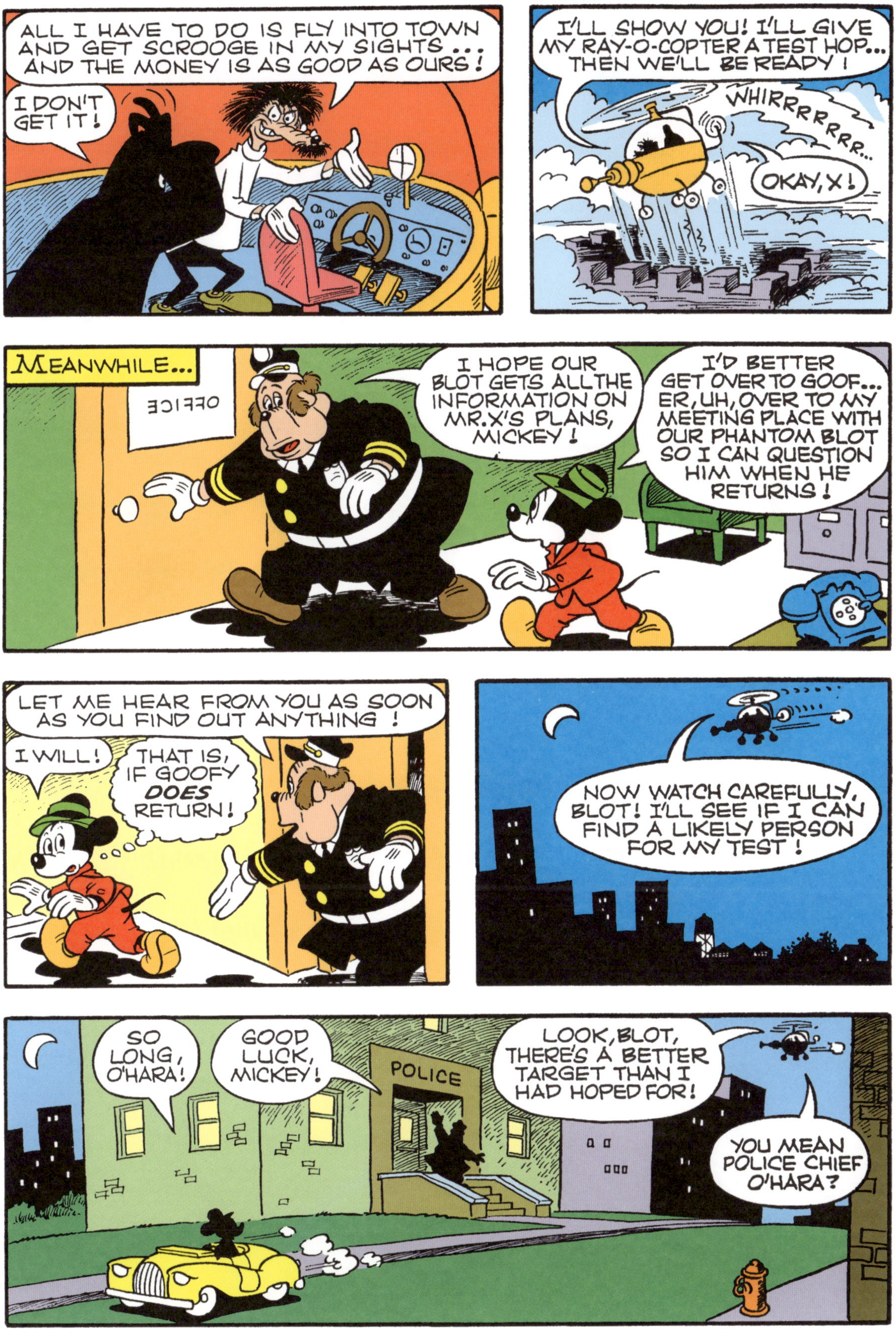
ALL I HAVE TO DO IS FLY INTO TOWN AND GET SCROOGE IN MY SIGHTS ... AND THE MONEY IS AS GOOD AS OURS!
I DON'T GET IT!
I'LL SHOW YOU! I'LL GIVE MY RAY-O-COPTER A TEST HOP... THEN WE'LL BE READY!
WHIRRRRRRRRR...
OKAY, X!
MEANWHILE...
OFFICE
I HOPE OUR BLOT GETS ALL THE INFORMATION ON MR. X'S PLANS, MICKEY!
I'D BETTER GET OVER TO GOOF... ER, UH, OVER TO MY MEETING PLACE WITH OUR PHANTOM BLOT SO I CAN QUESTION HIM WHEN HE RETURNS!
LET ME HEAR FROM YOU AS SOON AS YOU FIND OUT ANYTHING!
I WILL!
THAT IS, IF GOOFY DOES RETURN!
NOW WATCH CAREFULLY, BLOT! I'LL SEE IF I CAN FIND A LIKELY PERSON FOR MY TEST!
SO LONG, O'HARA!
GOOD LUCK, MICKEY!
POLICE
LOOK, BLOT, THERE'S A BETTER TARGET THAN I HAD HOPED FOR!
YOU MEAN POLICE CHIEF O'HARA?

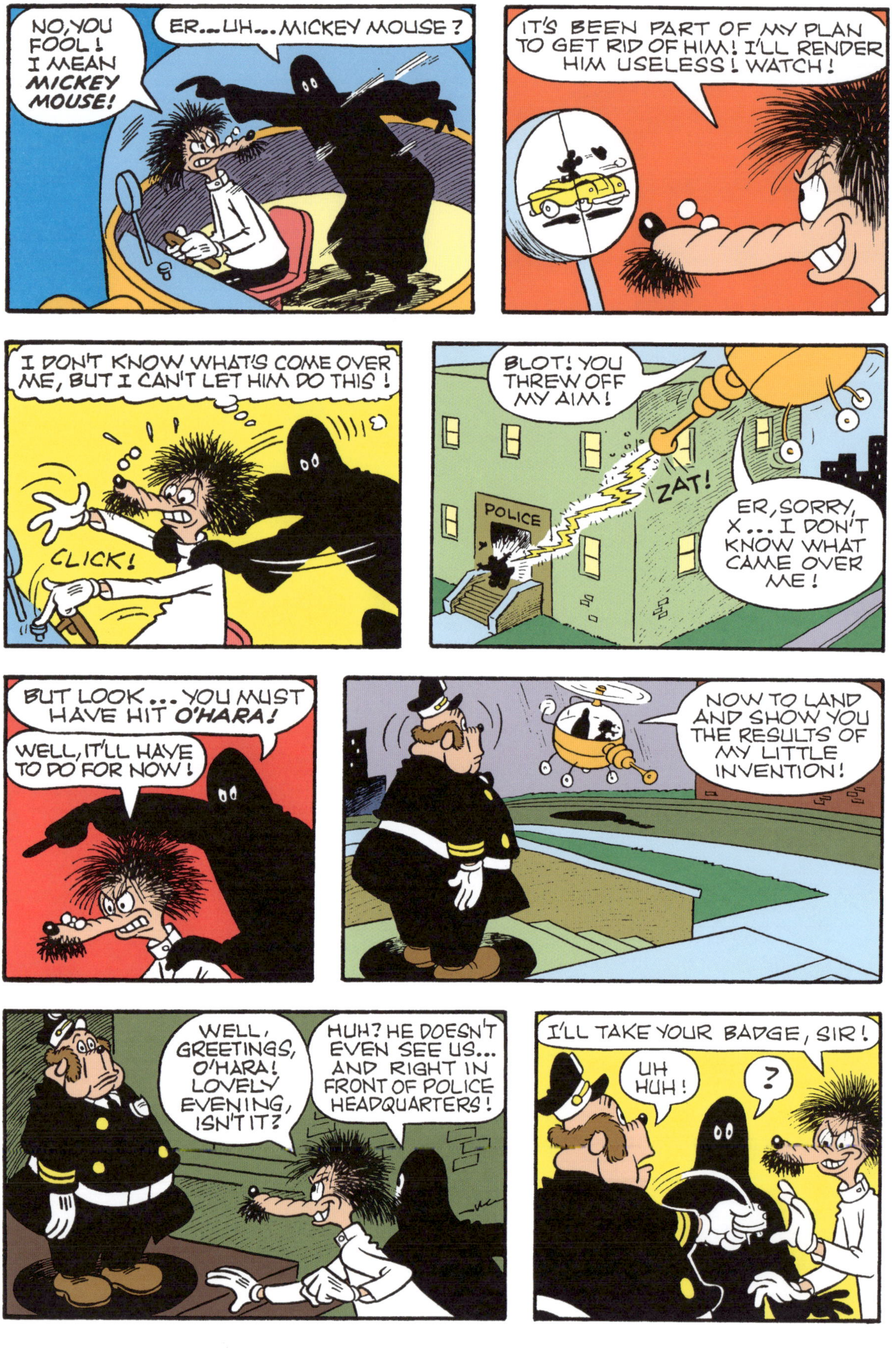
ER...UH...MICKEY MOUSE?
NO, YOU FOOL! I MEAN MICKEY MOUSE!
IT'S BEEN PART OF MY PLAN TO GET RID OF HIM! I'LL RENDER HIM USELESS! WATCH!
I DON'T KNOW WHAT'S COME OVER ME, BUT I CAN'T LET HIM DO THIS!
CLICK!
BLOT! YOU THREW OFF MY AIM!
POLICE
ZAT!
ER, SORRY, X... I DON'T KNOW WHAT CAME OVER ME!
BUT LOOK... YOU MUST HAVE HIT O'HARA!
WELL, IT'LL HAVE TO DO FOR NOW!
NOW TO LAND AND SHOW YOU THE RESULTS OF MY LITTLE INVENTION!
WELL, GREETINGS, O'HARA! LOVELY EVENING, ISN'T IT?
HUH? HE DOESN'T EVEN SEE US... AND RIGHT IN FRONT OF POLICE HEADQUARTERS!
I'LL TAKE YOUR BADGE, SIR!
UH HUH!
?

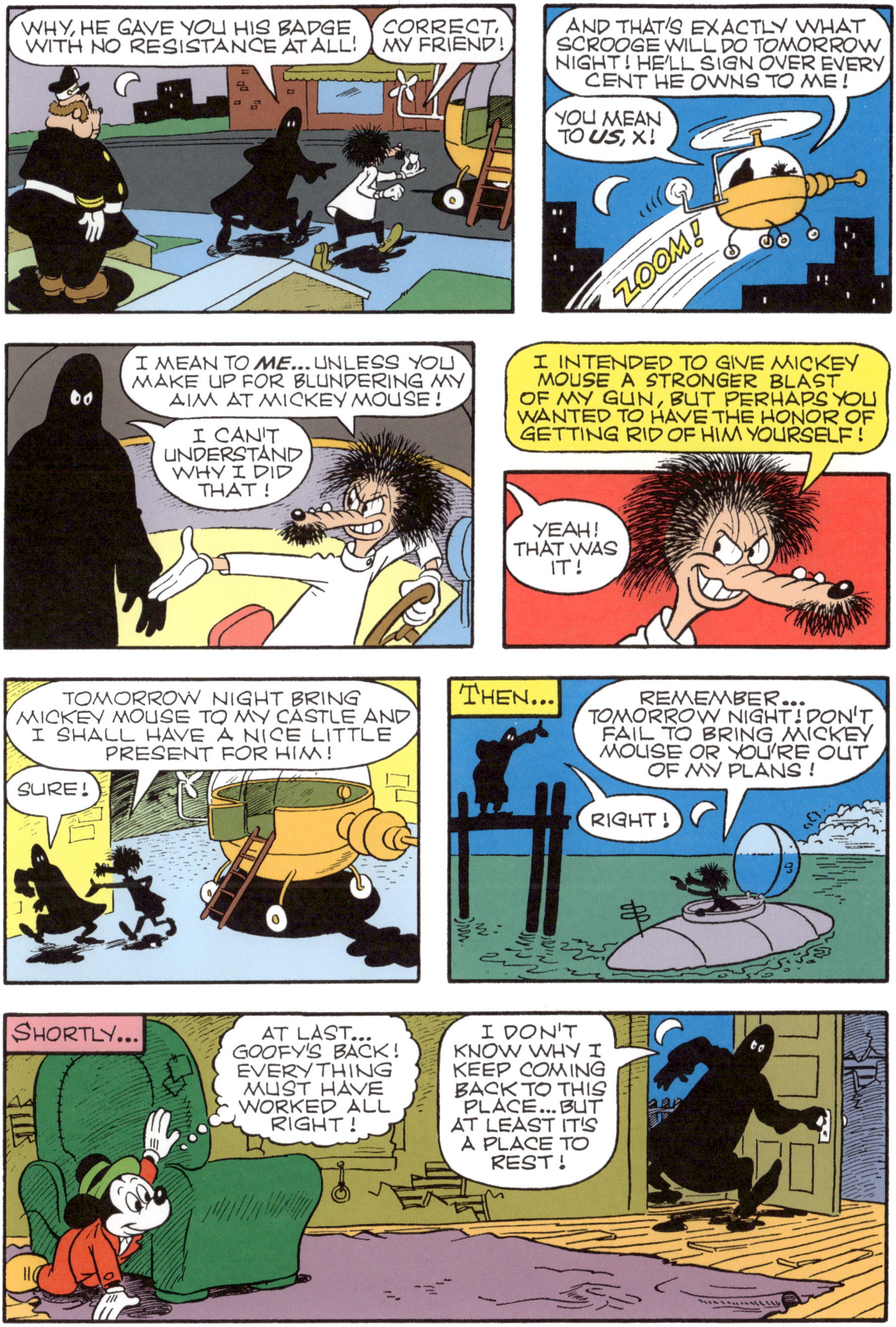

WHY, HE GAVE YOU HIS BADGE WITH NO RESISTANCE AT ALL!
CORRECT, MY FRIEND!
AND THAT'S EXACTLY WHAT SCROOGE WILL DO TOMORROW NIGHT! HE'LL SIGN OVER EVERY CENT HE OWNS TO ME!
YOU MEAN TO US, X!
ZOOM!
I MEAN TO ME... UNLESS YOU MAKE UP FOR BLUNDERING MY AIM AT MICKEY MOUSE!
I CAN'T UNDERSTAND WHY I DID THAT!
I INTENDED TO GIVE MICKEY MOUSE A STRONGER BLAST OF MY GUN, BUT PERHAPS YOU WANTED TO HAVE THE HONOR OF GETTING RID OF HIM YOURSELF!
YEAH! THAT WAS IT!
TOMORROW NIGHT BRING MICKEY MOUSE TO MY CASTLE AND I SHALL HAVE A NICE LITTLE PRESENT FOR HIM!
SURE!
THEN...
REMEMBER... TOMORROW NIGHT! DON'T FAIL TO BRING MICKEY MOUSE OR YOU'RE OUT OF MY PLANS!
RIGHT!
SHORTLY...
AT LAST... GOOFY'S BACK! EVERYTHING MUST HAVE WORKED ALL RIGHT!
I DON'T KNOW WHY I KEEP COMING BACK TO THIS PLACE... BUT AT LEAST IT'S A PLACE TO REST!

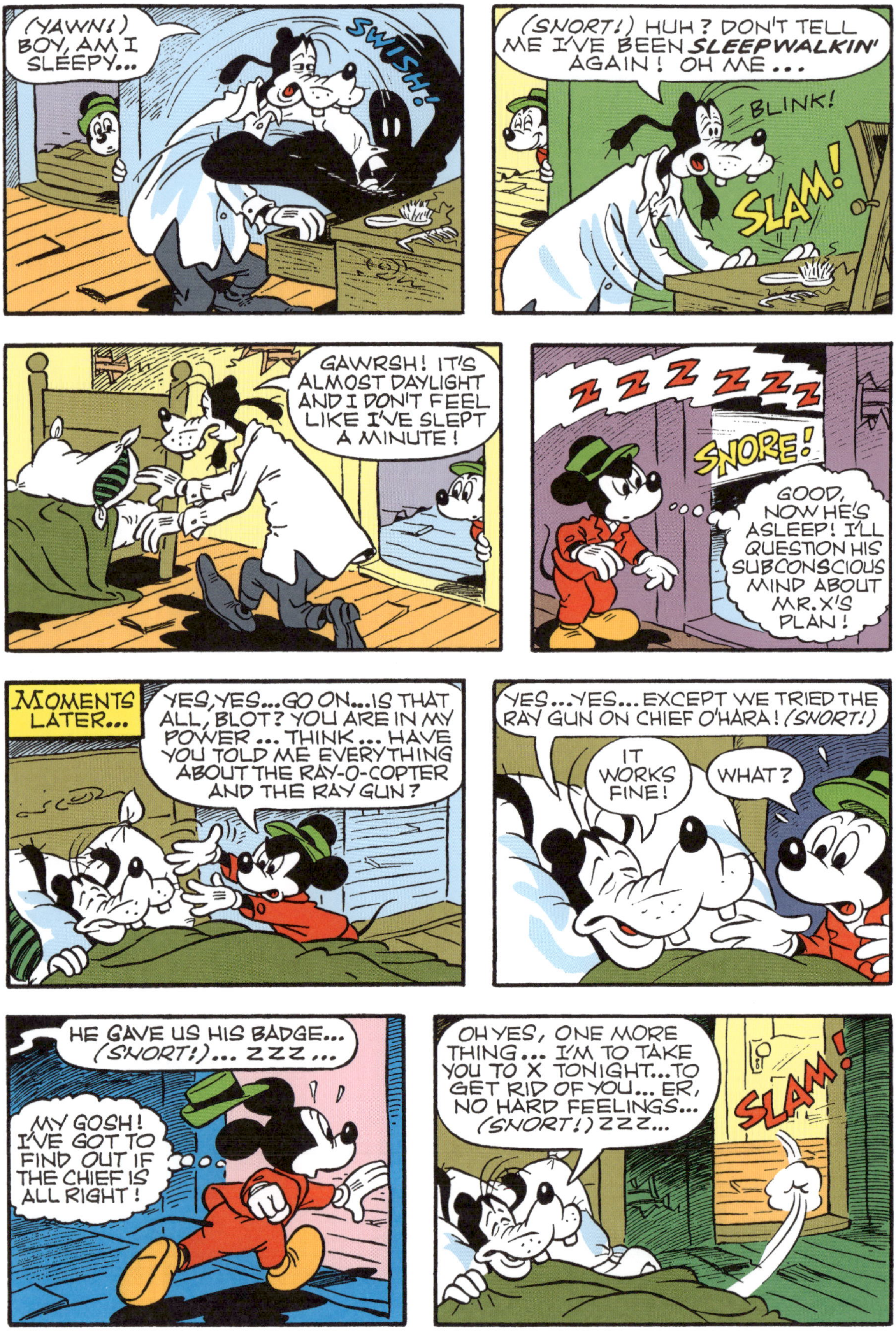
(YAWN!) BOY, AM I SLEEPY...
SWISH!
(SNORT!) HUH? DON'T TELL ME I'VE BEEN **SLEEPWALKIN'** AGAIN! OH ME...
BLINK!
SLAM!
GAWRSH! IT'S ALMOST DAYLIGHT AND I DON'T FEEL LIKE I'VE SLEPT A MINUTE!
Z Z Z Z Z Z
SNORE!
GOOD, NOW HE'S ASLEEP! I'LL QUESTION HIS SUBCONSCIOUS MIND ABOUT MR. X'S PLAN!
MOMENTS LATER...
YES, YES... GO ON... IS THAT ALL, BLOT? YOU ARE IN MY POWER... THINK... HAVE YOU TOLD ME EVERYTHING ABOUT THE RAY-O-COPTER AND THE RAY GUN?
YES... YES... EXCEPT WE TRIED THE RAY GUN ON CHIEF O'HARA! (SNORT!)
IT WORKS FINE!
WHAT?
HE GAVE US HIS BADGE... (SNORT!)... ZZZ...
MY GOSH! I'VE GOT TO FIND OUT IF THE CHIEF IS ALL RIGHT!
OH YES, ONE MORE THING... I'M TO TAKE YOU TO X TONIGHT... TO GET RID OF YOU... ER, NO HARD FEELINGS... (SNORT!) ZZZ...
SLAM!

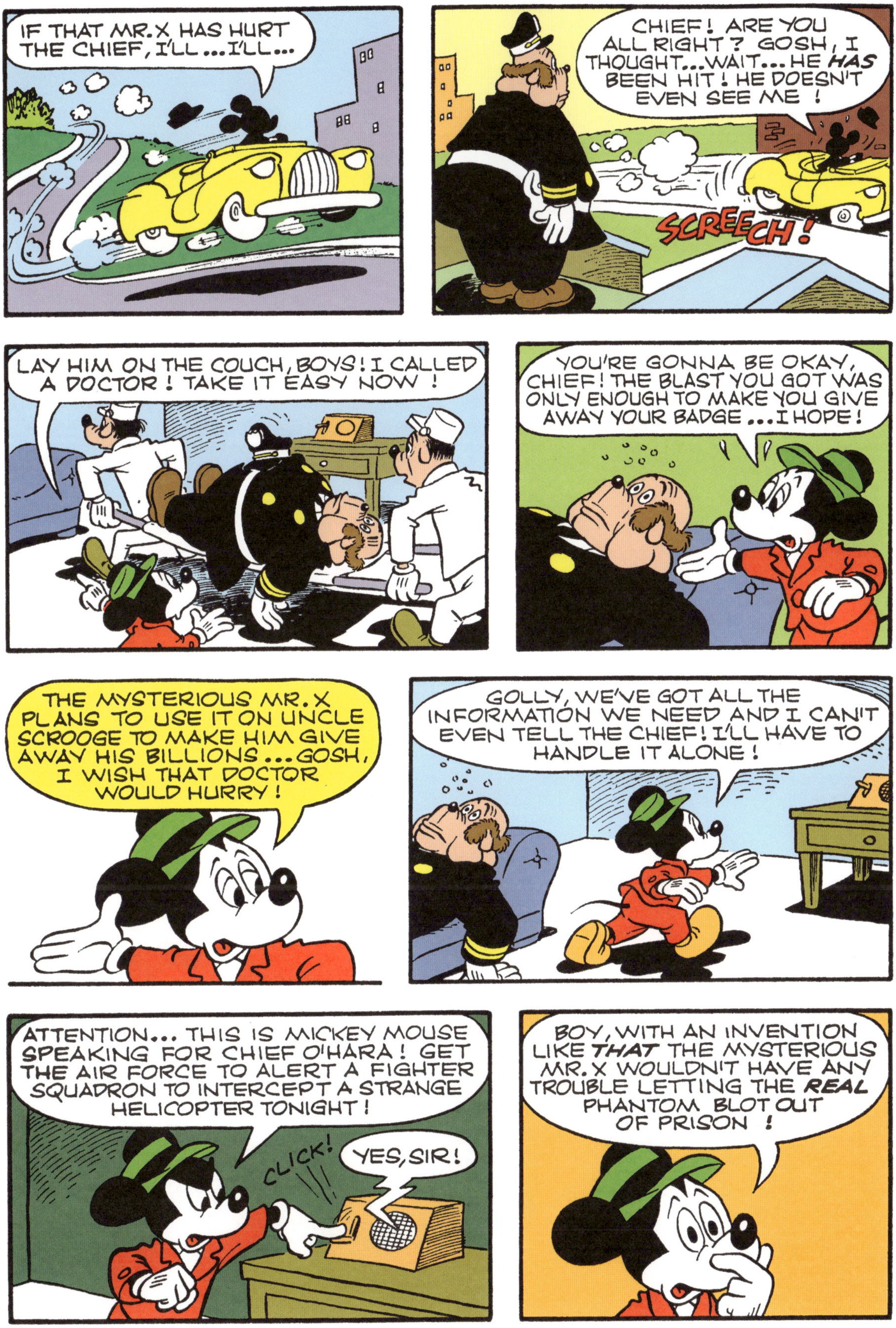
IF THAT MR. X HAS HURT THE CHIEF, I'LL ... I'LL ...
CHIEF! ARE YOU ALL RIGHT? GOSH, I THOUGHT... WAIT... HE *HAS* BEEN HIT! HE DOESN'T EVEN SEE ME!
SCREECH!
LAY HIM ON THE COUCH, BOYS! I CALLED A DOCTOR! TAKE IT EASY NOW!
YOU'RE GONNA BE OKAY, CHIEF! THE BLAST YOU GOT WAS ONLY ENOUGH TO MAKE YOU GIVE AWAY YOUR BADGE ... I HOPE!
THE MYSTERIOUS MR. X PLANS TO USE IT ON UNCLE SCROOGE TO MAKE HIM GIVE AWAY HIS BILLIONS ... GOSH, I WISH THAT DOCTOR WOULD HURRY!
GOLLY, WE'VE GOT ALL THE INFORMATION WE NEED AND I CAN'T EVEN TELL THE CHIEF! I'LL HAVE TO HANDLE IT ALONE!
ATTENTION... THIS IS MICKEY MOUSE SPEAKING FOR CHIEF O'HARA! GET THE AIR FORCE TO ALERT A FIGHTER SQUADRON TO INTERCEPT A STRANGE HELICOPTER TONIGHT!
CLICK!
YES, SIR!
BOY, WITH AN INVENTION LIKE *THAT* THE MYSTERIOUS MR. X WOULDN'T HAVE ANY TROUBLE LETTING THE *REAL* PHANTOM BLOT OUT OF PRISON!

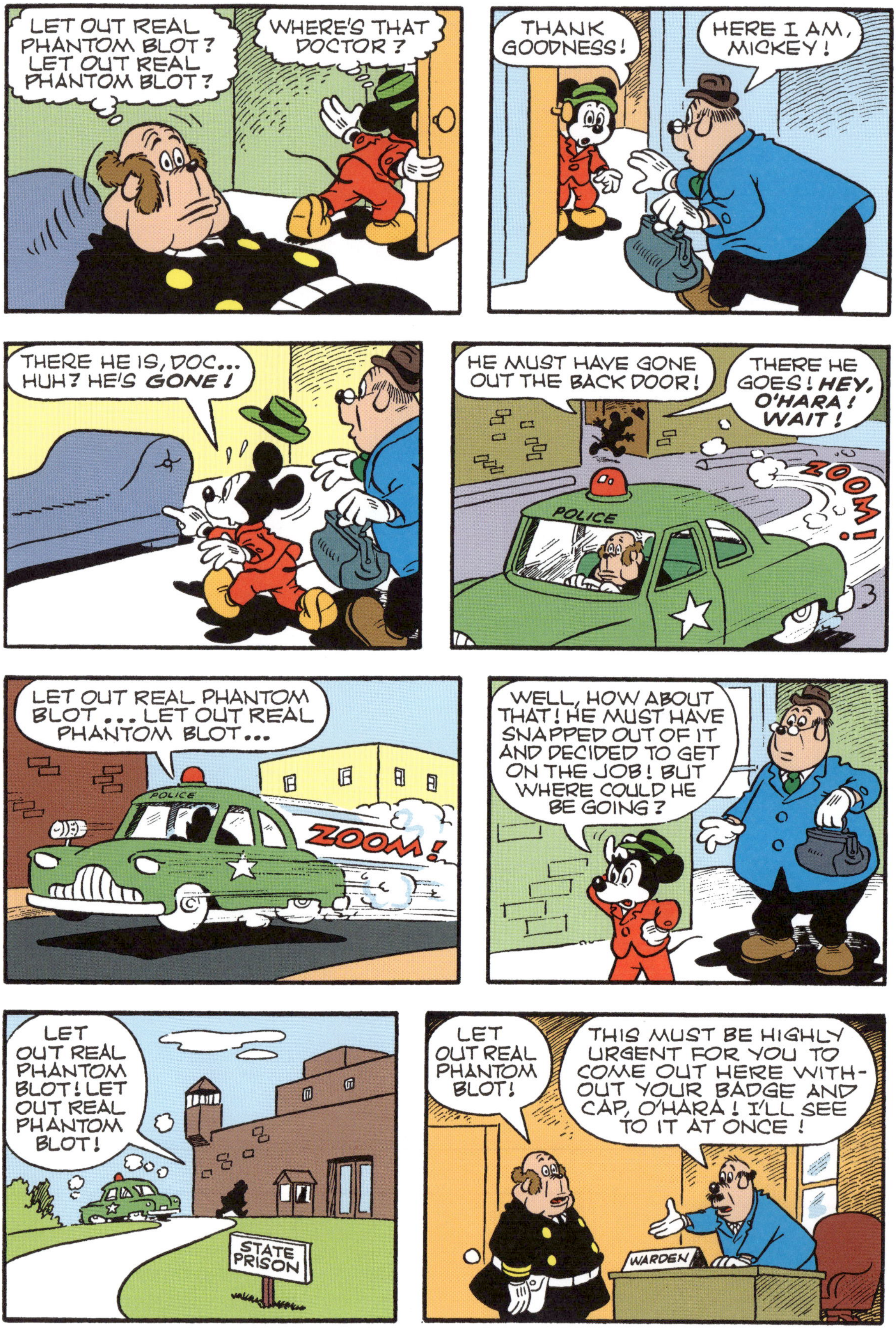
LET OUT REAL PHANTOM BLOT? LET OUT REAL PHANTOM BLOT?
WHERE'S THAT DOCTOR?
THANK GOODNESS!
HERE I AM, MICKEY!
THERE HE IS, DOC... HUH? HE'S GONE!
HE MUST HAVE GONE OUT THE BACK DOOR!
THERE HE GOES! HEY, O'HARA! WAIT!
POLICE
ZOOM!
LET OUT REAL PHANTOM BLOT... LET OUT REAL PHANTOM BLOT...
POLICE
ZOOM!
WELL, HOW ABOUT THAT! HE MUST HAVE SNAPPED OUT OF IT AND DECIDED TO GET ON THE JOB! BUT WHERE COULD HE BE GOING?
LET OUT REAL PHANTOM BLOT! LET OUT REAL PHANTOM BLOT!
STATE PRISON
LET OUT REAL PHANTOM BLOT!
THIS MUST BE HIGHLY URGENT FOR YOU TO COME OUT HERE WITH-OUT YOUR BADGE AND CAP, O'HARA! I'LL SEE TO IT AT ONCE!
WARDEN

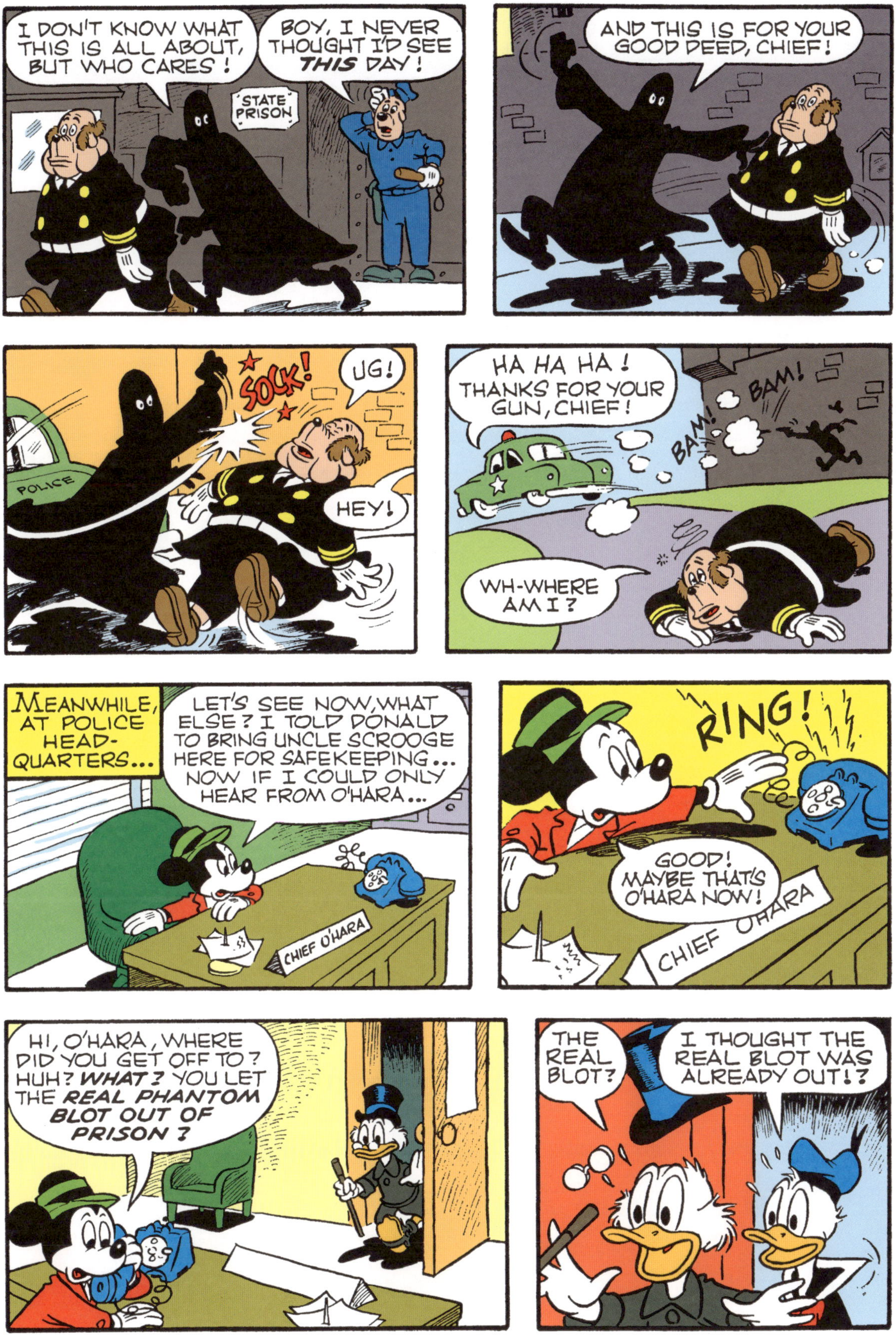

I DON'T KNOW WHAT THIS IS ALL ABOUT, BUT WHO CARES!
BOY, I NEVER THOUGHT I'D SEE **THIS** DAY!
STATE PRISON
AND THIS IS FOR YOUR GOOD DEED, CHIEF!
SOCK!
UG!
POLICE
HEY!
HA HA HA! THANKS FOR YOUR GUN, CHIEF!
BAM!
BAM!
WH-WHERE AM I?
MEANWHILE, AT POLICE HEAD-QUARTERS...
LET'S SEE NOW, WHAT ELSE? I TOLD DONALD TO BRING UNCLE SCROOGE HERE FOR SAFEKEEPING... NOW IF I COULD ONLY HEAR FROM O'HARA...
CHIEF O'HARA
RING!
GOOD! MAYBE THAT'S O'HARA NOW!
CHIEF O'HARA
HI, O'HARA, WHERE DID YOU GET OFF TO? HUH? ***WHAT?*** YOU LET THE ***REAL PHANTOM BLOT OUT OF PRISON?***
THE REAL BLOT?
I THOUGHT THE REAL BLOT WAS ALREADY OUT!?

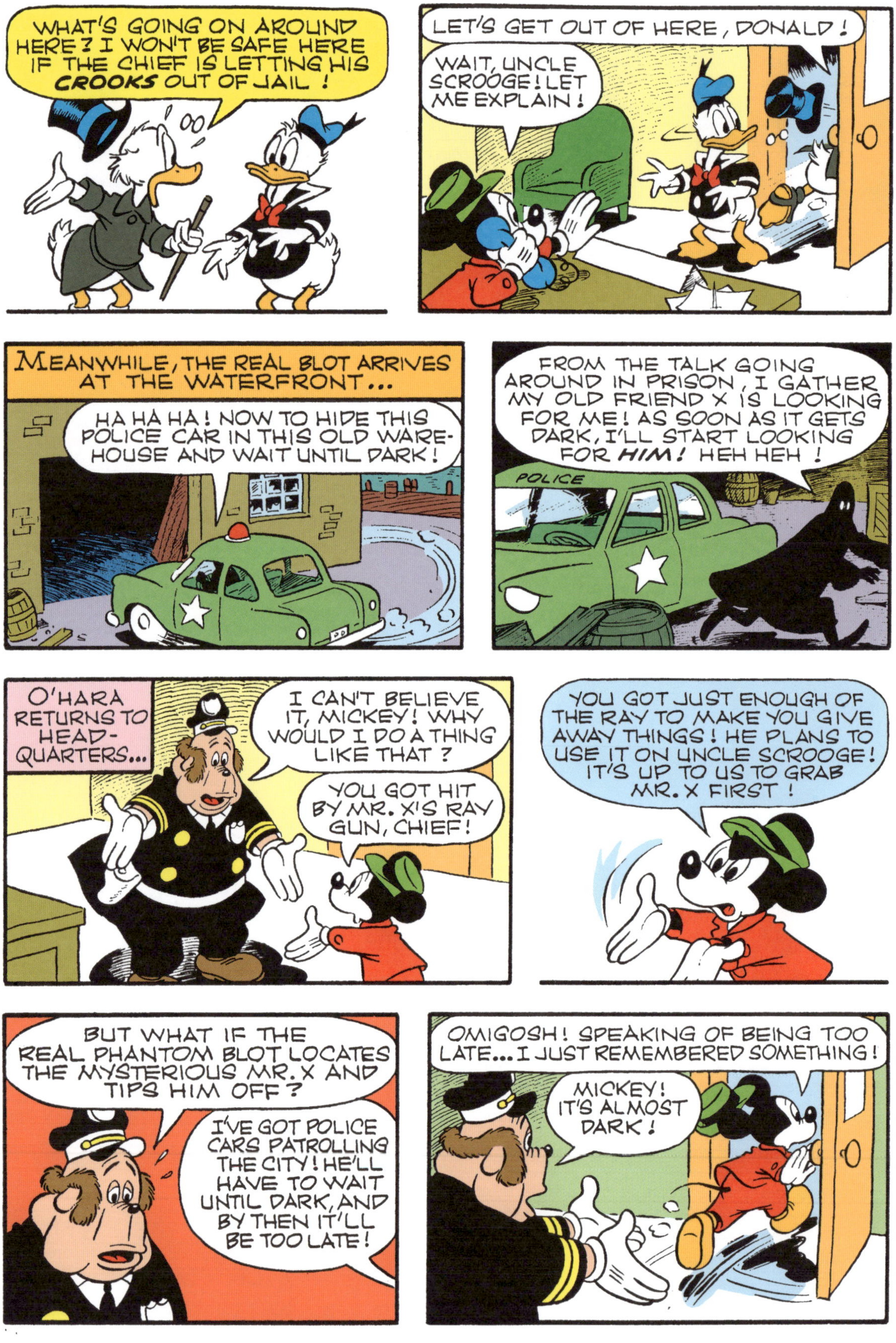
WHAT'S GOING ON AROUND HERE? I WON'T BE SAFE HERE IF THE CHIEF IS LETTING HIS CROOKS OUT OF JAIL!
LET'S GET OUT OF HERE, DONALD!
WAIT, UNCLE SCROOGE! LET ME EXPLAIN!
MEANWHILE, THE REAL BLOT ARRIVES AT THE WATERFRONT...
HA HA HA! NOW TO HIDE THIS POLICE CAR IN THIS OLD WAREHOUSE AND WAIT UNTIL DARK!
FROM THE TALK GOING AROUND IN PRISON, I GATHER MY OLD FRIEND X IS LOOKING FOR ME! AS SOON AS IT GETS DARK, I'LL START LOOKING FOR HIM! HEH HEH!
POLICE
O'HARA RETURNS TO HEADQUARTERS...
I CAN'T BELIEVE IT, MICKEY! WHY WOULD I DO A THING LIKE THAT?
YOU GOT HIT BY MR. X'S RAY GUN, CHIEF!
YOU GOT JUST ENOUGH OF THE RAY TO MAKE YOU GIVE AWAY THINGS! HE PLANS TO USE IT ON UNCLE SCROOGE! IT'S UP TO US TO GRAB MR. X FIRST!
BUT WHAT IF THE REAL PHANTOM BLOT LOCATES THE MYSTERIOUS MR. X AND TIPS HIM OFF?
I'VE GOT POLICE CARS PATROLLING THE CITY! HE'LL HAVE TO WAIT UNTIL DARK, AND BY THEN IT'LL BE TOO LATE!
OMIGOSH! SPEAKING OF BEING TOO LATE... I JUST REMEMBERED SOMETHING!
MICKEY! IT'S ALMOST DARK!

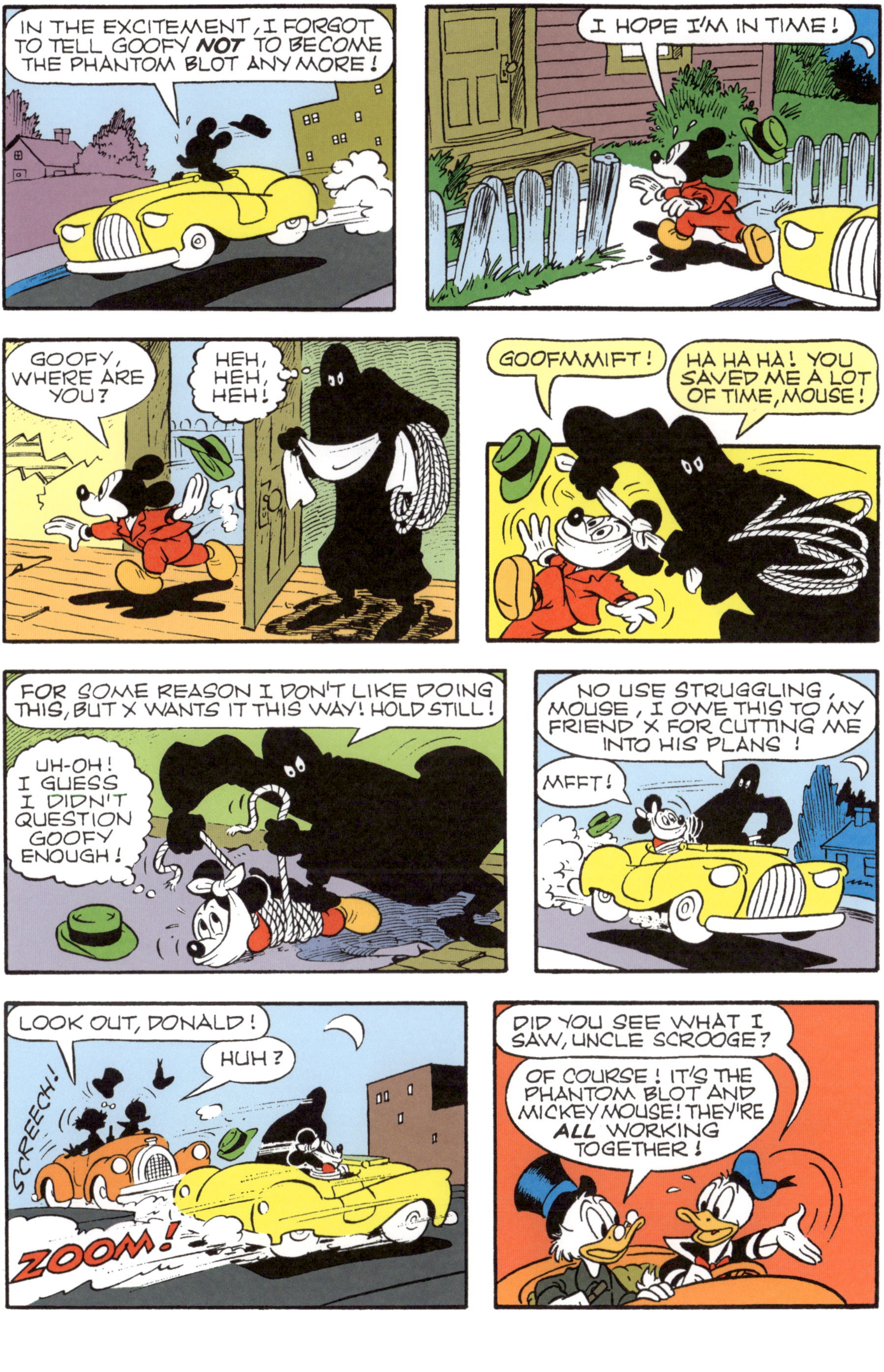
IN THE EXCITEMENT, I FORGOT TO TELL GOOFY **NOT** TO BECOME THE PHANTOM BLOT ANY MORE!
I HOPE I'M IN TIME!
GOOFY, WHERE ARE YOU?
HEH, HEH, HEH!
GOOFMMIFT!
HA HA HA! YOU SAVED ME A LOT OF TIME, MOUSE!
FOR SOME REASON I DON'T LIKE DOING THIS, BUT X WANTS IT THIS WAY! HOLD STILL!
UH-OH! I GUESS I DIDN'T QUESTION GOOFY ENOUGH!
NO USE STRUGGLING, MOUSE, I OWE THIS TO MY FRIEND X FOR CUTTING ME INTO HIS PLANS!
MFFT!
LOOK OUT, DONALD!
HUH?
SCREECH!
ZOOM!
DID YOU SEE WHAT I SAW, UNCLE SCROOGE?
OF COURSE! IT'S THE PHANTOM BLOT AND MICKEY MOUSE! THEY'RE **ALL** WORKING TOGETHER!

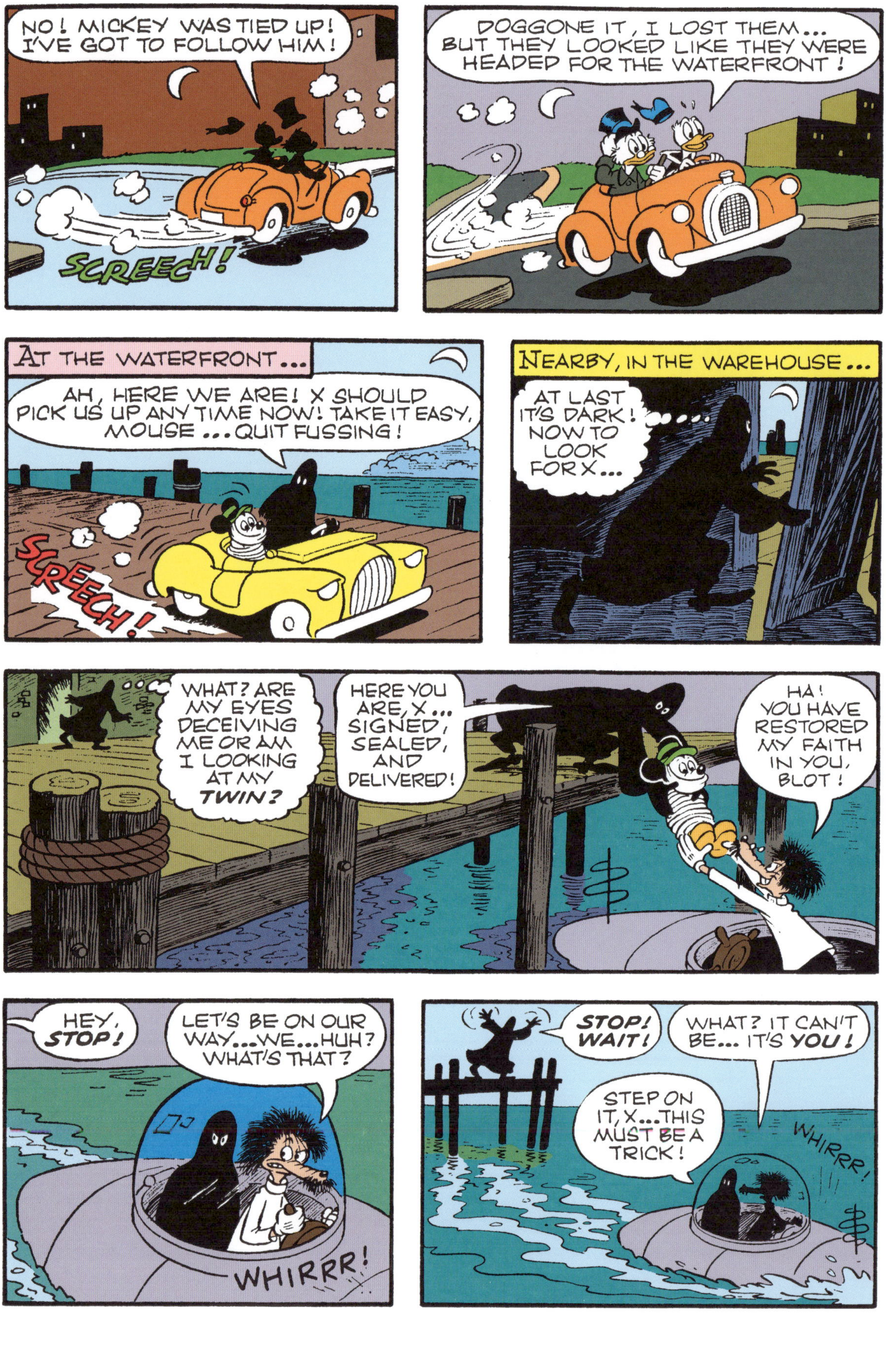
NO! MICKEY WAS TIED UP! I'VE GOT TO FOLLOW HIM!
SCREECH!
DOGGONE IT, I LOST THEM... BUT THEY LOOKED LIKE THEY WERE HEADED FOR THE WATERFRONT!
AT THE WATERFRONT...
AH, HERE WE ARE! X SHOULD PICK US UP ANY TIME NOW! TAKE IT EASY, MOUSE... QUIT FUSSING!
SCREECH!
NEARBY, IN THE WAREHOUSE...
AT LAST IT'S DARK! NOW TO LOOK FOR X...
WHAT? ARE MY EYES DECEIVING ME OR AM I LOOKING AT MY TWIN?
HERE YOU ARE, X... SIGNED, SEALED, AND DELIVERED!
HA! YOU HAVE RESTORED MY FAITH IN YOU, BLOT!
HEY, STOP!
LET'S BE ON OUR WAY... WE... HUH? WHAT'S THAT?
WHIRRR!
STOP! WAIT!
WHAT? IT CAN'T BE... IT'S YOU!
STEP ON IT, X... THIS MUST BE A TRICK!
WHIRRR!

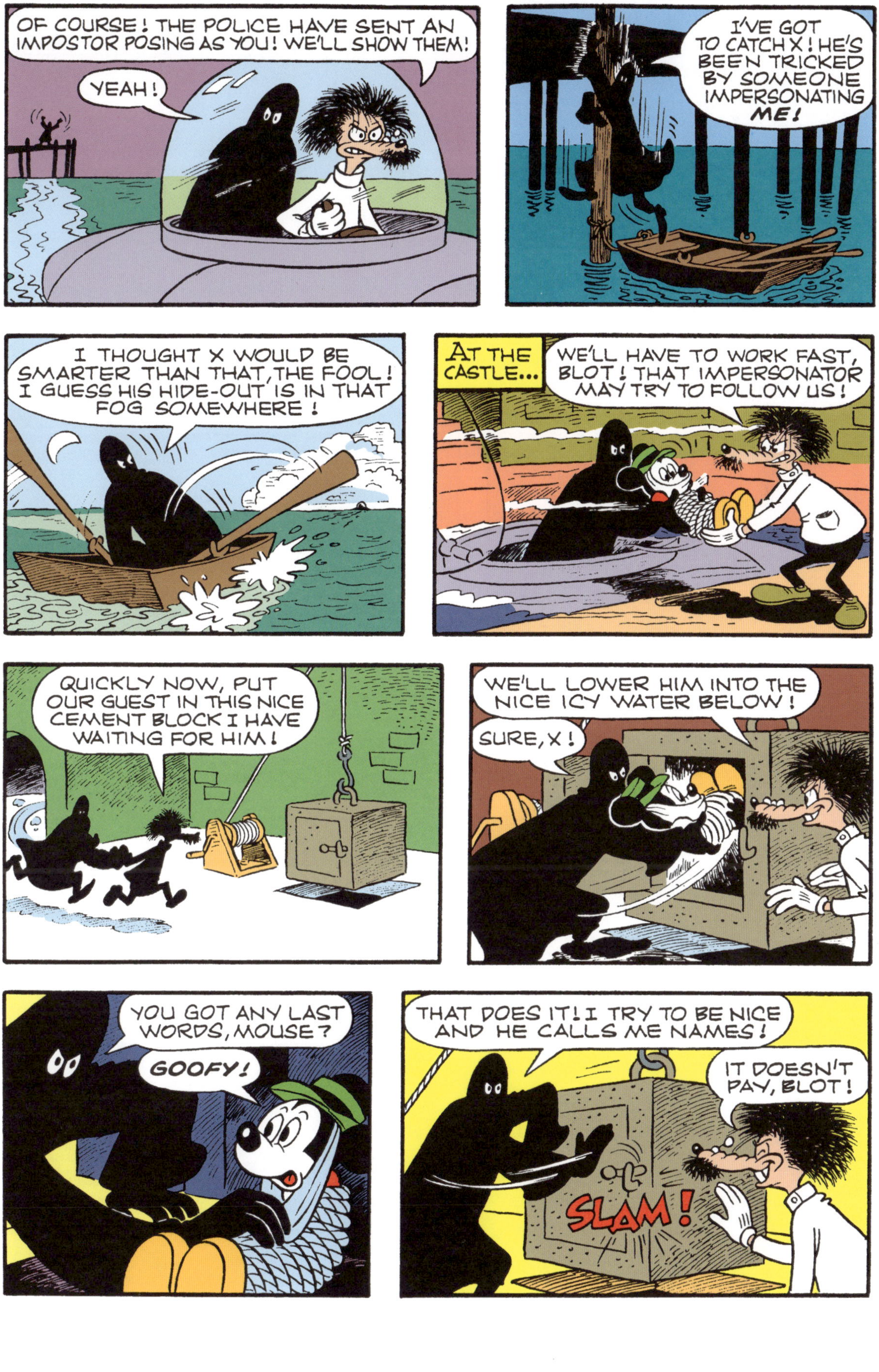
OF COURSE! THE POLICE HAVE SENT AN IMPOSTOR POSING AS YOU! WE'LL SHOW THEM!
YEAH!
I'VE GOT TO CATCH X! HE'S BEEN TRICKED BY SOMEONE IMPERSONATING ME!
I THOUGHT X WOULD BE SMARTER THAN THAT, THE FOOL! I GUESS HIS HIDE-OUT IS IN THAT FOG SOMEWHERE!
AT THE CASTLE...
WE'LL HAVE TO WORK FAST, BLOT! THAT IMPERSONATOR MAY TRY TO FOLLOW US!
QUICKLY NOW, PUT OUR GUEST IN THIS NICE CEMENT BLOCK I HAVE WAITING FOR HIM!
WE'LL LOWER HIM INTO THE NICE ICY WATER BELOW!
SURE, X!
YOU GOT ANY LAST WORDS, MOUSE?
GOOFY!
THAT DOES IT! I TRY TO BE NICE AND HE CALLS ME NAMES!
IT DOESN'T PAY, BLOT!
SLAM!

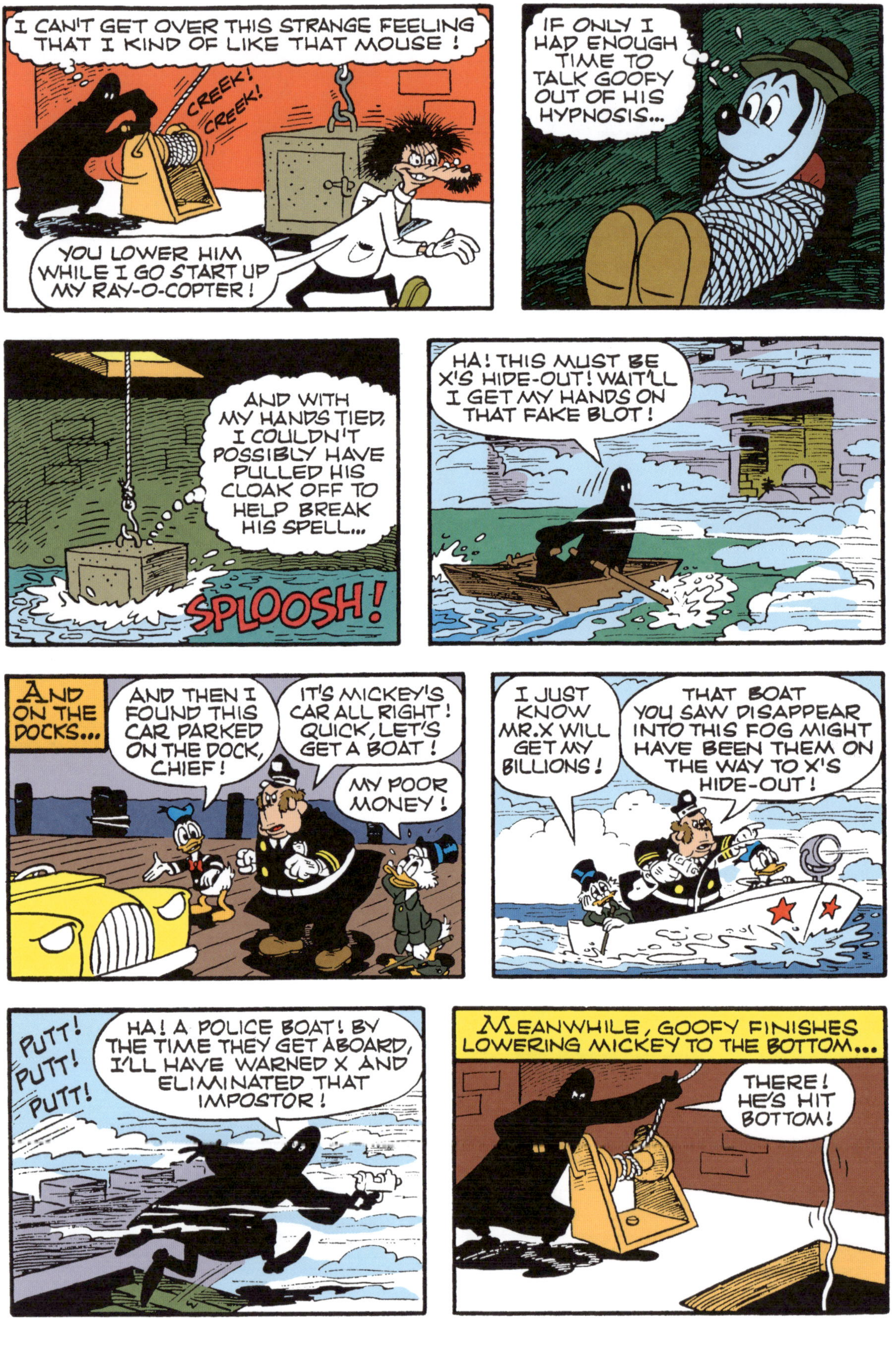

I CAN'T GET OVER THIS STRANGE FEELING THAT I KIND OF LIKE THAT MOUSE !
CREEK! CREEK!
YOU LOWER HIM WHILE I GO START UP MY RAY-O-COPTER !
IF ONLY I HAD ENOUGH TIME TO TALK GOOFY OUT OF HIS HYPNOSIS...
AND WITH MY HANDS TIED, I COULDN'T POSSIBLY HAVE PULLED HIS CLOAK OFF TO HELP BREAK HIS SPELL...
SPLOOSH !
HA! THIS MUST BE X'S HIDE-OUT! WAIT'LL I GET MY HANDS ON THAT FAKE BLOT !
AND ON THE DOCKS...
AND THEN I FOUND THIS CAR PARKED ON THE DOCK, CHIEF !
IT'S MICKEY'S CAR ALL RIGHT ! QUICK, LET'S GET A BOAT !
MY POOR MONEY !
I JUST KNOW MR.X WILL GET MY BILLIONS !
THAT BOAT YOU SAW DISAPPEAR INTO THIS FOG MIGHT HAVE BEEN THEM ON THE WAY TO X'S HIDE-OUT !
PUTT! PUTT! PUTT!
HA! A POLICE BOAT! BY THE TIME THEY GET ABOARD, I'LL HAVE WARNED X AND ELIMINATED THAT IMPOSTOR !
MEANWHILE, GOOFY FINISHES LOWERING MICKEY TO THE BOTTOM...
THERE! HE'S HIT BOTTOM!

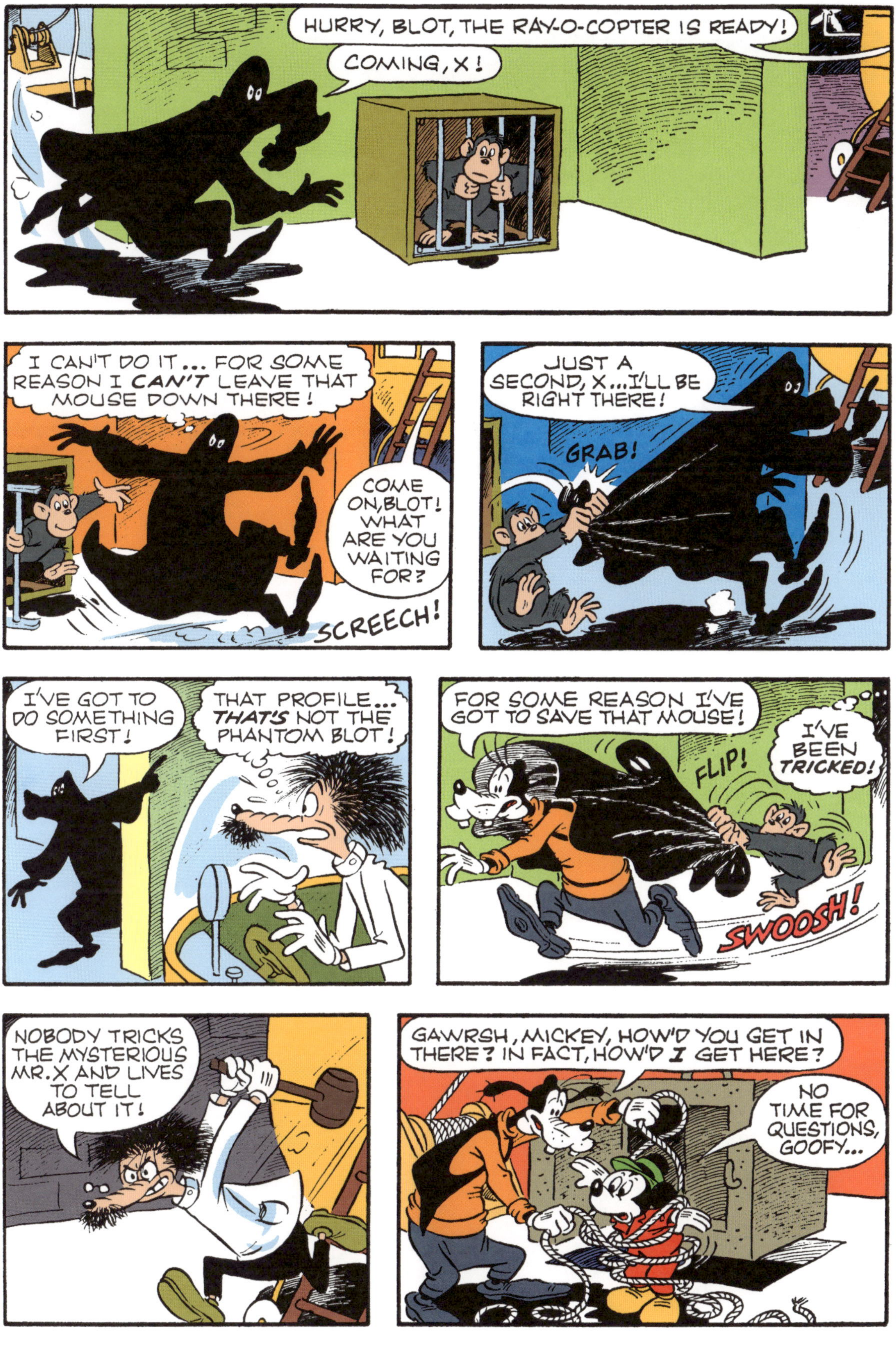
HURRY, BLOT, THE RAY-O-COPTER IS READY!
COMING, X!
I CAN'T DO IT... FOR SOME REASON I CAN'T LEAVE THAT MOUSE DOWN THERE!
COME ON, BLOT! WHAT ARE YOU WAITING FOR?
SCREECH!
JUST A SECOND, X...I'LL BE RIGHT THERE!
GRAB!
I'VE GOT TO DO SOMETHING FIRST!
THAT PROFILE... THAT'S NOT THE PHANTOM BLOT!
FOR SOME REASON I'VE GOT TO SAVE THAT MOUSE!
FLIP!
I'VE BEEN TRICKED!
SWOOSH!
NOBODY TRICKS THE MYSTERIOUS MR. X AND LIVES TO TELL ABOUT IT!
GAWRSH, MICKEY, HOW'D YOU GET IN THERE? IN FACT, HOW'D I GET HERE?
NO TIME FOR QUESTIONS, GOOFY...

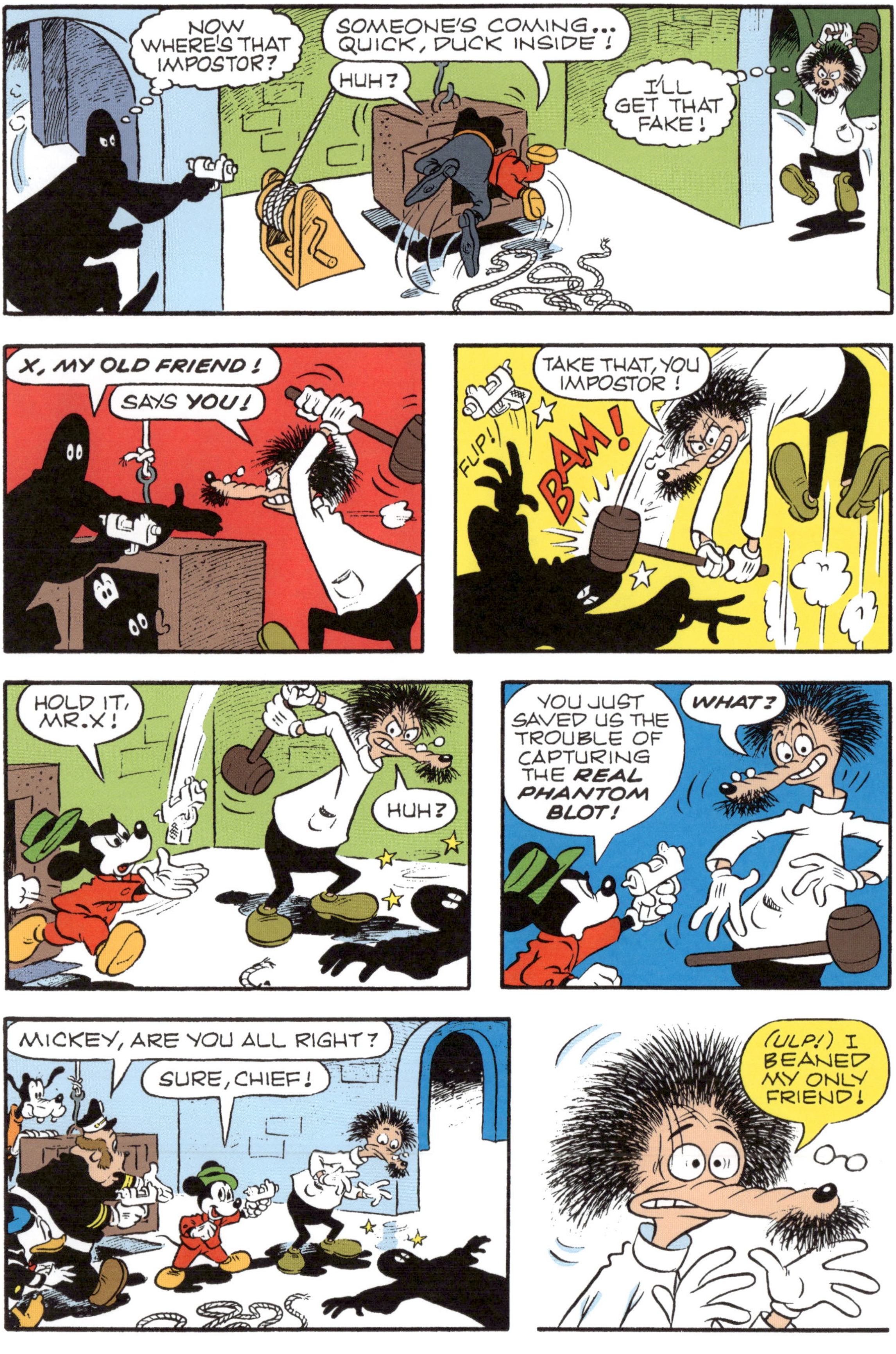
NOW WHERE'S THAT IMPOSTOR?
SOMEONE'S COMING... QUICK, DUCK INSIDE!
HUH?
I'LL GET THAT FAKE!
X, MY OLD FRIEND!
SAYS YOU!
TAKE THAT, YOU IMPOSTOR!
FLIP!
BAM!
HOLD IT, MR. X!
HUH?
YOU JUST SAVED US THE TROUBLE OF CAPTURING THE REAL PHANTOM BLOT!
WHAT?
MICKEY, ARE YOU ALL RIGHT?
SURE, CHIEF!
(ULP!) I BEANED MY ONLY FRIEND!

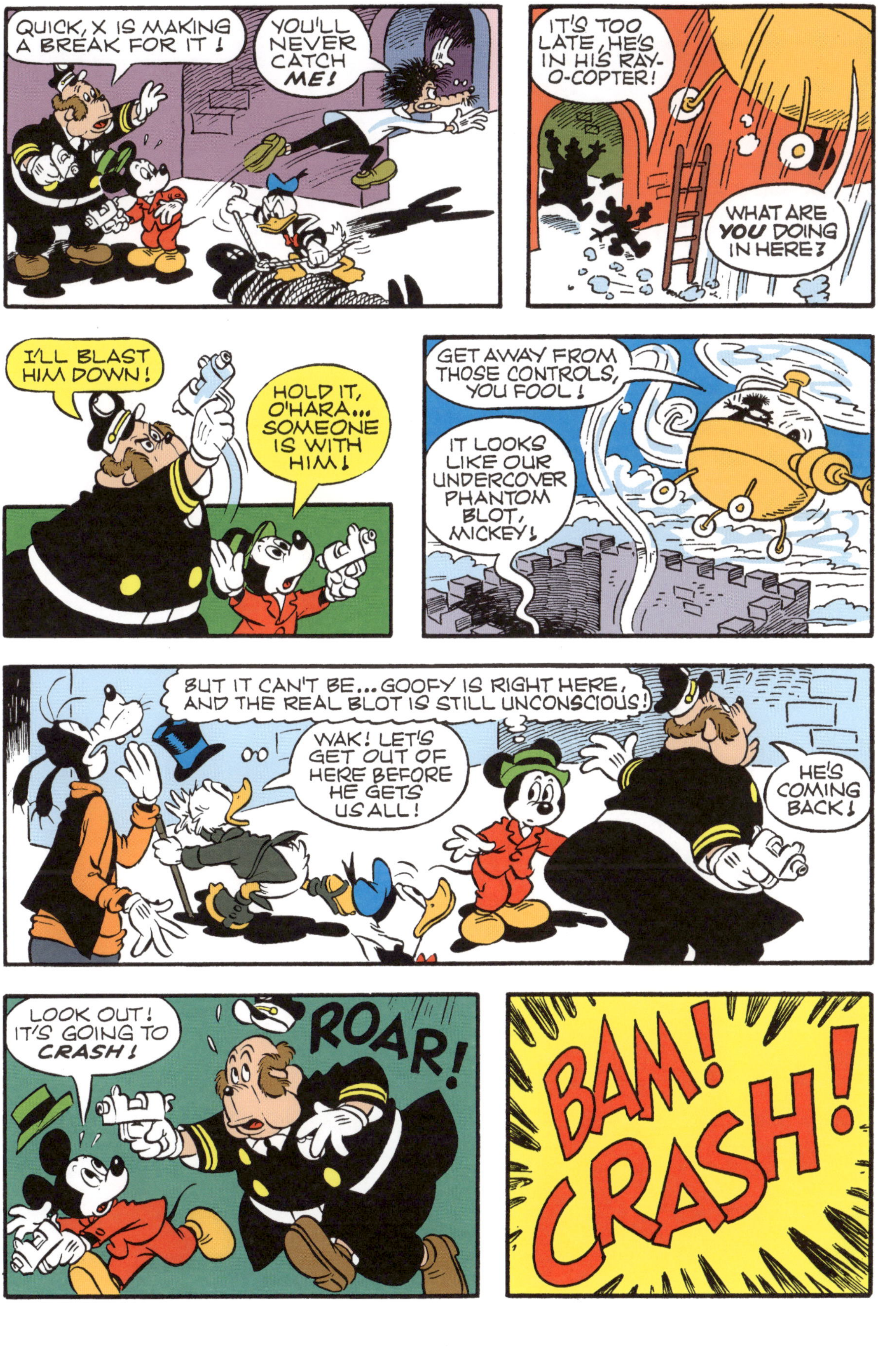
QUICK, X IS MAKING A BREAK FOR IT!
YOU'LL NEVER CATCH ME!
IT'S TOO LATE, HE'S IN HIS RAY-O-COPTER!
WHAT ARE YOU DOING IN HERE?
I'LL BLAST HIM DOWN!
HOLD IT, O'HARA... SOMEONE IS WITH HIM!
GET AWAY FROM THOSE CONTROLS, YOU FOOL!
IT LOOKS LIKE OUR UNDERCOVER PHANTOM BLOT, MICKEY!
BUT IT CAN'T BE... GOOFY IS RIGHT HERE, AND THE REAL BLOT IS STILL UNCONSCIOUS!
WAK! LET'S GET OUT OF HERE BEFORE HE GETS US ALL!
HE'S COMING BACK!
LOOK OUT! IT'S GOING TO CRASH!
ROAR!
BAM! CRASH!

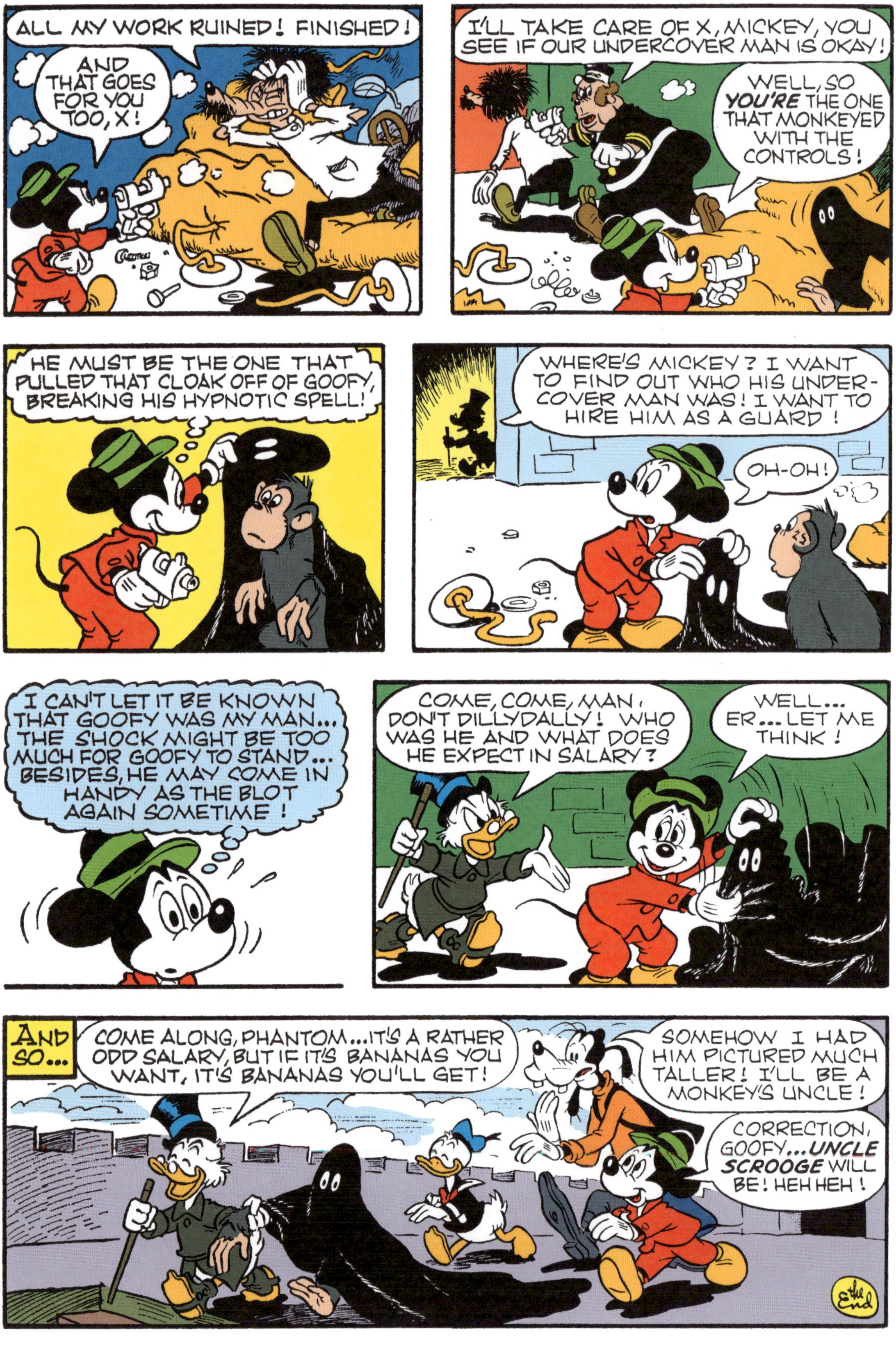
ALL MY WORK RUINED! FINISHED!
AND THAT GOES FOR YOU TOO, X!
I'LL TAKE CARE OF X, MICKEY, YOU SEE IF OUR UNDERCOVER MAN IS OKAY!
WELL, SO YOU'RE THE ONE THAT MONKEYED WITH THE CONTROLS!
HE MUST BE THE ONE THAT PULLED THAT CLOAK OFF OF GOOFY, BREAKING HIS HYPNOTIC SPELL!
WHERE'S MICKEY? I WANT TO FIND OUT WHO HIS UNDER-COVER MAN WAS! I WANT TO HIRE HIM AS A GUARD!
OH-OH!
I CAN'T LET IT BE KNOWN THAT GOOFY WAS MY MAN... THE SHOCK MIGHT BE TOO MUCH FOR GOOFY TO STAND... BESIDES, HE MAY COME IN HANDY AS THE BLOT AGAIN SOMETIME!
COME, COME, MAN, DON'T DILLYDALLY! WHO WAS HE AND WHAT DOES HE EXPECT IN SALARY?
WELL... ER... LET ME THINK!
AND SO...
COME ALONG, PHANTOM... IT'S A RATHER ODD SALARY, BUT IF IT'S BANANAS YOU WANT, IT'S BANANAS YOU'LL GET!
SOMEHOW I HAD HIM PICTURED MUCH TALLER! I'LL BE A MONKEY'S UNCLE!
CORRECTION, GOOFY... UNCLE SCROOGE WILL BE! HEH HEH!
The End

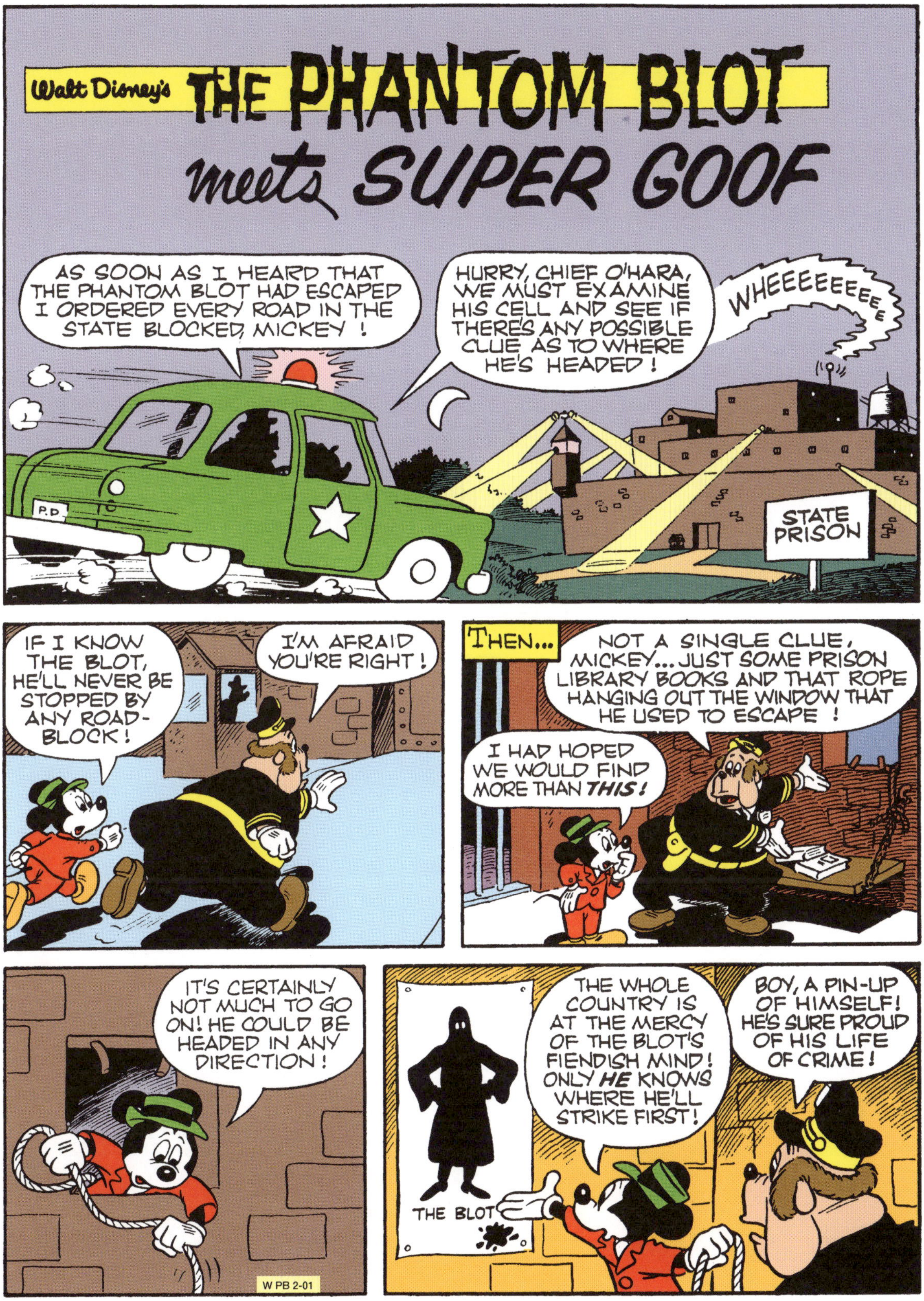
Walt Disney's THE PHANTOM BLOT meets SUPER GOOF
AS SOON AS I HEARD THAT THE PHANTOM BLOT HAD ESCAPED I ORDERED EVERY ROAD IN THE STATE BLOCKED, MICKEY !
HURRY, CHIEF O'HARA, WE MUST EXAMINE HIS CELL AND SEE IF THERE'S ANY POSSIBLE CLUE AS TO WHERE HE'S HEADED !
WHEEEEEEEEEE
P.D.
STATE PRISON
IF I KNOW THE BLOT, HE'LL NEVER BE STOPPED BY ANY ROAD-BLOCK !
I'M AFRAID YOU'RE RIGHT !
THEN...
NOT A SINGLE CLUE, MICKEY... JUST SOME PRISON LIBRARY BOOKS AND THAT ROPE HANGING OUT THE WINDOW THAT HE USED TO ESCAPE !
I HAD HOPED WE WOULD FIND MORE THAN THIS !
IT'S CERTAINLY NOT MUCH TO GO ON! HE COULD BE HEADED IN ANY DIRECTION !
W PB 2-01
THE WHOLE COUNTRY IS AT THE MERCY OF THE BLOT'S FIENDISH MIND! ONLY HE KNOWS WHERE HE'LL STRIKE FIRST!
BOY, A PIN-UP OF HIMSELF! HE'S SURE PROUD OF HIS LIFE OF CRIME!
THE BLOT

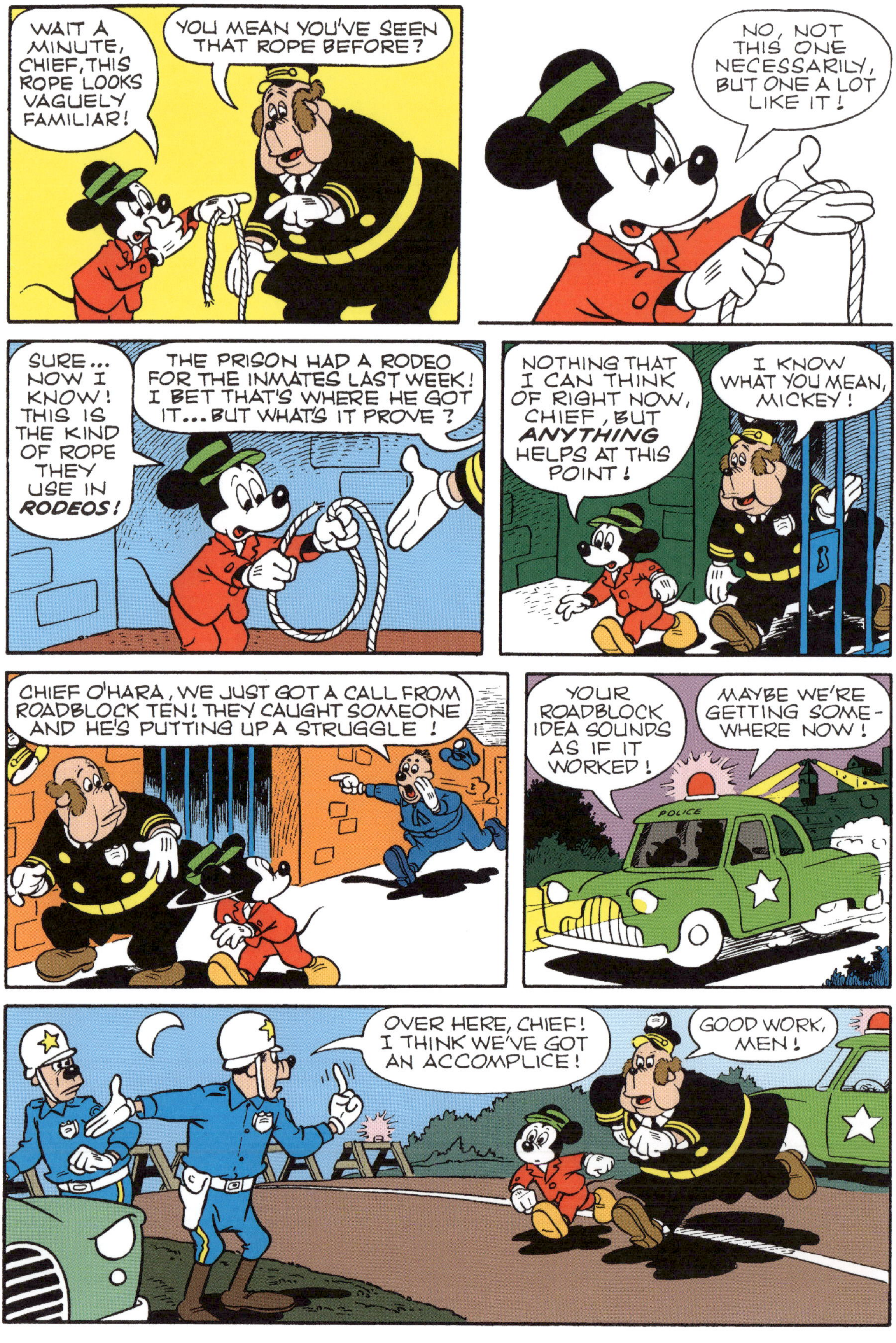
WAIT A MINUTE, CHIEF, THIS ROPE LOOKS VAGUELY FAMILIAR!
YOU MEAN YOU'VE SEEN THAT ROPE BEFORE?
NO, NOT THIS ONE NECESSARILY, BUT ONE A LOT LIKE IT!
SURE... NOW I KNOW! THIS IS THE KIND OF ROPE THEY USE IN **RODEOS!**
THE PRISON HAD A RODEO FOR THE INMATES LAST WEEK! I BET THAT'S WHERE HE GOT IT... BUT WHAT'S IT PROVE?
NOTHING THAT I CAN THINK OF RIGHT NOW, CHIEF, BUT **ANYTHING** HELPS AT THIS POINT!
I KNOW WHAT YOU MEAN, MICKEY!
CHIEF O'HARA, WE JUST GOT A CALL FROM ROADBLOCK TEN! THEY CAUGHT SOMEONE AND HE'S PUTTING UP A STRUGGLE!
YOUR ROADBLOCK IDEA SOUNDS AS IF IT WORKED!
MAYBE WE'RE GETTING SOMEWHERE NOW!
POLICE
OVER HERE, CHIEF! I THINK WE'VE GOT AN ACCOMPLICE!
GOOD WORK, MEN!

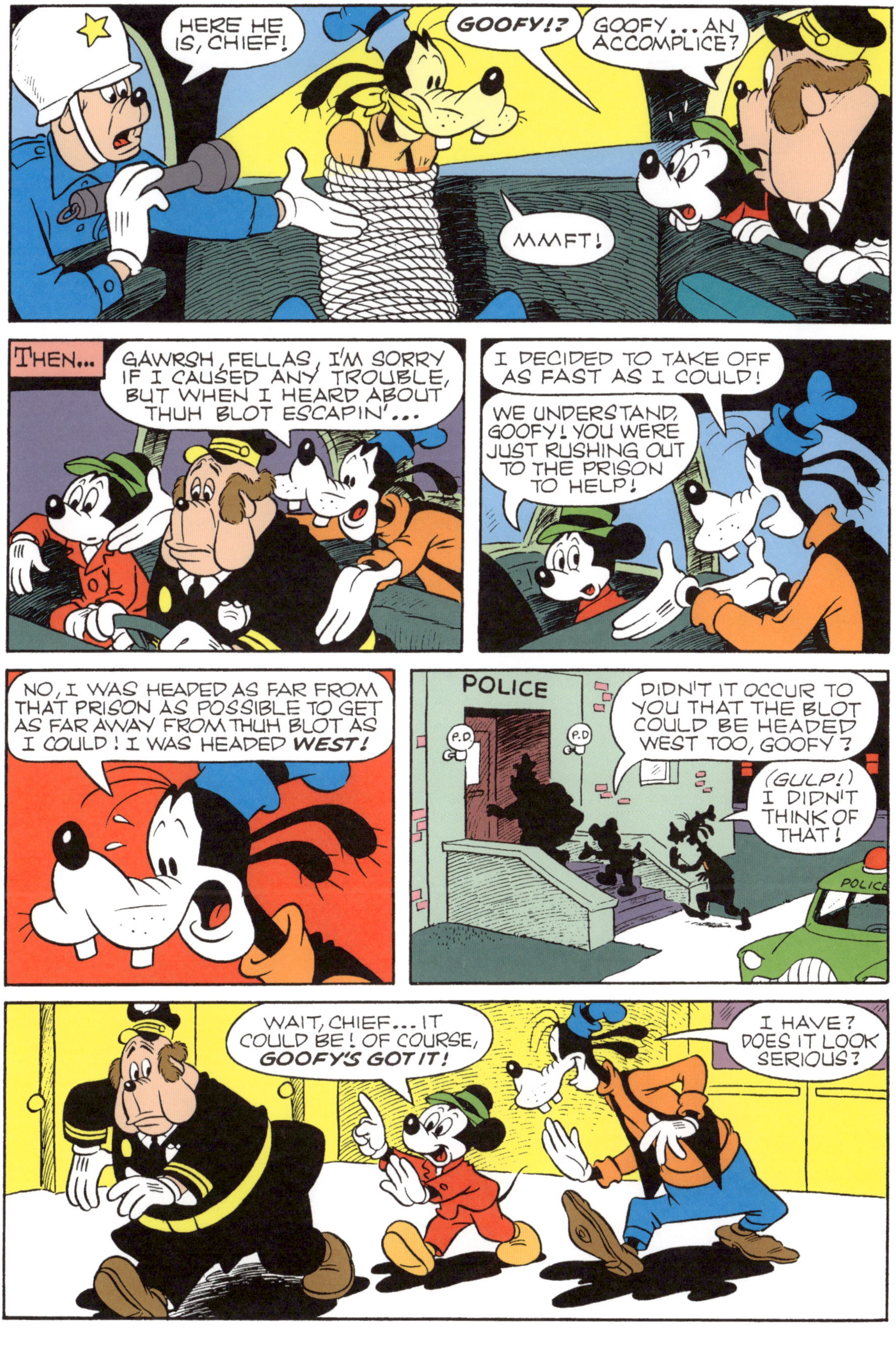
HERE HE IS, CHIEF!
GOOFY!?
GOOFY... AN ACCOMPLICE?
MMFT!
THEN...
GAWRSH, FELLAS, I'M SORRY IF I CAUSED ANY TROUBLE, BUT WHEN I HEARD ABOUT THUH BLOT ESCAPIN'...
I DECIDED TO TAKE OFF AS FAST AS I COULD!
WE UNDERSTAND, GOOFY! YOU WERE JUST RUSHING OUT TO THE PRISON TO HELP!
NO, I WAS HEADED AS FAR FROM THAT PRISON AS POSSIBLE TO GET AS FAR AWAY FROM THUH BLOT AS I COULD! I WAS HEADED *WEST!*
POLICE
P.D.
P.D.
DIDN'T IT OCCUR TO YOU THAT THE BLOT COULD BE HEADED WEST TOO, GOOFY?
(GULP!) I DIDN'T THINK OF THAT!
POLICE
WAIT, CHIEF... IT COULD BE! OF COURSE, **GOOFY'S GOT IT!**
I HAVE? DOES IT LOOK SERIOUS?

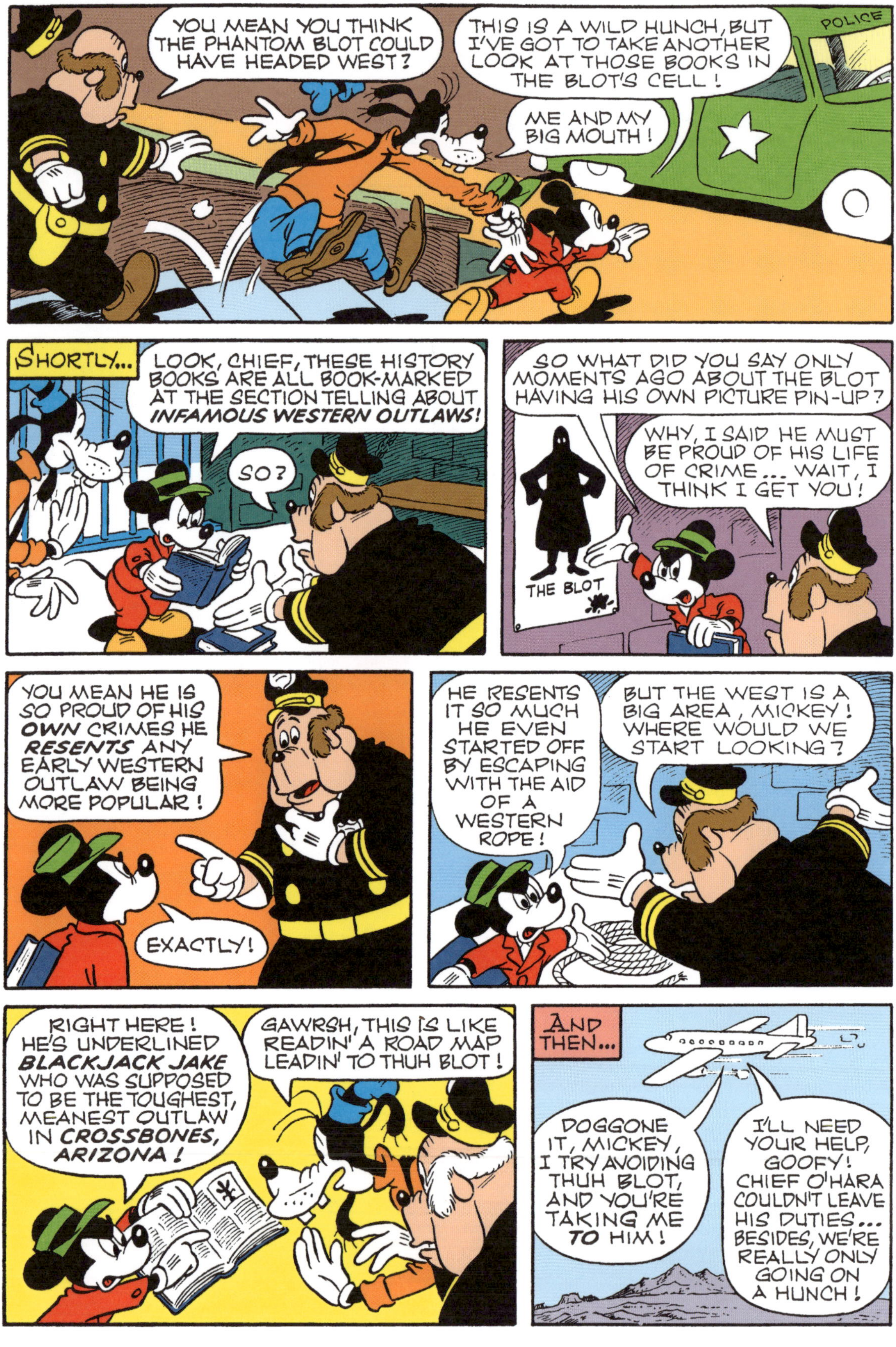
YOU MEAN YOU THINK THE PHANTOM BLOT COULD HAVE HEADED WEST?
THIS IS A WILD HUNCH, BUT I'VE GOT TO TAKE ANOTHER LOOK AT THOSE BOOKS IN THE BLOT'S CELL!
ME AND MY BIG MOUTH!
POLICE
SHORTLY...
LOOK, CHIEF, THESE HISTORY BOOKS ARE ALL BOOK-MARKED AT THE SECTION TELLING ABOUT INFAMOUS WESTERN OUTLAWS!
SO?
SO WHAT DID YOU SAY ONLY MOMENTS AGO ABOUT THE BLOT HAVING HIS OWN PICTURE PIN-UP?
WHY, I SAID HE MUST BE PROUD OF HIS LIFE OF CRIME... WAIT, I THINK I GET YOU!
THE BLOT
YOU MEAN HE IS SO PROUD OF HIS OWN CRIMES HE RESENTS ANY EARLY WESTERN OUTLAW BEING MORE POPULAR!
EXACTLY!
HE RESENTS IT SO MUCH HE EVEN STARTED OFF BY ESCAPING WITH THE AID OF A WESTERN ROPE!
BUT THE WEST IS A BIG AREA, MICKEY! WHERE WOULD WE START LOOKING?
RIGHT HERE! HE'S UNDERLINED BLACKJACK JAKE WHO WAS SUPPOSED TO BE THE TOUGHEST, MEANEST OUTLAW IN CROSSBONES, ARIZONA!
GAWRSH, THIS IS LIKE READIN' A ROAD MAP LEADIN' TO THUH BLOT!
AND THEN...
DOGGONE IT, MICKEY, I TRY AVOIDING THUH BLOT, AND YOU'RE TAKING ME TO HIM!
I'LL NEED YOUR HELP, GOOFY! CHIEF O'HARA COULDN'T LEAVE HIS DUTIES... BESIDES, WE'RE REALLY ONLY GOING ON A HUNCH!

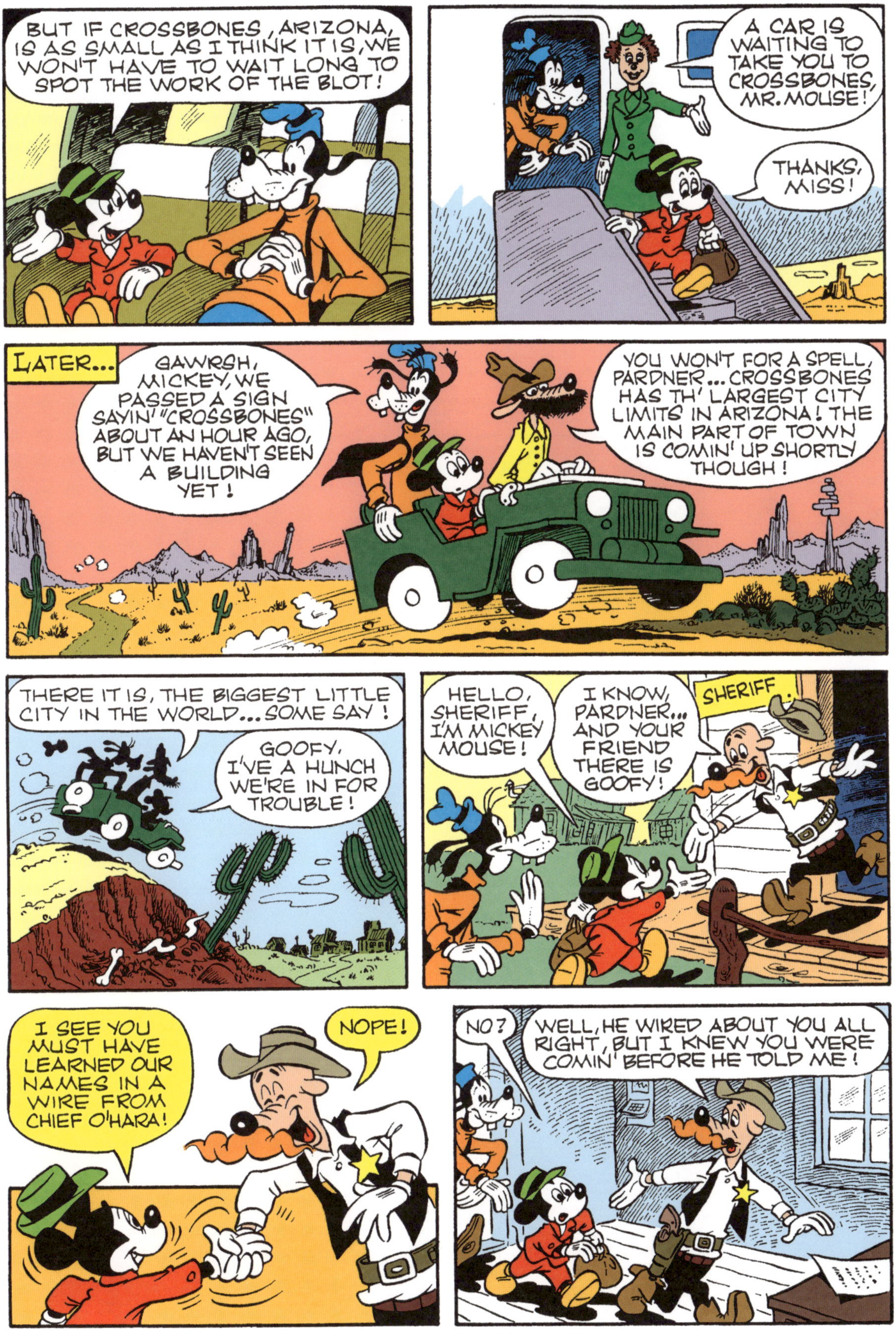
BUT IF CROSSBONES, ARIZONA, IS AS SMALL AS I THINK IT IS, WE WON'T HAVE TO WAIT LONG TO SPOT THE WORK OF THE BLOT!
A CAR IS WAITING TO TAKE YOU TO CROSSBONES, MR. MOUSE!
THANKS, MISS!
LATER...
GAWRSH, MICKEY, WE PASSED A SIGN SAYIN' "CROSSBONES" ABOUT AN HOUR AGO, BUT WE HAVEN'T SEEN A BUILDING YET!
YOU WON'T FOR A SPELL, PARDNER... CROSSBONES HAS TH' LARGEST CITY LIMITS IN ARIZONA! THE MAIN PART OF TOWN IS COMIN' UP SHORTLY THOUGH!
THERE IT IS, THE BIGGEST LITTLE CITY IN THE WORLD... SOME SAY!
GOOFY, I'VE A HUNCH WE'RE IN FOR TROUBLE!
HELLO, SHERIFF, I'M MICKEY MOUSE!
I KNOW, PARDNER... AND YOUR FRIEND THERE IS GOOFY!
SHERIFF
I SEE YOU MUST HAVE LEARNED OUR NAMES IN A WIRE FROM CHIEF O'HARA!
NOPE!
NO?
WELL, HE WIRED ABOUT YOU ALL RIGHT, BUT I KNEW YOU WERE COMIN' BEFORE HE TOLD ME!

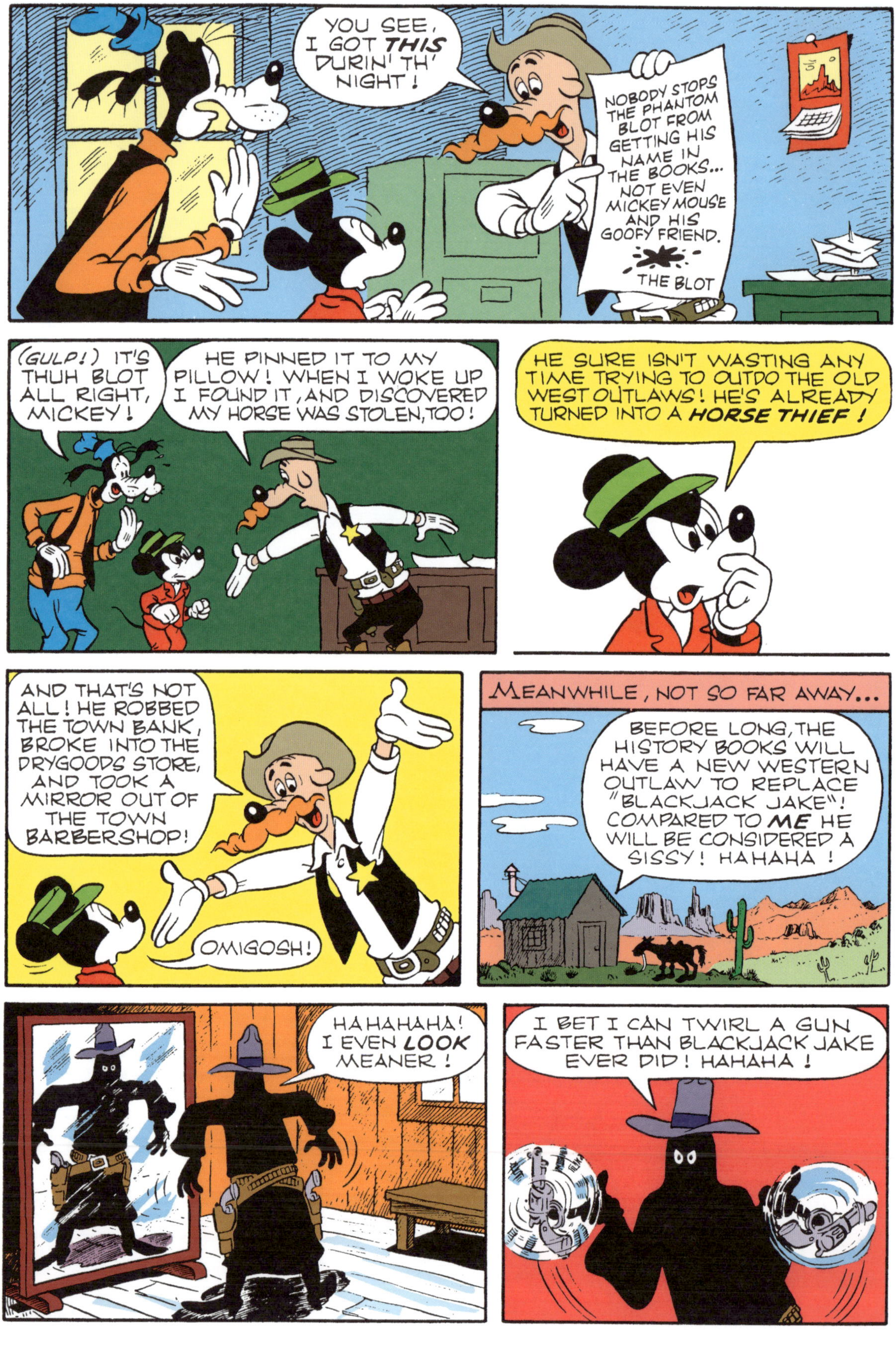
YOU SEE, I GOT THIS DURIN' TH' NIGHT!
NOBODY STOPS THE PHANTOM BLOT FROM GETTING HIS NAME IN THE BOOKS... NOT EVEN MICKEY MOUSE AND HIS GOOFY FRIEND.
THE BLOT
(GULP!) IT'S THUH BLOT ALL RIGHT, MICKEY!
HE PINNED IT TO MY PILLOW! WHEN I WOKE UP I FOUND IT, AND DISCOVERED MY HORSE WAS STOLEN, TOO!
HE SURE ISN'T WASTING ANY TIME TRYING TO OUTDO THE OLD WEST OUTLAWS! HE'S ALREADY TURNED INTO A HORSE THIEF!
AND THAT'S NOT ALL! HE ROBBED THE TOWN BANK, BROKE INTO THE DRYGOODS STORE, AND TOOK A MIRROR OUT OF THE TOWN BARBERSHOP!
OMIGOSH!
MEANWHILE, NOT SO FAR AWAY...
BEFORE LONG, THE HISTORY BOOKS WILL HAVE A NEW WESTERN OUTLAW TO REPLACE "BLACKJACK JAKE"! COMPARED TO ME HE WILL BE CONSIDERED A SISSY! HAHAHA!
HAHAHAHA! I EVEN LOOK MEANER!
I BET I CAN TWIRL A GUN FASTER THAN BLACKJACK JAKE EVER DID! HAHAHA!

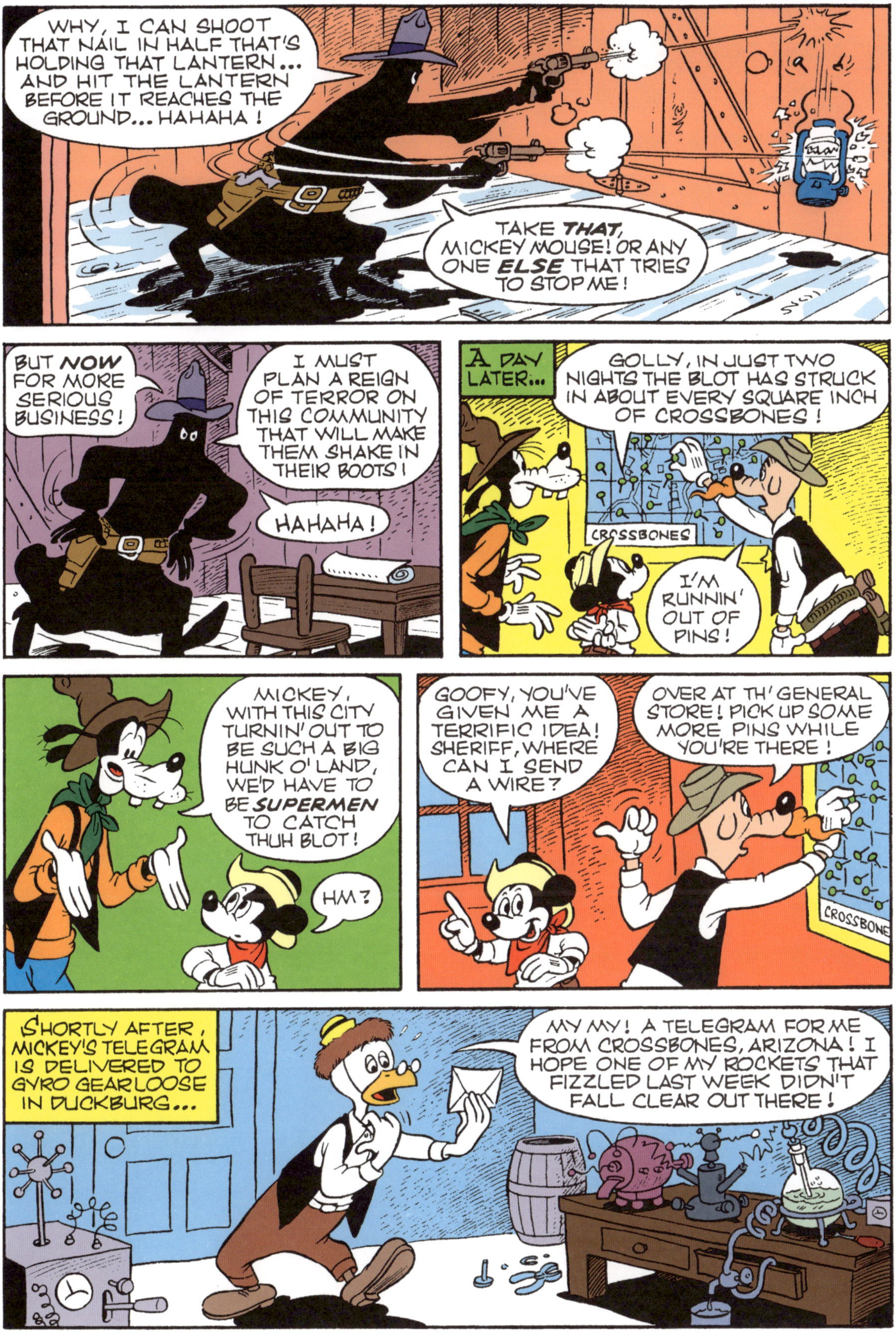
WHY, I CAN SHOOT THAT NAIL IN HALF THAT'S HOLDING THAT LANTERN... AND HIT THE LANTERN BEFORE IT REACHES THE GROUND... HAHAHA!
TAKE THAT, MICKEY MOUSE! OR ANY ONE ELSE THAT TRIES TO STOP ME!
BUT NOW FOR MORE SERIOUS BUSINESS!
I MUST PLAN A REIGN OF TERROR ON THIS COMMUNITY THAT WILL MAKE THEM SHAKE IN THEIR BOOTS!
HAHAHA!
A DAY LATER...
GOLLY, IN JUST TWO NIGHTS THE BLOT HAS STRUCK IN ABOUT EVERY SQUARE INCH OF CROSSBONES!
CROSSBONES
I'M RUNNIN' OUT OF PINS!
MICKEY, WITH THIS CITY TURNIN' OUT TO BE SUCH A BIG HUNK O' LAND, WE'D HAVE TO BE SUPERMEN TO CATCH THUH BLOT!
HM?
GOOFY, YOU'VE GIVEN ME A TERRIFIC IDEA! SHERIFF, WHERE CAN I SEND A WIRE?
OVER AT TH' GENERAL STORE! PICK UP SOME MORE PINS WHILE YOU'RE THERE!
CROSSBONE
SHORTLY AFTER, MICKEY'S TELEGRAM IS DELIVERED TO GYRO GEARLOOSE IN DUCKBURG...
MY MY! A TELEGRAM FOR ME FROM CROSSBONES, ARIZONA! I HOPE ONE OF MY ROCKETS THAT FIZZLED LAST WEEK DIDN'T FALL CLEAR OUT THERE!

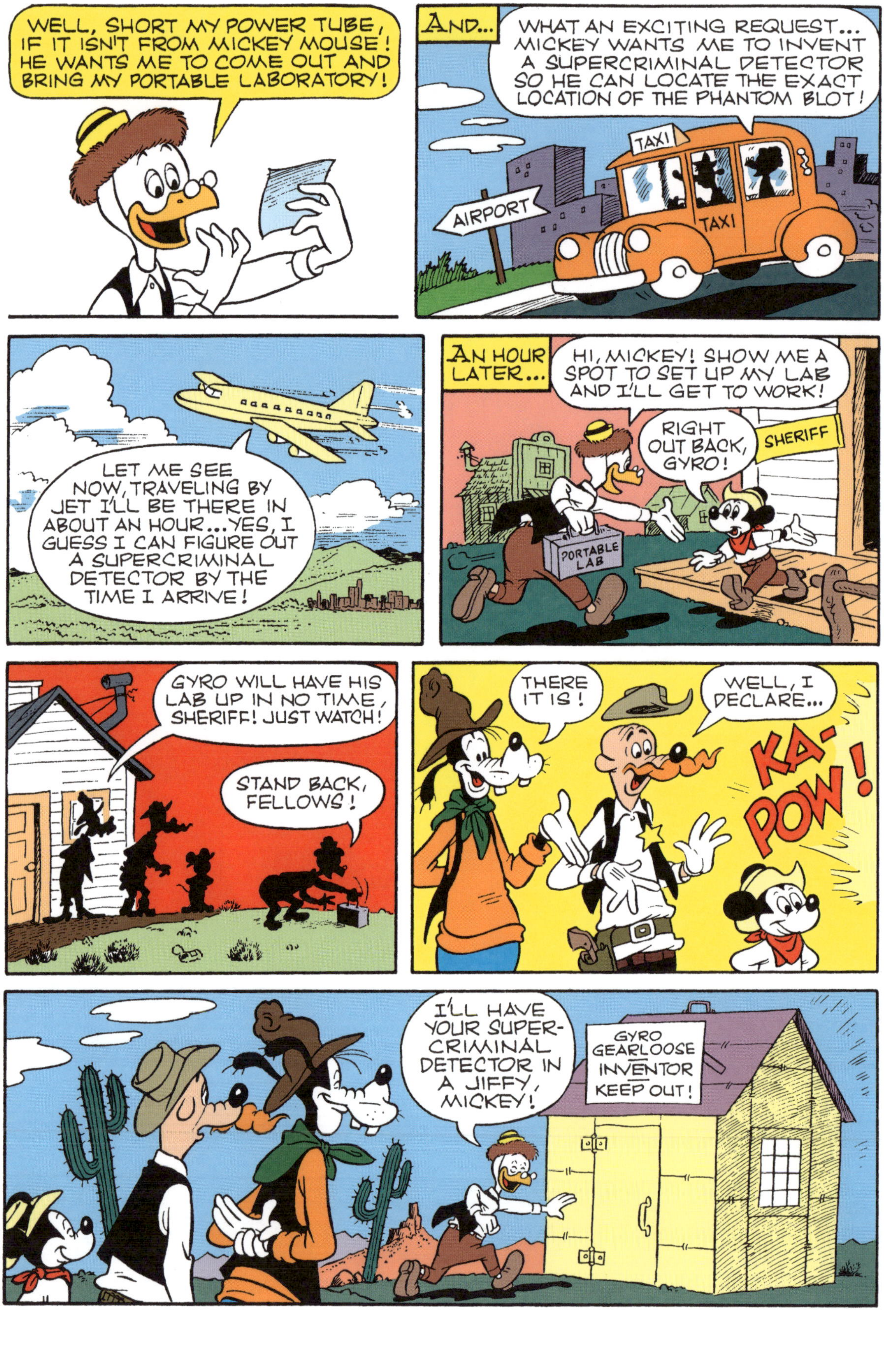
WELL, SHORT MY POWER TUBE, IF IT ISN'T FROM MICKEY MOUSE! HE WANTS ME TO COME OUT AND BRING MY PORTABLE LABORATORY!
AND...
WHAT AN EXCITING REQUEST... MICKEY WANTS ME TO INVENT A SUPERCRIMINAL DETECTOR SO HE CAN LOCATE THE EXACT LOCATION OF THE PHANTOM BLOT!
TAXI
AIRPORT
TAXI
LET ME SEE NOW, TRAVELING BY JET I'LL BE THERE IN ABOUT AN HOUR... YES, I GUESS I CAN FIGURE OUT A SUPERCRIMINAL DETECTOR BY THE TIME I ARRIVE!
AN HOUR LATER...
HI, MICKEY! SHOW ME A SPOT TO SET UP MY LAB AND I'LL GET TO WORK!
RIGHT OUT BACK, GYRO!
SHERIFF
PORTABLE LAB
GYRO WILL HAVE HIS LAB UP IN NO TIME, SHERIFF! JUST WATCH!
STAND BACK, FELLOWS!
THERE IT IS!
WELL, I DECLARE...
KA-POW!
I'LL HAVE YOUR SUPER-CRIMINAL DETECTOR IN A JIFFY, MICKEY!
GYRO GEARLOOSE INVENTOR KEEP OUT!

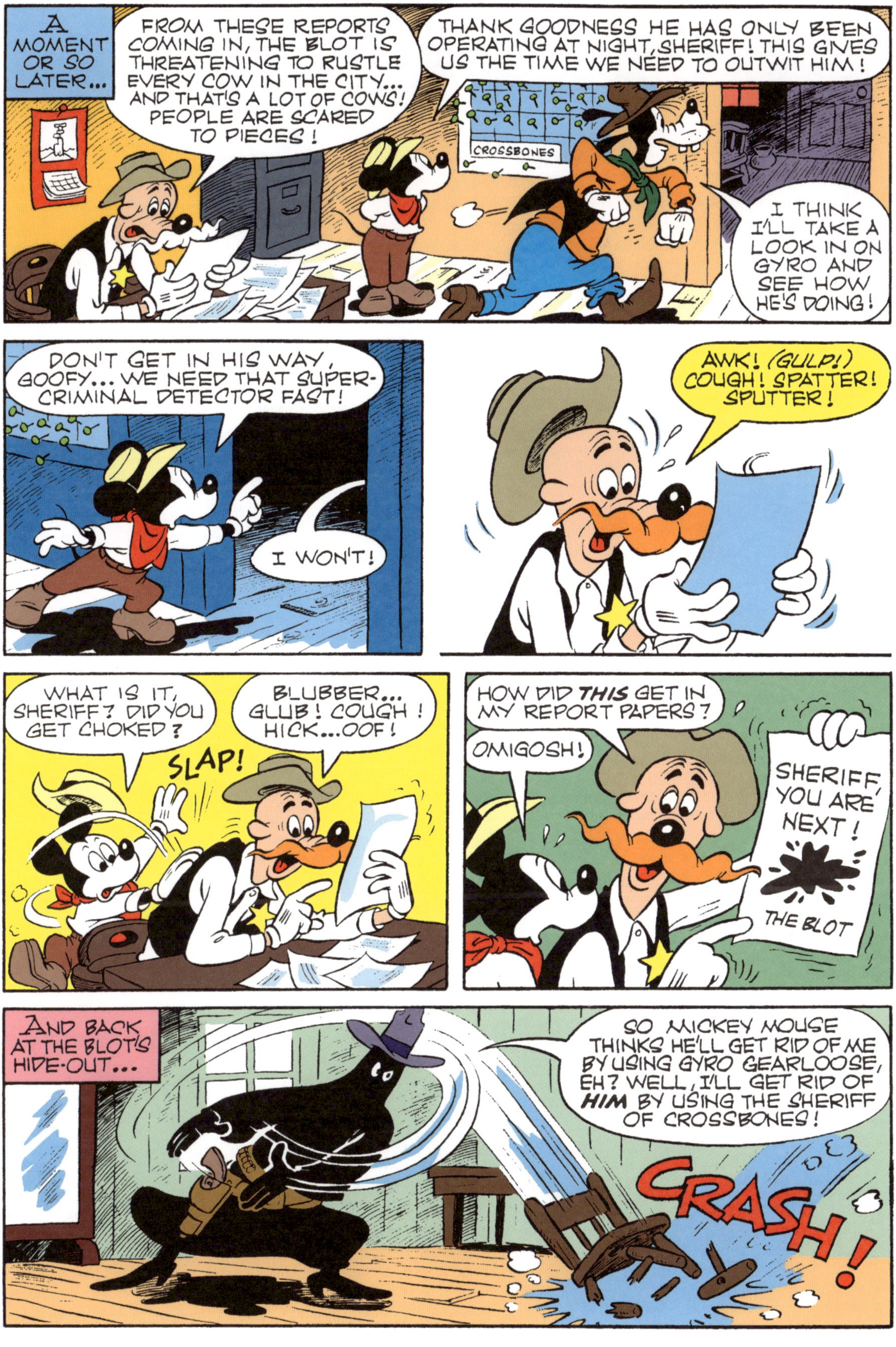
A MOMENT OR SO LATER...
FROM THESE REPORTS COMING IN, THE BLOT IS THREATENING TO RUSTLE EVERY COW IN THE CITY... AND THAT'S A LOT OF COWS! PEOPLE ARE SCARED TO PIECES!
THANK GOODNESS HE HAS ONLY BEEN OPERATING AT NIGHT, SHERIFF! THIS GIVES US THE TIME WE NEED TO OUTWIT HIM!
CROSSBONES
I THINK I'LL TAKE A LOOK IN ON GYRO AND SEE HOW HE'S DOING!
DON'T GET IN HIS WAY, GOOFY... WE NEED THAT SUPER-CRIMINAL DETECTOR FAST!
I WON'T!
AWK! (GULP!) COUGH! SPATTER! SPUTTER!
WHAT IS IT, SHERIFF? DID YOU GET CHOKED?
BLUBBER... GLUB! COUGH! HICK...OOF!
SLAP!
HOW DID THIS GET IN MY REPORT PAPERS?
OMIGOSH!
SHERIFF, YOU ARE NEXT!
THE BLOT
AND BACK AT THE BLOT'S HIDE-OUT...
SO MICKEY MOUSE THINKS HE'LL GET RID OF ME BY USING GYRO GEARLOOSE, EH? WELL, I'LL GET RID OF HIM BY USING THE SHERIFF OF CROSSBONES!
CRASH!

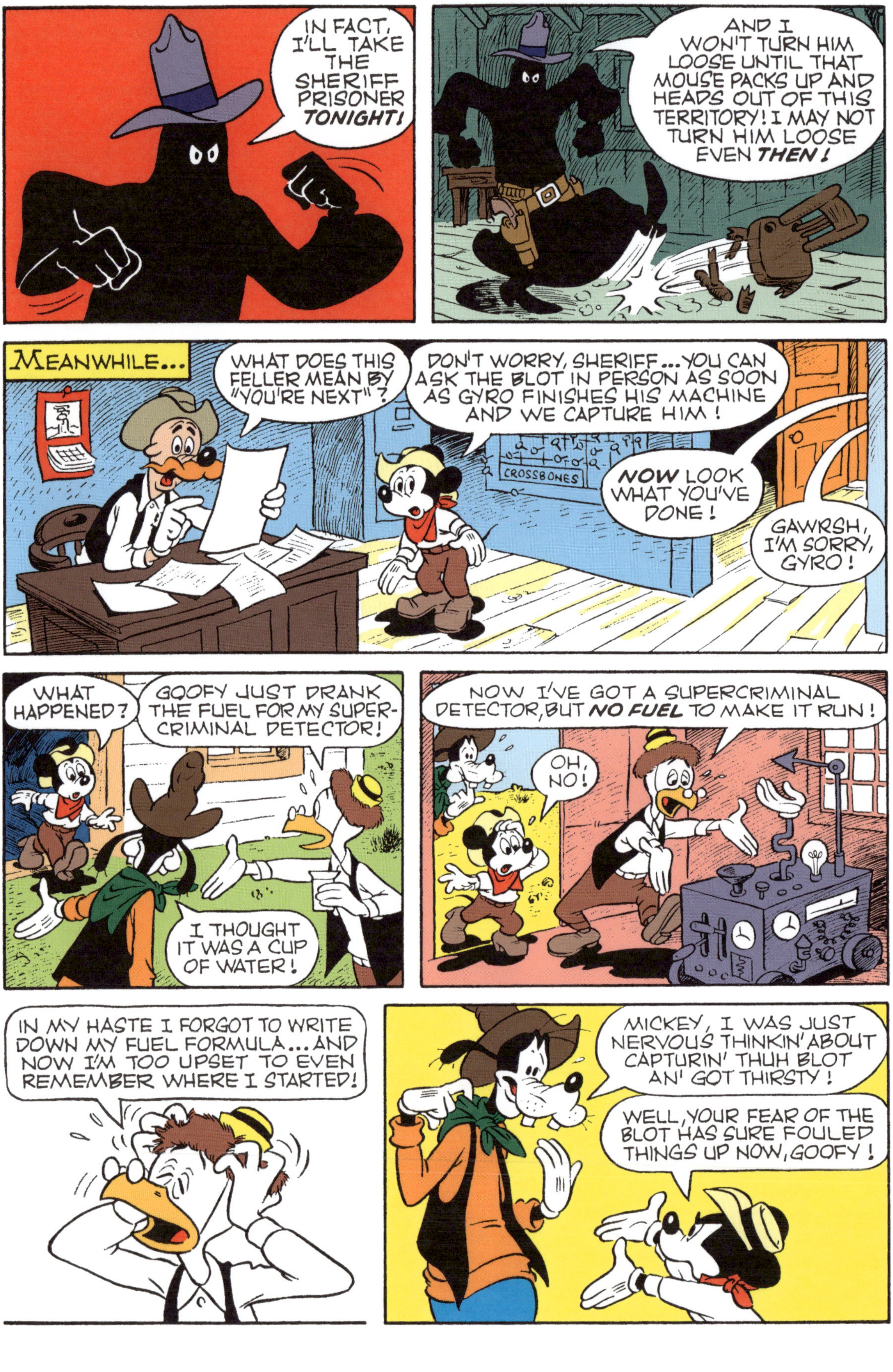
IN FACT, I'LL TAKE THE SHERIFF PRISONER TONIGHT!
AND I WON'T TURN HIM LOOSE UNTIL THAT MOUSE PACKS UP AND HEADS OUT OF THIS TERRITORY! I MAY NOT TURN HIM LOOSE EVEN THEN!
MEANWHILE...
WHAT DOES THIS FELLER MEAN BY "YOU'RE NEXT"?
DON'T WORRY, SHERIFF... YOU CAN ASK THE BLOT IN PERSON AS SOON AS GYRO FINISHES HIS MACHINE AND WE CAPTURE HIM!
CROSSBONES
NOW LOOK WHAT YOU'VE DONE!
GAWRSH, I'M SORRY, GYRO!
WHAT HAPPENED?
GOOFY JUST DRANK THE FUEL FOR MY SUPER-CRIMINAL DETECTOR!
I THOUGHT IT WAS A CUP OF WATER!
NOW I'VE GOT A SUPERCRIMINAL DETECTOR, BUT NO FUEL TO MAKE IT RUN!
OH NO!
IN MY HASTE I FORGOT TO WRITE DOWN MY FUEL FORMULA... AND NOW I'M TOO UPSET TO EVEN REMEMBER WHERE I STARTED!
MICKEY, I WAS JUST NERVOUS THINKIN' ABOUT CAPTURIN' THUH BLOT AN' GOT THIRSTY!
WELL, YOUR FEAR OF THE BLOT HAS SURE FOULED THINGS UP NOW, GOOFY!

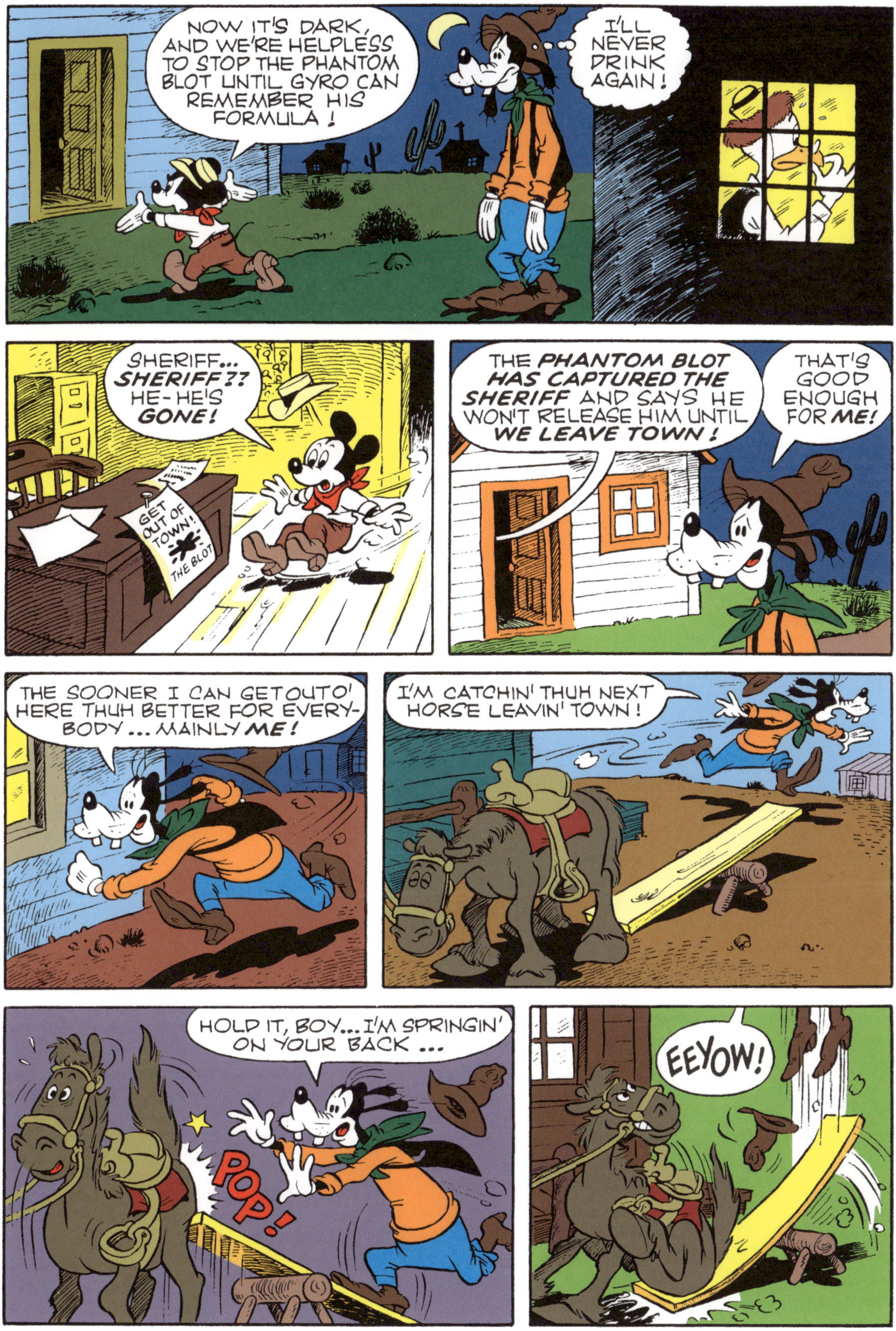

NOW IT'S DARK, AND WE'RE HELPLESS TO STOP THE PHANTOM BLOT UNTIL GYRO CAN REMEMBER HIS FORMULA !
I'LL NEVER DRINK AGAIN !
SHERIFF... SHERIFF?? HE- HE'S GONE!
GET OUT OF TOWN! THE BLOT
THE PHANTOM BLOT HAS CAPTURED THE SHERIFF AND SAYS HE WON'T RELEASE HIM UNTIL WE LEAVE TOWN !
THAT'S GOOD ENOUGH FOR ME!
THE SOONER I CAN GET OUTO' HERE THUH BETTER FOR EVERY-BODY ... MAINLY ME!
I'M CATCHIN' THUH NEXT HORSE LEAVIN' TOWN !
HOLD IT, BOY... I'M SPRINGIN' ON YOUR BACK ...
POP!
EEYOW!

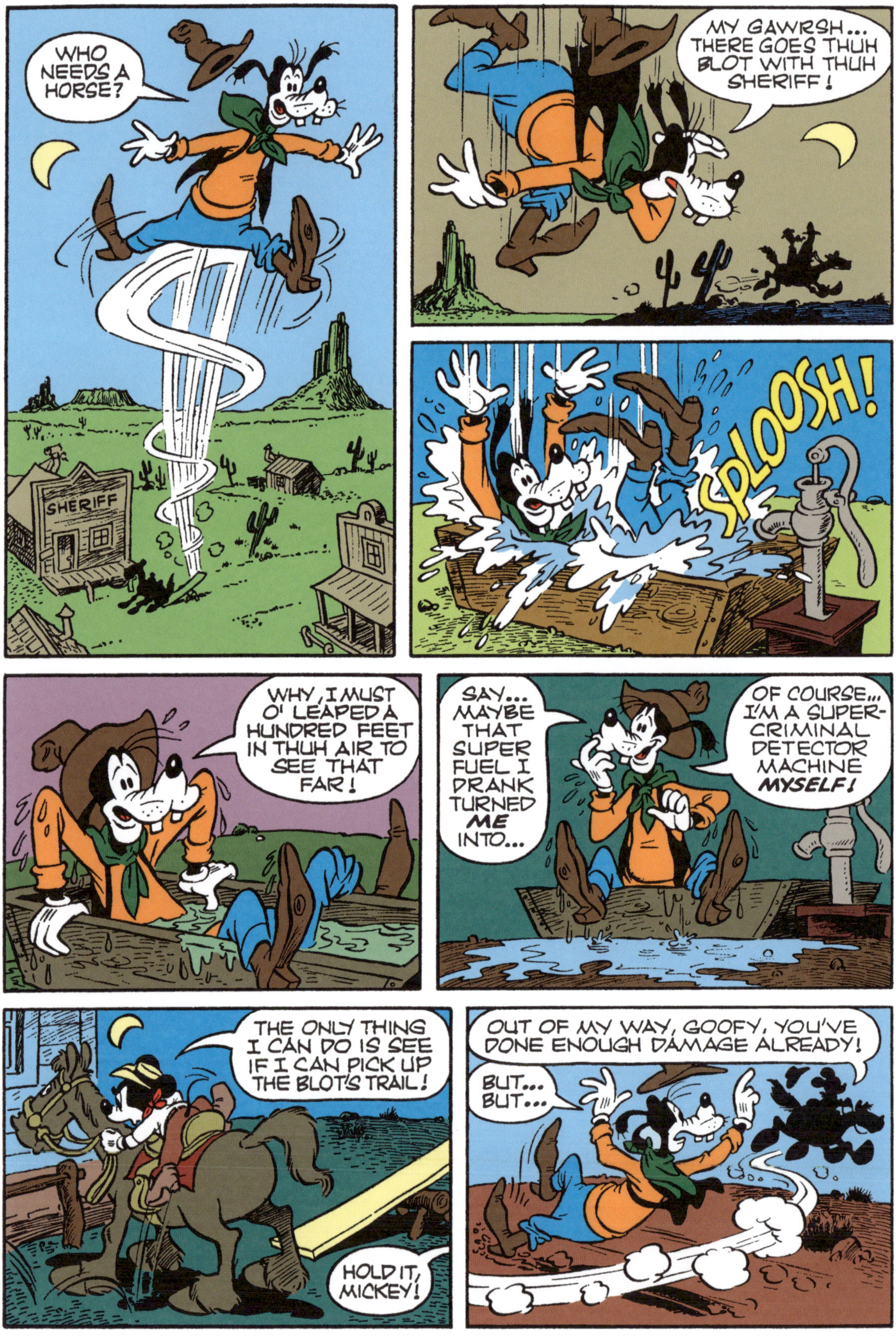
WHO NEEDS A HORSE?
MY GAWRSH... THERE GOES THUH BLOT WITH THUH SHERIFF!
SHERIFF
SPLOOSH!
WHY, I MUST O' LEAPED A HUNDRED FEET IN THUH AIR TO SEE THAT FAR!
SAY... MAYBE THAT SUPER FUEL I DRANK TURNED ME INTO...
OF COURSE... I'M A SUPER-CRIMINAL DETECTOR MACHINE MYSELF!
THE ONLY THING I CAN DO IS SEE IF I CAN PICK UP THE BLOT'S TRAIL!
HOLD IT, MICKEY!
OUT OF MY WAY, GOOFY, YOU'VE DONE ENOUGH DAMAGE ALREADY!
BUT... BUT...

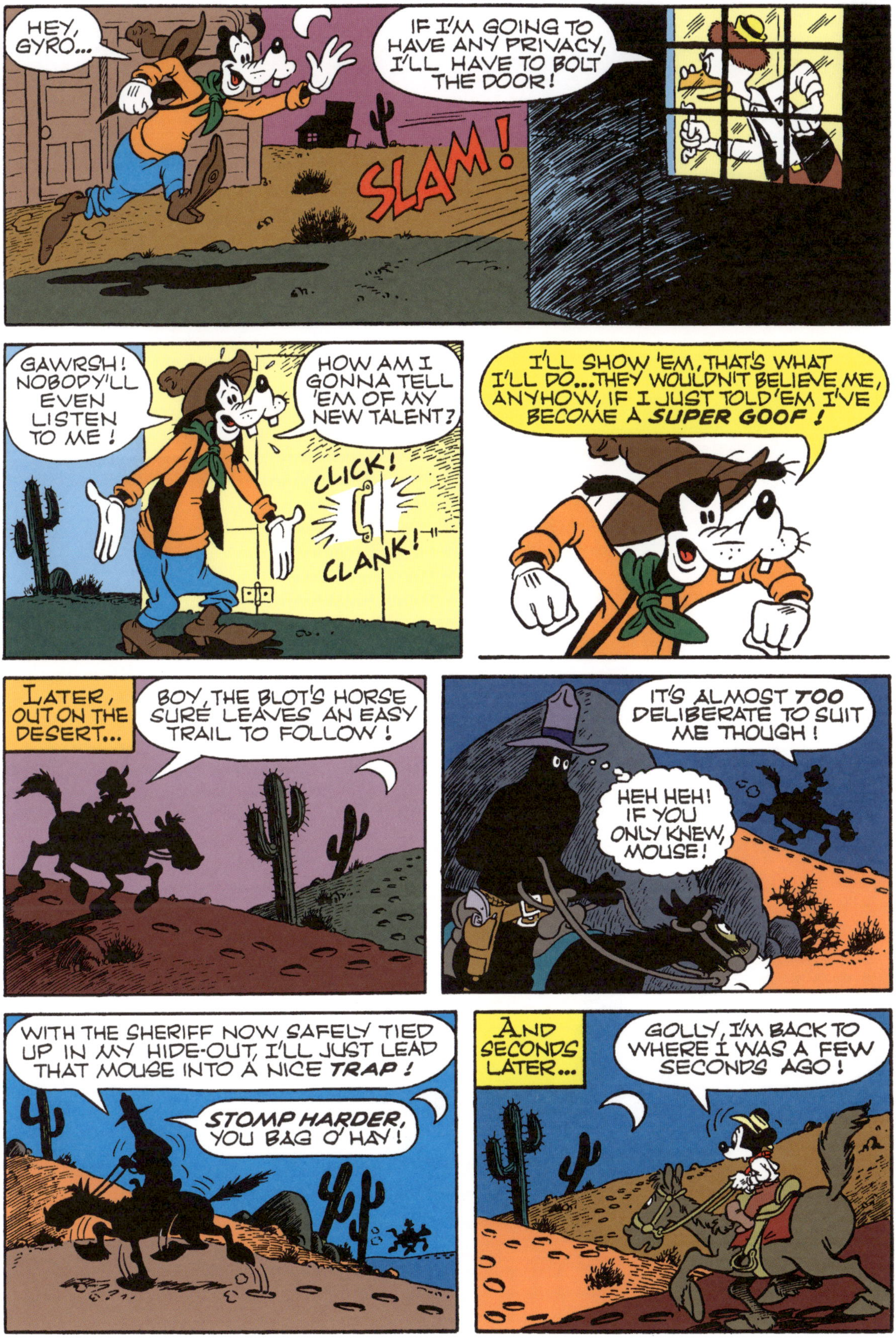
HEY, GYRO...
IF I'M GOING TO HAVE ANY PRIVACY, I'LL HAVE TO BOLT THE DOOR!
SLAM!
GAWRSH! NOBODY'LL EVEN LISTEN TO ME!
HOW AM I GONNA TELL 'EM OF MY NEW TALENT?
CLICK!
CLANK!
I'LL SHOW 'EM, THAT'S WHAT I'LL DO...THEY WOULDN'T BELIEVE ME, ANYHOW, IF I JUST TOLD 'EM I'VE BECOME A **SUPER GOOF!**
LATER, OUT ON THE DESERT...
BOY, THE BLOT'S HORSE SURE LEAVES AN EASY TRAIL TO FOLLOW!
IT'S ALMOST **TOO** DELIBERATE TO SUIT ME THOUGH!
HEH HEH! IF YOU ONLY KNEW, MOUSE!
WITH THE SHERIFF NOW SAFELY TIED UP IN MY HIDE-OUT, I'LL JUST LEAD THAT MOUSE INTO A NICE **TRAP!**
STOMP HARDER, YOU BAG O' HAY!
AND SECONDS LATER...
GOLLY, I'M BACK TO WHERE I WAS A FEW SECONDS AGO!

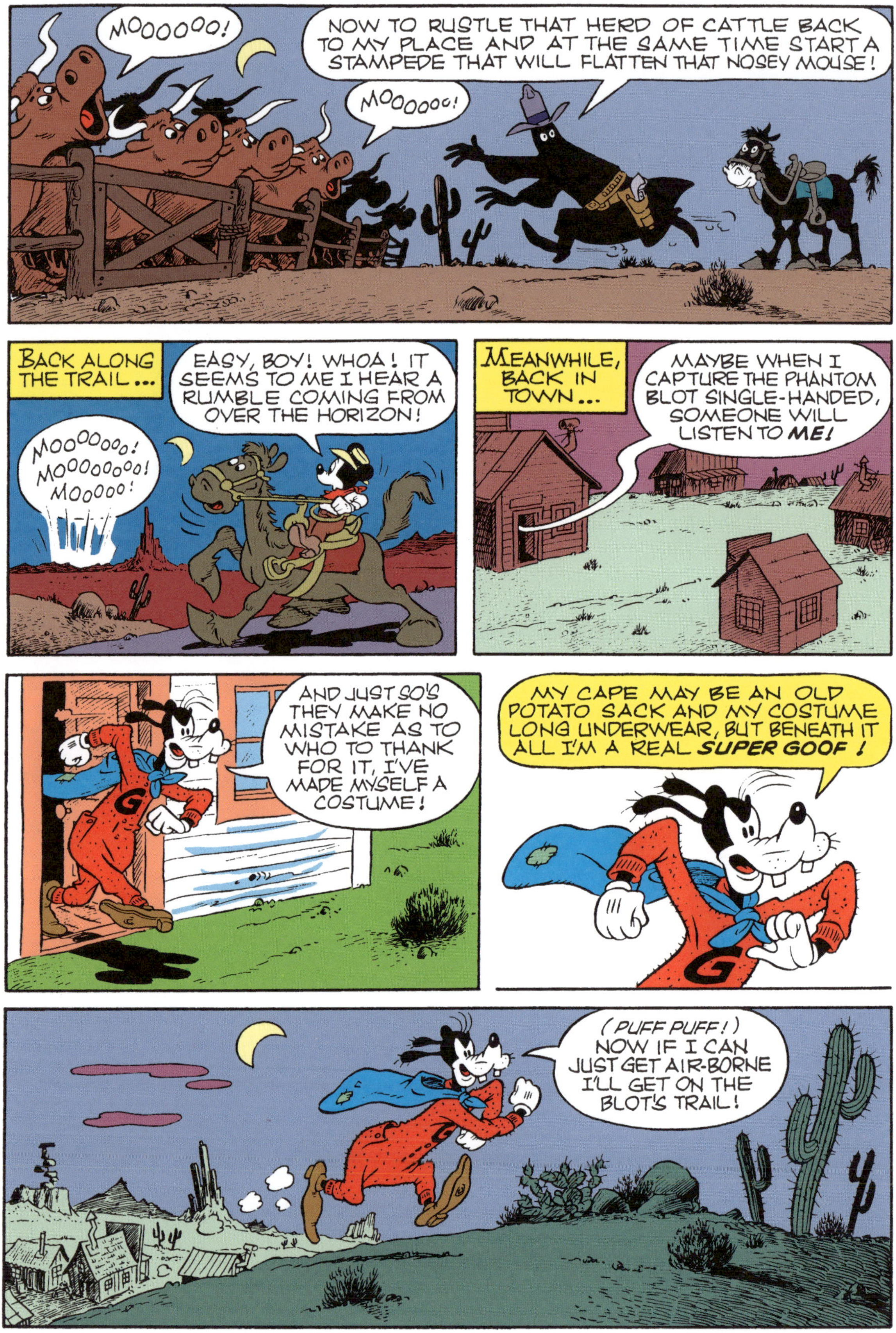
MOOOOOO!
NOW TO RUSTLE THAT HERD OF CATTLE BACK TO MY PLACE AND AT THE SAME TIME START A STAMPEDE THAT WILL FLATTEN THAT NOSEY MOUSE!
MOOOOOO!
BACK ALONG THE TRAIL...
EASY, BOY! WHOA! IT SEEMS TO ME I HEAR A RUMBLE COMING FROM OVER THE HORIZON!
MOOOOOOO! MOOOOOOOOO! MOOOOOO!
MEANWHILE, BACK IN TOWN...
MAYBE WHEN I CAPTURE THE PHANTOM BLOT SINGLE-HANDED, SOMEONE WILL LISTEN TO ME!
AND JUST SO'S THEY MAKE NO MISTAKE AS TO WHO TO THANK FOR IT, I'VE MADE MYSELF A COSTUME!
MY CAPE MAY BE AN OLD POTATO SACK AND MY COSTUME LONG UNDERWEAR, BUT BENEATH IT ALL I'M A REAL SUPER GOOF!
(PUFF PUFF!) NOW IF I CAN JUST GET AIR-BORNE I'LL GET ON THE BLOT'S TRAIL!

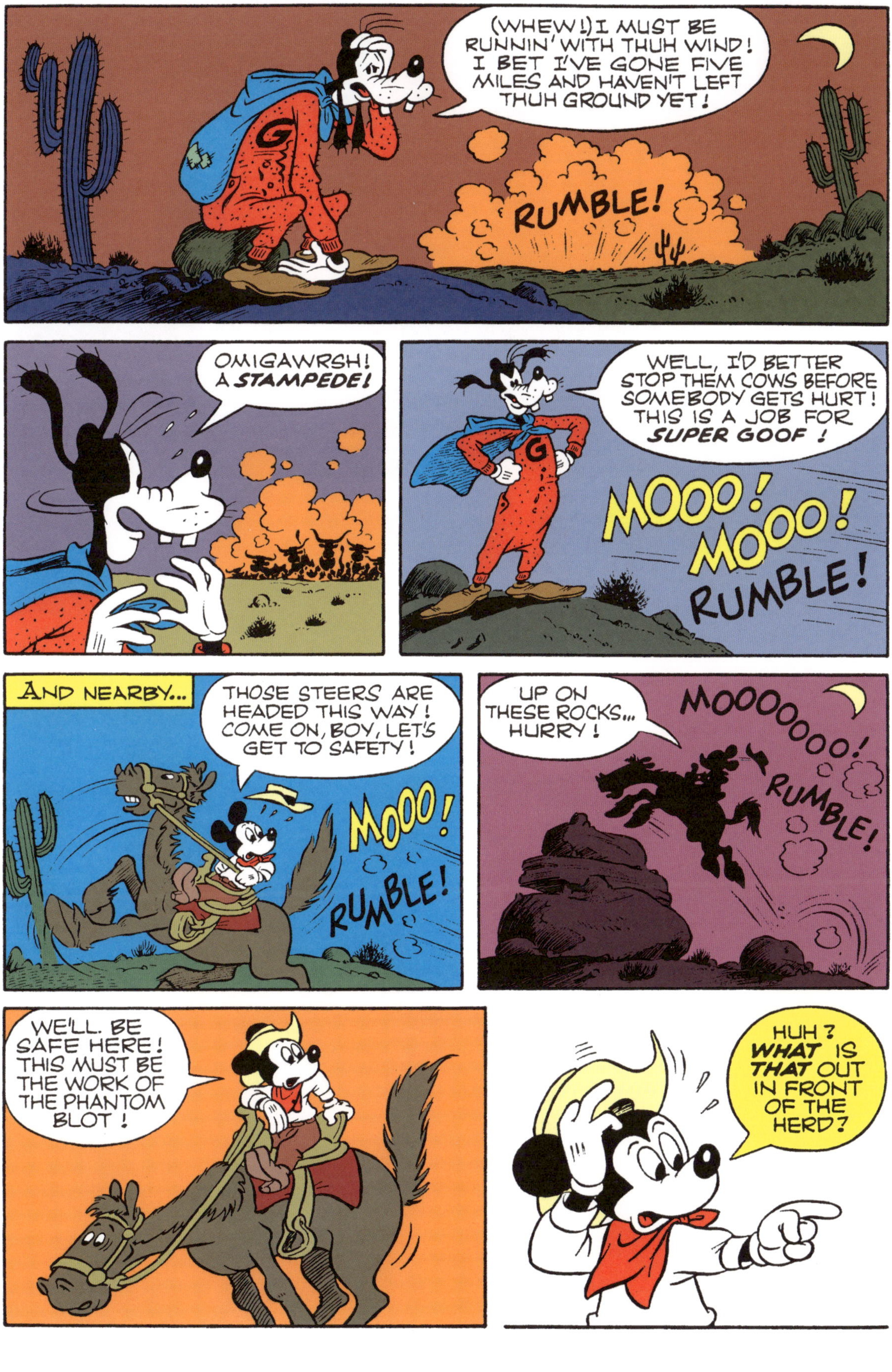
(WHEW!) I MUST BE RUNNIN' WITH THUH WIND! I BET I'VE GONE FIVE MILES AND HAVEN'T LEFT THUH GROUND YET!
RUMBLE!
OMIGAWRSH! A **STAMPEDE!**
WELL, I'D BETTER STOP THEM COWS BEFORE SOMEBODY GETS HURT! THIS IS A JOB FOR **SUPER GOOF!**
MOOO! MOOO!
RUMBLE!
AND NEARBY...
THOSE STEERS ARE HEADED THIS WAY! COME ON, BOY, LET'S GET TO SAFETY!
MOOO!
RUMBLE!
UP ON THESE ROCKS... HURRY!
MOOOOOOOO!
RUMBLE!
WE'LL. BE SAFE HERE! THIS MUST BE THE WORK OF THE PHANTOM BLOT!
HUH? **WHAT** IS **THAT** OUT IN FRONT OF THE HERD?

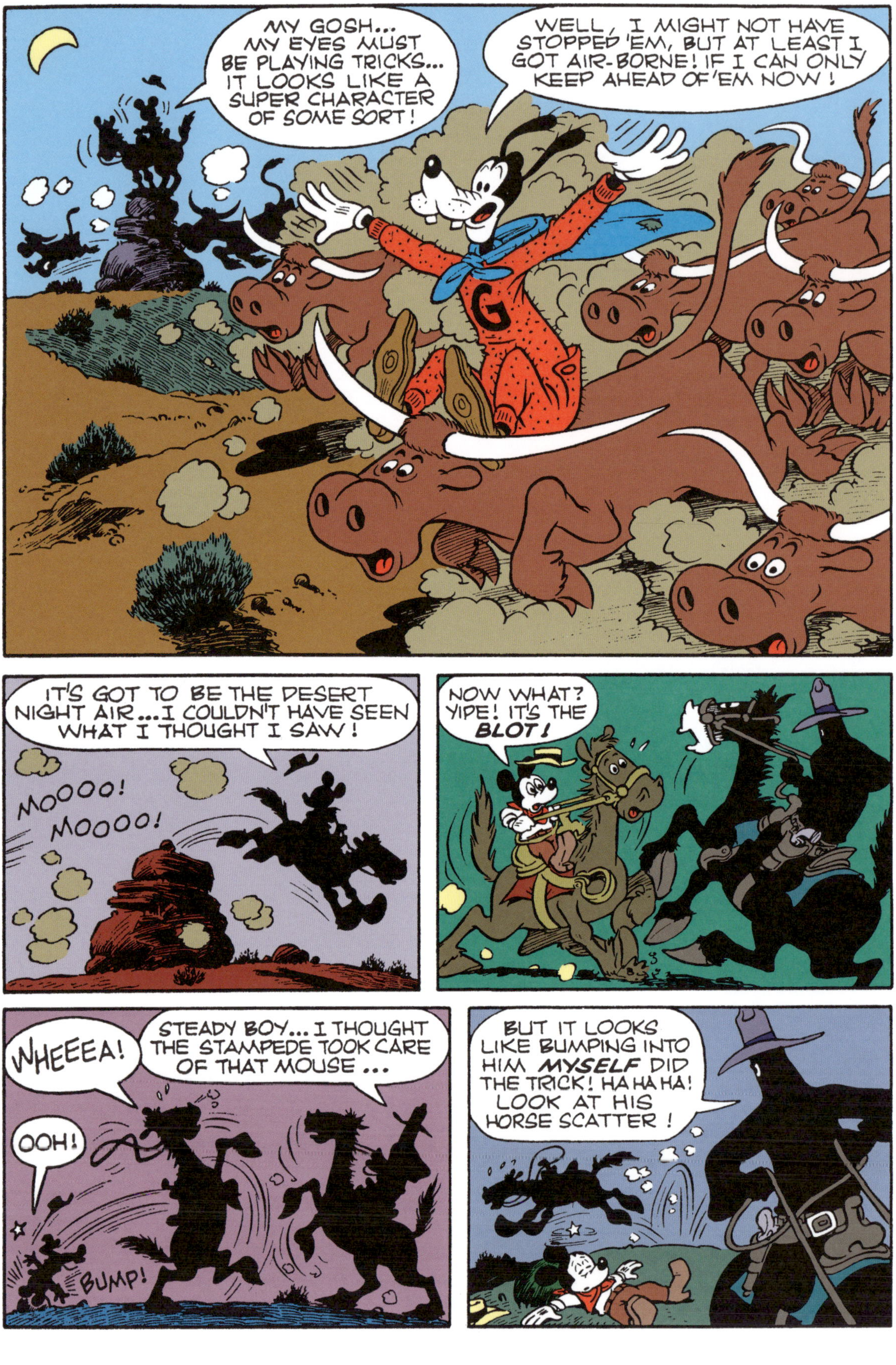
MY GOSH... MY EYES MUST BE PLAYING TRICKS... IT LOOKS LIKE A SUPER CHARACTER OF SOME SORT!
WELL, I MIGHT NOT HAVE STOPPED 'EM, BUT AT LEAST I GOT AIR-BORNE! IF I CAN ONLY KEEP AHEAD OF 'EM NOW!
IT'S GOT TO BE THE DESERT NIGHT AIR... I COULDN'T HAVE SEEN WHAT I THOUGHT I SAW!
MOOOO! MOOOO!
NOW WHAT? YIPE! IT'S THE BLOT!
WHEEEA!
STEADY BOY... I THOUGHT THE STAMPEDE TOOK CARE OF THAT MOUSE...
OOH!
BUMP!
BUT IT LOOKS LIKE BUMPING INTO HIM MYSELF DID THE TRICK! HA HA HA! LOOK AT HIS HORSE SCATTER!

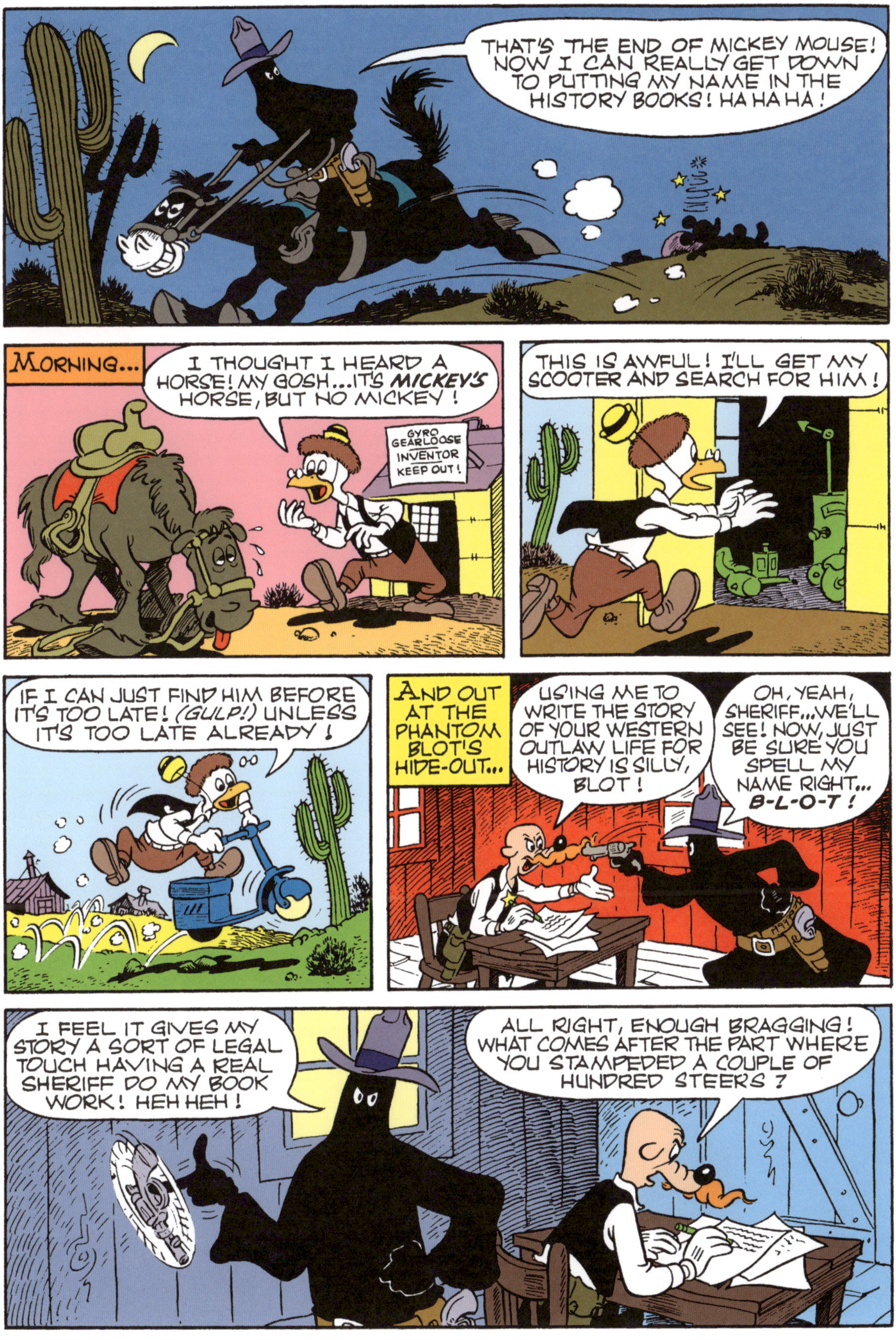
THAT'S THE END OF MICKEY MOUSE! NOW I CAN REALLY GET DOWN TO PUTTING MY NAME IN THE HISTORY BOOKS! HA HA HA!
MORNING...
I THOUGHT I HEARD A HORSE! MY GOSH...IT'S MICKEY'S HORSE, BUT NO MICKEY!
GYRO GEARLOOSE INVENTOR KEEP OUT!
THIS IS AWFUL! I'LL GET MY SCOOTER AND SEARCH FOR HIM!
IF I CAN JUST FIND HIM BEFORE IT'S TOO LATE! (GULP!) UNLESS IT'S TOO LATE ALREADY!
AND OUT AT THE PHANTOM BLOT'S HIDE-OUT...
USING ME TO WRITE THE STORY OF YOUR WESTERN OUTLAW LIFE FOR HISTORY IS SILLY, BLOT!
OH, YEAH, SHERIFF...WE'LL SEE! NOW, JUST BE SURE YOU SPELL MY NAME RIGHT... B-L-O-T!
I FEEL IT GIVES MY STORY A SORT OF LEGAL TOUCH HAVING A REAL SHERIFF DO MY BOOK WORK! HEH HEH!
ALL RIGHT, ENOUGH BRAGGING! WHAT COMES AFTER THE PART WHERE YOU STAMPEDED A COUPLE OF HUNDRED STEERS?

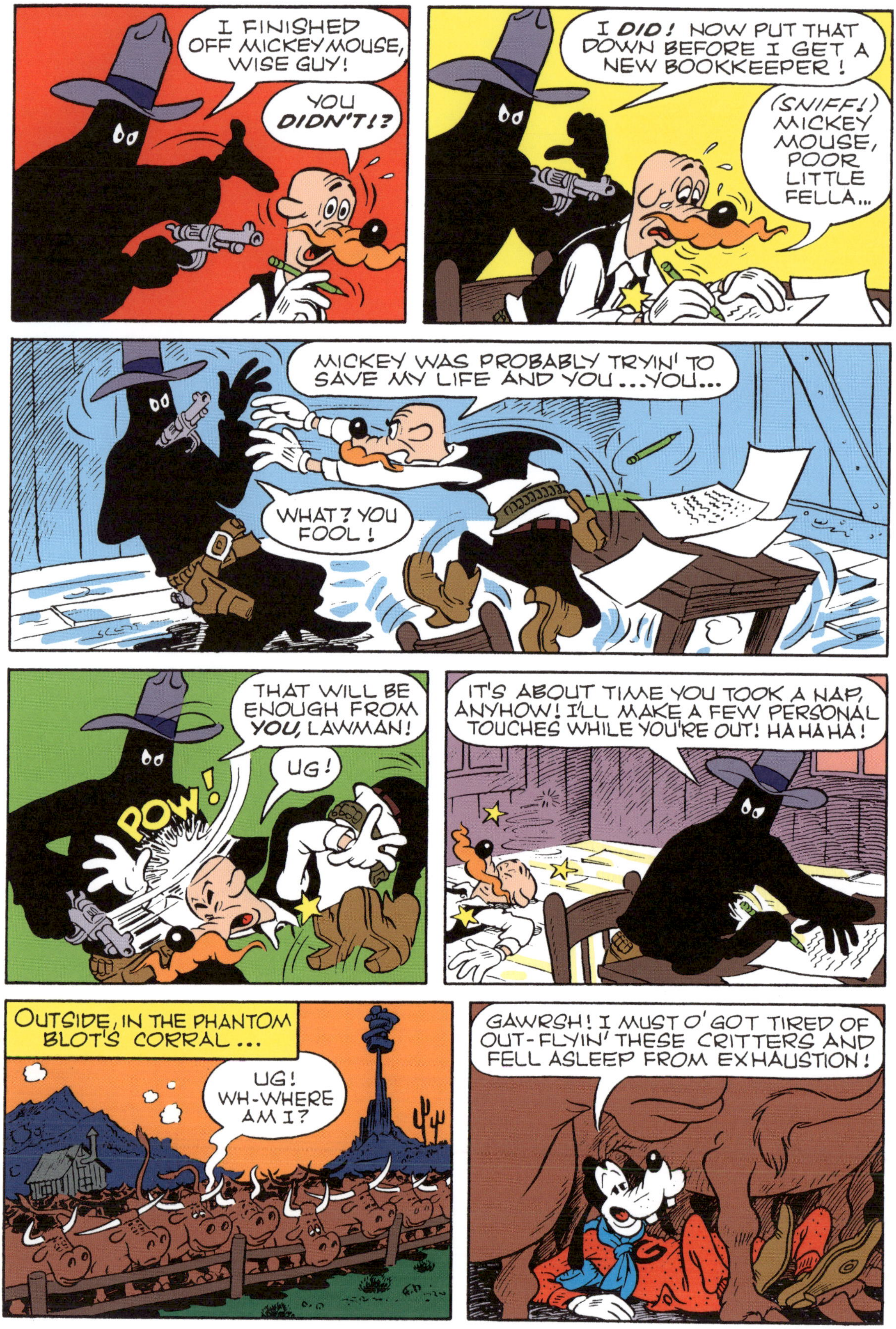
I FINISHED OFF MICKEY MOUSE, WISE GUY!
YOU DIDN'T!?
I DID! NOW PUT THAT DOWN BEFORE I GET A NEW BOOKKEEPER!
(SNIFF!) MICKEY MOUSE, POOR LITTLE FELLA...
MICKEY WAS PROBABLY TRYIN' TO SAVE MY LIFE AND YOU ...YOU...
WHAT? YOU FOOL!
THAT WILL BE ENOUGH FROM YOU, LAWMAN!
POW!
UG!
IT'S ABOUT TIME YOU TOOK A NAP, ANYHOW! I'LL MAKE A FEW PERSONAL TOUCHES WHILE YOU'RE OUT! HA HA HA!
OUTSIDE, IN THE PHANTOM BLOT'S CORRAL...
UG! WH-WHERE AM I?
GAWRSH! I MUST O' GOT TIRED OF OUT-FLYIN' THESE CRITTERS AND FELL ASLEEP FROM EXHAUSTION!

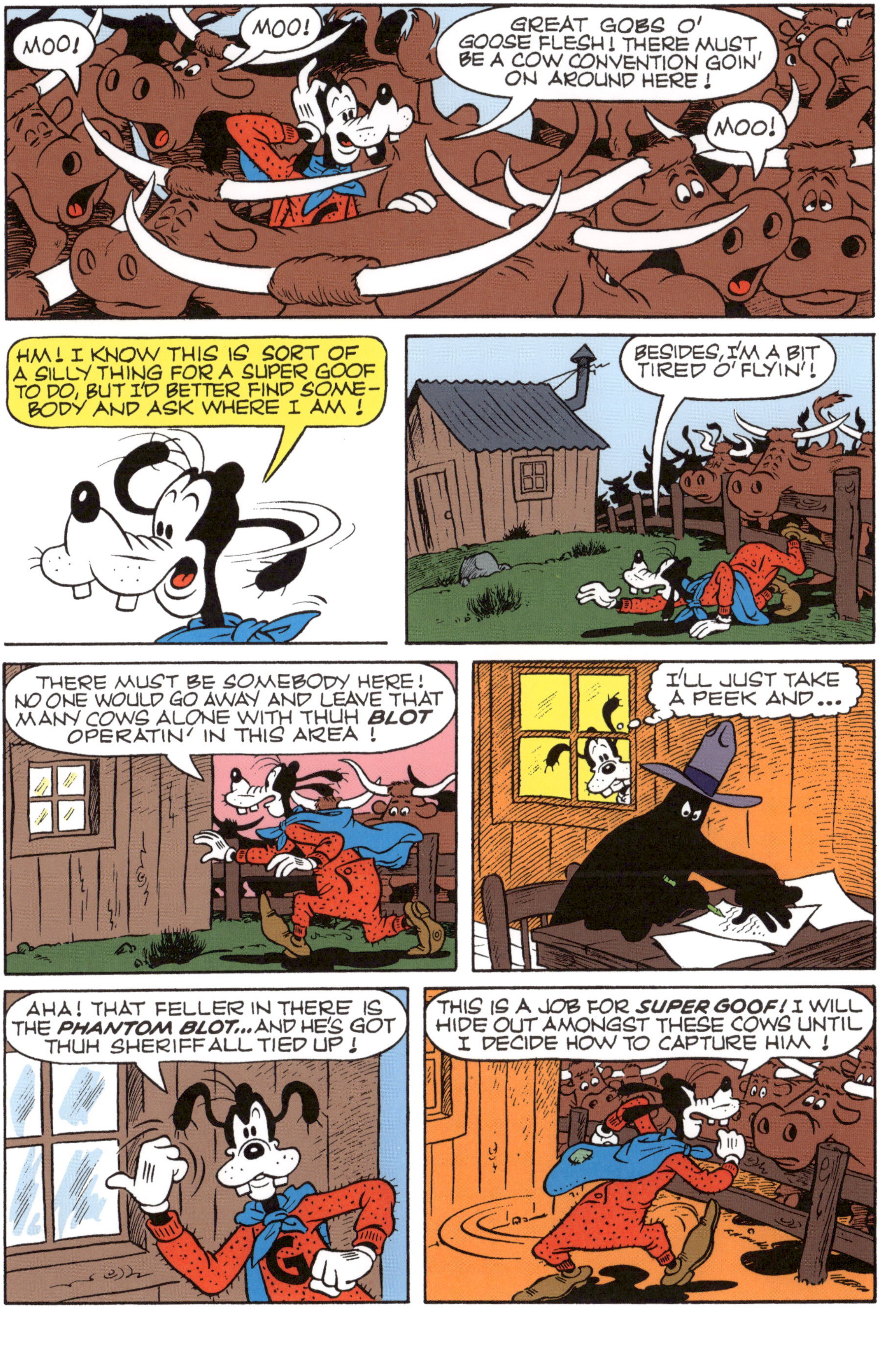
MOO!
MOO!
GREAT GOBS O' GOOSE FLESH! THERE MUST BE A COW CONVENTION GOIN' ON AROUND HERE!
MOO!
HM! I KNOW THIS IS SORT OF A SILLY THING FOR A SUPER GOOF TO DO, BUT I'D BETTER FIND SOMEBODY AND ASK WHERE I AM!
BESIDES, I'M A BIT TIRED O' FLYIN'!
THERE MUST BE SOMEBODY HERE! NO ONE WOULD GO AWAY AND LEAVE THAT MANY COWS ALONE WITH THUH *BLOT* OPERATIN' IN THIS AREA!
I'LL JUST TAKE A PEEK AND...
AHA! THAT FELLER IN THERE IS THE *PHANTOM BLOT*... AND HE'S GOT THUH SHERIFF ALL TIED UP!
THIS IS A JOB FOR *SUPER GOOF!* I WILL HIDE OUT AMONGST THESE COWS UNTIL I DECIDE HOW TO CAPTURE HIM!

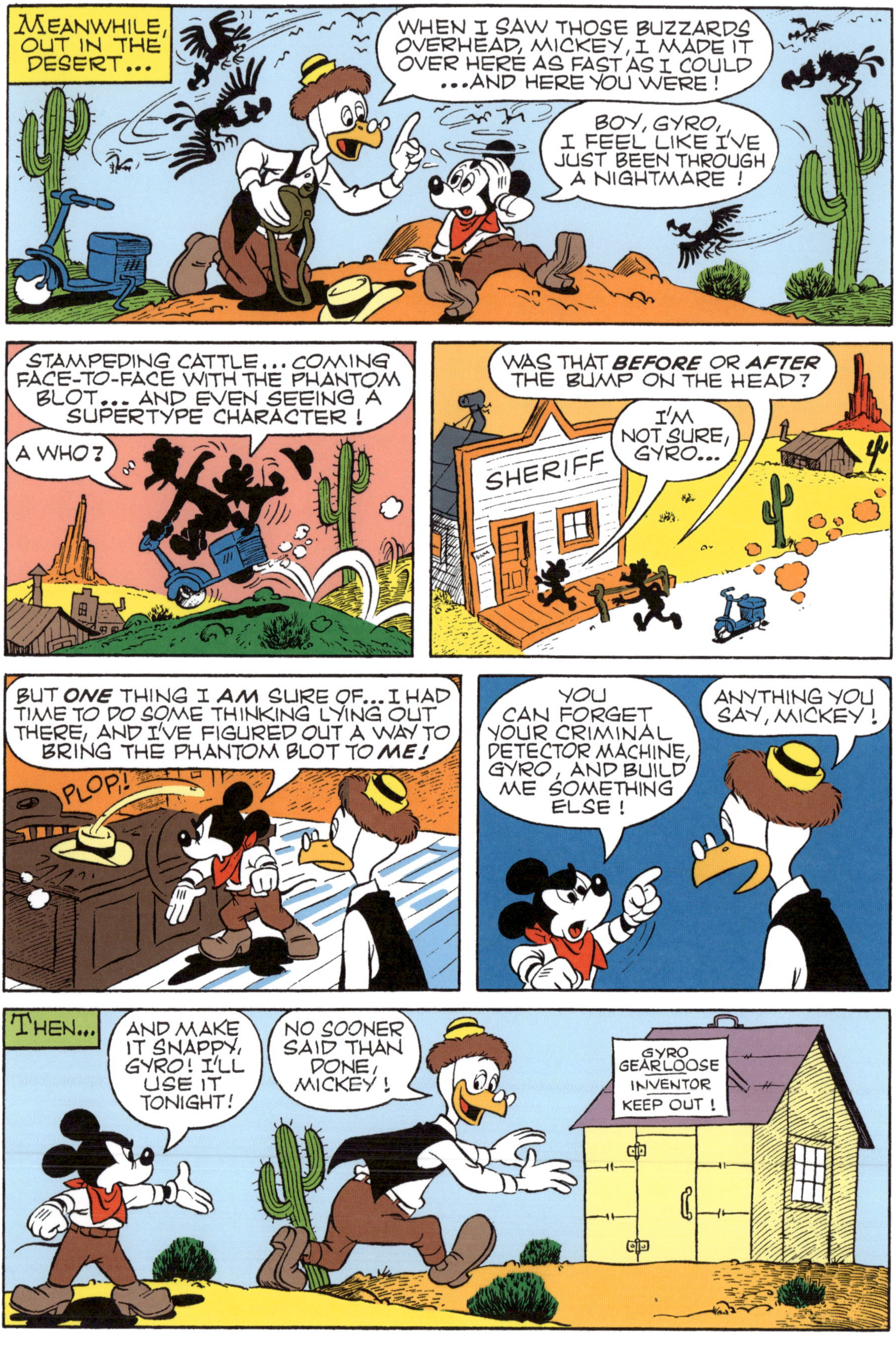
MEANWHILE, OUT IN THE DESERT...
WHEN I SAW THOSE BUZZARDS OVERHEAD, MICKEY, I MADE IT OVER HERE AS FAST AS I COULD ...AND HERE YOU WERE!
BOY, GYRO, I FEEL LIKE I'VE JUST BEEN THROUGH A NIGHTMARE!
STAMPEDING CATTLE... COMING FACE-TO-FACE WITH THE PHANTOM BLOT... AND EVEN SEEING A SUPERTYPE CHARACTER!
A WHO?
WAS THAT BEFORE OR AFTER THE BUMP ON THE HEAD?
I'M NOT SURE, GYRO...
SHERIFF
BUT ONE THING I AM SURE OF... I HAD TIME TO DO SOME THINKING LYING OUT THERE, AND I'VE FIGURED OUT A WAY TO BRING THE PHANTOM BLOT TO ME!
PLOP!
YOU CAN FORGET YOUR CRIMINAL DETECTOR MACHINE, GYRO, AND BUILD ME SOMETHING ELSE!
ANYTHING YOU SAY, MICKEY!
THEN...
AND MAKE IT SNAPPY, GYRO! I'LL USE IT TONIGHT!
NO SOONER SAID THAN DONE, MICKEY!
GYRO GEARLOOSE INVENTOR KEEP OUT!

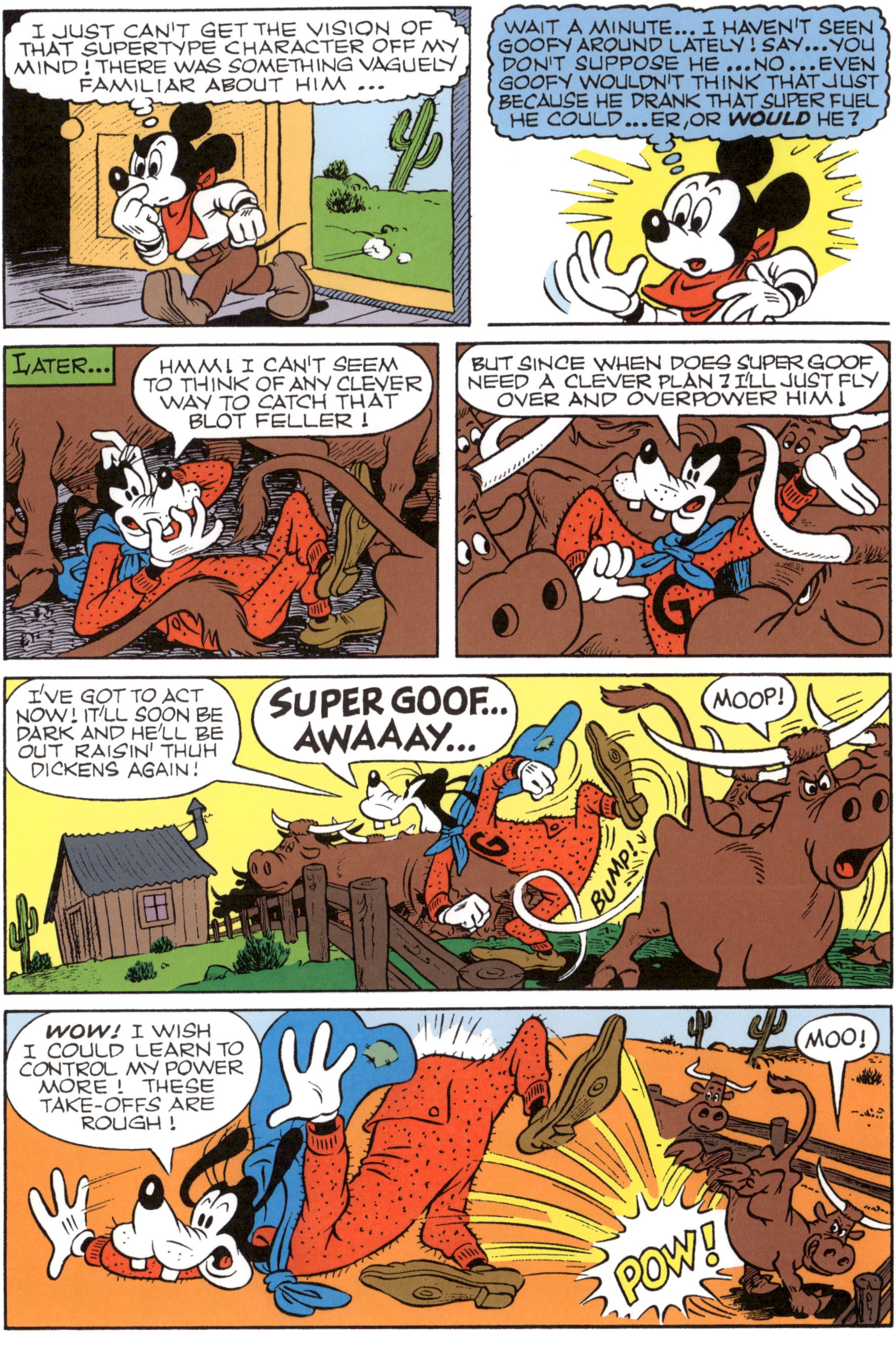
I JUST CAN'T GET THE VISION OF THAT SUPERTYPE CHARACTER OFF MY MIND! THERE WAS SOMETHING VAGUELY FAMILIAR ABOUT HIM ...
WAIT A MINUTE... I HAVEN'T SEEN GOOFY AROUND LATELY! SAY... YOU DON'T SUPPOSE HE ...NO ...EVEN GOOFY WOULDN'T THINK THAT JUST BECAUSE HE DRANK THAT SUPER FUEL HE COULD...ER, OR WOULD HE?
LATER...
HMM! I CAN'T SEEM TO THINK OF ANY CLEVER WAY TO CATCH THAT BLOT FELLER!
BUT SINCE WHEN DOES SUPER GOOF NEED A CLEVER PLAN? I'LL JUST FLY OVER AND OVERPOWER HIM!
I'VE GOT TO ACT NOW! IT'LL SOON BE DARK AND HE'LL BE OUT RAISIN' THUH DICKENS AGAIN!
SUPER GOOF... AWAAAY...
MOOP!
BUMP!
WOW! I WISH I COULD LEARN TO CONTROL MY POWER MORE! THESE TAKE-OFFS ARE ROUGH!
MOO!
POW!

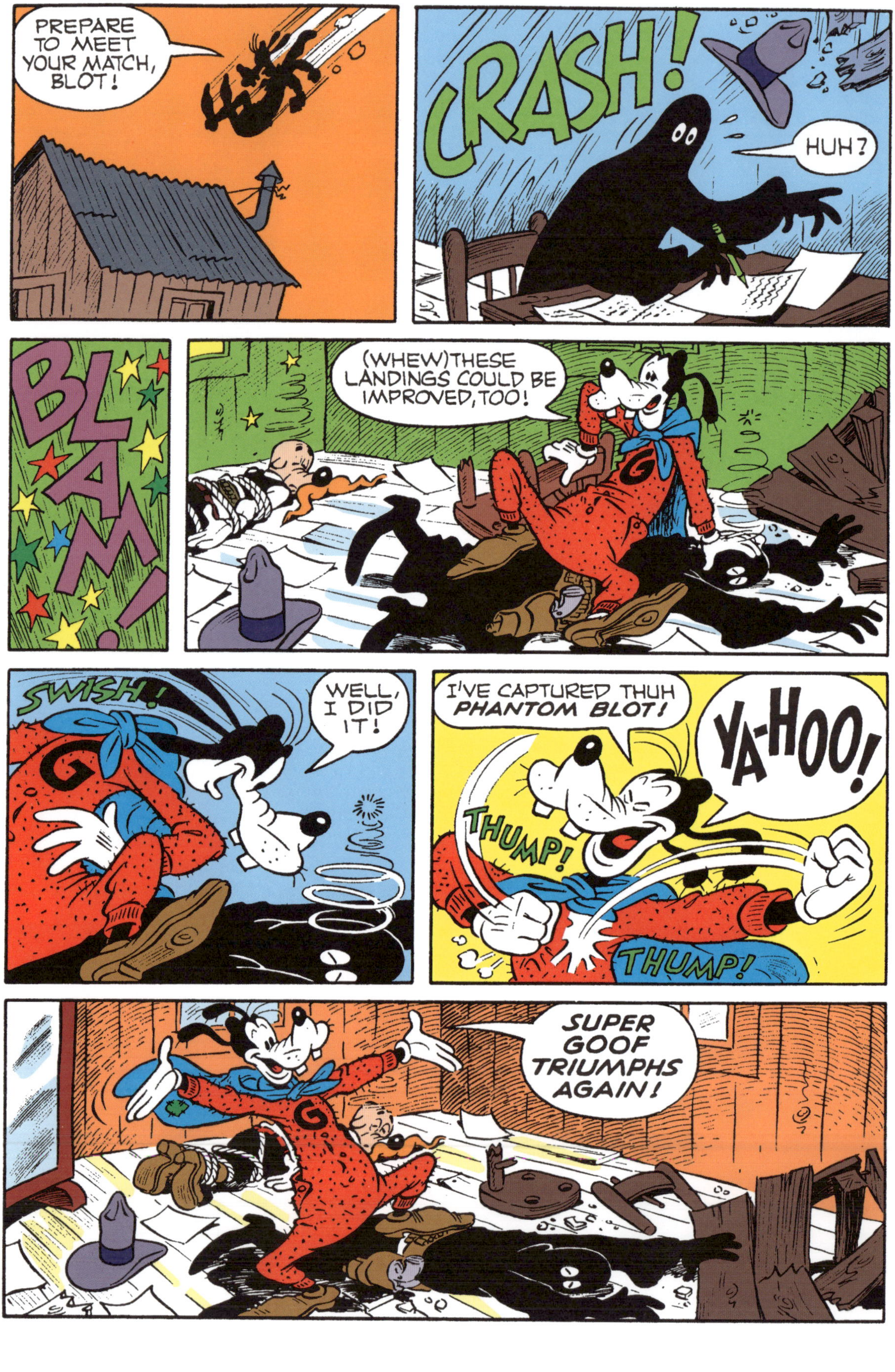
PREPARE TO MEET YOUR MATCH, BLOT!
CRASH!
HUH?
BLAM!
(WHEW) THESE LANDINGS COULD BE IMPROVED, TOO!
SWISH!
WELL, I DID IT!
I'VE CAPTURED THUH PHANTOM BLOT!
YA-HOO!
THUMP!
THUMP!
SUPER GOOF TRIUMPHS AGAIN!

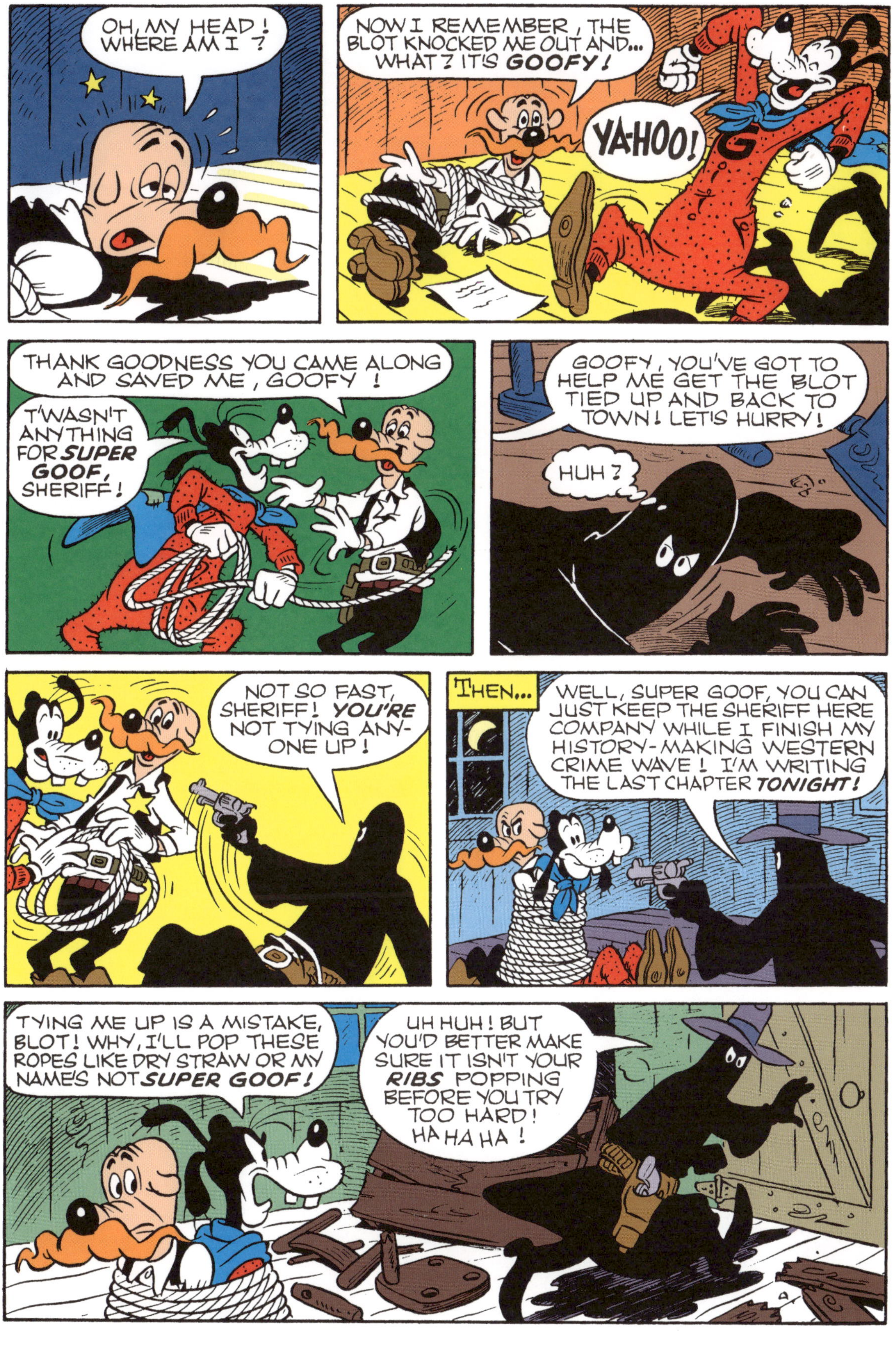
OH, MY HEAD! WHERE AM I ?
NOW I REMEMBER, THE BLOT KNOCKED ME OUT AND... WHAT? IT'S GOOFY!
YA-HOO!
THANK GOODNESS YOU CAME ALONG AND SAVED ME, GOOFY!
T'WASN'T ANYTHING FOR SUPER GOOF, SHERIFF!
GOOFY, YOU'VE GOT TO HELP ME GET THE BLOT TIED UP AND BACK TO TOWN! LET'S HURRY!
HUH?
NOT SO FAST, SHERIFF! YOU'RE NOT TYING ANY-ONE UP!
THEN...
WELL, SUPER GOOF, YOU CAN JUST KEEP THE SHERIFF HERE COMPANY WHILE I FINISH MY HISTORY-MAKING WESTERN CRIME WAVE! I'M WRITING THE LAST CHAPTER TONIGHT!
TYING ME UP IS A MISTAKE, BLOT! WHY, I'LL POP THESE ROPES LIKE DRY STRAW OR MY NAME'S NOT SUPER GOOF!
UH HUH! BUT YOU'D BETTER MAKE SURE IT ISN'T YOUR RIBS POPPING BEFORE YOU TRY TOO HARD! HA HA HA!

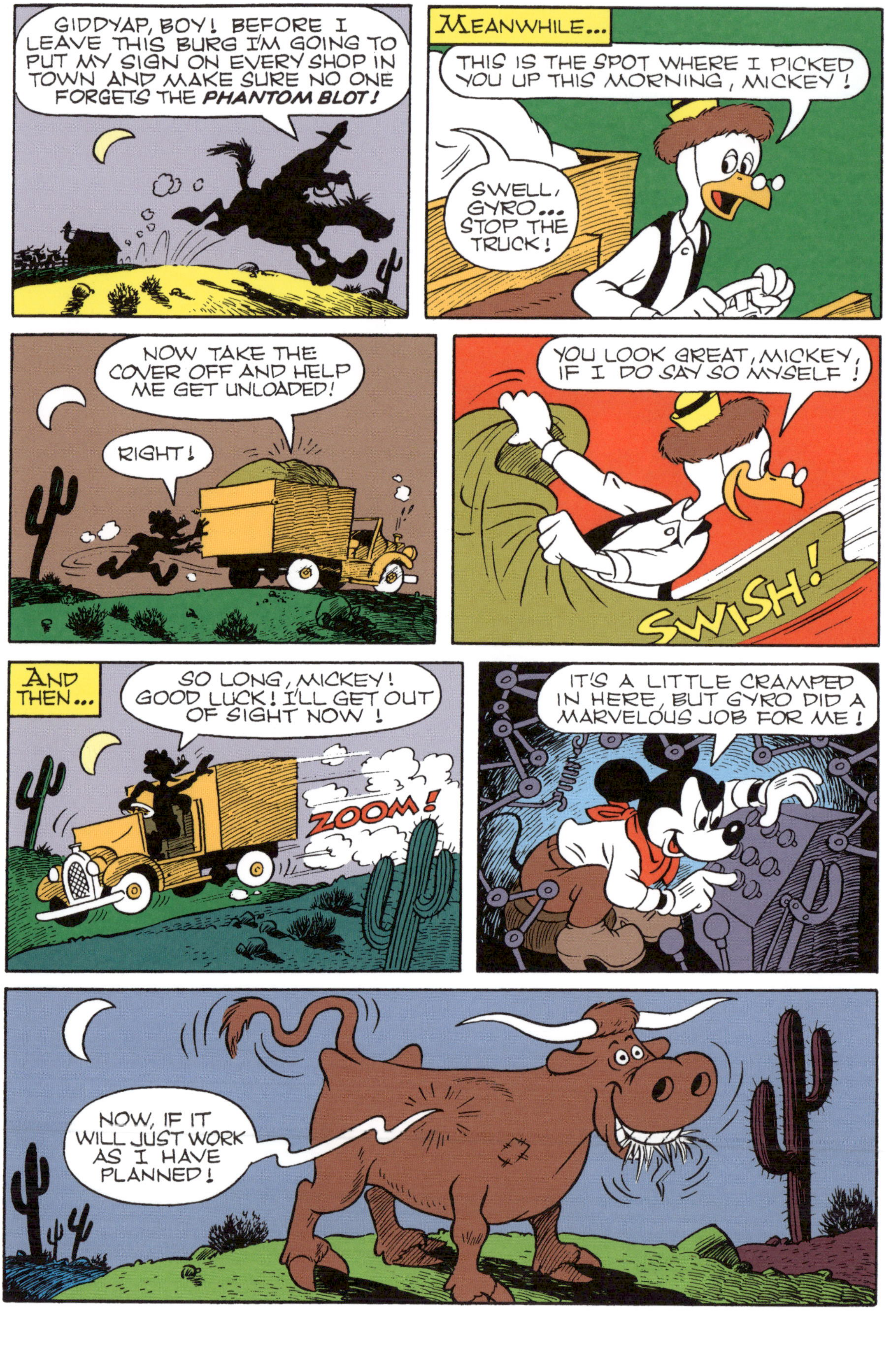
GIDDYAP, BOY! BEFORE I LEAVE THIS BURG I'M GOING TO PUT MY SIGN ON EVERY SHOP IN TOWN AND MAKE SURE NO ONE FORGETS THE PHANTOM BLOT!
MEANWHILE...
THIS IS THE SPOT WHERE I PICKED YOU UP THIS MORNING, MICKEY!
SWELL, GYRO... STOP THE TRUCK!
NOW TAKE THE COVER OFF AND HELP ME GET UNLOADED!
RIGHT!
YOU LOOK GREAT, MICKEY, IF I DO SAY SO MYSELF!
SWISH!
AND THEN...
SO LONG, MICKEY! GOOD LUCK! I'LL GET OUT OF SIGHT NOW!
ZOOM!
IT'S A LITTLE CRAMPED IN HERE, BUT GYRO DID A MARVELOUS JOB FOR ME!
NOW, IF IT WILL JUST WORK AS I HAVE PLANNED!

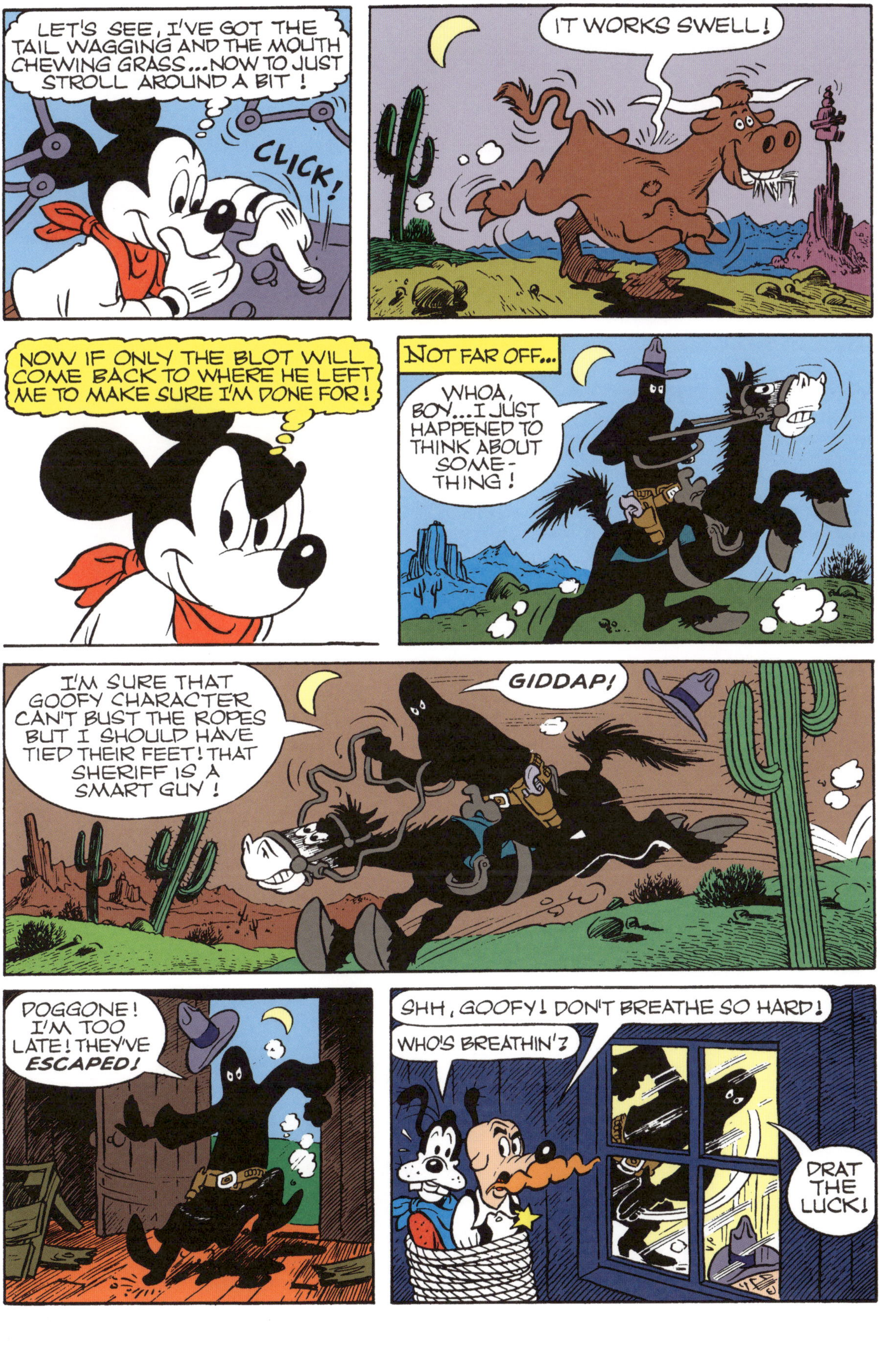
LET'S SEE, I'VE GOT THE TAIL WAGGING AND THE MOUTH CHEWING GRASS...NOW TO JUST STROLL AROUND A BIT!
CLICK!
IT WORKS SWELL!
NOW IF ONLY THE BLOT WILL COME BACK TO WHERE HE LEFT ME TO MAKE SURE I'M DONE FOR!
NOT FAR OFF...
WHOA, BOY...I JUST HAPPENED TO THINK ABOUT SOME-THING!
I'M SURE THAT GOOFY CHARACTER CAN'T BUST THE ROPES BUT I SHOULD HAVE TIED THEIR FEET! THAT SHERIFF IS A SMART GUY!
GIDDAP!
DOGGONE! I'M TOO LATE! THEY'VE ESCAPED!
SHH, GOOFY! DON'T BREATHE SO HARD!
WHO'S BREATHIN'?
DRAT THE LUCK!

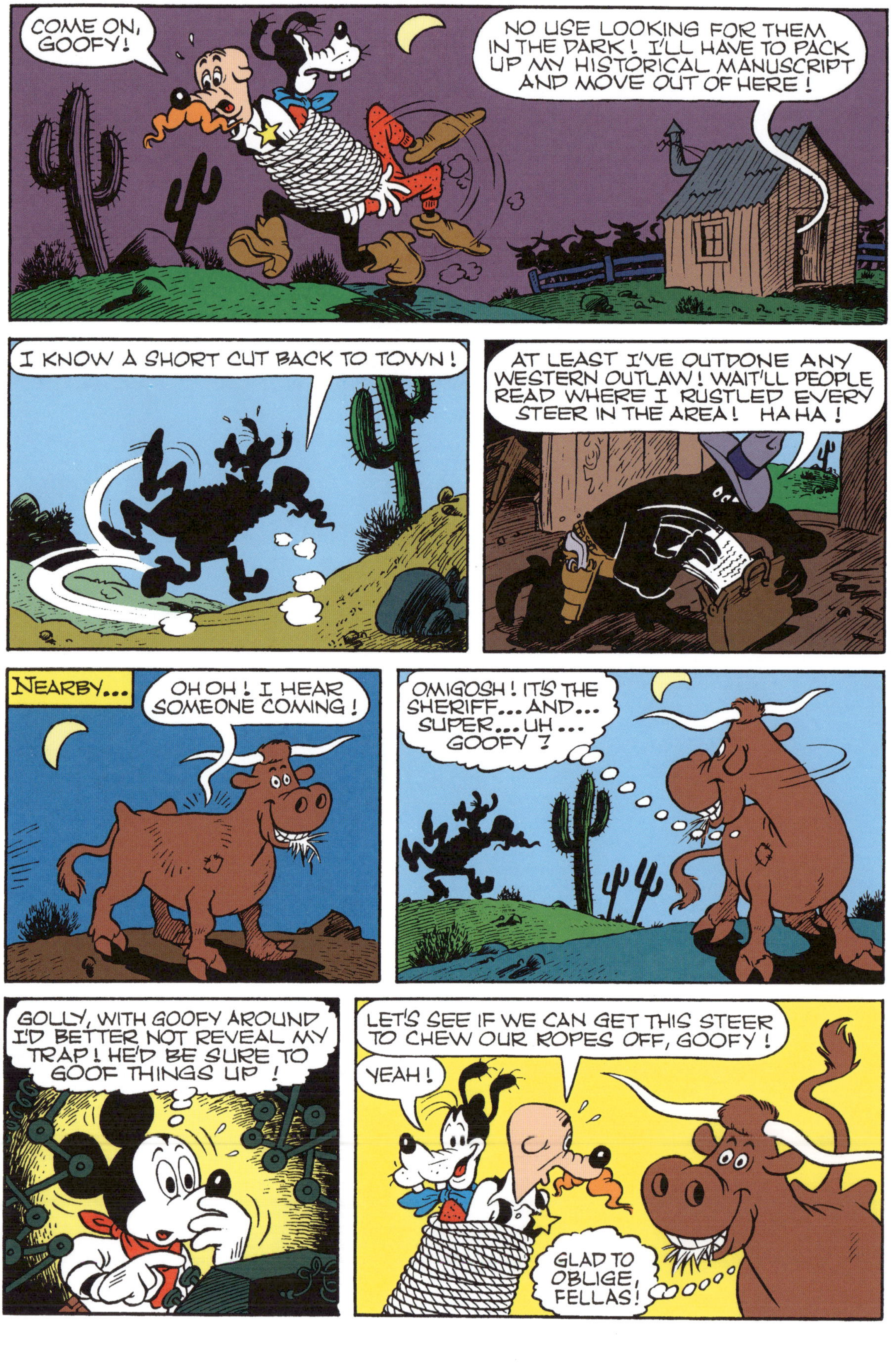
COME ON, GOOFY!
NO USE LOOKING FOR THEM IN THE DARK! I'LL HAVE TO PACK UP MY HISTORICAL MANUSCRIPT AND MOVE OUT OF HERE!
I KNOW A SHORT CUT BACK TO TOWN!
AT LEAST I'VE OUTDONE ANY WESTERN OUTLAW! WAIT'LL PEOPLE READ WHERE I RUSTLED EVERY STEER IN THE AREA! HA HA!
NEARBY...
OH OH! I HEAR SOMEONE COMING!
OMIGOSH! IT'S THE SHERIFF... AND... SUPER... UH... GOOFY?
GOLLY, WITH GOOFY AROUND I'D BETTER NOT REVEAL MY TRAP! HE'D BE SURE TO GOOF THINGS UP!
LET'S SEE IF WE CAN GET THIS STEER TO CHEW OUR ROPES OFF, GOOFY!
YEAH!
GLAD TO OBLIGE, FELLAS!

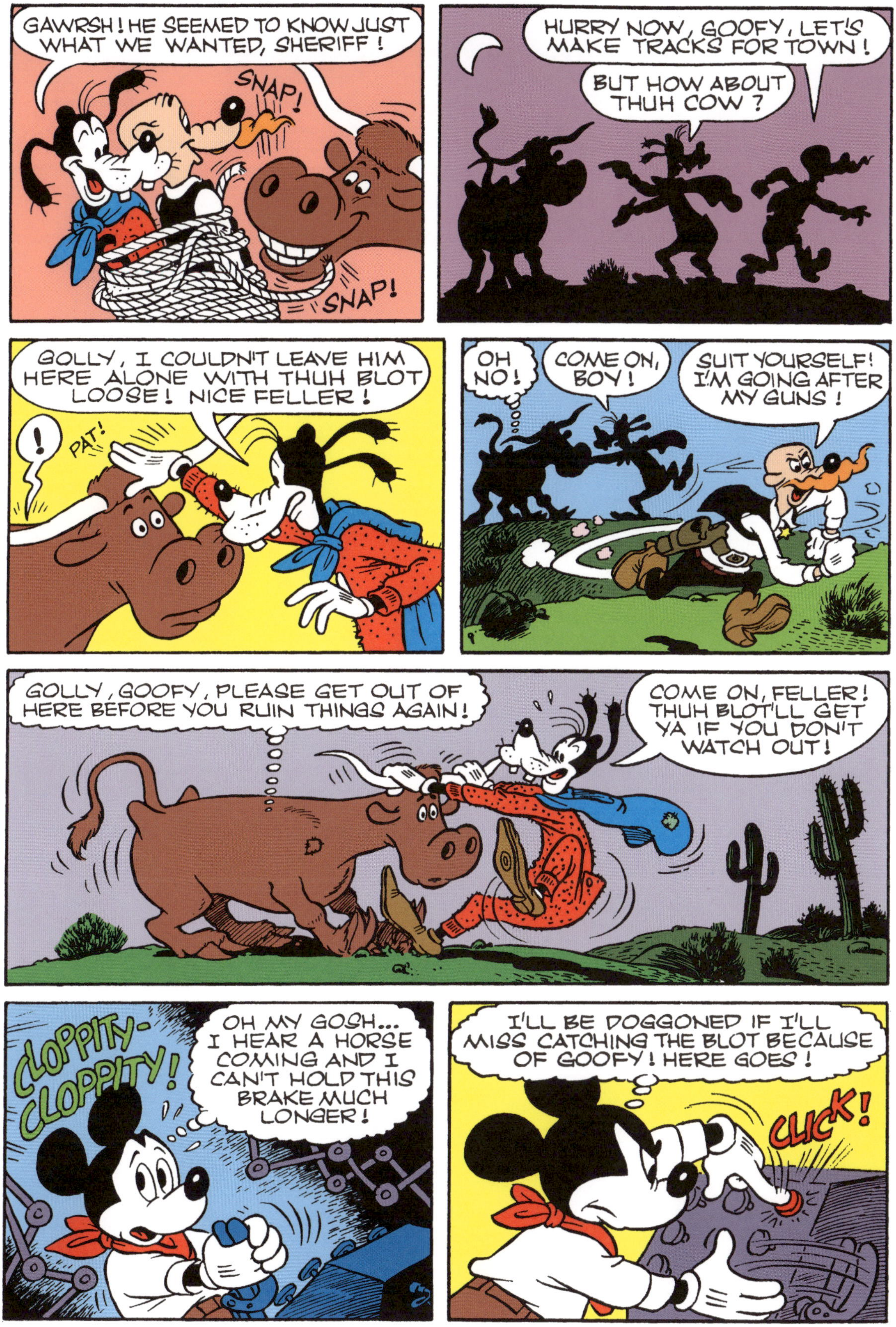
GAWRSH! HE SEEMED TO KNOW JUST WHAT WE WANTED, SHERIFF!
SNAP!
SNAP!
HURRY NOW, GOOFY, LET'S MAKE TRACKS FOR TOWN!
BUT HOW ABOUT THUH COW?
GOLLY, I COULDN'T LEAVE HIM HERE ALONE WITH THUH BLOT LOOSE! NICE FELLER!
PAT!
!
OH NO!
COME ON, BOY!
SUIT YOURSELF! I'M GOING AFTER MY GUNS!
GOLLY, GOOFY, PLEASE GET OUT OF HERE BEFORE YOU RUIN THINGS AGAIN!
COME ON, FELLER! THUH BLOT'LL GET YA IF YOU DON'T WATCH OUT!
CLOPPITY-CLOPPITY!
OH MY GOSH... I HEAR A HORSE COMING AND I CAN'T HOLD THIS BRAKE MUCH LONGER!
I'LL BE DOGGONED IF I'LL MISS CATCHING THE BLOT BECAUSE OF GOOFY! HERE GOES!
CLICK!

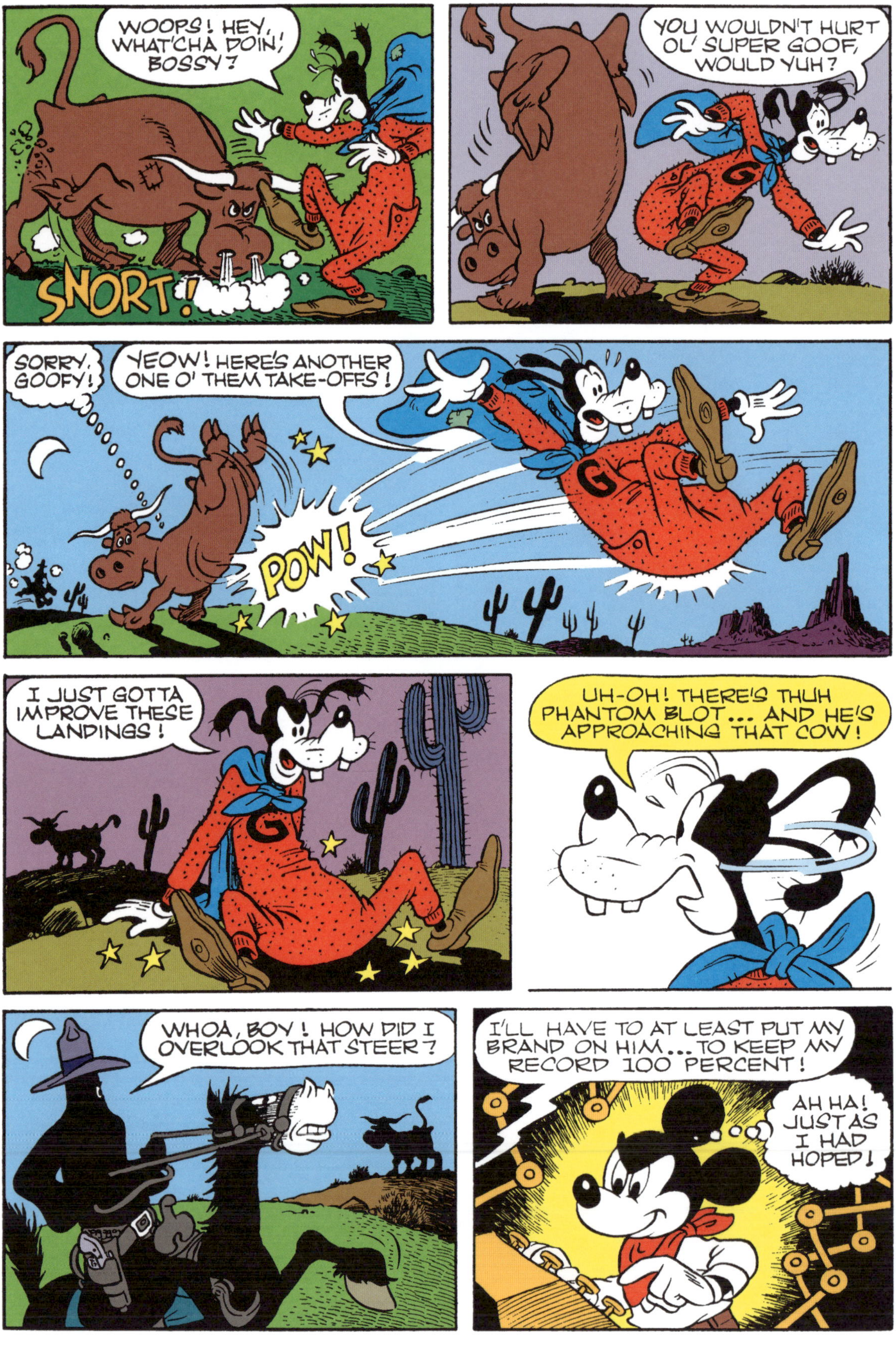

WOOPS! HEY, WHAT'CHA DOIN', BOSSY?
SNORT!
YOU WOULDN'T HURT OL' SUPER GOOF, WOULD YUH?
SORRY, GOOFY!
YEOW! HERE'S ANOTHER ONE O' THEM TAKE-OFFS!
POW!
I JUST GOTTA IMPROVE THESE LANDINGS!
UH-OH! THERE'S THUH PHANTOM BLOT... AND HE'S APPROACHING THAT COW!
WHOA, BOY! HOW DID I OVERLOOK THAT STEER?
I'LL HAVE TO AT LEAST PUT MY BRAND ON HIM... TO KEEP MY RECORD 100 PERCENT!
AH HA! JUST AS I HAD HOPED!

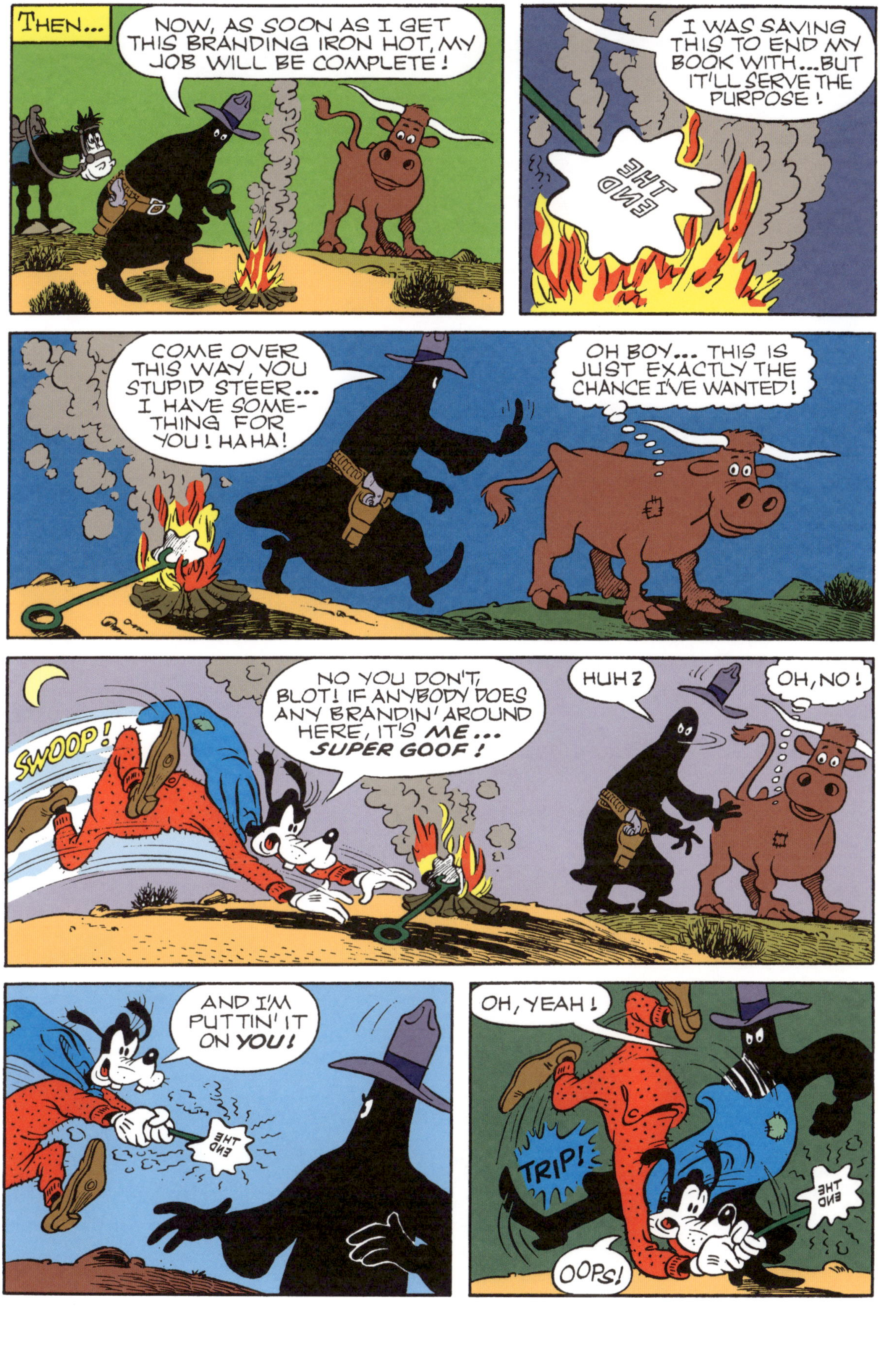
THEN...
NOW, AS SOON AS I GET THIS BRANDING IRON HOT, MY JOB WILL BE COMPLETE!
I WAS SAVING THIS TO END MY BOOK WITH...BUT IT'LL SERVE THE PURPOSE!
THE END
COME OVER THIS WAY, YOU STUPID STEER... I HAVE SOMETHING FOR YOU! HAHA!
OH BOY... THIS IS JUST EXACTLY THE CHANCE I'VE WANTED!
SWOOP!
NO YOU DON'T, BLOT! IF ANYBODY DOES ANY BRANDIN' AROUND HERE, IT'S ME... SUPER GOOF!
HUH?
OH, NO!
AND I'M PUTTIN' IT ON YOU!
THE END
OH, YEAH!
TRIP!
THE END
OOPS!

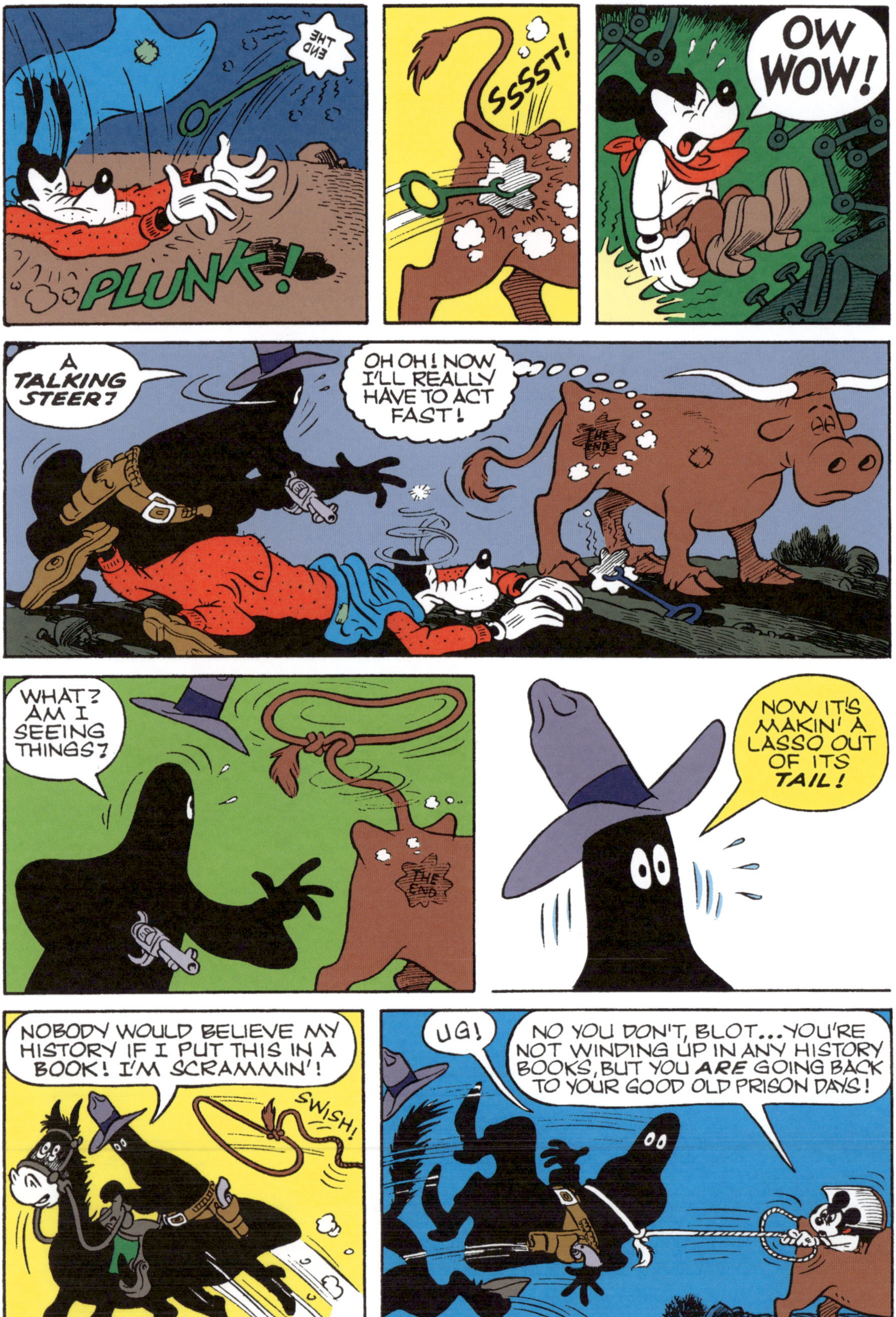
THE END
PLUNK!
SSSST!
OW WOW!
A TALKING STEER?
OH OH! NOW I'LL REALLY HAVE TO ACT FAST!
THE END
WHAT? AM I SEEING THINGS?
THE END
NOW IT'S MAKIN' A LASSO OUT OF ITS TAIL!
NOBODY WOULD BELIEVE MY HISTORY IF I PUT THIS IN A BOOK! I'M SCRAMMIN'!
SWISH!
UG!
NO YOU DON'T, BLOT... YOU'RE NOT WINDING UP IN ANY HISTORY BOOKS, BUT YOU ARE GOING BACK TO YOUR GOOD OLD PRISON DAYS!

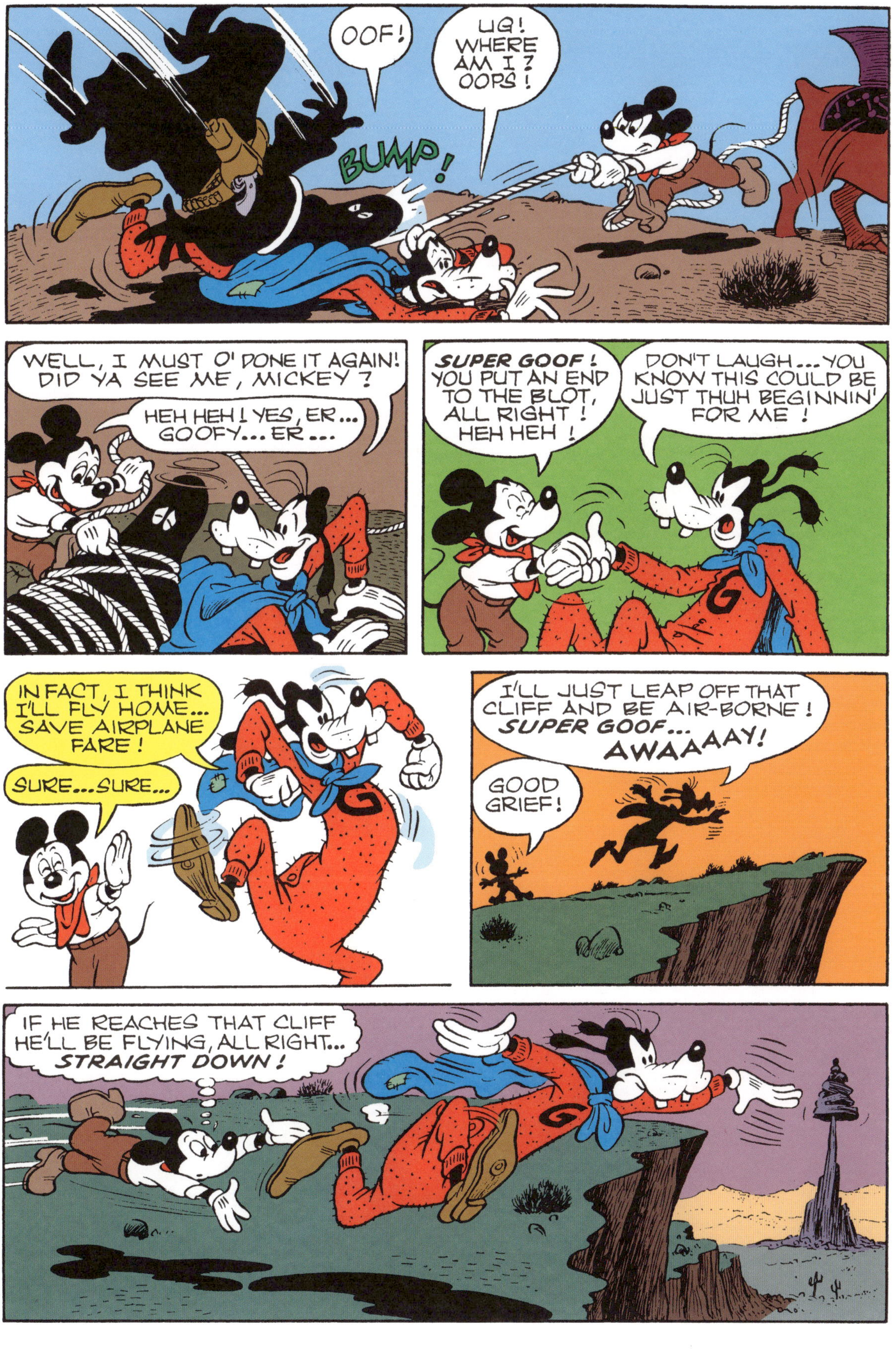
OOF!
UG! WHERE AM I? OOPS!
BUMP!
WELL, I MUST O' DONE IT AGAIN! DID YA SEE ME, MICKEY?
HEH HEH! YES, ER... GOOFY... ER...
SUPER GOOF! YOU PUT AN END TO THE BLOT, ALL RIGHT! HEH HEH!
DON'T LAUGH... YOU KNOW THIS COULD BE JUST THUH BEGINNIN' FOR ME!
IN FACT, I THINK I'LL FLY HOME... SAVE AIRPLANE FARE!
SURE... SURE...
I'LL JUST LEAP OFF THAT CLIFF AND BE AIR-BORNE! SUPER GOOF... AWAAAAY!
GOOD GRIEF!
IF HE REACHES THAT CLIFF HE'LL BE FLYING, ALL RIGHT... STRAIGHT DOWN!

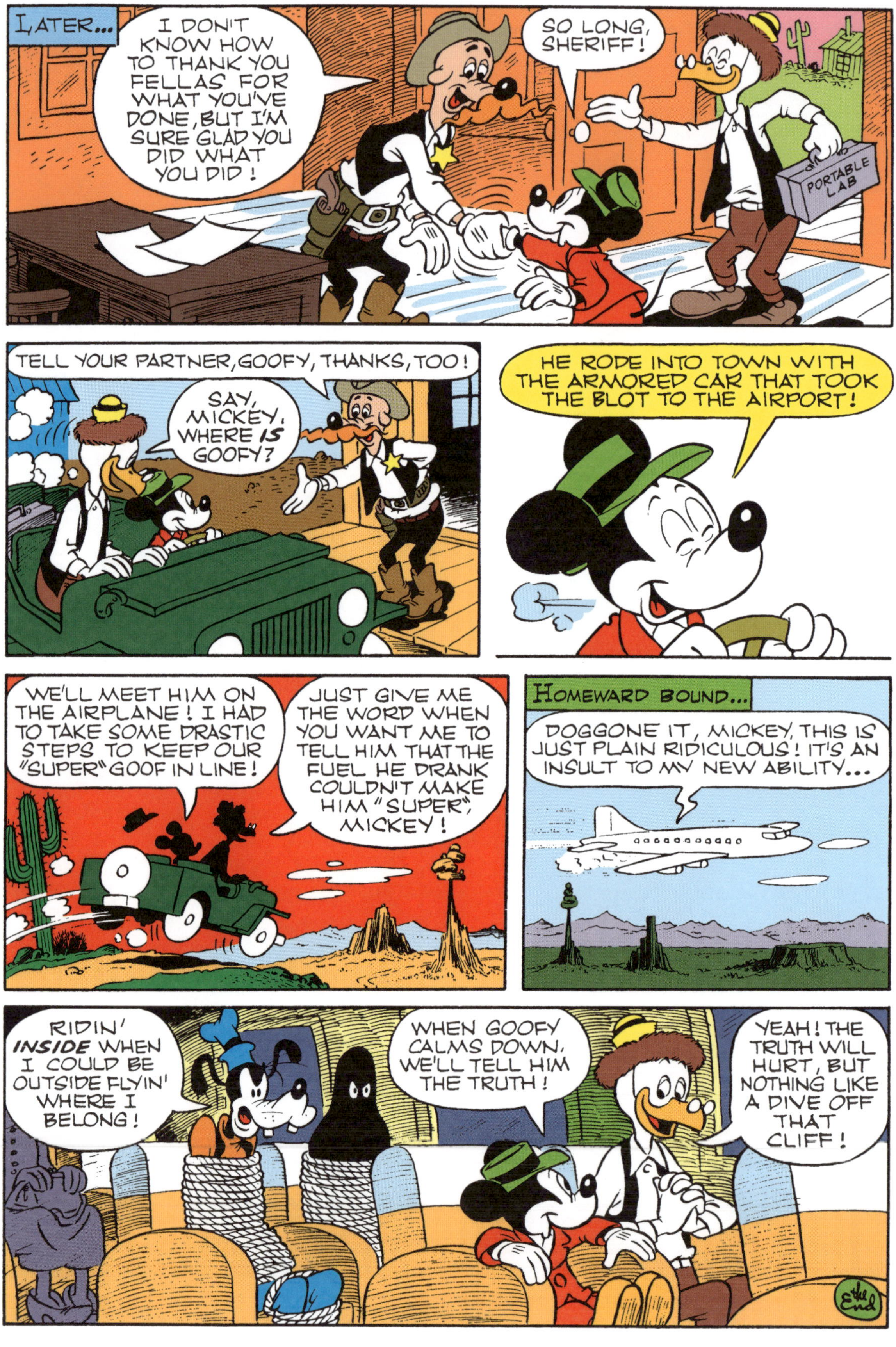
LATER...
I DON'T KNOW HOW TO THANK YOU FELLAS FOR WHAT YOU'VE DONE, BUT I'M SURE GLAD YOU DID WHAT YOU DID!
SO LONG, SHERIFF!
PORTABLE LAB
TELL YOUR PARTNER, GOOFY, THANKS, TOO!
SAY, MICKEY, WHERE IS GOOFY?
HE RODE INTO TOWN WITH THE ARMORED CAR THAT TOOK THE BLOT TO THE AIRPORT!
WE'LL MEET HIM ON THE AIRPLANE! I HAD TO TAKE SOME DRASTIC STEPS TO KEEP OUR "SUPER" GOOF IN LINE!
JUST GIVE ME THE WORD WHEN YOU WANT ME TO TELL HIM THAT THE FUEL HE DRANK COULDN'T MAKE HIM "SUPER", MICKEY!
HOMEWARD BOUND...
DOGGONE IT, MICKEY, THIS IS JUST PLAIN RIDICULOUS! IT'S AN INSULT TO MY NEW ABILITY...
RIDIN' INSIDE WHEN I COULD BE OUTSIDE FLYIN' WHERE I BELONG!
WHEN GOOFY CALMS DOWN, WE'LL TELL HIM THE TRUTH!
YEAH! THE TRUTH WILL HURT, BUT NOTHING LIKE A DIVE OFF THAT CLIFF!
The End

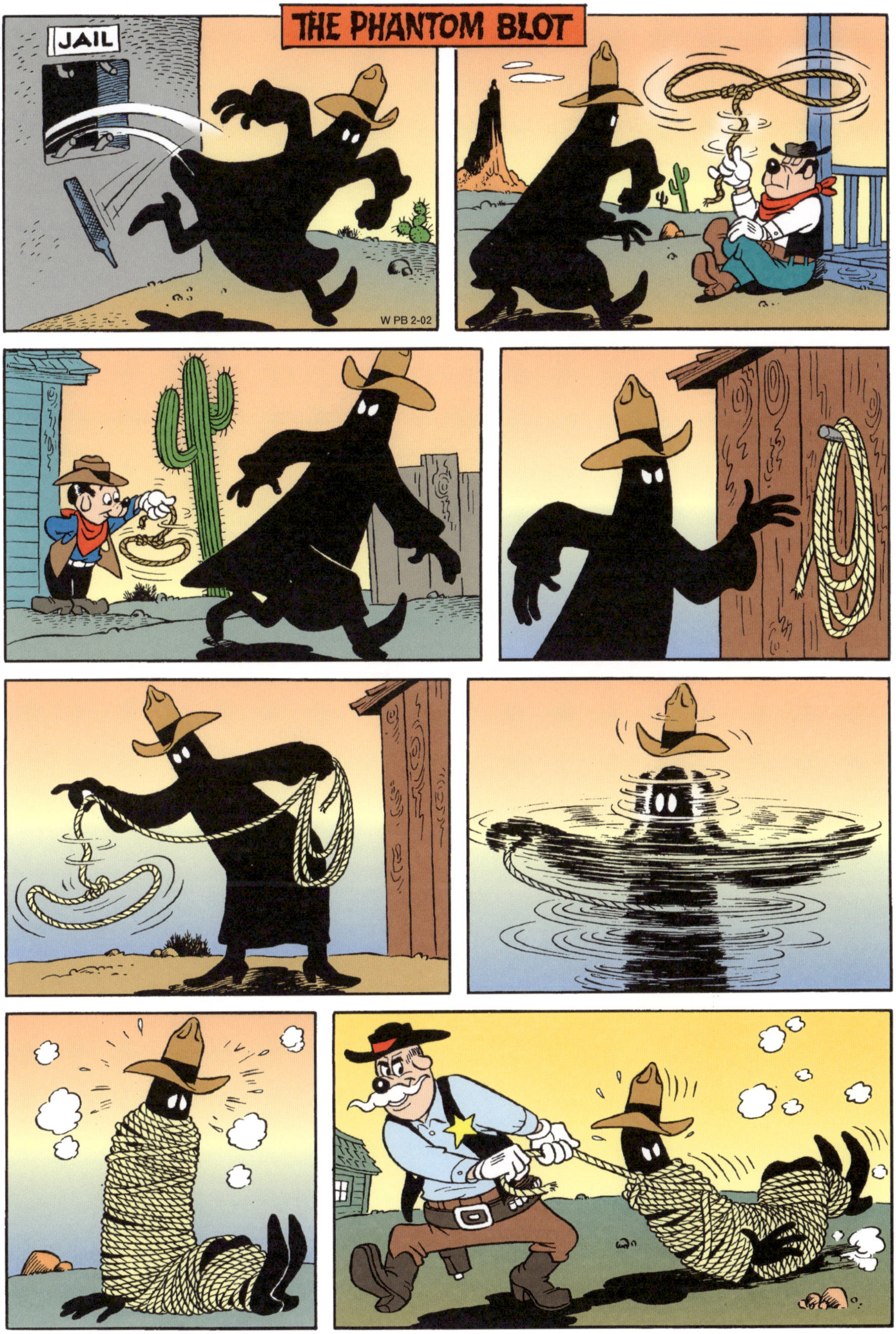
THE PHANTOM BLOT
JAIL
W PB 2-02

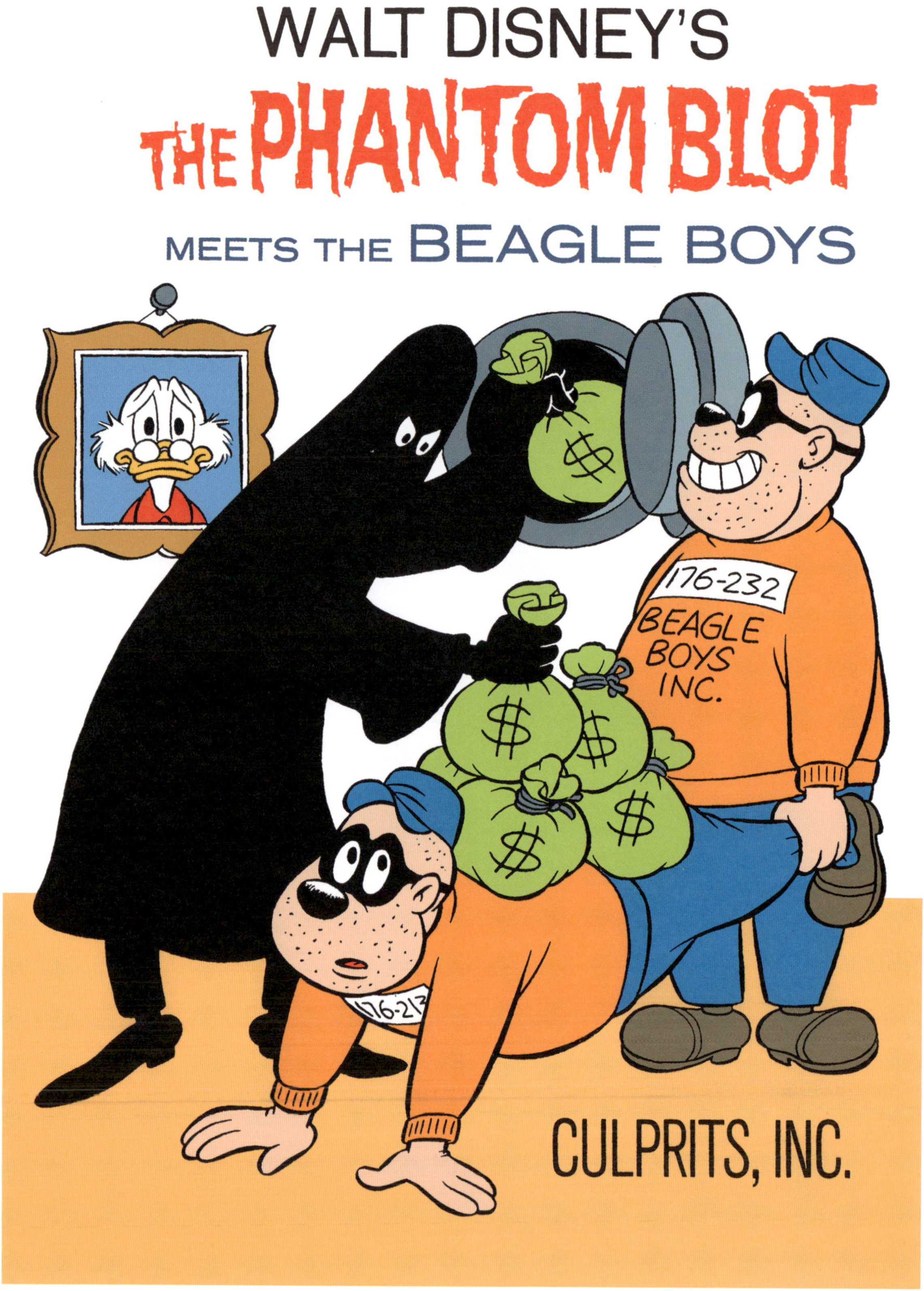
WALT DISNEY'S
THE PHANTOM BLOT
MEETS THE BEAGLE BOYS
176-232
BEAGLE BOYS INC.
CULPRITS, INC.

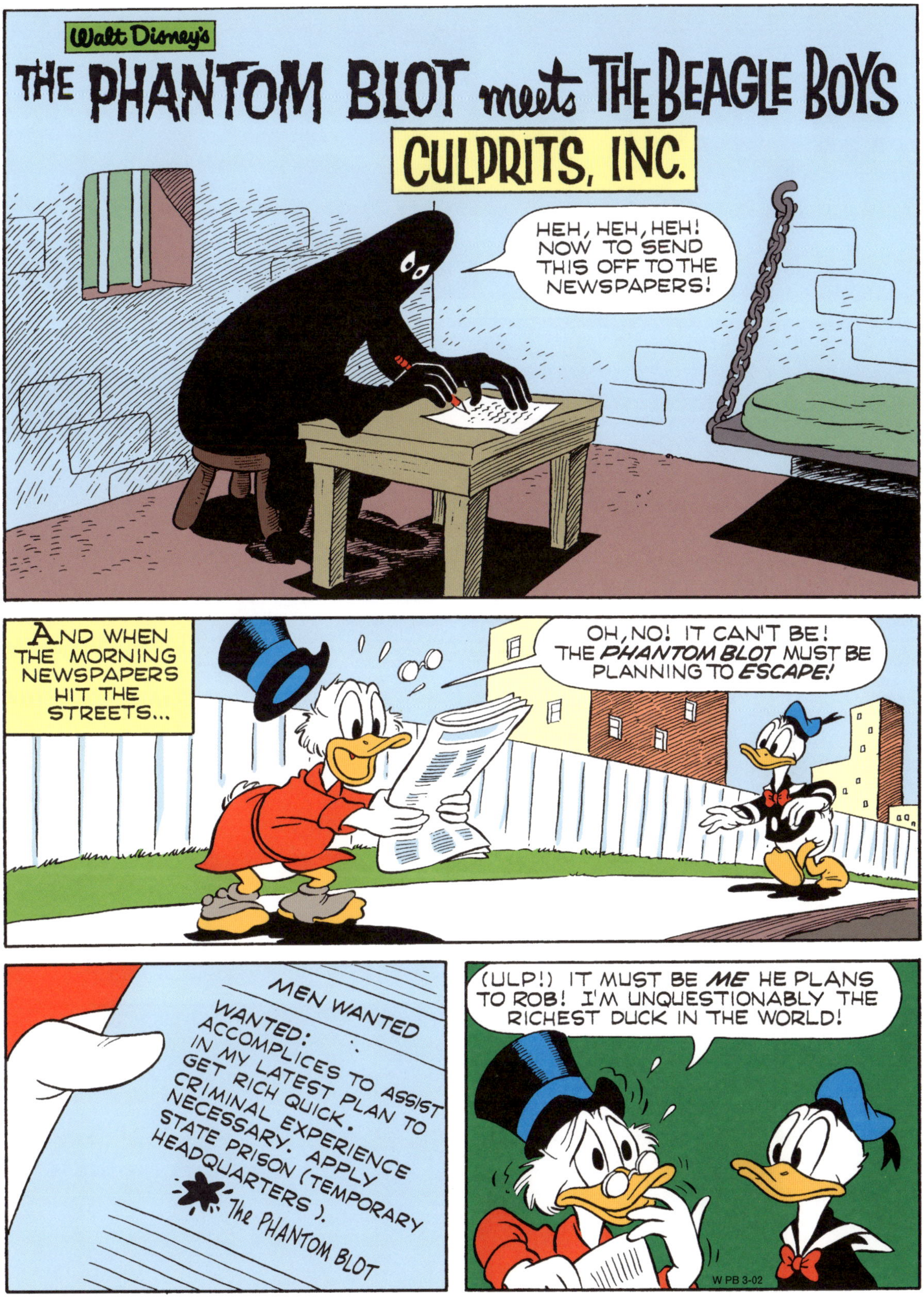
Walt Disney's
THE PHANTOM BLOT meets THE BEAGLE BOYS
CULPRITS, INC.
HEH, HEH, HEH! NOW TO SEND THIS OFF TO THE NEWSPAPERS!
AND WHEN THE MORNING NEWSPAPERS HIT THE STREETS...
OH, NO! IT CAN'T BE! THE PHANTOM BLOT MUST BE PLANNING TO ESCAPE!
MEN WANTED
WANTED: ACCOMPLICES TO ASSIST IN MY LATEST PLAN TO GET RICH QUICK. CRIMINAL EXPERIENCE NECESSARY. APPLY STATE PRISON (TEMPORARY HEADQUARTERS).
The PHANTOM BLOT
(ULP!) IT MUST BE ME HE PLANS TO ROB! I'M UNQUESTIONABLY THE RICHEST DUCK IN THE WORLD!
W PB 3-02

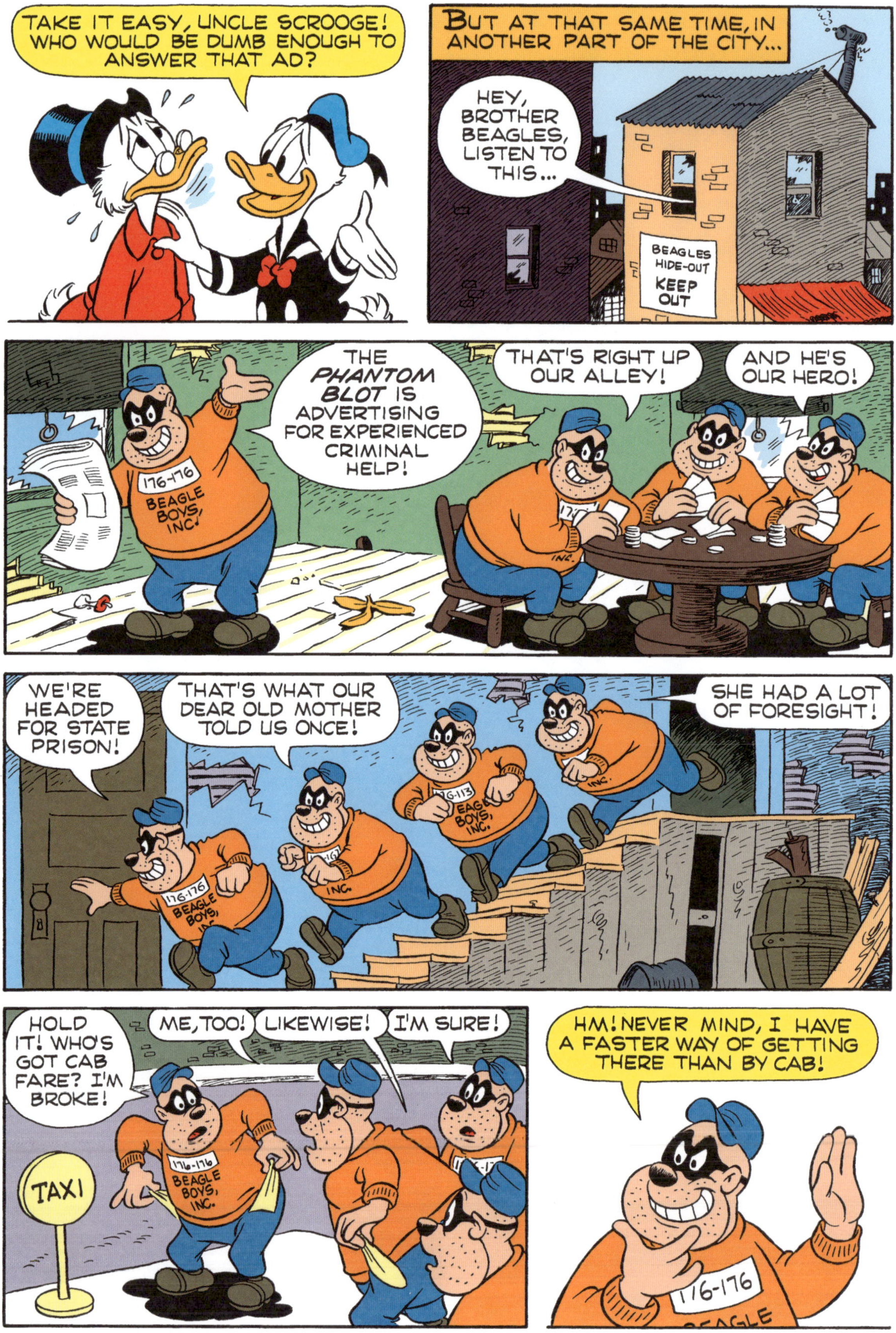
TAKE IT EASY, UNCLE SCROOGE! WHO WOULD BE DUMB ENOUGH TO ANSWER THAT AD?
BUT AT THAT SAME TIME, IN ANOTHER PART OF THE CITY...
HEY, BROTHER BEAGLES, LISTEN TO THIS...
BEAGLES HIDE-OUT KEEP OUT
THE PHANTOM BLOT IS ADVERTISING FOR EXPERIENCED CRIMINAL HELP!
176-176 BEAGLE BOYS, INC.
THAT'S RIGHT UP OUR ALLEY!
AND HE'S OUR HERO!
WE'RE HEADED FOR STATE PRISON!
THAT'S WHAT OUR DEAR OLD MOTHER TOLD US ONCE!
SHE HAD A LOT OF FORESIGHT!
HOLD IT! WHO'S GOT CAB FARE? I'M BROKE!
ME, TOO!
LIKEWISE!
I'M SURE!
TAXI
HM! NEVER MIND, I HAVE A FASTER WAY OF GETTING THERE THAN BY CAB!

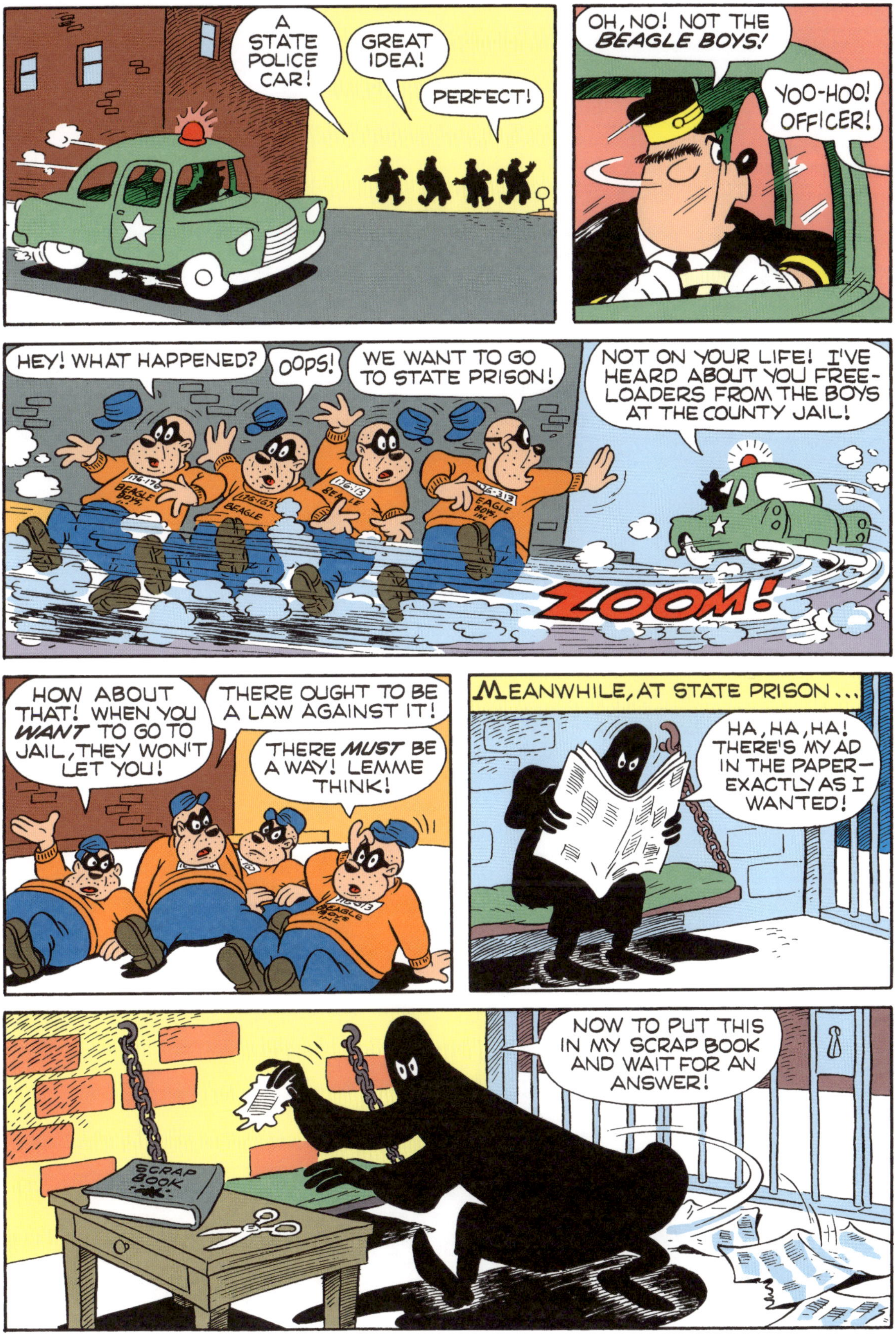
A STATE POLICE CAR!
GREAT IDEA!
PERFECT!
OH, NO! NOT THE *BEAGLE BOYS!*
YOO-HOO! OFFICER!
HEY! WHAT HAPPENED?
OOPS!
WE WANT TO GO TO STATE PRISON!
NOT ON YOUR LIFE! I'VE HEARD ABOUT YOU FREE-LOADERS FROM THE BOYS AT THE COUNTY JAIL!
ZOOM!
HOW ABOUT THAT! WHEN YOU *WANT* TO GO TO JAIL, THEY WON'T LET YOU!
THERE OUGHT TO BE A LAW AGAINST IT!
THERE *MUST* BE A WAY! LEMME THINK!
MEANWHILE, AT STATE PRISON...
HA, HA, HA! THERE'S MY AD IN THE PAPER— EXACTLY AS I WANTED!
NOW TO PUT THIS IN MY SCRAP BOOK AND WAIT FOR AN ANSWER!
SCRAP BOOK

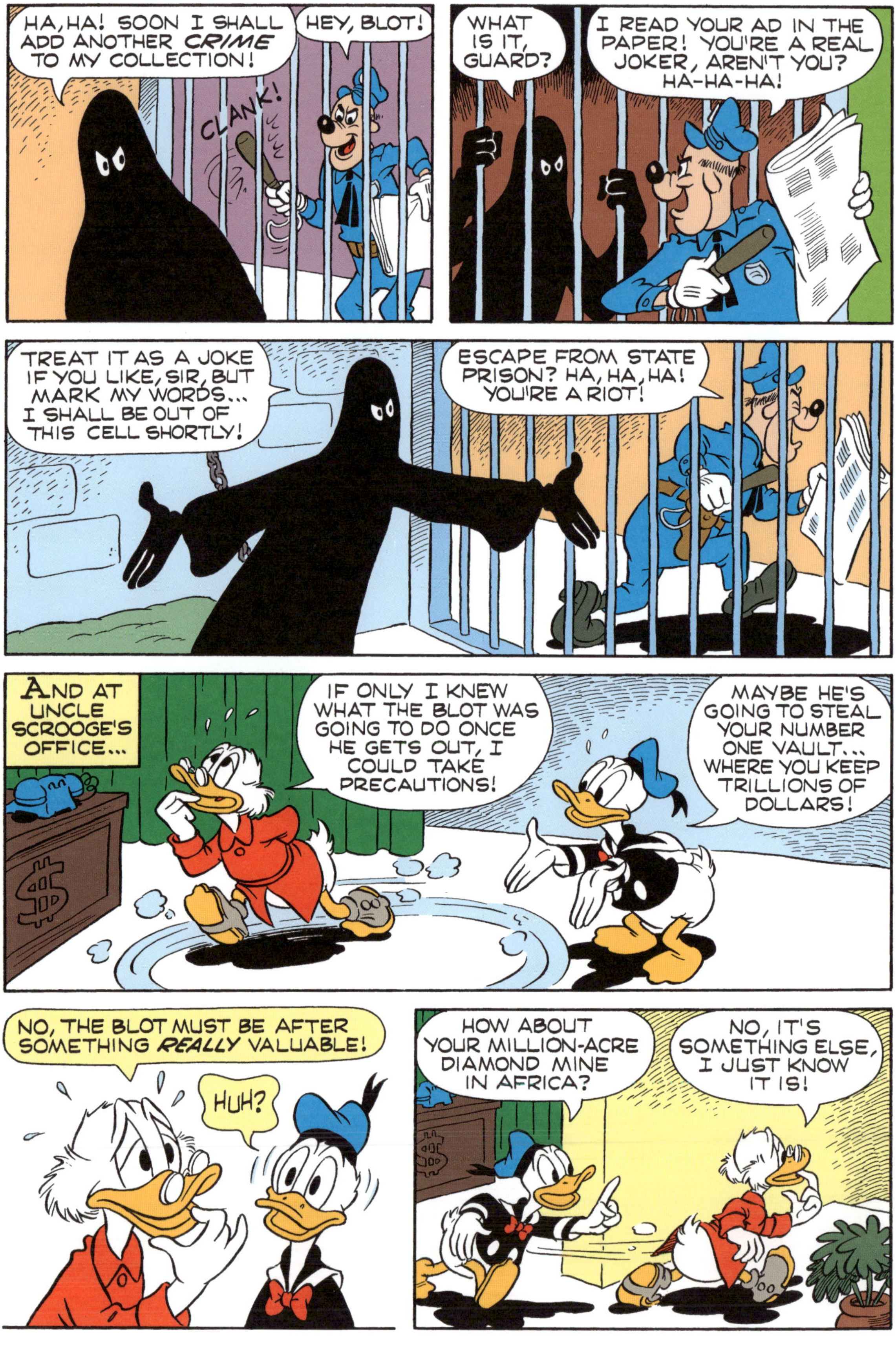

HA, HA! SOON I SHALL ADD ANOTHER CRIME TO MY COLLECTION!
HEY, BLOT!
CLANK!
WHAT IS IT, GUARD?
I READ YOUR AD IN THE PAPER! YOU'RE A REAL JOKER, AREN'T YOU? HA-HA-HA!
TREAT IT AS A JOKE IF YOU LIKE, SIR, BUT MARK MY WORDS... I SHALL BE OUT OF THIS CELL SHORTLY!
ESCAPE FROM STATE PRISON? HA, HA, HA! YOU'RE A RIOT!
AND AT UNCLE SCROOGE'S OFFICE...
IF ONLY I KNEW WHAT THE BLOT WAS GOING TO DO ONCE HE GETS OUT, I COULD TAKE PRECAUTIONS!
MAYBE HE'S GOING TO STEAL YOUR NUMBER ONE VAULT... WHERE YOU KEEP TRILLIONS OF DOLLARS!
NO, THE BLOT MUST BE AFTER SOMETHING REALLY VALUABLE!
HUH?
HOW ABOUT YOUR MILLION-ACRE DIAMOND MINE IN AFRICA?
NO, IT'S SOMETHING ELSE, I JUST KNOW IT IS!

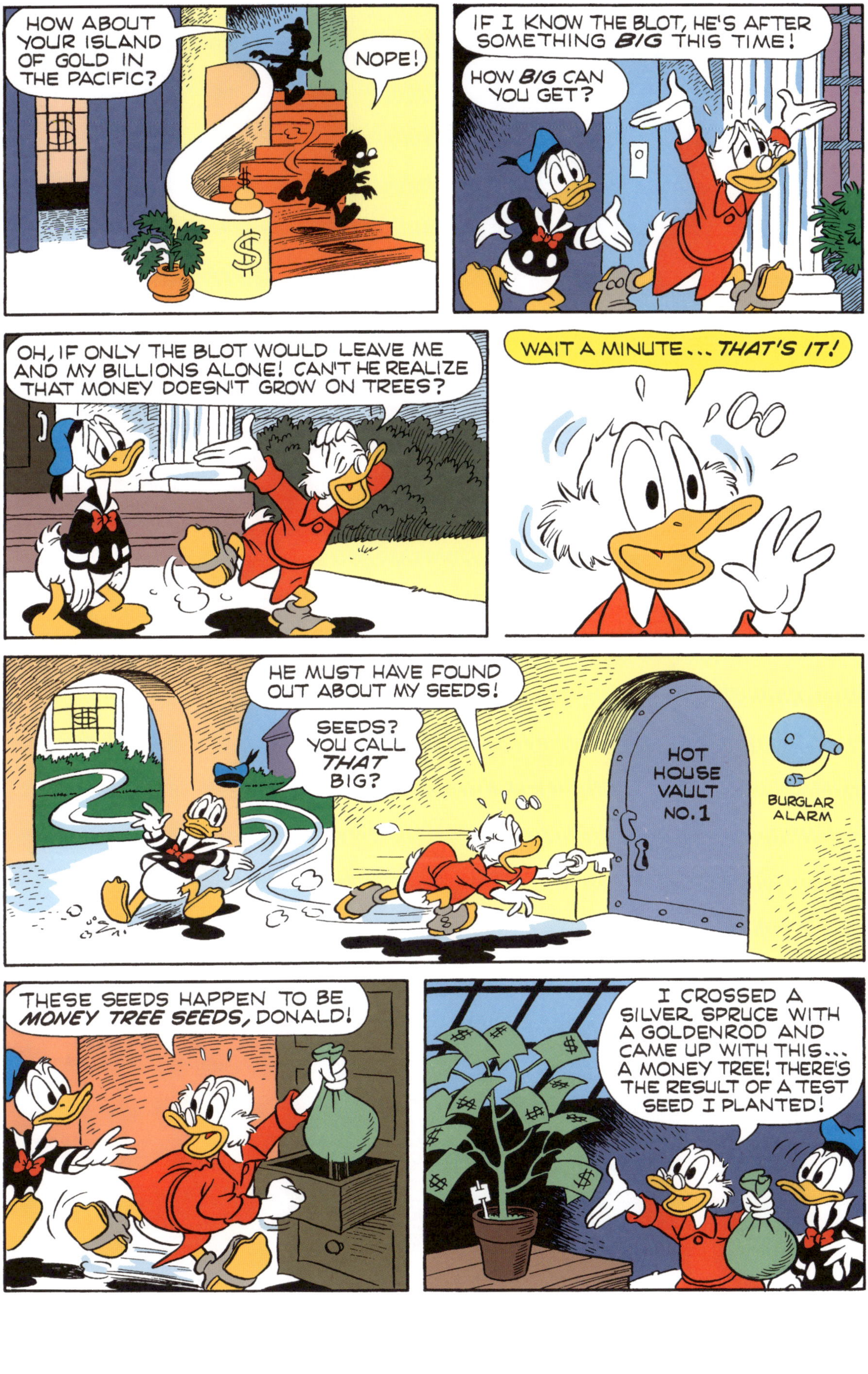
HOW ABOUT YOUR ISLAND OF GOLD IN THE PACIFIC?
NOPE!
IF I KNOW THE BLOT, HE'S AFTER SOMETHING BIG THIS TIME!
HOW BIG CAN YOU GET?
OH, IF ONLY THE BLOT WOULD LEAVE ME AND MY BILLIONS ALONE! CAN'T HE REALIZE THAT MONEY DOESN'T GROW ON TREES?
WAIT A MINUTE... THAT'S IT!
HE MUST HAVE FOUND OUT ABOUT MY SEEDS!
SEEDS? YOU CALL THAT BIG?
HOT HOUSE VAULT NO. 1
BURGLAR ALARM
THESE SEEDS HAPPEN TO BE MONEY TREE SEEDS, DONALD!
I CROSSED A SILVER SPRUCE WITH A GOLDENROD AND CAME UP WITH THIS... A MONEY TREE! THERE'S THE RESULT OF A TEST SEED I PLANTED!

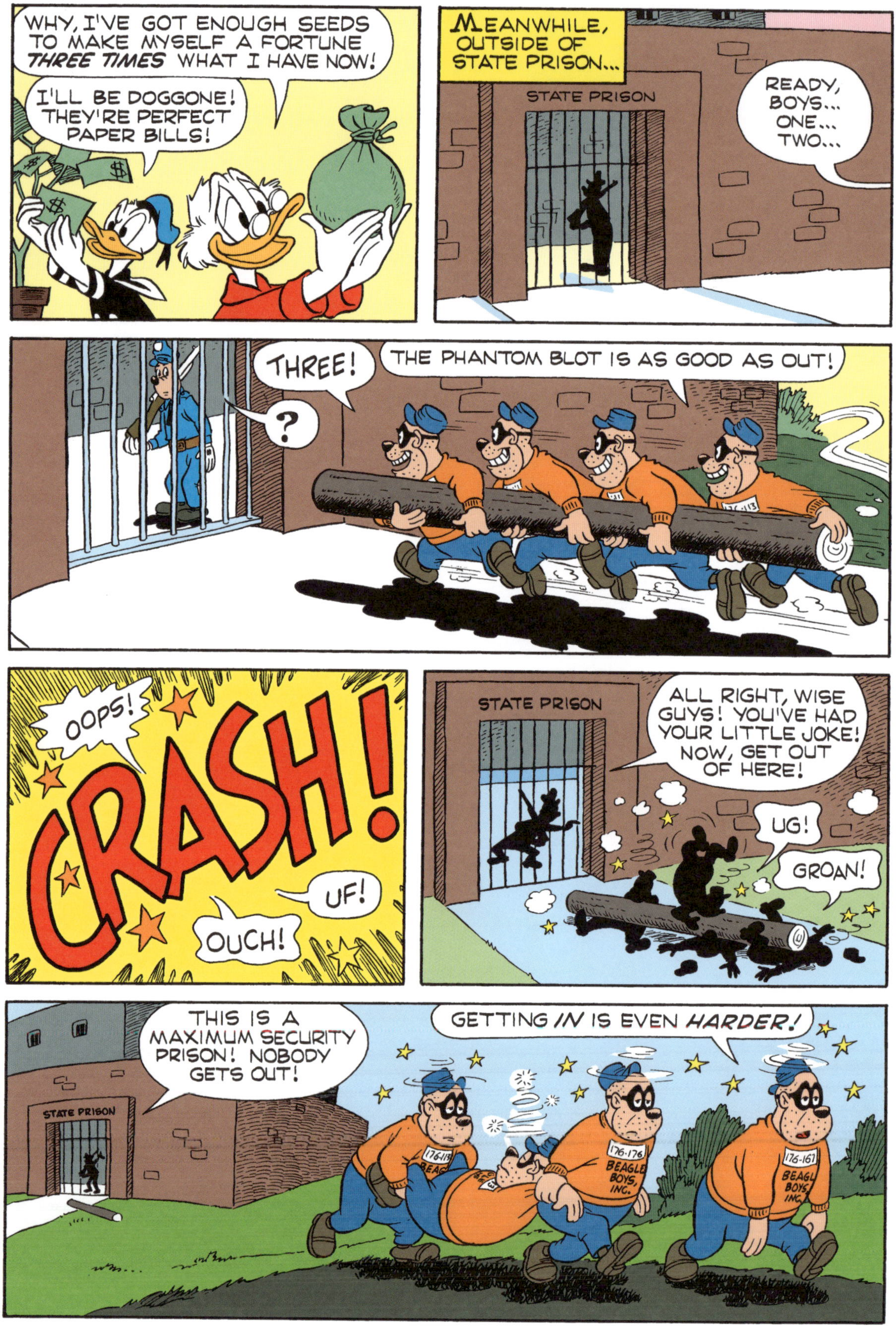
WHY, I'VE GOT ENOUGH SEEDS TO MAKE MYSELF A FORTUNE *THREE TIMES* WHAT I HAVE NOW!
I'LL BE DOGGONE! THEY'RE PERFECT PAPER BILLS!
MEANWHILE, OUTSIDE OF STATE PRISON...
STATE PRISON
READY, BOYS... ONE... TWO...
THREE!
THE PHANTOM BLOT IS AS GOOD AS OUT!
?
OOPS!
CRASH!
UF!
OUCH!
STATE PRISON
ALL RIGHT, WISE GUYS! YOU'VE HAD YOUR LITTLE JOKE! NOW, GET OUT OF HERE!
UG!
GROAN!
THIS IS A MAXIMUM SECURITY PRISON! NOBODY GETS OUT!
GETTING *IN* IS EVEN *HARDER!*
STATE PRISON
176-176
BEAGLE BOYS, INC.
176-167
BEAGLE BOYS, INC.

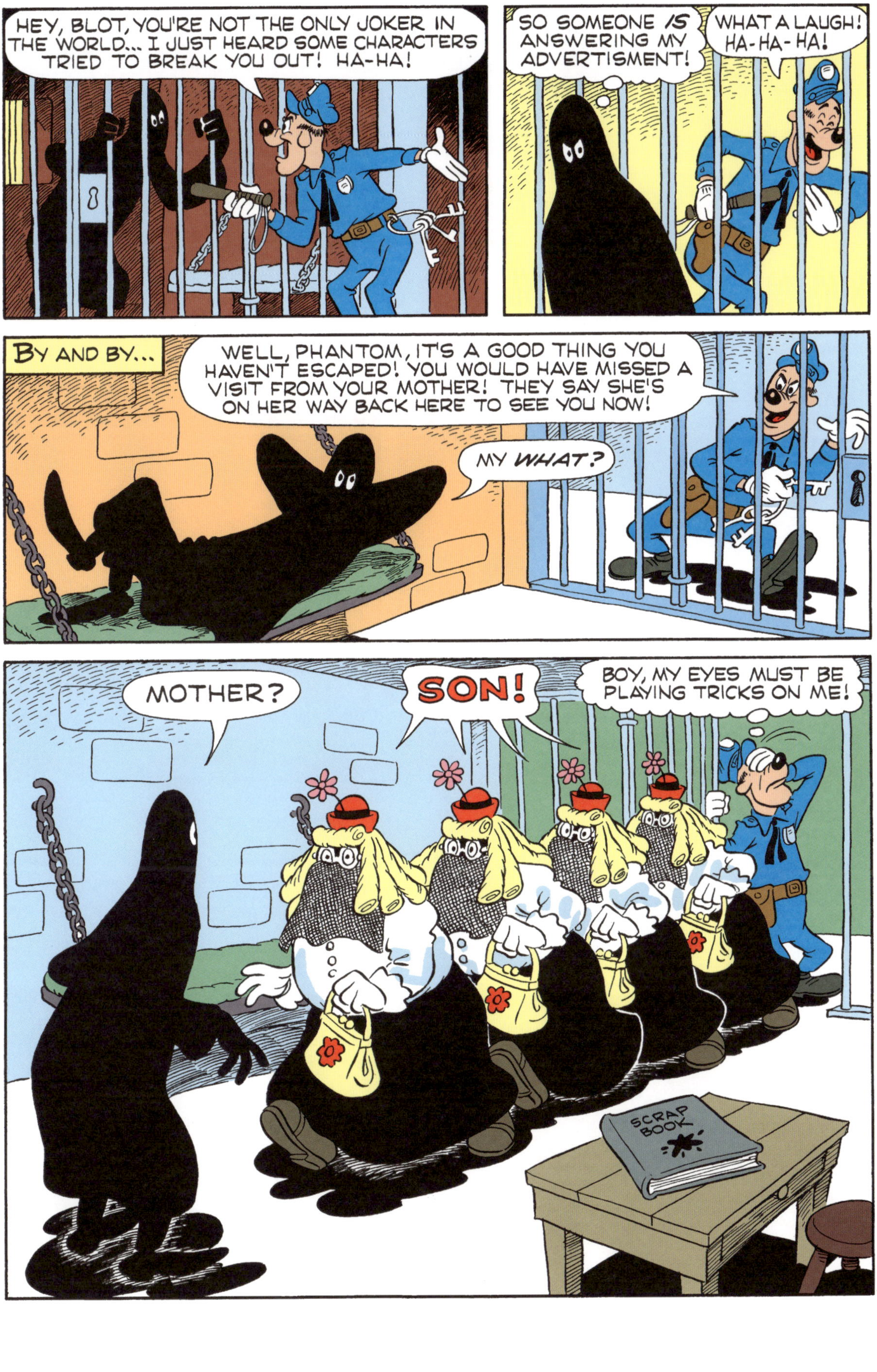
HEY, BLOT, YOU'RE NOT THE ONLY JOKER IN THE WORLD... I JUST HEARD SOME CHARACTERS TRIED TO BREAK YOU OUT! HA-HA!
SO SOMEONE *IS* ANSWERING MY ADVERTISMENT!
WHAT A LAUGH! HA-HA-HA!
BY AND BY...
WELL, PHANTOM, IT'S A GOOD THING YOU HAVEN'T ESCAPED! YOU WOULD HAVE MISSED A VISIT FROM YOUR MOTHER! THEY SAY SHE'S ON HER WAY BACK HERE TO SEE YOU NOW!
MY *WHAT?*
MOTHER?
SON!
BOY, MY EYES MUST BE PLAYING TRICKS ON ME!
SCRAP BOOK

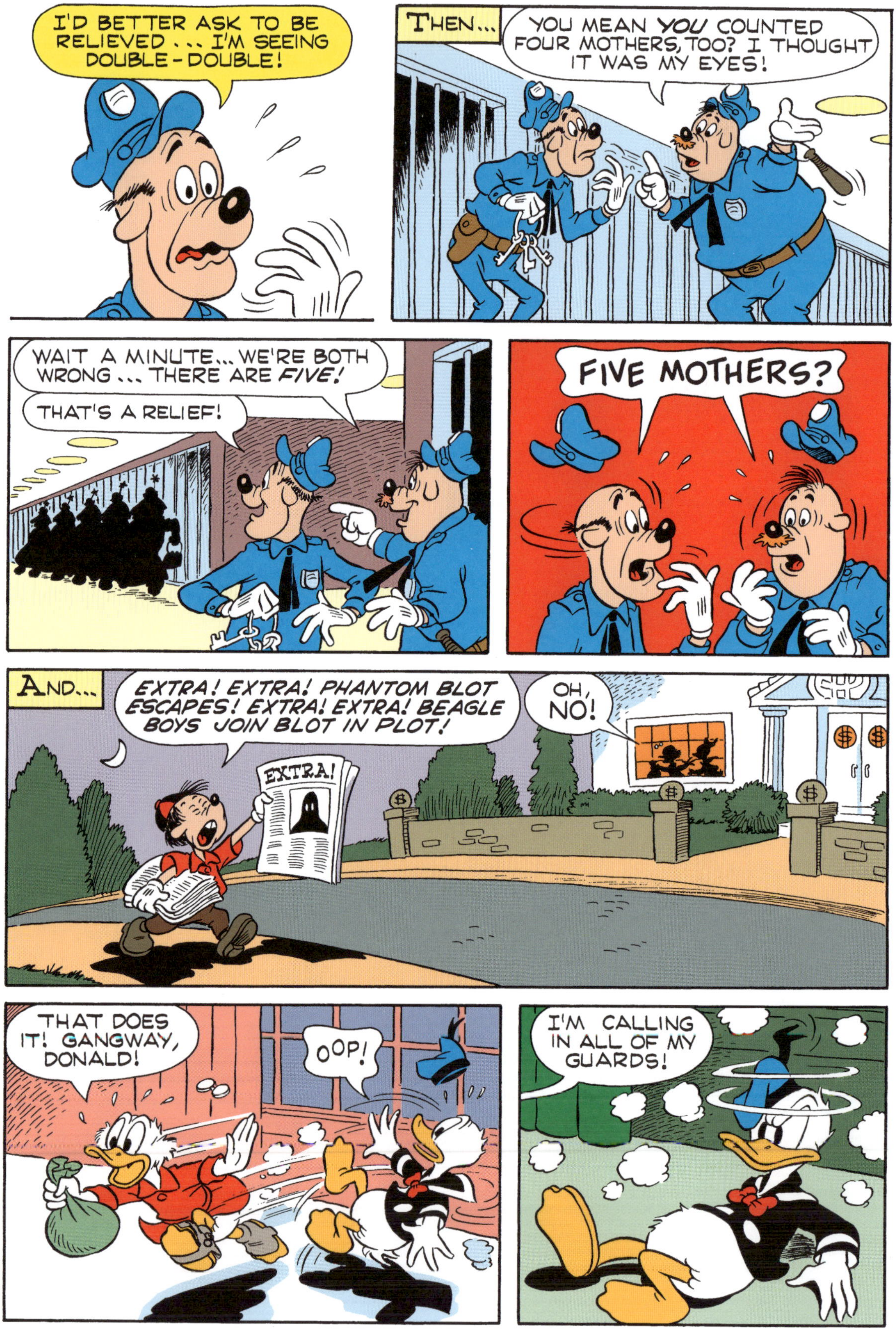
I'D BETTER ASK TO BE RELIEVED . . . I'M SEEING DOUBLE-DOUBLE!
THEN...
YOU MEAN YOU COUNTED FOUR MOTHERS, TOO? I THOUGHT IT WAS MY EYES!
WAIT A MINUTE... WE'RE BOTH WRONG . . . THERE ARE FIVE!
THAT'S A RELIEF!
FIVE MOTHERS?
AND...
EXTRA! EXTRA! PHANTOM BLOT ESCAPES! EXTRA! EXTRA! BEAGLE BOYS JOIN BLOT IN PLOT!
EXTRA!
OH, NO!
THAT DOES IT! GANGWAY, DONALD!
OOP!
I'M CALLING IN ALL OF MY GUARDS!

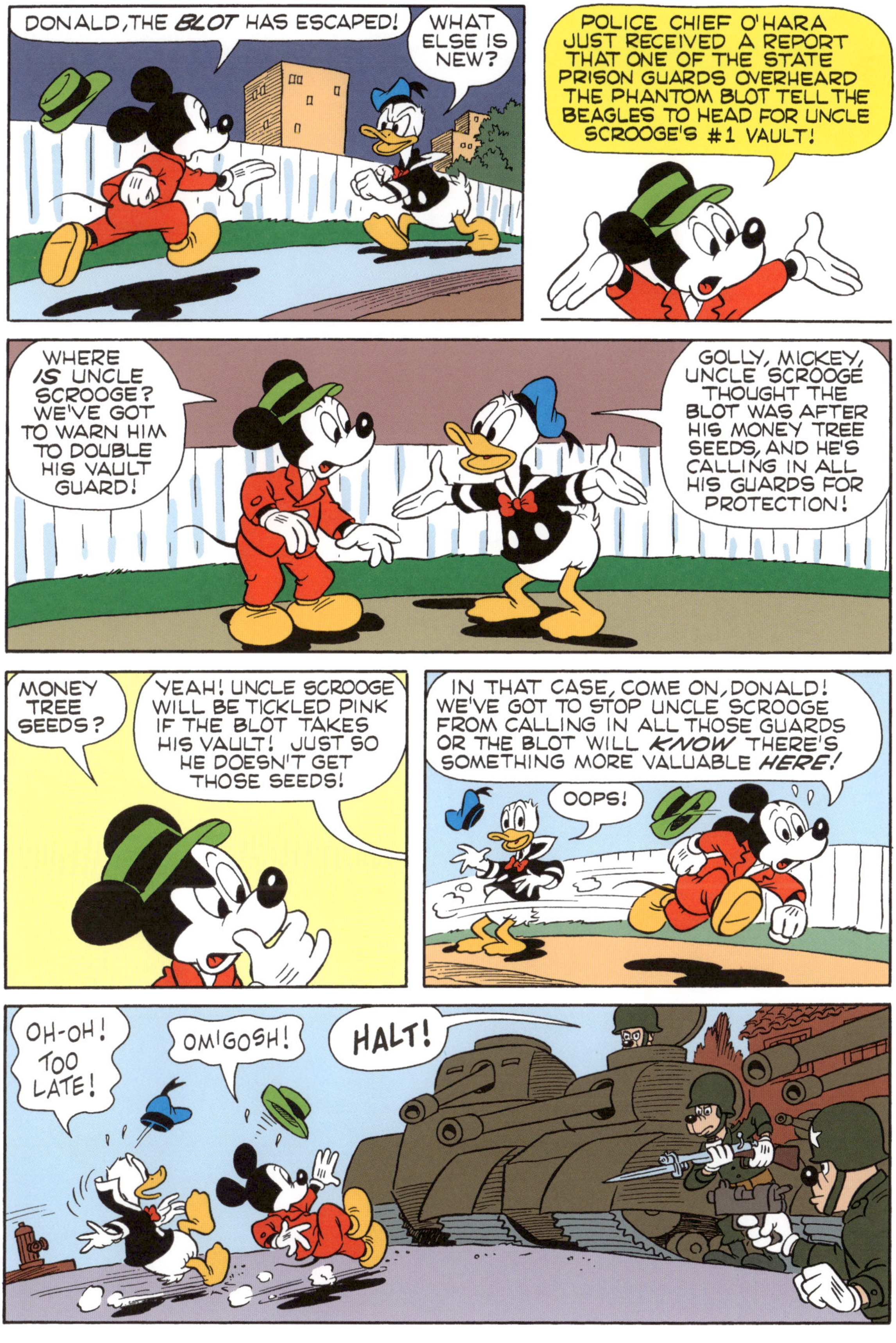
DONALD, THE BLOT HAS ESCAPED!
WHAT ELSE IS NEW?
POLICE CHIEF O'HARA JUST RECEIVED A REPORT THAT ONE OF THE STATE PRISON GUARDS OVERHEARD THE PHANTOM BLOT TELL THE BEAGLES TO HEAD FOR UNCLE SCROOGE'S #1 VAULT!
WHERE IS UNCLE SCROOGE? WE'VE GOT TO WARN HIM TO DOUBLE HIS VAULT GUARD!
GOLLY, MICKEY, UNCLE SCROOGE THOUGHT THE BLOT WAS AFTER HIS MONEY TREE SEEDS, AND HE'S CALLING IN ALL HIS GUARDS FOR PROTECTION!
MONEY TREE SEEDS?
YEAH! UNCLE SCROOGE WILL BE TICKLED PINK IF THE BLOT TAKES HIS VAULT! JUST SO HE DOESN'T GET THOSE SEEDS!
IN THAT CASE, COME ON, DONALD! WE'VE GOT TO STOP UNCLE SCROOGE FROM CALLING IN ALL THOSE GUARDS OR THE BLOT WILL KNOW THERE'S SOMETHING MORE VALUABLE HERE!
OOPS!
OH-OH! TOO LATE!
OMIGOSH!
HALT!

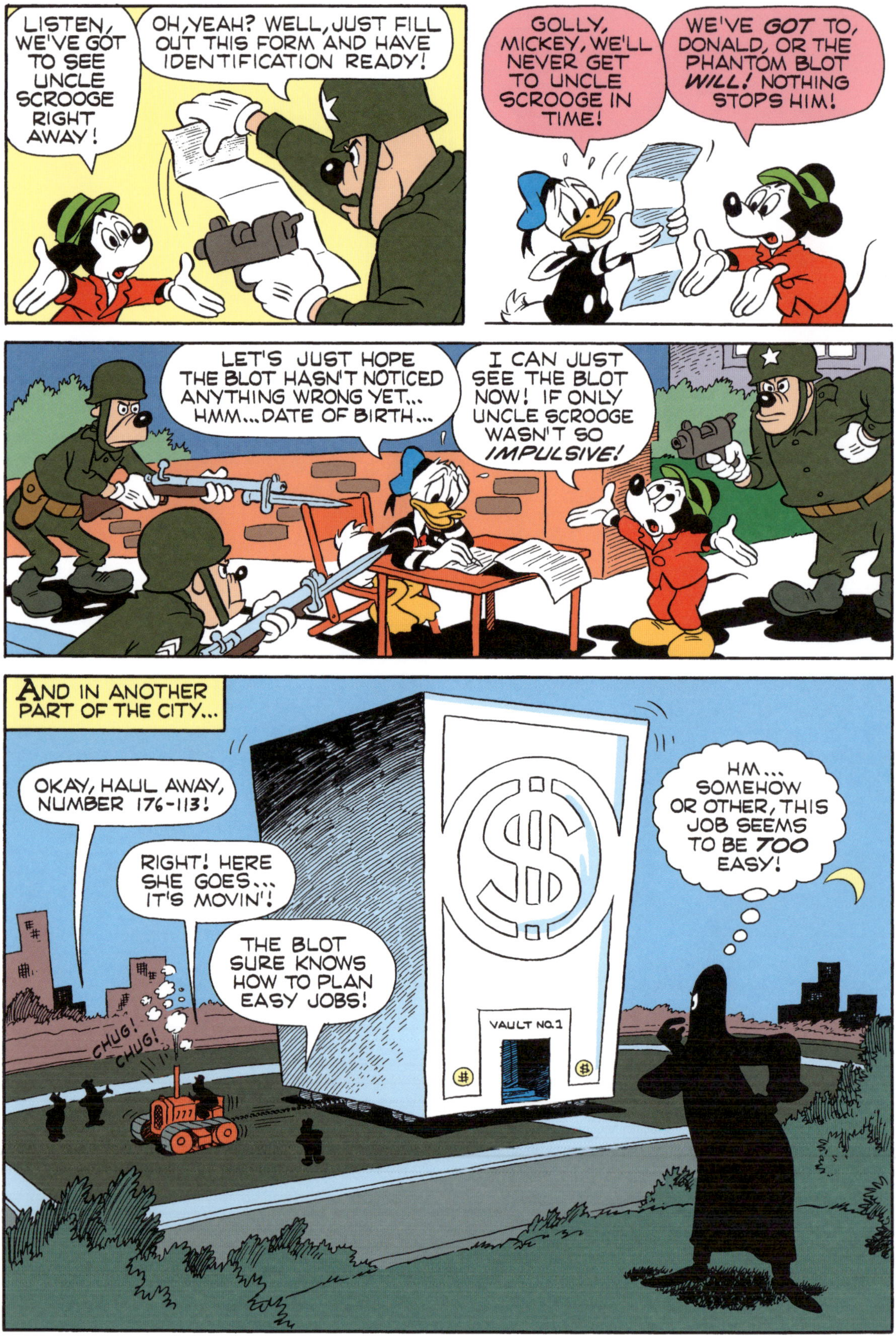

LISTEN, WE'VE GOT TO SEE UNCLE SCROOGE RIGHT AWAY!
OH, YEAH? WELL, JUST FILL OUT THIS FORM AND HAVE IDENTIFICATION READY!
GOLLY, MICKEY, WE'LL NEVER GET TO UNCLE SCROOGE IN TIME!
WE'VE *GOT* TO, DONALD, OR THE PHANTOM BLOT *WILL!* NOTHING STOPS HIM!
LET'S JUST HOPE THE BLOT HASN'T NOTICED ANYTHING WRONG YET... HMM... DATE OF BIRTH...
I CAN JUST SEE THE BLOT NOW! IF ONLY UNCLE SCROOGE WASN'T SO *IMPULSIVE!*
AND IN ANOTHER PART OF THE CITY...
OKAY, HAUL AWAY, NUMBER 176-113!
RIGHT! HERE SHE GOES... IT'S MOVIN'!
THE BLOT SURE KNOWS HOW TO PLAN EASY JOBS!
CHUG! CHUG!
VAULT NO. 1
HM... SOMEHOW OR OTHER, THIS JOB SEEMS TO BE *TOO* EASY!

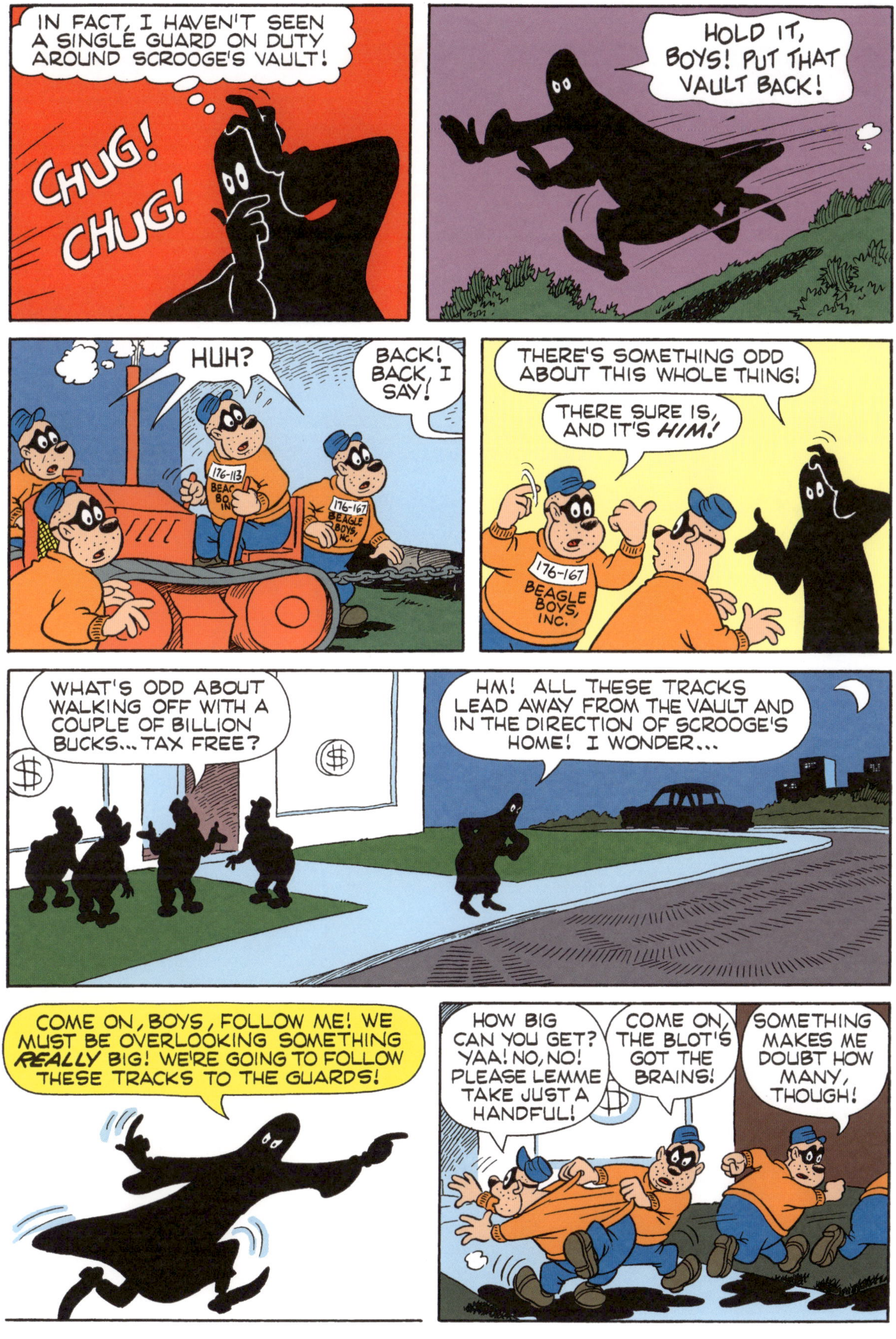
IN FACT, I HAVEN'T SEEN A SINGLE GUARD ON DUTY AROUND SCROOGE'S VAULT!
CHUG! CHUG!
HOLD IT, BOYS! PUT THAT VAULT BACK!
HUH?
BACK! BACK, I SAY!
176-113
176-167 BEAGLE BOYS, INC.
THERE'S SOMETHING ODD ABOUT THIS WHOLE THING!
THERE SURE IS, AND IT'S HIM!
176-167 BEAGLE BOYS, INC.
WHAT'S ODD ABOUT WALKING OFF WITH A COUPLE OF BILLION BUCKS... TAX FREE?
HM! ALL THESE TRACKS LEAD AWAY FROM THE VAULT AND IN THE DIRECTION OF SCROOGE'S HOME! I WONDER...
COME ON, BOYS, FOLLOW ME! WE MUST BE OVERLOOKING SOMETHING REALLY BIG! WE'RE GOING TO FOLLOW THESE TRACKS TO THE GUARDS!
HOW BIG CAN YOU GET? YAA! NO, NO! PLEASE LEMME TAKE JUST A HANDFUL!
COME ON, THE BLOT'S GOT THE BRAINS!
SOMETHING MAKES ME DOUBT HOW MANY, THOUGH!

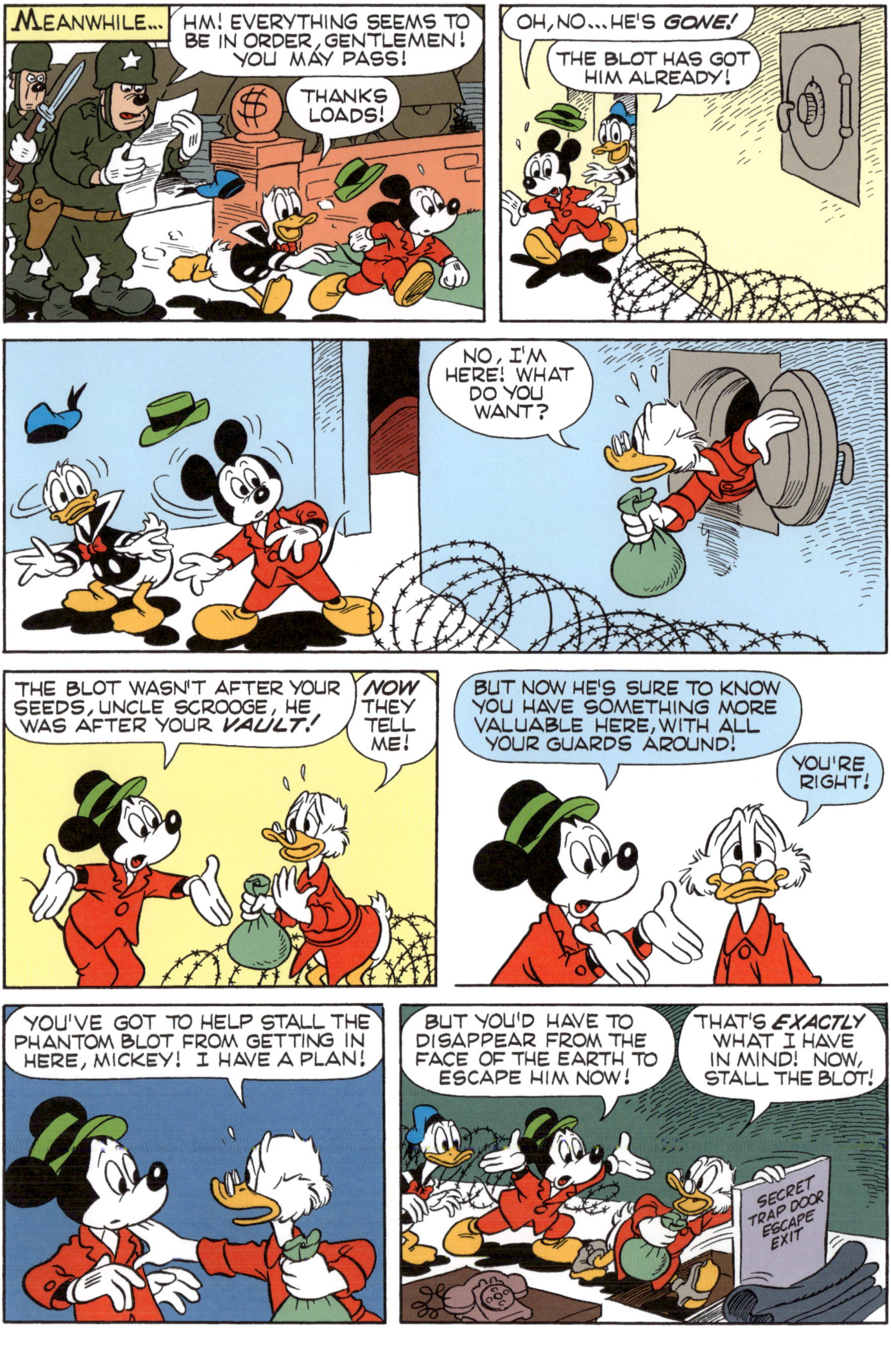
MEANWHILE...
HM! EVERYTHING SEEMS TO BE IN ORDER, GENTLEMEN! YOU MAY PASS!
THANKS LOADS!
OH, NO...HE'S *GONE!*
THE BLOT HAS GOT HIM ALREADY!
NO, I'M HERE! WHAT DO YOU WANT?
THE BLOT WASN'T AFTER YOUR SEEDS, UNCLE SCROOGE, HE WAS AFTER YOUR *VAULT!*
NOW THEY TELL ME!
BUT NOW HE'S SURE TO KNOW YOU HAVE SOMETHING MORE VALUABLE HERE, WITH ALL YOUR GUARDS AROUND!
YOU'RE RIGHT!
YOU'VE GOT TO HELP STALL THE PHANTOM BLOT FROM GETTING IN HERE, MICKEY! I HAVE A PLAN!
BUT YOU'D HAVE TO DISAPPEAR FROM THE FACE OF THE EARTH TO ESCAPE HIM NOW!
THAT'S *EXACTLY* WHAT I HAVE IN MIND! NOW, STALL THE BLOT!
SECRET TRAP DOOR ESCAPE EXIT

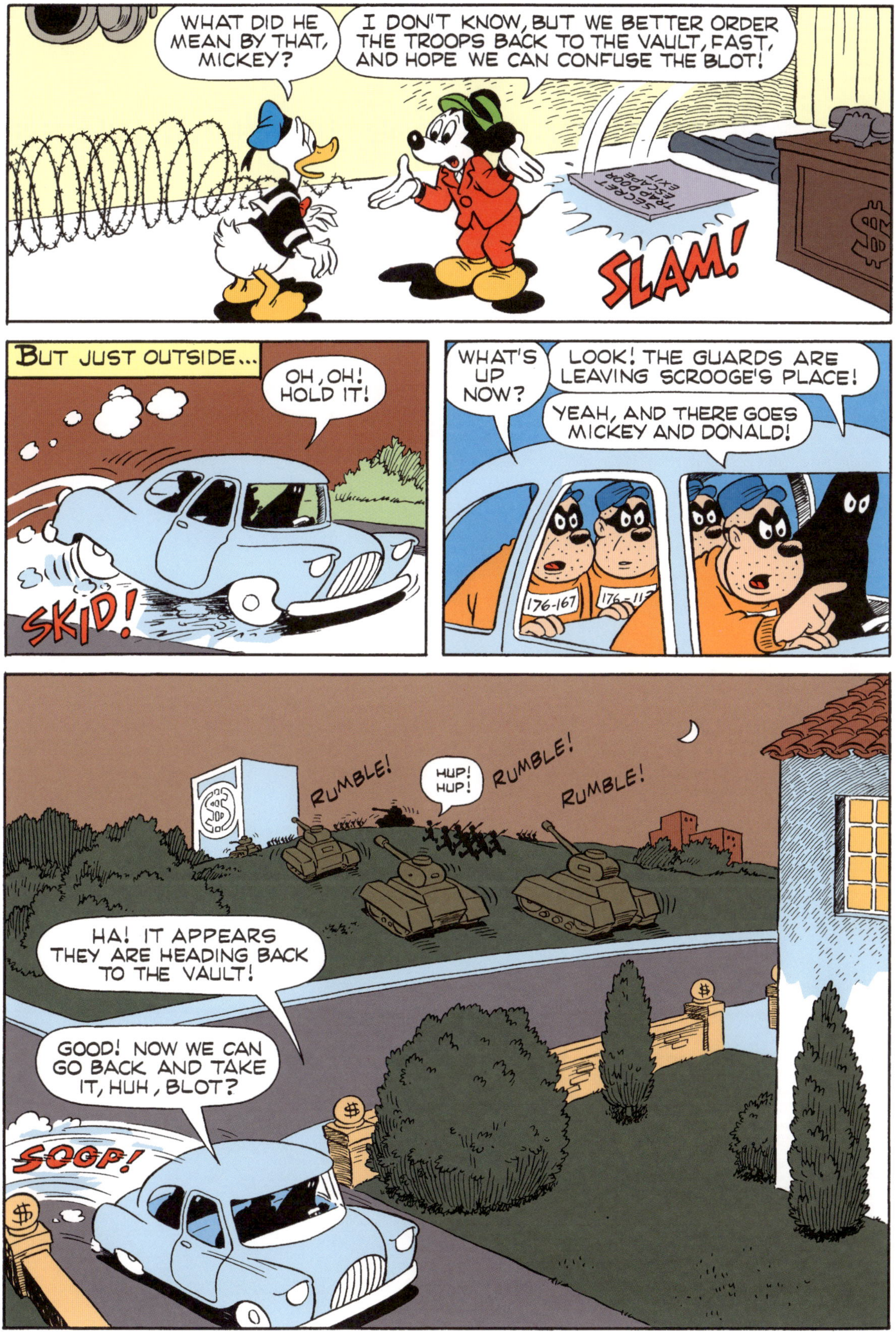
WHAT DID HE MEAN BY THAT, MICKEY?
I DON'T KNOW, BUT WE BETTER ORDER THE TROOPS BACK TO THE VAULT, FAST, AND HOPE WE CAN CONFUSE THE BLOT!
SECRET TRAPDOOR ESCAPE EXIT
SLAM!
BUT JUST OUTSIDE...
OH, OH! HOLD IT!
SKID!
WHAT'S UP NOW?
LOOK! THE GUARDS ARE LEAVING SCROOGE'S PLACE!
YEAH, AND THERE GOES MICKEY AND DONALD!
176-167
RUMBLE!
HUP! HUP!
RUMBLE!
RUMBLE!
HA! IT APPEARS THEY ARE HEADING BACK TO THE VAULT!
GOOD! NOW WE CAN GO BACK AND TAKE IT, HUH, BLOT?
SOOP!

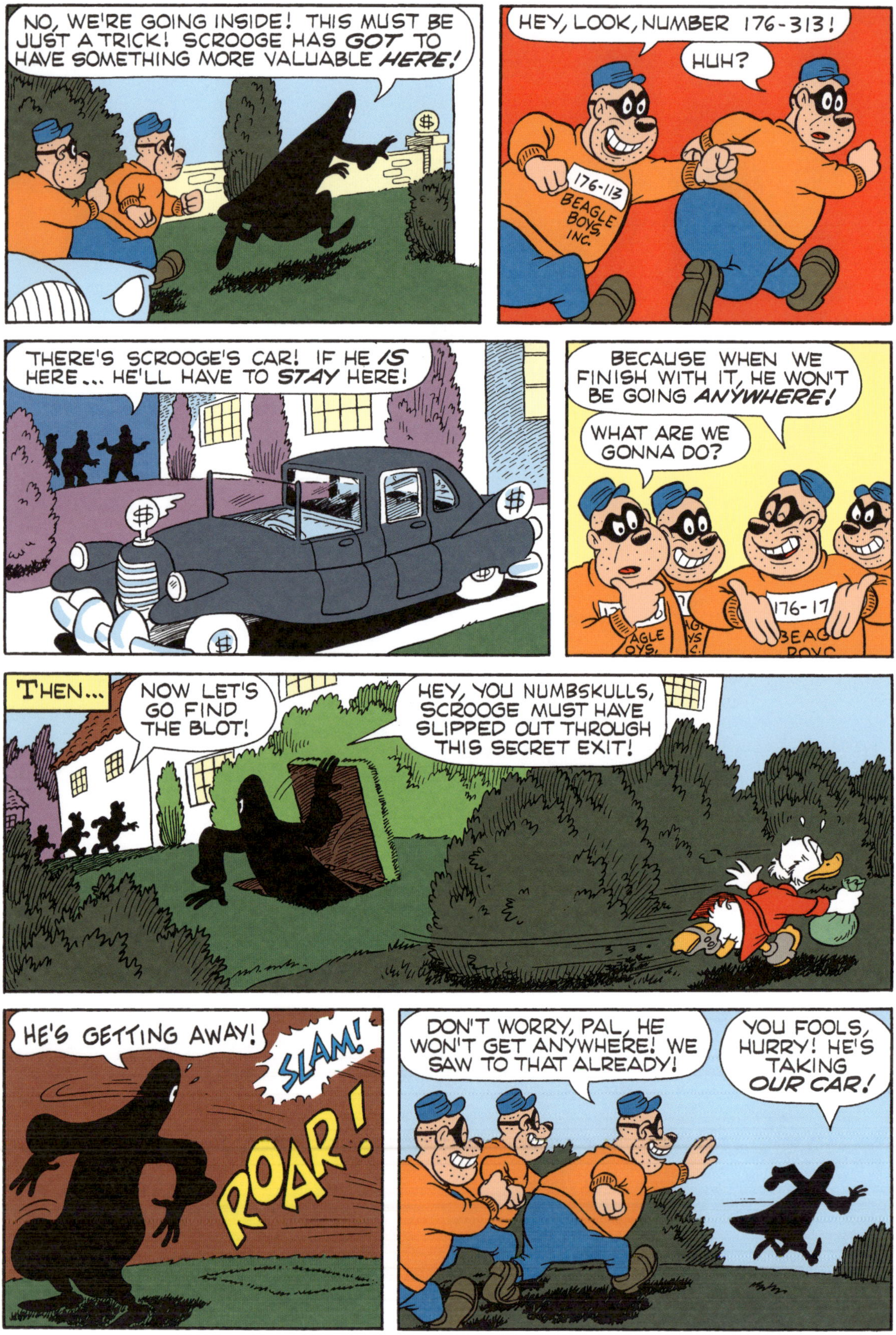
NO, WE'RE GOING INSIDE! THIS MUST BE JUST A TRICK! SCROOGE HAS GOT TO HAVE SOMETHING MORE VALUABLE HERE!
HEY, LOOK, NUMBER 176-313!
HUH?
176-113 BEAGLE BOYS, INC.
THERE'S SCROOGE'S CAR! IF HE IS HERE... HE'LL HAVE TO STAY HERE!
WHAT ARE WE GONNA DO?
BECAUSE WHEN WE FINISH WITH IT, HE WON'T BE GOING ANYWHERE!
THEN...
NOW LET'S GO FIND THE BLOT!
HEY, YOU NUMBSKULLS, SCROOGE MUST HAVE SLIPPED OUT THROUGH THIS SECRET EXIT!
HE'S GETTING AWAY!
SLAM!
ROAR!
DON'T WORRY, PAL, HE WON'T GET ANYWHERE! WE SAW TO THAT ALREADY!
YOU FOOLS, HURRY! HE'S TAKING OUR CAR!

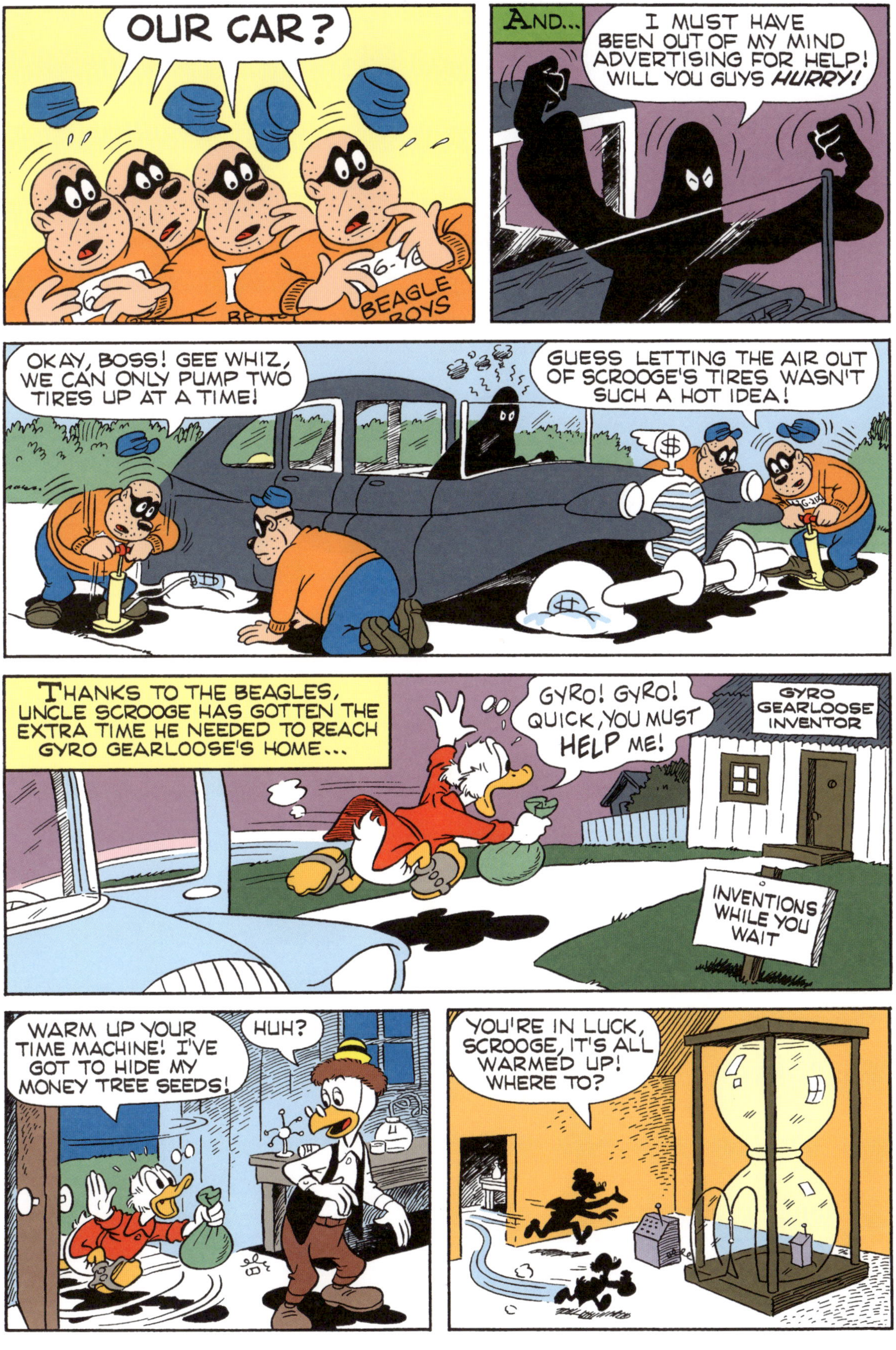
OUR CAR?
BEAGLE BOYS
AND...
I MUST HAVE BEEN OUT OF MY MIND ADVERTISING FOR HELP! WILL YOU GUYS HURRY!
OKAY, BOSS! GEE WHIZ, WE CAN ONLY PUMP TWO TIRES UP AT A TIME!
GUESS LETTING THE AIR OUT OF SCROOGE'S TIRES WASN'T SUCH A HOT IDEA!
THANKS TO THE BEAGLES, UNCLE SCROOGE HAS GOTTEN THE EXTRA TIME HE NEEDED TO REACH GYRO GEARLOOSE'S HOME...
GYRO! GYRO! QUICK, YOU MUST HELP ME!
GYRO GEARLOOSE INVENTOR
INVENTIONS WHILE YOU WAIT
WARM UP YOUR TIME MACHINE! I'VE GOT TO HIDE MY MONEY TREE SEEDS!
HUH?
YOU'RE IN LUCK, SCROOGE, IT'S ALL WARMED UP! WHERE TO?

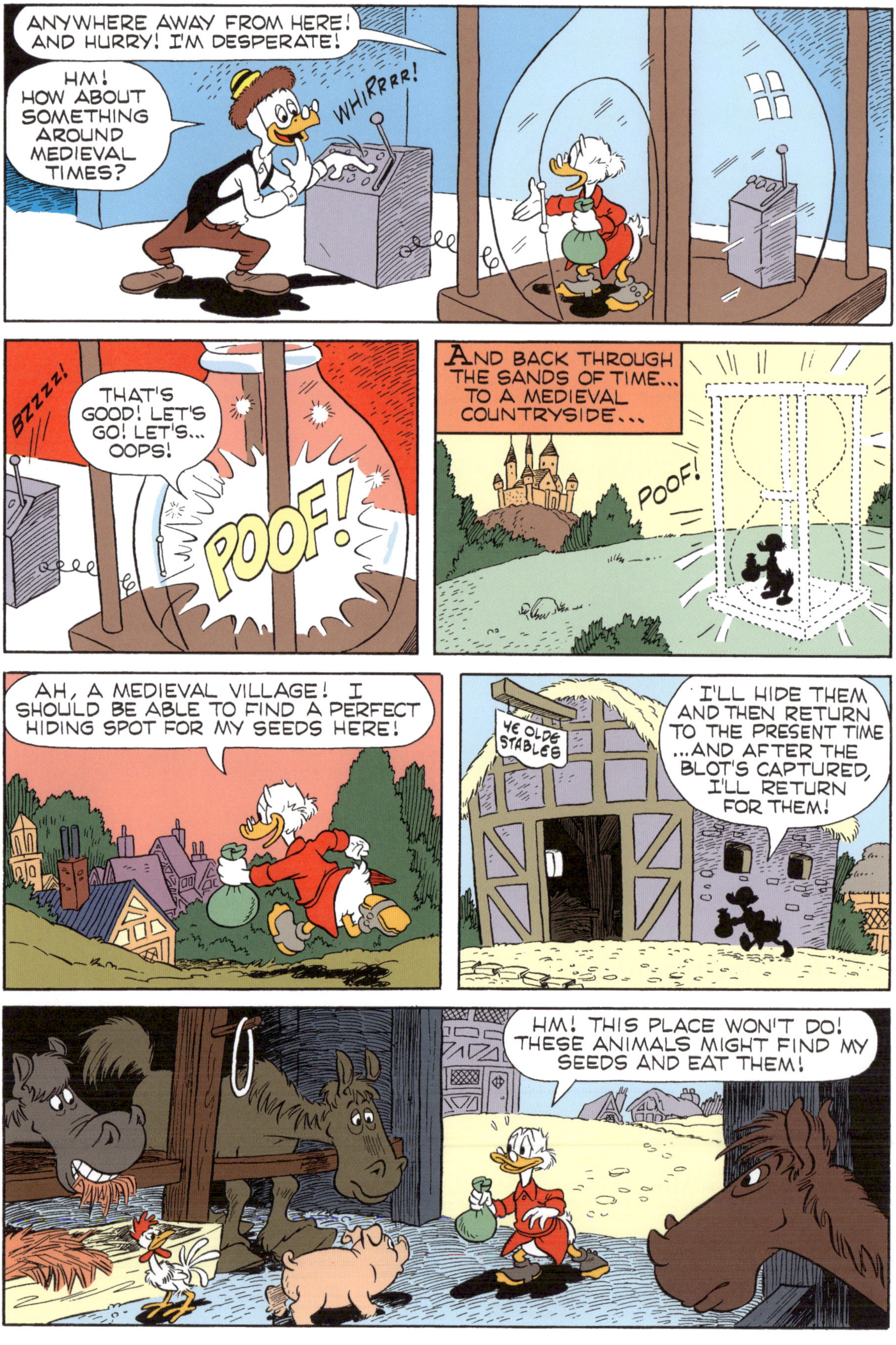

ANYWHERE AWAY FROM HERE! AND HURRY! I'M DESPERATE!
HM! HOW ABOUT SOMETHING AROUND MEDIEVAL TIMES?
WHIRRRR!
BZZZZ!
THAT'S GOOD! LET'S GO! LET'S... OOPS!
POOF!
AND BACK THROUGH THE SANDS OF TIME... TO A MEDIEVAL COUNTRYSIDE...
POOF!
AH, A MEDIEVAL VILLAGE! I SHOULD BE ABLE TO FIND A PERFECT HIDING SPOT FOR MY SEEDS HERE!
YE OLDE STABLES
I'LL HIDE THEM AND THEN RETURN TO THE PRESENT TIME ...AND AFTER THE BLOT'S CAPTURED, I'LL RETURN FOR THEM!
HM! THIS PLACE WON'T DO! THESE ANIMALS MIGHT FIND MY SEEDS AND EAT THEM!

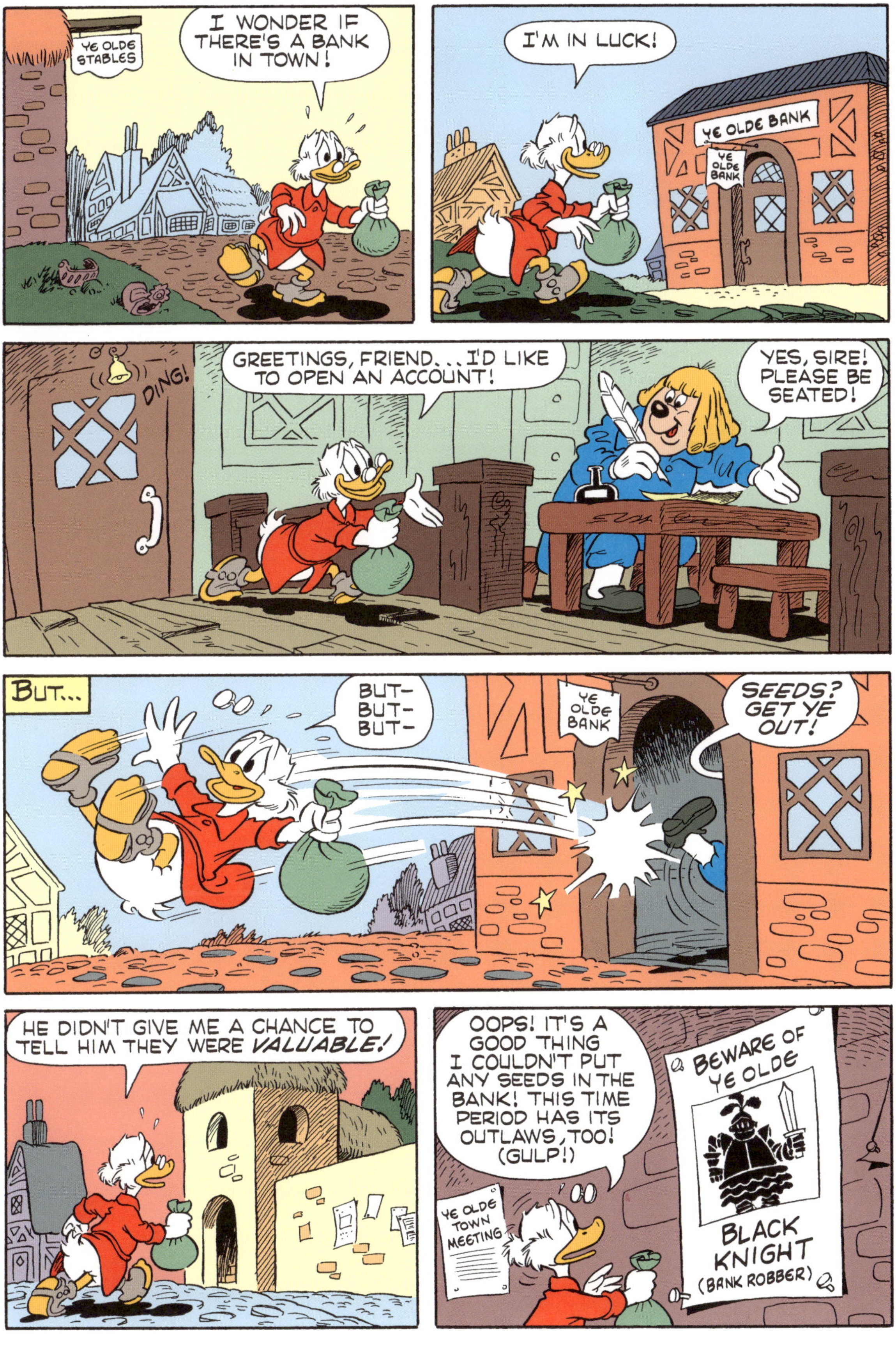
YE OLDE STABLES
I WONDER IF THERE'S A BANK IN TOWN!
I'M IN LUCK!
YE OLDE BANK
YE OLDE BANK
DING!
GREETINGS, FRIEND...I'D LIKE TO OPEN AN ACCOUNT!
YES, SIRE! PLEASE BE SEATED!
BUT...
BUT- BUT- BUT-
YE OLDE BANK
SEEDS? GET YE OUT!
HE DIDN'T GIVE ME A CHANCE TO TELL HIM THEY WERE *VALUABLE!*
OOPS! IT'S A GOOD THING I COULDN'T PUT ANY SEEDS IN THE BANK! THIS TIME PERIOD HAS ITS OUTLAWS, TOO! (GULP!)
YE OLDE TOWN MEETING
BEWARE OF YE OLDE
BLACK KNIGHT (BANK ROBBER)

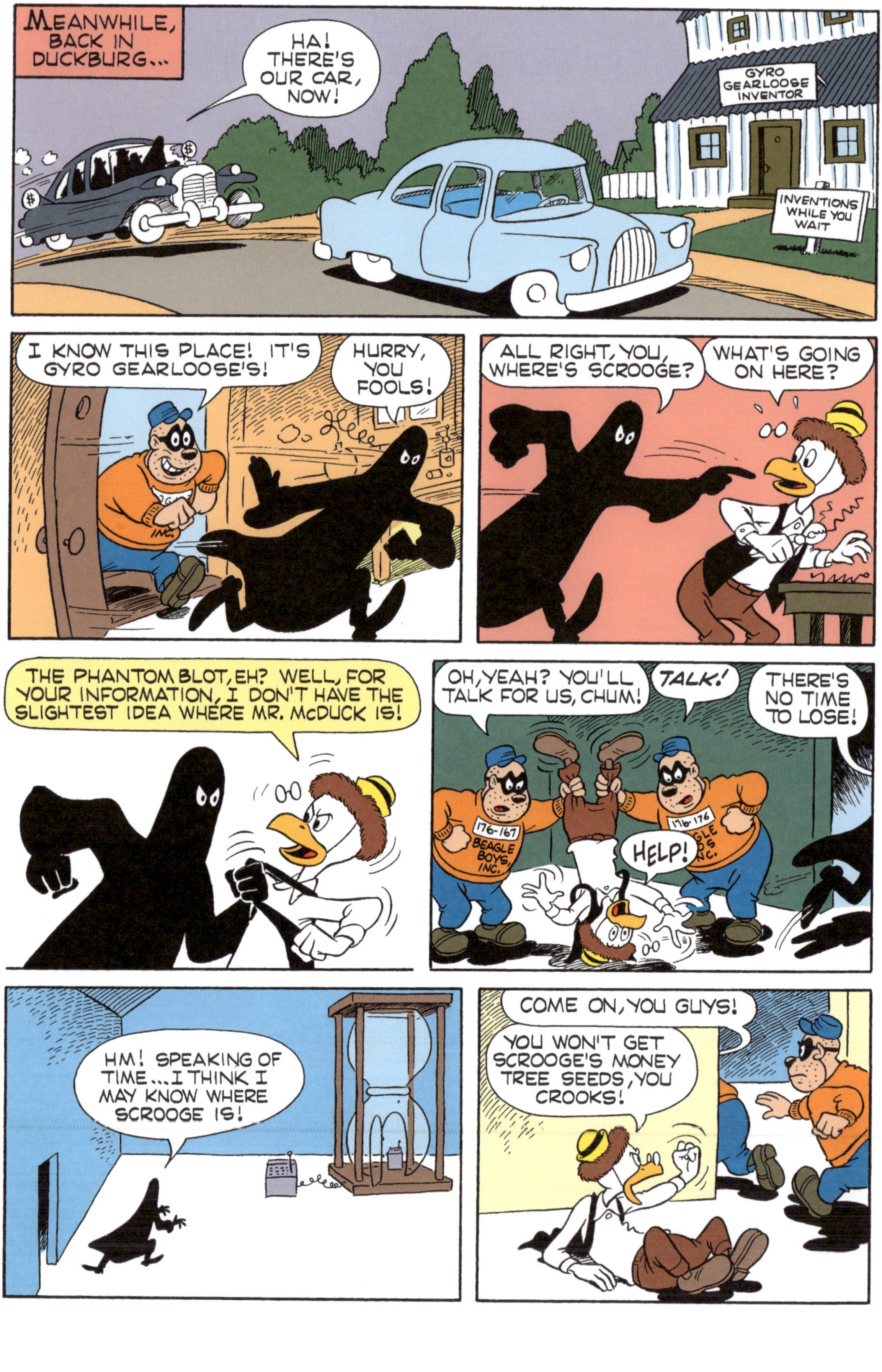
MEANWHILE, BACK IN DUCKBURG...
HA! THERE'S OUR CAR, NOW!
GYRO GEARLOOSE INVENTOR
INVENTIONS WHILE YOU WAIT
I KNOW THIS PLACE! IT'S GYRO GEARLOOSE'S!
HURRY, YOU FOOLS!
ALL RIGHT, YOU, WHERE'S SCROOGE?
WHAT'S GOING ON HERE?
THE PHANTOM BLOT, EH? WELL, FOR YOUR INFORMATION, I DON'T HAVE THE SLIGHTEST IDEA WHERE MR. McDUCK IS!
OH, YEAH? YOU'LL TALK FOR US, CHUM!
TALK!
THERE'S NO TIME TO LOSE!
176-167
BEAGLE BOYS, INC.
176-176
HELP!
HM! SPEAKING OF TIME...I THINK I MAY KNOW WHERE SCROOGE IS!
COME ON, YOU GUYS!
YOU WON'T GET SCROOGE'S MONEY TREE SEEDS, YOU CROOKS!

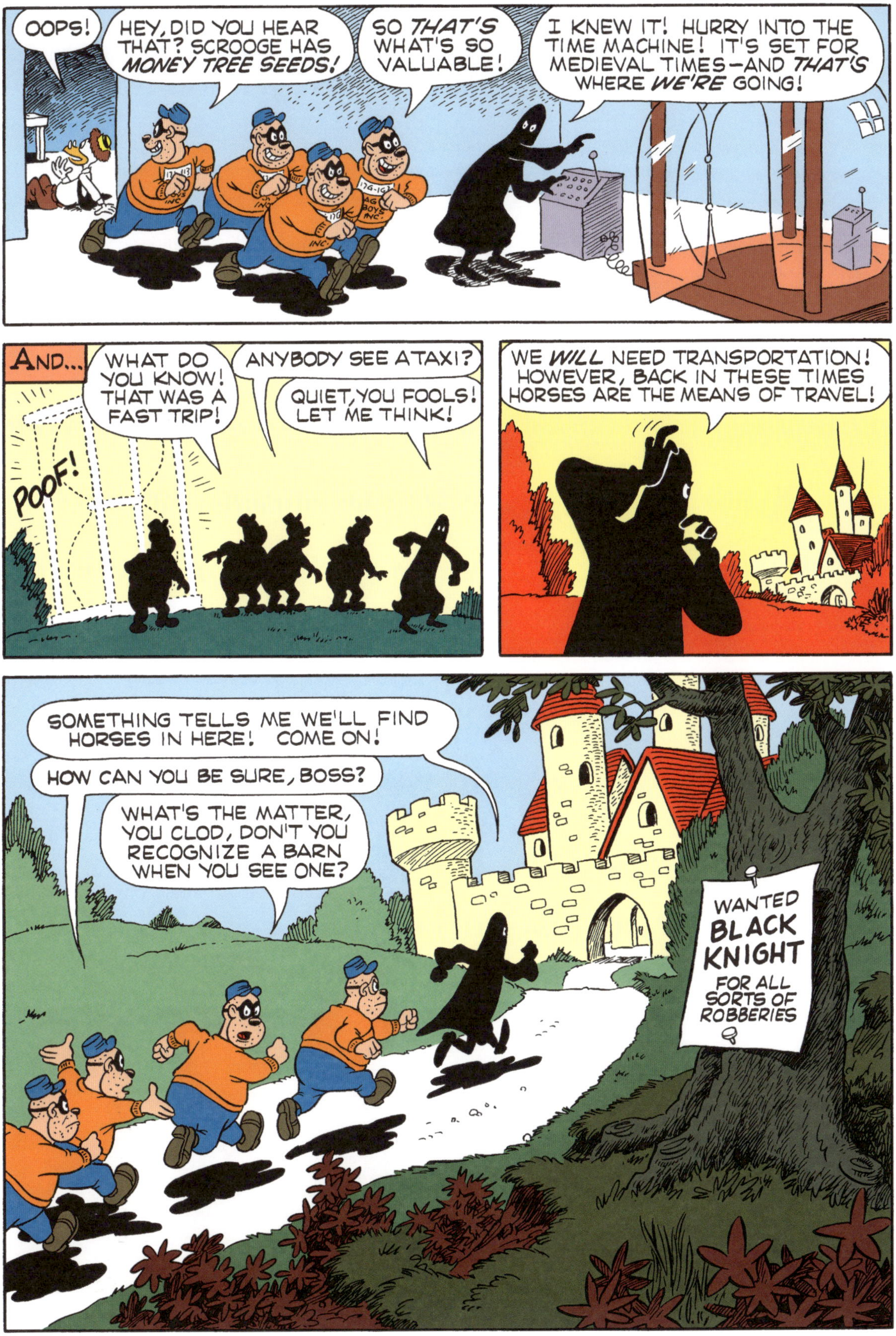

OOPS!
HEY, DID YOU HEAR THAT? SCROOGE HAS MONEY TREE SEEDS!
SO THAT'S WHAT'S SO VALUABLE!
I KNEW IT! HURRY INTO THE TIME MACHINE! IT'S SET FOR MEDIEVAL TIMES—AND THAT'S WHERE WE'RE GOING!
AND...
WHAT DO YOU KNOW! THAT WAS A FAST TRIP!
ANYBODY SEE A TAXI?
QUIET, YOU FOOLS! LET ME THINK!
POOF!
WE WILL NEED TRANSPORTATION! HOWEVER, BACK IN THESE TIMES HORSES ARE THE MEANS OF TRAVEL!
SOMETHING TELLS ME WE'LL FIND HORSES IN HERE! COME ON!
HOW CAN YOU BE SURE, BOSS?
WHAT'S THE MATTER, YOU CLOD, DON'T YOU RECOGNIZE A BARN WHEN YOU SEE ONE?
WANTED BLACK KNIGHT FOR ALL SORTS OF ROBBERIES

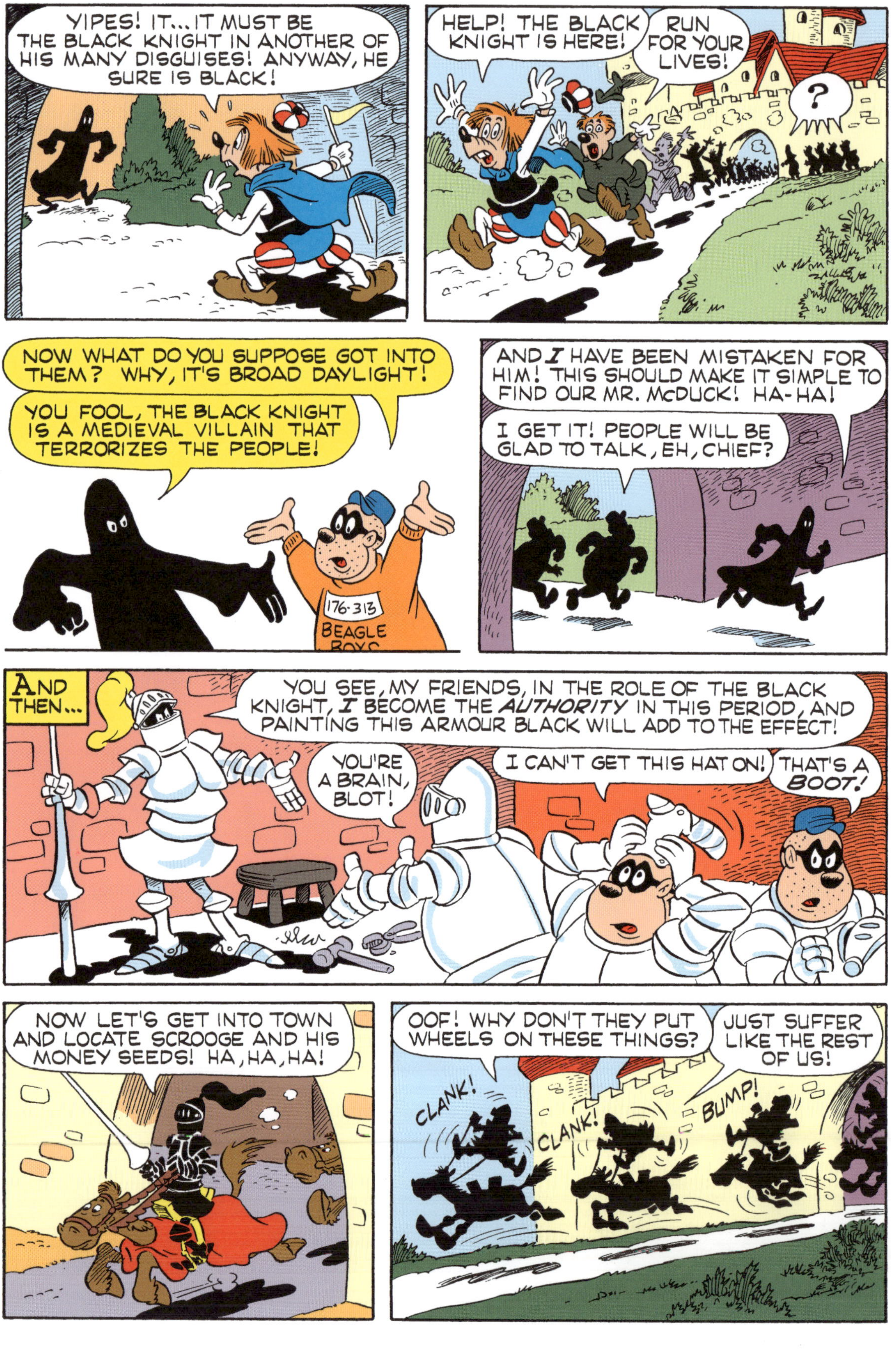
YIPES! IT... IT MUST BE THE BLACK KNIGHT IN ANOTHER OF HIS MANY DISGUISES! ANYWAY, HE SURE IS BLACK!
HELP! THE BLACK KNIGHT IS HERE!
RUN FOR YOUR LIVES!
?
NOW WHAT DO YOU SUPPOSE GOT INTO THEM? WHY, IT'S BROAD DAYLIGHT!
YOU FOOL, THE BLACK KNIGHT IS A MEDIEVAL VILLAIN THAT TERRORIZES THE PEOPLE!
176-313
BEAGLE BOYS
AND I HAVE BEEN MISTAKEN FOR HIM! THIS SHOULD MAKE IT SIMPLE TO FIND OUR MR. McDUCK! HA-HA!
I GET IT! PEOPLE WILL BE GLAD TO TALK, EH, CHIEF?
AND THEN...
YOU SEE, MY FRIENDS, IN THE ROLE OF THE BLACK KNIGHT, I BECOME THE AUTHORITY IN THIS PERIOD, AND PAINTING THIS ARMOUR BLACK WILL ADD TO THE EFFECT!
YOU'RE A BRAIN, BLOT!
I CAN'T GET THIS HAT ON!
THAT'S A BOOT!
NOW LET'S GET INTO TOWN AND LOCATE SCROOGE AND HIS MONEY SEEDS! HA, HA, HA!
OOF! WHY DON'T THEY PUT WHEELS ON THESE THINGS?
JUST SUFFER LIKE THE REST OF US!
CLANK!
CLANK!
BUMP!

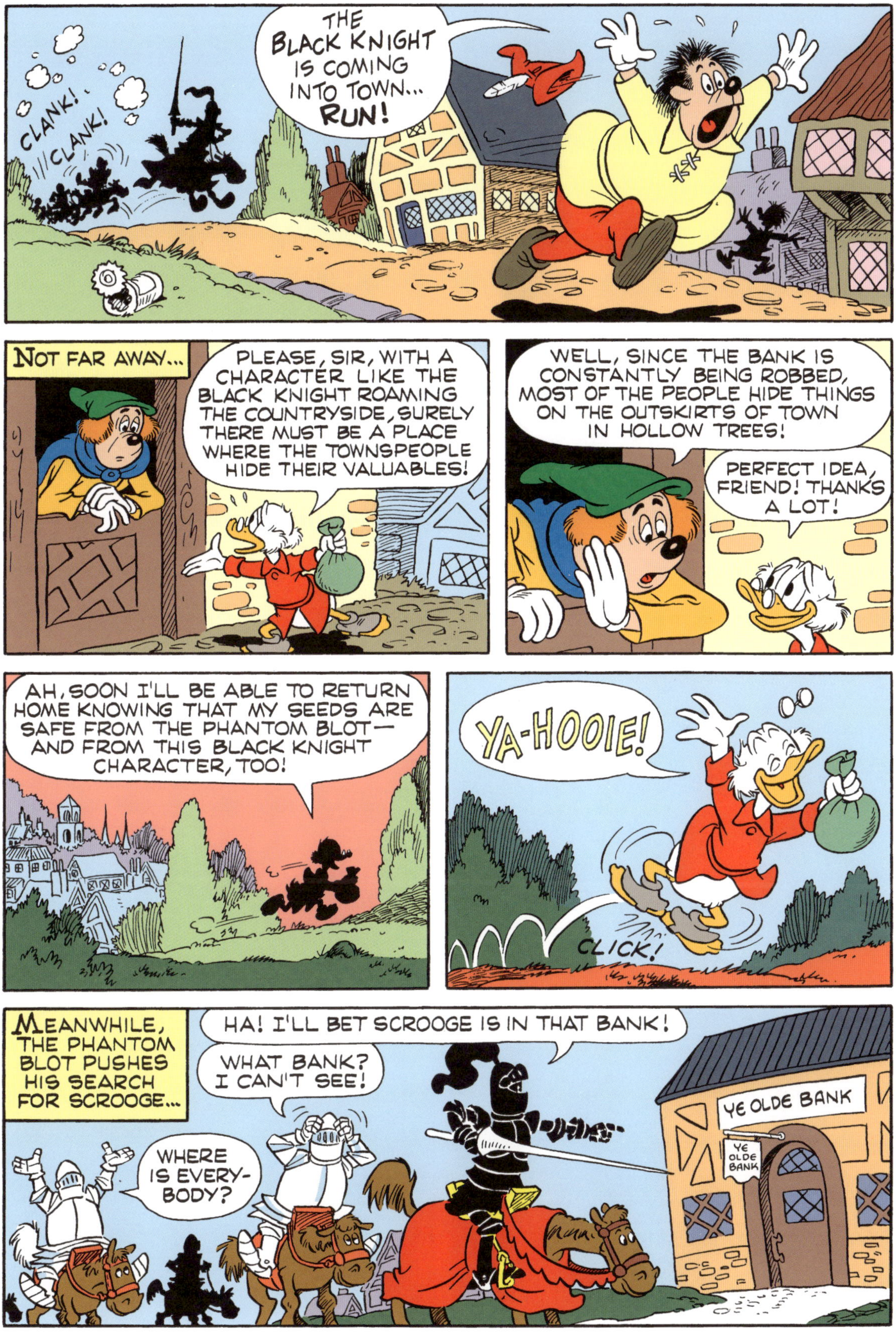

CLANK! CLANK!
THE BLACK KNIGHT IS COMING INTO TOWN... RUN!
NOT FAR AWAY...
PLEASE, SIR, WITH A CHARACTER LIKE THE BLACK KNIGHT ROAMING THE COUNTRYSIDE, SURELY THERE MUST BE A PLACE WHERE THE TOWNSPEOPLE HIDE THEIR VALUABLES!
WELL, SINCE THE BANK IS CONSTANTLY BEING ROBBED, MOST OF THE PEOPLE HIDE THINGS ON THE OUTSKIRTS OF TOWN IN HOLLOW TREES!
PERFECT IDEA, FRIEND! THANKS A LOT!
AH, SOON I'LL BE ABLE TO RETURN HOME KNOWING THAT MY SEEDS ARE SAFE FROM THE PHANTOM BLOT— AND FROM THIS BLACK KNIGHT CHARACTER, TOO!
YA-HOOIE!
CLICK!
MEANWHILE, THE PHANTOM BLOT PUSHES HIS SEARCH FOR SCROOGE...
HA! I'LL BET SCROOGE IS IN THAT BANK!
WHAT BANK? I CAN'T SEE!
WHERE IS EVERY-BODY?
YE OLDE BANK
YE OLDE BANK

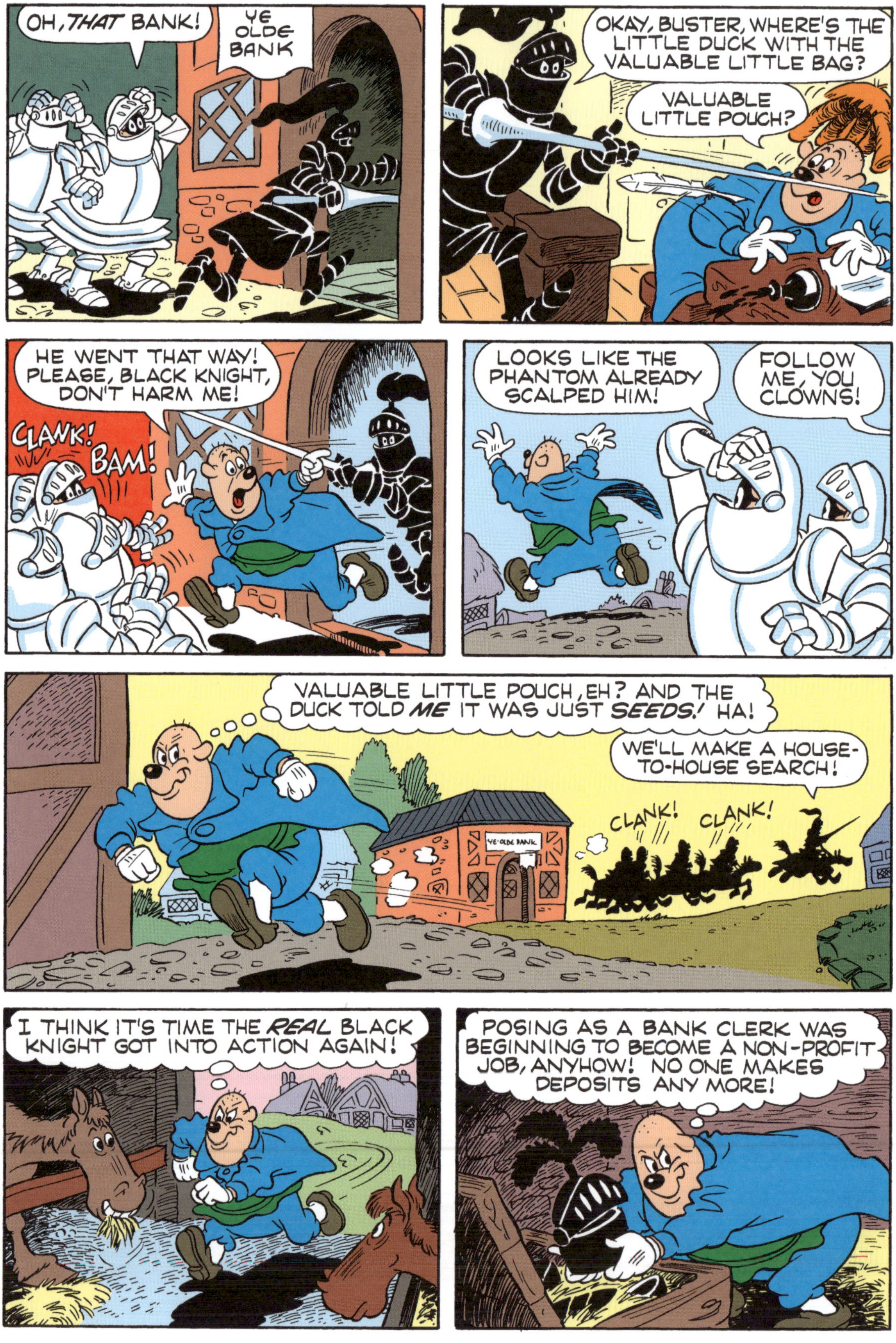
OH, *THAT* BANK!
YE OLDE BANK
OKAY, BUSTER, WHERE'S THE LITTLE DUCK WITH THE VALUABLE LITTLE BAG?
VALUABLE LITTLE POUCH?
HE WENT THAT WAY! PLEASE, BLACK KNIGHT, DON'T HARM ME!
CLANK! BAM!
LOOKS LIKE THE PHANTOM ALREADY SCALPED HIM!
FOLLOW ME, YOU CLOWNS!
VALUABLE LITTLE POUCH, EH? AND THE DUCK TOLD *ME* IT WAS JUST *SEEDS!* HA!
WE'LL MAKE A HOUSE-TO-HOUSE SEARCH!
YE OLDE BANK
CLANK! CLANK!
I THINK IT'S TIME THE *REAL* BLACK KNIGHT GOT INTO ACTION AGAIN!
POSING AS A BANK CLERK WAS BEGINNING TO BECOME A NON-PROFIT JOB, ANYHOW! NO ONE MAKES DEPOSITS ANY MORE!

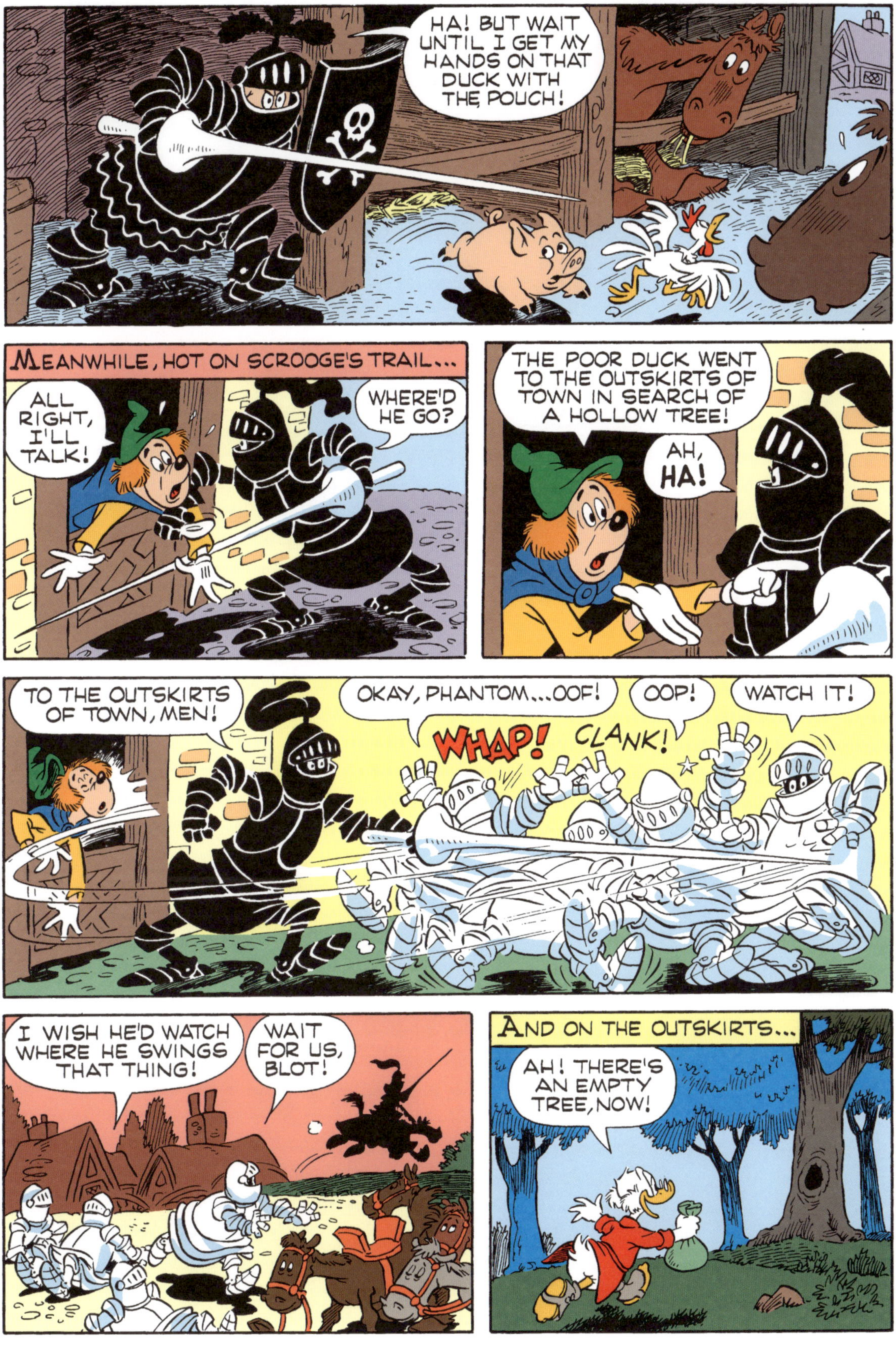
HA! BUT WAIT UNTIL I GET MY HANDS ON THAT DUCK WITH THE POUCH!
MEANWHILE, HOT ON SCROOGE'S TRAIL...
ALL RIGHT, I'LL TALK!
WHERE'D HE GO?
THE POOR DUCK WENT TO THE OUTSKIRTS OF TOWN IN SEARCH OF A HOLLOW TREE!
AH, HA!
TO THE OUTSKIRTS OF TOWN, MEN!
OKAY, PHANTOM...OOF!
OOP!
WATCH IT!
WHAP!
CLANK!
I WISH HE'D WATCH WHERE HE SWINGS THAT THING!
WAIT FOR US, BLOT!
AND ON THE OUTSKIRTS...
AH! THERE'S AN EMPTY TREE, NOW!

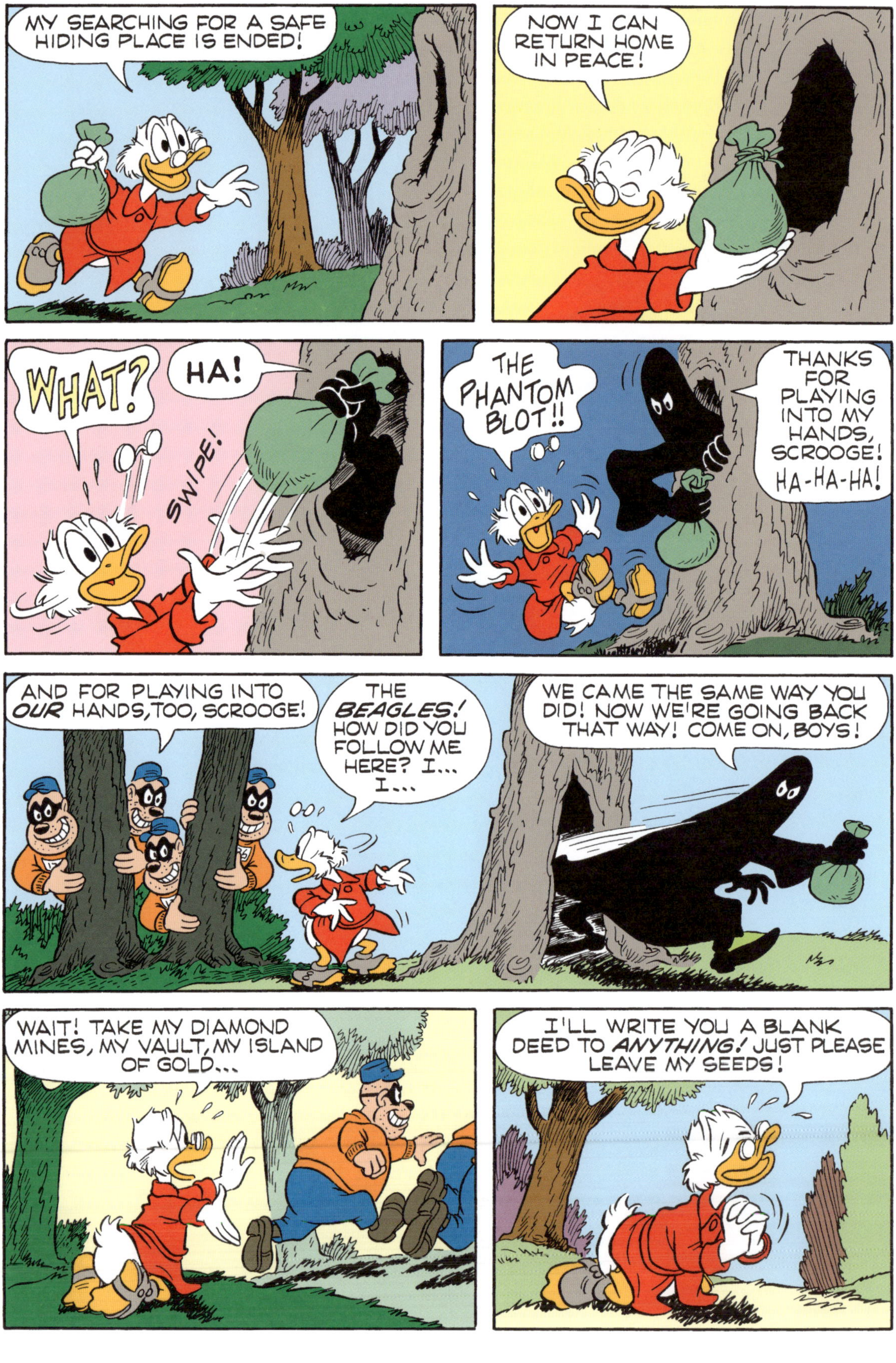
MY SEARCHING FOR A SAFE HIDING PLACE IS ENDED!
NOW I CAN RETURN HOME IN PEACE!
WHAT?
HA!
SWIPE!
THE PHANTOM BLOT!!
THANKS FOR PLAYING INTO MY HANDS, SCROOGE! HA-HA-HA!
AND FOR PLAYING INTO *OUR* HANDS, TOO, SCROOGE!
THE *BEAGLES!* HOW DID YOU FOLLOW ME HERE? I... I...
WE CAME THE SAME WAY YOU DID! NOW WE'RE GOING BACK THAT WAY! COME ON, BOYS!
WAIT! TAKE MY DIAMOND MINES, MY VAULT, MY ISLAND OF GOLD...
I'LL WRITE YOU A BLANK DEED TO *ANYTHING!* JUST PLEASE LEAVE MY SEEDS!

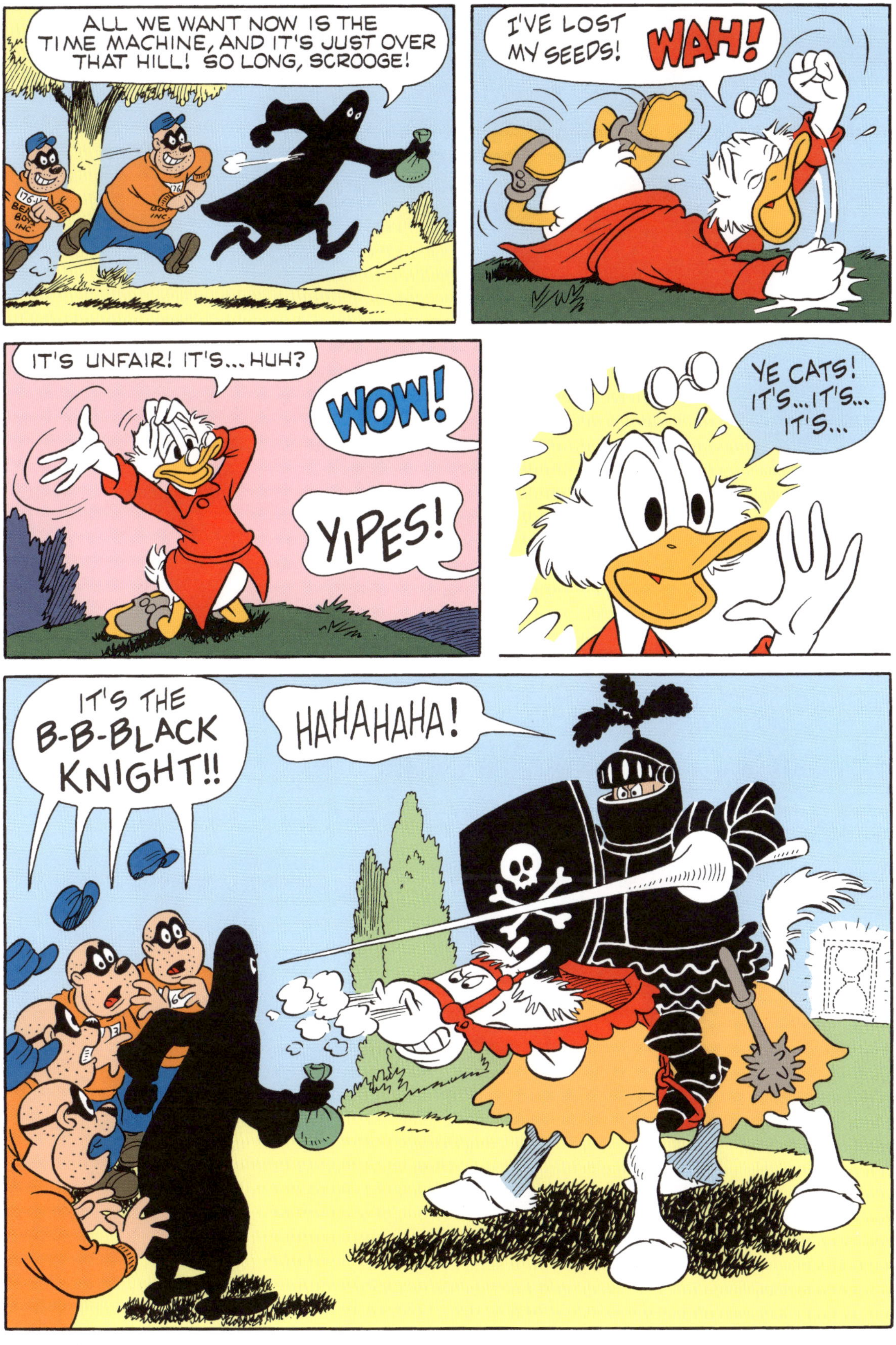
ALL WE WANT NOW IS THE TIME MACHINE, AND IT'S JUST OVER THAT HILL! SO LONG, SCROOGE!
I'VE LOST MY SEEDS!
WAH!
IT'S UNFAIR! IT'S... HUH?
WOW!
YIPES!
YE CATS! IT'S...IT'S... IT'S...
IT'S THE B-B-BLACK KNIGHT!!
HAHAHAHA!

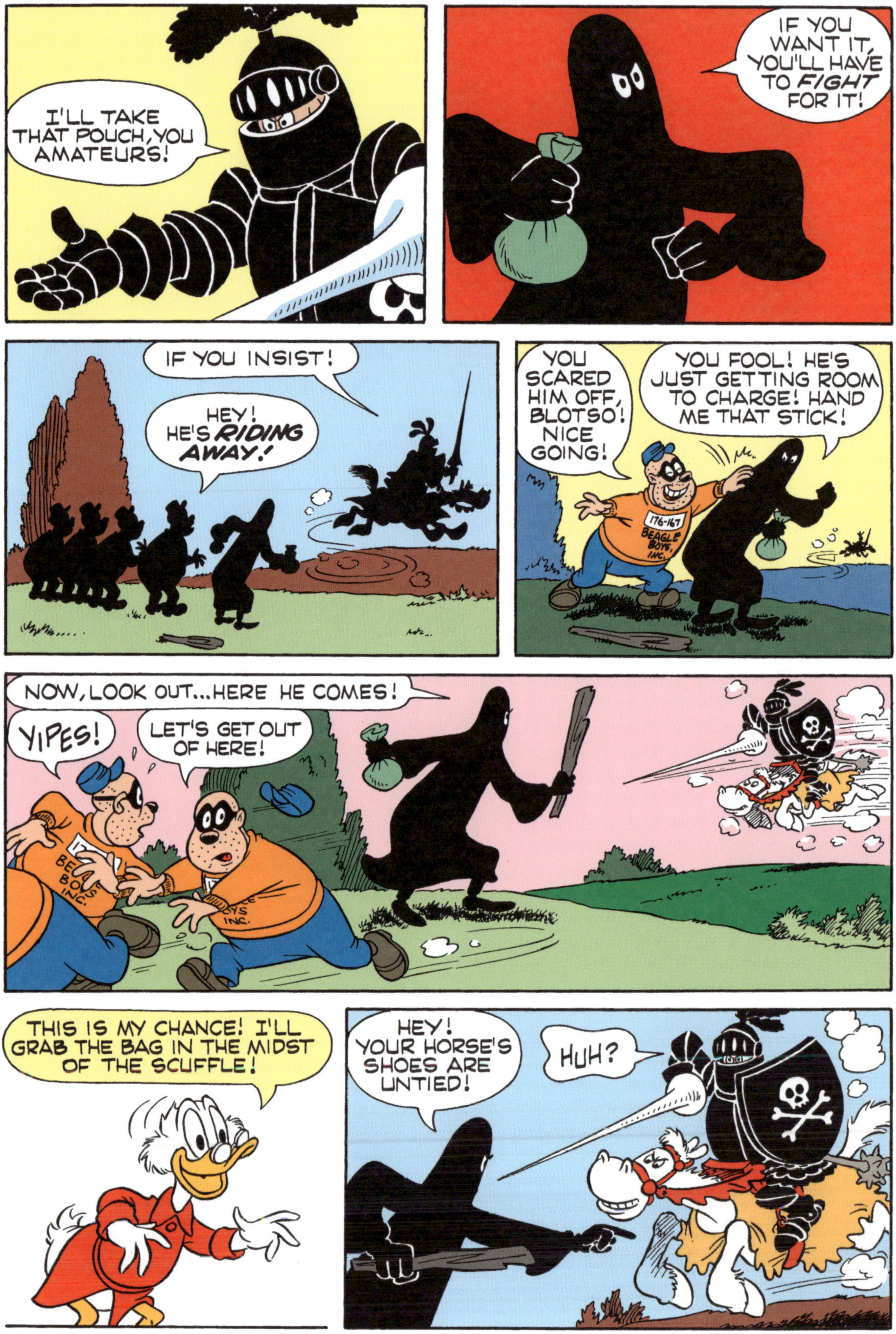

I'LL TAKE THAT POUCH, YOU AMATEURS!
IF YOU WANT IT, YOU'LL HAVE TO *FIGHT* FOR IT!
IF YOU INSIST!
HEY! HE'S *RIDING AWAY!*
YOU SCARED HIM OFF, BLOTSO! NICE GOING!
YOU FOOL! HE'S JUST GETTING ROOM TO CHARGE! HAND ME THAT STICK!
176-167
BEAGLE BOYS, INC.
NOW, LOOK OUT...HERE HE COMES!
YIPES!
LET'S GET OUT OF HERE!
THIS IS MY CHANCE! I'LL GRAB THE BAG IN THE MIDST OF THE SCUFFLE!
HEY! YOUR HORSE'S SHOES ARE UNTIED!
HUH?

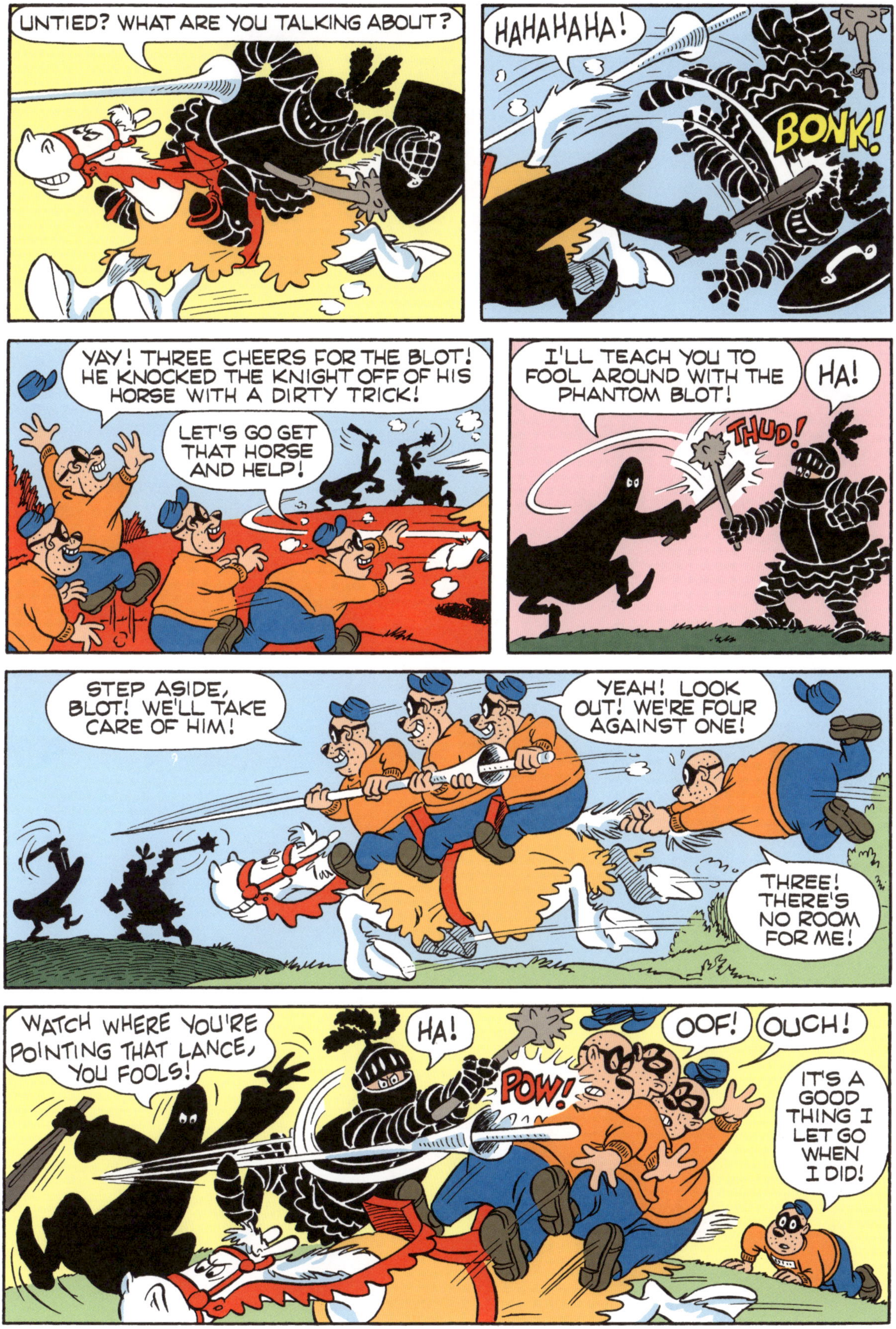
UNTIED? WHAT ARE YOU TALKING ABOUT?
HAHAHAHA!
BONK!
YAY! THREE CHEERS FOR THE BLOT! HE KNOCKED THE KNIGHT OFF OF HIS HORSE WITH A DIRTY TRICK!
LET'S GO GET THAT HORSE AND HELP!
I'LL TEACH YOU TO FOOL AROUND WITH THE PHANTOM BLOT!
HA!
THUD!
STEP ASIDE, BLOT! WE'LL TAKE CARE OF HIM!
YEAH! LOOK OUT! WE'RE FOUR AGAINST ONE!
THREE! THERE'S NO ROOM FOR ME!
WATCH WHERE YOU'RE POINTING THAT LANCE, YOU FOOLS!
HA!
POW!
OOF!
OUCH!
IT'S A GOOD THING I LET GO WHEN I DID!

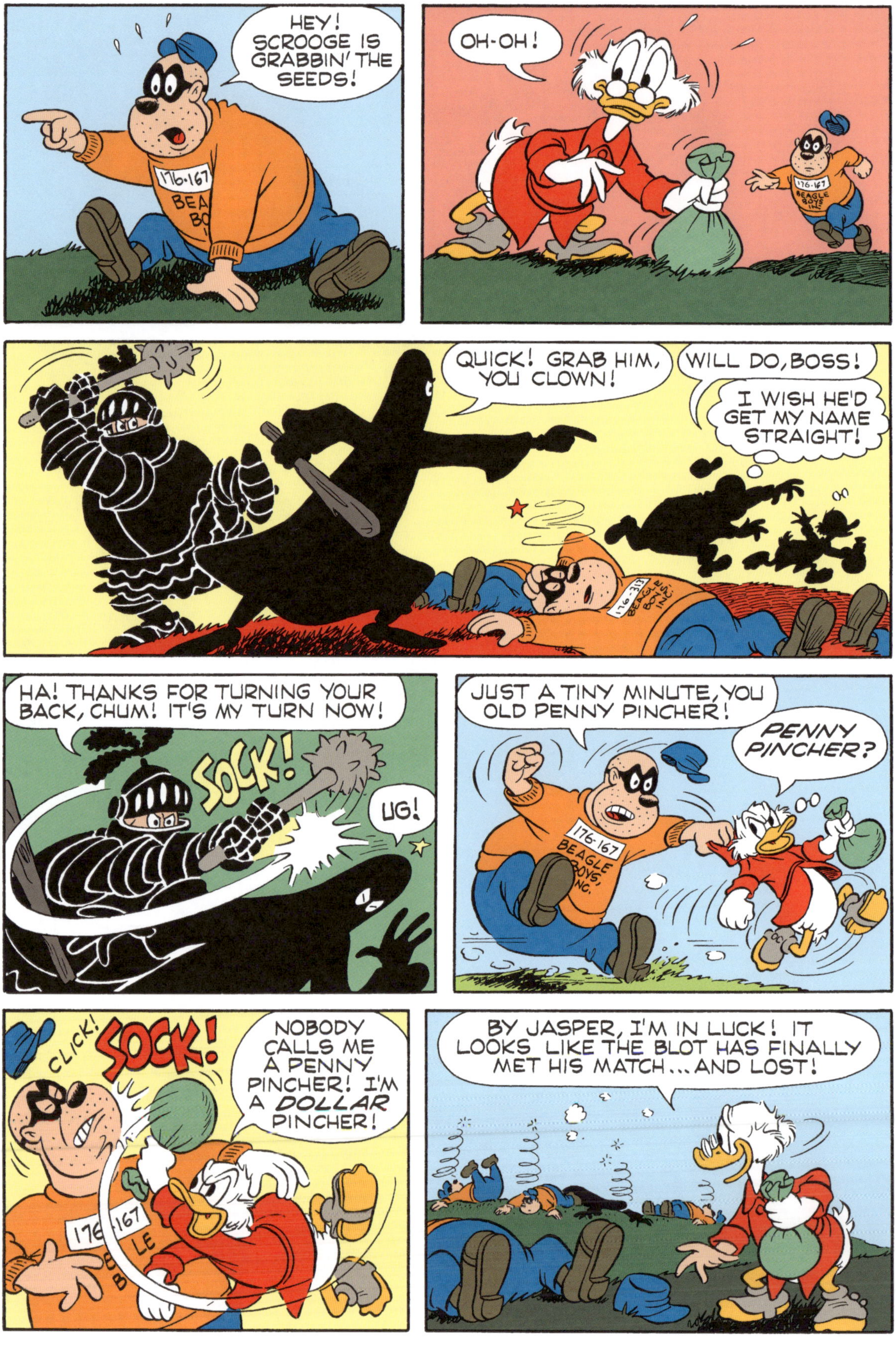
HEY! SCROOGE IS GRABBIN' THE SEEDS!
OH-OH!
QUICK! GRAB HIM, YOU CLOWN!
WILL DO, BOSS!
I WISH HE'D GET MY NAME STRAIGHT!
HA! THANKS FOR TURNING YOUR BACK, CHUM! IT'S MY TURN NOW!
SOCK!
UG!
JUST A TINY MINUTE, YOU OLD PENNY PINCHER!
PENNY PINCHER?
CLICK!
SOCK!
NOBODY CALLS ME A PENNY PINCHER! I'M A *DOLLAR* PINCHER!
BY JASPER, I'M IN LUCK! IT LOOKS LIKE THE BLOT HAS FINALLY MET HIS MATCH... AND LOST!

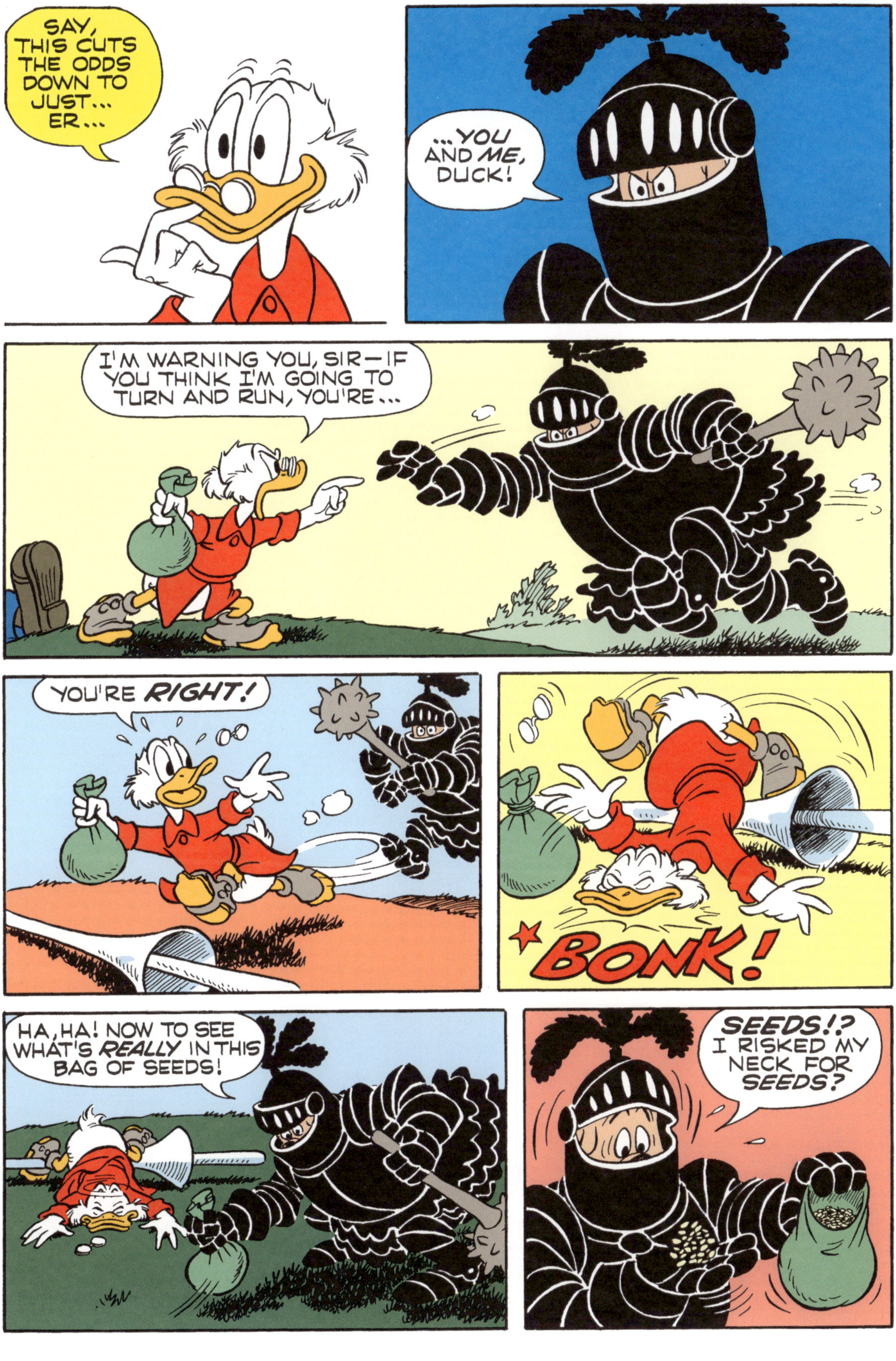
SAY, THIS CUTS THE ODDS DOWN TO JUST... ER...
...YOU AND ME, DUCK!
I'M WARNING YOU, SIR—IF YOU THINK I'M GOING TO TURN AND RUN, YOU'RE...
YOU'RE RIGHT!
BONK!
HA, HA! NOW TO SEE WHAT'S REALLY IN THIS BAG OF SEEDS!
SEEDS!? I RISKED MY NECK FOR SEEDS?

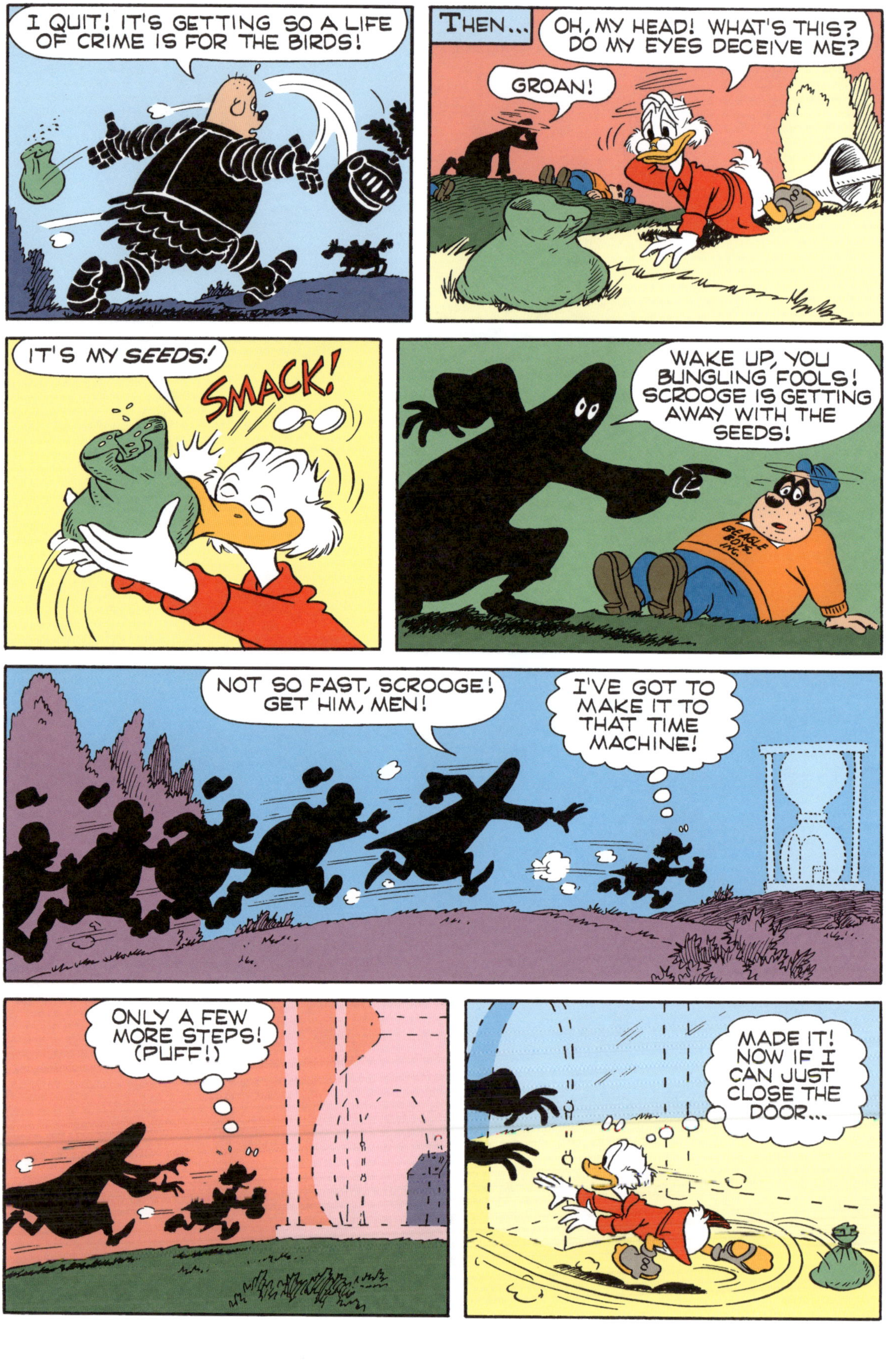
I QUIT! IT'S GETTING SO A LIFE OF CRIME IS FOR THE BIRDS!
THEN...
OH, MY HEAD! WHAT'S THIS? DO MY EYES DECEIVE ME?
GROAN!
IT'S MY SEEDS!
SMACK!
WAKE UP, YOU BUNGLING FOOLS! SCROOGE IS GETTING AWAY WITH THE SEEDS!
BEAGLE BOYS, INC.
NOT SO FAST, SCROOGE! GET HIM, MEN!
I'VE GOT TO MAKE IT TO THAT TIME MACHINE!
ONLY A FEW MORE STEPS! (PUFF!)
MADE IT! NOW IF I CAN JUST CLOSE THE DOOR...

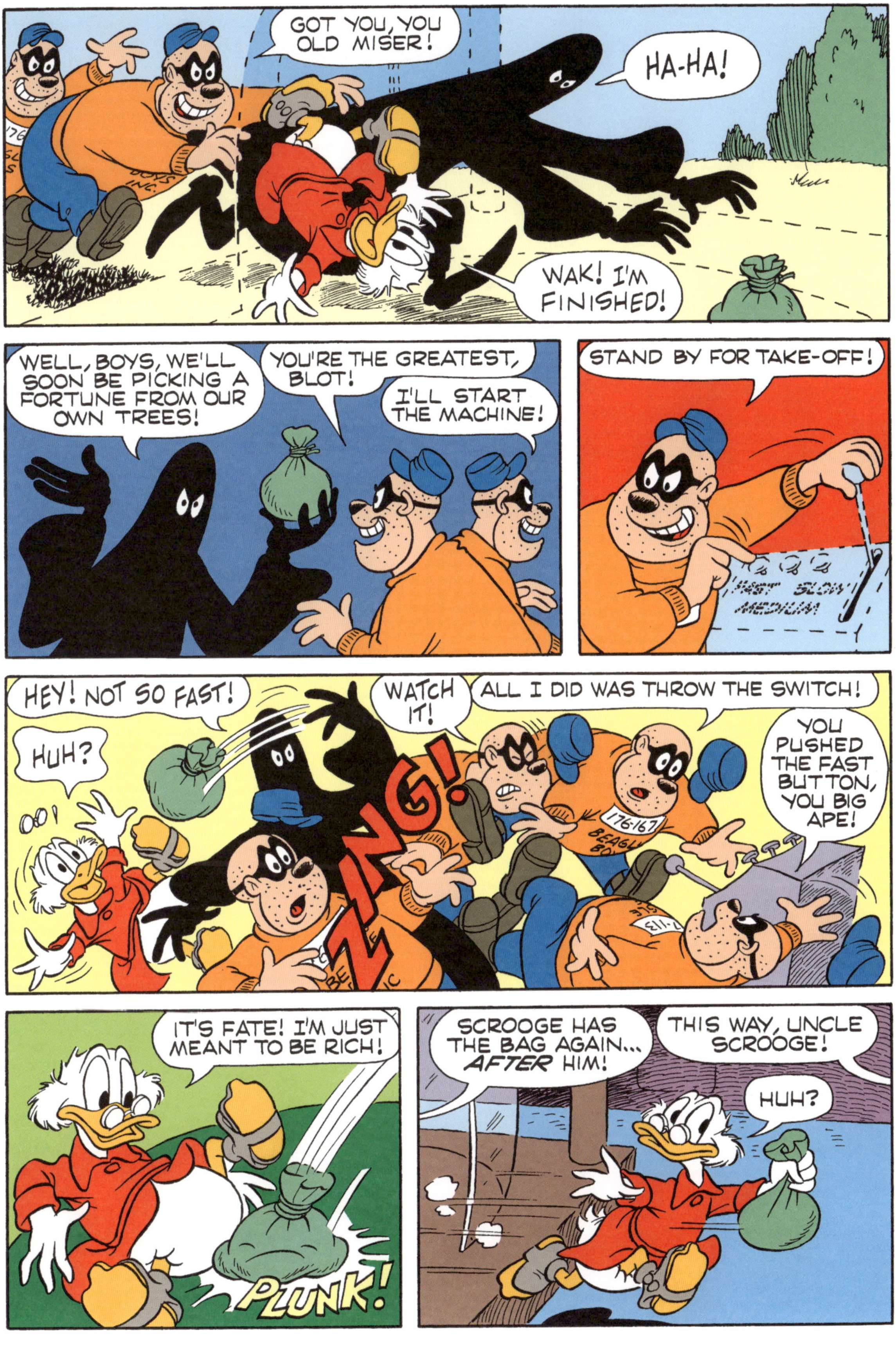
GOT YOU, YOU OLD MISER!
HA-HA!
WAK! I'M FINISHED!
WELL, BOYS, WE'LL SOON BE PICKING A FORTUNE FROM OUR OWN TREES!
YOU'RE THE GREATEST, BLOT!
I'LL START THE MACHINE!
STAND BY FOR TAKE-OFF!
FAST SLOW MEDIUM
HEY! NOT SO FAST!
HUH?
WATCH IT!
ALL I DID WAS THROW THE SWITCH!
YOU PUSHED THE FAST BUTTON, YOU BIG APE!
ZING!
IT'S FATE! I'M JUST MEANT TO BE RICH!
PLUNK!
SCROOGE HAS THE BAG AGAIN... AFTER HIM!
THIS WAY, UNCLE SCROOGE!
HUH?

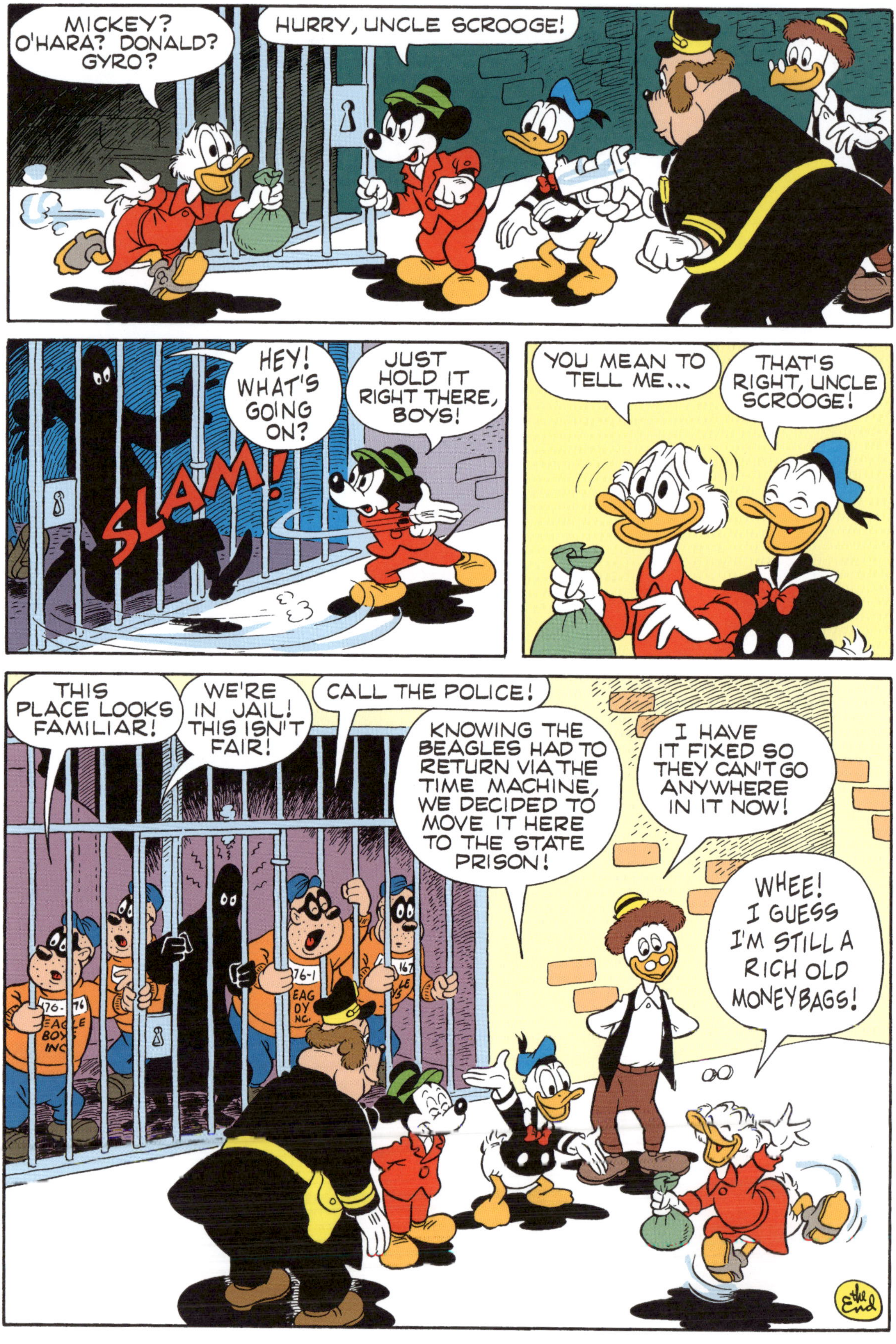
MICKEY? O'HARA? DONALD? GYRO?
HURRY, UNCLE SCROOGE!
HEY! WHAT'S GOING ON?
JUST HOLD IT RIGHT THERE, BOYS!
SLAM!
YOU MEAN TO TELL ME...
THAT'S RIGHT, UNCLE SCROOGE!
THIS PLACE LOOKS FAMILIAR!
WE'RE IN JAIL! THIS ISN'T FAIR!
CALL THE POLICE!
KNOWING THE BEAGLES HAD TO RETURN VIA THE TIME MACHINE, WE DECIDED TO MOVE IT HERE TO THE STATE PRISON!
I HAVE IT FIXED SO THEY CAN'T GO ANYWHERE IN IT NOW!
WHEE! I GUESS I'M STILL A RICH OLD MONEYBAGS!
the End

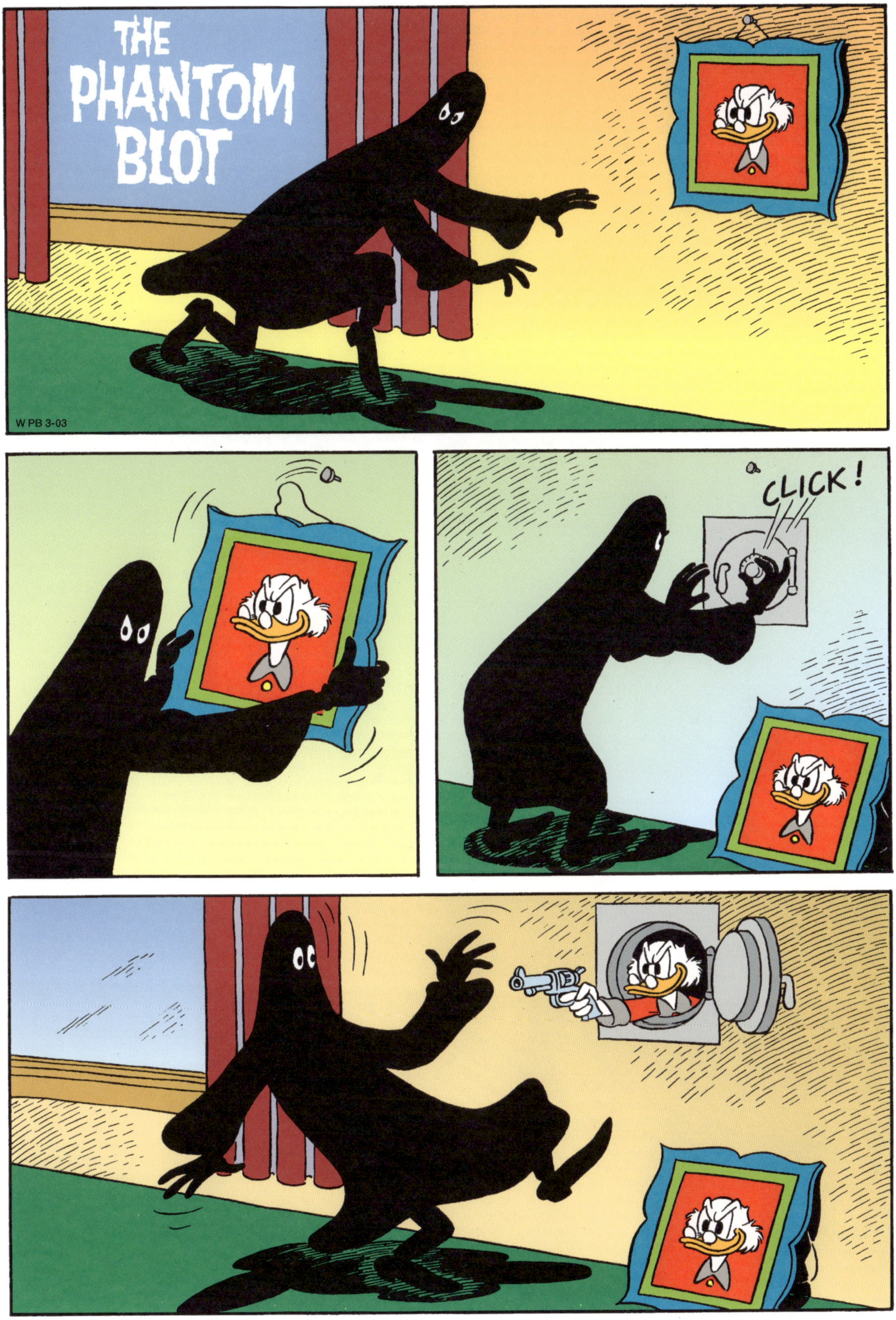
THE PHANTOM BLOT
W PB 3-03
CLICK!

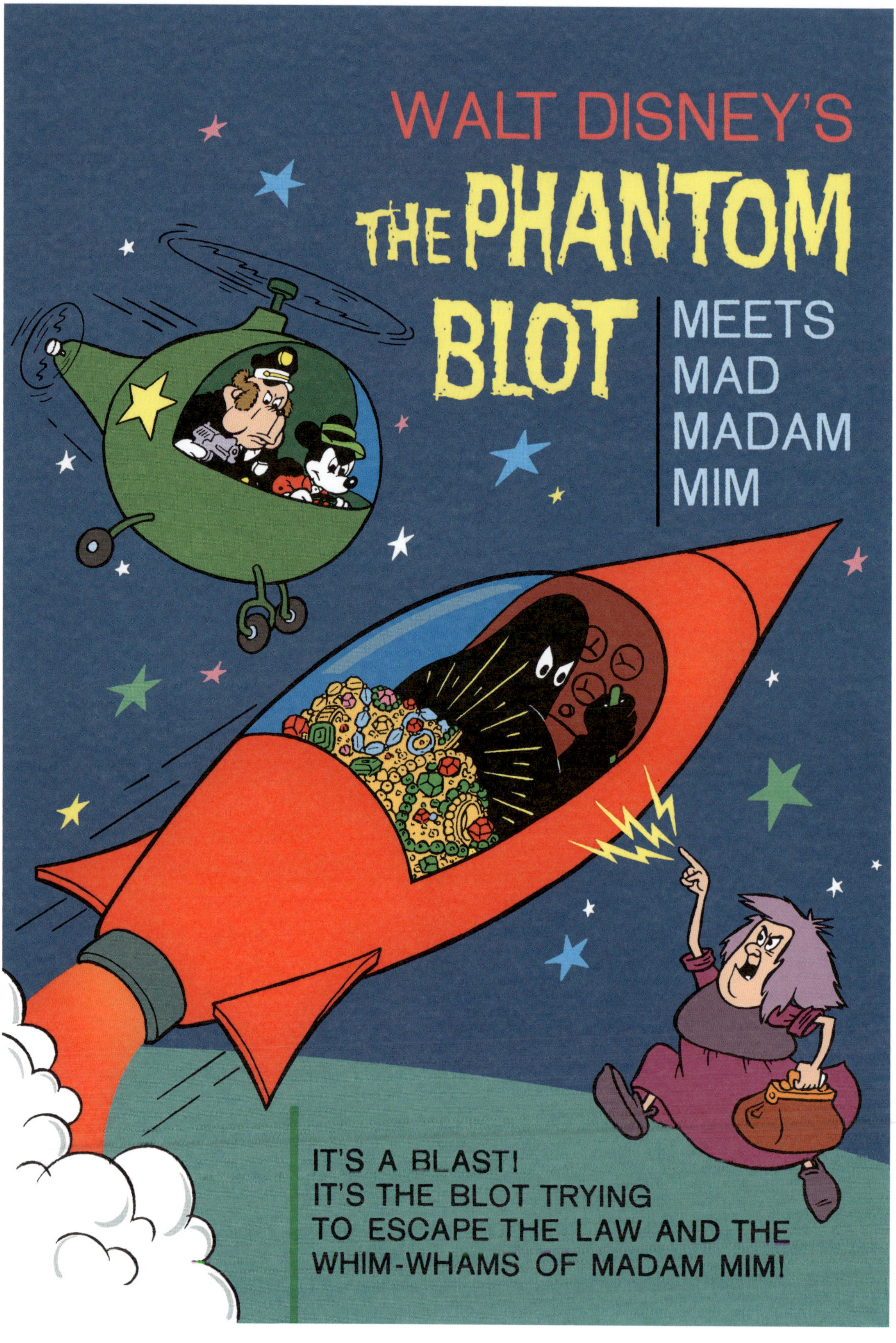

WALT DISNEY'S
THE PHANTOM BLOT
MEETS MAD MADAM MIM
IT'S A BLAST!
IT'S THE BLOT TRYING
TO ESCAPE THE LAW AND THE
WHIM-WHAMS OF MADAM MIM!

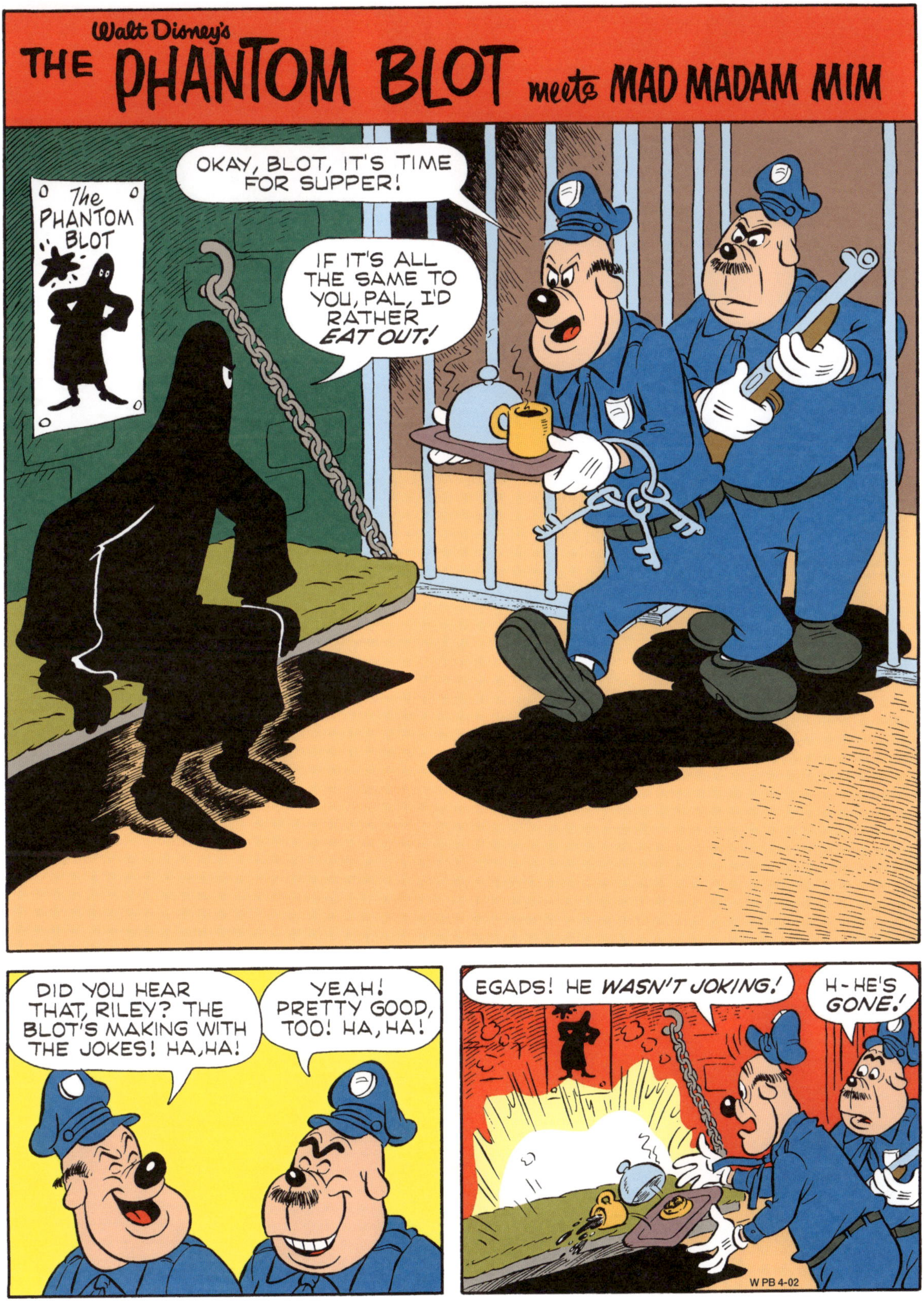
Walt Disney's
THE PHANTOM BLOT meets MAD MADAM MIM
The PHANTOM BLOT
OKAY, BLOT, IT'S TIME FOR SUPPER!
IF IT'S ALL THE SAME TO YOU, PAL, I'D RATHER EAT OUT!
DID YOU HEAR THAT, RILEY? THE BLOT'S MAKING WITH THE JOKES! HA, HA!
YEAH! PRETTY GOOD, TOO! HA, HA!
EGADS! HE WASN'T JOKING!
H-HE'S GONE!
W PB 4-02

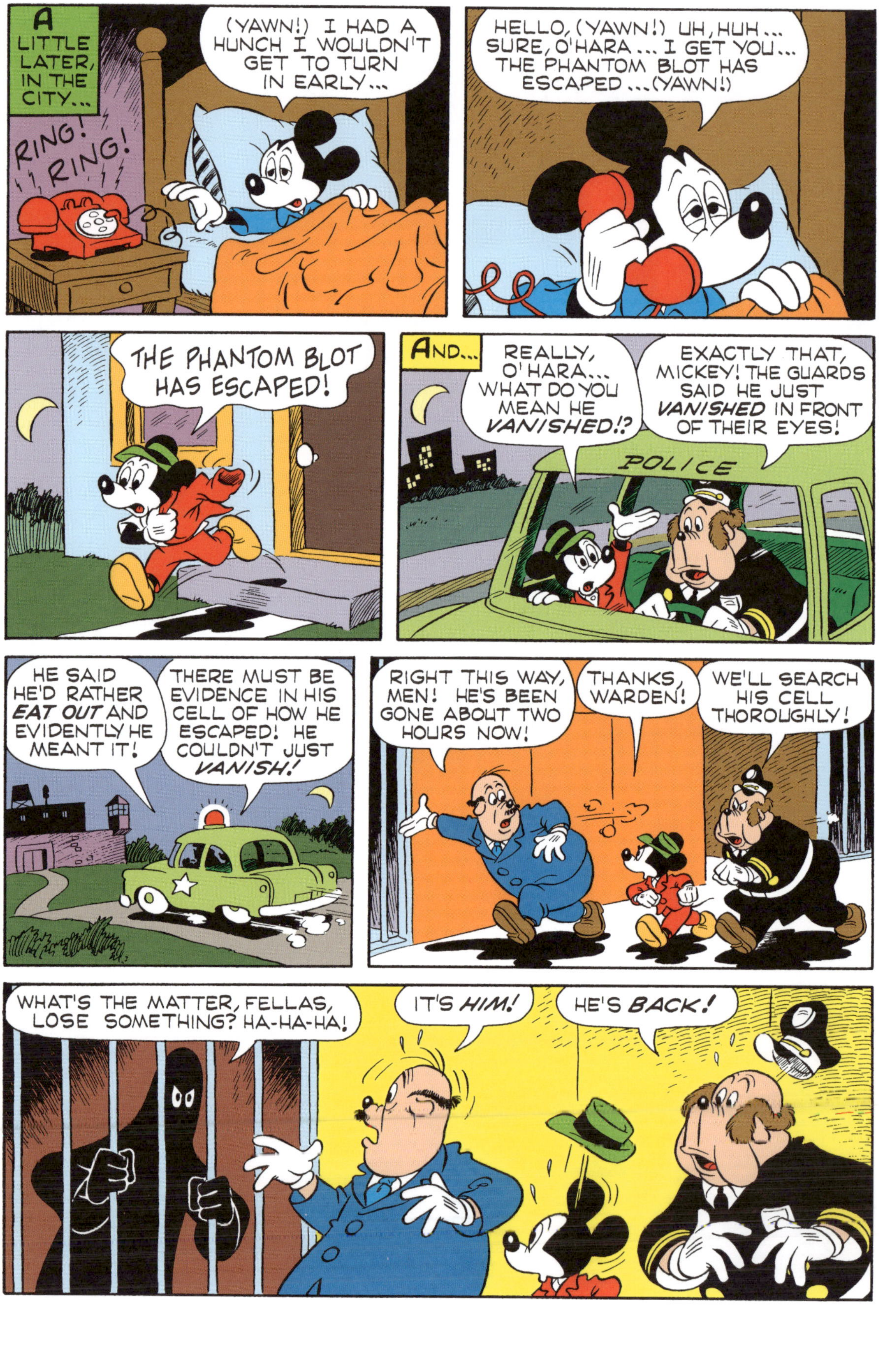
A LITTLE LATER, IN THE CITY...
(YAWN!) I HAD A HUNCH I WOULDN'T GET TO TURN IN EARLY...
RING! RING!
HELLO, (YAWN!) UH, HUH... SURE, O'HARA... I GET YOU... THE PHANTOM BLOT HAS ESCAPED...(YAWN!)
THE PHANTOM BLOT HAS ESCAPED!
AND...
REALLY, O'HARA... WHAT DO YOU MEAN HE VANISHED!?
EXACTLY THAT, MICKEY! THE GUARDS SAID HE JUST VANISHED IN FRONT OF THEIR EYES!
POLICE
HE SAID HE'D RATHER EAT OUT AND EVIDENTLY HE MEANT IT!
THERE MUST BE EVIDENCE IN HIS CELL OF HOW HE ESCAPED! HE COULDN'T JUST VANISH!
RIGHT THIS WAY, MEN! HE'S BEEN GONE ABOUT TWO HOURS NOW!
THANKS, WARDEN!
WE'LL SEARCH HIS CELL THOROUGHLY!
WHAT'S THE MATTER, FELLAS, LOSE SOMETHING? HA-HA-HA!
IT'S HIM!
HE'S BACK!

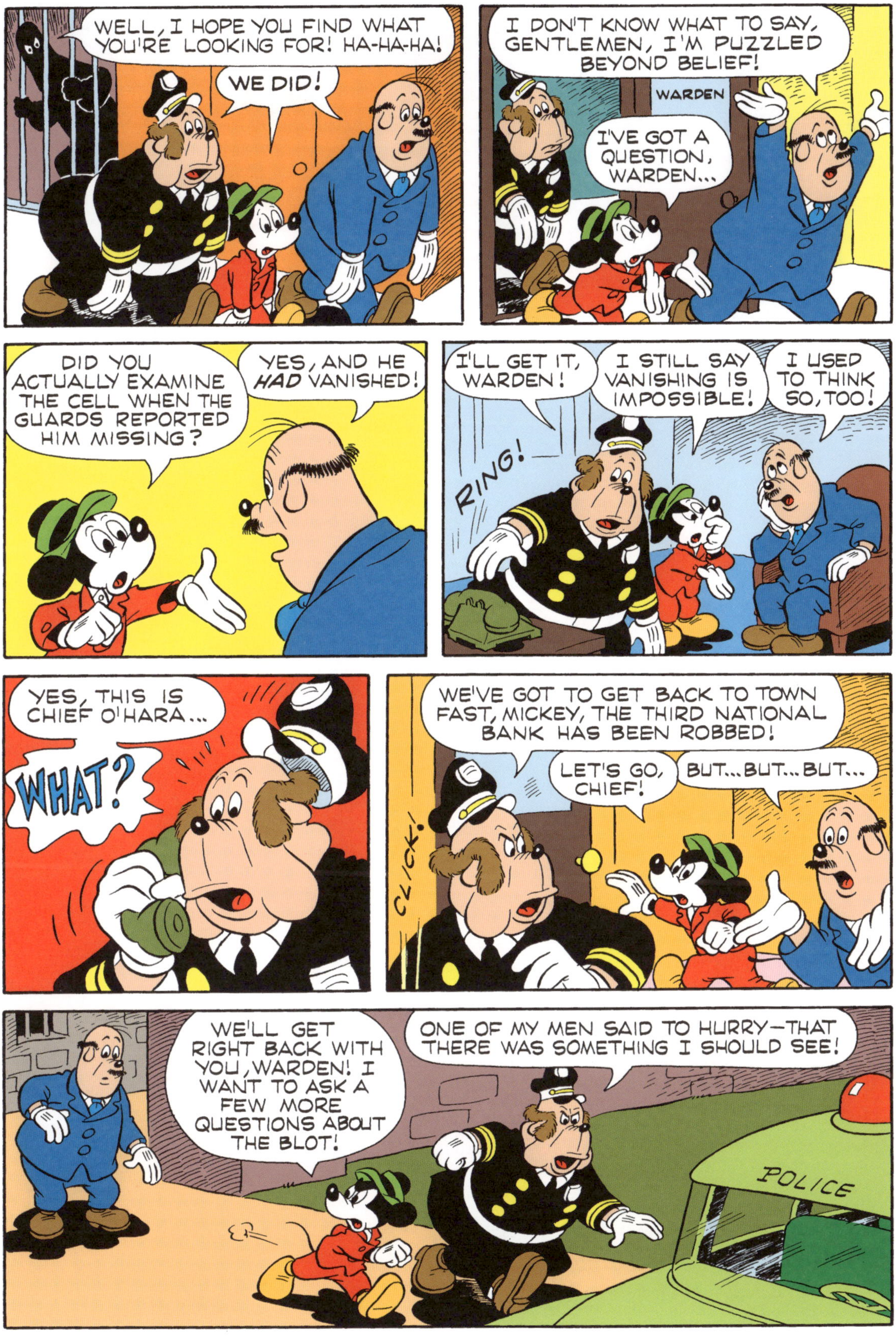
WELL, I HOPE YOU FIND WHAT YOU'RE LOOKING FOR! HA-HA-HA!
WE DID!
I DON'T KNOW WHAT TO SAY, GENTLEMEN, I'M PUZZLED BEYOND BELIEF!
WARDEN
I'VE GOT A QUESTION, WARDEN...
DID YOU ACTUALLY EXAMINE THE CELL WHEN THE GUARDS REPORTED HIM MISSING?
YES, AND HE *HAD* VANISHED!
I'LL GET IT, WARDEN!
I STILL SAY VANISHING IS IMPOSSIBLE!
I USED TO THINK SO, TOO!
RING!
YES, THIS IS CHIEF O'HARA...
WHAT?
WE'VE GOT TO GET BACK TO TOWN FAST, MICKEY, THE THIRD NATIONAL BANK HAS BEEN ROBBED!
LET'S GO, CHIEF!
BUT...BUT...BUT...
CLICK!
WE'LL GET RIGHT BACK WITH YOU, WARDEN! I WANT TO ASK A FEW MORE QUESTIONS ABOUT THE BLOT!
ONE OF MY MEN SAID TO HURRY—THAT THERE WAS SOMETHING I SHOULD SEE!
POLICE

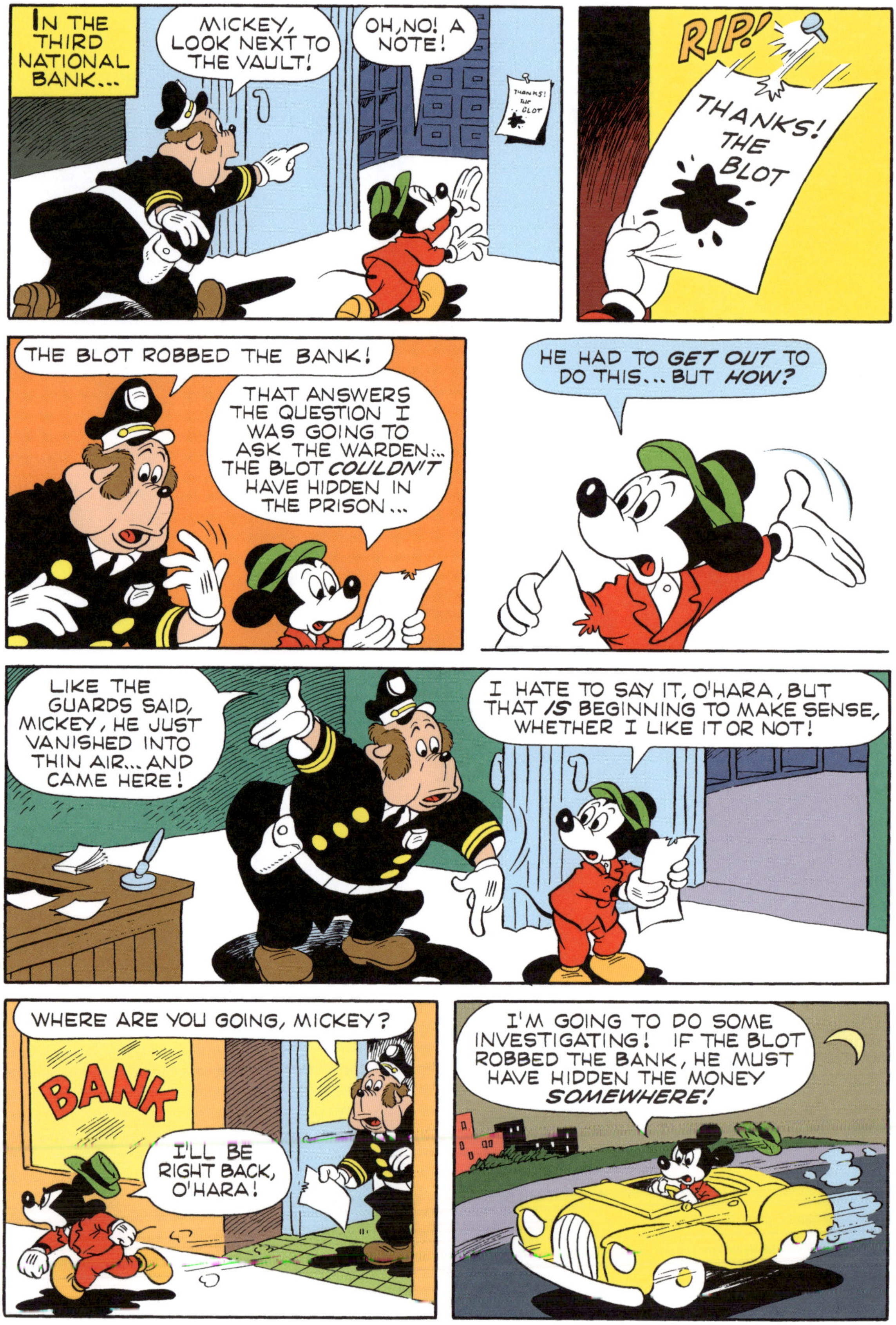
IN THE THIRD NATIONAL BANK...
MICKEY, LOOK NEXT TO THE VAULT!
OH, NO! A NOTE!
THANKS! THE BLOT
RIP!
THANKS! THE BLOT
THE BLOT ROBBED THE BANK!
THAT ANSWERS THE QUESTION I WAS GOING TO ASK THE WARDEN... THE BLOT COULDN'T HAVE HIDDEN IN THE PRISON...
HE HAD TO GET OUT TO DO THIS... BUT HOW?
LIKE THE GUARDS SAID, MICKEY, HE JUST VANISHED INTO THIN AIR... AND CAME HERE!
I HATE TO SAY IT, O'HARA, BUT THAT IS BEGINNING TO MAKE SENSE, WHETHER I LIKE IT OR NOT!
WHERE ARE YOU GOING, MICKEY?
BANK
I'LL BE RIGHT BACK, O'HARA!
I'M GOING TO DO SOME INVESTIGATING! IF THE BLOT ROBBED THE BANK, HE MUST HAVE HIDDEN THE MONEY SOMEWHERE!

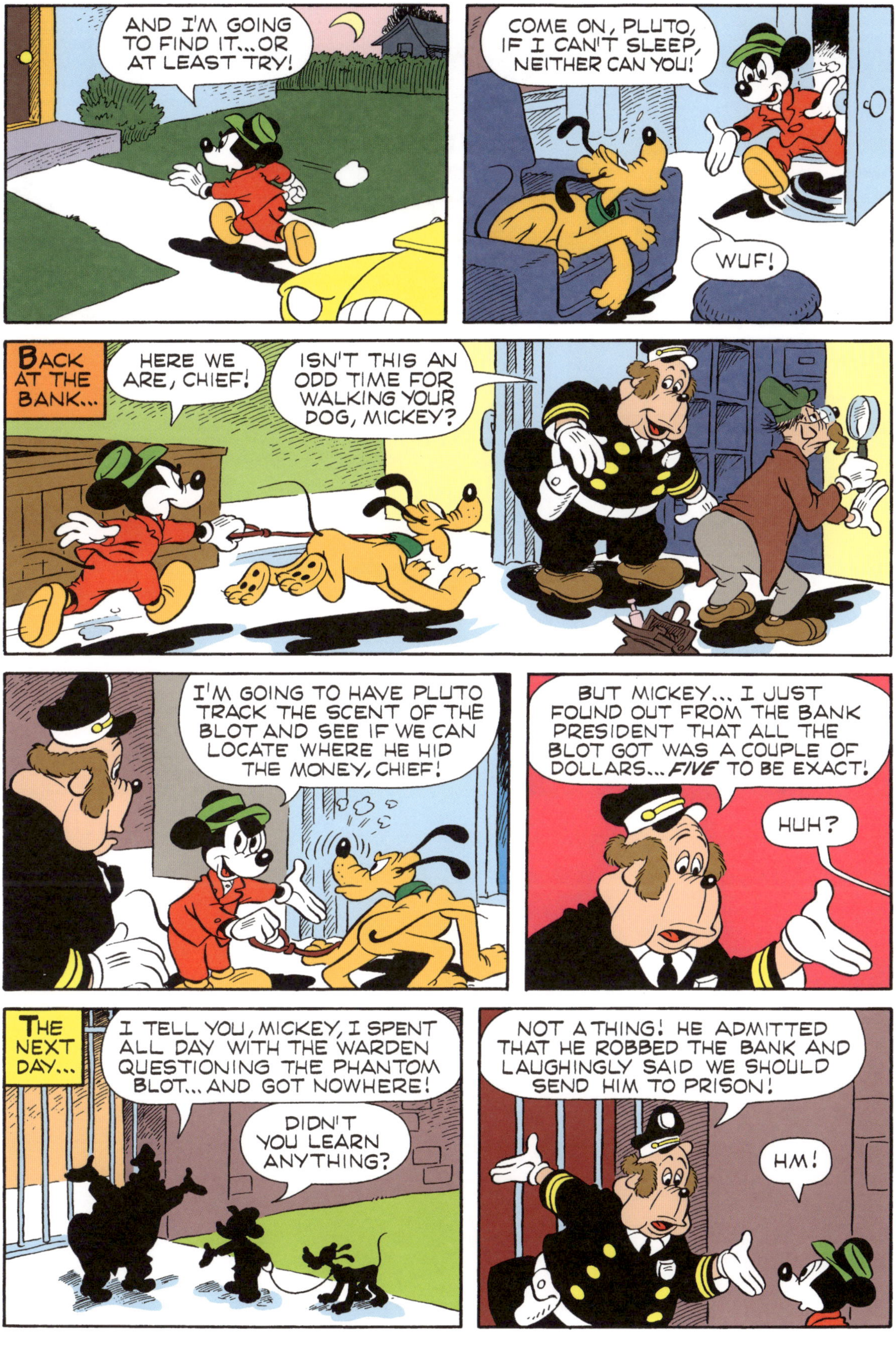
AND I'M GOING TO FIND IT...OR AT LEAST TRY!
COME ON, PLUTO, IF I CAN'T SLEEP, NEITHER CAN YOU!
WUF!
BACK AT THE BANK...
HERE WE ARE, CHIEF!
ISN'T THIS AN ODD TIME FOR WALKING YOUR DOG, MICKEY?
I'M GOING TO HAVE PLUTO TRACK THE SCENT OF THE BLOT AND SEE IF WE CAN LOCATE WHERE HE HID THE MONEY, CHIEF!
BUT MICKEY... I JUST FOUND OUT FROM THE BANK PRESIDENT THAT ALL THE BLOT GOT WAS A COUPLE OF DOLLARS... FIVE TO BE EXACT!
HUH?
THE NEXT DAY...
I TELL YOU, MICKEY, I SPENT ALL DAY WITH THE WARDEN QUESTIONING THE PHANTOM BLOT... AND GOT NOWHERE!
DIDN'T YOU LEARN ANYTHING?
NOT A THING! HE ADMITTED THAT HE ROBBED THE BANK AND LAUGHINGLY SAID WE SHOULD SEND HIM TO PRISON!
HM!

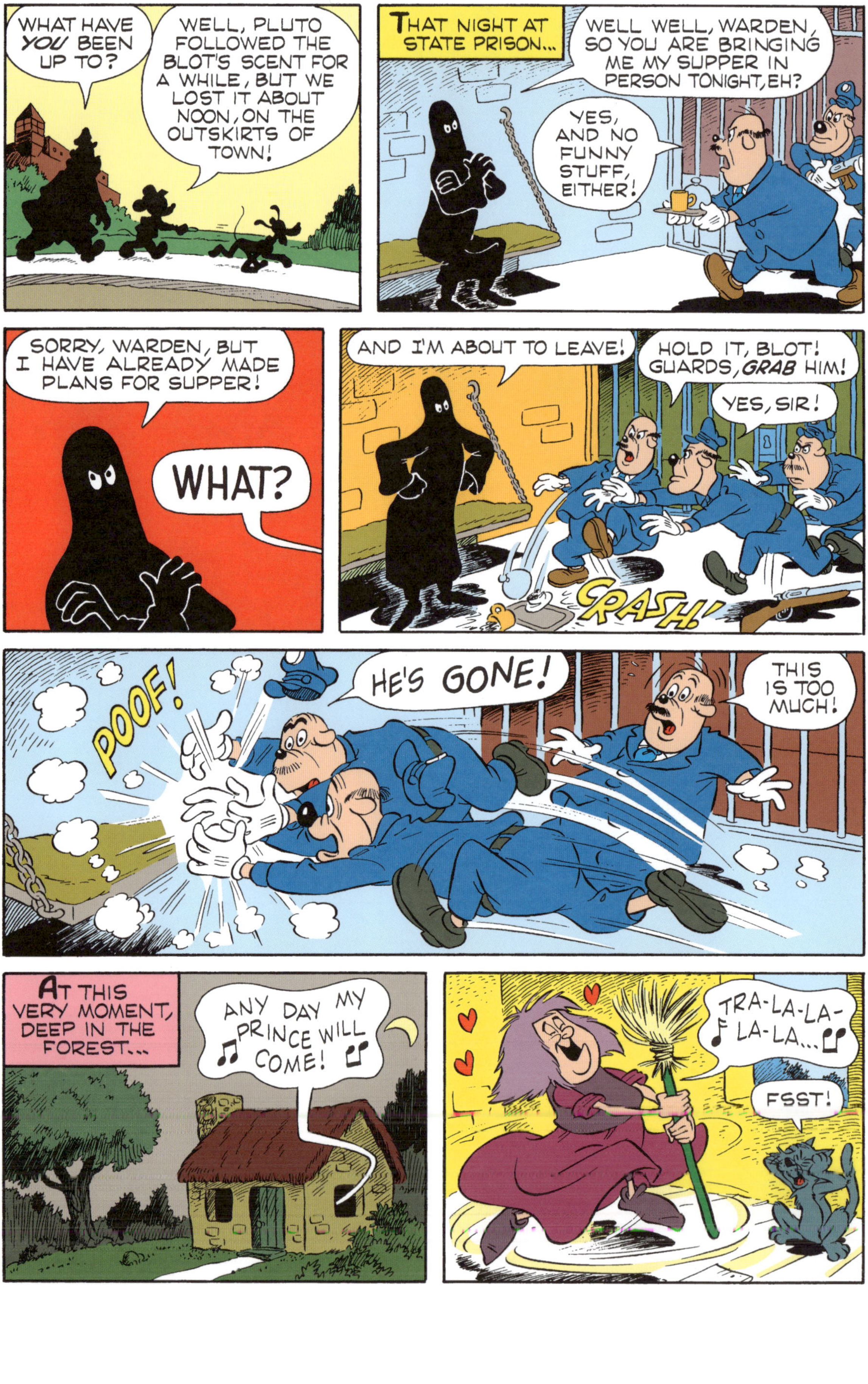
WHAT HAVE YOU BEEN UP TO?
WELL, PLUTO FOLLOWED THE BLOT'S SCENT FOR A WHILE, BUT WE LOST IT ABOUT NOON, ON THE OUTSKIRTS OF TOWN!
THAT NIGHT AT STATE PRISON...
WELL WELL, WARDEN, SO YOU ARE BRINGING ME MY SUPPER IN PERSON TONIGHT, EH?
YES, AND NO FUNNY STUFF, EITHER!
SORRY, WARDEN, BUT I HAVE ALREADY MADE PLANS FOR SUPPER!
WHAT?
AND I'M ABOUT TO LEAVE!
HOLD IT, BLOT! GUARDS, GRAB HIM!
YES, SIR!
CRASH!
POOF!
HE'S GONE!
THIS IS TOO MUCH!
AT THIS VERY MOMENT, DEEP IN THE FOREST...
ANY DAY MY PRINCE WILL COME!
TRA-LA-LA-LA-LA...
FSST!

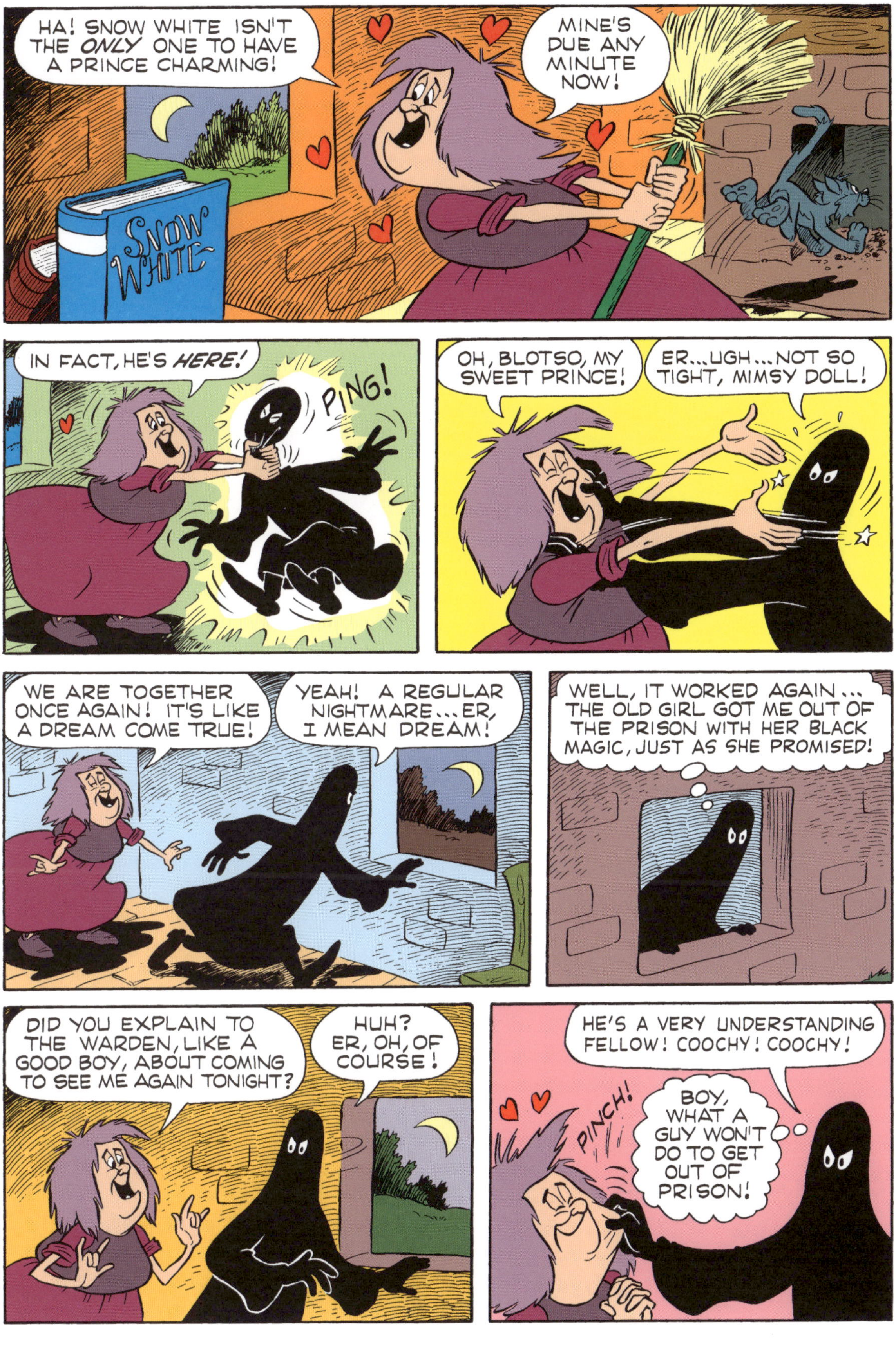
HA! SNOW WHITE ISN'T THE *ONLY* ONE TO HAVE A PRINCE CHARMING!
MINE'S DUE ANY MINUTE NOW!
SNOW WHITE
IN FACT, HE'S ***HERE!***
PING!
OH, BLOTSO, MY SWEET PRINCE!
ER...UGH...NOT SO TIGHT, MIMSY DOLL!
WE ARE TOGETHER ONCE AGAIN! IT'S LIKE A DREAM COME TRUE!
YEAH! A REGULAR NIGHTMARE...ER, I MEAN DREAM!
WELL, IT WORKED AGAIN... THE OLD GIRL GOT ME OUT OF THE PRISON WITH HER BLACK MAGIC, JUST AS SHE PROMISED!
DID YOU EXPLAIN TO THE WARDEN, LIKE A GOOD BOY, ABOUT COMING TO SEE ME AGAIN TONIGHT?
HUH? ER, OH, OF COURSE!
HE'S A VERY UNDERSTANDING FELLOW! COOCHY! COOCHY!
PINCH!
BOY, WHAT A GUY WON'T DO TO GET OUT OF PRISON!

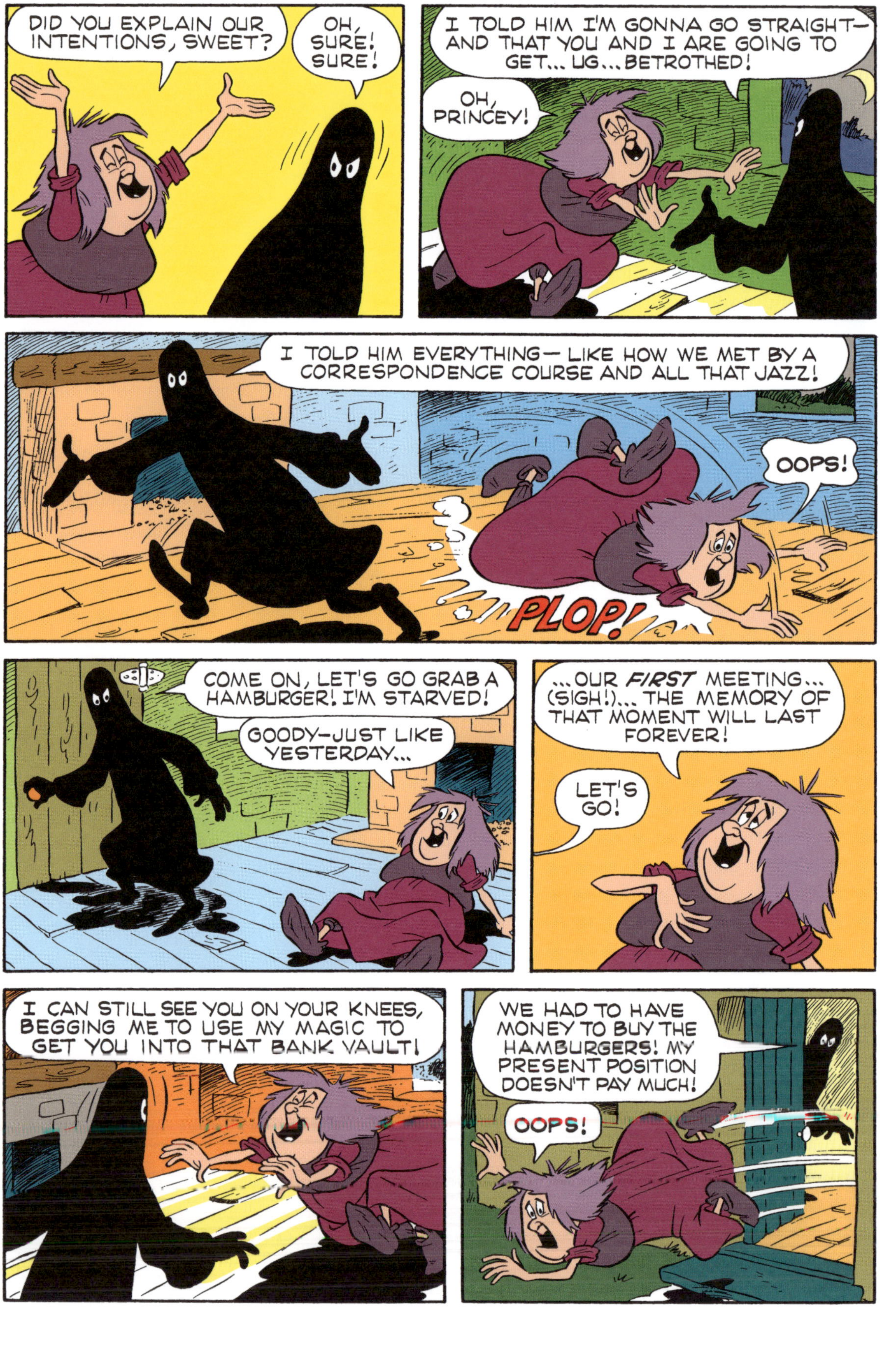
DID YOU EXPLAIN OUR INTENTIONS, SWEET?
OH, SURE! SURE!
I TOLD HIM I'M GONNA GO STRAIGHT— AND THAT YOU AND I ARE GOING TO GET... UG... BETROTHED!
OH, PRINCEY!
I TOLD HIM EVERYTHING— LIKE HOW WE MET BY A CORRESPONDENCE COURSE AND ALL THAT JAZZ!
OOPS!
PLOP!
COME ON, LET'S GO GRAB A HAMBURGER! I'M STARVED!
GOODY—JUST LIKE YESTERDAY...
...OUR *FIRST* MEETING... (SIGH!)... THE MEMORY OF THAT MOMENT WILL LAST FOREVER!
LET'S GO!
I CAN STILL SEE YOU ON YOUR KNEES, BEGGING ME TO USE MY MAGIC TO GET YOU INTO THAT BANK VAULT!
WE HAD TO HAVE MONEY TO BUY THE HAMBURGERS! MY PRESENT POSITION DOESN'T PAY MUCH!
OOPS!

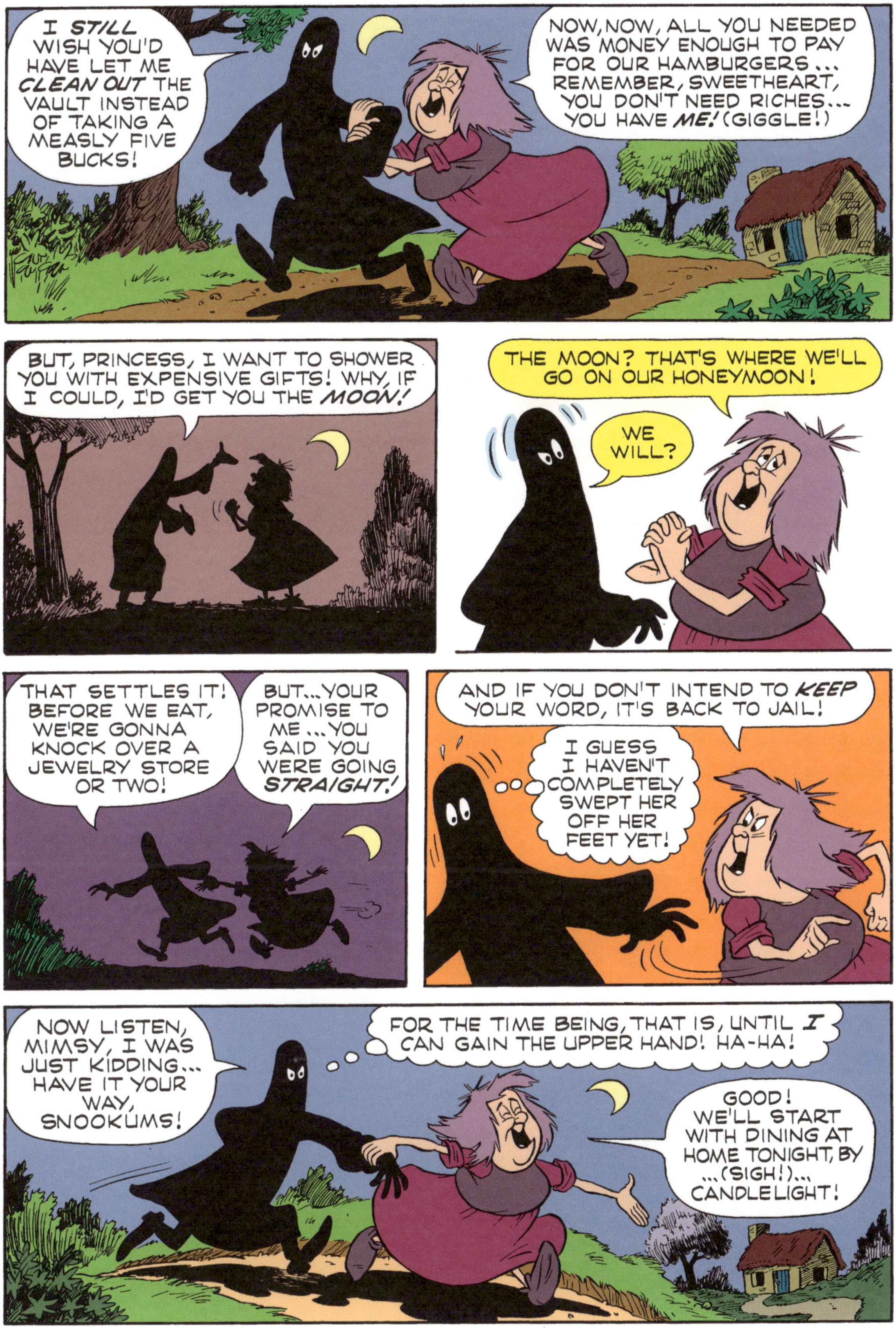

I STILL WISH YOU'D HAVE LET ME CLEAN OUT THE VAULT INSTEAD OF TAKING A MEASLY FIVE BUCKS!
NOW, NOW, ALL YOU NEEDED WAS MONEY ENOUGH TO PAY FOR OUR HAMBURGERS... REMEMBER, SWEETHEART, YOU DON'T NEED RICHES... YOU HAVE ME! (GIGGLE!)
BUT, PRINCESS, I WANT TO SHOWER YOU WITH EXPENSIVE GIFTS! WHY, IF I COULD, I'D GET YOU THE MOON!
THE MOON? THAT'S WHERE WE'LL GO ON OUR HONEYMOON!
WE WILL?
THAT SETTLES IT! BEFORE WE EAT, WE'RE GONNA KNOCK OVER A JEWELRY STORE OR TWO!
BUT...YOUR PROMISE TO ME...YOU SAID YOU WERE GOING STRAIGHT!
AND IF YOU DON'T INTEND TO KEEP YOUR WORD, IT'S BACK TO JAIL!
I GUESS I HAVEN'T COMPLETELY SWEPT HER OFF HER FEET YET!
NOW LISTEN, MIMSY, I WAS JUST KIDDING... HAVE IT YOUR WAY, SNOOKUMS!
FOR THE TIME BEING, THAT IS, UNTIL I CAN GAIN THE UPPER HAND! HA-HA!
GOOD! WE'LL START WITH DINING AT HOME TONIGHT, BY ...(SIGH!)... CANDLELIGHT!

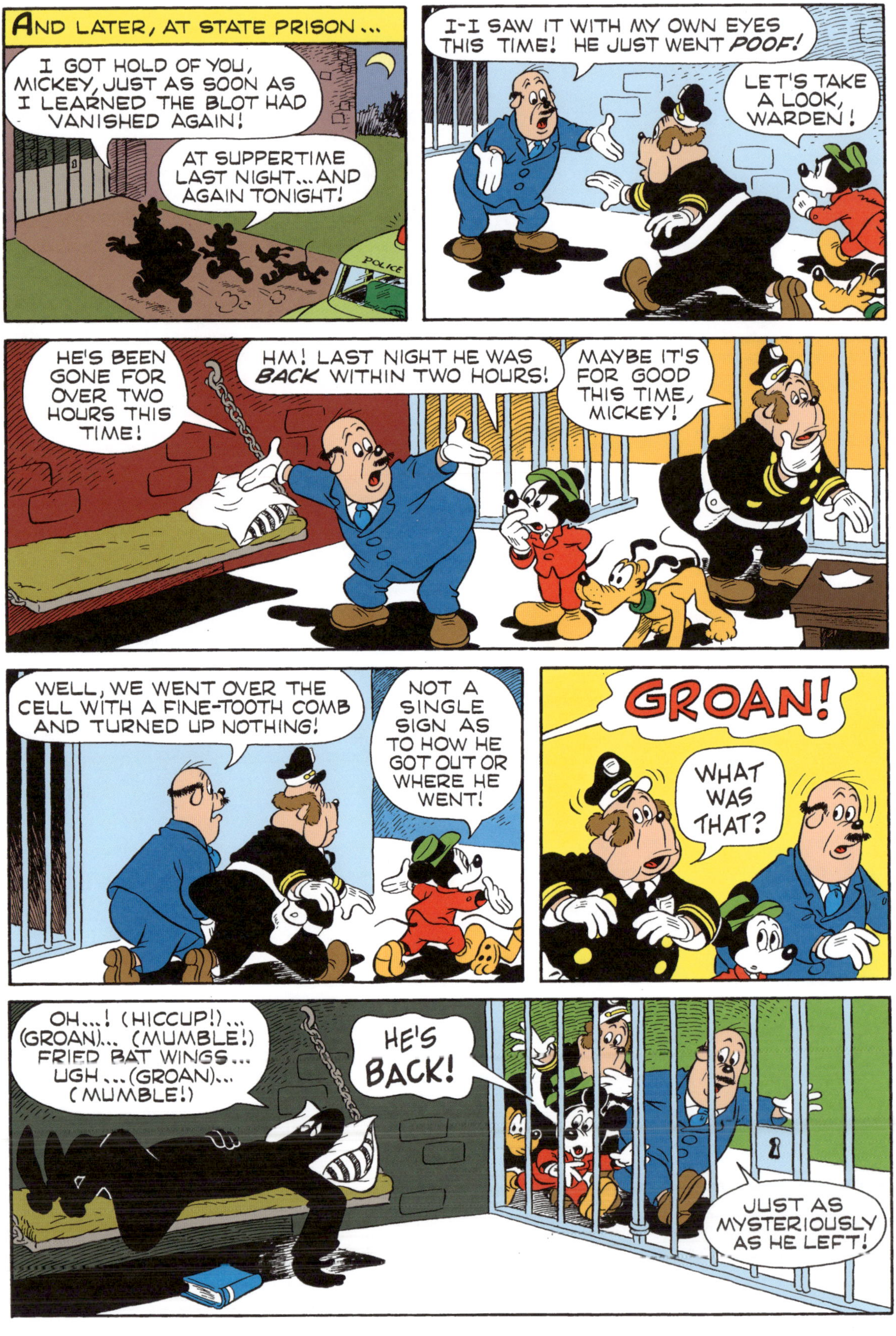
AND LATER, AT STATE PRISON ...
I GOT HOLD OF YOU, MICKEY, JUST AS SOON AS I LEARNED THE BLOT HAD VANISHED AGAIN!
AT SUPPERTIME LAST NIGHT... AND AGAIN TONIGHT!
POLICE
I-I SAW IT WITH MY OWN EYES THIS TIME! HE JUST WENT POOF!
LET'S TAKE A LOOK, WARDEN!
HE'S BEEN GONE FOR OVER TWO HOURS THIS TIME!
HM! LAST NIGHT HE WAS BACK WITHIN TWO HOURS!
MAYBE IT'S FOR GOOD THIS TIME, MICKEY!
WELL, WE WENT OVER THE CELL WITH A FINE-TOOTH COMB AND TURNED UP NOTHING!
NOT A SINGLE SIGN AS TO HOW HE GOT OUT OR WHERE HE WENT!
GROAN!
WHAT WAS THAT?
OH...! (HICCUP!)... (GROAN)... (MUMBLE!) FRIED BAT WINGS... UGH... (GROAN)... (MUMBLE!)
HE'S BACK!
JUST AS MYSTERIOUSLY AS HE LEFT!

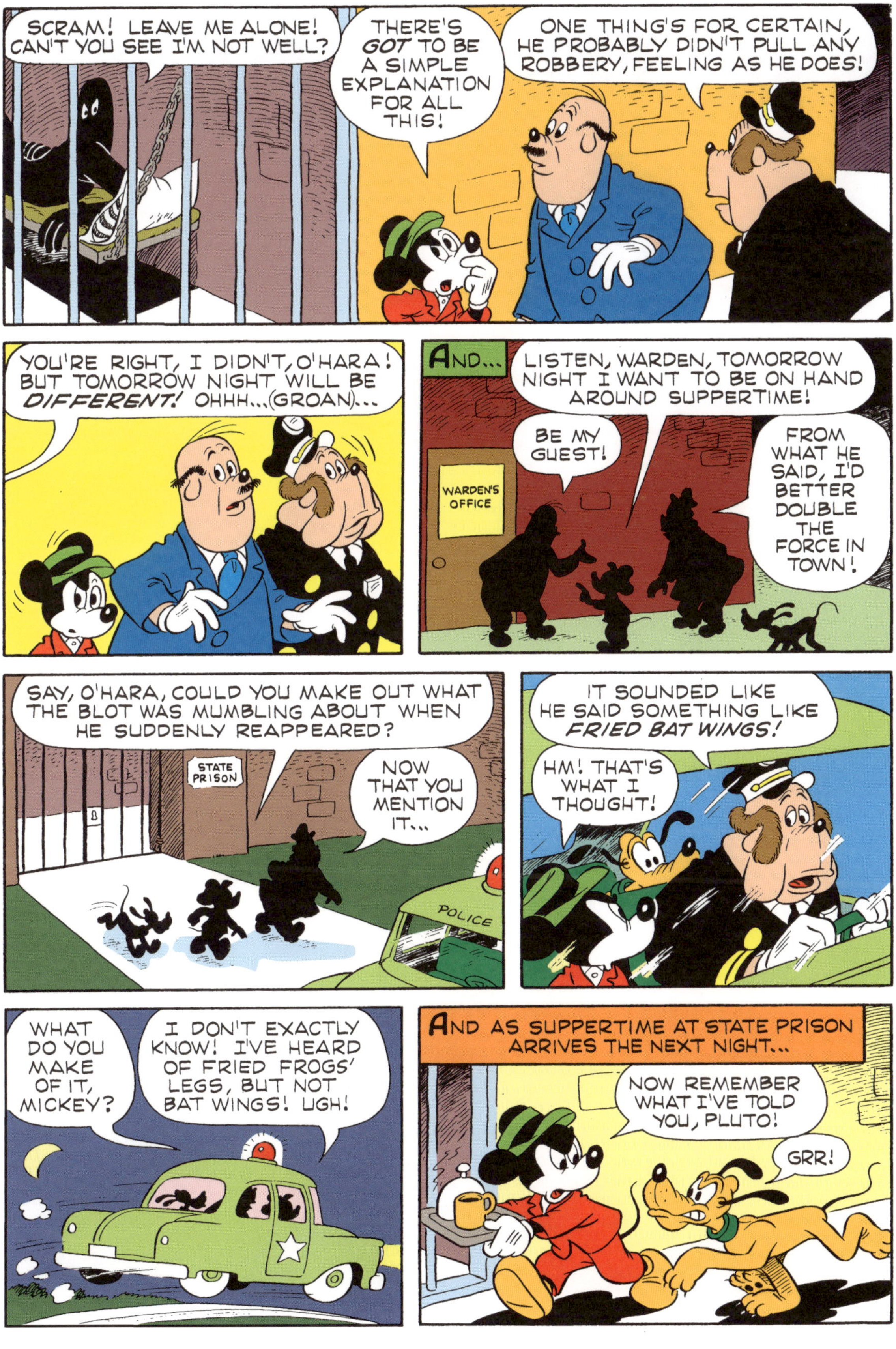
SCRAM! LEAVE ME ALONE! CAN'T YOU SEE I'M NOT WELL?
THERE'S *GOT* TO BE A SIMPLE EXPLANATION FOR ALL THIS!
ONE THING'S FOR CERTAIN, HE PROBABLY DIDN'T PULL ANY ROBBERY, FEELING AS HE DOES!
YOU'RE RIGHT, I DIDN'T, O'HARA! BUT TOMORROW NIGHT WILL BE *DIFFERENT!* OHHH...(GROAN)...
AND...
LISTEN, WARDEN, TOMORROW NIGHT I WANT TO BE ON HAND AROUND SUPPERTIME!
BE MY GUEST!
WARDEN'S OFFICE
FROM WHAT HE SAID, I'D BETTER DOUBLE THE FORCE IN TOWN!
SAY, O'HARA, COULD YOU MAKE OUT WHAT THE BLOT WAS MUMBLING ABOUT WHEN HE SUDDENLY REAPPEARED?
STATE PRISON
NOW THAT YOU MENTION IT...
POLICE
IT SOUNDED LIKE HE SAID SOMETHING LIKE *FRIED BAT WINGS!*
HM! THAT'S WHAT I THOUGHT!
WHAT DO YOU MAKE OF IT, MICKEY?
I DON'T EXACTLY KNOW! I'VE HEARD OF FRIED FROGS' LEGS, BUT NOT BAT WINGS! UGH!
AND AS SUPPERTIME AT STATE PRISON ARRIVES THE NEXT NIGHT...
NOW REMEMBER WHAT I'VE TOLD YOU, PLUTO!
GRR!

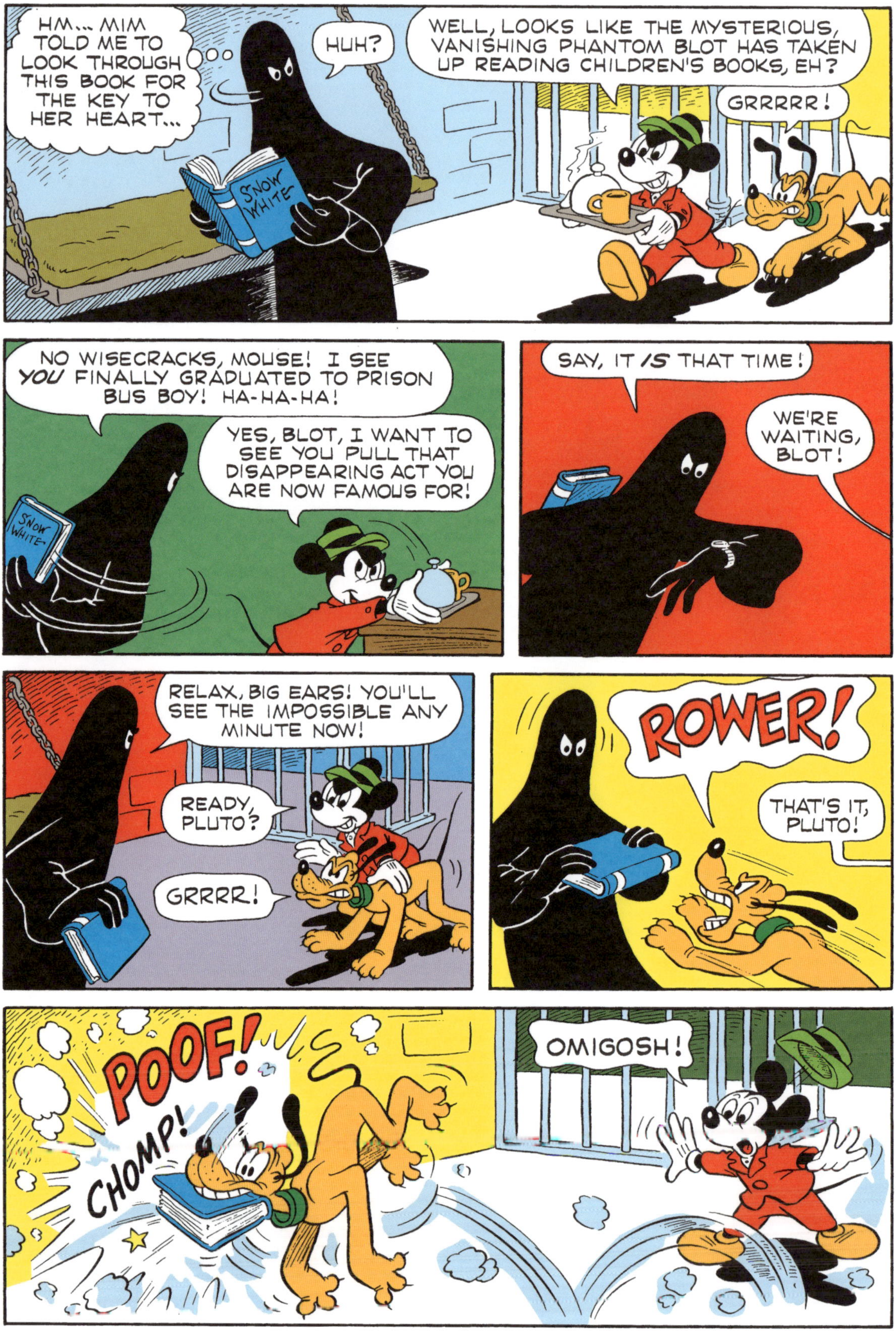
HM... MIM TOLD ME TO LOOK THROUGH THIS BOOK FOR THE KEY TO HER HEART...
SNOW WHITE
HUH?
WELL, LOOKS LIKE THE MYSTERIOUS, VANISHING PHANTOM BLOT HAS TAKEN UP READING CHILDREN'S BOOKS, EH?
GRRRRR!
NO WISECRACKS, MOUSE! I SEE YOU FINALLY GRADUATED TO PRISON BUS BOY! HA-HA-HA!
YES, BLOT, I WANT TO SEE YOU PULL THAT DISAPPEARING ACT YOU ARE NOW FAMOUS FOR!
SNOW WHITE
SAY, IT IS THAT TIME!
WE'RE WAITING, BLOT!
RELAX, BIG EARS! YOU'LL SEE THE IMPOSSIBLE ANY MINUTE NOW!
READY, PLUTO?
GRRRR!
ROWER!
THAT'S IT, PLUTO!
POOF!
CHOMP!
OMIGOSH!

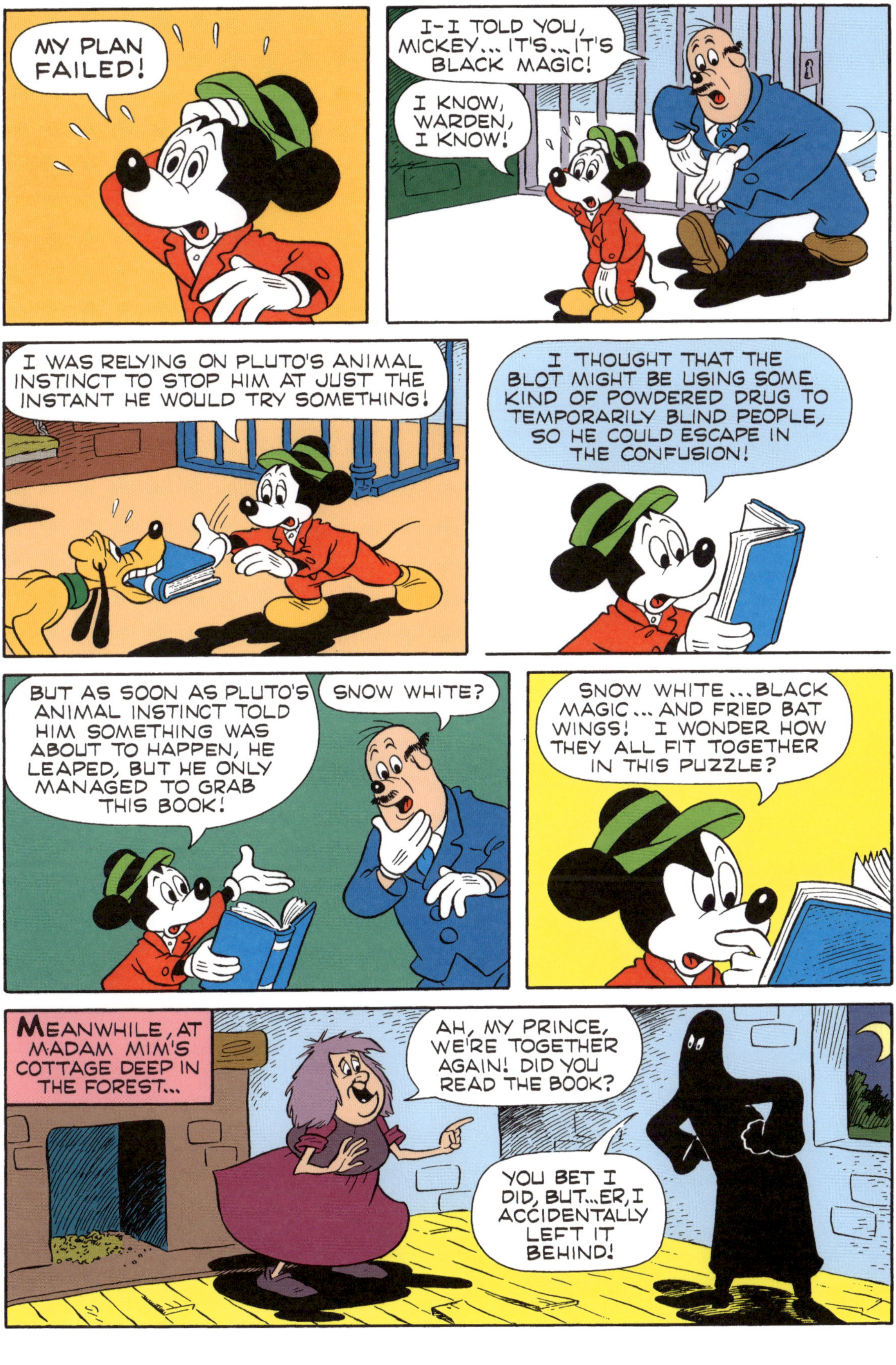
MY PLAN FAILED!
I-I TOLD YOU, MICKEY... IT'S... IT'S BLACK MAGIC!
I KNOW, WARDEN, I KNOW!
I WAS RELYING ON PLUTO'S ANIMAL INSTINCT TO STOP HIM AT JUST THE INSTANT HE WOULD TRY SOMETHING!
I THOUGHT THAT THE BLOT MIGHT BE USING SOME KIND OF POWDERED DRUG TO TEMPORARILY BLIND PEOPLE, SO HE COULD ESCAPE IN THE CONFUSION!
BUT AS SOON AS PLUTO'S ANIMAL INSTINCT TOLD HIM SOMETHING WAS ABOUT TO HAPPEN, HE LEAPED, BUT HE ONLY MANAGED TO GRAB THIS BOOK!
SNOW WHITE?
SNOW WHITE... BLACK MAGIC... AND FRIED BAT WINGS! I WONDER HOW THEY ALL FIT TOGETHER IN THIS PUZZLE?
MEANWHILE, AT MADAM MIM'S COTTAGE DEEP IN THE FOREST...
AH, MY PRINCE, WE'RE TOGETHER AGAIN! DID YOU READ THE BOOK?
YOU BET I DID, BUT...ER, I ACCIDENTALLY LEFT IT BEHIND!

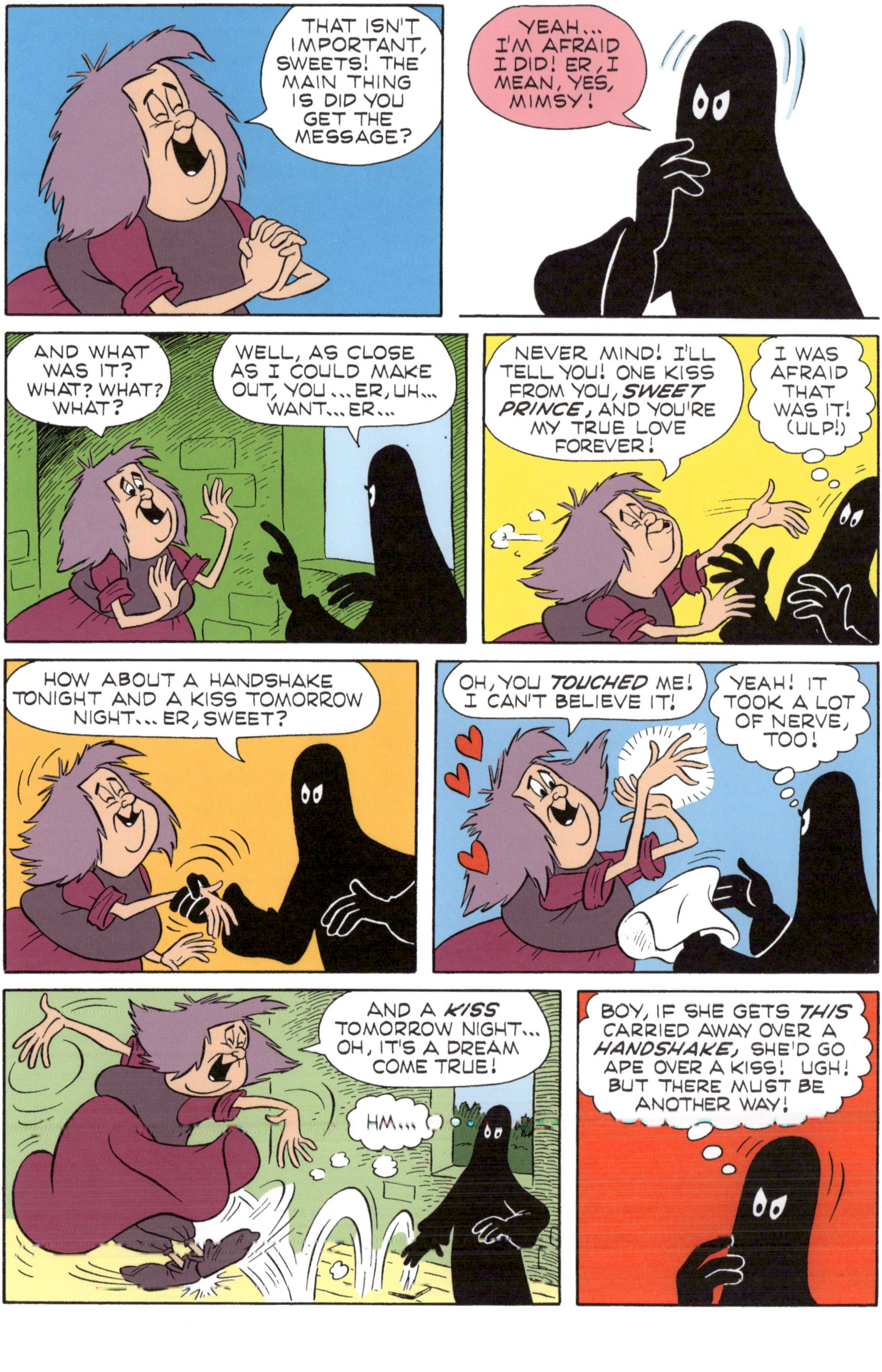
THAT ISN'T IMPORTANT, SWEETS! THE MAIN THING IS DID YOU GET THE MESSAGE?
YEAH... I'M AFRAID I DID! ER, I MEAN, YES, MIMSY!
AND WHAT WAS IT? WHAT? WHAT? WHAT?
WELL, AS CLOSE AS I COULD MAKE OUT, YOU... ER, UH... WANT... ER...
NEVER MIND! I'LL TELL YOU! ONE KISS FROM YOU, SWEET PRINCE, AND YOU'RE MY TRUE LOVE FOREVER!
I WAS AFRAID THAT WAS IT! (ULP!)
HOW ABOUT A HANDSHAKE TONIGHT AND A KISS TOMORROW NIGHT... ER, SWEET?
OH, YOU TOUCHED ME! I CAN'T BELIEVE IT!
YEAH! IT TOOK A LOT OF NERVE, TOO!
AND A KISS TOMORROW NIGHT... OH, IT'S A DREAM COME TRUE!
HM...
BOY, IF SHE GETS THIS CARRIED AWAY OVER A HANDSHAKE, SHE'D GO APE OVER A KISS! UGH! BUT THERE MUST BE ANOTHER WAY!

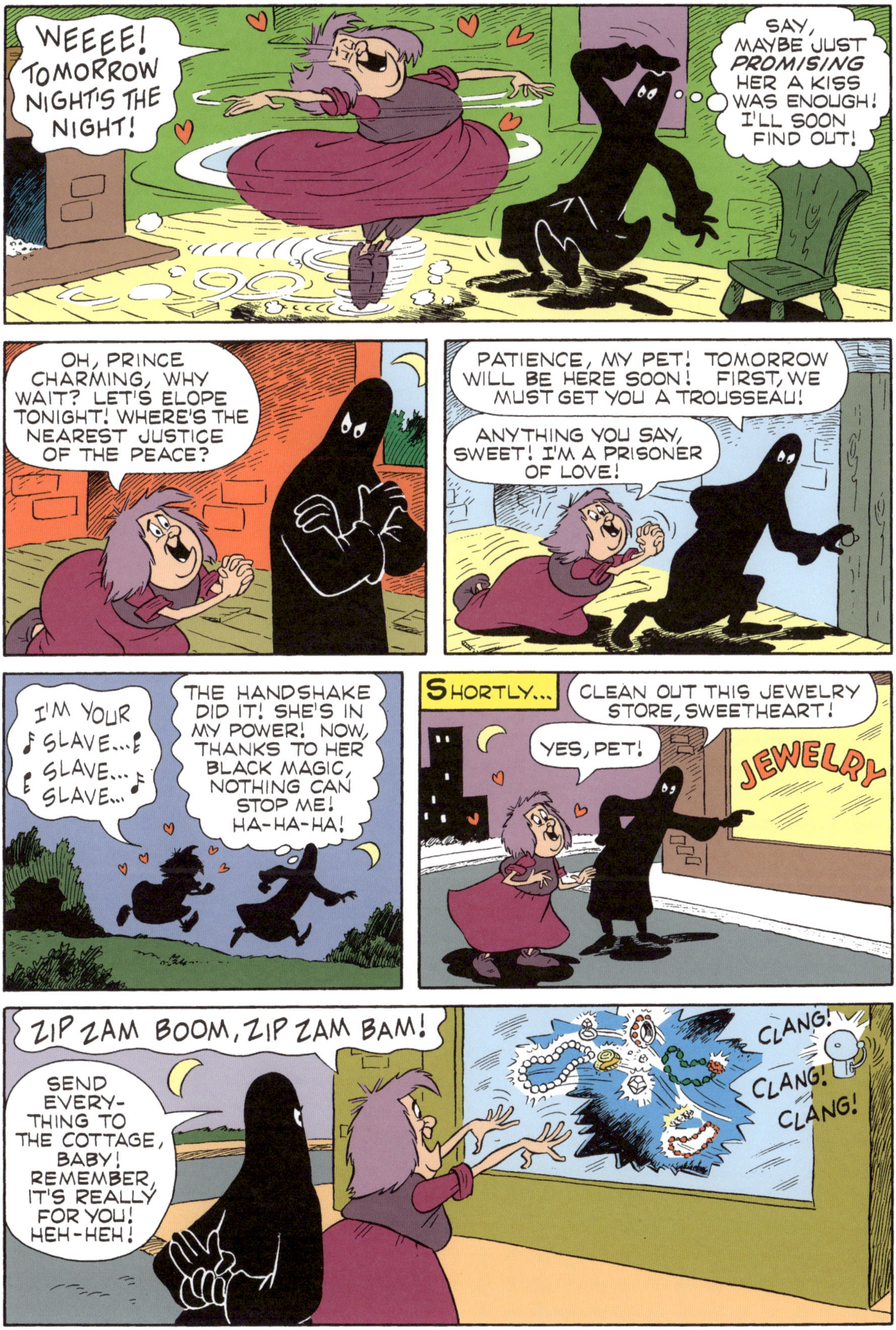
WEEEE! TOMORROW NIGHT'S THE NIGHT!
SAY, MAYBE JUST PROMISING HER A KISS WAS ENOUGH! I'LL SOON FIND OUT!
OH, PRINCE CHARMING, WHY WAIT? LET'S ELOPE TONIGHT! WHERE'S THE NEAREST JUSTICE OF THE PEACE?
PATIENCE, MY PET! TOMORROW WILL BE HERE SOON! FIRST, WE MUST GET YOU A TROUSSEAU!
ANYTHING YOU SAY, SWEET! I'M A PRISONER OF LOVE!
I'M YOUR SLAVE... SLAVE... SLAVE...
THE HANDSHAKE DID IT! SHE'S IN MY POWER! NOW, THANKS TO HER BLACK MAGIC, NOTHING CAN STOP ME! HA-HA-HA!
SHORTLY...
CLEAN OUT THIS JEWELRY STORE, SWEETHEART!
YES, PET!
JEWELRY
ZIP ZAM BOOM, ZIP ZAM BAM!
SEND EVERY-THING TO THE COTTAGE, BABY! REMEMBER, IT'S REALLY FOR YOU! HEH-HEH!
CLANG!
CLANG!
CLANG!

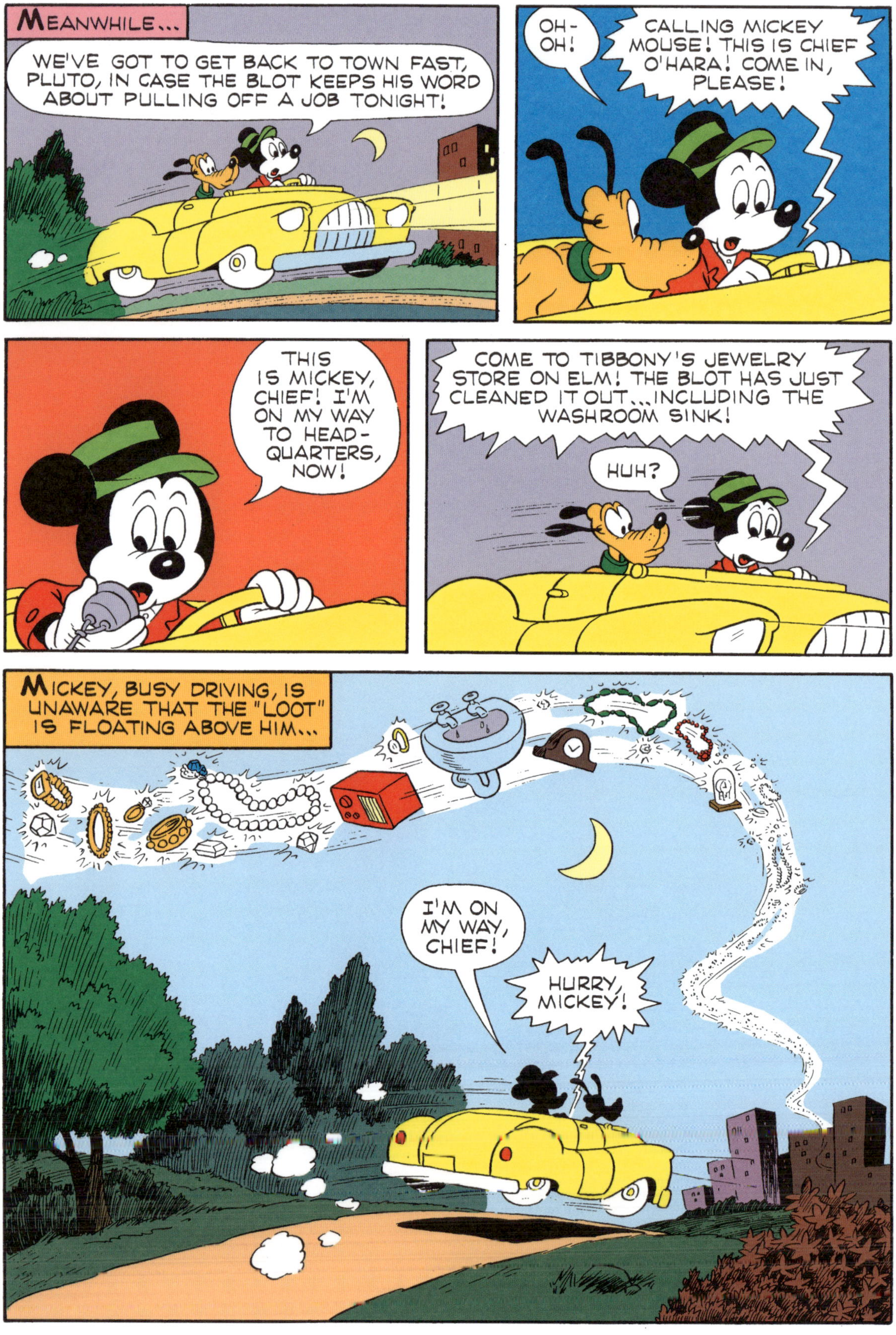
MEANWHILE...
WE'VE GOT TO GET BACK TO TOWN FAST, PLUTO, IN CASE THE BLOT KEEPS HIS WORD ABOUT PULLING OFF A JOB TONIGHT!
OH-OH!
CALLING MICKEY MOUSE! THIS IS CHIEF O'HARA! COME IN, PLEASE!
THIS IS MICKEY, CHIEF! I'M ON MY WAY TO HEAD-QUARTERS, NOW!
COME TO TIBBONY'S JEWELRY STORE ON ELM! THE BLOT HAS JUST CLEANED IT OUT...INCLUDING THE WASHROOM SINK!
HUH?
MICKEY, BUSY DRIVING, IS UNAWARE THAT THE "LOOT" IS FLOATING ABOVE HIM...
I'M ON MY WAY, CHIEF!
HURRY, MICKEY!

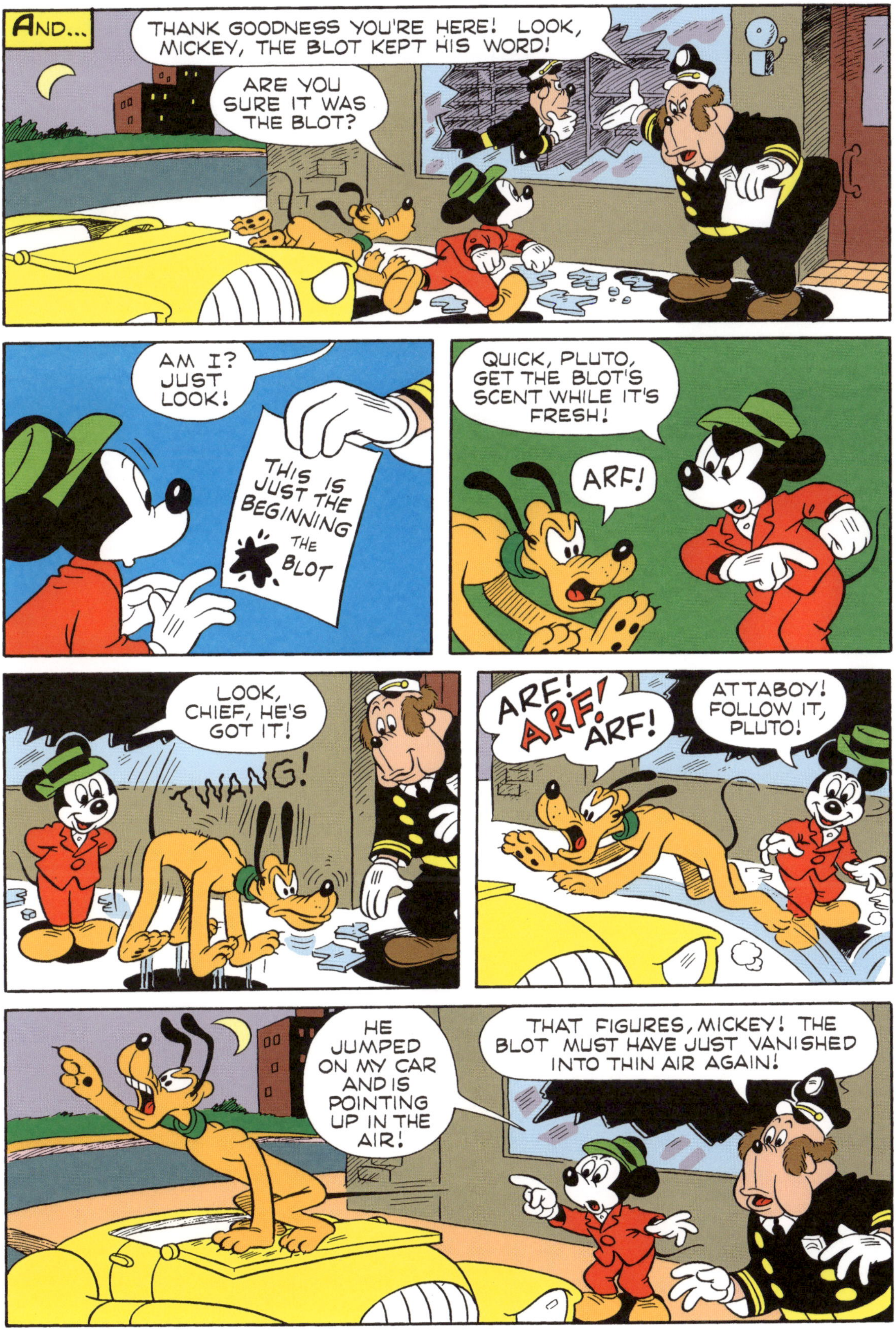
AND...
THANK GOODNESS YOU'RE HERE! LOOK, MICKEY, THE BLOT KEPT HIS WORD!
ARE YOU SURE IT WAS THE BLOT?
AM I? JUST LOOK!
THIS IS JUST THE BEGINNING THE BLOT
QUICK, PLUTO, GET THE BLOT'S SCENT WHILE IT'S FRESH!
ARF!
LOOK, CHIEF, HE'S GOT IT!
TWANG!
ARF! ARF! ARF!
ATTABOY! FOLLOW IT, PLUTO!
HE JUMPED ON MY CAR AND IS POINTING UP IN THE AIR!
THAT FIGURES, MICKEY! THE BLOT MUST HAVE JUST VANISHED INTO THIN AIR AGAIN!

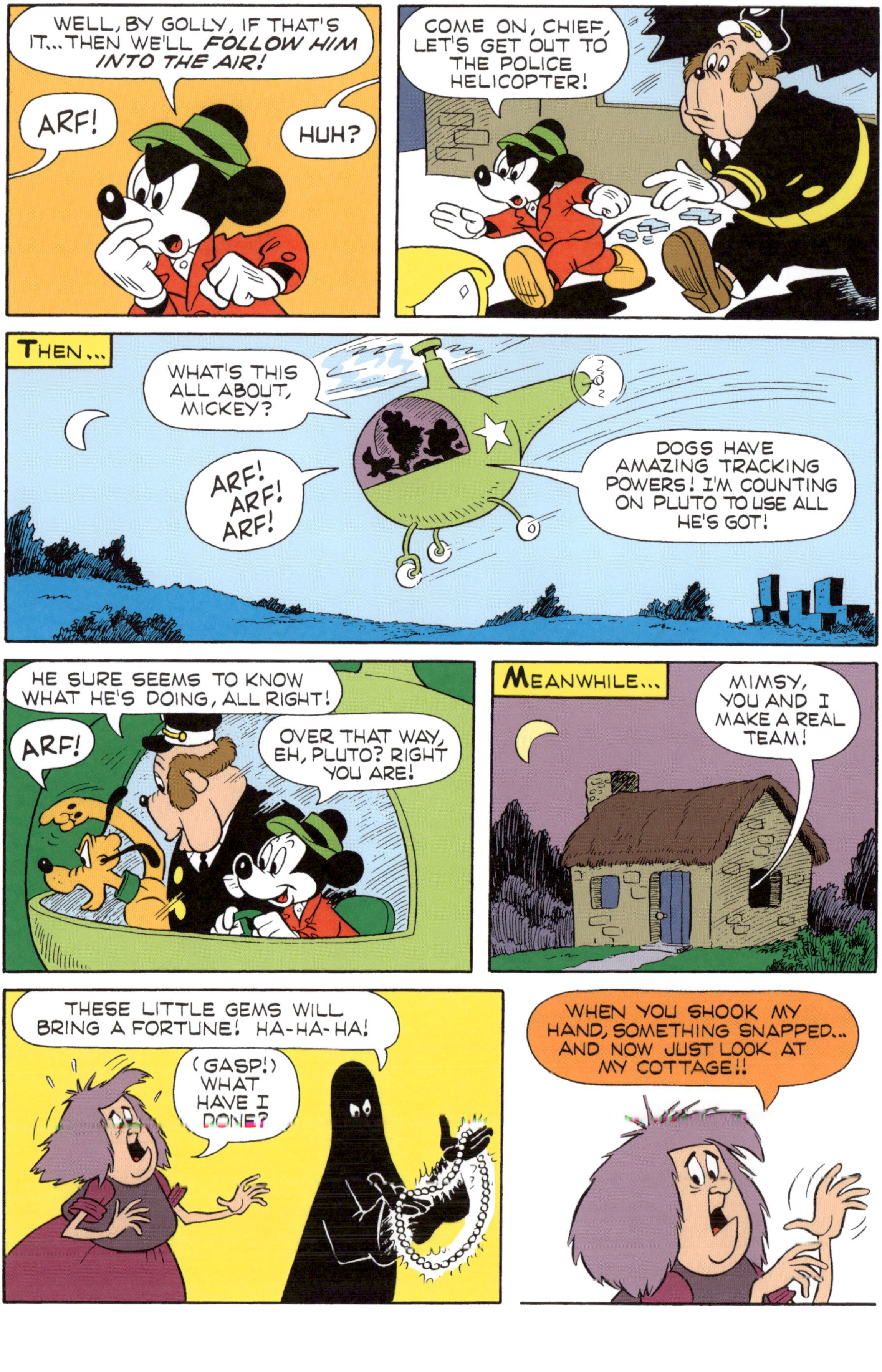
WELL, BY GOLLY, IF THAT'S IT...THEN WE'LL FOLLOW HIM INTO THE AIR!
ARF!
HUH?
COME ON, CHIEF, LET'S GET OUT TO THE POLICE HELICOPTER!
THEN...
WHAT'S THIS ALL ABOUT, MICKEY?
ARF! ARF! ARF!
DOGS HAVE AMAZING TRACKING POWERS! I'M COUNTING ON PLUTO TO USE ALL HE'S GOT!
HE SURE SEEMS TO KNOW WHAT HE'S DOING, ALL RIGHT!
ARF!
OVER THAT WAY, EH, PLUTO? RIGHT YOU ARE!
MEANWHILE...
MIMSY, YOU AND I MAKE A REAL TEAM!
THESE LITTLE GEMS WILL BRING A FORTUNE! HA-HA-HA!
(GASP!) WHAT HAVE I DONE?
WHEN YOU SHOOK MY HAND, SOMETHING SNAPPED... AND NOW JUST LOOK AT MY COTTAGE!!

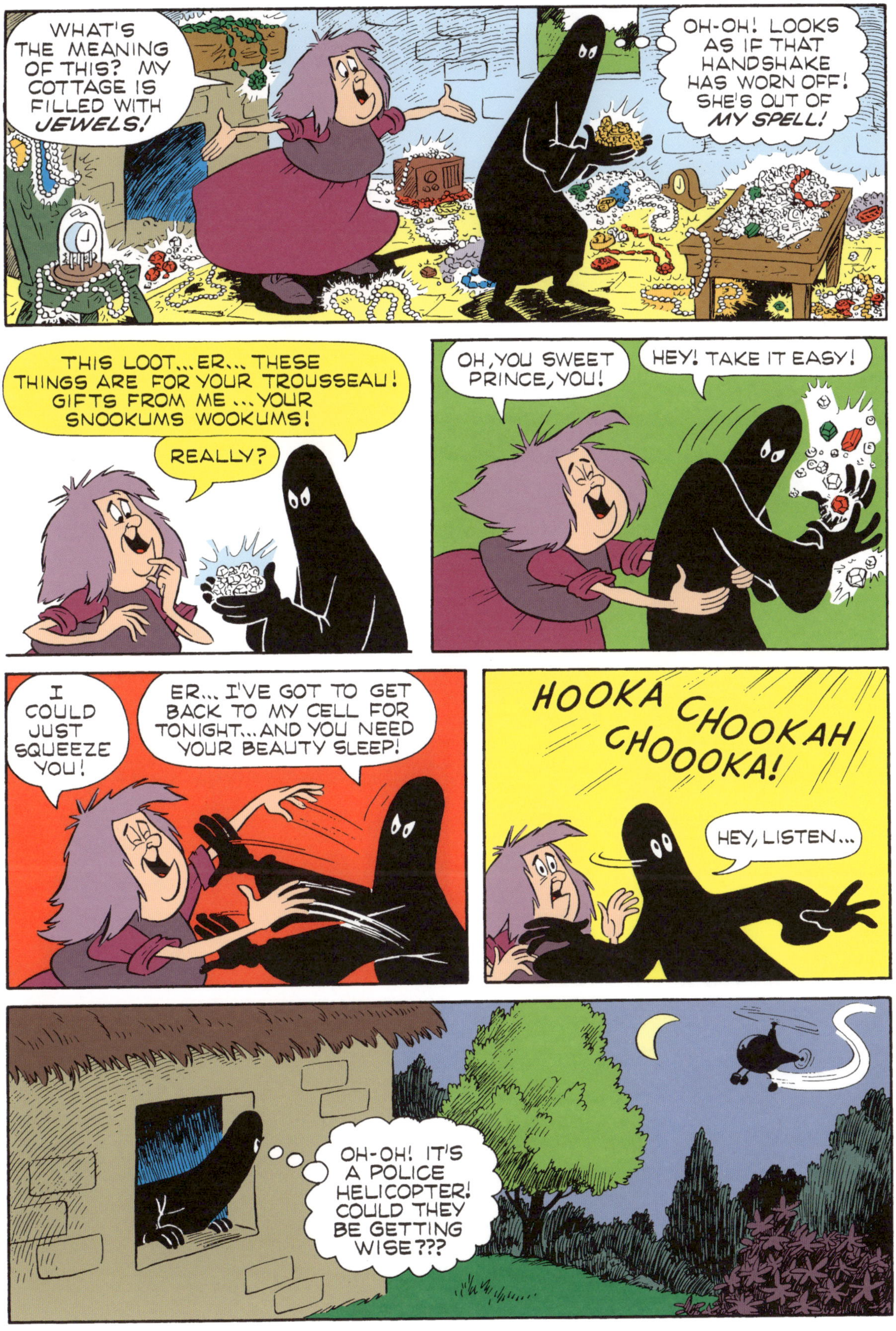
WHAT'S THE MEANING OF THIS? MY COTTAGE IS FILLED WITH *JEWELS!*
OH-OH! LOOKS AS IF THAT HANDSHAKE HAS WORN OFF! SHE'S OUT OF *MY SPELL!*
THIS LOOT... ER... THESE THINGS ARE FOR YOUR TROUSSEAU! GIFTS FROM ME... YOUR SNOOKUMS WOOKUMS!
REALLY?
OH, YOU SWEET PRINCE, YOU!
HEY! TAKE IT EASY!
I COULD JUST SQUEEZE YOU!
ER... I'VE GOT TO GET BACK TO MY CELL FOR TONIGHT... AND YOU NEED YOUR BEAUTY SLEEP!
HOOKA CHOOKAH CHOOOKA!
HEY, LISTEN...
OH-OH! IT'S A POLICE HELICOPTER! COULD THEY BE GETTING WISE???

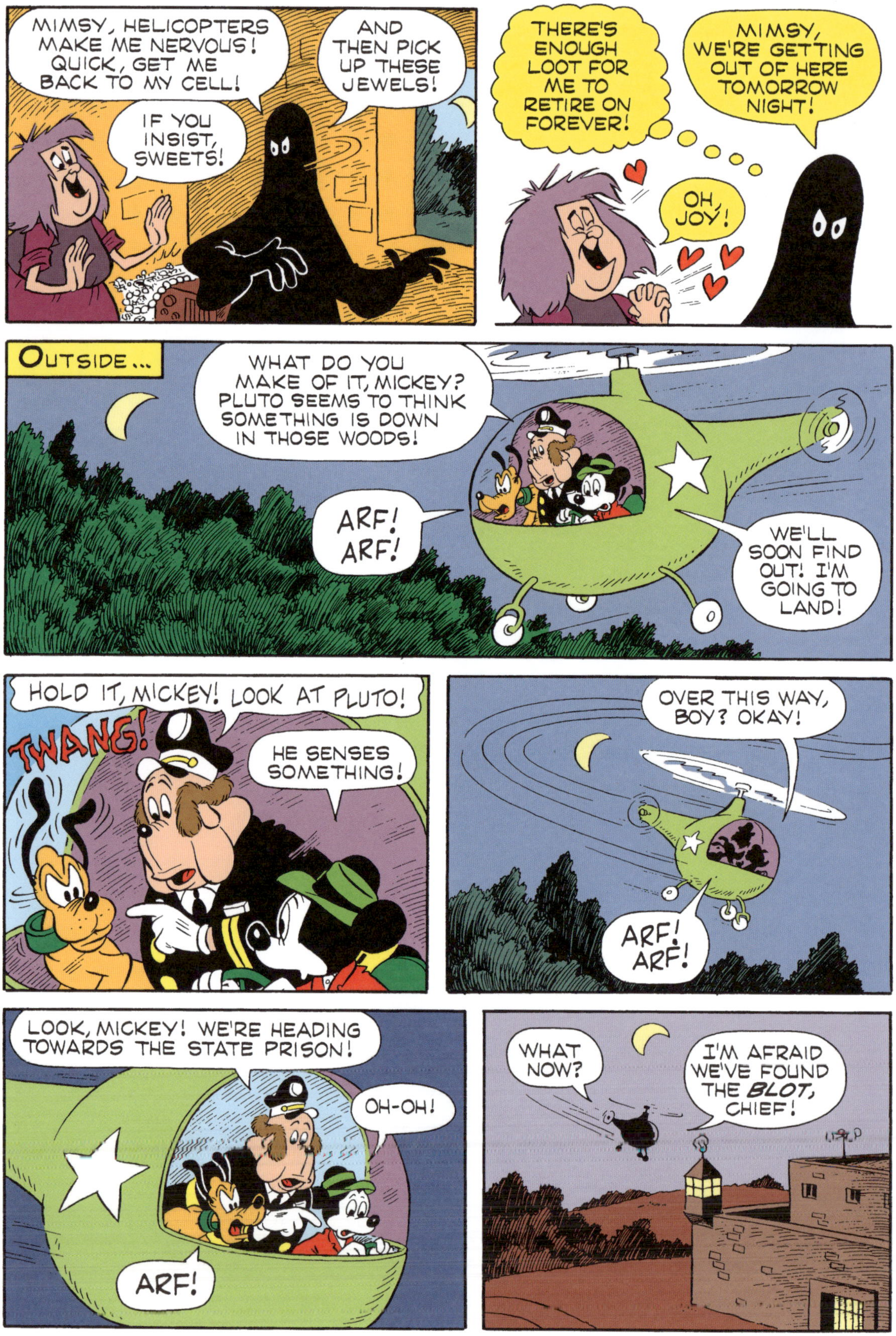
MIMSY, HELICOPTERS MAKE ME NERVOUS! QUICK, GET ME BACK TO MY CELL!
AND THEN PICK UP THESE JEWELS!
IF YOU INSIST, SWEETS!
THERE'S ENOUGH LOOT FOR ME TO RETIRE ON FOREVER!
MIMSY, WE'RE GETTING OUT OF HERE TOMORROW NIGHT!
OH, JOY!
OUTSIDE...
WHAT DO YOU MAKE OF IT, MICKEY? PLUTO SEEMS TO THINK SOMETHING IS DOWN IN THOSE WOODS!
ARF! ARF!
WE'LL SOON FIND OUT! I'M GOING TO LAND!
HOLD IT, MICKEY! LOOK AT PLUTO!
TWANG!
HE SENSES SOMETHING!
OVER THIS WAY, BOY? OKAY!
ARF! ARF!
LOOK, MICKEY! WE'RE HEADING TOWARDS THE STATE PRISON!
OH-OH!
ARF!
WHAT NOW?
I'M AFRAID WE'VE FOUND THE *BLOT*, CHIEF!

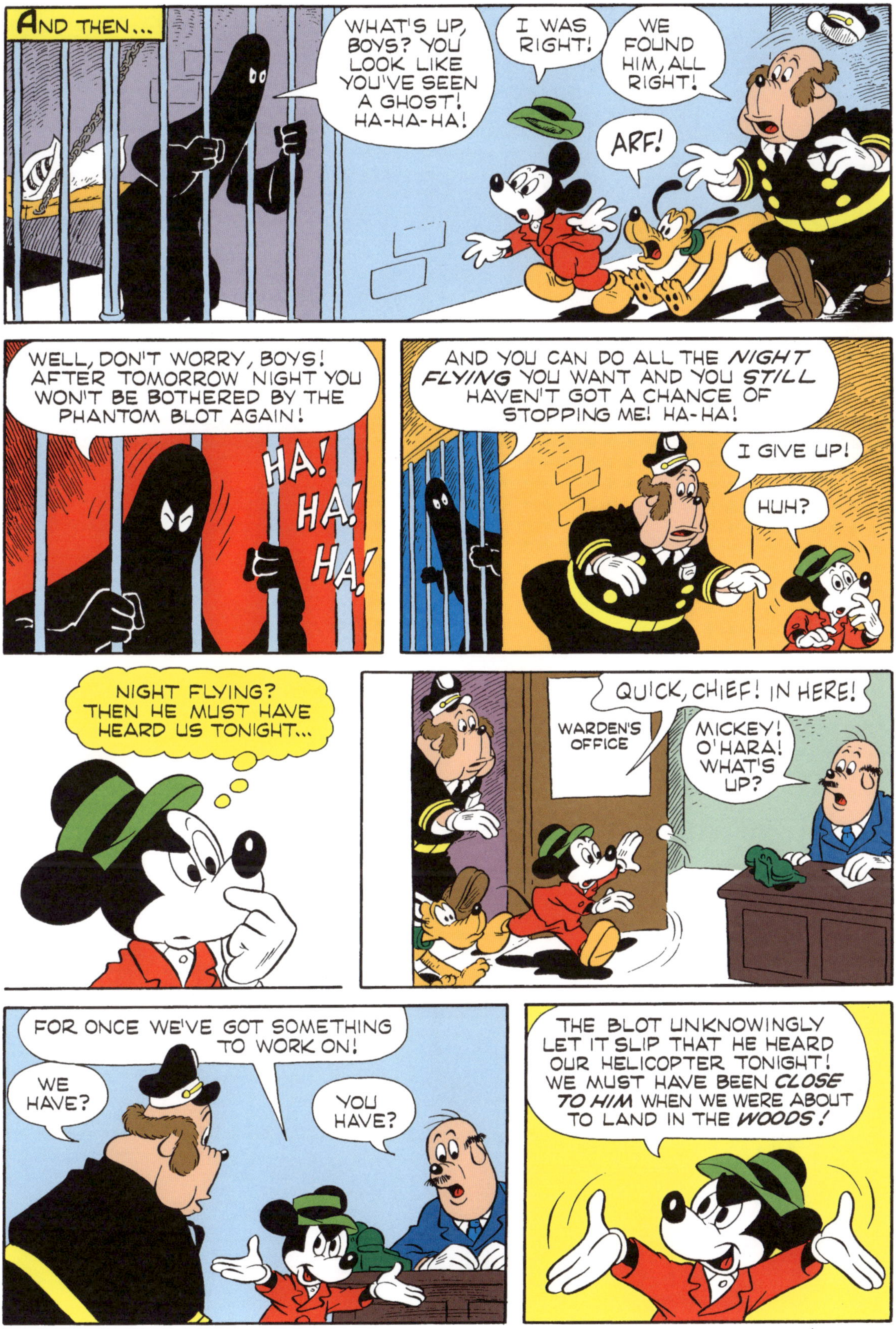
AND THEN...
WHAT'S UP, BOYS? YOU LOOK LIKE YOU'VE SEEN A GHOST! HA-HA-HA!
I WAS RIGHT!
WE FOUND HIM, ALL RIGHT!
ARF!
WELL, DON'T WORRY, BOYS! AFTER TOMORROW NIGHT YOU WON'T BE BOTHERED BY THE PHANTOM BLOT AGAIN!
HA! HA! HA!
AND YOU CAN DO ALL THE NIGHT FLYING YOU WANT AND YOU STILL HAVEN'T GOT A CHANCE OF STOPPING ME! HA-HA!
I GIVE UP!
HUH?
NIGHT FLYING? THEN HE MUST HAVE HEARD US TONIGHT...
QUICK, CHIEF! IN HERE!
WARDEN'S OFFICE
MICKEY! O'HARA! WHAT'S UP?
FOR ONCE WE'VE GOT SOMETHING TO WORK ON!
WE HAVE?
YOU HAVE?
THE BLOT UNKNOWINGLY LET IT SLIP THAT HE HEARD OUR HELICOPTER TONIGHT! WE MUST HAVE BEEN CLOSE TO HIM WHEN WE WERE ABOUT TO LAND IN THE WOODS!

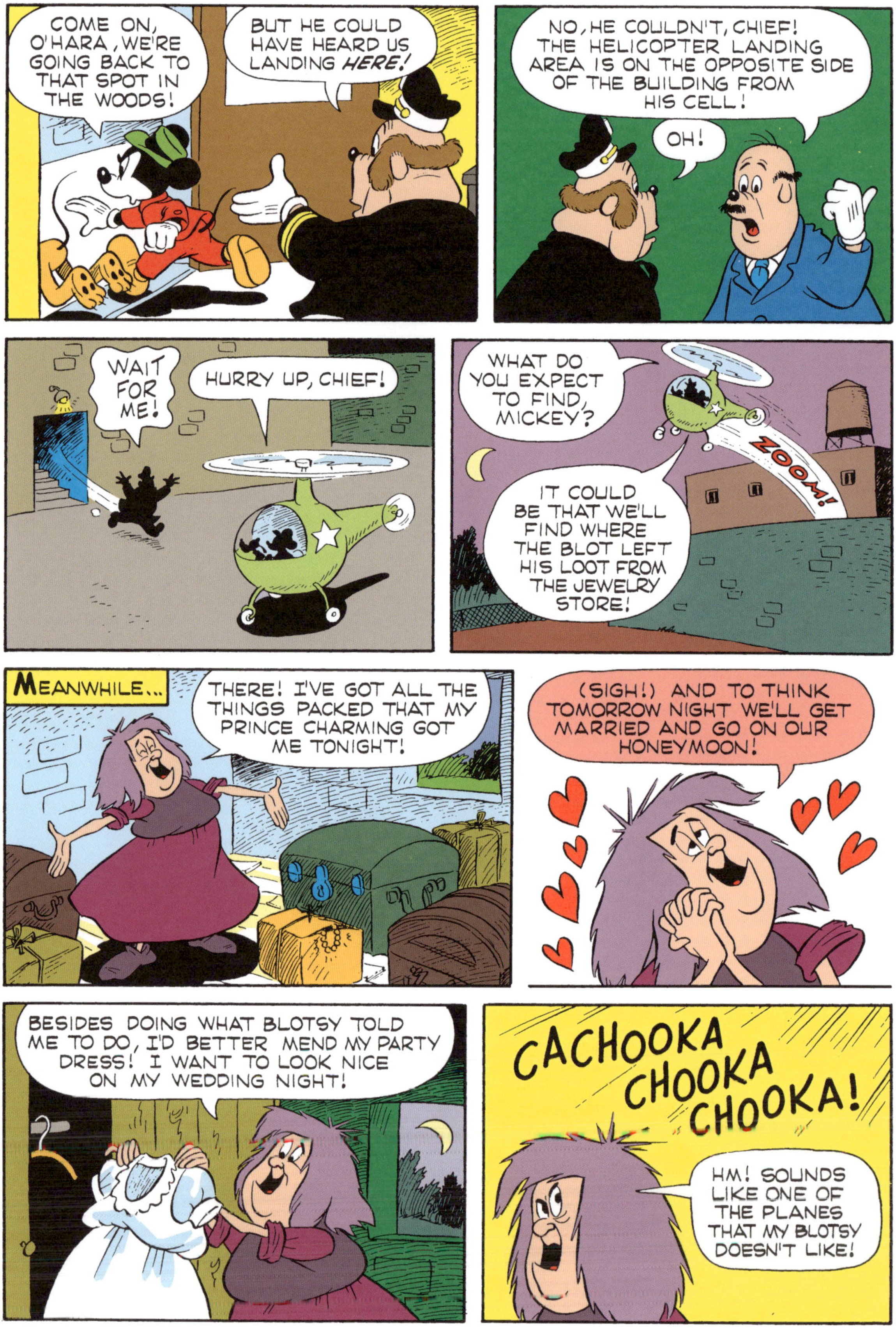
COME ON, O'HARA, WE'RE GOING BACK TO THAT SPOT IN THE WOODS!
BUT HE COULD HAVE HEARD US LANDING HERE!
NO, HE COULDN'T, CHIEF! THE HELICOPTER LANDING AREA IS ON THE OPPOSITE SIDE OF THE BUILDING FROM HIS CELL!
OH!
WAIT FOR ME!
HURRY UP, CHIEF!
WHAT DO YOU EXPECT TO FIND, MICKEY?
ZOOM!
IT COULD BE THAT WE'LL FIND WHERE THE BLOT LEFT HIS LOOT FROM THE JEWELRY STORE!
MEANWHILE...
THERE! I'VE GOT ALL THE THINGS PACKED THAT MY PRINCE CHARMING GOT ME TONIGHT!
(SIGH!) AND TO THINK TOMORROW NIGHT WE'LL GET MARRIED AND GO ON OUR HONEYMOON!
BESIDES DOING WHAT BLOTSY TOLD ME TO DO, I'D BETTER MEND MY PARTY DRESS! I WANT TO LOOK NICE ON MY WEDDING NIGHT!
CACHOOKA CHOOKA CHOOKA!
HM! SOUNDS LIKE ONE OF THE PLANES THAT MY BLOTSY DOESN'T LIKE!

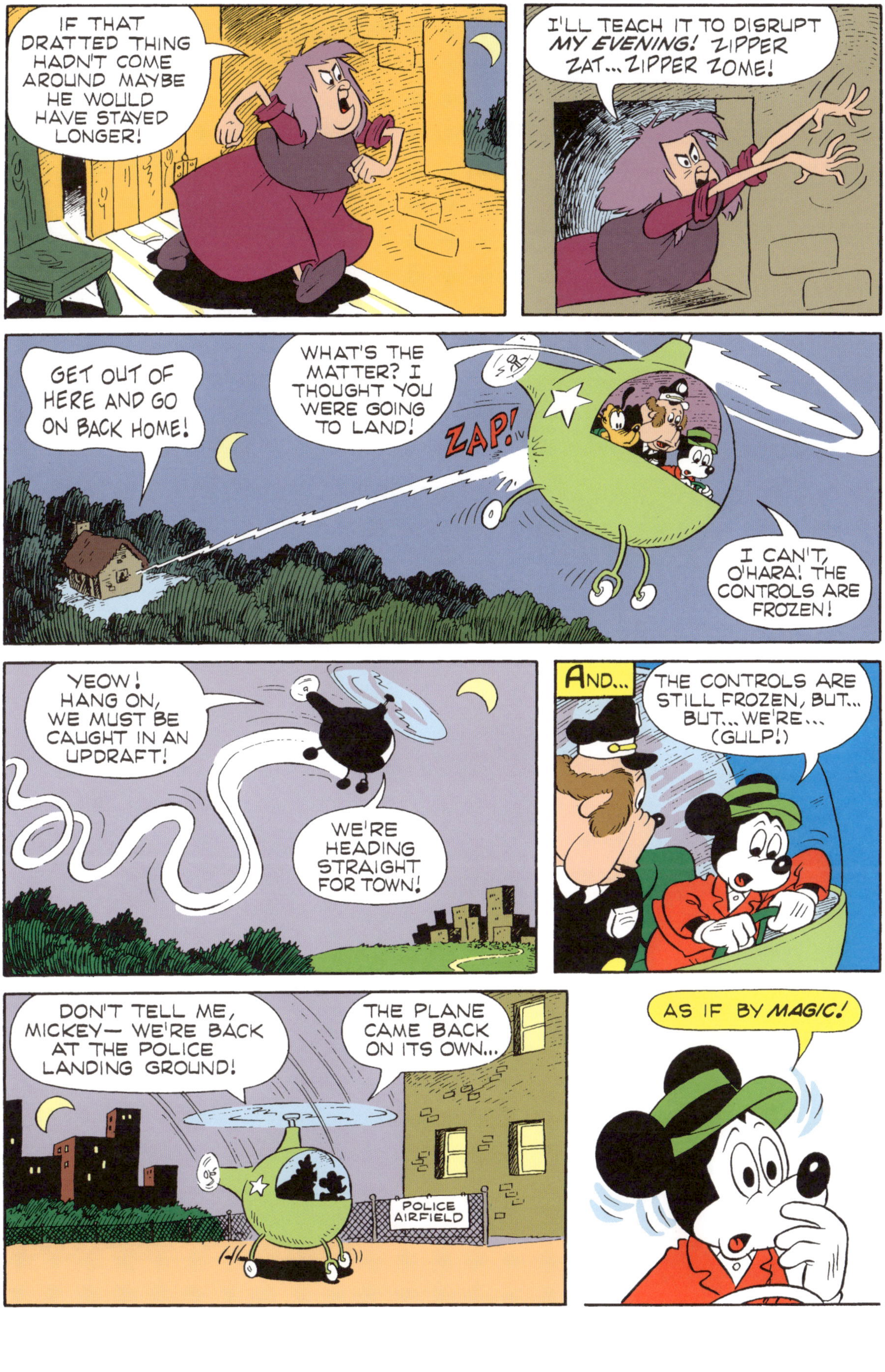

IF THAT DRATTED THING HADN'T COME AROUND MAYBE HE WOULD HAVE STAYED LONGER!
I'LL TEACH IT TO DISRUPT MY EVENING! ZIPPER ZAT... ZIPPER ZOME!
GET OUT OF HERE AND GO ON BACK HOME!
WHAT'S THE MATTER? I THOUGHT YOU WERE GOING TO LAND!
ZAP!
I CAN'T, O'HARA! THE CONTROLS ARE FROZEN!
YEOW! HANG ON, WE MUST BE CAUGHT IN AN UPDRAFT!
WE'RE HEADING STRAIGHT FOR TOWN!
AND...
THE CONTROLS ARE STILL FROZEN, BUT... BUT... WE'RE... (GULP!)
DON'T TELL ME, MICKEY— WE'RE BACK AT THE POLICE LANDING GROUND!
THE PLANE CAME BACK ON ITS OWN...
POLICE AIRFIELD
AS IF BY MAGIC!

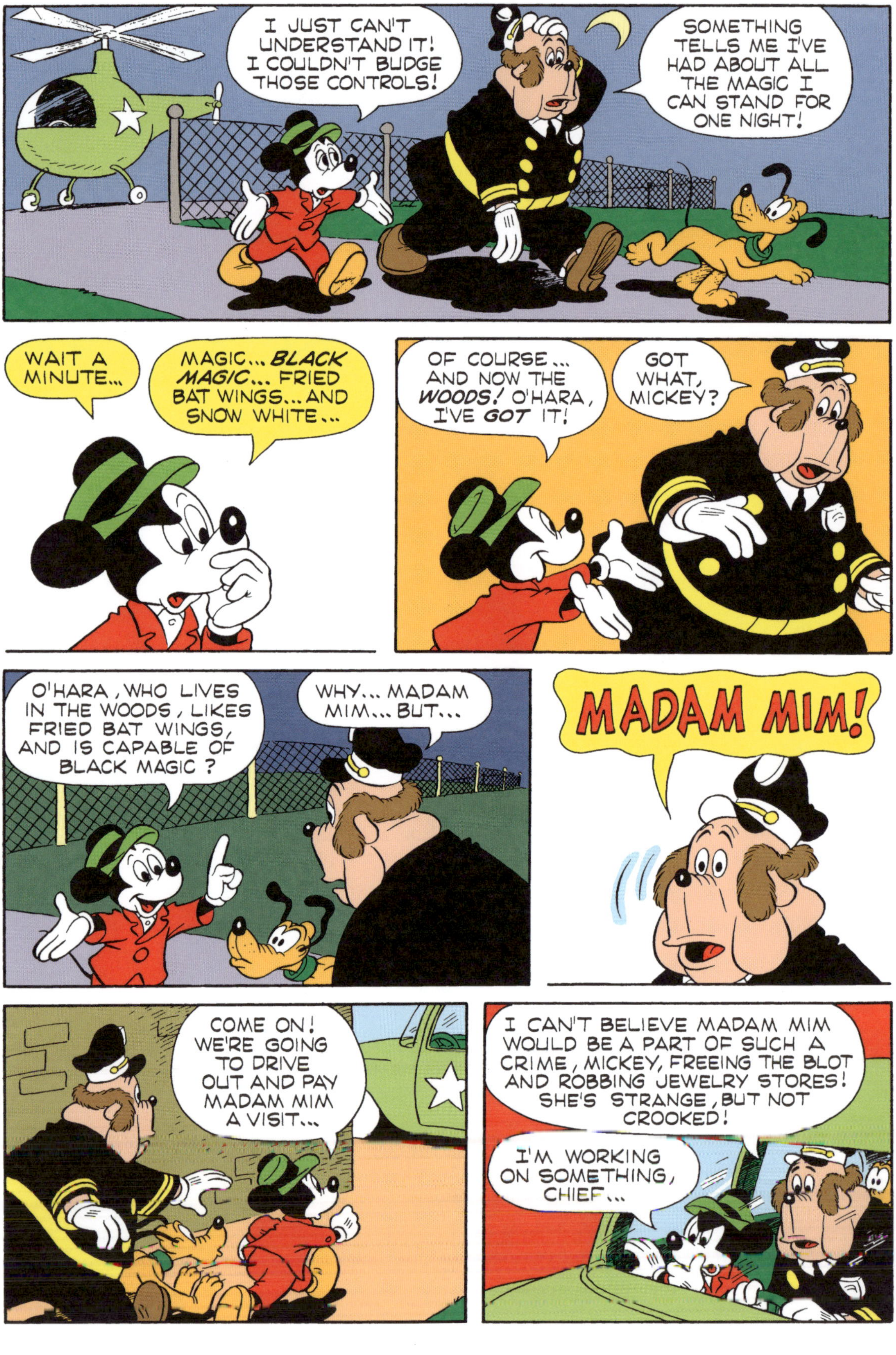
I JUST CAN'T UNDERSTAND IT! I COULDN'T BUDGE THOSE CONTROLS!
SOMETHING TELLS ME I'VE HAD ABOUT ALL THE MAGIC I CAN STAND FOR ONE NIGHT!
WAIT A MINUTE...
MAGIC... BLACK MAGIC... FRIED BAT WINGS... AND SNOW WHITE...
OF COURSE... AND NOW THE WOODS! O'HARA, I'VE GOT IT!
GOT WHAT, MICKEY?
O'HARA, WHO LIVES IN THE WOODS, LIKES FRIED BAT WINGS, AND IS CAPABLE OF BLACK MAGIC?
WHY... MADAM MIM... BUT...
MADAM MIM!
COME ON! WE'RE GOING TO DRIVE OUT AND PAY MADAM MIM A VISIT...
I CAN'T BELIEVE MADAM MIM WOULD BE A PART OF SUCH A CRIME, MICKEY, FREEING THE BLOT AND ROBBING JEWELRY STORES! SHE'S STRANGE, BUT NOT CROOKED!
I'M WORKING ON SOMETHING, CHIEF...

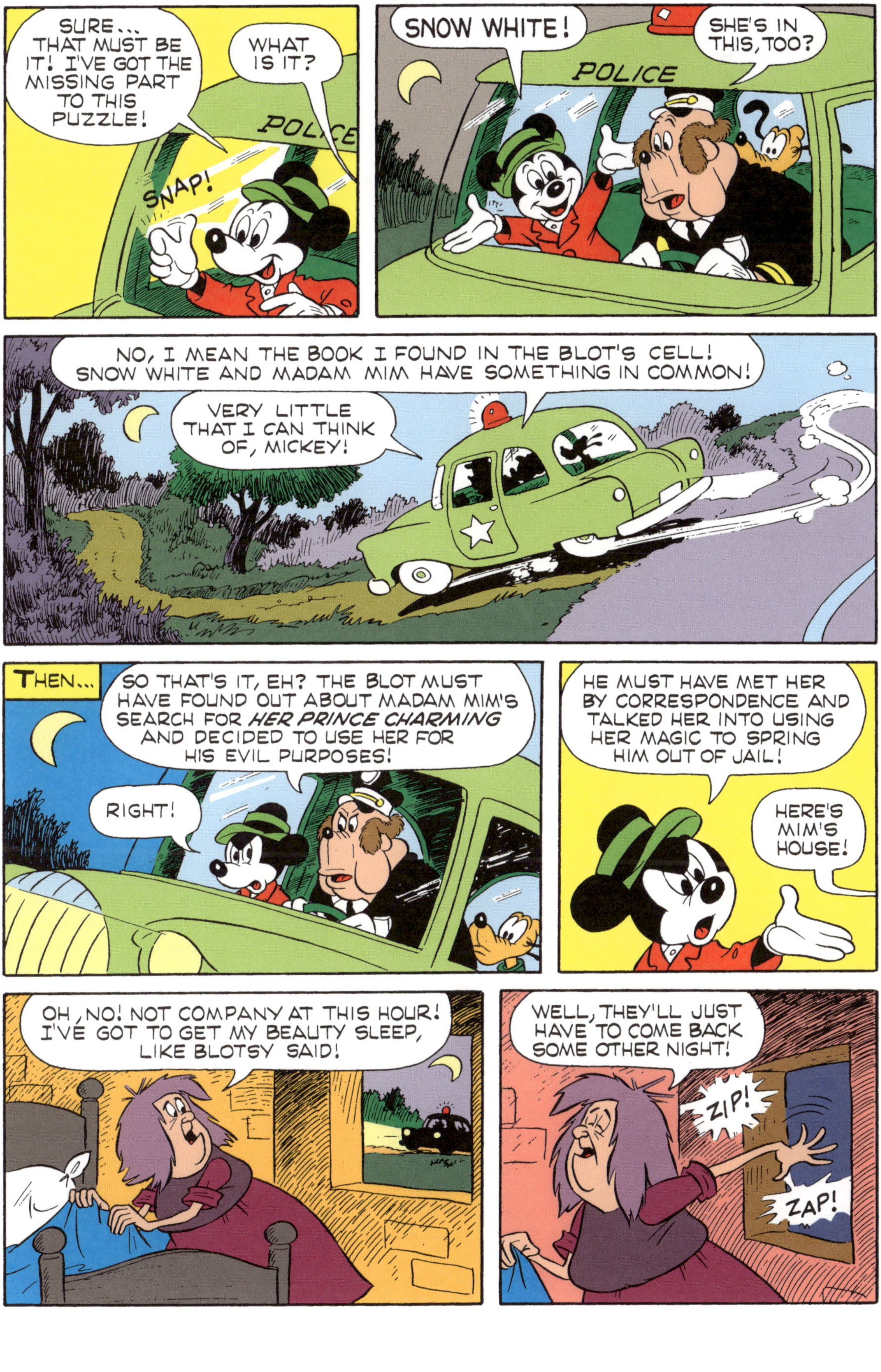
SURE... THAT MUST BE IT! I'VE GOT THE MISSING PART TO THIS PUZZLE!
WHAT IS IT?
POLICE
SNAP!
SNOW WHITE!
SHE'S IN THIS, TOO?
POLICE
NO, I MEAN THE BOOK I FOUND IN THE BLOT'S CELL! SNOW WHITE AND MADAM MIM HAVE SOMETHING IN COMMON!
VERY LITTLE THAT I CAN THINK OF, MICKEY!
THEN...
SO THAT'S IT, EH? THE BLOT MUST HAVE FOUND OUT ABOUT MADAM MIM'S SEARCH FOR *HER PRINCE CHARMING* AND DECIDED TO USE HER FOR HIS EVIL PURPOSES!
RIGHT!
HE MUST HAVE MET HER BY CORRESPONDENCE AND TALKED HER INTO USING HER MAGIC TO SPRING HIM OUT OF JAIL!
HERE'S MIM'S HOUSE!
OH, NO! NOT COMPANY AT THIS HOUR! I'VE GOT TO GET MY BEAUTY SLEEP, LIKE BLOTSY SAID!
WELL, THEY'LL JUST HAVE TO COME BACK SOME OTHER NIGHT!
ZIP!
ZAP!

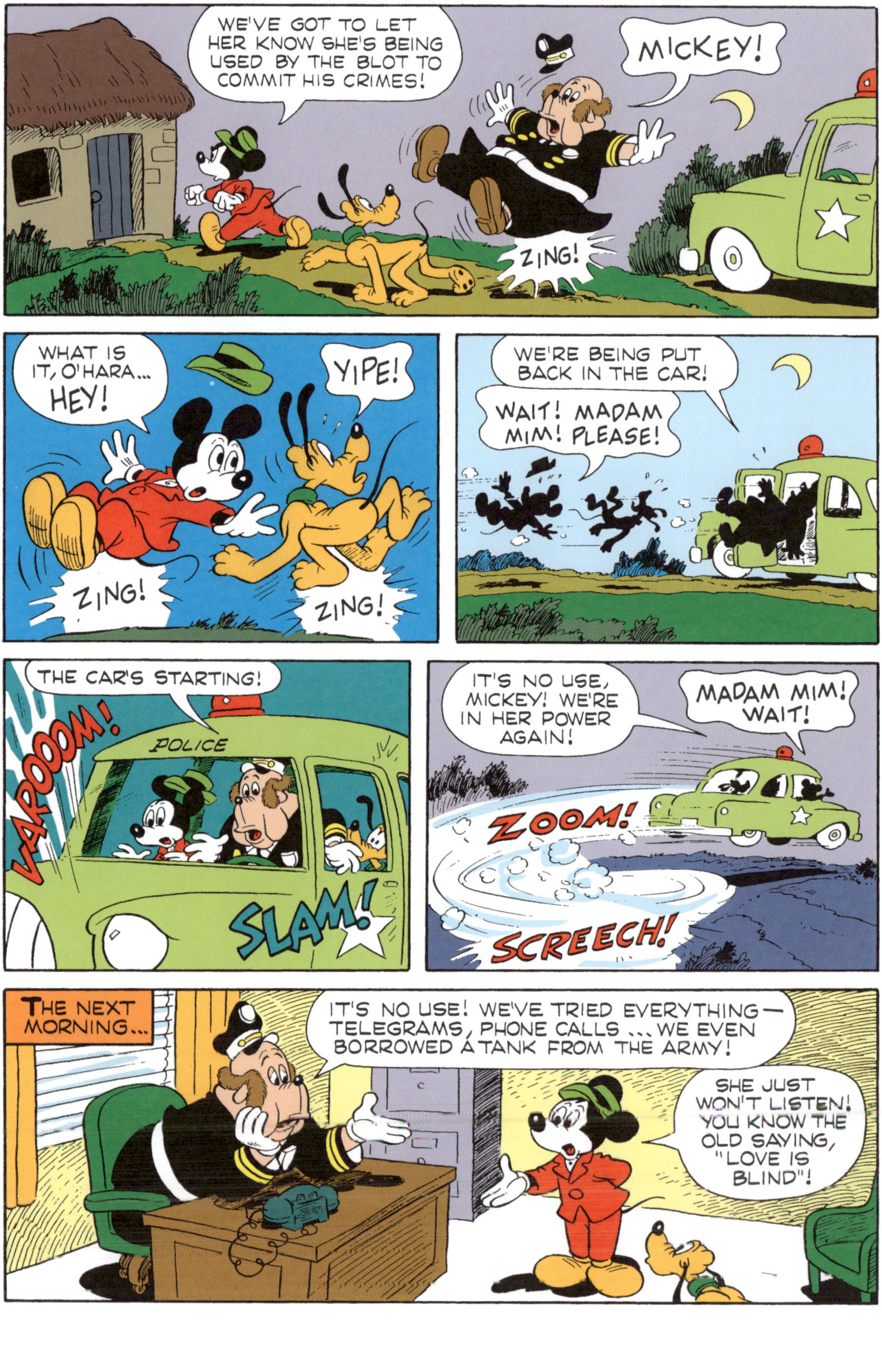
WE'VE GOT TO LET HER KNOW SHE'S BEING USED BY THE BLOT TO COMMIT HIS CRIMES!
MICKEY!
ZING!
WHAT IS IT, O'HARA... HEY!
YIPE!
ZING!
ZING!
WE'RE BEING PUT BACK IN THE CAR!
WAIT! MADAM MIM! PLEASE!
THE CAR'S STARTING!
VAROOOM!
POLICE
SLAM!
IT'S NO USE, MICKEY! WE'RE IN HER POWER AGAIN!
MADAM MIM! WAIT!
ZOOM!
SCREECH!
THE NEXT MORNING...
IT'S NO USE! WE'VE TRIED EVERYTHING— TELEGRAMS, PHONE CALLS ... WE EVEN BORROWED A TANK FROM THE ARMY!
SHE JUST WON'T LISTEN! YOU KNOW THE OLD SAYING, "LOVE IS BLIND"!

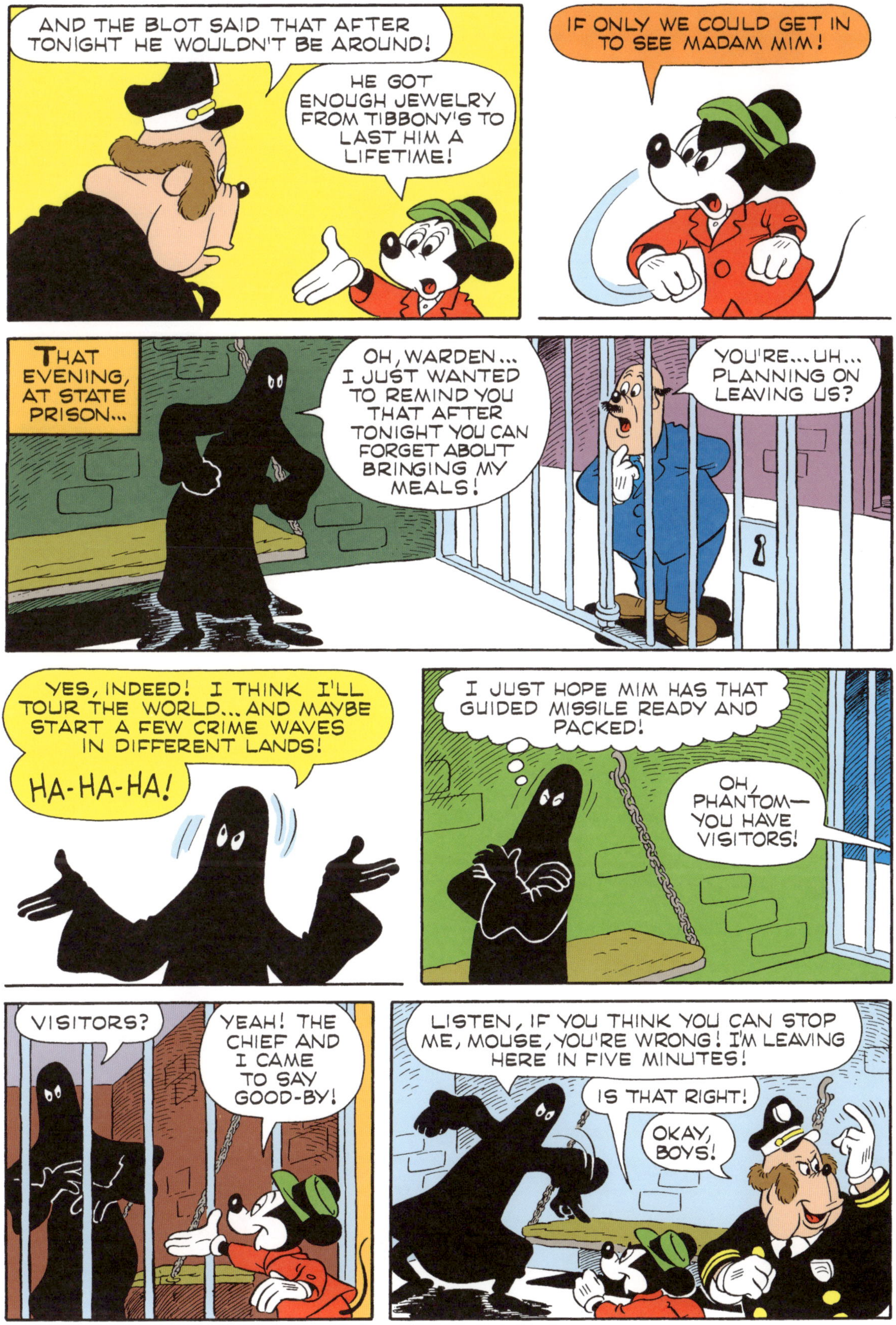

AND THE BLOT SAID THAT AFTER TONIGHT HE WOULDN'T BE AROUND!
HE GOT ENOUGH JEWELRY FROM TIBBONY'S TO LAST HIM A LIFETIME!
IF ONLY WE COULD GET IN TO SEE MADAM MIM!
THAT EVENING, AT STATE PRISON...
OH, WARDEN... I JUST WANTED TO REMIND YOU THAT AFTER TONIGHT YOU CAN FORGET ABOUT BRINGING MY MEALS!
YOU'RE... UH... PLANNING ON LEAVING US?
YES, INDEED! I THINK I'LL TOUR THE WORLD... AND MAYBE START A FEW CRIME WAVES IN DIFFERENT LANDS!
HA-HA-HA!
I JUST HOPE MIM HAS THAT GUIDED MISSILE READY AND PACKED!
OH, PHANTOM— YOU HAVE VISITORS!
VISITORS?
YEAH! THE CHIEF AND I CAME TO SAY GOOD-BY!
LISTEN, IF YOU THINK YOU CAN STOP ME, MOUSE, YOU'RE WRONG! I'M LEAVING HERE IN FIVE MINUTES!
IS THAT RIGHT!
OKAY, BOYS!

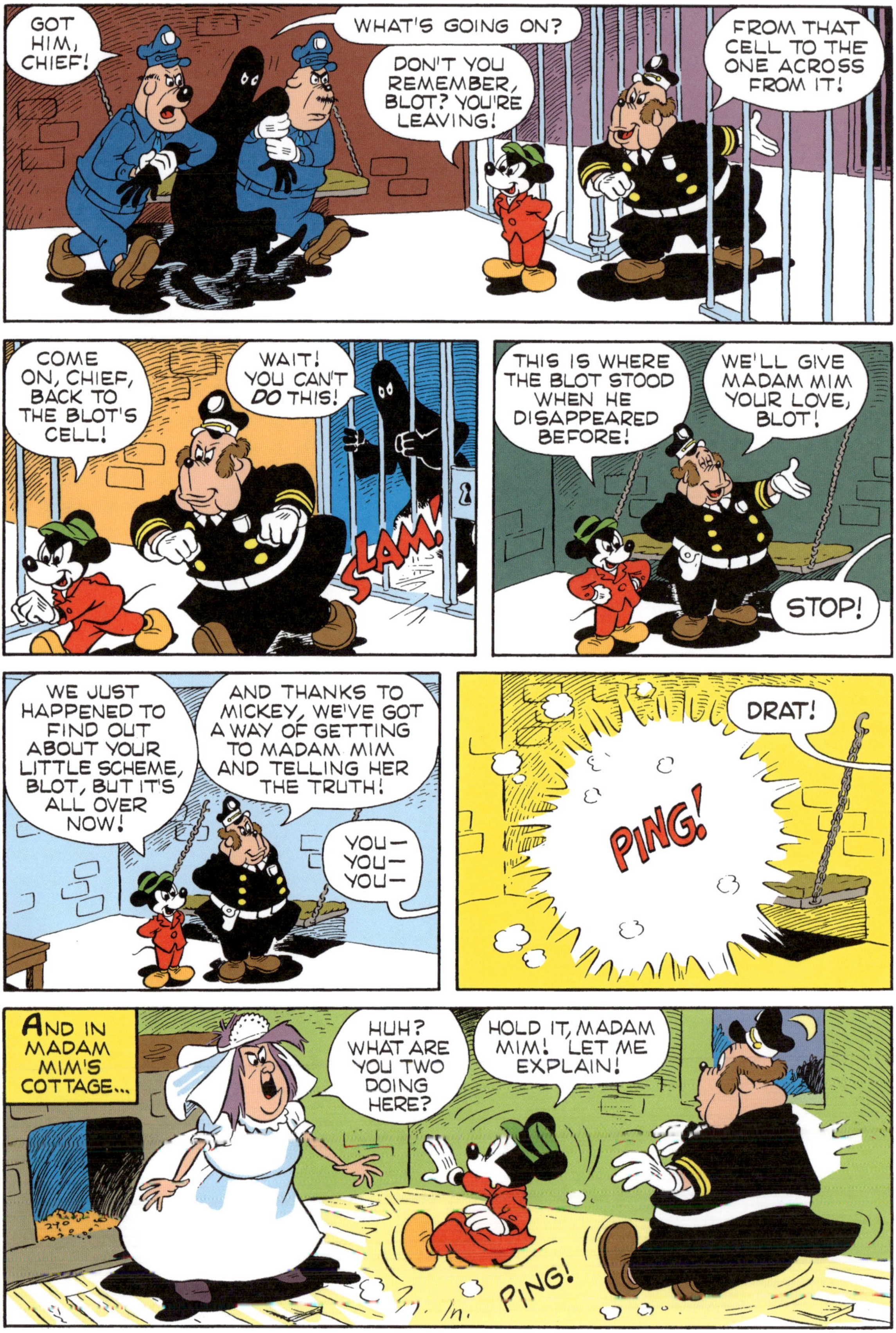
GOT HIM, CHIEF!
WHAT'S GOING ON?
DON'T YOU REMEMBER, BLOT? YOU'RE LEAVING!
FROM THAT CELL TO THE ONE ACROSS FROM IT!
COME ON, CHIEF, BACK TO THE BLOT'S CELL!
WAIT! YOU CAN'T DO THIS!
SLAM!
THIS IS WHERE THE BLOT STOOD WHEN HE DISAPPEARED BEFORE!
WE'LL GIVE MADAM MIM YOUR LOVE, BLOT!
STOP!
WE JUST HAPPENED TO FIND OUT ABOUT YOUR LITTLE SCHEME, BLOT, BUT IT'S ALL OVER NOW!
AND THANKS TO MICKEY, WE'VE GOT A WAY OF GETTING TO MADAM MIM AND TELLING HER THE TRUTH!
YOU— YOU— YOU—
DRAT!
PING!
AND IN MADAM MIM'S COTTAGE...
HUH? WHAT ARE YOU TWO DOING HERE?
HOLD IT, MADAM MIM! LET ME EXPLAIN!
PING!

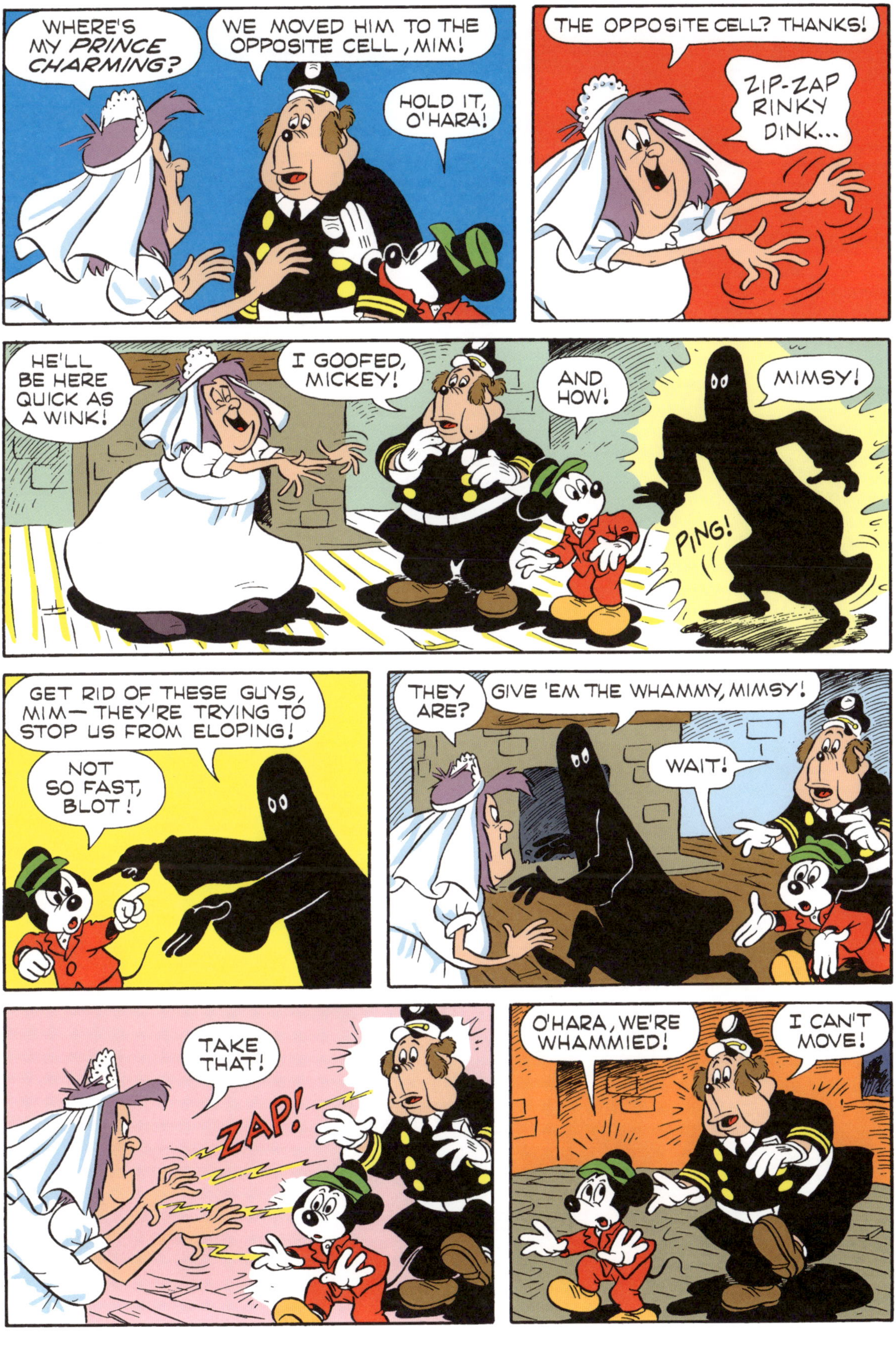
WHERE'S MY *PRINCE CHARMING*?
WE MOVED HIM TO THE OPPOSITE CELL, MIM!
HOLD IT, O'HARA!
THE OPPOSITE CELL? THANKS!
ZIP-ZAP RINKY DINK...
HE'LL BE HERE QUICK AS A WINK!
I GOOFED, MICKEY!
AND HOW!
MIMSY!
PING!
GET RID OF THESE GUYS, MIM— THEY'RE TRYING TO STOP US FROM ELOPING!
NOT SO FAST, BLOT!
THEY ARE?
GIVE 'EM THE WHAMMY, MIMSY!
WAIT!
TAKE THAT!
ZAP!
O'HARA, WE'RE WHAMMIED!
I CAN'T MOVE!

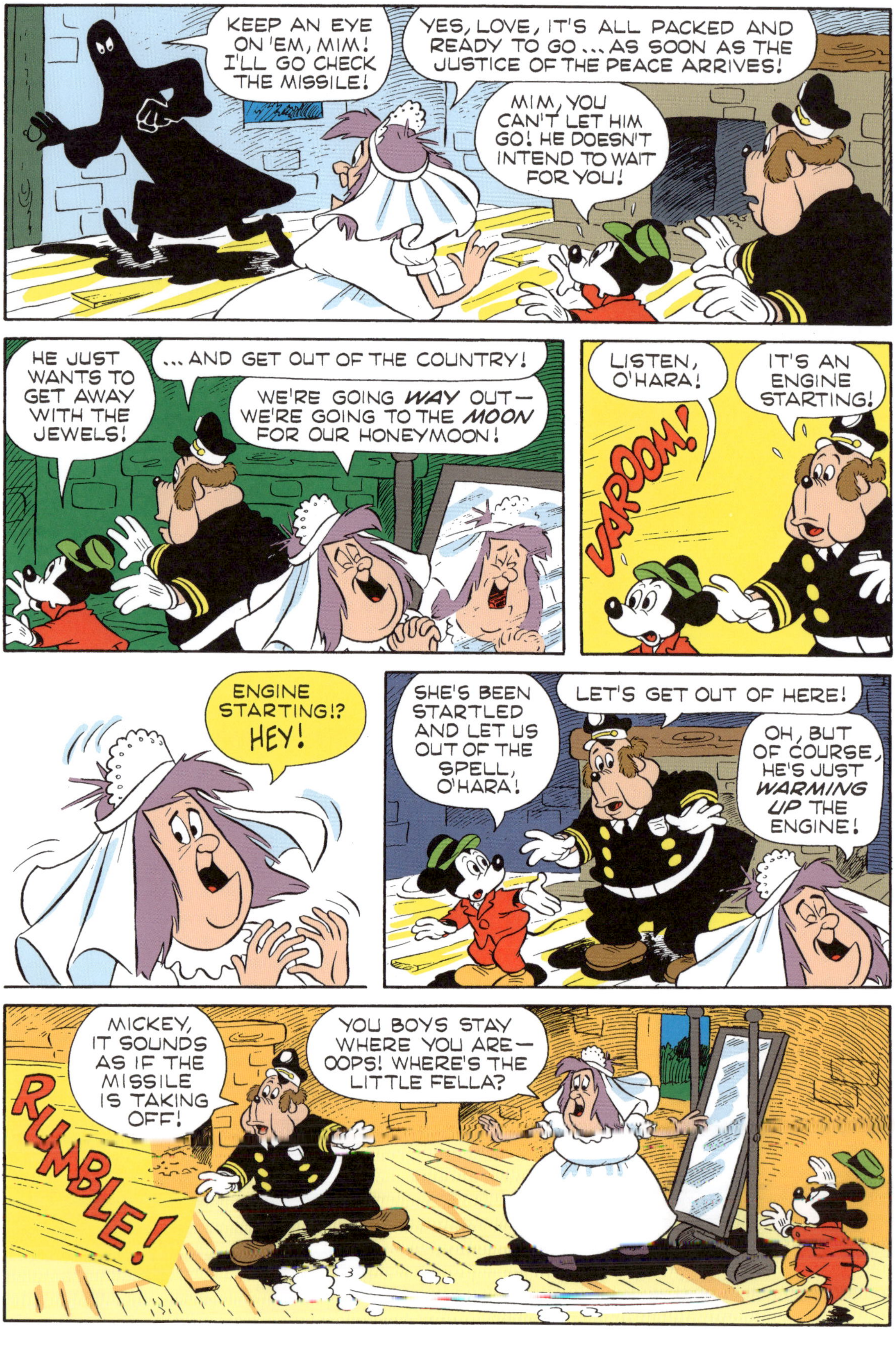
KEEP AN EYE ON 'EM, MIM! I'LL GO CHECK THE MISSILE!
YES, LOVE, IT'S ALL PACKED AND READY TO GO ... AS SOON AS THE JUSTICE OF THE PEACE ARRIVES!
MIM, YOU CAN'T LET HIM GO! HE DOESN'T INTEND TO WAIT FOR YOU!
HE JUST WANTS TO GET AWAY WITH THE JEWELS!
... AND GET OUT OF THE COUNTRY!
WE'RE GOING *WAY* OUT— WE'RE GOING TO THE *MOON* FOR OUR HONEYMOON!
LISTEN, O'HARA!
VAROOM!
IT'S AN ENGINE STARTING!
ENGINE STARTING!? HEY!
SHE'S BEEN STARTLED AND LET US OUT OF THE SPELL, O'HARA!
LET'S GET OUT OF HERE!
OH, BUT OF COURSE, HE'S JUST *WARMING UP* THE ENGINE!
MICKEY, IT SOUNDS AS IF THE MISSILE IS TAKING OFF!
RUMBLE!
YOU BOYS STAY WHERE YOU ARE— OOPS! WHERE'S THE LITTLE FELLA?

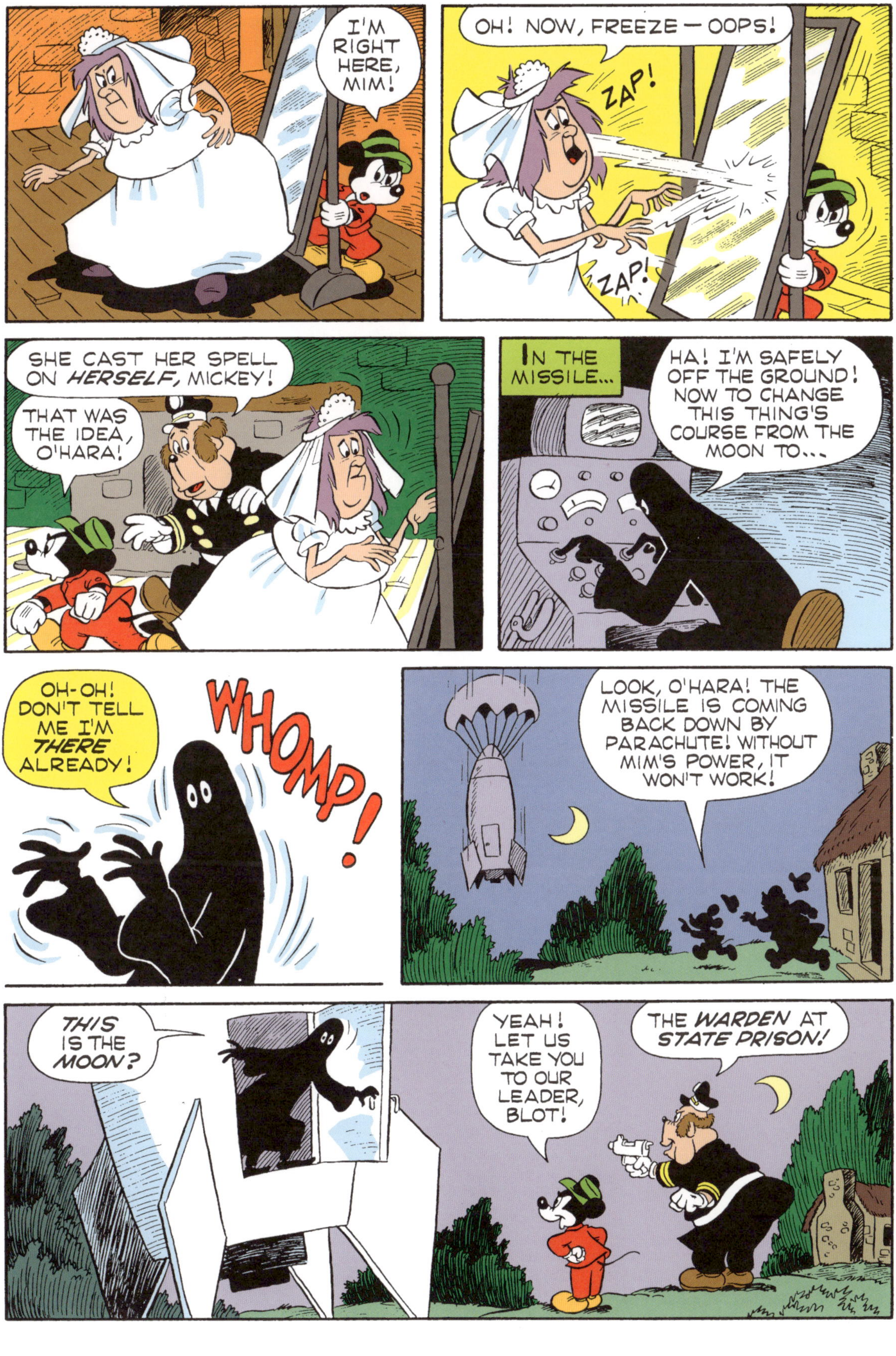

I'M RIGHT HERE, MIM!
OH! NOW, FREEZE — OOPS!
ZAP!
ZAP!
SHE CAST HER SPELL ON *HERSELF,* MICKEY!
THAT WAS THE IDEA, O'HARA!
IN THE MISSILE...
HA! I'M SAFELY OFF THE GROUND! NOW TO CHANGE THIS THING'S COURSE FROM THE MOON TO...
OH-OH! DON'T TELL ME I'M *THERE* ALREADY!
WHOMP!
LOOK, O'HARA! THE MISSILE IS COMING BACK DOWN BY PARACHUTE! WITHOUT MIM'S POWER, IT WON'T WORK!
THIS IS THE *MOON?*
YEAH! LET US TAKE YOU TO OUR LEADER, BLOT!
THE *WARDEN* AT *STATE PRISON!*

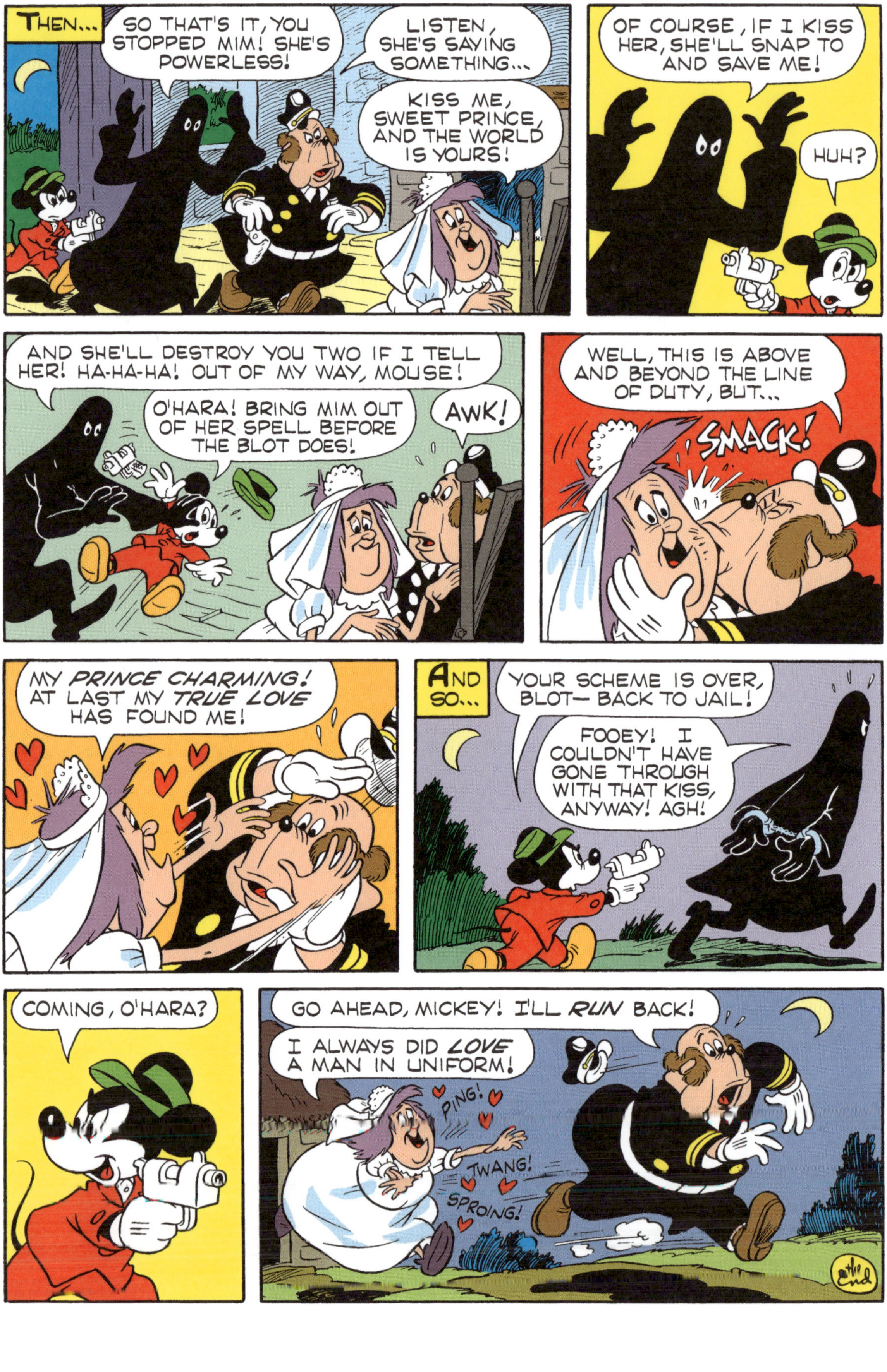
THEN...
SO THAT'S IT, YOU STOPPED MIM! SHE'S POWERLESS!
LISTEN, SHE'S SAYING SOMETHING...
KISS ME, SWEET PRINCE, AND THE WORLD IS YOURS!
OF COURSE, IF I KISS HER, SHE'LL SNAP TO AND SAVE ME!
HUH?
AND SHE'LL DESTROY YOU TWO IF I TELL HER! HA-HA-HA! OUT OF MY WAY, MOUSE!
O'HARA! BRING MIM OUT OF HER SPELL BEFORE THE BLOT DOES!
AWK!
WELL, THIS IS ABOVE AND BEYOND THE LINE OF DUTY, BUT...
SMACK!
MY PRINCE CHARMING! AT LAST MY TRUE LOVE HAS FOUND ME!
AND SO...
YOUR SCHEME IS OVER, BLOT— BACK TO JAIL!
FOOEY! I COULDN'T HAVE GONE THROUGH WITH THAT KISS, ANYWAY! AGH!
COMING, O'HARA?
GO AHEAD, MICKEY! I'LL RUN BACK!
I ALWAYS DID LOVE A MAN IN UNIFORM!
PING!
TWANG!
SPROING!
the end

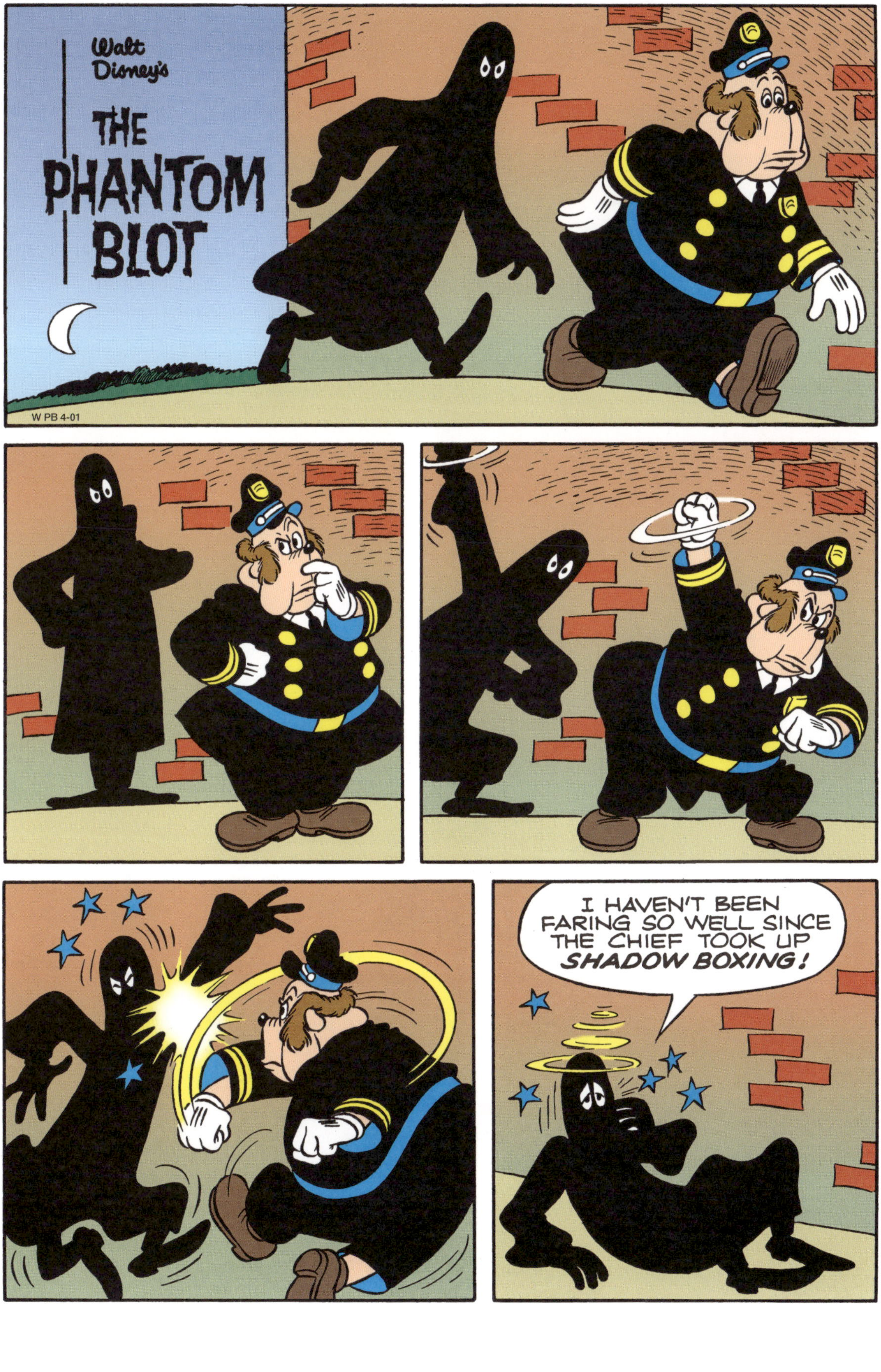
Walt Disney's
THE PHANTOM BLOT
W PB 4-01
I HAVEN'T BEEN FARING SO WELL SINCE THE CHIEF TOOK UP *SHADOW BOXING!*

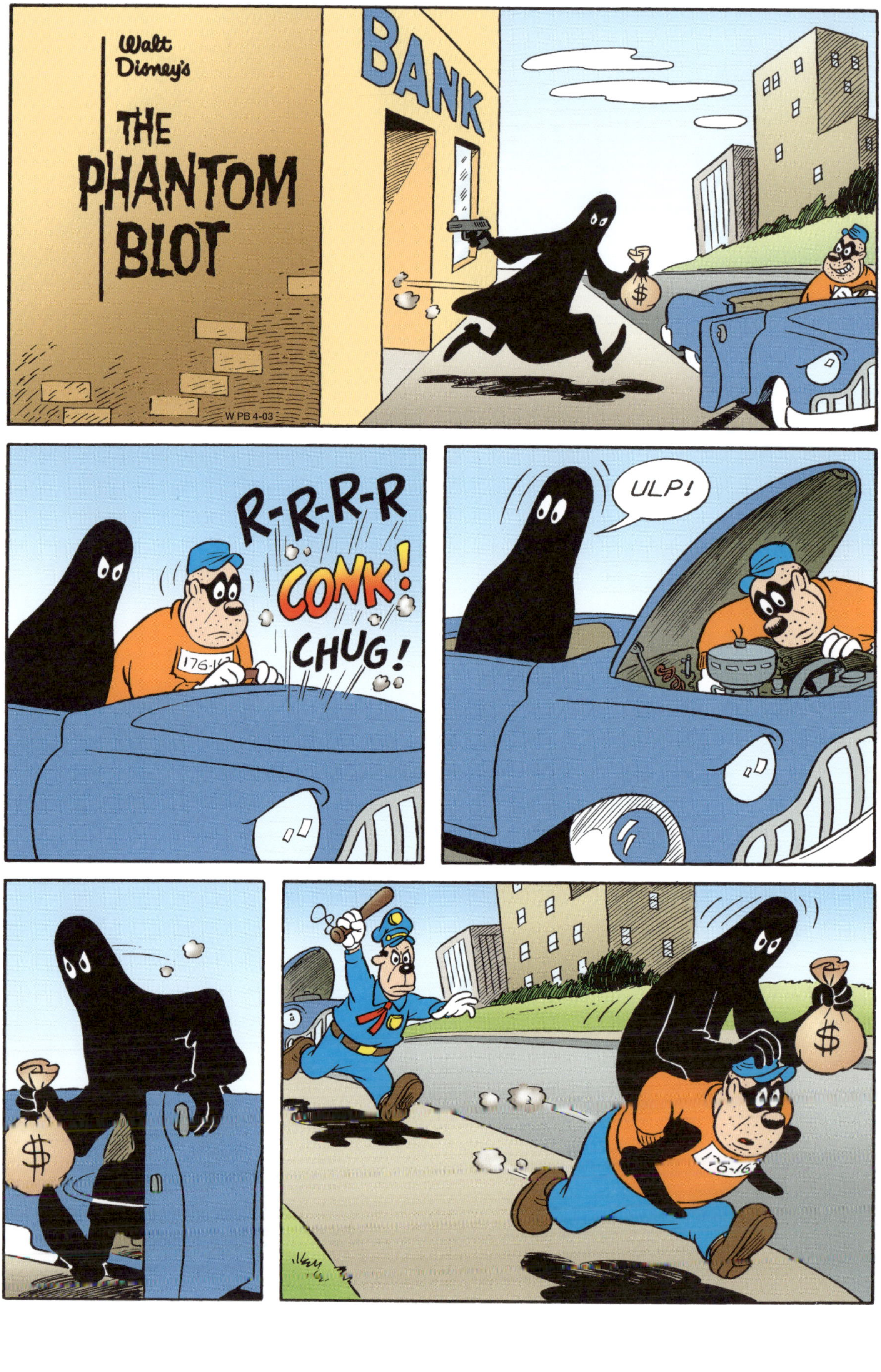
Walt Disney's
THE PHANTOM BLOT
BANK
W PB 4-03
R-R-R-R
CONK!
CHUG!
ULP!

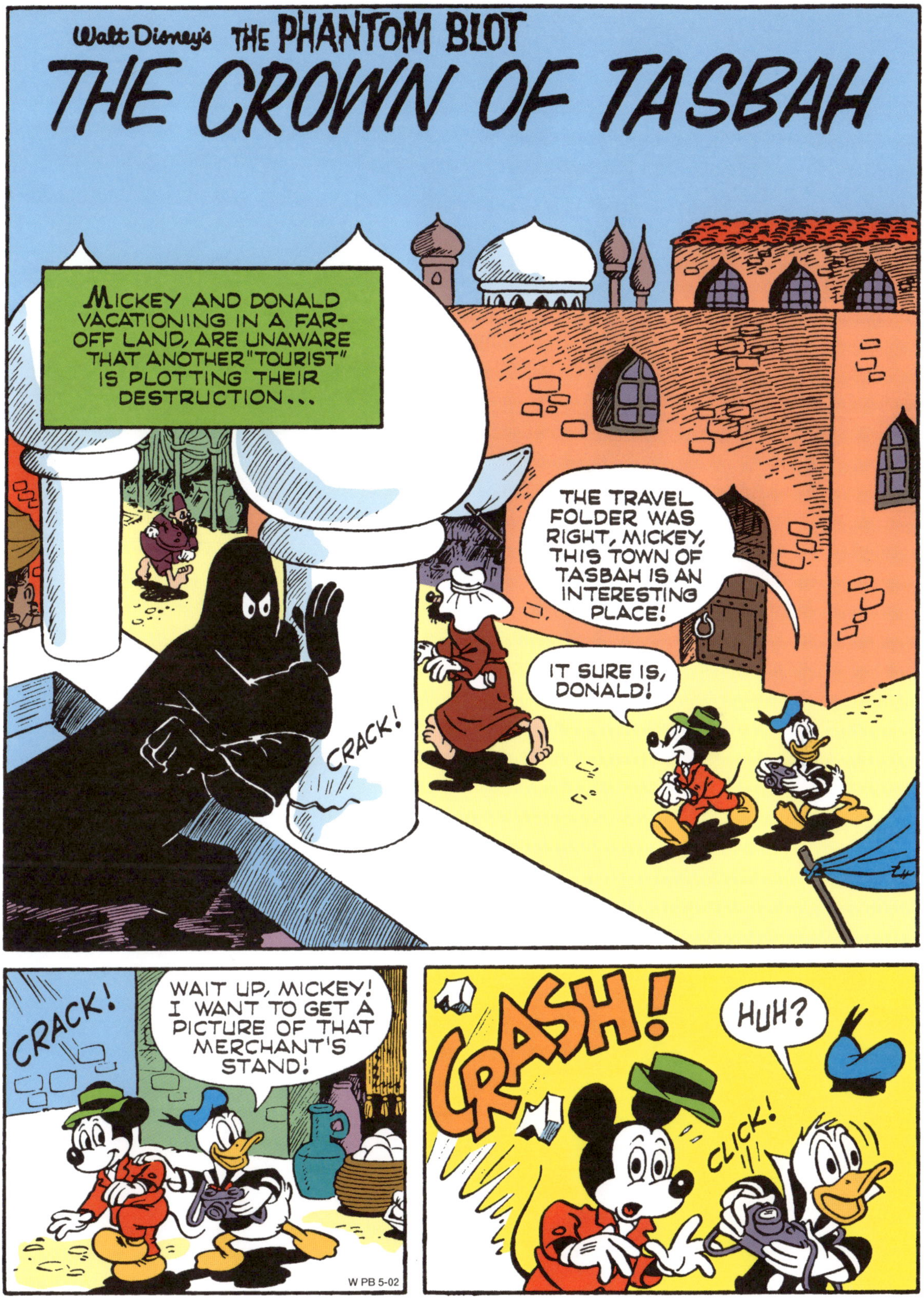
Walt Disney's THE PHANTOM BLOT
THE CROWN OF TASBAH
MICKEY AND DONALD VACATIONING IN A FAR-OFF LAND, ARE UNAWARE THAT ANOTHER "TOURIST" IS PLOTTING THEIR DESTRUCTION...
THE TRAVEL FOLDER WAS RIGHT, MICKEY, THIS TOWN OF TASBAH IS AN INTERESTING PLACE!
IT SURE IS, DONALD!
CRACK!
CRACK!
WAIT UP, MICKEY! I WANT TO GET A PICTURE OF THAT MERCHANT'S STAND!
W PB 5-02
CRASH!
HUH?
CLICK!

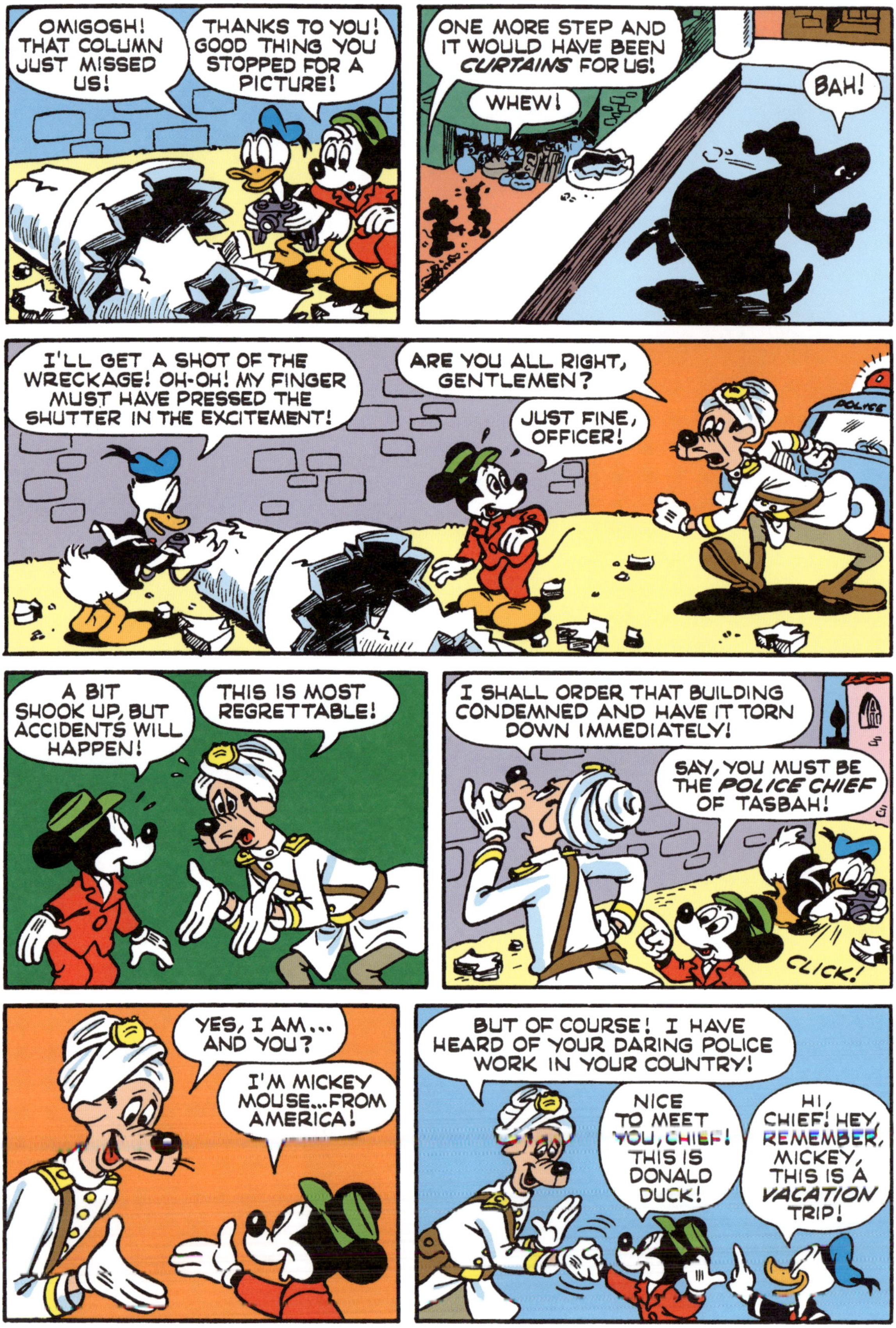
OMIGOSH! THAT COLUMN JUST MISSED US!
THANKS TO YOU! GOOD THING YOU STOPPED FOR A PICTURE!
ONE MORE STEP AND IT WOULD HAVE BEEN *CURTAINS* FOR US!
WHEW!
BAH!
I'LL GET A SHOT OF THE WRECKAGE! OH-OH! MY FINGER MUST HAVE PRESSED THE SHUTTER IN THE EXCITEMENT!
ARE YOU ALL RIGHT, GENTLEMEN?
JUST FINE, OFFICER!
POLICE
A BIT SHOOK UP, BUT ACCIDENTS WILL HAPPEN!
THIS IS MOST REGRETTABLE!
I SHALL ORDER THAT BUILDING CONDEMNED AND HAVE IT TORN DOWN IMMEDIATELY!
SAY, YOU MUST BE THE *POLICE CHIEF* OF TASBAH!
CLICK!
YES, I AM... AND YOU?
I'M MICKEY MOUSE...FROM AMERICA!
BUT OF COURSE! I HAVE HEARD OF YOUR DARING POLICE WORK IN YOUR COUNTRY!
NICE TO MEET YOU, CHIEF! THIS IS DONALD DUCK!
HI, CHIEF! HEY, REMEMBER, MICKEY, THIS IS A *VACATION* TRIP!

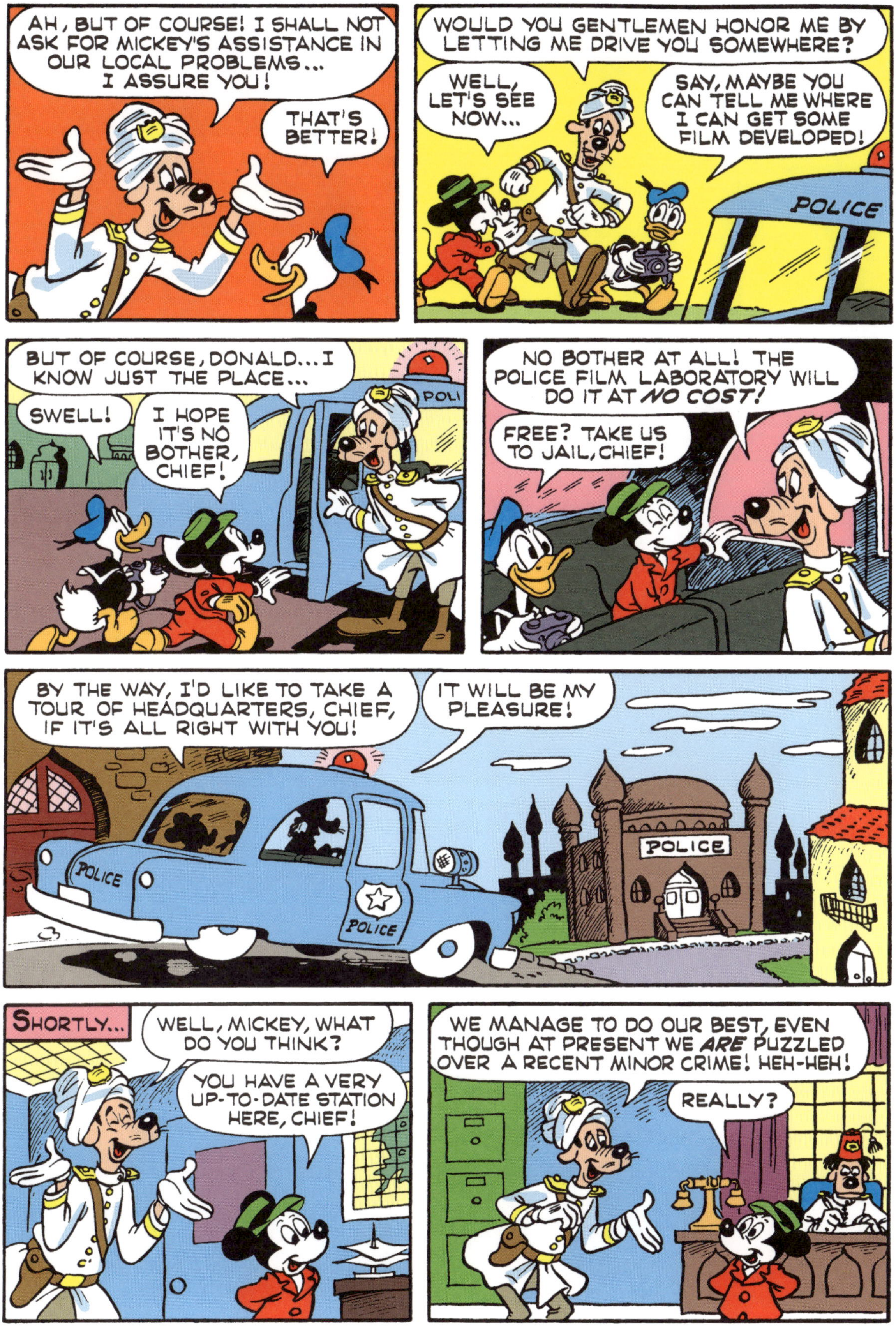
AH, BUT OF COURSE! I SHALL NOT ASK FOR MICKEY'S ASSISTANCE IN OUR LOCAL PROBLEMS... I ASSURE YOU!
THAT'S BETTER!
WOULD YOU GENTLEMEN HONOR ME BY LETTING ME DRIVE YOU SOMEWHERE?
WELL, LET'S SEE NOW...
SAY, MAYBE YOU CAN TELL ME WHERE I CAN GET SOME FILM DEVELOPED!
POLICE
BUT OF COURSE, DONALD... I KNOW JUST THE PLACE...
SWELL!
I HOPE IT'S NO BOTHER, CHIEF!
POLI
NO BOTHER AT ALL! THE POLICE FILM LABORATORY WILL DO IT AT NO COST!
FREE? TAKE US TO JAIL, CHIEF!
BY THE WAY, I'D LIKE TO TAKE A TOUR OF HEADQUARTERS, CHIEF, IF IT'S ALL RIGHT WITH YOU!
IT WILL BE MY PLEASURE!
POLICE
POLICE
POLICE
POLICE
SHORTLY...
WELL, MICKEY, WHAT DO YOU THINK?
YOU HAVE A VERY UP-TO-DATE STATION HERE, CHIEF!
WE MANAGE TO DO OUR BEST, EVEN THOUGH AT PRESENT WE ARE PUZZLED OVER A RECENT MINOR CRIME! HEH-HEH!
REALLY?

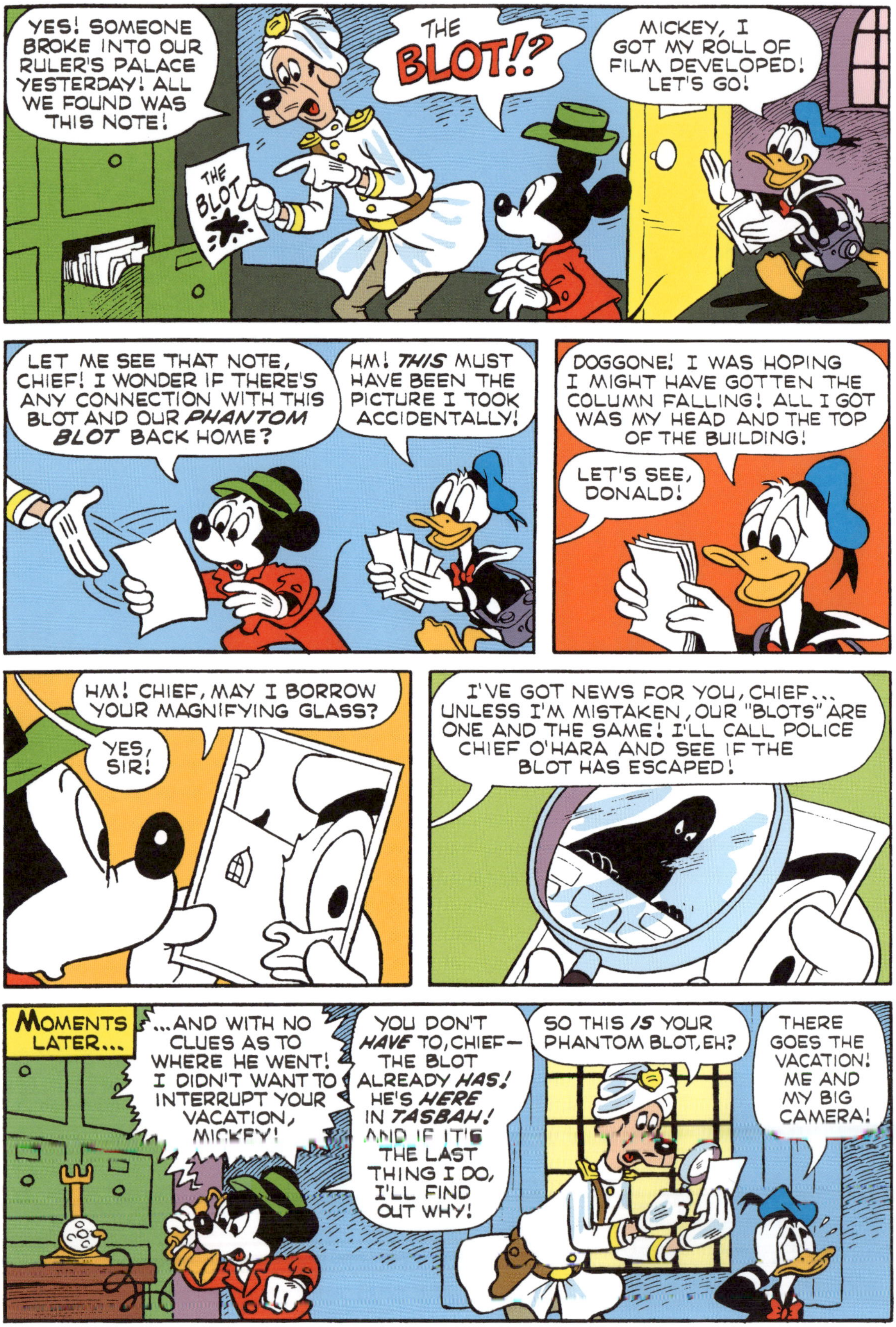
YES! SOMEONE BROKE INTO OUR RULER'S PALACE YESTERDAY! ALL WE FOUND WAS THIS NOTE!
THE BLOT
THE BLOT!?
MICKEY, I GOT MY ROLL OF FILM DEVELOPED! LET'S GO!
LET ME SEE THAT NOTE, CHIEF! I WONDER IF THERE'S ANY CONNECTION WITH THIS BLOT AND OUR *PHANTOM BLOT* BACK HOME?
HM! *THIS* MUST HAVE BEEN THE PICTURE I TOOK ACCIDENTALLY!
DOGGONE! I WAS HOPING I MIGHT HAVE GOTTEN THE COLUMN FALLING! ALL I GOT WAS MY HEAD AND THE TOP OF THE BUILDING!
LET'S SEE, DONALD!
HM! CHIEF, MAY I BORROW YOUR MAGNIFYING GLASS?
YES, SIR!
I'VE GOT NEWS FOR YOU, CHIEF... UNLESS I'M MISTAKEN, OUR "BLOTS" ARE ONE AND THE SAME! I'LL CALL POLICE CHIEF O'HARA AND SEE IF THE BLOT HAS ESCAPED!
MOMENTS LATER...
...AND WITH NO CLUES AS TO WHERE HE WENT! I DIDN'T WANT TO INTERRUPT YOUR VACATION, MICKEY!
YOU DON'T *HAVE* TO, CHIEF— THE BLOT ALREADY *HAS!* HE'S *HERE* IN *TASBAH!* AND IF IT'S THE LAST THING I DO, I'LL FIND OUT WHY!
SO THIS *IS* YOUR PHANTOM BLOT, EH?
THERE GOES THE VACATION! ME AND MY BIG CAMERA!

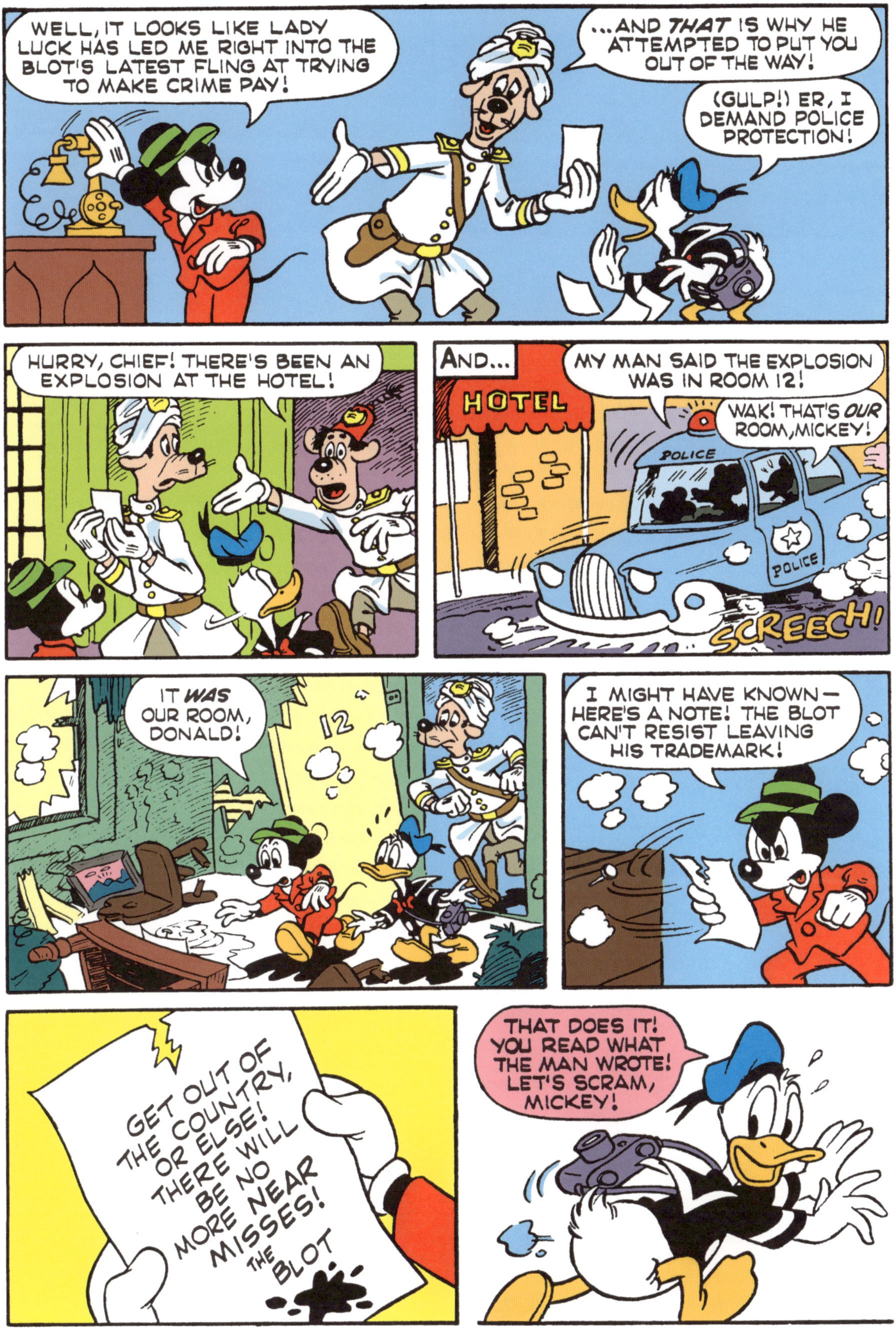
WELL, IT LOOKS LIKE LADY LUCK HAS LED ME RIGHT INTO THE BLOT'S LATEST FLING AT TRYING TO MAKE CRIME PAY!
...AND THAT IS WHY HE ATTEMPTED TO PUT YOU OUT OF THE WAY!
(GULP!) ER, I DEMAND POLICE PROTECTION!
HURRY, CHIEF! THERE'S BEEN AN EXPLOSION AT THE HOTEL!
AND...
HOTEL
MY MAN SAID THE EXPLOSION WAS IN ROOM 12!
WAK! THAT'S OUR ROOM, MICKEY!
POLICE
POLICE
SCREECH!
IT WAS OUR ROOM, DONALD!
12
I MIGHT HAVE KNOWN— HERE'S A NOTE! THE BLOT CAN'T RESIST LEAVING HIS TRADEMARK!
GET OUT OF THE COUNTRY, OR ELSE! THERE WILL BE NO MORE NEAR MISSES!
THE BLOT
THAT DOES IT! YOU READ WHAT THE MAN WROTE! LET'S SCRAM, MICKEY!

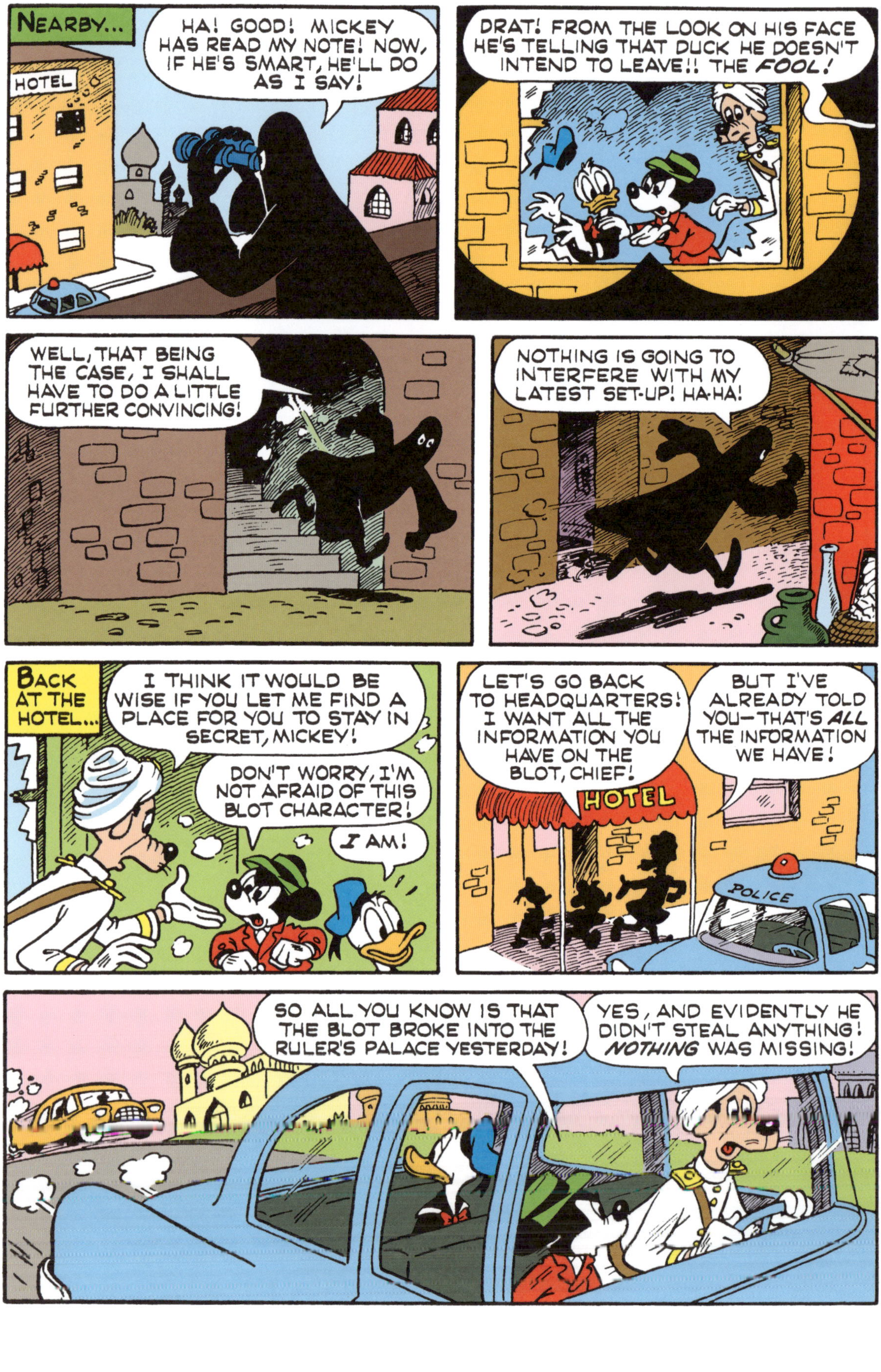
NEARBY...
HA! GOOD! MICKEY HAS READ MY NOTE! NOW, IF HE'S SMART, HE'LL DO AS I SAY!
HOTEL
DRAT! FROM THE LOOK ON HIS FACE HE'S TELLING THAT DUCK HE DOESN'T INTEND TO LEAVE!! THE FOOL!
WELL, THAT BEING THE CASE, I SHALL HAVE TO DO A LITTLE FURTHER CONVINCING!
NOTHING IS GOING TO INTERFERE WITH MY LATEST SET-UP! HA-HA!
BACK AT THE HOTEL...
I THINK IT WOULD BE WISE IF YOU LET ME FIND A PLACE FOR YOU TO STAY IN SECRET, MICKEY!
DON'T WORRY, I'M NOT AFRAID OF THIS BLOT CHARACTER!
I AM!
LET'S GO BACK TO HEADQUARTERS! I WANT ALL THE INFORMATION YOU HAVE ON THE BLOT, CHIEF!
BUT I'VE ALREADY TOLD YOU—THAT'S ALL THE INFORMATION WE HAVE!
HOTEL
POLICE
SO ALL YOU KNOW IS THAT THE BLOT BROKE INTO THE RULER'S PALACE YESTERDAY!
YES, AND EVIDENTLY HE DIDN'T STEAL ANYTHING! NOTHING WAS MISSING!

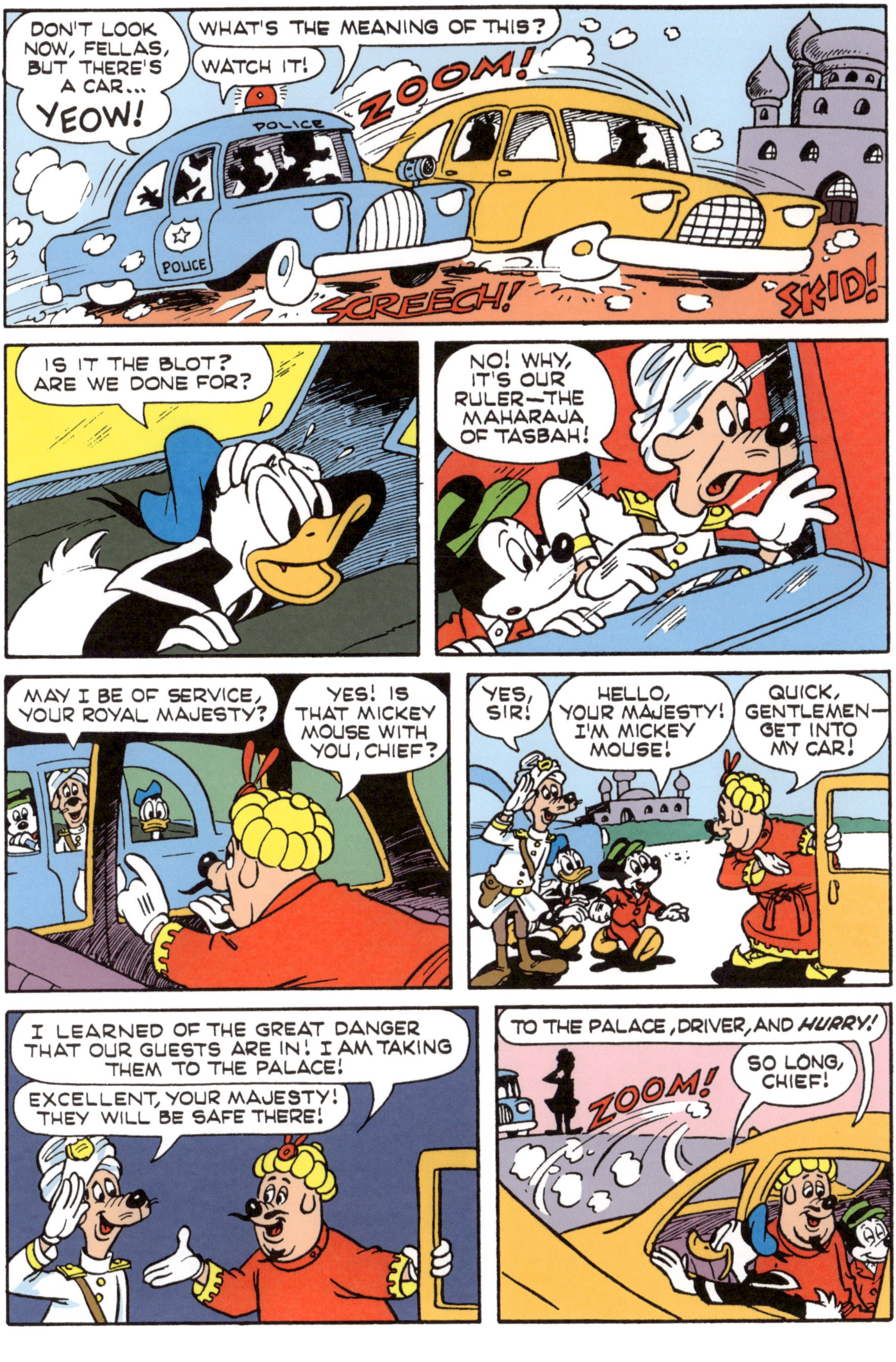

DON'T LOOK NOW, FELLAS, BUT THERE'S A CAR... YEOW!
WHAT'S THE MEANING OF THIS?
WATCH IT!
ZOOM!
POLICE
SCREECH!
SKID!
IS IT THE BLOT? ARE WE DONE FOR?
NO! WHY, IT'S OUR RULER—THE MAHARAJA OF TASBAH!
MAY I BE OF SERVICE, YOUR ROYAL MAJESTY?
YES! IS THAT MICKEY MOUSE WITH YOU, CHIEF?
YES, SIR!
HELLO, YOUR MAJESTY! I'M MICKEY MOUSE!
QUICK, GENTLEMEN—GET INTO MY CAR!
I LEARNED OF THE GREAT DANGER THAT OUR GUESTS ARE IN! I AM TAKING THEM TO THE PALACE!
EXCELLENT, YOUR MAJESTY! THEY WILL BE SAFE THERE!
TO THE PALACE, DRIVER, AND HURRY!
SO LONG, CHIEF!
ZOOM!

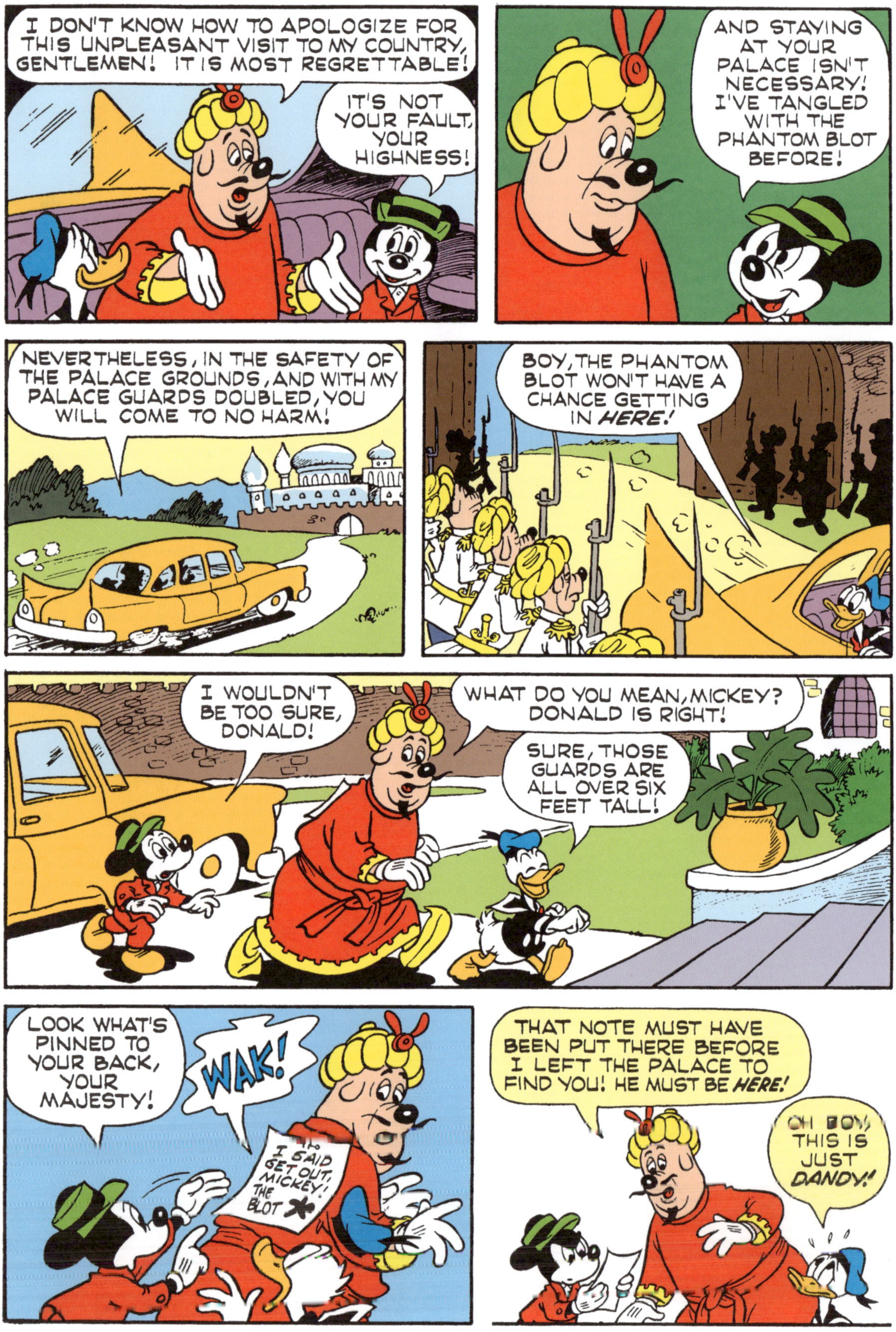
I DON'T KNOW HOW TO APOLOGIZE FOR THIS UNPLEASANT VISIT TO MY COUNTRY, GENTLEMEN! IT IS MOST REGRETTABLE!
IT'S NOT YOUR FAULT, YOUR HIGHNESS!
AND STAYING AT YOUR PALACE ISN'T NECESSARY! I'VE TANGLED WITH THE PHANTOM BLOT BEFORE!
NEVERTHELESS, IN THE SAFETY OF THE PALACE GROUNDS, AND WITH MY PALACE GUARDS DOUBLED, YOU WILL COME TO NO HARM!
BOY, THE PHANTOM BLOT WON'T HAVE A CHANCE GETTING IN *HERE!*
I WOULDN'T BE TOO SURE, DONALD!
WHAT DO YOU MEAN, MICKEY? DONALD IS RIGHT!
SURE, THOSE GUARDS ARE ALL OVER SIX FEET TALL!
LOOK WHAT'S PINNED TO YOUR BACK, YOUR MAJESTY!
WAK!
I SAID GET OUT, MICKEY! THE BLOT
THAT NOTE MUST HAVE BEEN PUT THERE BEFORE I LEFT THE PALACE TO FIND YOU! HE MUST BE *HERE!*
OH BOY THIS IS JUST *DANDY!*

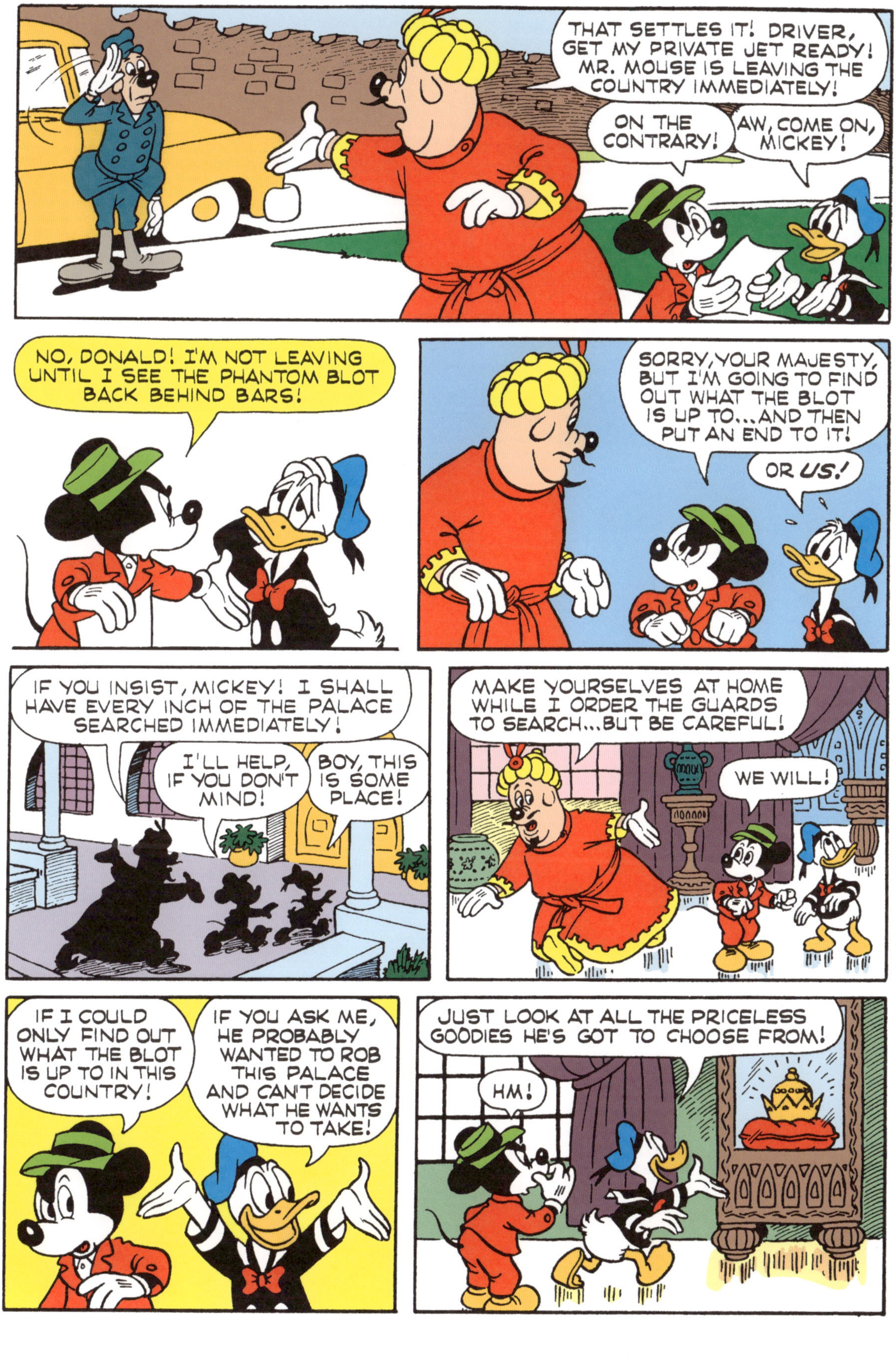
THAT SETTLES IT! DRIVER, GET MY PRIVATE JET READY! MR. MOUSE IS LEAVING THE COUNTRY IMMEDIATELY!
ON THE CONTRARY!
AW, COME ON, MICKEY!
NO, DONALD! I'M NOT LEAVING UNTIL I SEE THE PHANTOM BLOT BACK BEHIND BARS!
SORRY, YOUR MAJESTY, BUT I'M GOING TO FIND OUT WHAT THE BLOT IS UP TO...AND THEN PUT AN END TO IT!
OR US!
IF YOU INSIST, MICKEY! I SHALL HAVE EVERY INCH OF THE PALACE SEARCHED IMMEDIATELY!
I'LL HELP, IF YOU DON'T MIND!
BOY, THIS IS SOME PLACE!
MAKE YOURSELVES AT HOME WHILE I ORDER THE GUARDS TO SEARCH...BUT BE CAREFUL!
WE WILL!
IF I COULD ONLY FIND OUT WHAT THE BLOT IS UP TO IN THIS COUNTRY!
IF YOU ASK ME, HE PROBABLY WANTED TO ROB THIS PALACE AND CAN'T DECIDE WHAT HE WANTS TO TAKE!
JUST LOOK AT ALL THE PRICELESS GOODIES HE'S GOT TO CHOOSE FROM!
HM!

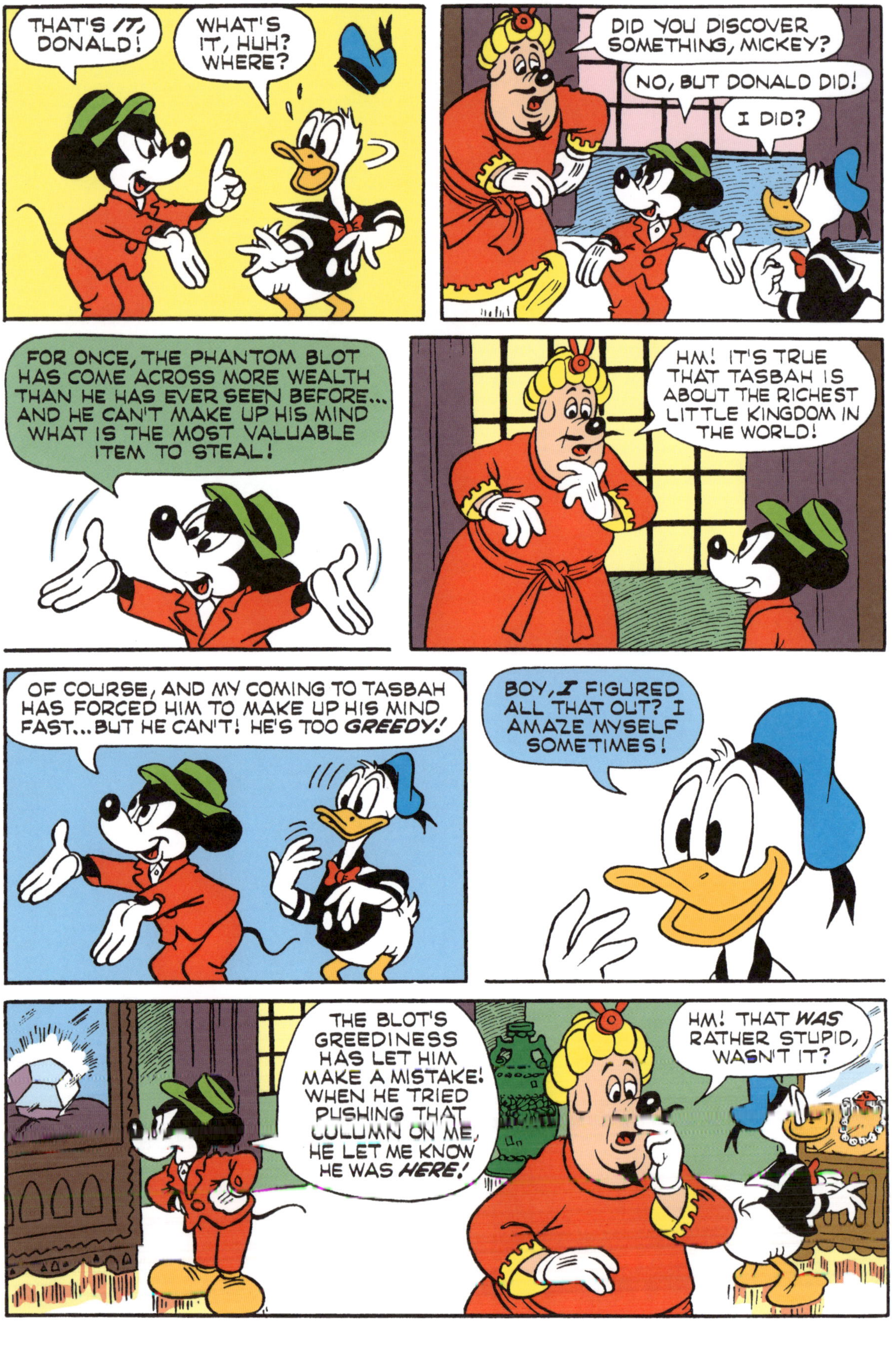
THAT'S *IT*, DONALD!
WHAT'S IT, HUH? WHERE?
DID YOU DISCOVER SOMETHING, MICKEY?
NO, BUT DONALD DID!
I DID?
FOR ONCE, THE PHANTOM BLOT HAS COME ACROSS MORE WEALTH THAN HE HAS EVER SEEN BEFORE... AND HE CAN'T MAKE UP HIS MIND WHAT IS THE MOST VALUABLE ITEM TO STEAL!
HM! IT'S TRUE THAT TASBAH IS ABOUT THE RICHEST LITTLE KINGDOM IN THE WORLD!
OF COURSE, AND MY COMING TO TASBAH HAS FORCED HIM TO MAKE UP HIS MIND FAST...BUT HE CAN'T! HE'S TOO *GREEDY!*
BOY, *I* FIGURED ALL THAT OUT? I AMAZE MYSELF SOMETIMES!
THE BLOT'S GREEDINESS HAS LET HIM MAKE A MISTAKE! WHEN HE TRIED PUSHING THAT COLUMN ON ME, HE LET ME KNOW HE WAS *HERE!*
HM! THAT *WAS* RATHER STUPID, WASN'T IT?

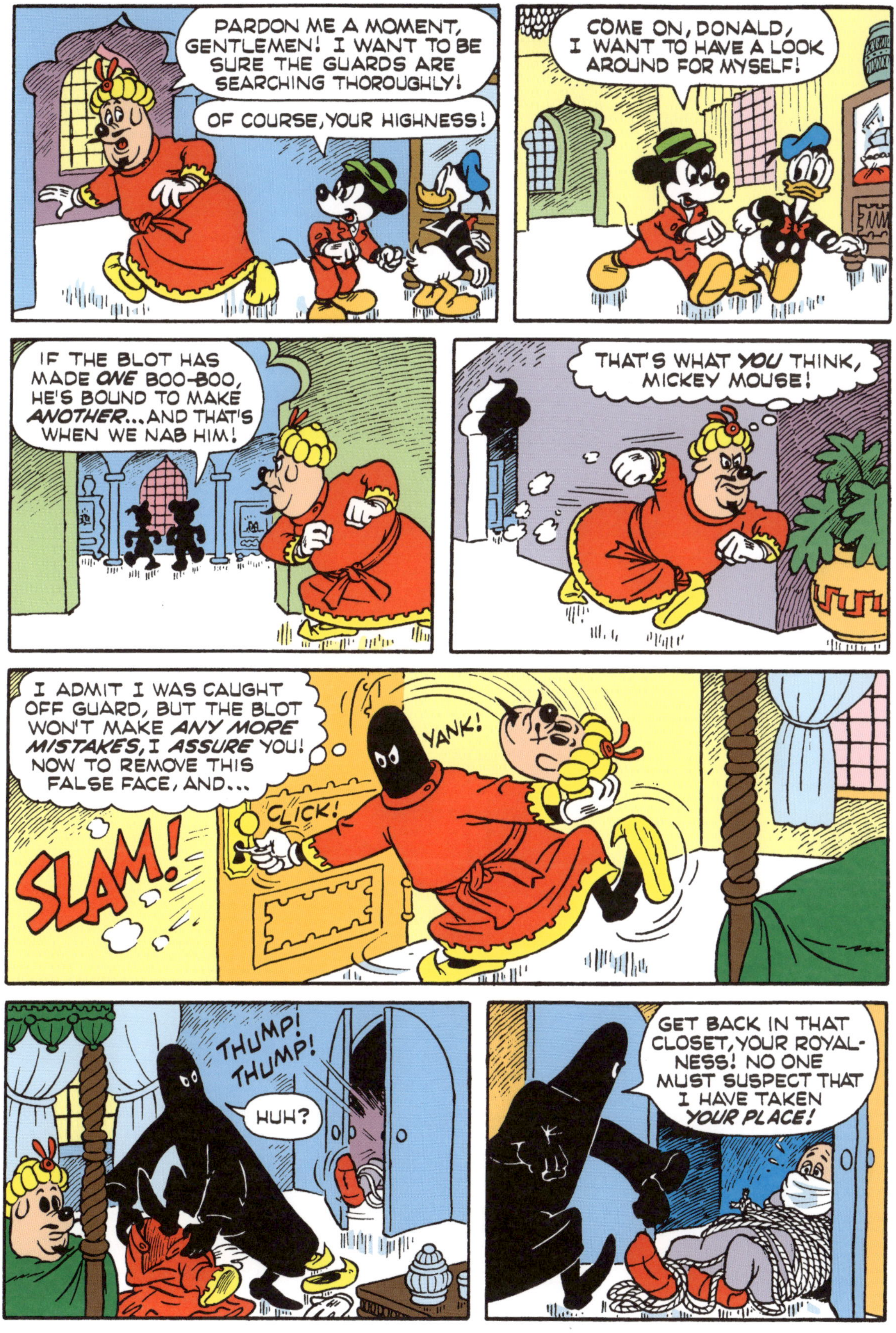

PARDON ME A MOMENT, GENTLEMEN! I WANT TO BE SURE THE GUARDS ARE SEARCHING THOROUGHLY!
OF COURSE, YOUR HIGHNESS!
COME ON, DONALD, I WANT TO HAVE A LOOK AROUND FOR MYSELF!
IF THE BLOT HAS MADE ONE BOO-BOO, HE'S BOUND TO MAKE ANOTHER... AND THAT'S WHEN WE NAB HIM!
THAT'S WHAT YOU THINK, MICKEY MOUSE!
I ADMIT I WAS CAUGHT OFF GUARD, BUT THE BLOT WON'T MAKE ANY MORE MISTAKES, I ASSURE YOU! NOW TO REMOVE THIS FALSE FACE, AND...
YANK!
CLICK!
SLAM!
THUMP! THUMP!
HUH?
GET BACK IN THAT CLOSET, YOUR ROYAL-NESS! NO ONE MUST SUSPECT THAT I HAVE TAKEN YOUR PLACE!

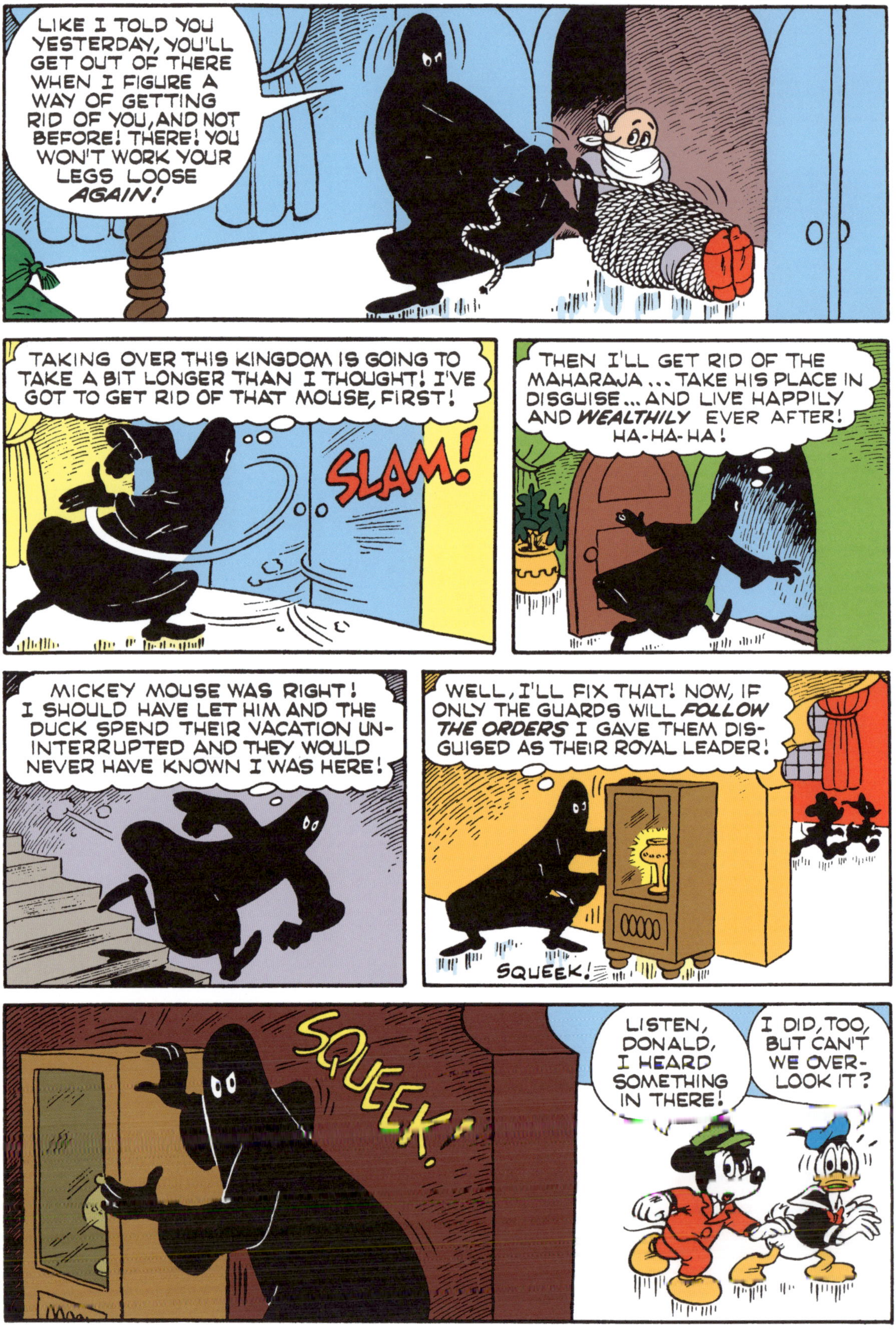

LIKE I TOLD YOU YESTERDAY, YOU'LL GET OUT OF THERE WHEN I FIGURE A WAY OF GETTING RID OF YOU, AND NOT BEFORE! THERE! YOU WON'T WORK YOUR LEGS LOOSE *AGAIN!*
TAKING OVER THIS KINGDOM IS GOING TO TAKE A BIT LONGER THAN I THOUGHT! I'VE GOT TO GET RID OF THAT MOUSE, FIRST!
SLAM!
THEN I'LL GET RID OF THE MAHARAJA ... TAKE HIS PLACE IN DISGUISE ... AND LIVE HAPPILY AND *WEALTHILY* EVER AFTER! HA-HA-HA!
MICKEY MOUSE WAS RIGHT! I SHOULD HAVE LET HIM AND THE DUCK SPEND THEIR VACATION UNINTERRUPTED AND THEY WOULD NEVER HAVE KNOWN I WAS HERE!
WELL, I'LL FIX THAT! NOW, IF ONLY THE GUARDS WILL *FOLLOW THE ORDERS* I GAVE THEM DISGUISED AS THEIR ROYAL LEADER!
SQUEEK!
SQUEEK!
LISTEN, DONALD, I HEARD SOMETHING IN THERE!
I DID, TOO, BUT CAN'T WE OVERLOOK IT?

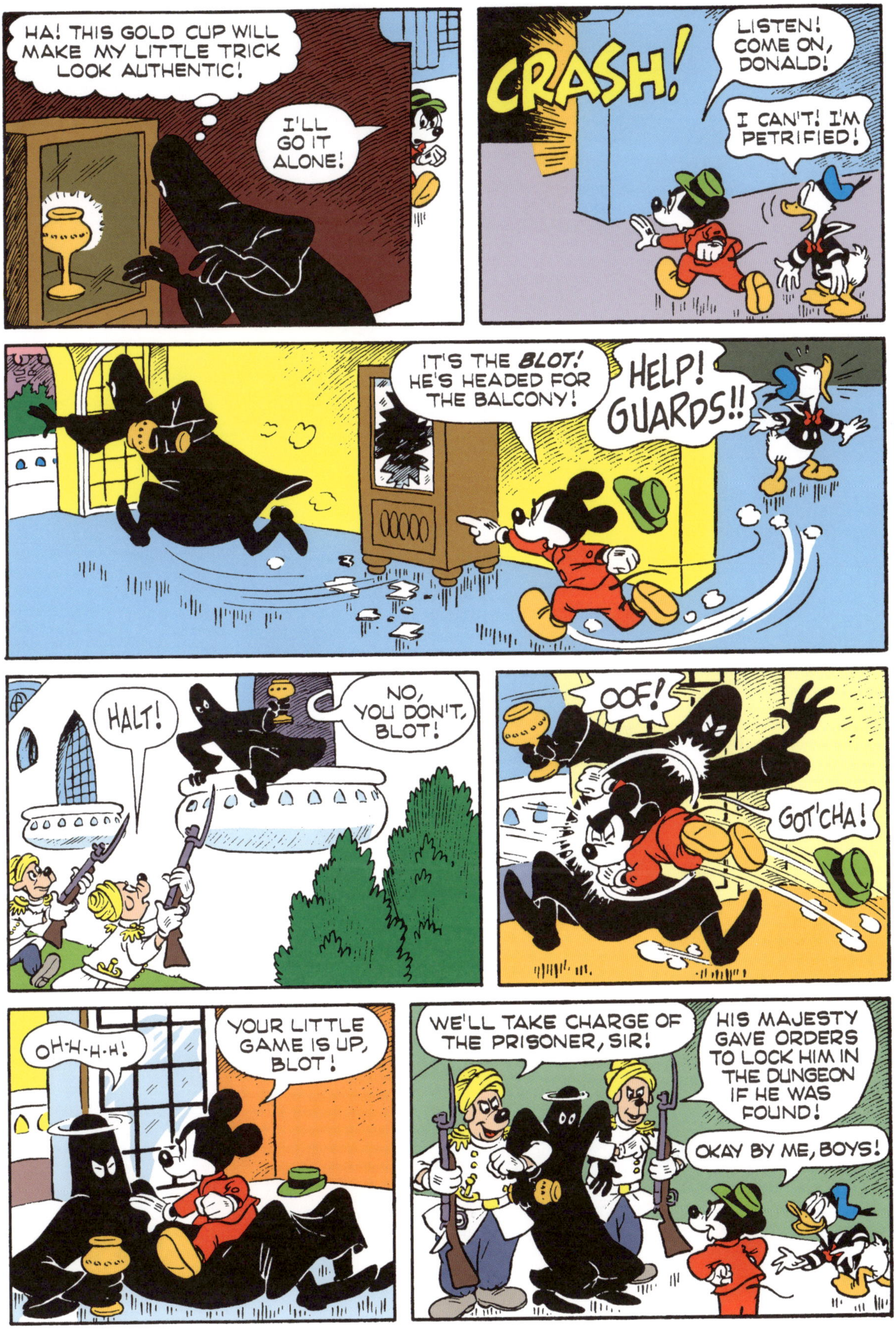
HA! THIS GOLD CUP WILL MAKE MY LITTLE TRICK LOOK AUTHENTIC!
I'LL GO IT ALONE!
CRASH!
LISTEN! COME ON, DONALD!
I CAN'T! I'M PETRIFIED!
IT'S THE BLOT! HE'S HEADED FOR THE BALCONY!
HELP! GUARDS!!
HALT!
NO, YOU DON'T, BLOT!
OOF!
GOT'CHA!
OH-H-H-H!
YOUR LITTLE GAME IS UP, BLOT!
WE'LL TAKE CHARGE OF THE PRISONER, SIR!
HIS MAJESTY GAVE ORDERS TO LOCK HIM IN THE DUNGEON IF HE WAS FOUND!
OKAY BY ME, BOYS!

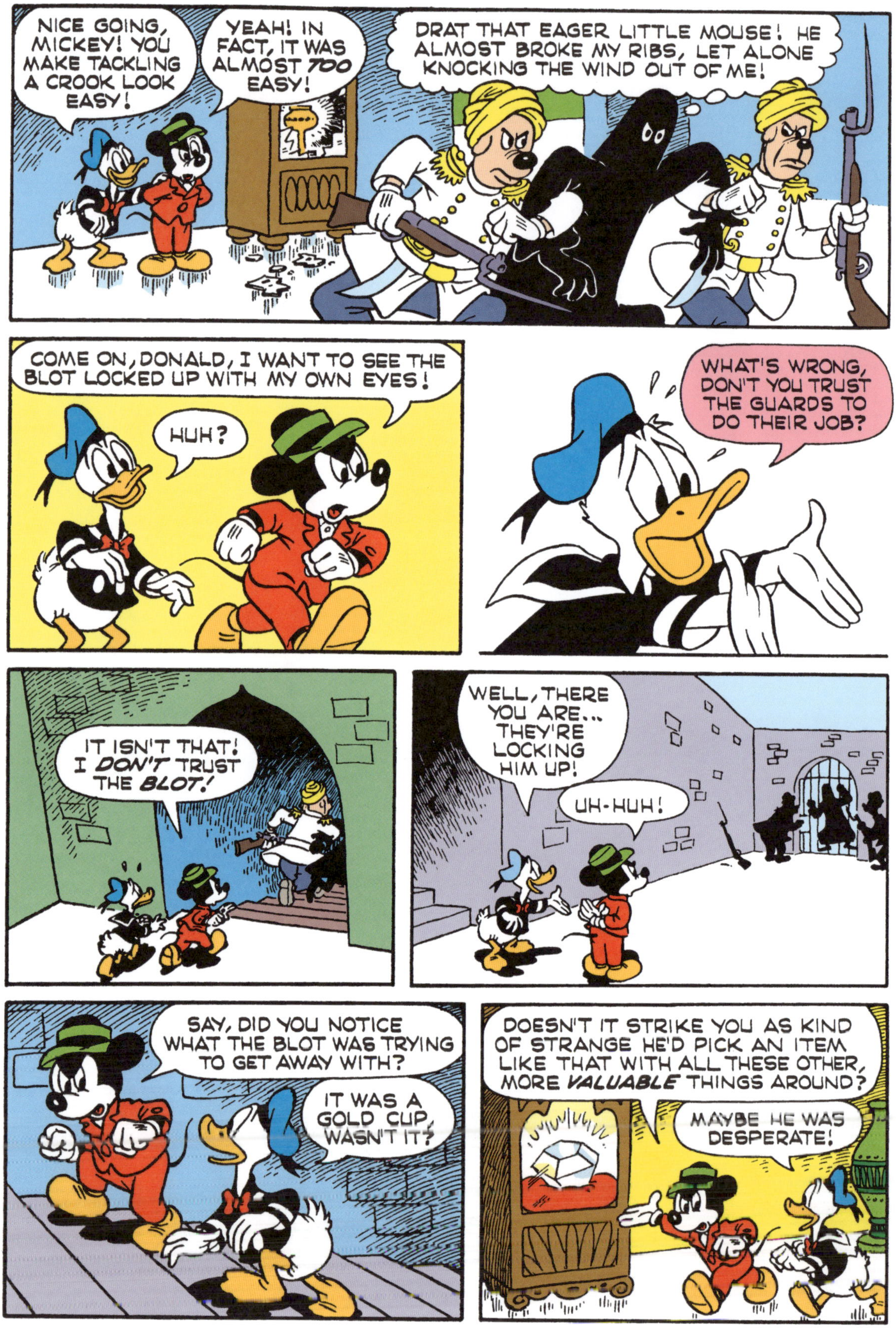
NICE GOING, MICKEY! YOU MAKE TACKLING A CROOK LOOK EASY!
YEAH! IN FACT, IT WAS ALMOST *TOO* EASY!
DRAT THAT EAGER LITTLE MOUSE! HE ALMOST BROKE MY RIBS, LET ALONE KNOCKING THE WIND OUT OF ME!
COME ON, DONALD, I WANT TO SEE THE BLOT LOCKED UP WITH MY OWN EYES!
HUH?
WHAT'S WRONG, DON'T YOU TRUST THE GUARDS TO DO THEIR JOB?
IT ISN'T THAT! I *DON'T* TRUST THE *BLOT!*
WELL, THERE YOU ARE... THEY'RE LOCKING HIM UP!
UH-HUH!
SAY, DID YOU NOTICE WHAT THE BLOT WAS TRYING TO GET AWAY WITH?
IT WAS A GOLD CUP, WASN'T IT?
DOESN'T IT STRIKE YOU AS KIND OF STRANGE HE'D PICK AN ITEM LIKE THAT WITH ALL THESE OTHER, MORE *VALUABLE* THINGS AROUND?
MAYBE HE WAS DESPERATE!

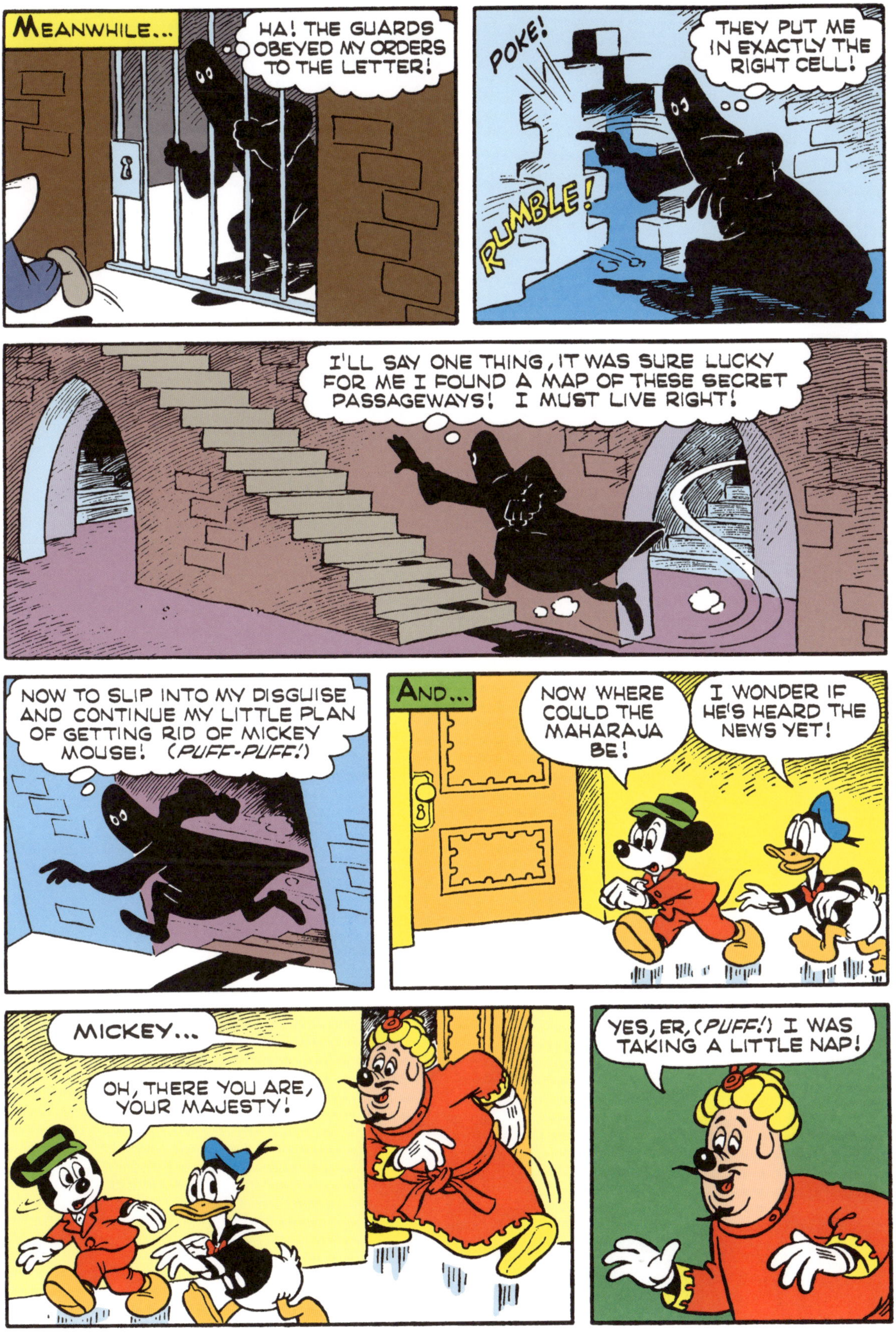
MEANWHILE...
HA! THE GUARDS OBEYED MY ORDERS TO THE LETTER!
POKE!
THEY PUT ME IN EXACTLY THE RIGHT CELL!
RUMBLE!
I'LL SAY ONE THING, IT WAS SURE LUCKY FOR ME I FOUND A MAP OF THESE SECRET PASSAGEWAYS! I MUST LIVE RIGHT!
NOW TO SLIP INTO MY DISGUISE AND CONTINUE MY LITTLE PLAN OF GETTING RID OF MICKEY MOUSE! (PUFF-PUFF!)
AND...
NOW WHERE COULD THE MAHARAJA BE!
I WONDER IF HE'S HEARD THE NEWS YET!
MICKEY...
OH, THERE YOU ARE, YOUR MAJESTY!
YES, ER, (PUFF!) I WAS TAKING A LITTLE NAP!

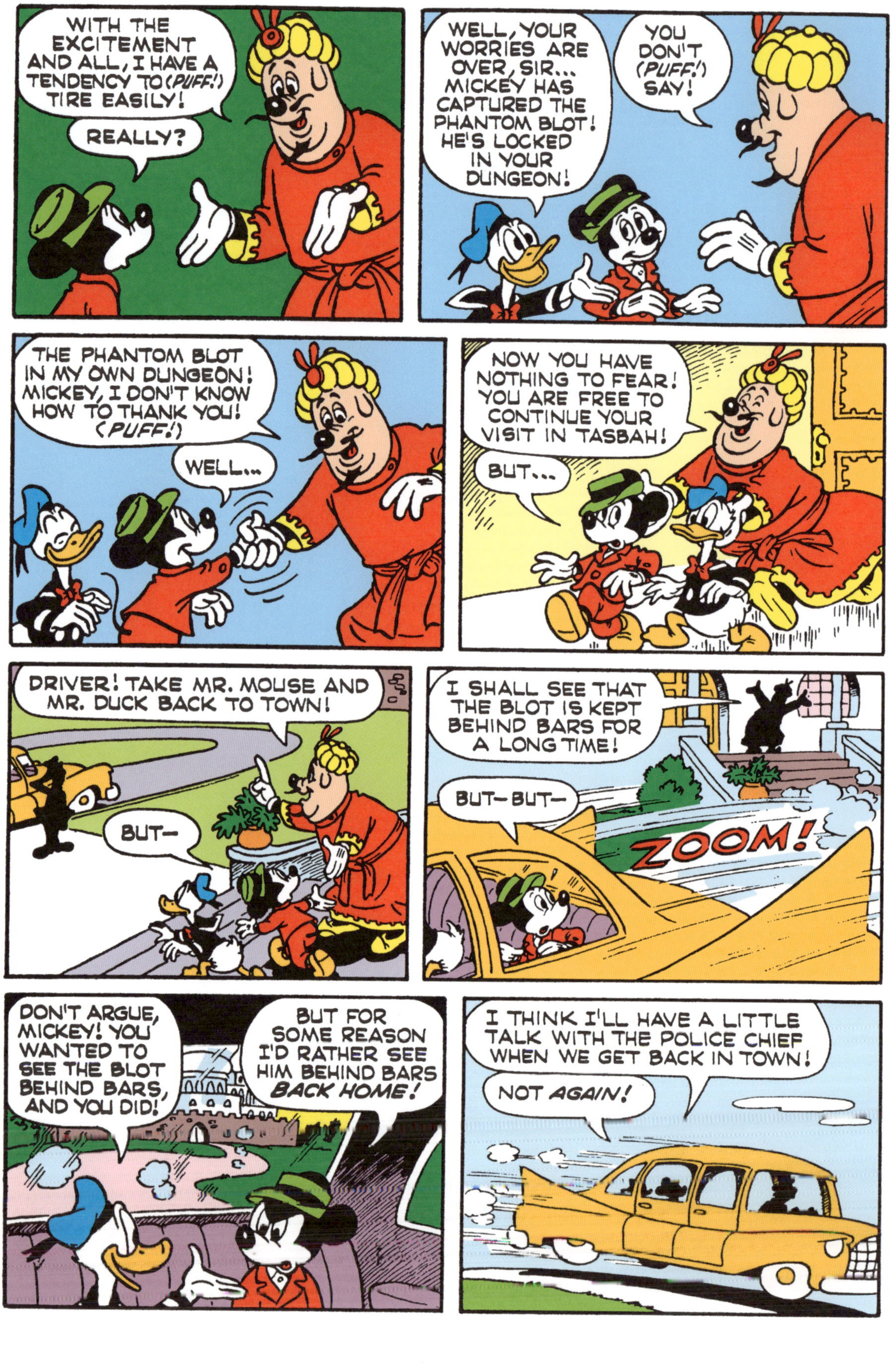

WITH THE EXCITEMENT AND ALL, I HAVE A TENDENCY TO (PUFF!) TIRE EASILY!
REALLY?
WELL, YOUR WORRIES ARE OVER, SIR... MICKEY HAS CAPTURED THE PHANTOM BLOT! HE'S LOCKED IN YOUR DUNGEON!
YOU DON'T (PUFF!) SAY!
THE PHANTOM BLOT IN MY OWN DUNGEON! MICKEY, I DON'T KNOW HOW TO THANK YOU! (PUFF!)
WELL...
NOW YOU HAVE NOTHING TO FEAR! YOU ARE FREE TO CONTINUE YOUR VISIT IN TASBAH!
BUT...
DRIVER! TAKE MR. MOUSE AND MR. DUCK BACK TO TOWN!
BUT—
I SHALL SEE THAT THE BLOT IS KEPT BEHIND BARS FOR A LONG TIME!
BUT—BUT—
ZOOM!
DON'T ARGUE, MICKEY! YOU WANTED TO SEE THE BLOT BEHIND BARS, AND YOU DID!
BUT FOR SOME REASON I'D RATHER SEE HIM BEHIND BARS BACK HOME!
I THINK I'LL HAVE A LITTLE TALK WITH THE POLICE CHIEF WHEN WE GET BACK IN TOWN!
NOT AGAIN!

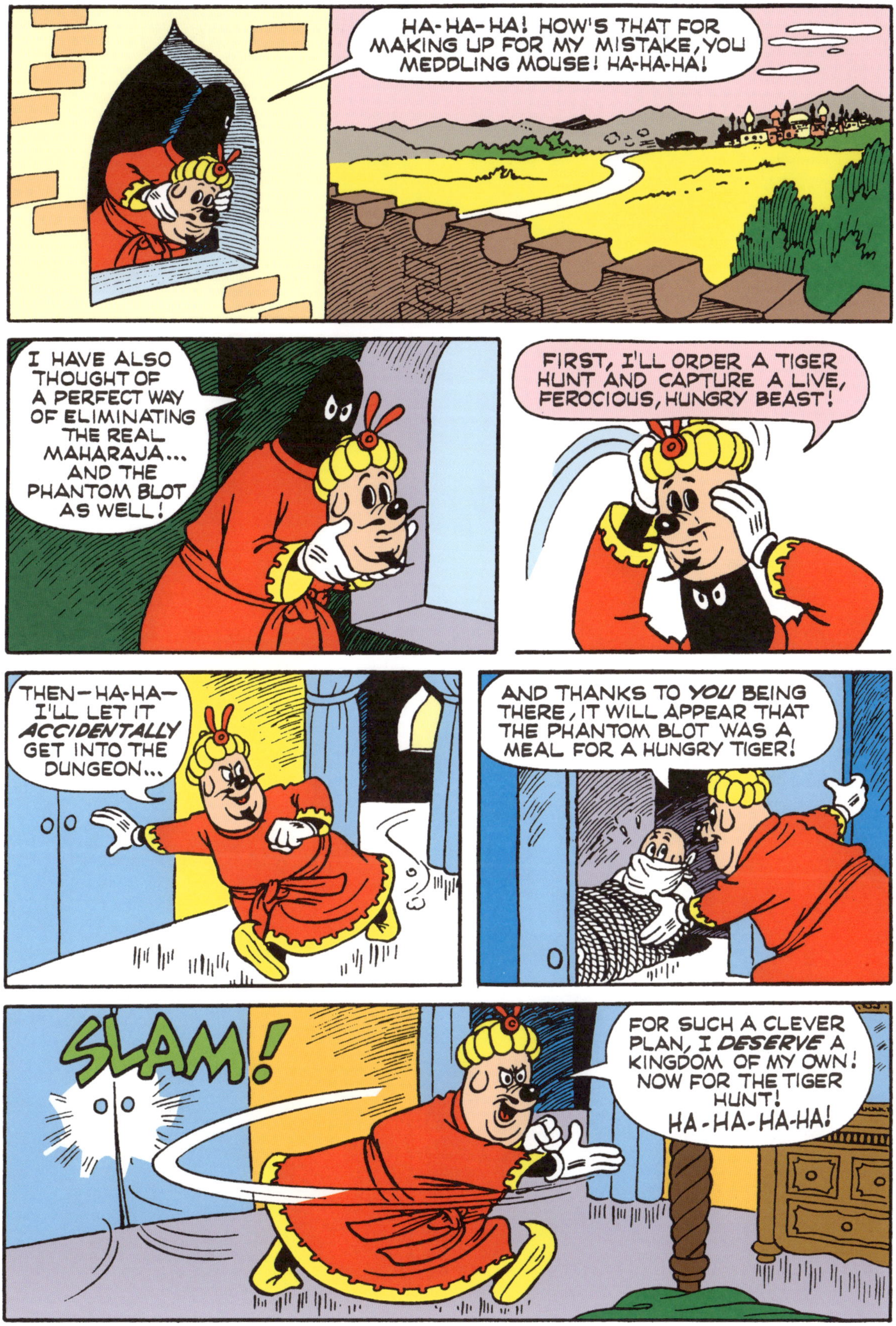
HA-HA-HA! HOW'S THAT FOR MAKING UP FOR MY MISTAKE, YOU MEDDLING MOUSE! HA-HA-HA!
I HAVE ALSO THOUGHT OF A PERFECT WAY OF ELIMINATING THE REAL MAHARAJA... AND THE PHANTOM BLOT AS WELL!
FIRST, I'LL ORDER A TIGER HUNT AND CAPTURE A LIVE, FEROCIOUS, HUNGRY BEAST!
THEN—HA-HA—I'LL LET IT *ACCIDENTALLY* GET INTO THE DUNGEON...
AND THANKS TO *YOU* BEING THERE, IT WILL APPEAR THAT THE PHANTOM BLOT WAS A MEAL FOR A HUNGRY TIGER!
SLAM!
FOR SUCH A CLEVER PLAN, I *DESERVE* A KINGDOM OF MY OWN! NOW FOR THE TIGER HUNT! HA-HA-HA-HA!

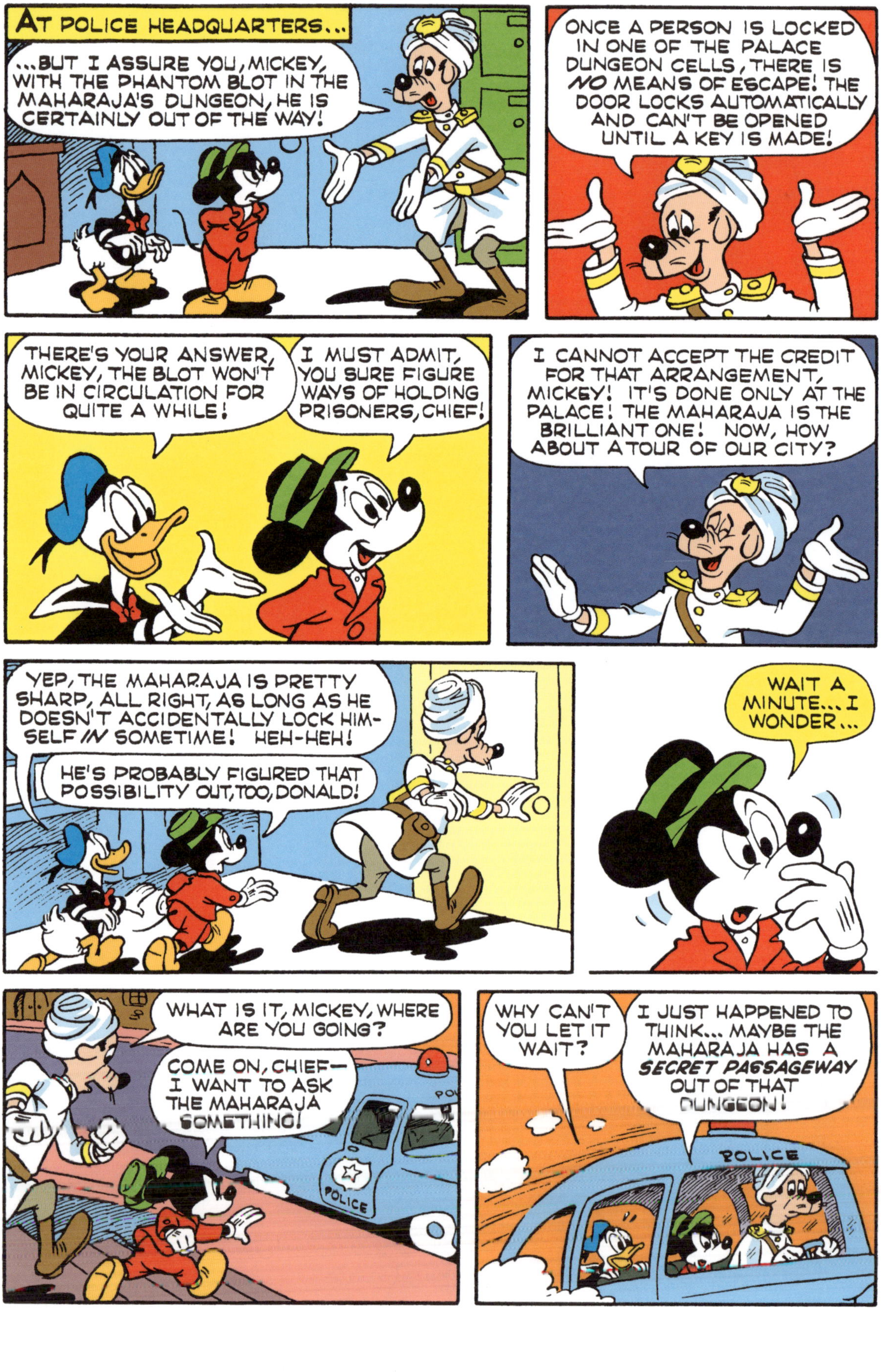
AT POLICE HEADQUARTERS...
...BUT I ASSURE YOU, MICKEY, WITH THE PHANTOM BLOT IN THE MAHARAJA'S DUNGEON, HE IS CERTAINLY OUT OF THE WAY!
ONCE A PERSON IS LOCKED IN ONE OF THE PALACE DUNGEON CELLS, THERE IS NO MEANS OF ESCAPE! THE DOOR LOCKS AUTOMATICALLY AND CAN'T BE OPENED UNTIL A KEY IS MADE!
THERE'S YOUR ANSWER, MICKEY, THE BLOT WON'T BE IN CIRCULATION FOR QUITE A WHILE!
I MUST ADMIT, YOU SURE FIGURE WAYS OF HOLDING PRISONERS, CHIEF!
I CANNOT ACCEPT THE CREDIT FOR THAT ARRANGEMENT, MICKEY! IT'S DONE ONLY AT THE PALACE! THE MAHARAJA IS THE BRILLIANT ONE! NOW, HOW ABOUT A TOUR OF OUR CITY?
YEP, THE MAHARAJA IS PRETTY SHARP, ALL RIGHT, AS LONG AS HE DOESN'T ACCIDENTALLY LOCK HIMSELF IN SOMETIME! HEH-HEH!
HE'S PROBABLY FIGURED THAT POSSIBILITY OUT, TOO, DONALD!
WAIT A MINUTE... I WONDER...
WHAT IS IT, MICKEY, WHERE ARE YOU GOING?
COME ON, CHIEF— I WANT TO ASK THE MAHARAJA SOMETHING!
POLICE
WHY CAN'T YOU LET IT WAIT?
I JUST HAPPENED TO THINK... MAYBE THE MAHARAJA HAS A SECRET PASSAGEWAY OUT OF THAT DUNGEON!
POLICE

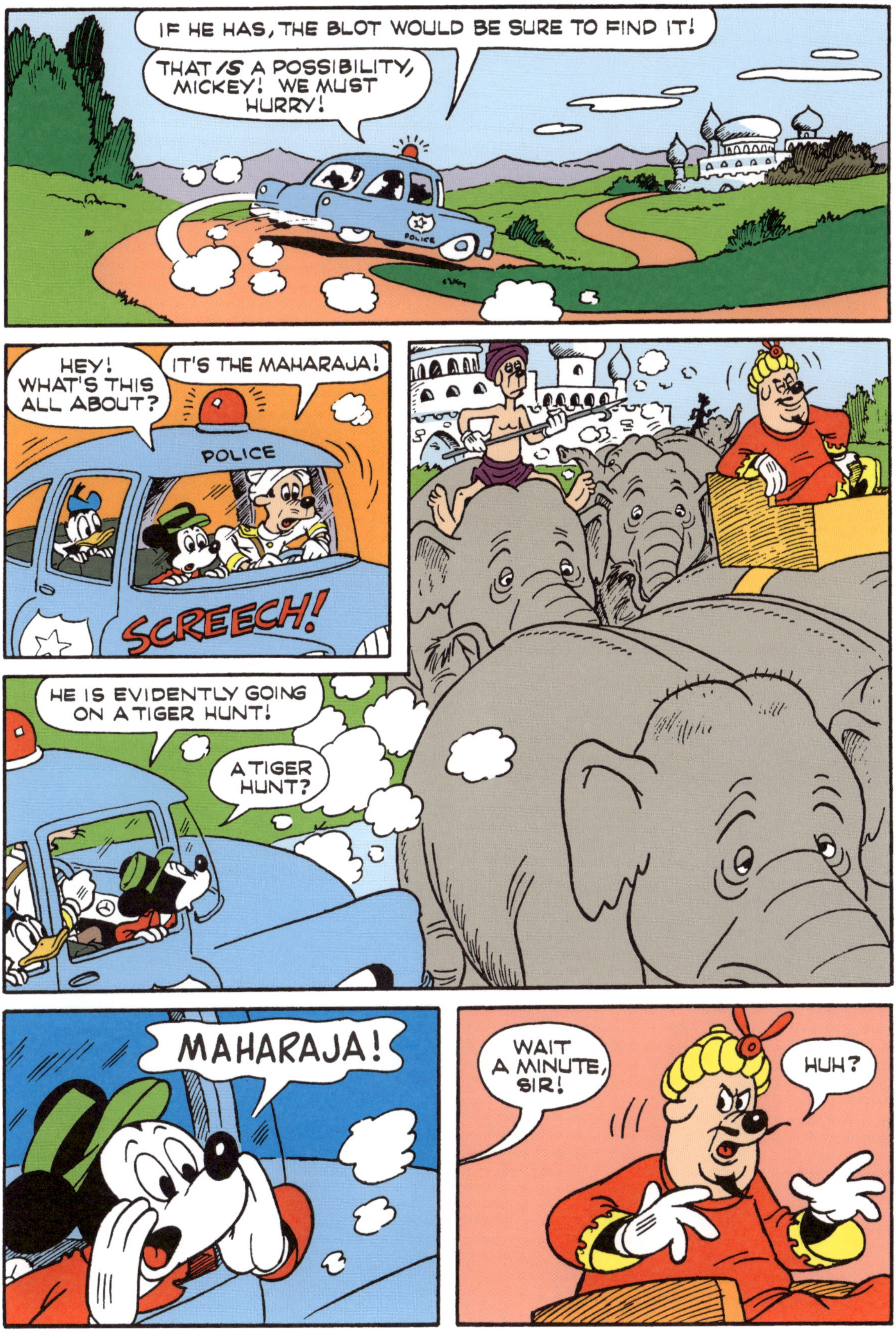

IF HE HAS, THE BLOT WOULD BE SURE TO FIND IT!
THAT IS A POSSIBILITY, MICKEY! WE MUST HURRY!
POLICE
HEY! WHAT'S THIS ALL ABOUT?
IT'S THE MAHARAJA!
POLICE
SCREECH!
HE IS EVIDENTLY GOING ON A TIGER HUNT!
A TIGER HUNT?
MAHARAJA!
WAIT A MINUTE, SIR!
HUH?

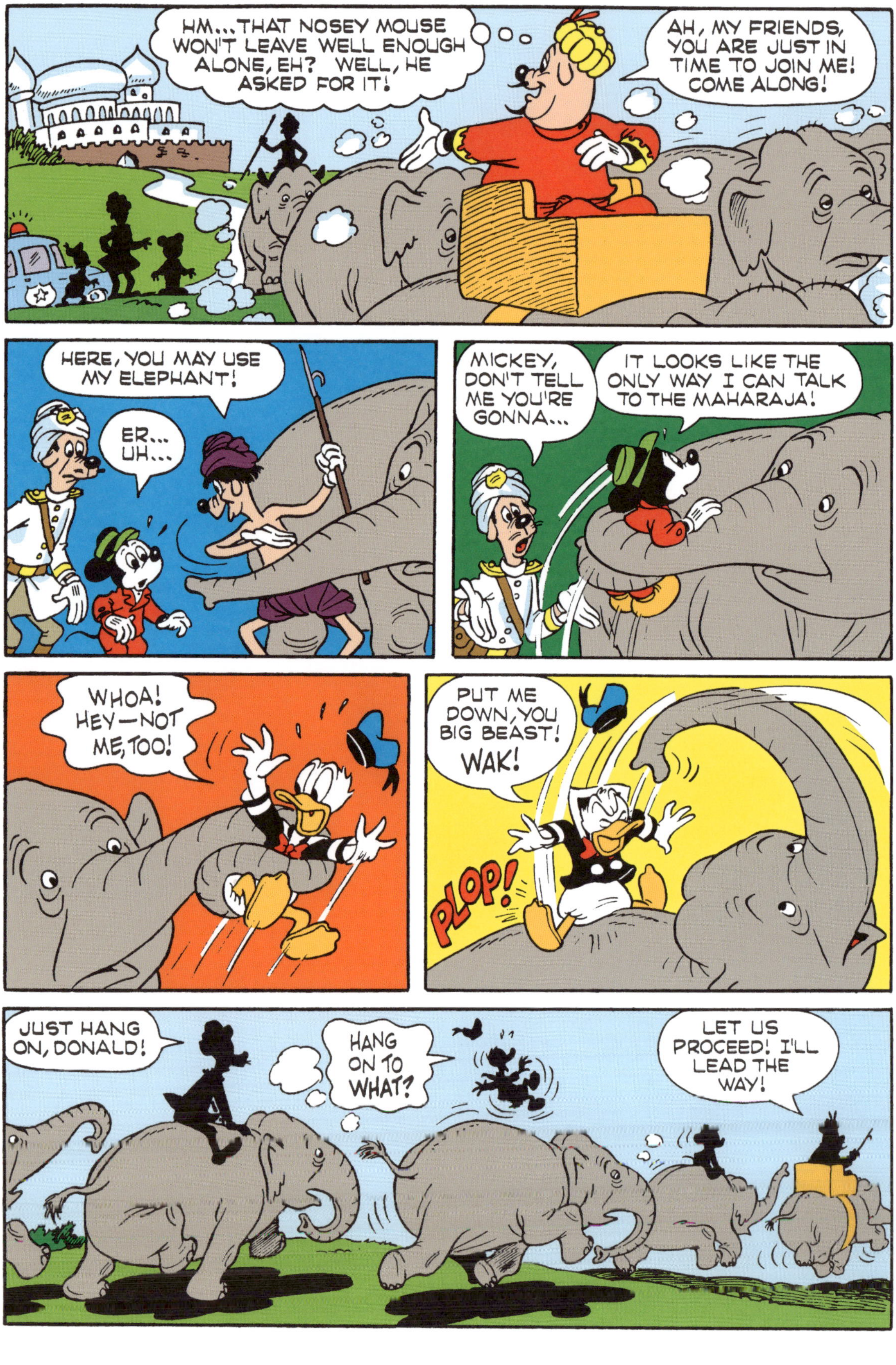
HM...THAT NOSEY MOUSE WON'T LEAVE WELL ENOUGH ALONE, EH? WELL, HE ASKED FOR IT!
AH, MY FRIENDS, YOU ARE JUST IN TIME TO JOIN ME! COME ALONG!
HERE, YOU MAY USE MY ELEPHANT!
ER... UH...
MICKEY, DON'T TELL ME YOU'RE GONNA...
IT LOOKS LIKE THE ONLY WAY I CAN TALK TO THE MAHARAJA!
WHOA! HEY—NOT ME, TOO!
PUT ME DOWN, YOU BIG BEAST! WAK!
PLOP!
JUST HANG ON, DONALD!
HANG ON TO WHAT?
LET US PROCEED! I'LL LEAD THE WAY!

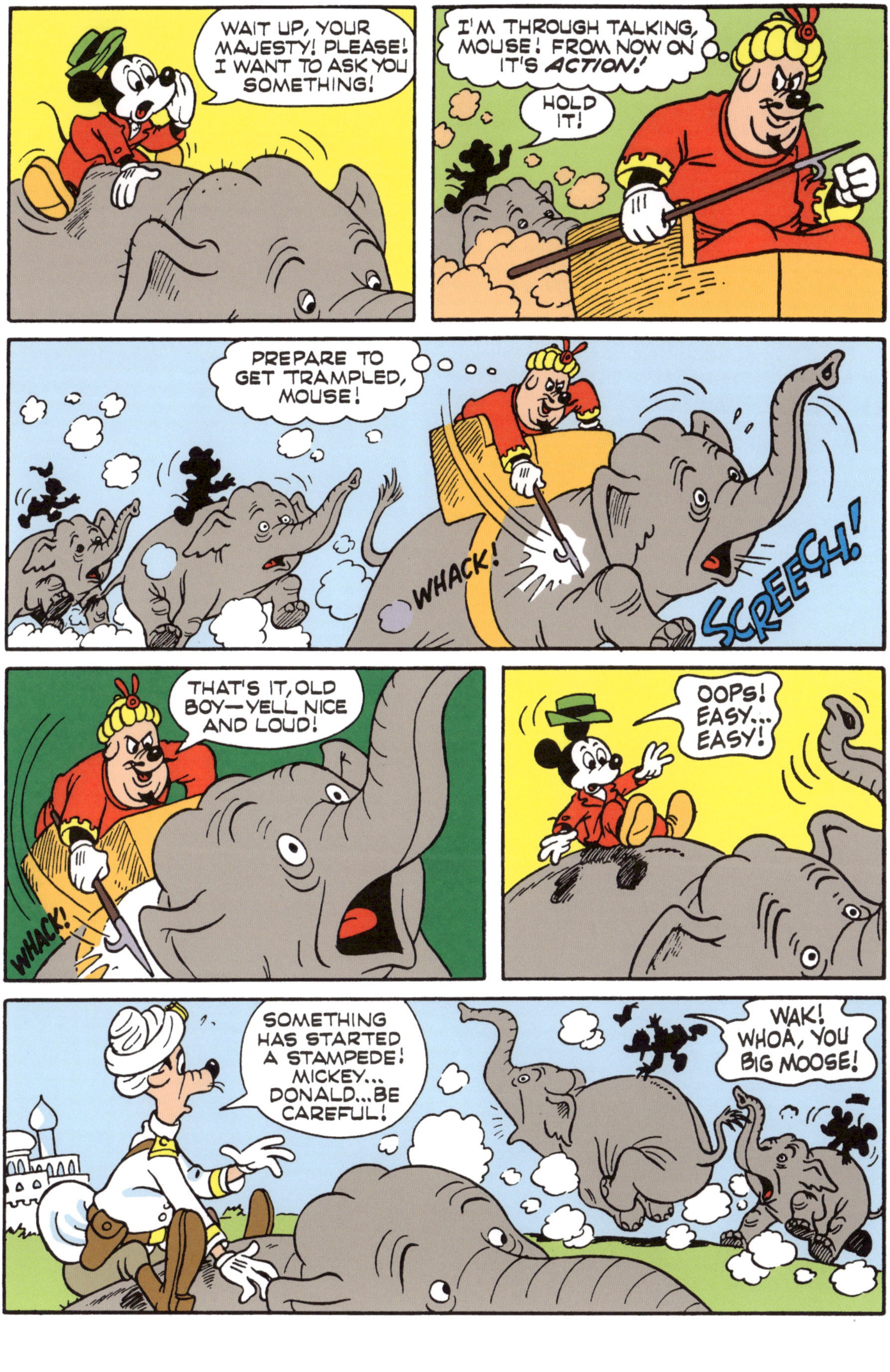
WAIT UP, YOUR MAJESTY! PLEASE! I WANT TO ASK YOU SOMETHING!
I'M THROUGH TALKING, MOUSE! FROM NOW ON IT'S ACTION!
HOLD IT!
PREPARE TO GET TRAMPLED, MOUSE!
WHACK!
SCREECH!
THAT'S IT, OLD BOY—YELL NICE AND LOUD!
WHACK!
OOPS! EASY... EASY!
SOMETHING HAS STARTED A STAMPEDE! MICKEY... DONALD...BE CAREFUL!
WAK! WHOA, YOU BIG MOOSE!

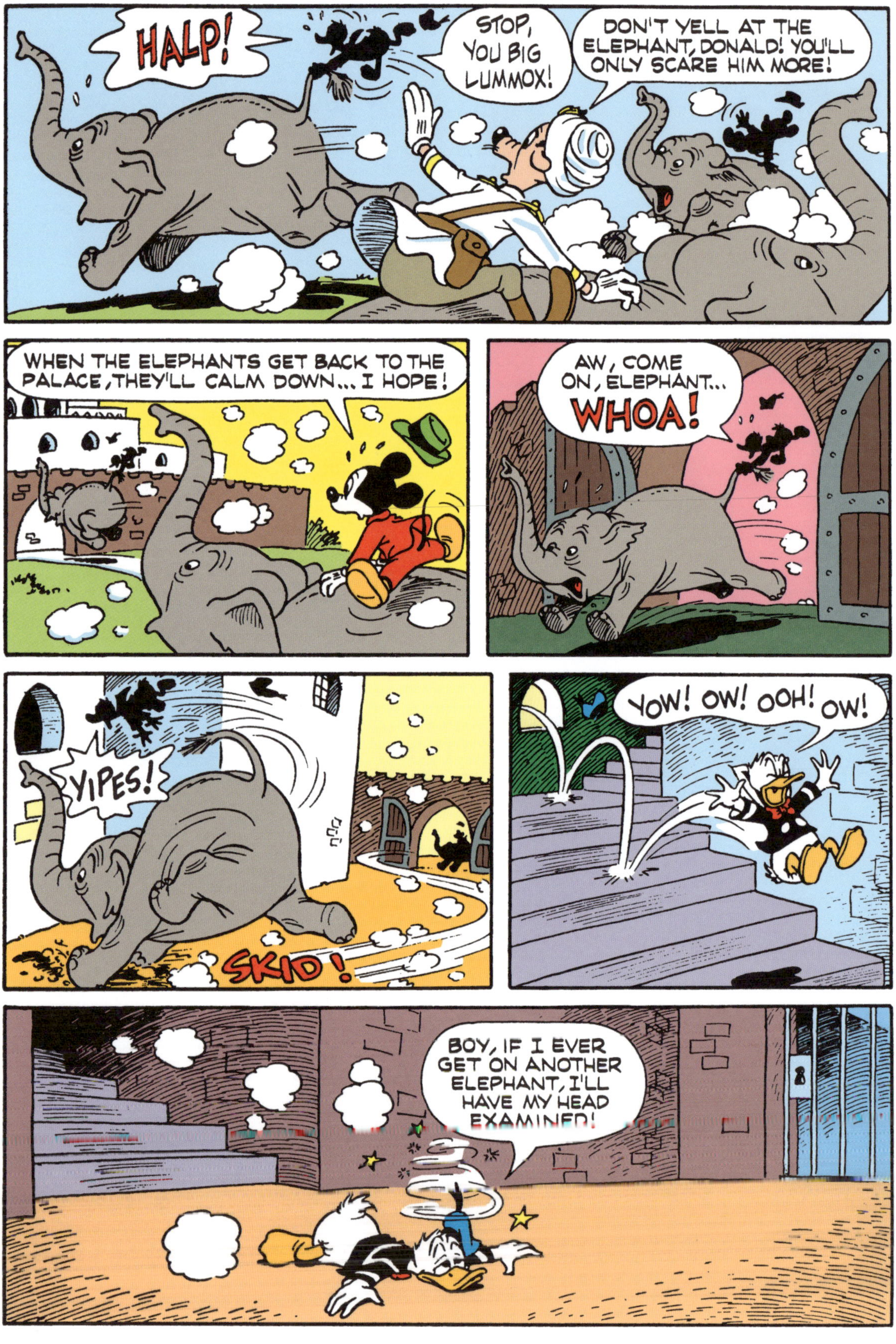
HALP!
STOP, YOU BIG LUMMOX!
DON'T YELL AT THE ELEPHANT, DONALD! YOU'LL ONLY SCARE HIM MORE!
WHEN THE ELEPHANTS GET BACK TO THE PALACE, THEY'LL CALM DOWN... I HOPE!
AW, COME ON, ELEPHANT...
WHOA!
YIPES!
SKID!
YOW! OW! OOH! OW!
BOY, IF I EVER GET ON ANOTHER ELEPHANT, I'LL HAVE MY HEAD EXAMINED!

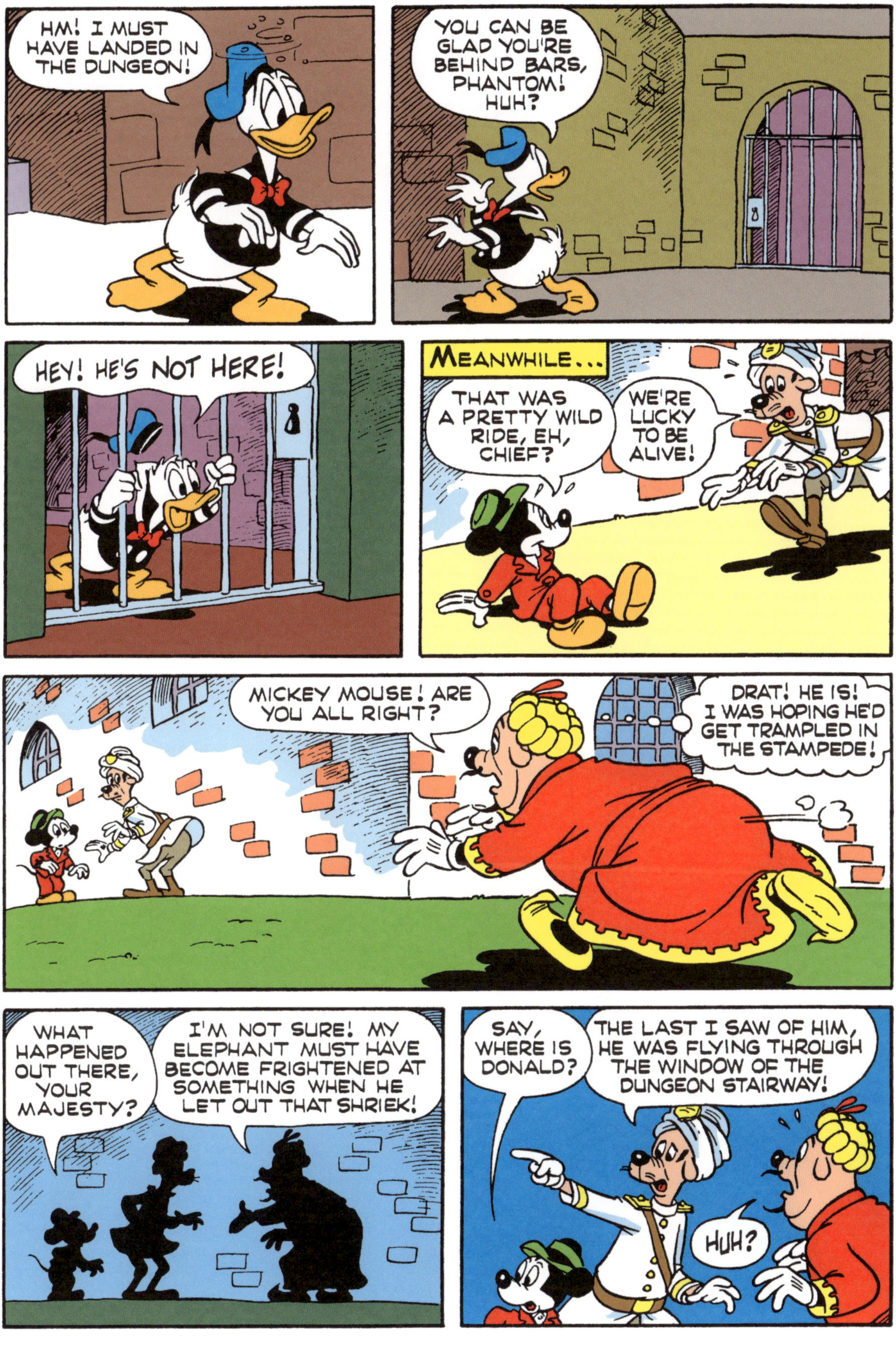
HM! I MUST HAVE LANDED IN THE DUNGEON!
YOU CAN BE GLAD YOU'RE BEHIND BARS, PHANTOM! HUH?
HEY! HE'S NOT HERE!
MEANWHILE...
THAT WAS A PRETTY WILD RIDE, EH, CHIEF?
WE'RE LUCKY TO BE ALIVE!
MICKEY MOUSE! ARE YOU ALL RIGHT?
DRAT! HE IS! I WAS HOPING HE'D GET TRAMPLED IN THE STAMPEDE!
WHAT HAPPENED OUT THERE, YOUR MAJESTY?
I'M NOT SURE! MY ELEPHANT MUST HAVE BECOME FRIGHTENED AT SOMETHING WHEN HE LET OUT THAT SHRIEK!
SAY, WHERE IS DONALD?
THE LAST I SAW OF HIM, HE WAS FLYING THROUGH THE WINDOW OF THE DUNGEON STAIRWAY!
HUH?

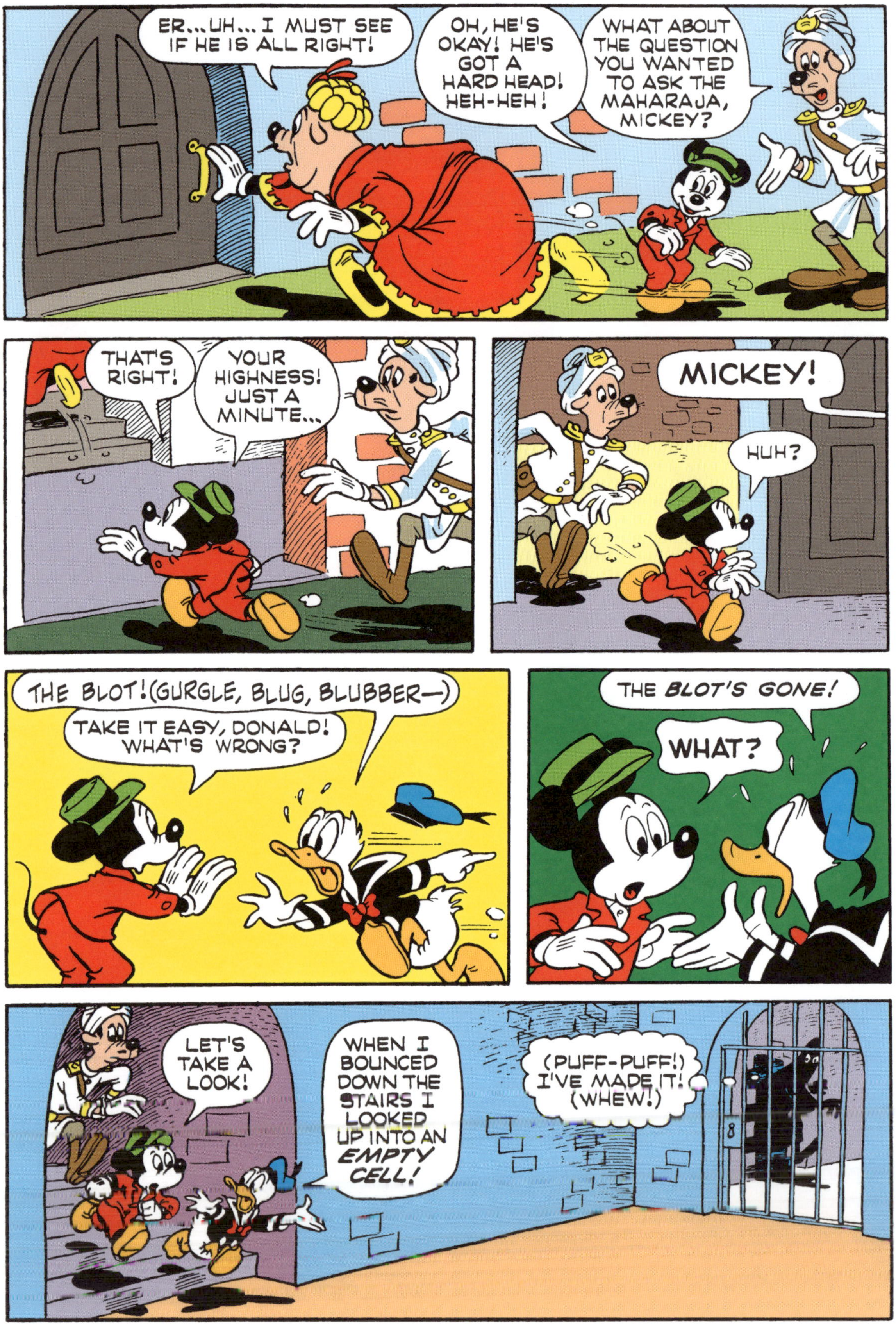
ER... UH... I MUST SEE IF HE IS ALL RIGHT!
OH, HE'S OKAY! HE'S GOT A HARD HEAD! HEH-HEH!
WHAT ABOUT THE QUESTION YOU WANTED TO ASK THE MAHARAJA, MICKEY?
THAT'S RIGHT!
YOUR HIGHNESS! JUST A MINUTE...
MICKEY!
HUH?
THE BLOT! (GURGLE, BLUG, BLUBBER—)
TAKE IT EASY, DONALD! WHAT'S WRONG?
THE BLOT'S GONE!
WHAT?
LET'S TAKE A LOOK!
WHEN I BOUNCED DOWN THE STAIRS I LOOKED UP INTO AN EMPTY CELL!
(PUFF-PUFF!) I'VE MADE IT! (WHEW!)
8

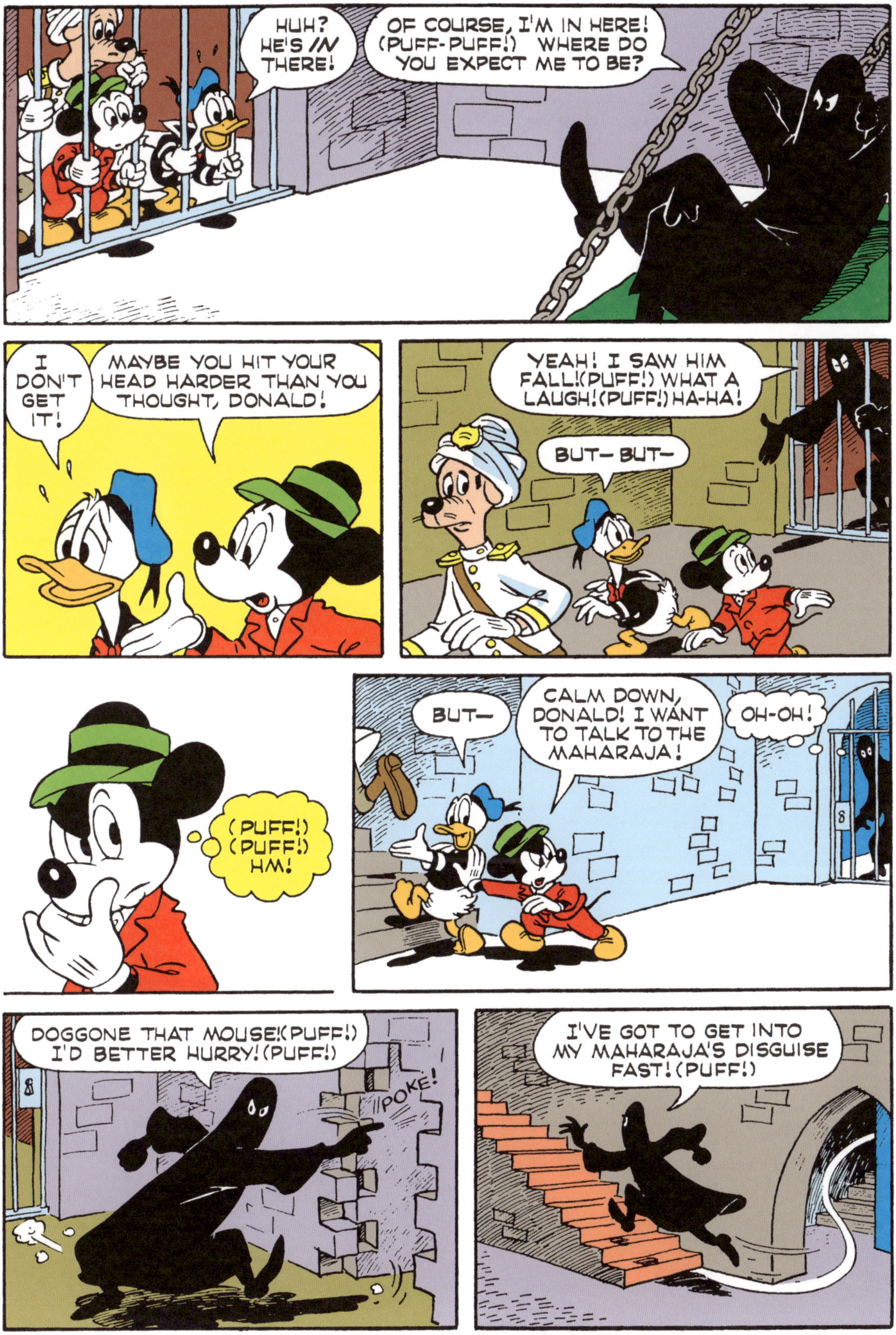
HUH? HE'S IN THERE!
OF COURSE, I'M IN HERE! (PUFF-PUFF!) WHERE DO YOU EXPECT ME TO BE?
I DON'T GET IT!
MAYBE YOU HIT YOUR HEAD HARDER THAN YOU THOUGHT, DONALD!
YEAH! I SAW HIM FALL! (PUFF!) WHAT A LAUGH! (PUFF!) HA-HA!
BUT— BUT—
(PUFF!) (PUFF!) HM!
BUT—
CALM DOWN, DONALD! I WANT TO TALK TO THE MAHARAJA!
OH-OH!
DOGGONE THAT MOUSE! (PUFF!) I'D BETTER HURRY! (PUFF!)
POKE!
I'VE GOT TO GET INTO MY MAHARAJA'S DISGUISE FAST! (PUFF!)

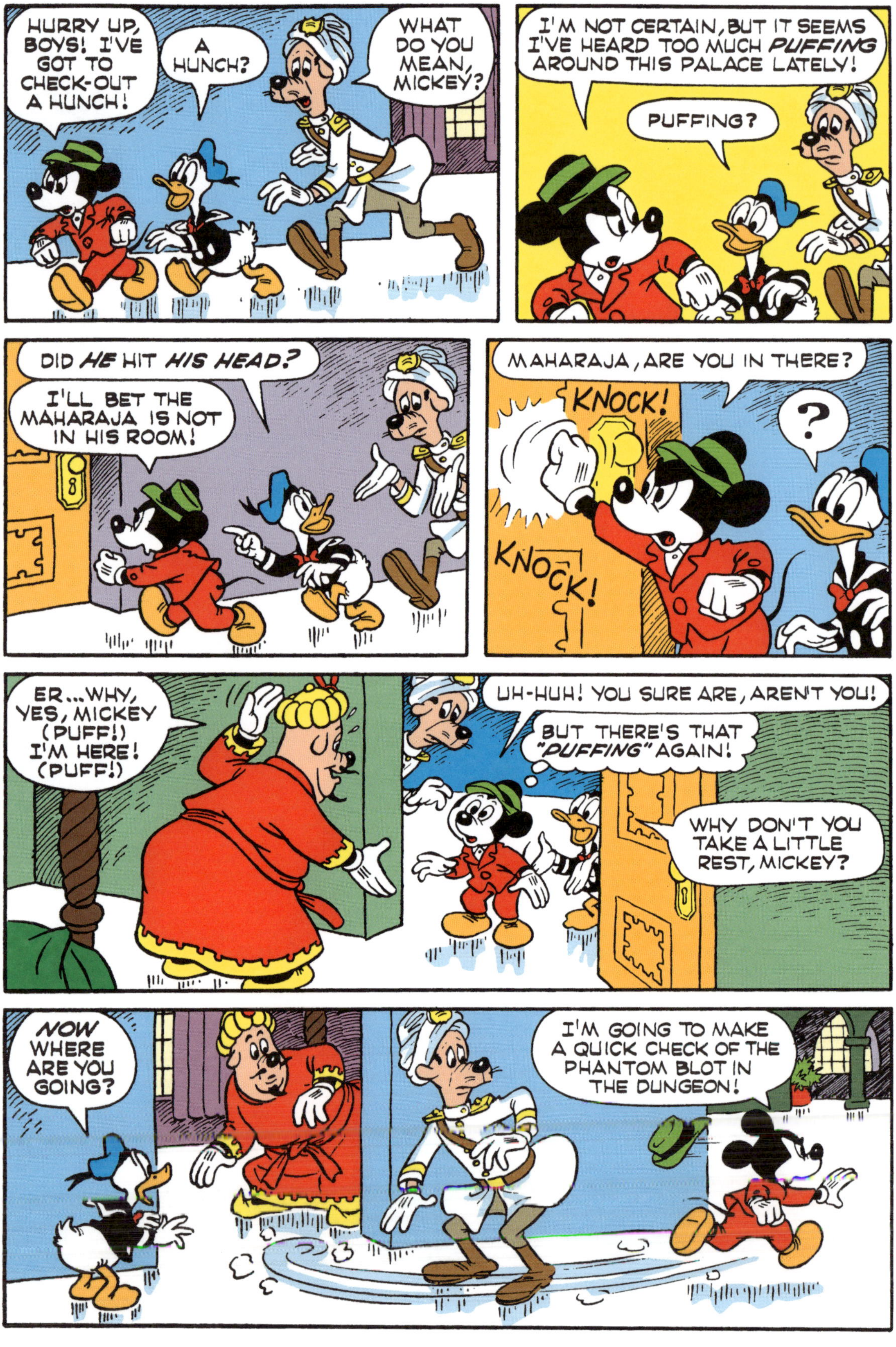

HURRY UP, BOYS! I'VE GOT TO CHECK-OUT A HUNCH!
A HUNCH?
WHAT DO YOU MEAN, MICKEY?
I'M NOT CERTAIN, BUT IT SEEMS I'VE HEARD TOO MUCH *PUFFING* AROUND THIS PALACE LATELY!
PUFFING?
DID *HE* HIT *HIS HEAD?*
I'LL BET THE MAHARAJA IS NOT IN HIS ROOM!
MAHARAJA, ARE YOU IN THERE?
KNOCK!
KNOCK!
?
ER...WHY, YES, MICKEY (PUFF!) I'M HERE! (PUFF!)
UH-HUH! YOU SURE ARE, AREN'T YOU!
BUT THERE'S THAT "*PUFFING*" AGAIN!
WHY DON'T YOU TAKE A LITTLE REST, MICKEY?
NOW WHERE ARE YOU GOING?
I'M GOING TO MAKE A QUICK CHECK OF THE PHANTOM BLOT IN THE DUNGEON!

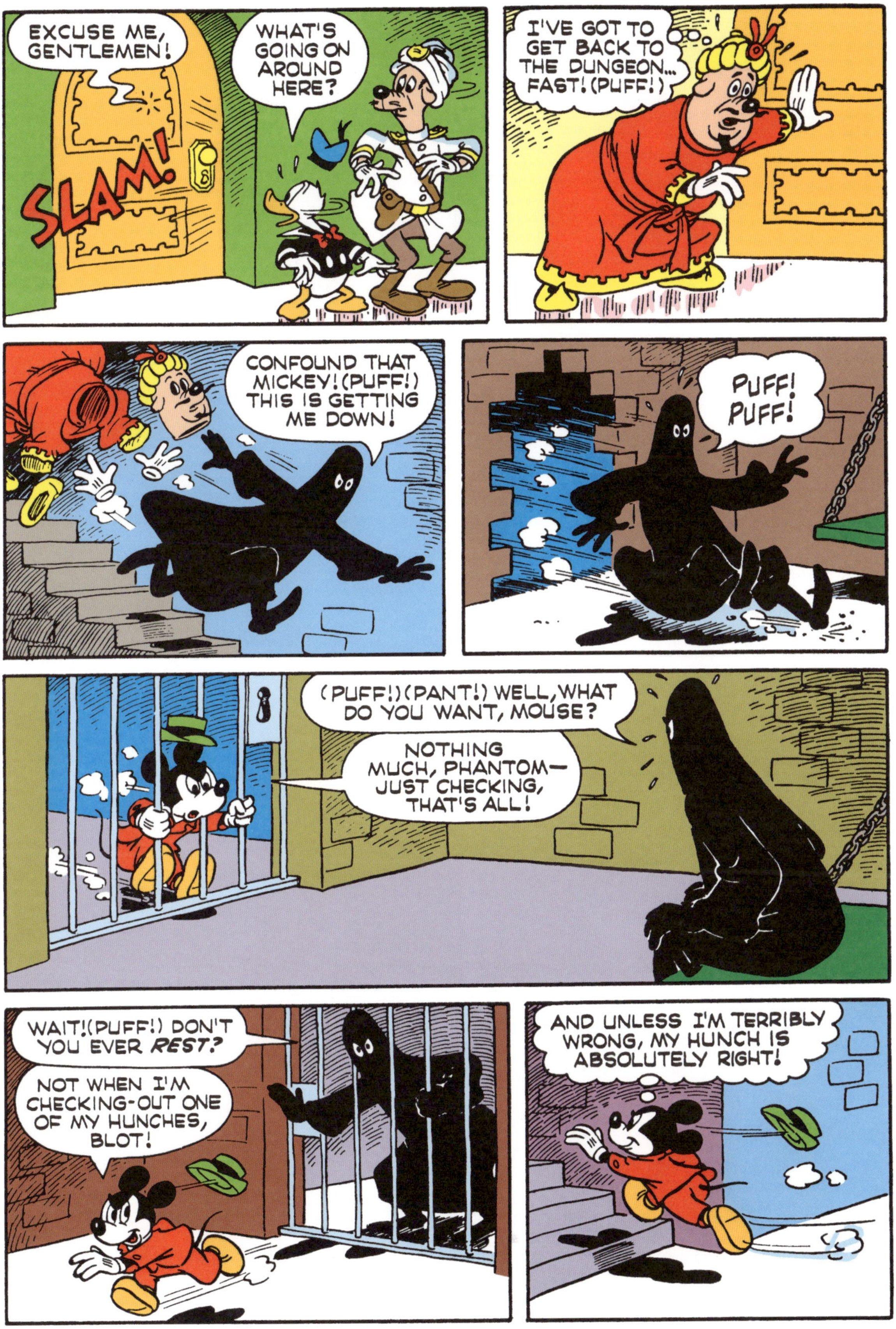
EXCUSE ME, GENTLEMEN!
WHAT'S GOING ON AROUND HERE?
SLAM!
I'VE GOT TO GET BACK TO THE DUNGEON... FAST! (PUFF!)
CONFOUND THAT MICKEY! (PUFF!) THIS IS GETTING ME DOWN!
PUFF! PUFF!
(PUFF!)(PANT!) WELL, WHAT DO YOU WANT, MOUSE?
NOTHING MUCH, PHANTOM— JUST CHECKING, THAT'S ALL!
WAIT! (PUFF!) DON'T YOU EVER *REST?*
NOT WHEN I'M CHECKING-OUT ONE OF MY HUNCHES, BLOT!
AND UNLESS I'M TERRIBLY WRONG, MY HUNCH IS ABSOLUTELY RIGHT!

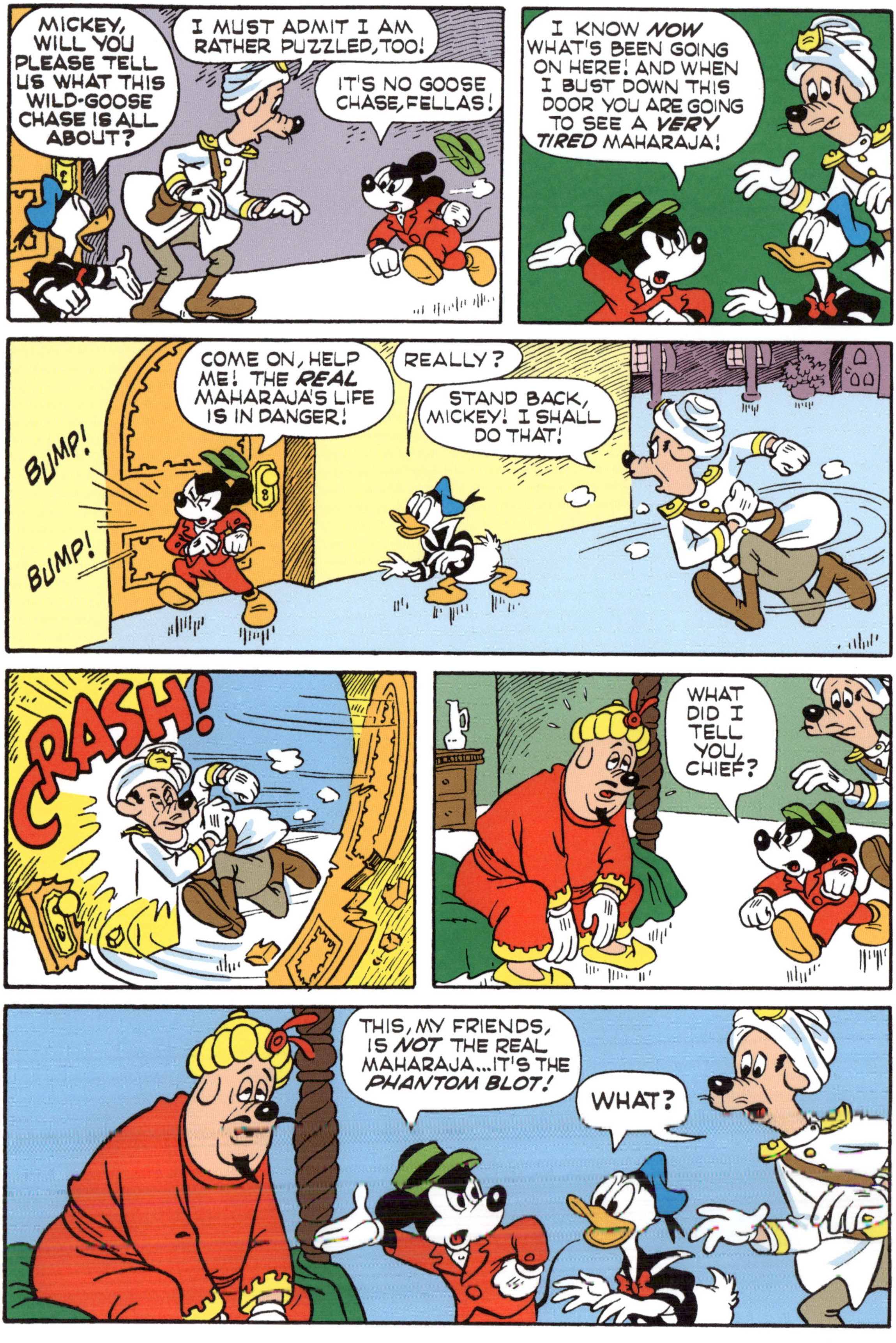
MICKEY, WILL YOU PLEASE TELL US WHAT THIS WILD-GOOSE CHASE IS ALL ABOUT?
I MUST ADMIT I AM RATHER PUZZLED, TOO!
IT'S NO GOOSE CHASE, FELLAS!
I KNOW NOW WHAT'S BEEN GOING ON HERE! AND WHEN I BUST DOWN THIS DOOR YOU ARE GOING TO SEE A VERY TIRED MAHARAJA!
BUMP!
BUMP!
COME ON, HELP ME! THE REAL MAHARAJA'S LIFE IS IN DANGER!
REALLY?
STAND BACK, MICKEY! I SHALL DO THAT!
CRASH!
WHAT DID I TELL YOU, CHIEF?
THIS, MY FRIENDS, IS NOT THE REAL MAHARAJA...IT'S THE PHANTOM BLOT!
WHAT?

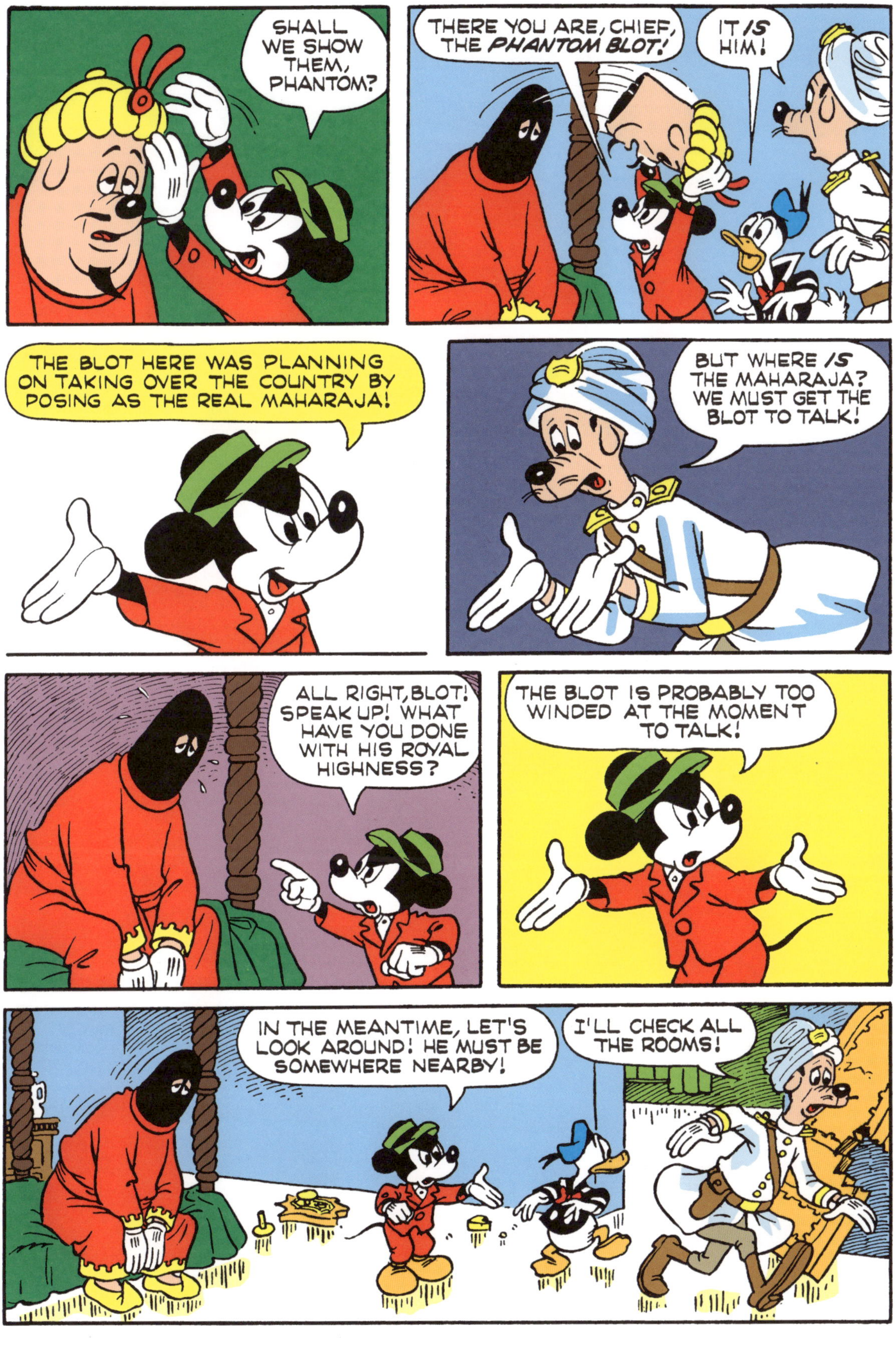
SHALL WE SHOW THEM, PHANTOM?
THERE YOU ARE, CHIEF, THE *PHANTOM BLOT!*
IT *IS* HIM!
THE BLOT HERE WAS PLANNING ON TAKING OVER THE COUNTRY BY POSING AS THE REAL MAHARAJA!
BUT WHERE *IS* THE MAHARAJA? WE MUST GET THE BLOT TO TALK!
ALL RIGHT, BLOT! SPEAK UP! WHAT HAVE YOU DONE WITH HIS ROYAL HIGHNESS?
THE BLOT IS PROBABLY TOO WINDED AT THE MOMENT TO TALK!
IN THE MEANTIME, LET'S LOOK AROUND! HE MUST BE SOMEWHERE NEARBY!
I'LL CHECK ALL THE ROOMS!

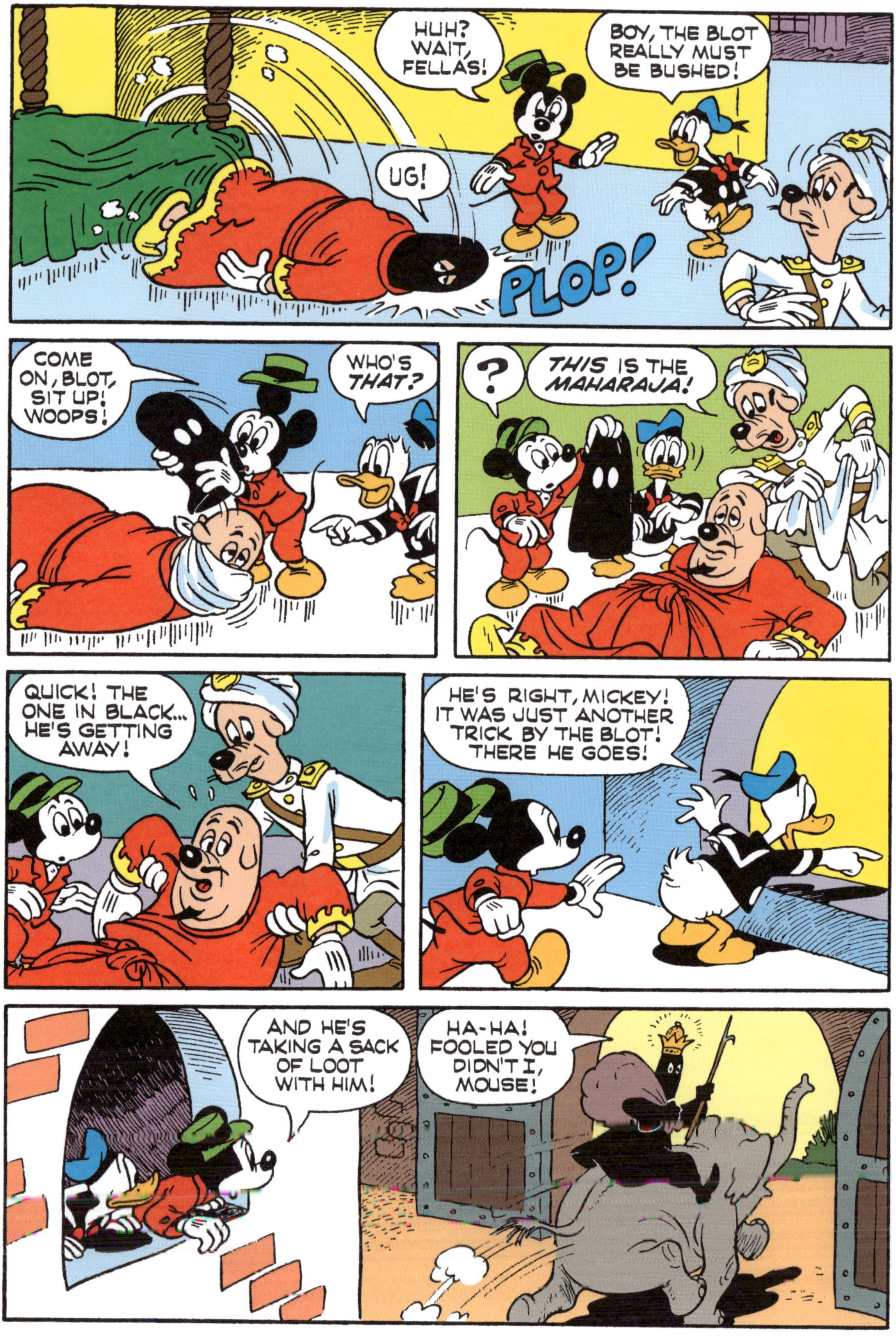
HUH? WAIT, FELLAS!
BOY, THE BLOT REALLY MUST BE BUSHED!
UG!
PLOP!
COME ON, BLOT, SIT UP! WOOPS!
WHO'S THAT?
?
THIS IS THE MAHARAJA!
QUICK! THE ONE IN BLACK... HE'S GETTING AWAY!
HE'S RIGHT, MICKEY! IT WAS JUST ANOTHER TRICK BY THE BLOT! THERE HE GOES!
AND HE'S TAKING A SACK OF LOOT WITH HIM!
HA-HA! FOOLED YOU DIDN'T I, MOUSE!

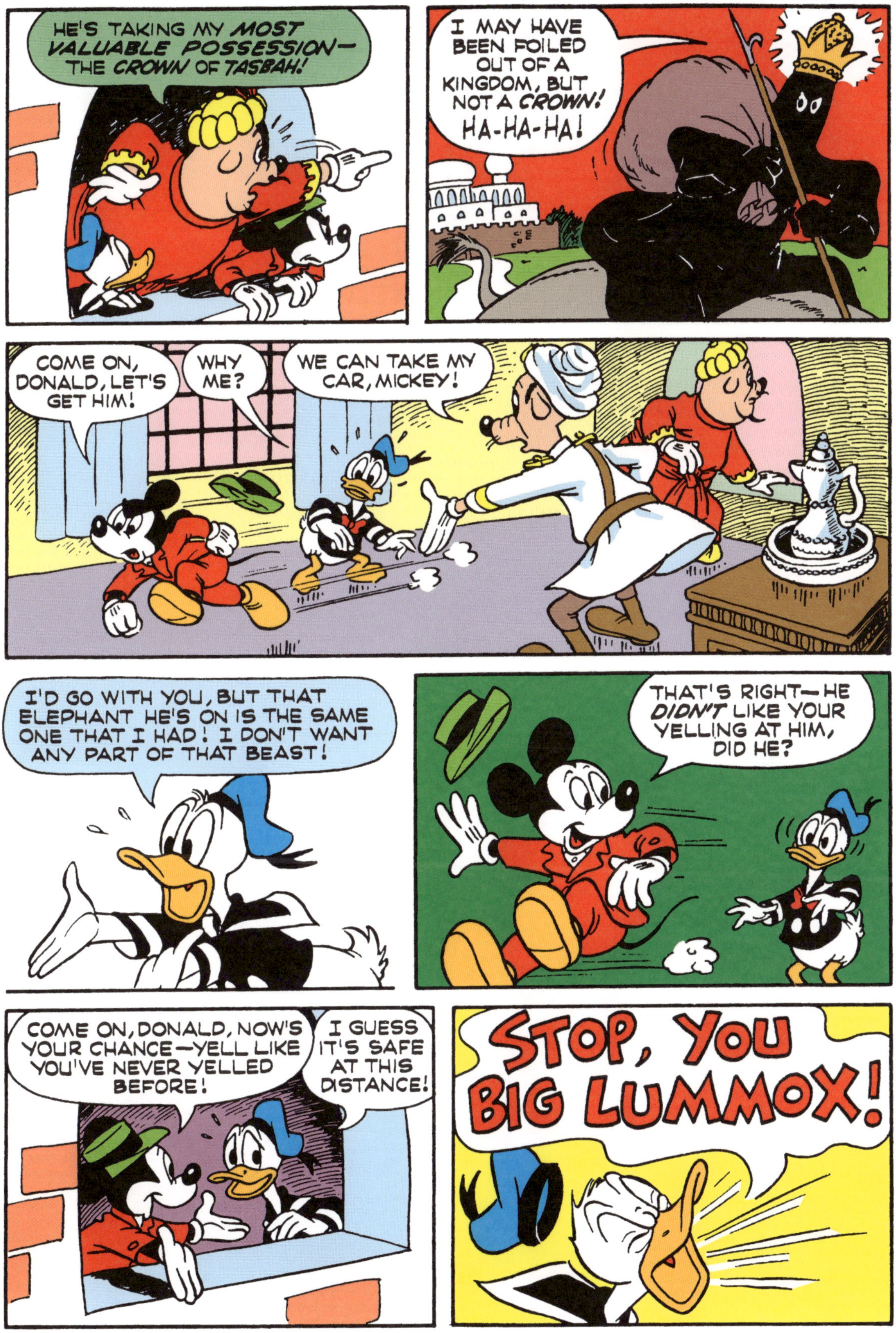
HE'S TAKING MY *MOST VALUABLE POSSESSION*— THE *CROWN* OF *TASBAH!*
I MAY HAVE BEEN FOILED OUT OF A KINGDOM, BUT NOT A *CROWN!* HA-HA-HA!
COME ON, DONALD, LET'S GET HIM!
WHY ME?
WE CAN TAKE MY CAR, MICKEY!
I'D GO WITH YOU, BUT THAT ELEPHANT HE'S ON IS THE SAME ONE THAT I HAD! I DON'T WANT ANY PART OF THAT BEAST!
THAT'S RIGHT—HE *DIDN'T* LIKE YOUR YELLING AT HIM, DID HE?
COME ON, DONALD, NOW'S YOUR CHANCE—YELL LIKE YOU'VE NEVER YELLED BEFORE!
I GUESS IT'S SAFE AT THIS DISTANCE!
STOP, YOU BIG LUMMOX!

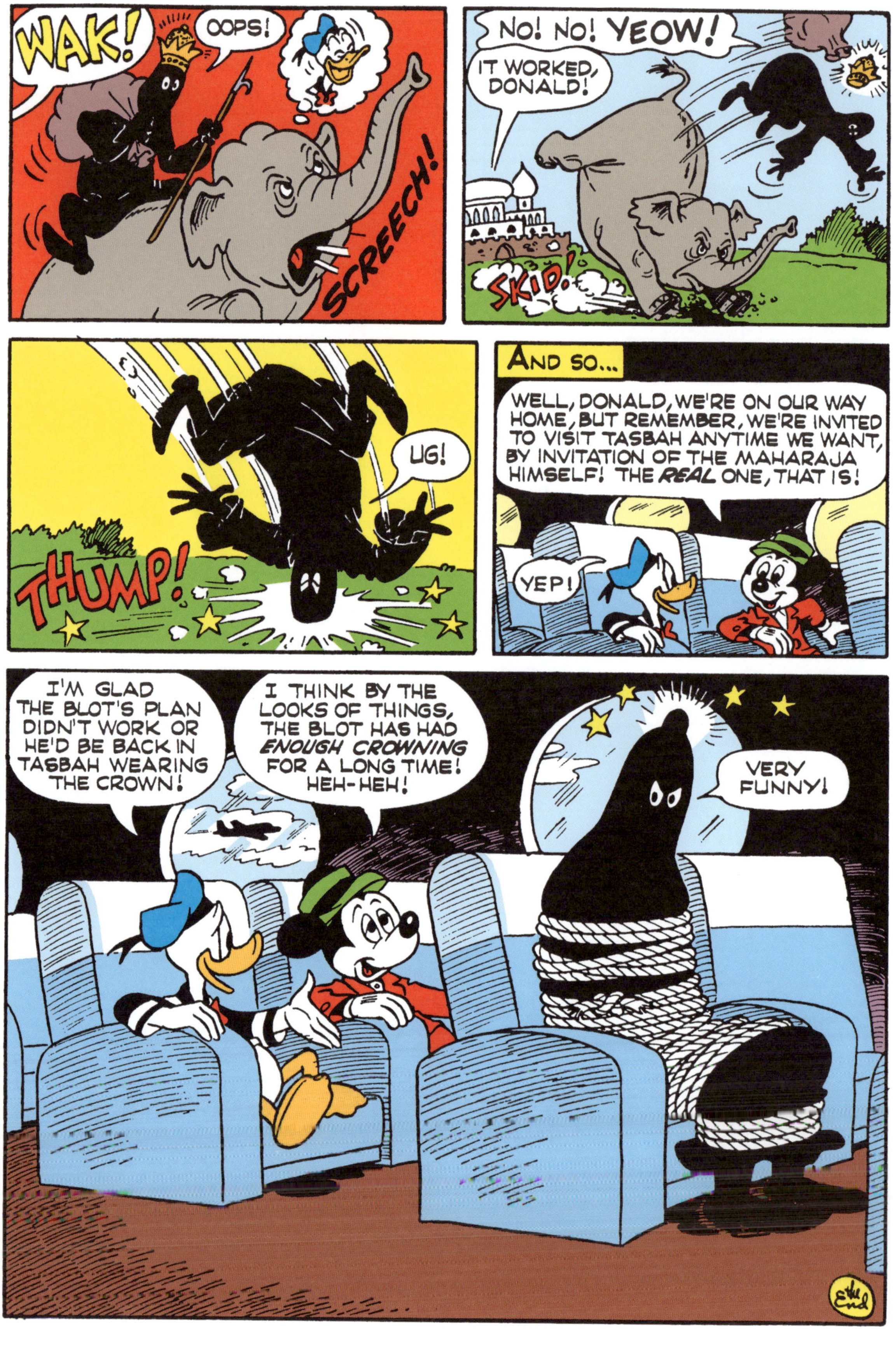
WAK!
OOPS!
SCREECH!
NO! NO! YEOW!
IT WORKED, DONALD!
SKID!
UG!
THUMP!
AND SO...
WELL, DONALD, WE'RE ON OUR WAY HOME, BUT REMEMBER, WE'RE INVITED TO VISIT TASBAH ANYTIME WE WANT, BY INVITATION OF THE MAHARAJA HIMSELF! THE *REAL* ONE, THAT IS!
YEP!
I'M GLAD THE BLOT'S PLAN DIDN'T WORK OR HE'D BE BACK IN TASBAH WEARING THE CROWN!
I THINK BY THE LOOKS OF THINGS, THE BLOT HAS HAD *ENOUGH CROWNING* FOR A LONG TIME! HEH-HEH!
VERY FUNNY!
The End

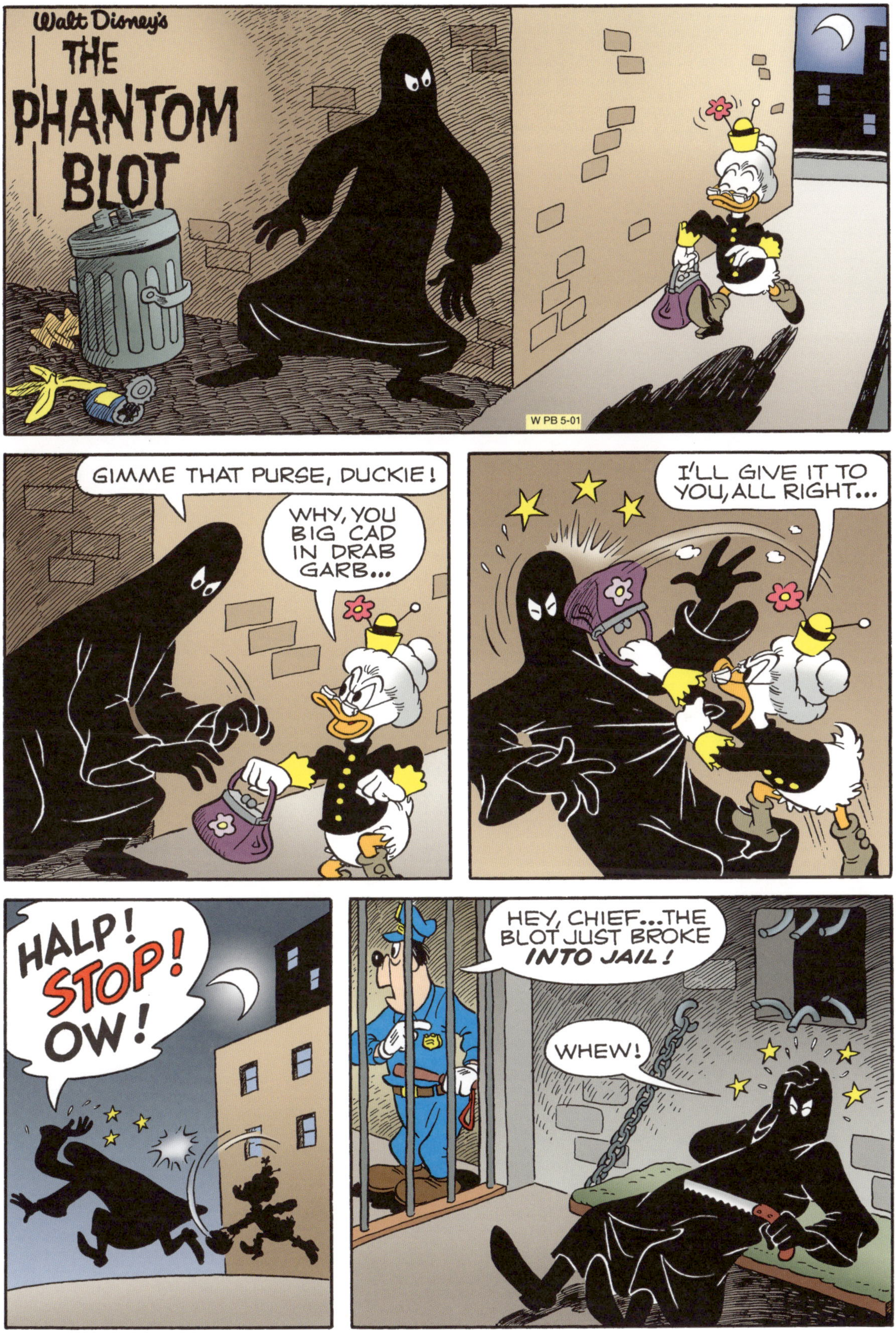
Walt Disney's
THE PHANTOM BLOT
W PB 5-01
GIMME THAT PURSE, DUCKIE!
WHY, YOU BIG CAD IN DRAB GARB...
I'LL GIVE IT TO YOU, ALL RIGHT...
HALP! STOP! OW!
HEY, CHIEF...THE BLOT JUST BROKE *INTO JAIL!*
WHEW!

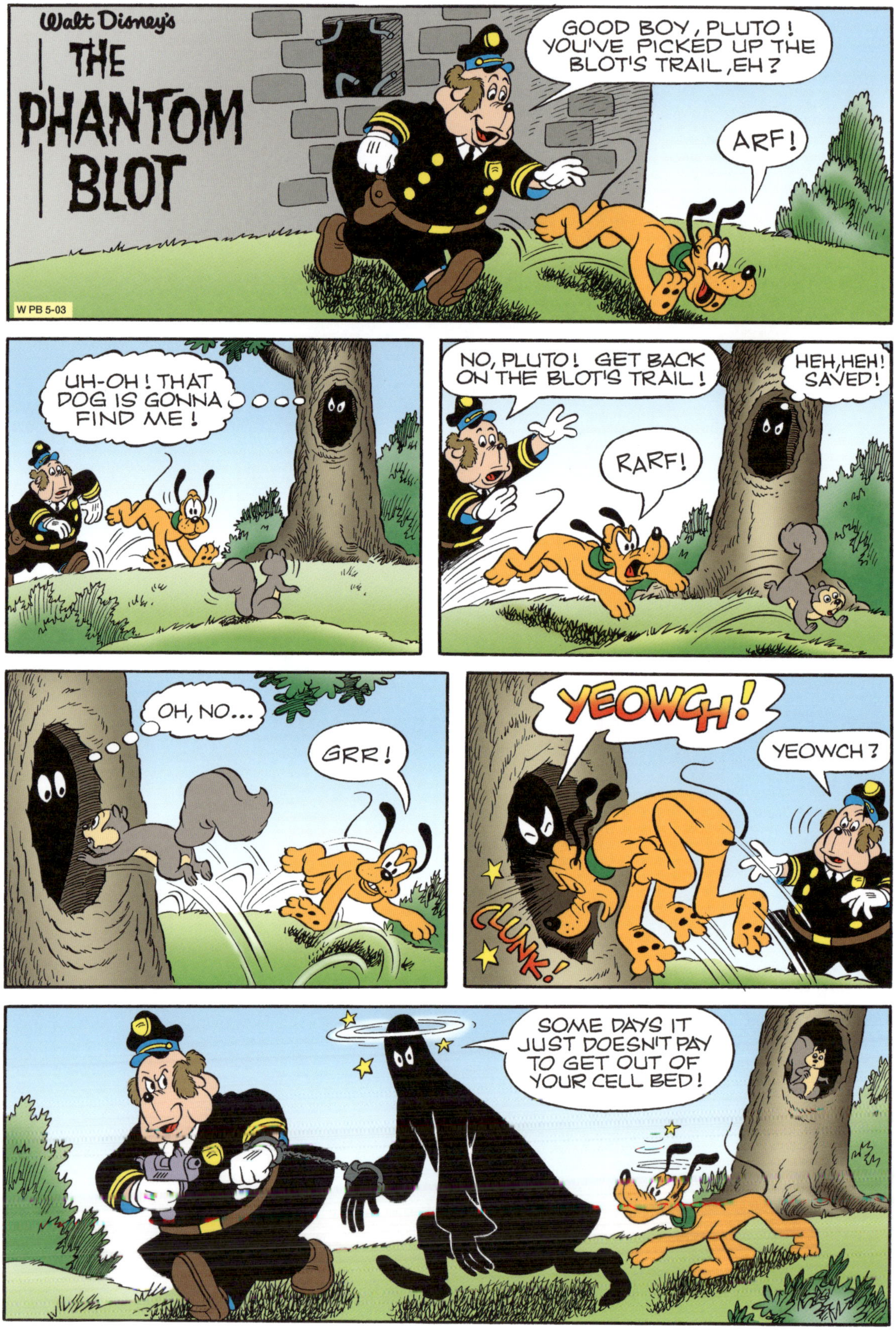
Walt Disney's
THE PHANTOM BLOT
GOOD BOY, PLUTO! YOU'VE PICKED UP THE BLOT'S TRAIL, EH?
ARF!
W PB 5-03
UH-OH! THAT DOG IS GONNA FIND ME!
NO, PLUTO! GET BACK ON THE BLOT'S TRAIL!
HEH, HEH! SAVED!
RARF!
OH, NO...
GRR!
YEOWCH!
YEOWCH?
CLUNK!
SOME DAYS IT JUST DOESN'T PAY TO GET OUT OF YOUR CELL BED!

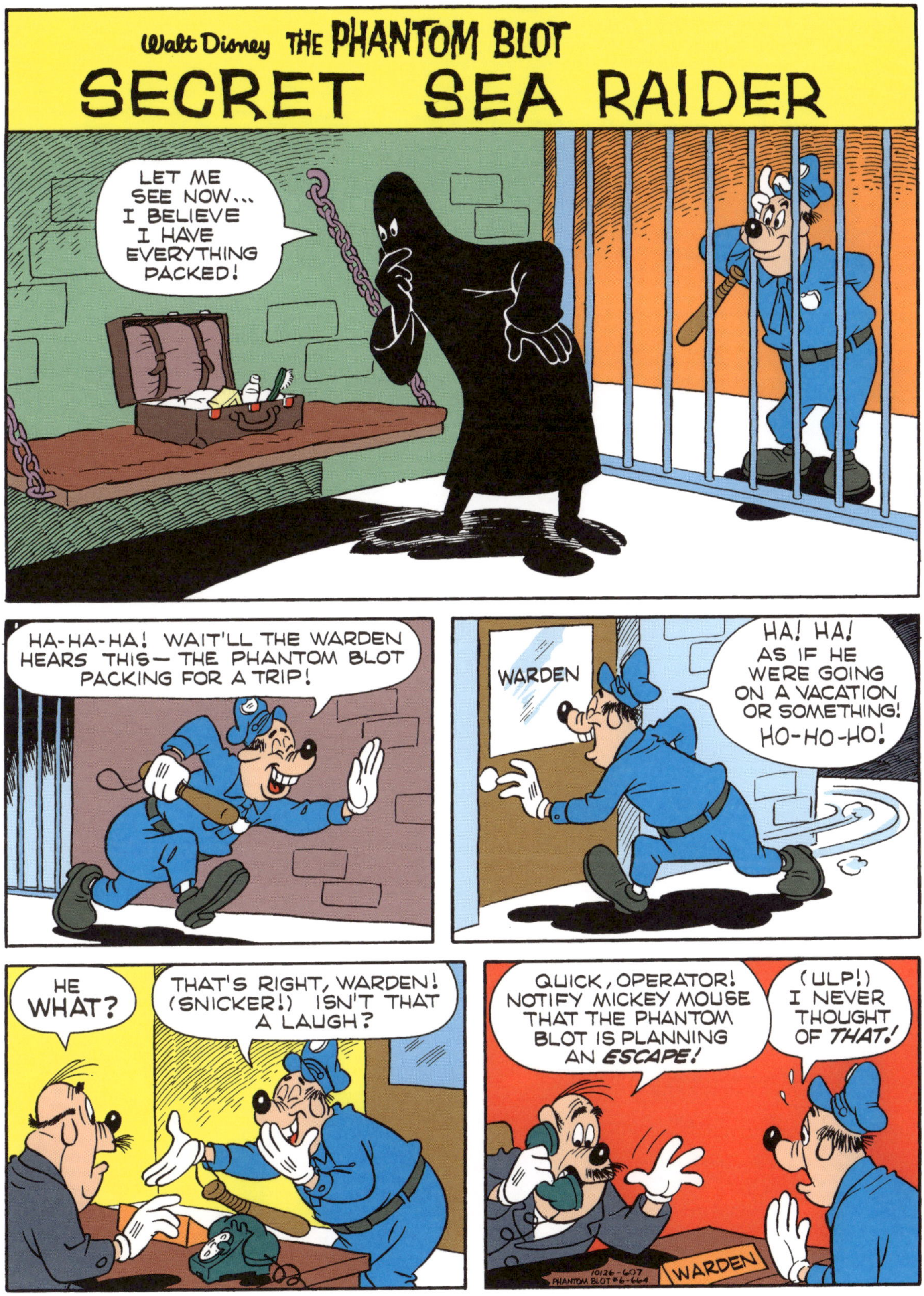
Walt Disney THE PHANTOM BLOT
SECRET SEA RAIDER
LET ME SEE NOW... I BELIEVE I HAVE EVERYTHING PACKED!
HA-HA-HA! WAIT'LL THE WARDEN HEARS THIS— THE PHANTOM BLOT PACKING FOR A TRIP!
WARDEN
HA! HA! AS IF HE WERE GOING ON A VACATION OR SOMETHING! HO-HO-HO!
HE WHAT?
THAT'S RIGHT, WARDEN! (SNICKER!) ISN'T THAT A LAUGH?
QUICK, OPERATOR! NOTIFY MICKEY MOUSE THAT THE PHANTOM BLOT IS PLANNING AN *ESCAPE!*
(ULP!) I NEVER THOUGHT OF *THAT!*
10126-607
PHANTOM BLOT #6-664
WARDEN

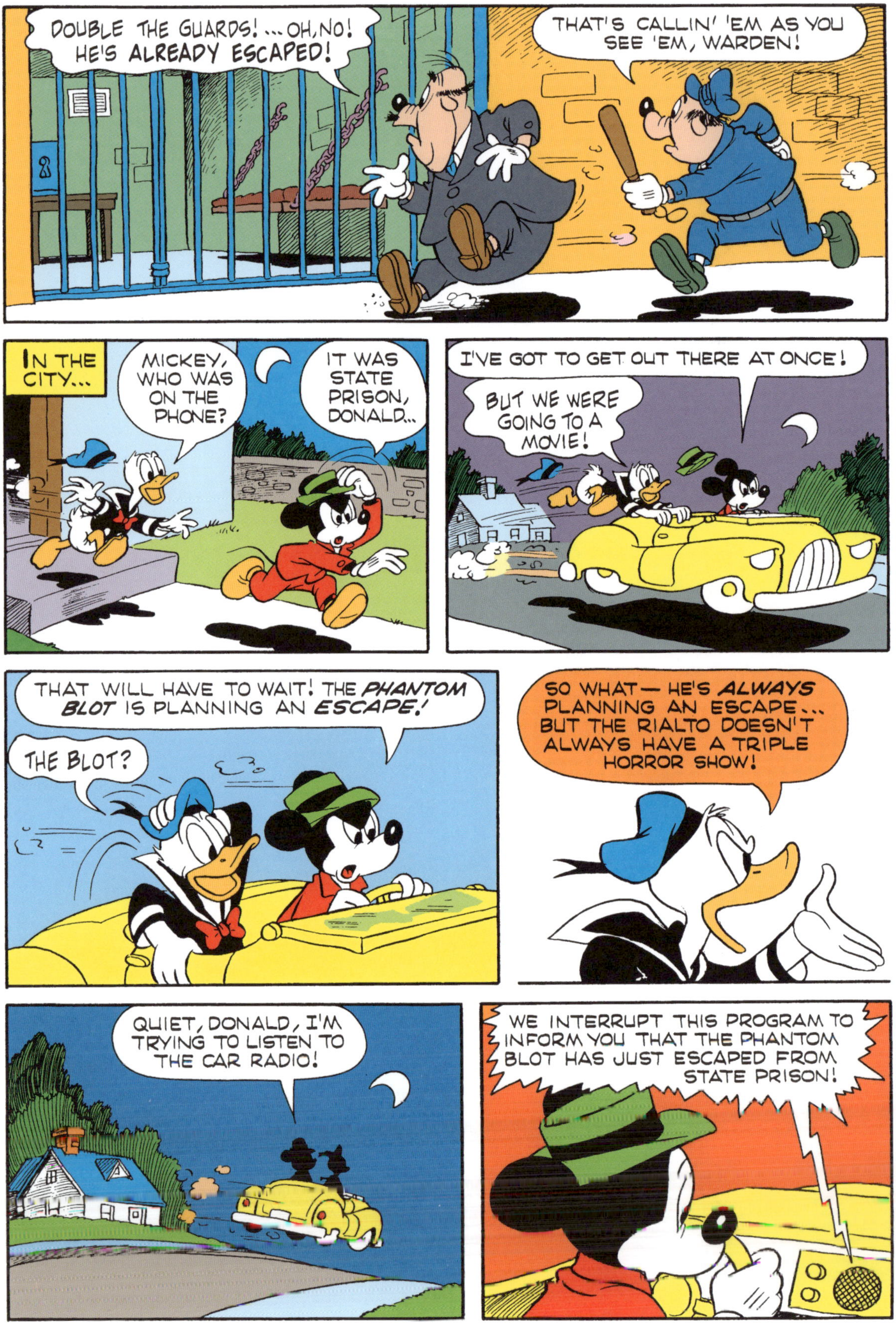
DOUBLE THE GUARDS! ...OH, NO! HE'S ALREADY ESCAPED!
THAT'S CALLIN' 'EM AS YOU SEE 'EM, WARDEN!
IN THE CITY...
MICKEY, WHO WAS ON THE PHONE?
IT WAS STATE PRISON, DONALD...
I'VE GOT TO GET OUT THERE AT ONCE!
BUT WE WERE GOING TO A MOVIE!
THAT WILL HAVE TO WAIT! THE *PHANTOM BLOT* IS PLANNING AN *ESCAPE!*
THE BLOT?
SO WHAT— HE'S *ALWAYS* PLANNING AN ESCAPE... BUT THE RIALTO DOESN'T ALWAYS HAVE A TRIPLE HORROR SHOW!
QUIET, DONALD, I'M TRYING TO LISTEN TO THE CAR RADIO!
WE INTERRUPT THIS PROGRAM TO INFORM YOU THAT THE PHANTOM BLOT HAS JUST ESCAPED FROM STATE PRISON!

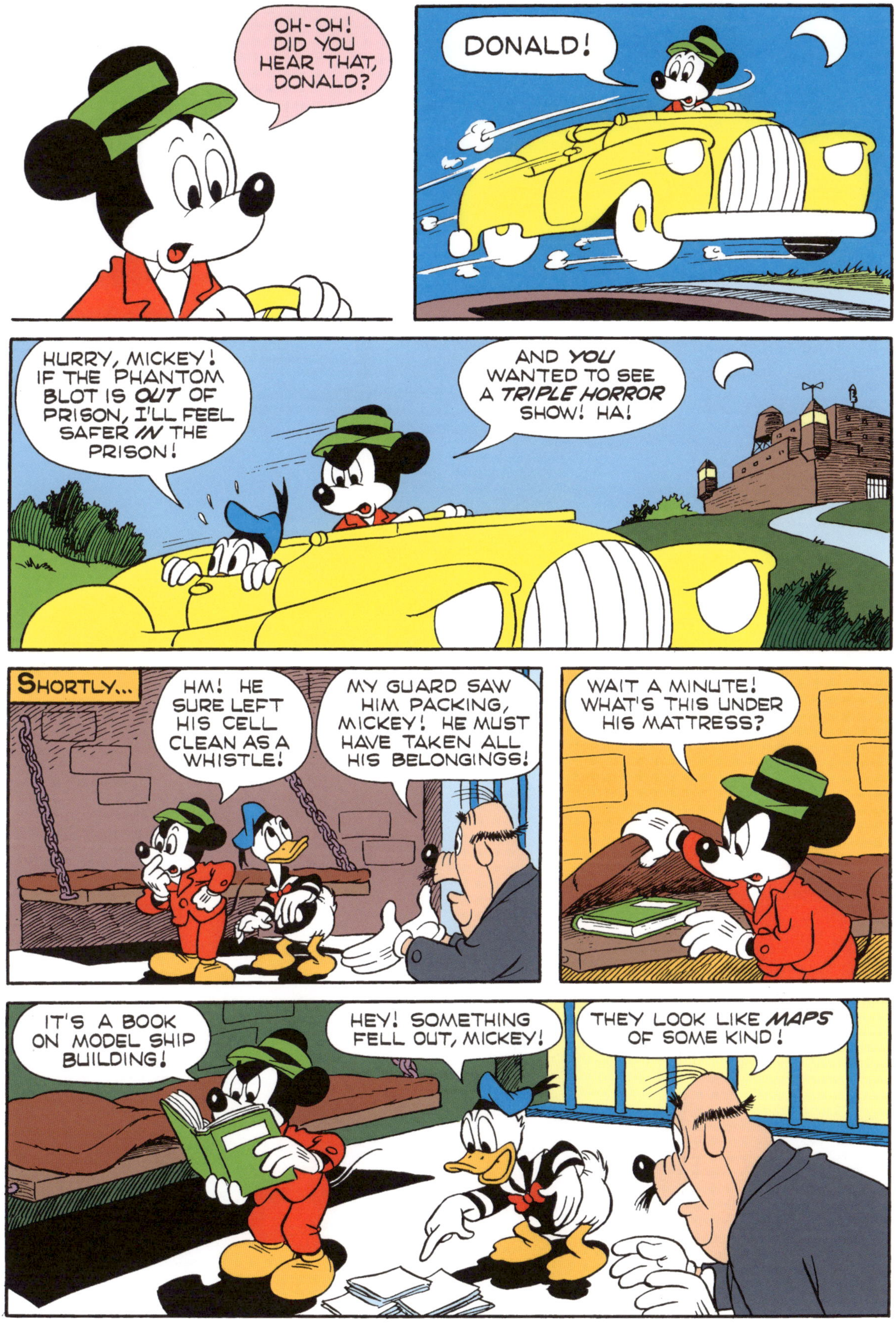
OH-OH! DID YOU HEAR THAT, DONALD?
DONALD!
HURRY, MICKEY! IF THE PHANTOM BLOT IS *OUT* OF PRISON, I'LL FEEL SAFER *IN* THE PRISON!
AND *YOU* WANTED TO SEE A *TRIPLE HORROR* SHOW! HA!
SHORTLY...
HM! HE SURE LEFT HIS CELL CLEAN AS A WHISTLE!
MY GUARD SAW HIM PACKING, MICKEY! HE MUST HAVE TAKEN ALL HIS BELONGINGS!
WAIT A MINUTE! WHAT'S THIS UNDER HIS MATTRESS?
IT'S A BOOK ON MODEL SHIP BUILDING!
HEY! SOMETHING FELL OUT, MICKEY!
THEY LOOK LIKE *MAPS* OF SOME KIND!

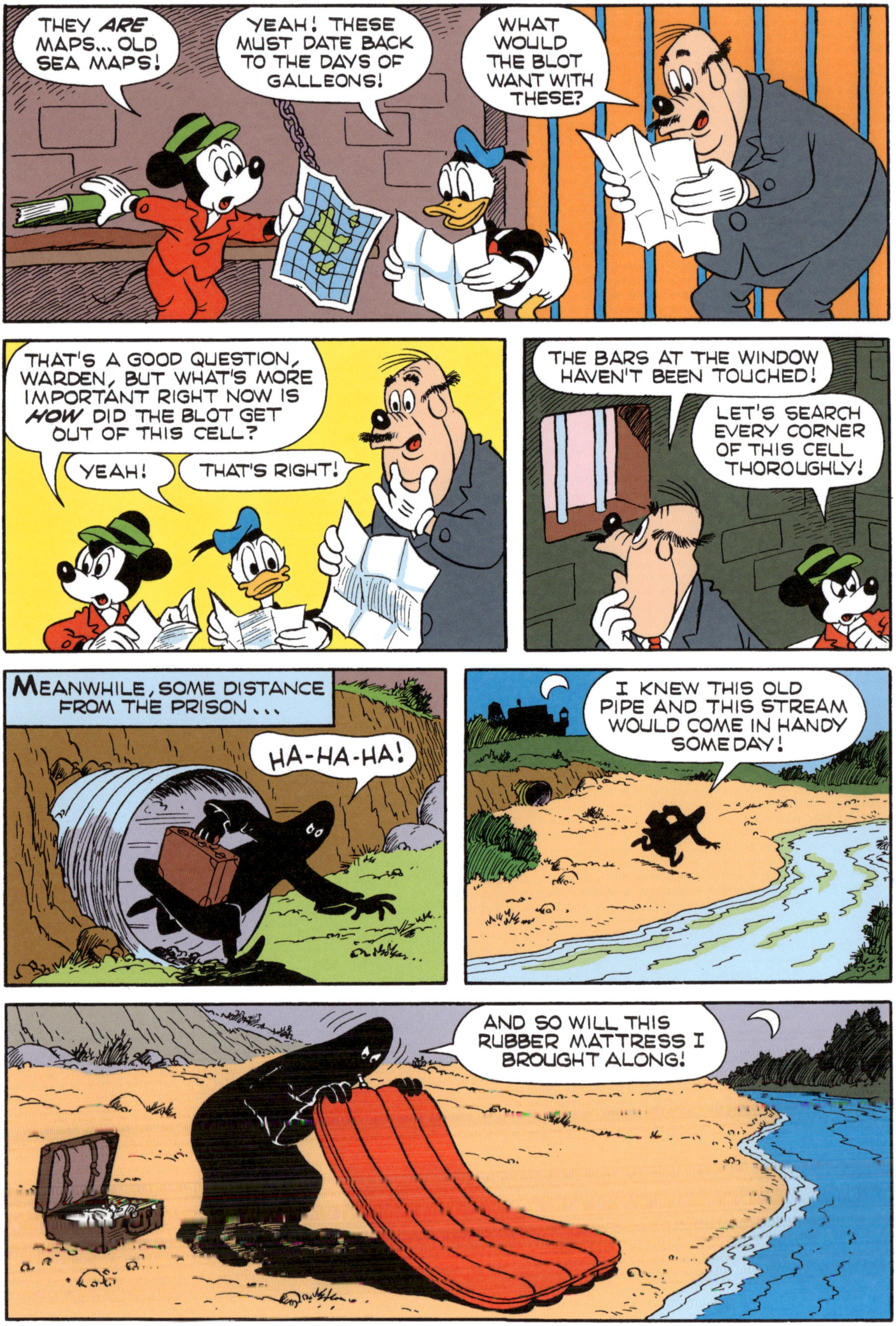
THEY ARE MAPS... OLD SEA MAPS!
YEAH! THESE MUST DATE BACK TO THE DAYS OF GALLEONS!
WHAT WOULD THE BLOT WANT WITH THESE?
THAT'S A GOOD QUESTION, WARDEN, BUT WHAT'S MORE IMPORTANT RIGHT NOW IS HOW DID THE BLOT GET OUT OF THIS CELL?
YEAH!
THAT'S RIGHT!
THE BARS AT THE WINDOW HAVEN'T BEEN TOUCHED!
LET'S SEARCH EVERY CORNER OF THIS CELL THOROUGHLY!
MEANWHILE, SOME DISTANCE FROM THE PRISON...
HA-HA-HA!
I KNEW THIS OLD PIPE AND THIS STREAM WOULD COME IN HANDY SOMEDAY!
AND SO WILL THIS RUBBER MATTRESS I BROUGHT ALONG!

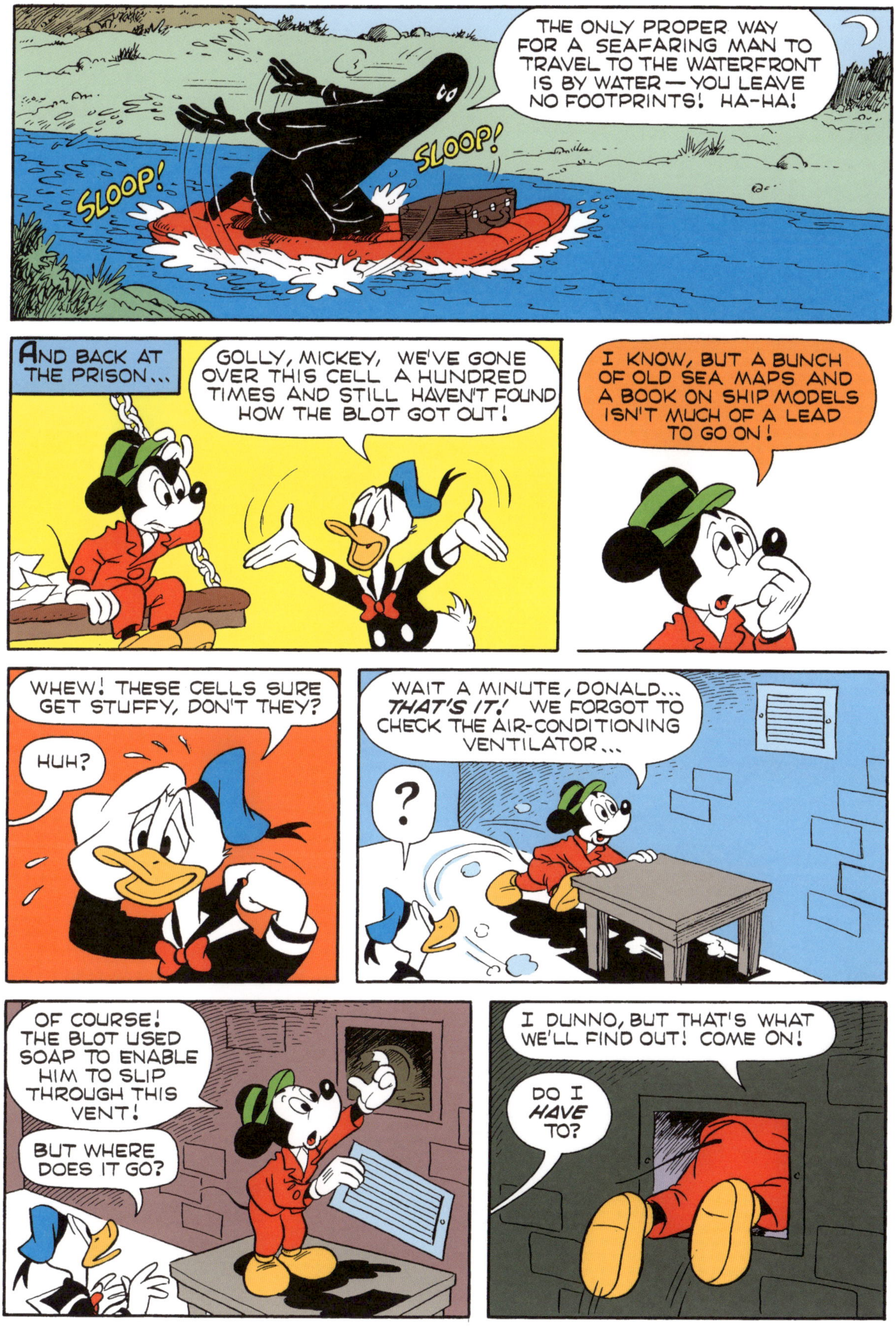
THE ONLY PROPER WAY FOR A SEAFARING MAN TO TRAVEL TO THE WATERFRONT IS BY WATER — YOU LEAVE NO FOOTPRINTS! HA-HA!
SLOOP!
SLOOP!
AND BACK AT THE PRISON...
GOLLY, MICKEY, WE'VE GONE OVER THIS CELL A HUNDRED TIMES AND STILL HAVEN'T FOUND HOW THE BLOT GOT OUT!
I KNOW, BUT A BUNCH OF OLD SEA MAPS AND A BOOK ON SHIP MODELS ISN'T MUCH OF A LEAD TO GO ON!
WHEW! THESE CELLS SURE GET STUFFY, DON'T THEY?
HUH?
WAIT A MINUTE, DONALD... THAT'S IT! WE FORGOT TO CHECK THE AIR-CONDITIONING VENTILATOR...
?
OF COURSE! THE BLOT USED SOAP TO ENABLE HIM TO SLIP THROUGH THIS VENT!
BUT WHERE DOES IT GO?
I DUNNO, BUT THAT'S WHAT WE'LL FIND OUT! COME ON!
DO I HAVE TO?

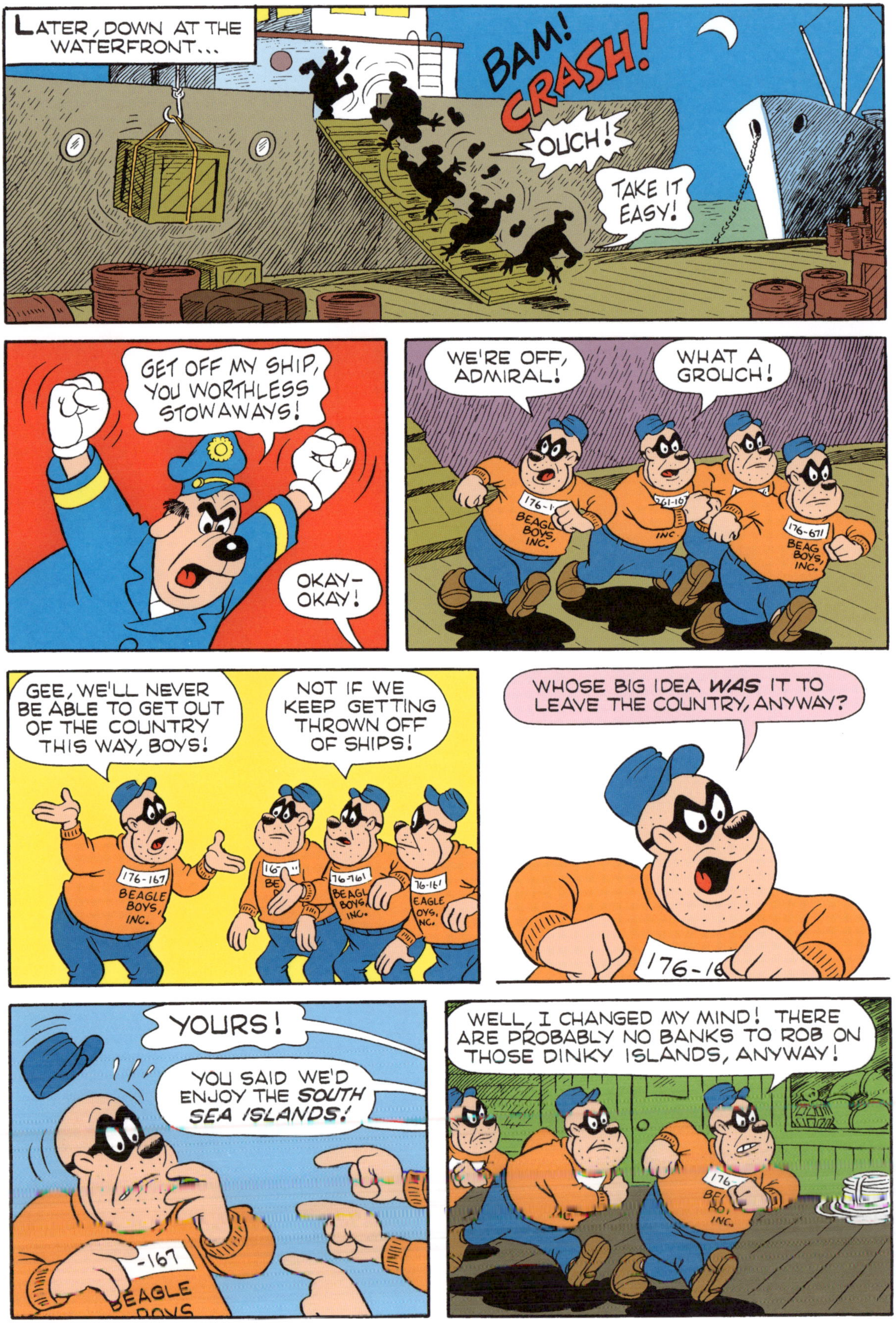
LATER, DOWN AT THE WATERFRONT...
BAM!
CRASH!
OUCH!
TAKE IT EASY!
GET OFF MY SHIP, YOU WORTHLESS STOWAWAYS!
OKAY-OKAY!
WE'RE OFF, ADMIRAL!
WHAT A GROUCH!
GEE, WE'LL NEVER BE ABLE TO GET OUT OF THE COUNTRY THIS WAY, BOYS!
NOT IF WE KEEP GETTING THROWN OFF OF SHIPS!
WHOSE BIG IDEA *WAS* IT TO LEAVE THE COUNTRY, ANYWAY?
YOURS!
YOU SAID WE'D ENJOY THE *SOUTH SEA ISLANDS!*
WELL, I CHANGED MY MIND! THERE ARE PROBABLY NO BANKS TO ROB ON THOSE DINKY ISLANDS, ANYWAY!

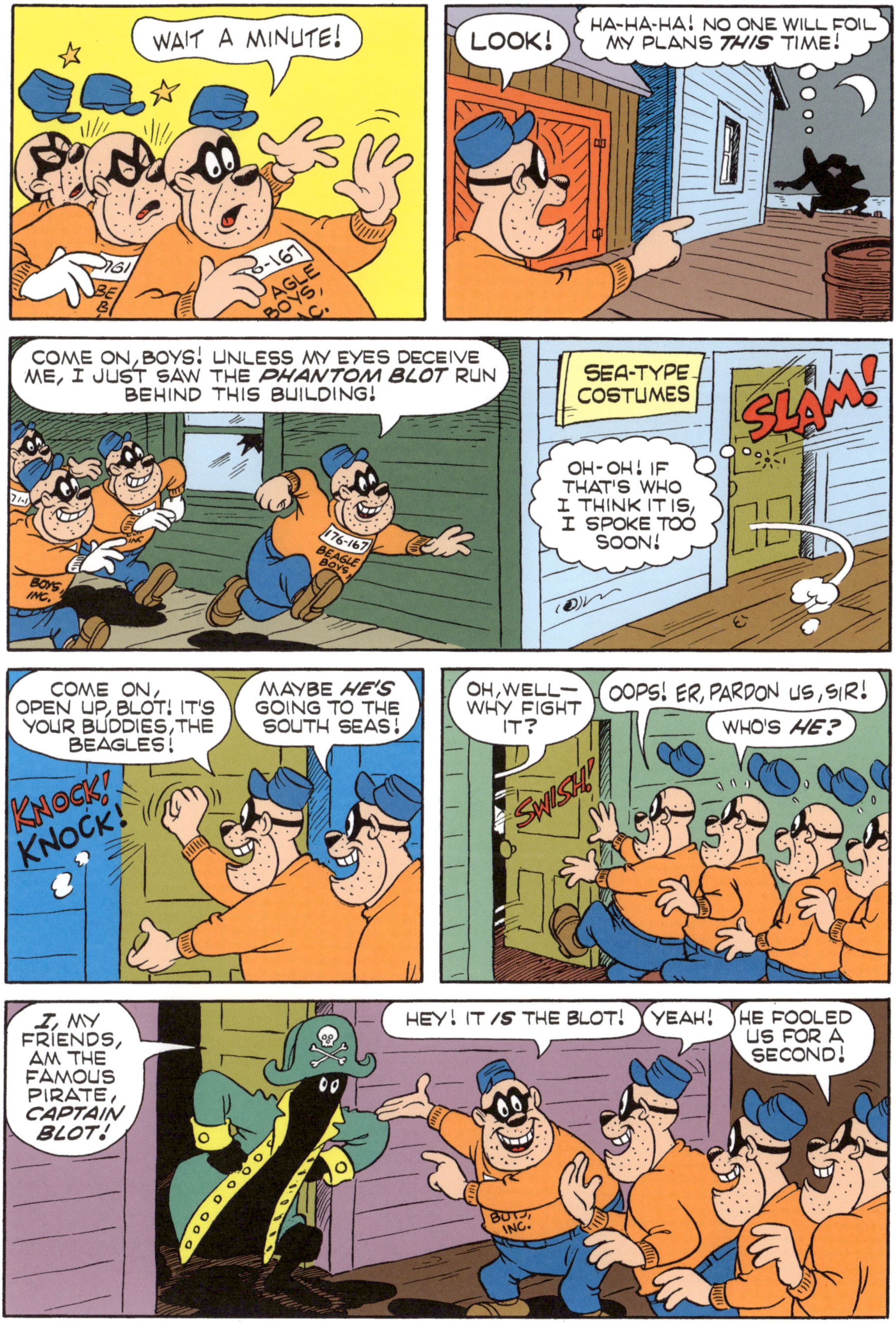
WAIT A MINUTE!
176-167
BEAGLE BOYS, INC.
LOOK!
HA-HA-HA! NO ONE WILL FOIL MY PLANS *THIS* TIME!
COME ON, BOYS! UNLESS MY EYES DECEIVE ME, I JUST SAW THE *PHANTOM BLOT* RUN BEHIND THIS BUILDING!
176-167
BEAGLE BOYS
SEA-TYPE COSTUMES
SLAM!
OH-OH! IF THAT'S WHO I THINK IT IS, I SPOKE TOO SOON!
COME ON, OPEN UP, BLOT! IT'S YOUR BUDDIES, THE BEAGLES!
MAYBE *HE'S* GOING TO THE SOUTH SEAS!
KNOCK! KNOCK!
OH, WELL— WHY FIGHT IT?
SWISH!
OOPS! ER, PARDON US, SIR!
WHO'S *HE?*
I, MY FRIENDS, AM THE FAMOUS PIRATE, *CAPTAIN BLOT*!
HEY! IT *IS* THE BLOT!
YEAH!
HE FOOLED US FOR A SECOND!

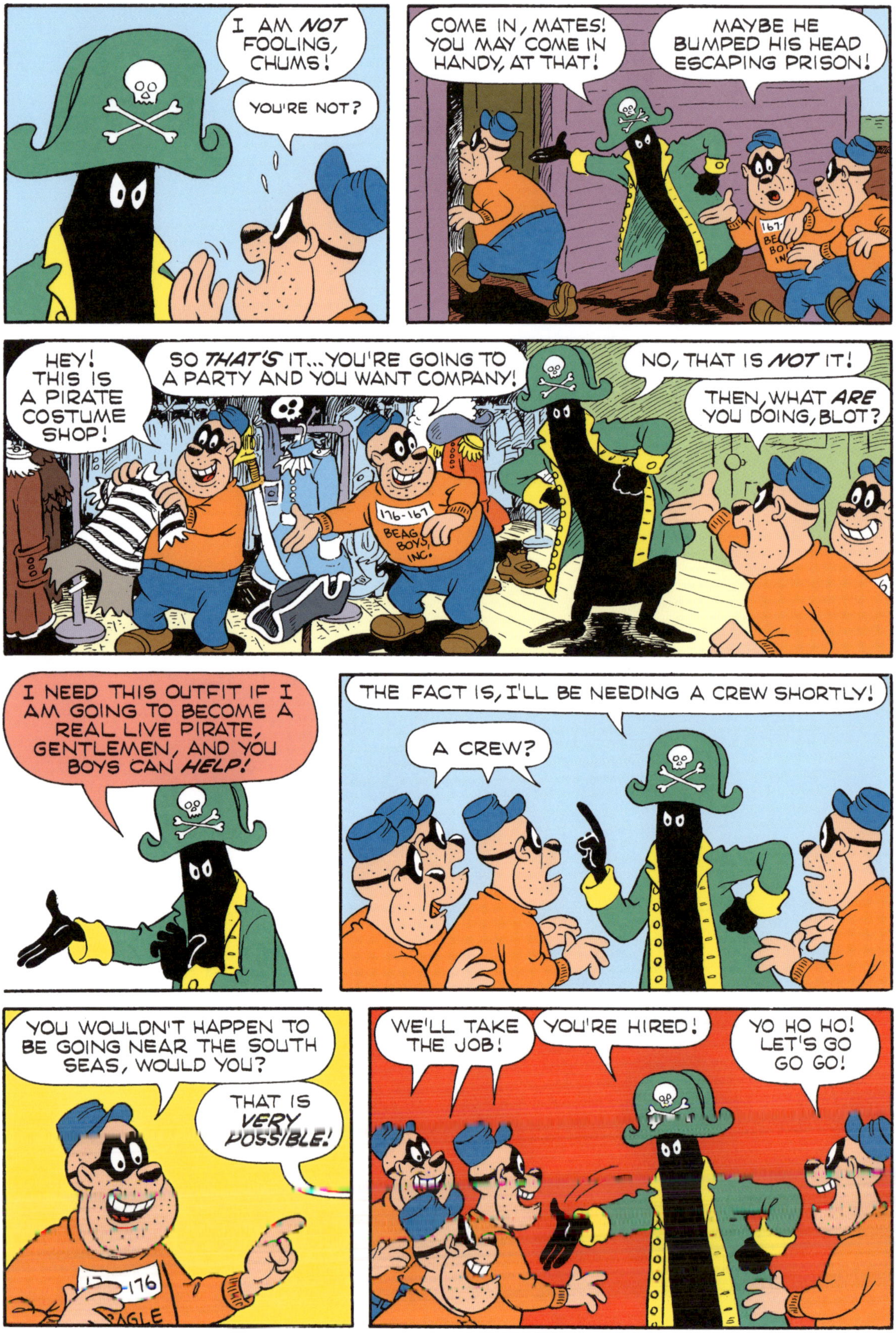
I AM NOT FOOLING, CHUMS!
YOU'RE NOT?
COME IN, MATES! YOU MAY COME IN HANDY, AT THAT!
MAYBE HE BUMPED HIS HEAD ESCAPING PRISON!
HEY! THIS IS A PIRATE COSTUME SHOP!
SO THAT'S IT... YOU'RE GOING TO A PARTY AND YOU WANT COMPANY!
176-167
BEAG BOYS, INC.
NO, THAT IS NOT IT!
THEN, WHAT ARE YOU DOING, BLOT?
I NEED THIS OUTFIT IF I AM GOING TO BECOME A REAL LIVE PIRATE, GENTLEMEN, AND YOU BOYS CAN HELP!
THE FACT IS, I'LL BE NEEDING A CREW SHORTLY!
A CREW?
YOU WOULDN'T HAPPEN TO BE GOING NEAR THE SOUTH SEAS, WOULD YOU?
THAT IS VERY POSSIBLE!
WE'LL TAKE THE JOB!
YOU'RE HIRED!
YO HO HO! LET'S GO GO GO!

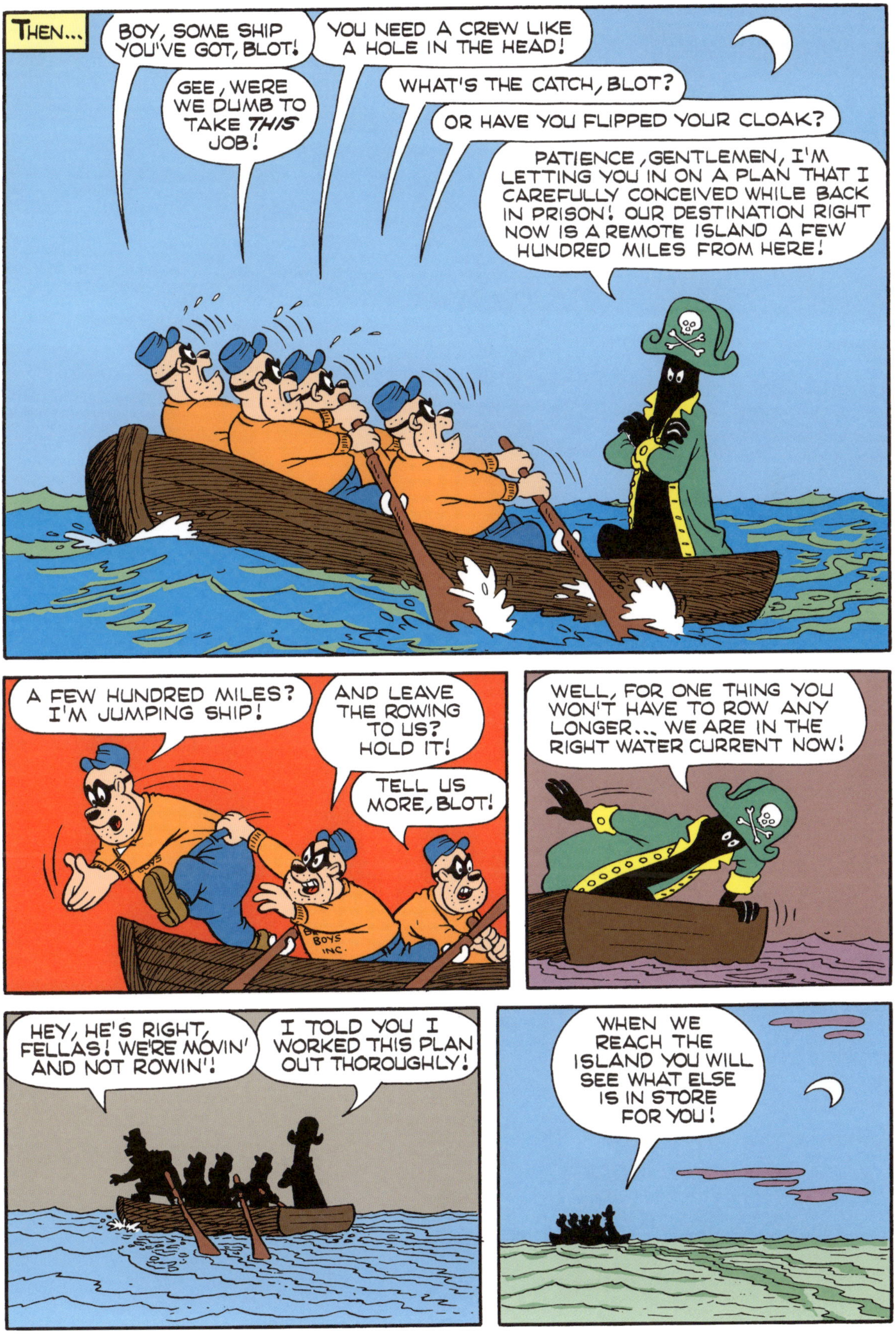
THEN...
BOY, SOME SHIP YOU'VE GOT, BLOT!
GEE, WERE WE DUMB TO TAKE *THIS* JOB!
YOU NEED A CREW LIKE A HOLE IN THE HEAD!
WHAT'S THE CATCH, BLOT?
OR HAVE YOU FLIPPED YOUR CLOAK?
PATIENCE, GENTLEMEN, I'M LETTING YOU IN ON A PLAN THAT I CAREFULLY CONCEIVED WHILE BACK IN PRISON! OUR DESTINATION RIGHT NOW IS A REMOTE ISLAND A FEW HUNDRED MILES FROM HERE!
A FEW HUNDRED MILES? I'M JUMPING SHIP!
AND LEAVE THE ROWING TO US? HOLD IT!
TELL US MORE, BLOT!
BOYS INC.
WELL, FOR ONE THING YOU WON'T HAVE TO ROW ANY LONGER... WE ARE IN THE RIGHT WATER CURRENT NOW!
HEY, HE'S RIGHT, FELLAS! WE'RE MOVIN' AND NOT ROWIN'!
I TOLD YOU I WORKED THIS PLAN OUT THOROUGHLY!
WHEN WE REACH THE ISLAND YOU WILL SEE WHAT ELSE IS IN STORE FOR YOU!

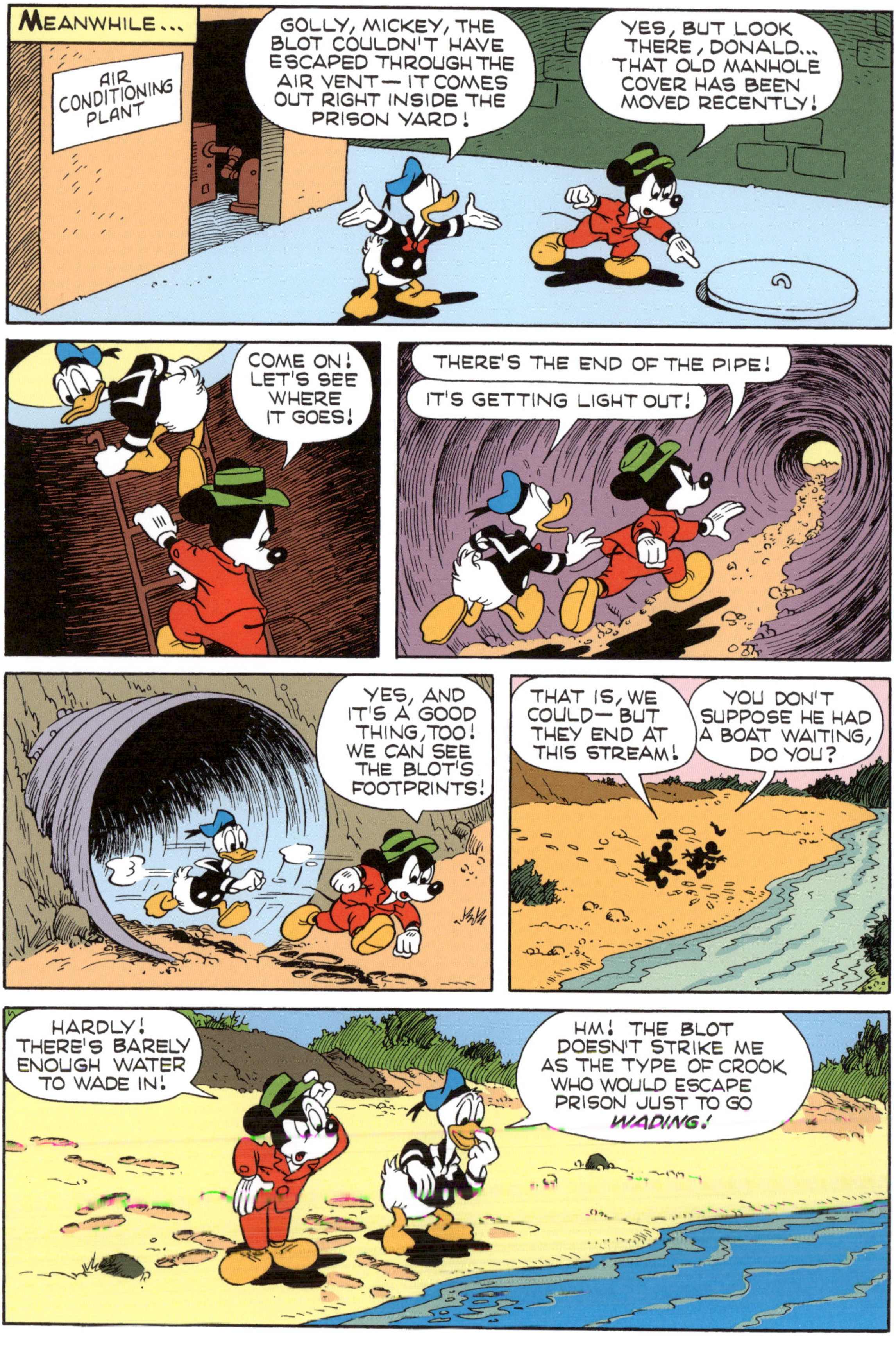

MEANWHILE...
AIR CONDITIONING PLANT
GOLLY, MICKEY, THE BLOT COULDN'T HAVE ESCAPED THROUGH THE AIR VENT — IT COMES OUT RIGHT INSIDE THE PRISON YARD!
YES, BUT LOOK THERE, DONALD... THAT OLD MANHOLE COVER HAS BEEN MOVED RECENTLY!
COME ON! LET'S SEE WHERE IT GOES!
THERE'S THE END OF THE PIPE!
IT'S GETTING LIGHT OUT!
YES, AND IT'S A GOOD THING, TOO! WE CAN SEE THE BLOT'S FOOTPRINTS!
THAT IS, WE COULD— BUT THEY END AT THIS STREAM!
YOU DON'T SUPPOSE HE HAD A BOAT WAITING, DO YOU?
HARDLY! THERE'S BARELY ENOUGH WATER TO WADE IN!
HM! THE BLOT DOESN'T STRIKE ME AS THE TYPE OF CROOK WHO WOULD ESCAPE PRISON JUST TO GO *WADING!*

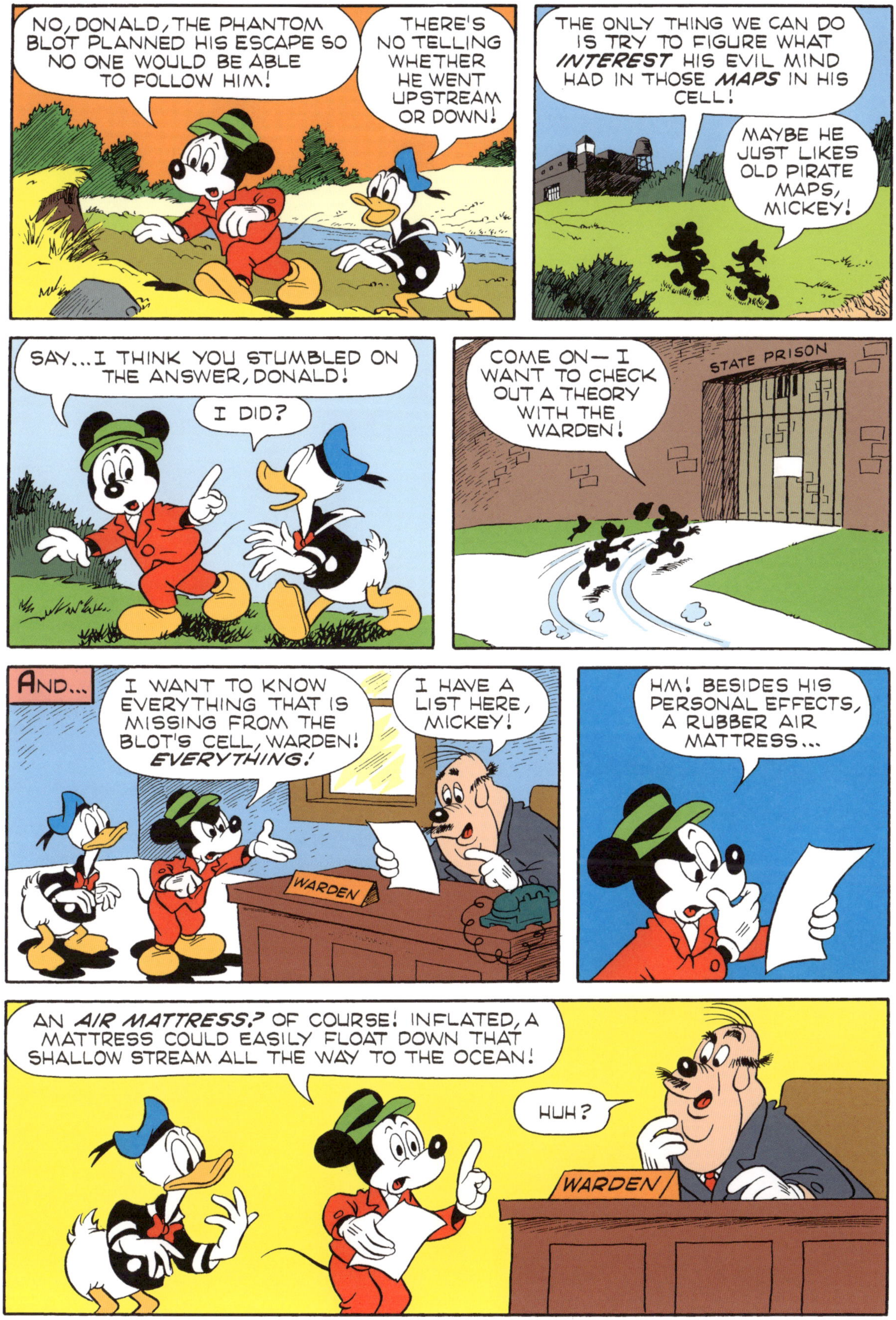
NO, DONALD, THE PHANTOM BLOT PLANNED HIS ESCAPE SO NO ONE WOULD BE ABLE TO FOLLOW HIM!
THERE'S NO TELLING WHETHER HE WENT UPSTREAM OR DOWN!
THE ONLY THING WE CAN DO IS TRY TO FIGURE WHAT *INTEREST* HIS EVIL MIND HAD IN THOSE *MAPS* IN HIS CELL!
MAYBE HE JUST LIKES OLD PIRATE MAPS, MICKEY!
SAY...I THINK YOU STUMBLED ON THE ANSWER, DONALD!
I DID?
COME ON— I WANT TO CHECK OUT A THEORY WITH THE WARDEN!
STATE PRISON
AND...
I WANT TO KNOW EVERYTHING THAT IS MISSING FROM THE BLOT'S CELL, WARDEN! *EVERYTHING!*
I HAVE A LIST HERE, MICKEY!
WARDEN
HM! BESIDES HIS PERSONAL EFFECTS, A RUBBER AIR MATTRESS...
AN *AIR MATTRESS?* OF COURSE! INFLATED, A MATTRESS COULD EASILY FLOAT DOWN THAT SHALLOW STREAM ALL THE WAY TO THE OCEAN!
HUH?
WARDEN

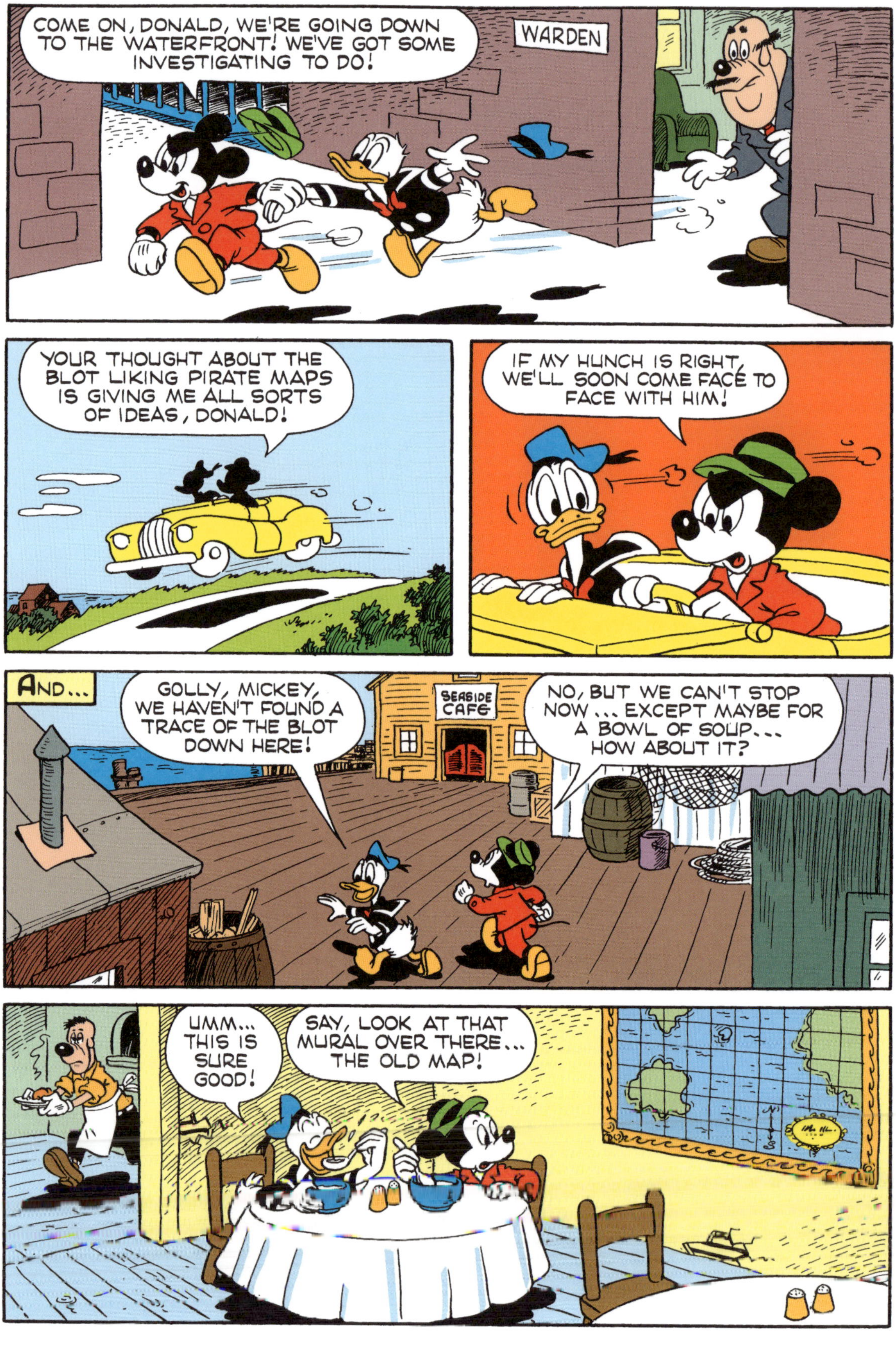
COME ON, DONALD, WE'RE GOING DOWN TO THE WATERFRONT! WE'VE GOT SOME INVESTIGATING TO DO!
WARDEN
YOUR THOUGHT ABOUT THE BLOT LIKING PIRATE MAPS IS GIVING ME ALL SORTS OF IDEAS, DONALD!
IF MY HUNCH IS RIGHT, WE'LL SOON COME FACE TO FACE WITH HIM!
AND...
GOLLY, MICKEY, WE HAVEN'T FOUND A TRACE OF THE BLOT DOWN HERE!
SEASIDE CAFE
NO, BUT WE CAN'T STOP NOW... EXCEPT MAYBE FOR A BOWL OF SOUP... HOW ABOUT IT?
UMM... THIS IS SURE GOOD!
SAY, LOOK AT THAT MURAL OVER THERE... THE OLD MAP!

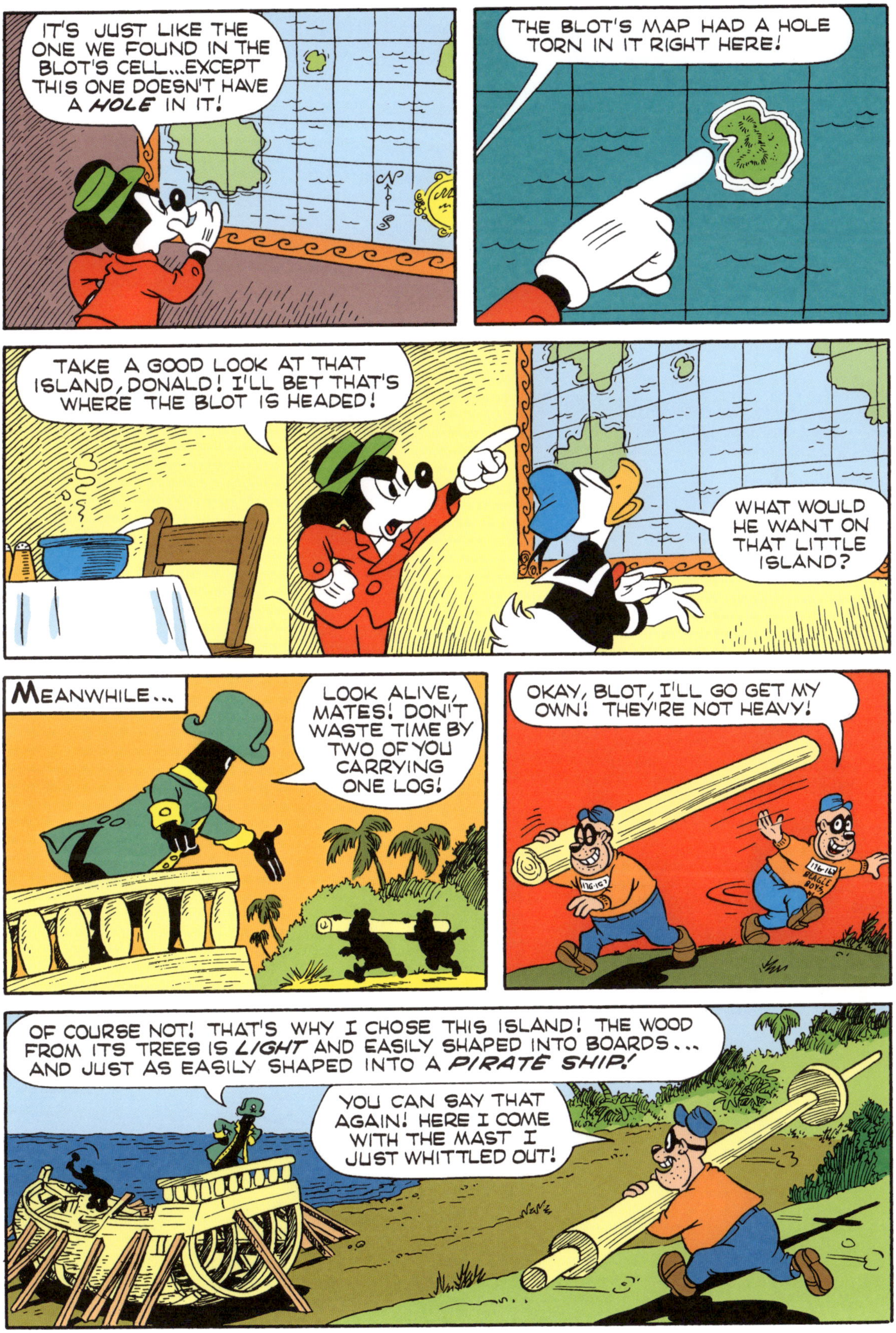

IT'S JUST LIKE THE ONE WE FOUND IN THE BLOT'S CELL...EXCEPT THIS ONE DOESN'T HAVE A *HOLE* IN IT!
THE BLOT'S MAP HAD A HOLE TORN IN IT RIGHT HERE!
TAKE A GOOD LOOK AT THAT ISLAND, DONALD! I'LL BET THAT'S WHERE THE BLOT IS HEADED!
WHAT WOULD HE WANT ON THAT LITTLE ISLAND?
MEANWHILE...
LOOK ALIVE, MATES! DON'T WASTE TIME BY TWO OF YOU CARRYING ONE LOG!
OKAY, BLOT, I'LL GO GET MY OWN! THEY'RE NOT HEAVY!
176-167
176-167
BEAGLE BOYS
OF COURSE NOT! THAT'S WHY I CHOSE THIS ISLAND! THE WOOD FROM ITS TREES IS *LIGHT* AND EASILY SHAPED INTO BOARDS... AND JUST AS EASILY SHAPED INTO A *PIRATE SHIP!*
YOU CAN SAY THAT AGAIN! HERE I COME WITH THE MAST I JUST WHITTLED OUT!

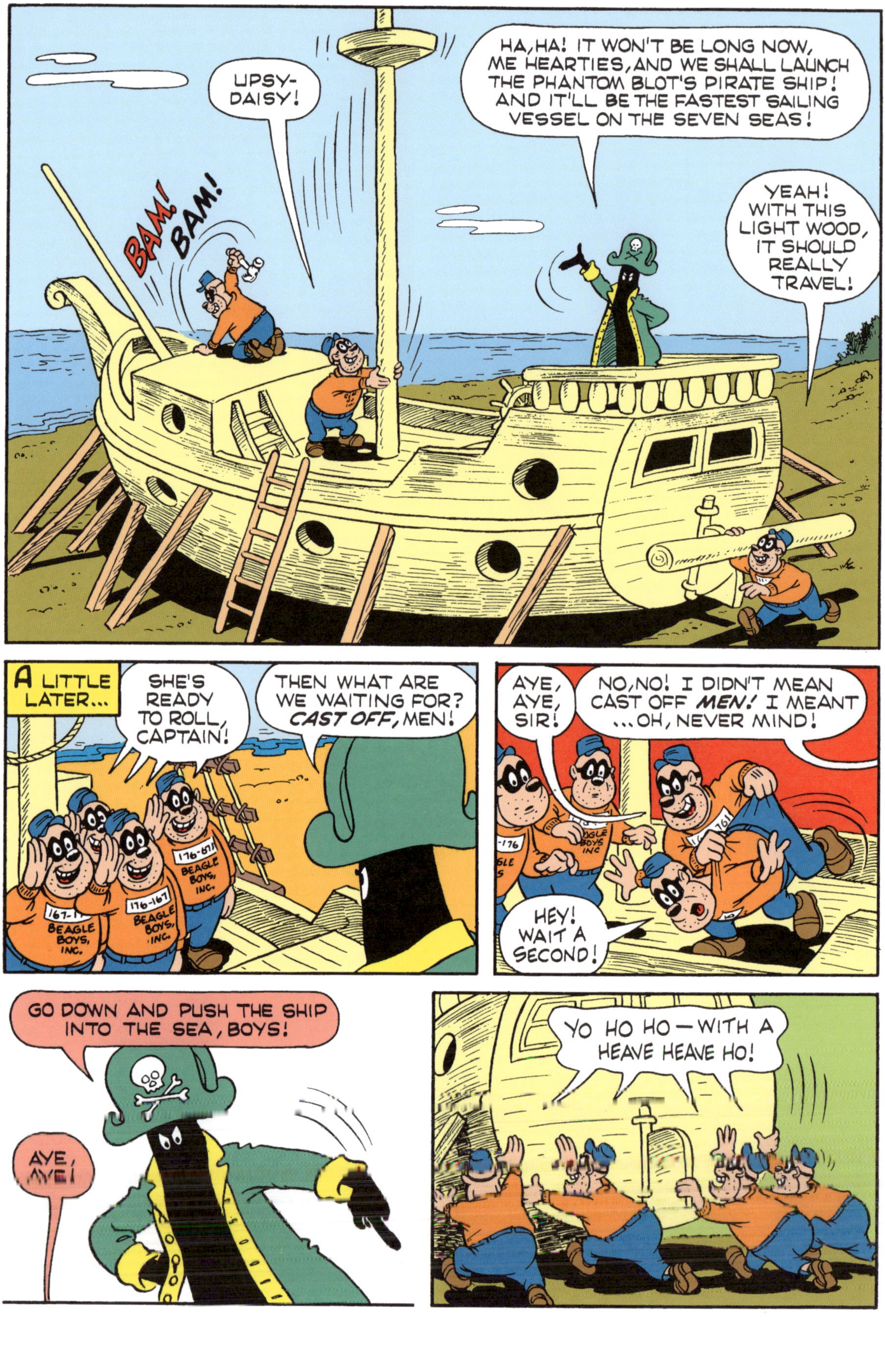
BAM!
BAM!
UPSY-DAISY!
HA, HA! IT WON'T BE LONG NOW, ME HEARTIES, AND WE SHALL LAUNCH THE PHANTOM BLOT'S PIRATE SHIP! AND IT'LL BE THE FASTEST SAILING VESSEL ON THE SEVEN SEAS!
YEAH! WITH THIS LIGHT WOOD, IT SHOULD REALLY TRAVEL!
A LITTLE LATER...
SHE'S READY TO ROLL, CAPTAIN!
THEN WHAT ARE WE WAITING FOR? *CAST OFF*, MEN!
176-167
BEAGLE BOYS, INC.
AYE, AYE, SIR!
NO, NO! I DIDN'T MEAN CAST OFF *MEN!* I MEANT ...OH, NEVER MIND!
HEY! WAIT A SECOND!
GO DOWN AND PUSH THE SHIP INTO THE SEA, BOYS!
AYE, AYE!
YO HO HO — WITH A HEAVE HEAVE HO!

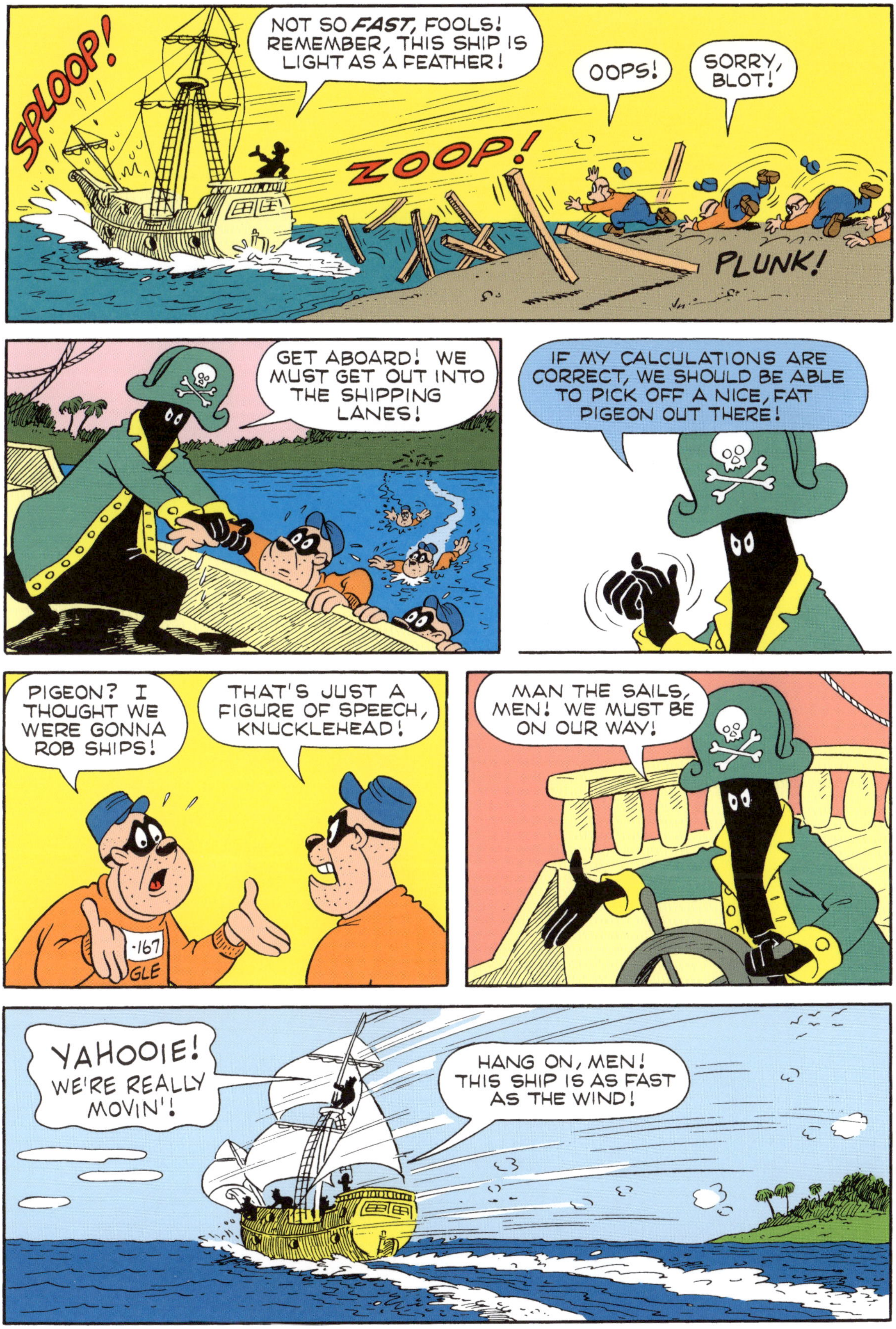
SPLOOP!
NOT SO FAST, FOOLS! REMEMBER, THIS SHIP IS LIGHT AS A FEATHER!
ZOOP!
OOPS!
SORRY, BLOT!
PLUNK!
GET ABOARD! WE MUST GET OUT INTO THE SHIPPING LANES!
IF MY CALCULATIONS ARE CORRECT, WE SHOULD BE ABLE TO PICK OFF A NICE, FAT PIGEON OUT THERE!
PIGEON? I THOUGHT WE WERE GONNA ROB SHIPS!
THAT'S JUST A FIGURE OF SPEECH, KNUCKLEHEAD!
-167
GLE
MAN THE SAILS, MEN! WE MUST BE ON OUR WAY!
YAHOOIE! WE'RE REALLY MOVIN'!
HANG ON, MEN! THIS SHIP IS AS FAST AS THE WIND!

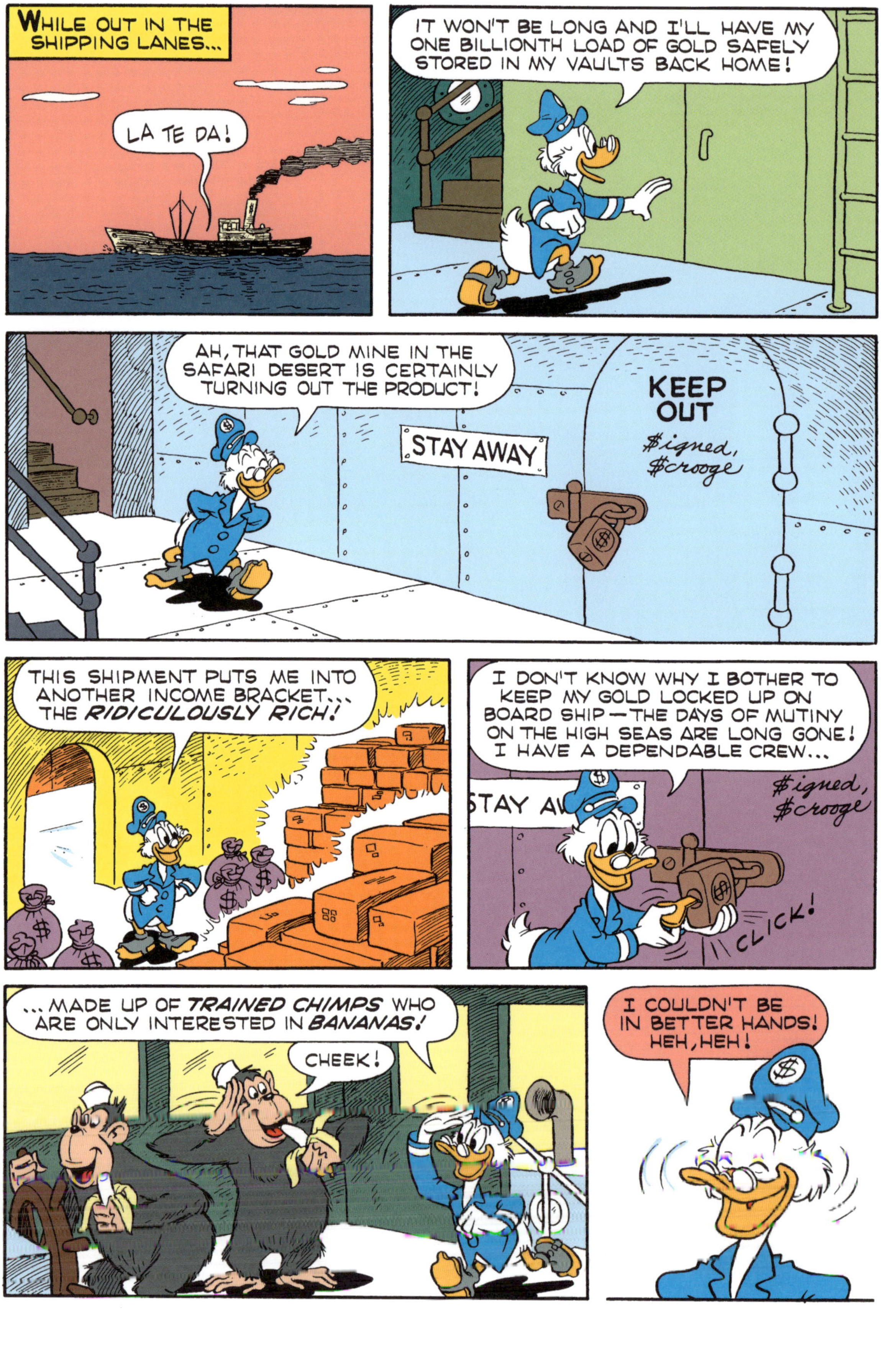
WHILE OUT IN THE SHIPPING LANES...
LA TE DA!
IT WON'T BE LONG AND I'LL HAVE MY ONE BILLIONTH LOAD OF GOLD SAFELY STORED IN MY VAULTS BACK HOME!
AH, THAT GOLD MINE IN THE SAFARI DESERT IS CERTAINLY TURNING OUT THE PRODUCT!
STAY AWAY
KEEP OUT
$igned, $crooge
THIS SHIPMENT PUTS ME INTO ANOTHER INCOME BRACKET... THE *RIDICULOUSLY RICH!*
I DON'T KNOW WHY I BOTHER TO KEEP MY GOLD LOCKED UP ON BOARD SHIP—THE DAYS OF MUTINY ON THE HIGH SEAS ARE LONG GONE! I HAVE A DEPENDABLE CREW...
$igned, $crooge
CLICK!
...MADE UP OF *TRAINED CHIMPS* WHO ARE ONLY INTERESTED IN *BANANAS!*
CHEEK!
I COULDN'T BE IN BETTER HANDS! HEH, HEH!

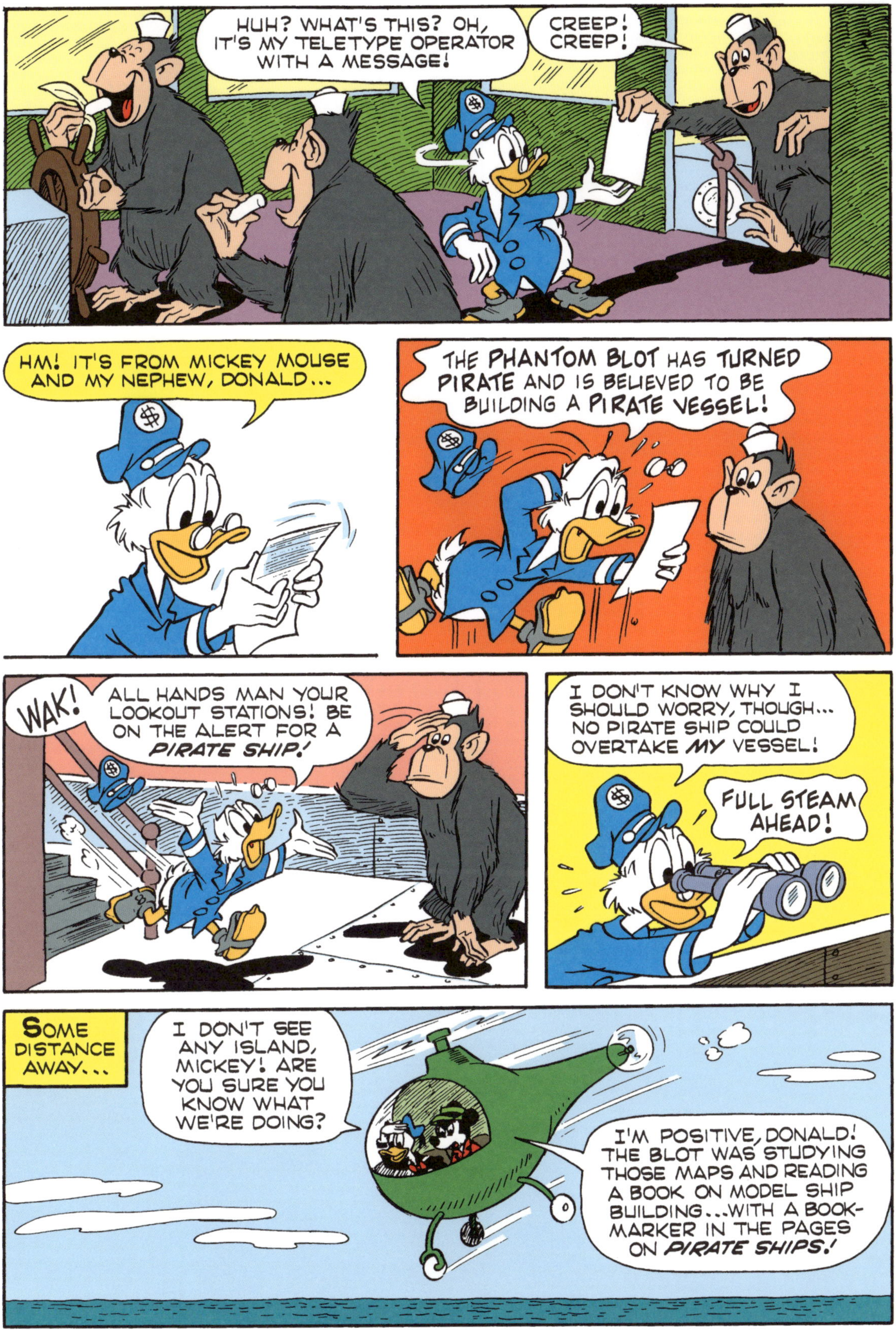
HUH? WHAT'S THIS? OH, IT'S MY TELETYPE OPERATOR WITH A MESSAGE!
CREEP! CREEP!
HM! IT'S FROM MICKEY MOUSE AND MY NEPHEW, DONALD...
THE PHANTOM BLOT HAS TURNED PIRATE AND IS BELIEVED TO BE BUILDING A PIRATE VESSEL!
WAK!
ALL HANDS MAN YOUR LOOKOUT STATIONS! BE ON THE ALERT FOR A PIRATE SHIP!
I DON'T KNOW WHY I SHOULD WORRY, THOUGH... NO PIRATE SHIP COULD OVERTAKE MY VESSEL!
FULL STEAM AHEAD!
SOME DISTANCE AWAY...
I DON'T SEE ANY ISLAND, MICKEY! ARE YOU SURE YOU KNOW WHAT WE'RE DOING?
I'M POSITIVE, DONALD! THE BLOT WAS STUDYING THOSE MAPS AND READING A BOOK ON MODEL SHIP BUILDING...WITH A BOOK-MARKER IN THE PAGES ON PIRATE SHIPS!

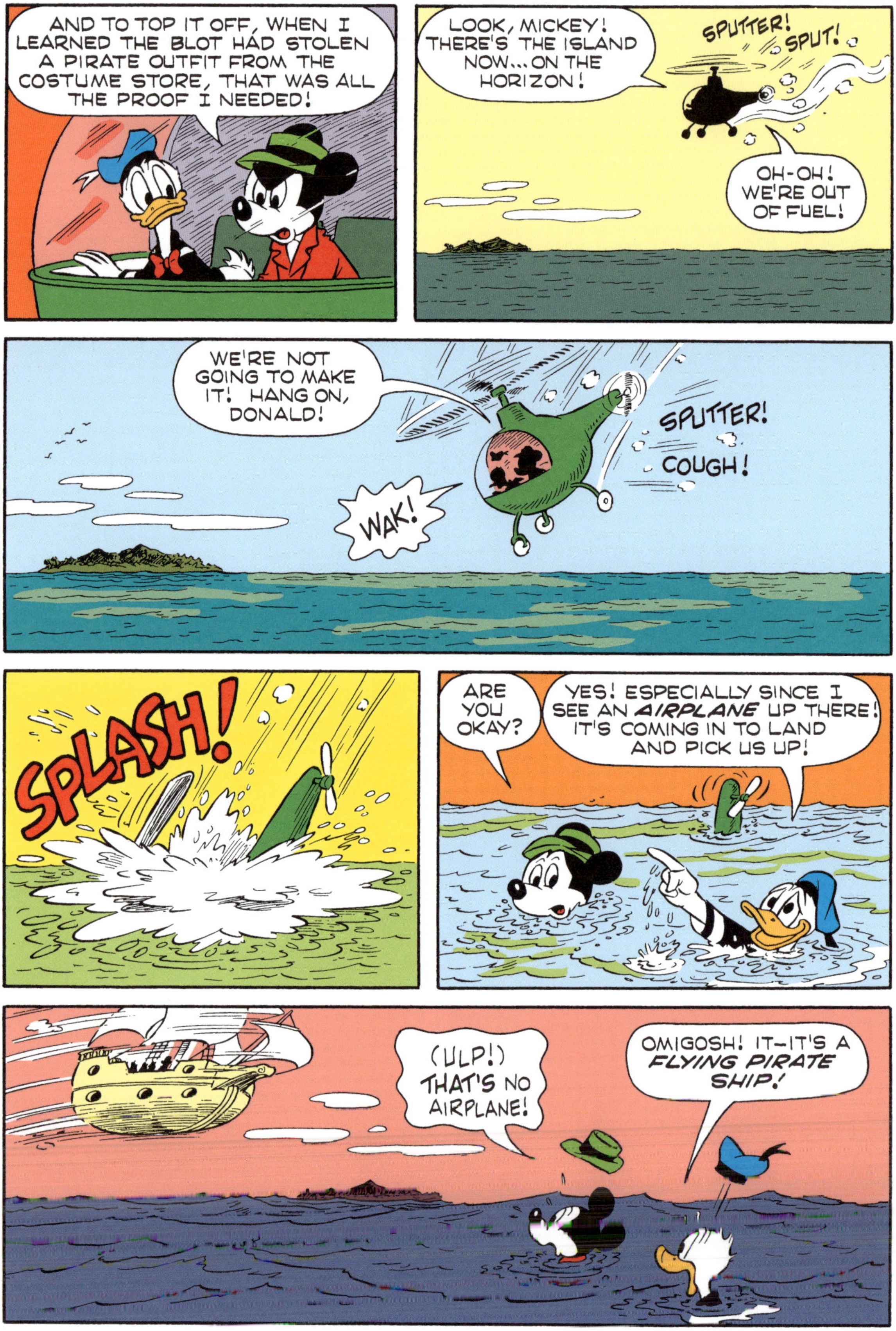
AND TO TOP IT OFF, WHEN I LEARNED THE BLOT HAD STOLEN A PIRATE OUTFIT FROM THE COSTUME STORE, THAT WAS ALL THE PROOF I NEEDED!
LOOK, MICKEY! THERE'S THE ISLAND NOW...ON THE HORIZON!
SPUTTER! SPUT!
OH-OH! WE'RE OUT OF FUEL!
WE'RE NOT GOING TO MAKE IT! HANG ON, DONALD!
SPUTTER!
COUGH!
WAK!
SPLASH!
ARE YOU OKAY?
YES! ESPECIALLY SINCE I SEE AN AIRPLANE UP THERE! IT'S COMING IN TO LAND AND PICK US UP!
(ULP!) THAT'S NO AIRPLANE!
OMIGOSH! IT-IT'S A FLYING PIRATE SHIP!

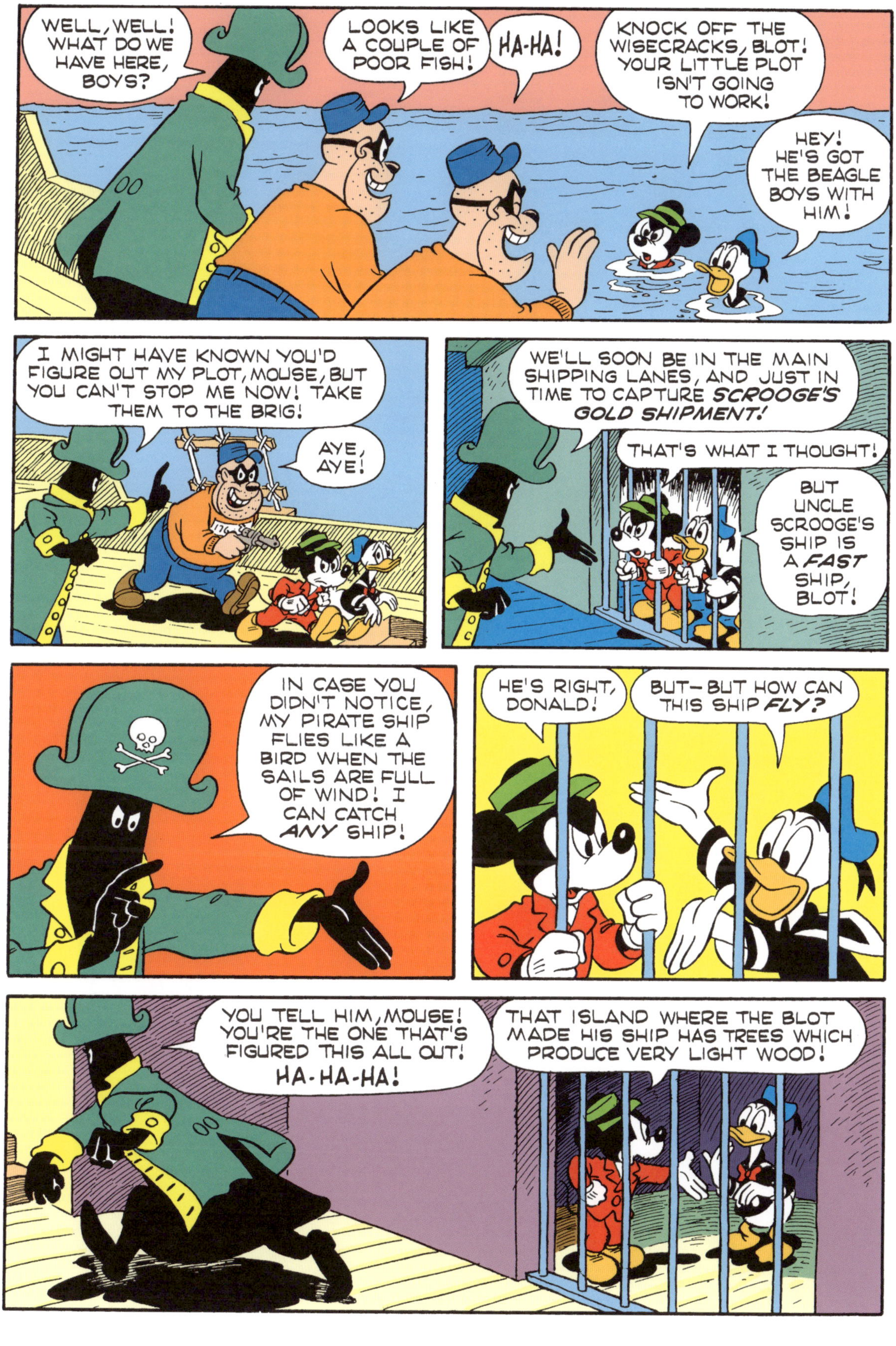
WELL, WELL! WHAT DO WE HAVE HERE, BOYS?
LOOKS LIKE A COUPLE OF POOR FISH!
HA-HA!
KNOCK OFF THE WISECRACKS, BLOT! YOUR LITTLE PLOT ISN'T GOING TO WORK!
HEY! HE'S GOT THE BEAGLE BOYS WITH HIM!
I MIGHT HAVE KNOWN YOU'D FIGURE OUT MY PLOT, MOUSE, BUT YOU CAN'T STOP ME NOW! TAKE THEM TO THE BRIG!
AYE, AYE!
WE'LL SOON BE IN THE MAIN SHIPPING LANES, AND JUST IN TIME TO CAPTURE *SCROOGE'S GOLD SHIPMENT!*
THAT'S WHAT I THOUGHT!
BUT UNCLE SCROOGE'S SHIP IS A *FAST* SHIP, BLOT!
IN CASE YOU DIDN'T NOTICE, MY PIRATE SHIP FLIES LIKE A BIRD WHEN THE SAILS ARE FULL OF WIND! I CAN CATCH *ANY* SHIP!
HE'S RIGHT, DONALD!
BUT—BUT HOW CAN THIS SHIP *FLY?*
YOU TELL HIM, MOUSE! YOU'RE THE ONE THAT'S FIGURED THIS ALL OUT! HA-HA-HA!
THAT ISLAND WHERE THE BLOT MADE HIS SHIP HAS TREES WHICH PRODUCE VERY LIGHT WOOD!

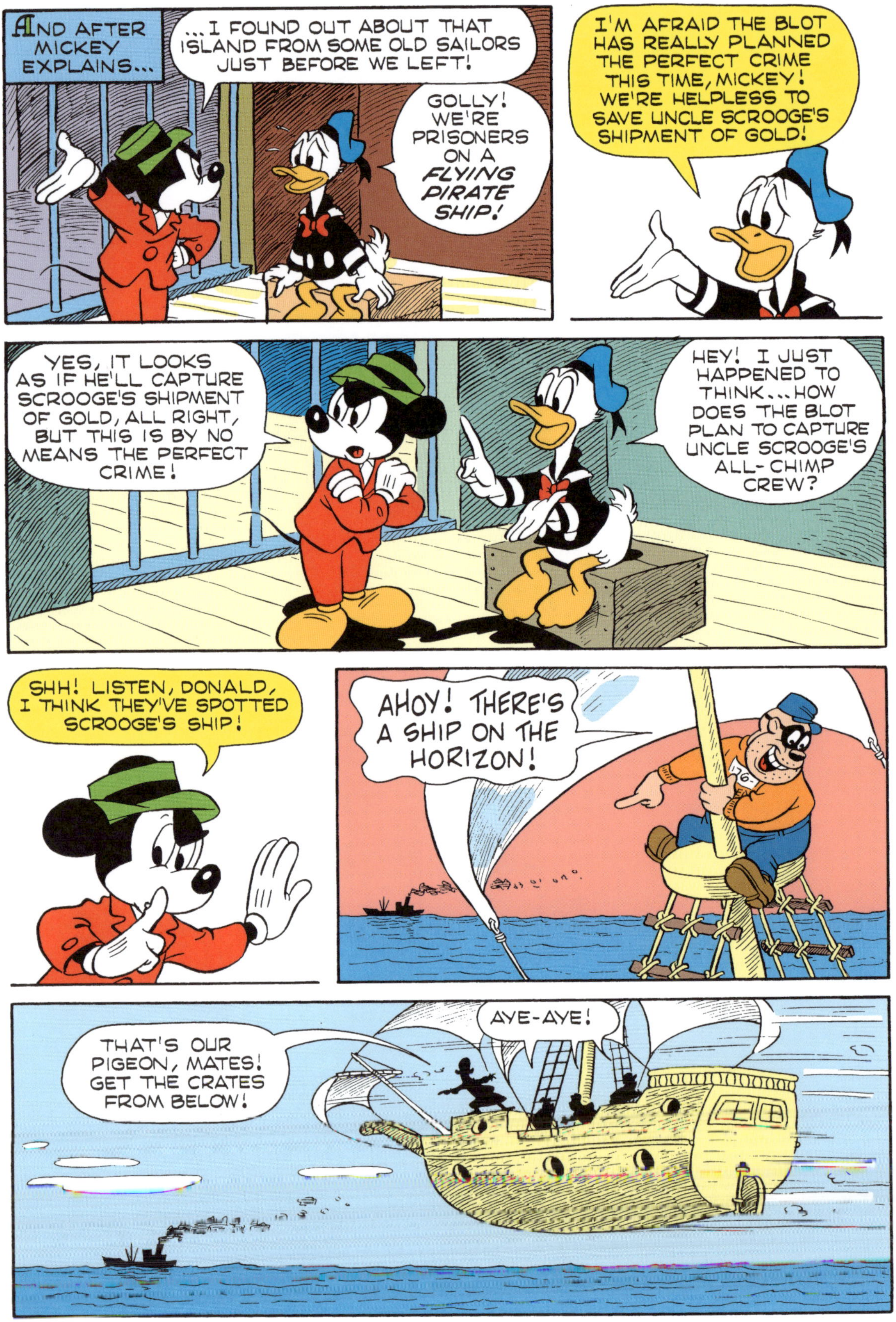
AND AFTER MICKEY EXPLAINS...
...I FOUND OUT ABOUT THAT ISLAND FROM SOME OLD SAILORS JUST BEFORE WE LEFT!
GOLLY! WE'RE PRISONERS ON A FLYING PIRATE SHIP!
I'M AFRAID THE BLOT HAS REALLY PLANNED THE PERFECT CRIME THIS TIME, MICKEY! WE'RE HELPLESS TO SAVE UNCLE SCROOGE'S SHIPMENT OF GOLD!
YES, IT LOOKS AS IF HE'LL CAPTURE SCROOGE'S SHIPMENT OF GOLD, ALL RIGHT, BUT THIS IS BY NO MEANS THE PERFECT CRIME!
HEY! I JUST HAPPENED TO THINK...HOW DOES THE BLOT PLAN TO CAPTURE UNCLE SCROOGE'S ALL-CHIMP CREW?
SHH! LISTEN, DONALD, I THINK THEY'VE SPOTTED SCROOGE'S SHIP!
AHOY! THERE'S A SHIP ON THE HORIZON!
THAT'S OUR PIGEON, MATES! GET THE CRATES FROM BELOW!
AYE-AYE!

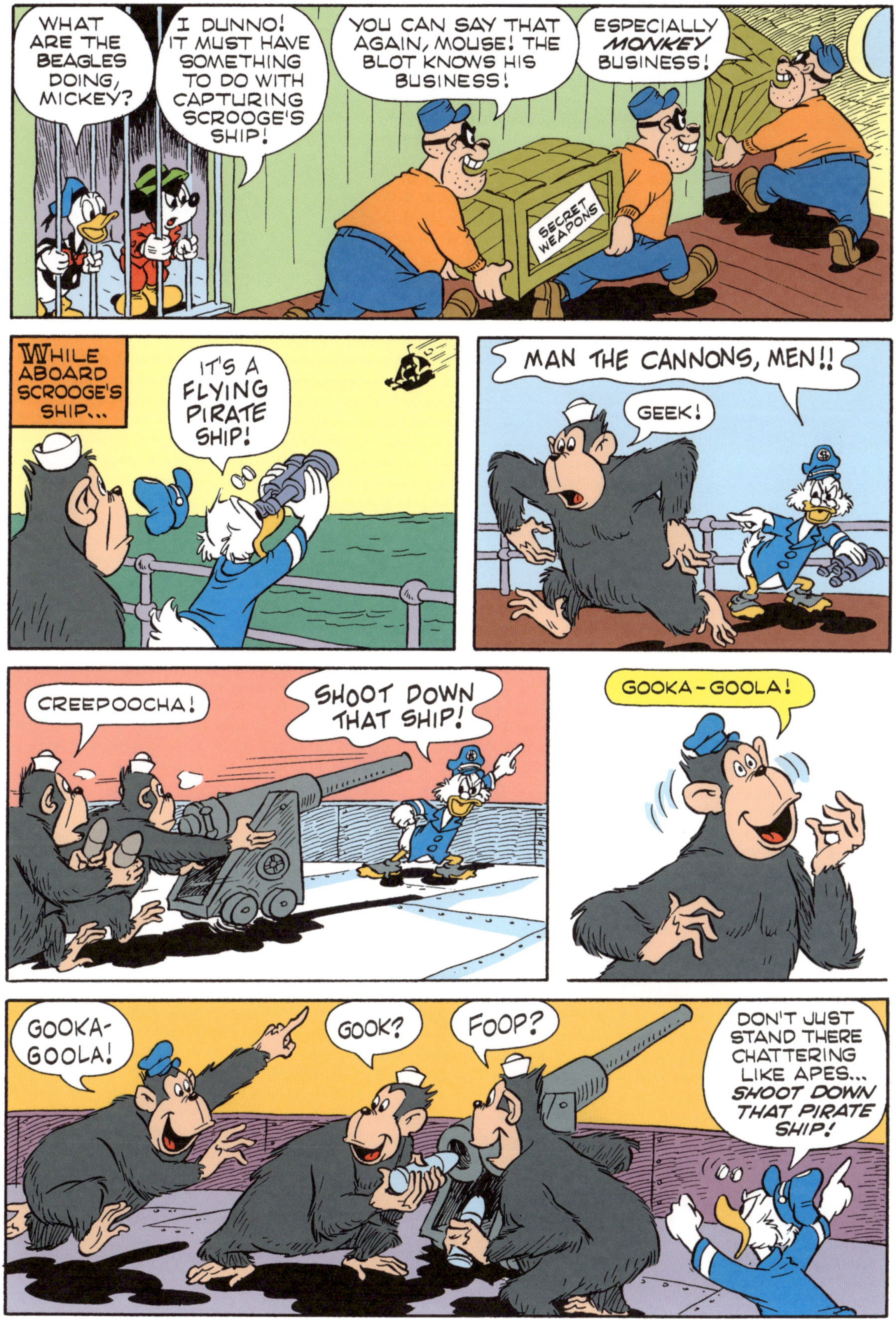

WHAT ARE THE BEAGLES DOING, MICKEY?
I DUNNO! IT MUST HAVE SOMETHING TO DO WITH CAPTURING SCROOGE'S SHIP!
YOU CAN SAY THAT AGAIN, MOUSE! THE BLOT KNOWS HIS BUSINESS!
ESPECIALLY MONKEY BUSINESS!
SECRET WEAPONS
WHILE ABOARD SCROOGE'S SHIP...
IT'S A FLYING PIRATE SHIP!
MAN THE CANNONS, MEN!!
GEEK!
CREEPOOCHA!
SHOOT DOWN THAT SHIP!
GOOKA-GOOLA!
GOOKA-GOOLA!
GOOK?
FOOP?
DON'T JUST STAND THERE CHATTERING LIKE APES... SHOOT DOWN THAT PIRATE SHIP!

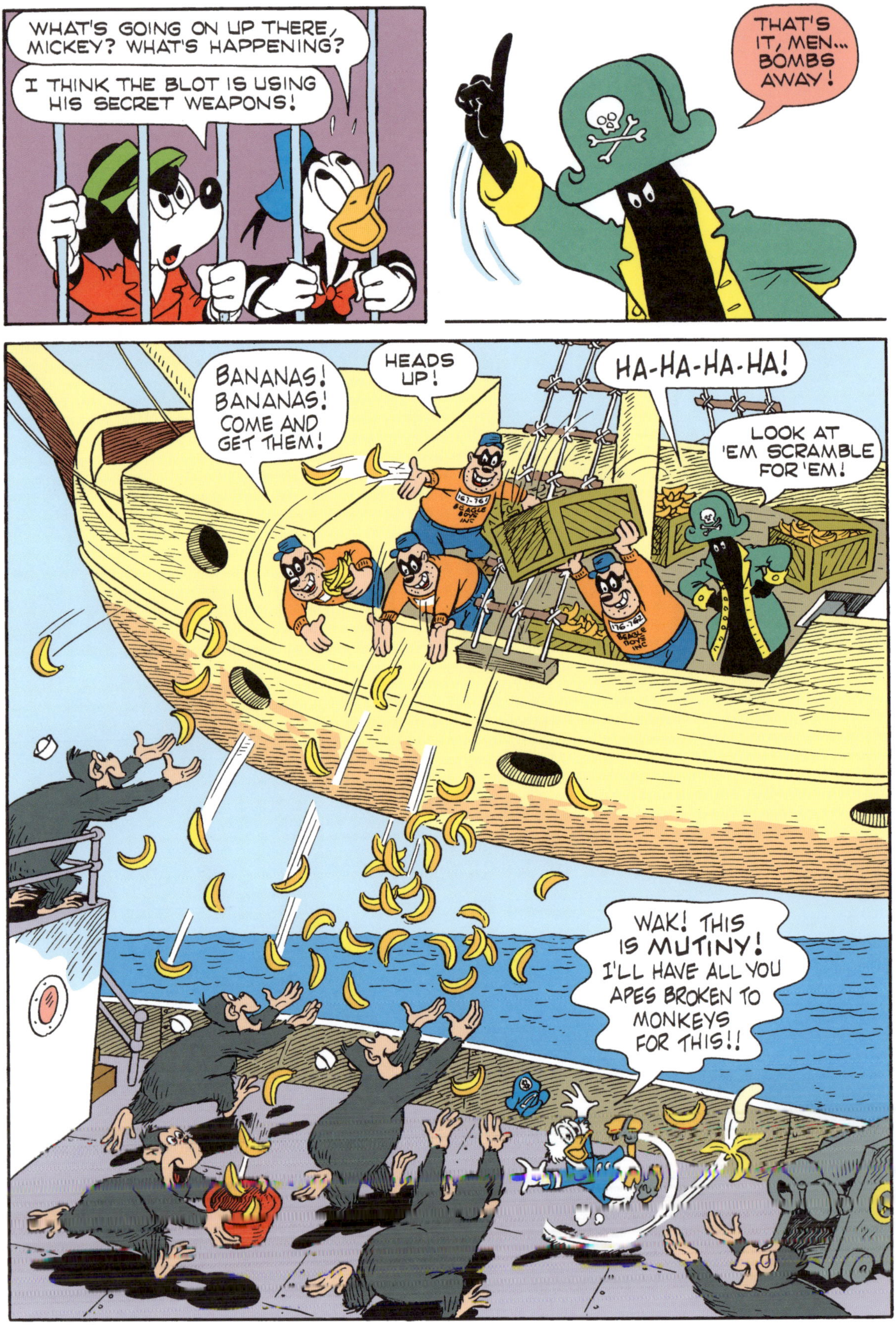
WHAT'S GOING ON UP THERE, MICKEY? WHAT'S HAPPENING?
I THINK THE BLOT IS USING HIS SECRET WEAPONS!
THAT'S IT, MEN... BOMBS AWAY!
BANANAS! BANANAS! COME AND GET THEM!
HEADS UP!
HA-HA-HA-HA!
LOOK AT 'EM SCRAMBLE FOR 'EM!
WAK! THIS IS MUTINY! I'LL HAVE ALL YOU APES BROKEN TO MONKEYS FOR THIS!!

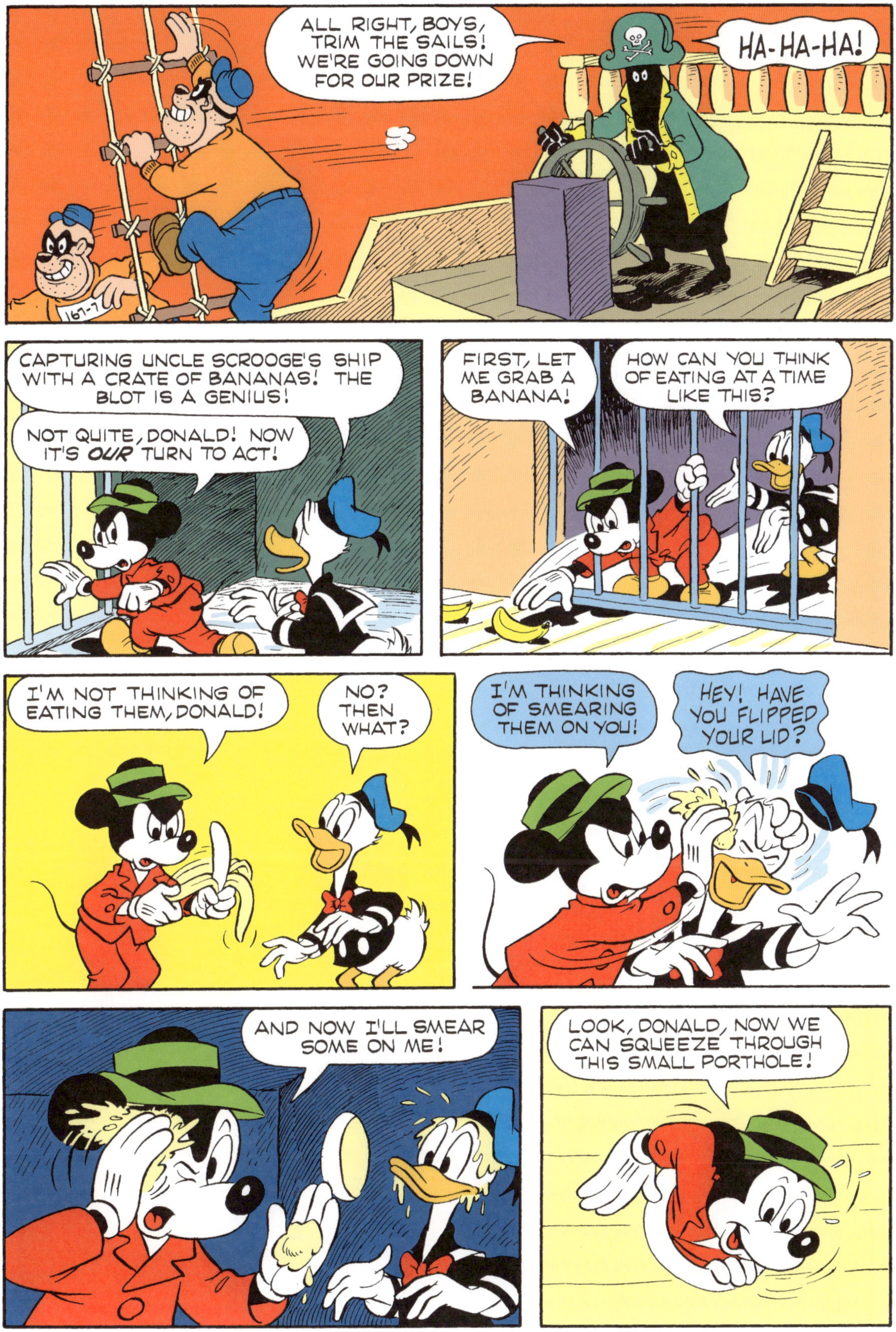
ALL RIGHT, BOYS, TRIM THE SAILS! WE'RE GOING DOWN FOR OUR PRIZE!
HA-HA-HA!
167-7
CAPTURING UNCLE SCROOGE'S SHIP WITH A CRATE OF BANANAS! THE BLOT IS A GENIUS!
NOT QUITE, DONALD! NOW IT'S OUR TURN TO ACT!
FIRST, LET ME GRAB A BANANA!
HOW CAN YOU THINK OF EATING AT A TIME LIKE THIS?
I'M NOT THINKING OF EATING THEM, DONALD!
NO? THEN WHAT?
I'M THINKING OF SMEARING THEM ON YOU!
HEY! HAVE YOU FLIPPED YOUR LID?
AND NOW I'LL SMEAR SOME ON ME!
LOOK, DONALD, NOW WE CAN SQUEEZE THROUGH THIS SMALL PORTHOLE!

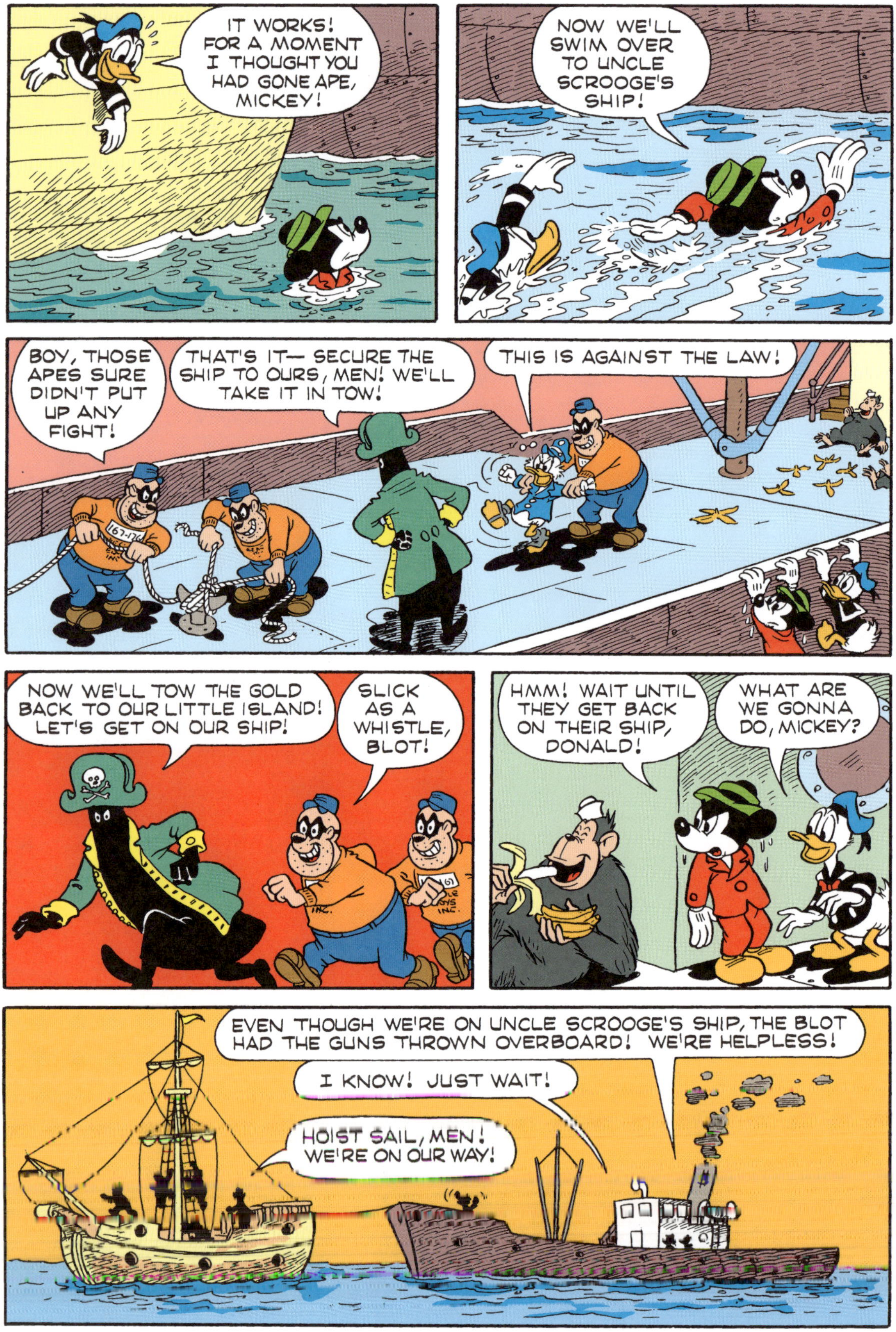

IT WORKS! FOR A MOMENT I THOUGHT YOU HAD GONE APE, MICKEY!
NOW WE'LL SWIM OVER TO UNCLE SCROOGE'S SHIP!
BOY, THOSE APES SURE DIDN'T PUT UP ANY FIGHT!
THAT'S IT— SECURE THE SHIP TO OURS, MEN! WE'LL TAKE IT IN TOW!
THIS IS AGAINST THE LAW!
NOW WE'LL TOW THE GOLD BACK TO OUR LITTLE ISLAND! LET'S GET ON OUR SHIP!
SLICK AS A WHISTLE, BLOT!
HMM! WAIT UNTIL THEY GET BACK ON THEIR SHIP, DONALD!
WHAT ARE WE GONNA DO, MICKEY?
EVEN THOUGH WE'RE ON UNCLE SCROOGE'S SHIP, THE BLOT HAD THE GUNS THROWN OVERBOARD! WE'RE HELPLESS!
I KNOW! JUST WAIT!
HOIST SAIL, MEN! WE'RE ON OUR WAY!

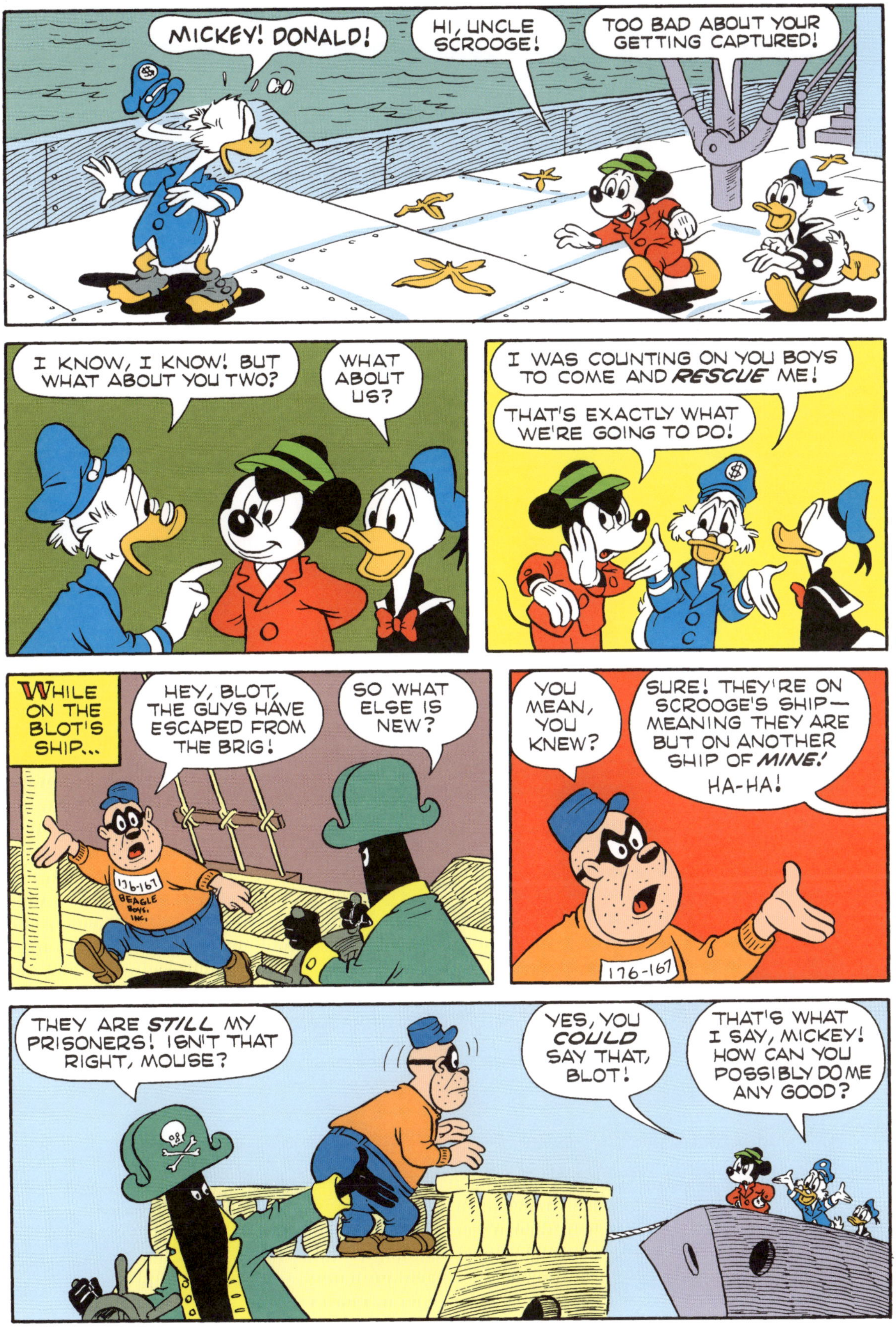
MICKEY! DONALD!
HI, UNCLE SCROOGE!
TOO BAD ABOUT YOUR GETTING CAPTURED!
I KNOW, I KNOW! BUT WHAT ABOUT YOU TWO?
WHAT ABOUT US?
I WAS COUNTING ON YOU BOYS TO COME AND RESCUE ME!
THAT'S EXACTLY WHAT WE'RE GOING TO DO!
WHILE ON THE BLOT'S SHIP...
HEY, BLOT, THE GUYS HAVE ESCAPED FROM THE BRIG!
SO WHAT ELSE IS NEW?
176-167
BEAGLE BOYS, INC.
YOU MEAN, YOU KNEW?
SURE! THEY'RE ON SCROOGE'S SHIP— MEANING THEY ARE BUT ON ANOTHER SHIP OF MINE!
HA-HA!
176-167
THEY ARE STILL MY PRISONERS! ISN'T THAT RIGHT, MOUSE?
YES, YOU COULD SAY THAT, BLOT!
THAT'S WHAT I SAY, MICKEY! HOW CAN YOU POSSIBLY DO ME ANY GOOD?

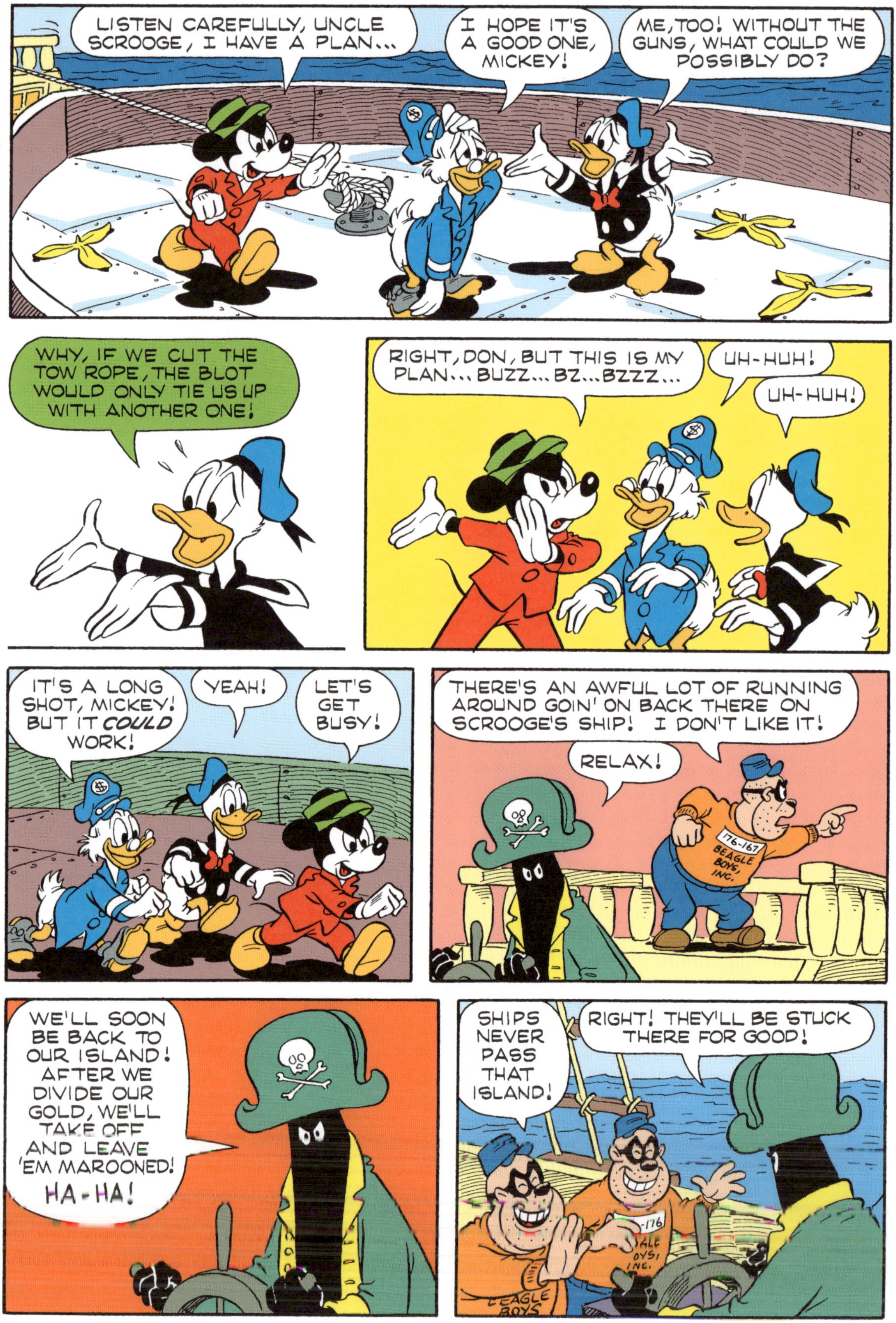

LISTEN CAREFULLY, UNCLE SCROOGE, I HAVE A PLAN...
I HOPE IT'S A GOOD ONE, MICKEY!
ME, TOO! WITHOUT THE GUNS, WHAT COULD WE POSSIBLY DO?
WHY, IF WE CUT THE TOW ROPE, THE BLOT WOULD ONLY TIE US UP WITH ANOTHER ONE!
RIGHT, DON, BUT THIS IS MY PLAN... BUZZ... BZ... BZZZ...
UH-HUH!
UH-HUH!
IT'S A LONG SHOT, MICKEY! BUT IT COULD WORK!
YEAH!
LET'S GET BUSY!
THERE'S AN AWFUL LOT OF RUNNING AROUND GOIN' ON BACK THERE ON SCROOGE'S SHIP! I DON'T LIKE IT!
RELAX!
176-167 BEAGLE BOYS, INC.
WE'LL SOON BE BACK TO OUR ISLAND! AFTER WE DIVIDE OUR GOLD, WE'LL TAKE OFF AND LEAVE 'EM MAROONED!
HA-HA!
SHIPS NEVER PASS THAT ISLAND!
RIGHT! THEY'LL BE STUCK THERE FOR GOOD!

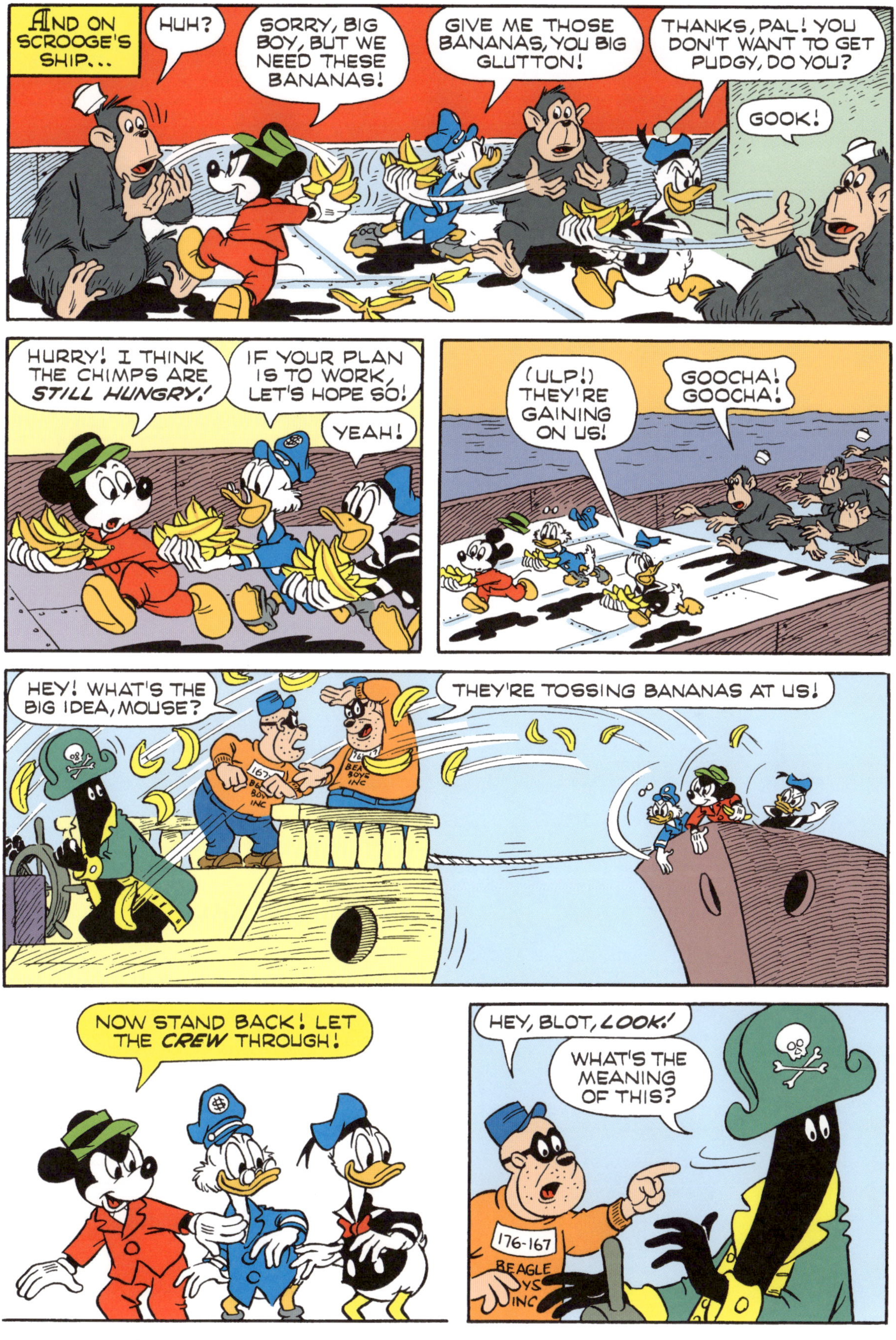
AND ON SCROOGE'S SHIP...
HUH?
SORRY, BIG BOY, BUT WE NEED THESE BANANAS!
GIVE ME THOSE BANANAS, YOU BIG GLUTTON!
THANKS, PAL! YOU DON'T WANT TO GET PUDGY, DO YOU?
GOOK!
HURRY! I THINK THE CHIMPS ARE STILL HUNGRY!
IF YOUR PLAN IS TO WORK, LET'S HOPE SO!
YEAH!
(ULP!) THEY'RE GAINING ON US!
GOOCHA! GOOCHA!
HEY! WHAT'S THE BIG IDEA, MOUSE?
THEY'RE TOSSING BANANAS AT US!
NOW STAND BACK! LET THE CREW THROUGH!
HEY, BLOT, LOOK!
WHAT'S THE MEANING OF THIS?
176-167
BEAGLE BOYS INC

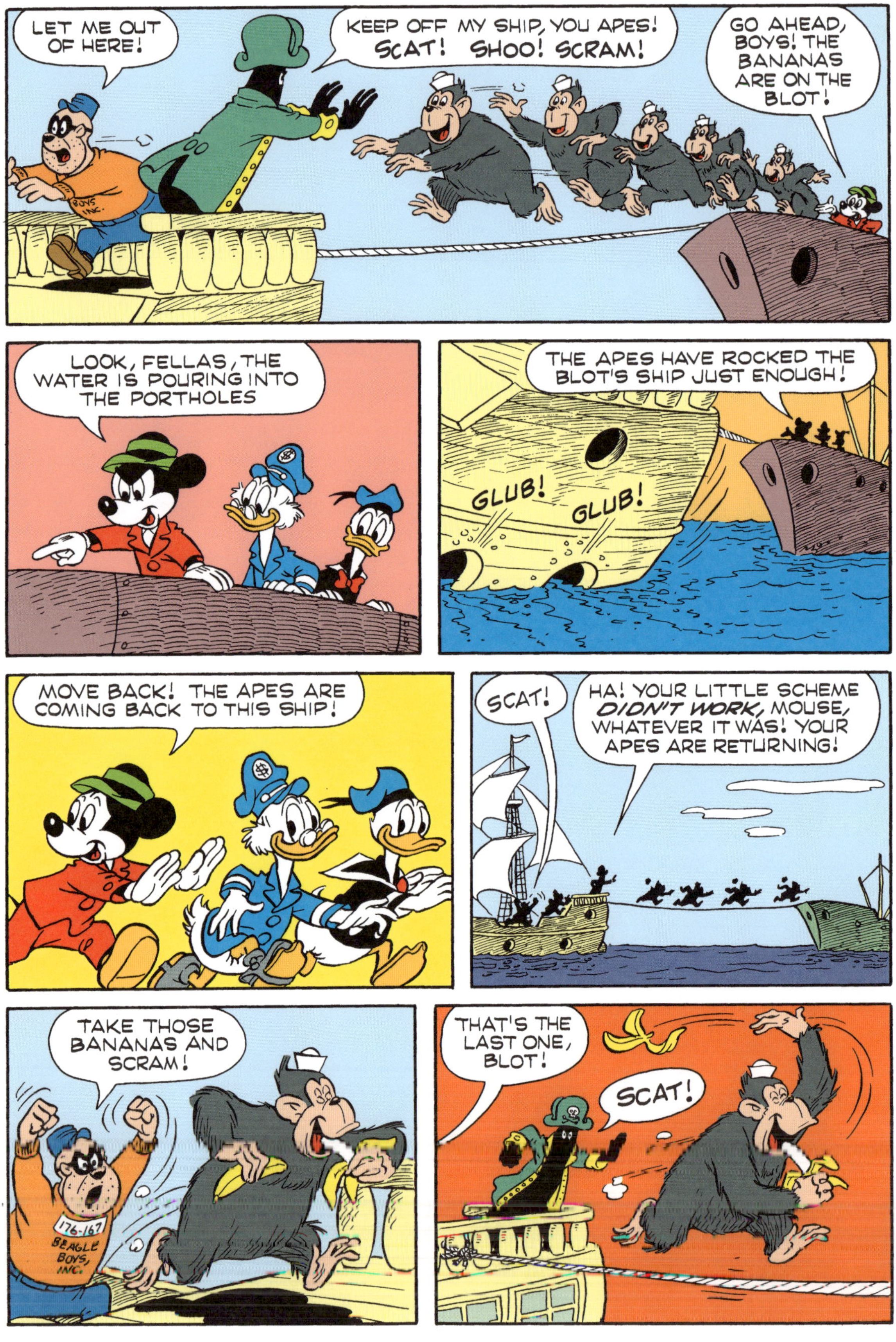
LET ME OUT OF HERE!
KEEP OFF MY SHIP, YOU APES! SCAT! SHOO! SCRAM!
GO AHEAD, BOYS! THE BANANAS ARE ON THE BLOT!
BOYS INC.
LOOK, FELLAS, THE WATER IS POURING INTO THE PORTHOLES
THE APES HAVE ROCKED THE BLOT'S SHIP JUST ENOUGH!
GLUB! GLUB!
MOVE BACK! THE APES ARE COMING BACK TO THIS SHIP!
SCAT!
HA! YOUR LITTLE SCHEME DIDN'T WORK, MOUSE, WHATEVER IT WAS! YOUR APES ARE RETURNING!
TAKE THOSE BANANAS AND SCRAM!
176-167
BEAGLE BOYS, INC.
THAT'S THE LAST ONE, BLOT!
SCAT!

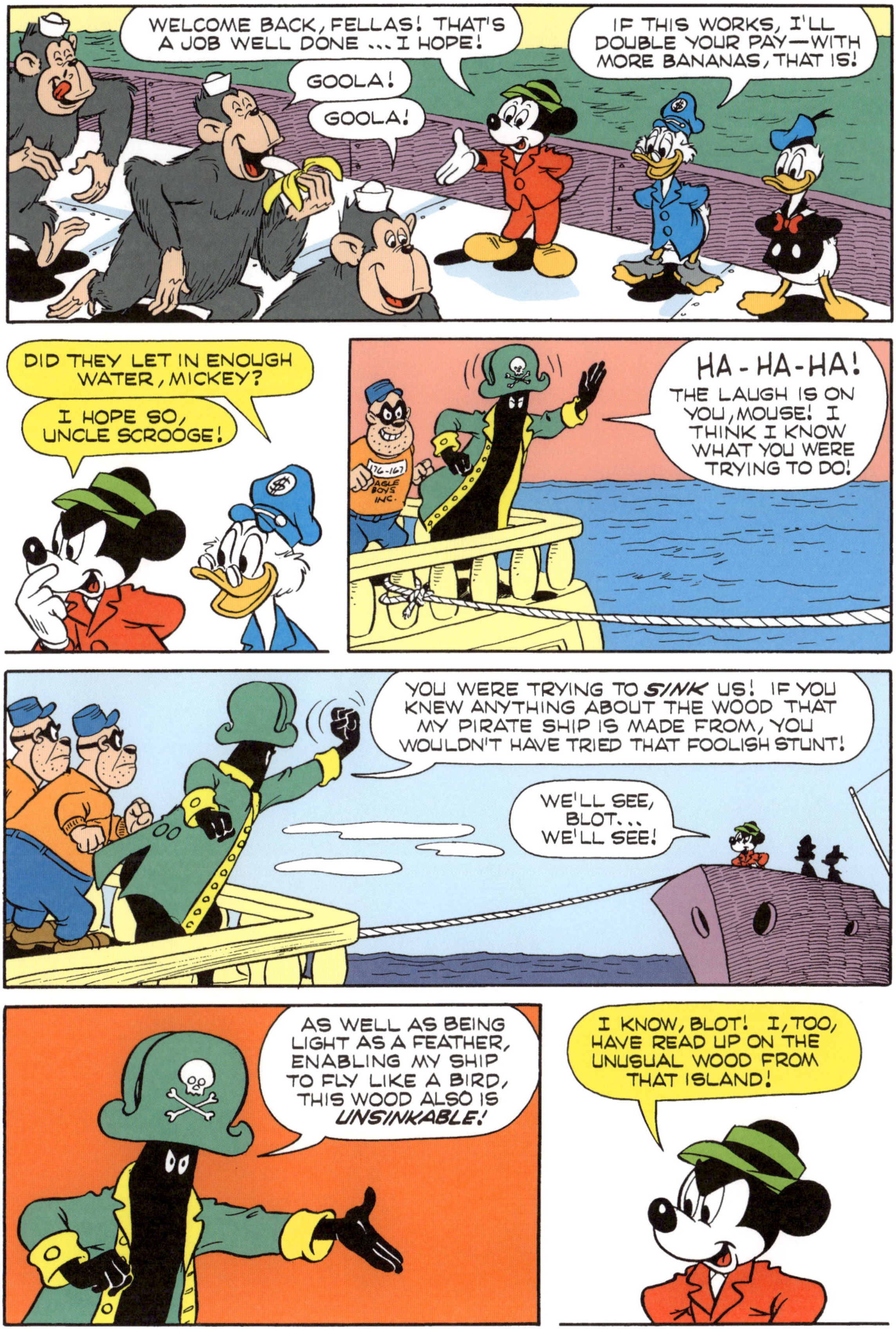

WELCOME BACK, FELLAS! THAT'S A JOB WELL DONE ... I HOPE!
GOOLA!
GOOLA!
IF THIS WORKS, I'LL DOUBLE YOUR PAY—WITH MORE BANANAS, THAT IS!
DID THEY LET IN ENOUGH WATER, MICKEY?
I HOPE SO, UNCLE SCROOGE!
HA-HA-HA! THE LAUGH IS ON YOU, MOUSE! I THINK I KNOW WHAT YOU WERE TRYING TO DO!
YOU WERE TRYING TO *SINK* US! IF YOU KNEW ANYTHING ABOUT THE WOOD THAT MY PIRATE SHIP IS MADE FROM, YOU WOULDN'T HAVE TRIED THAT FOOLISH STUNT!
WE'LL SEE, BLOT... WE'LL SEE!
AS WELL AS BEING LIGHT AS A FEATHER, ENABLING MY SHIP TO FLY LIKE A BIRD, THIS WOOD ALSO IS *UNSINKABLE!*
I KNOW, BLOT! I, TOO, HAVE READ UP ON THE UNUSUAL WOOD FROM THAT ISLAND!

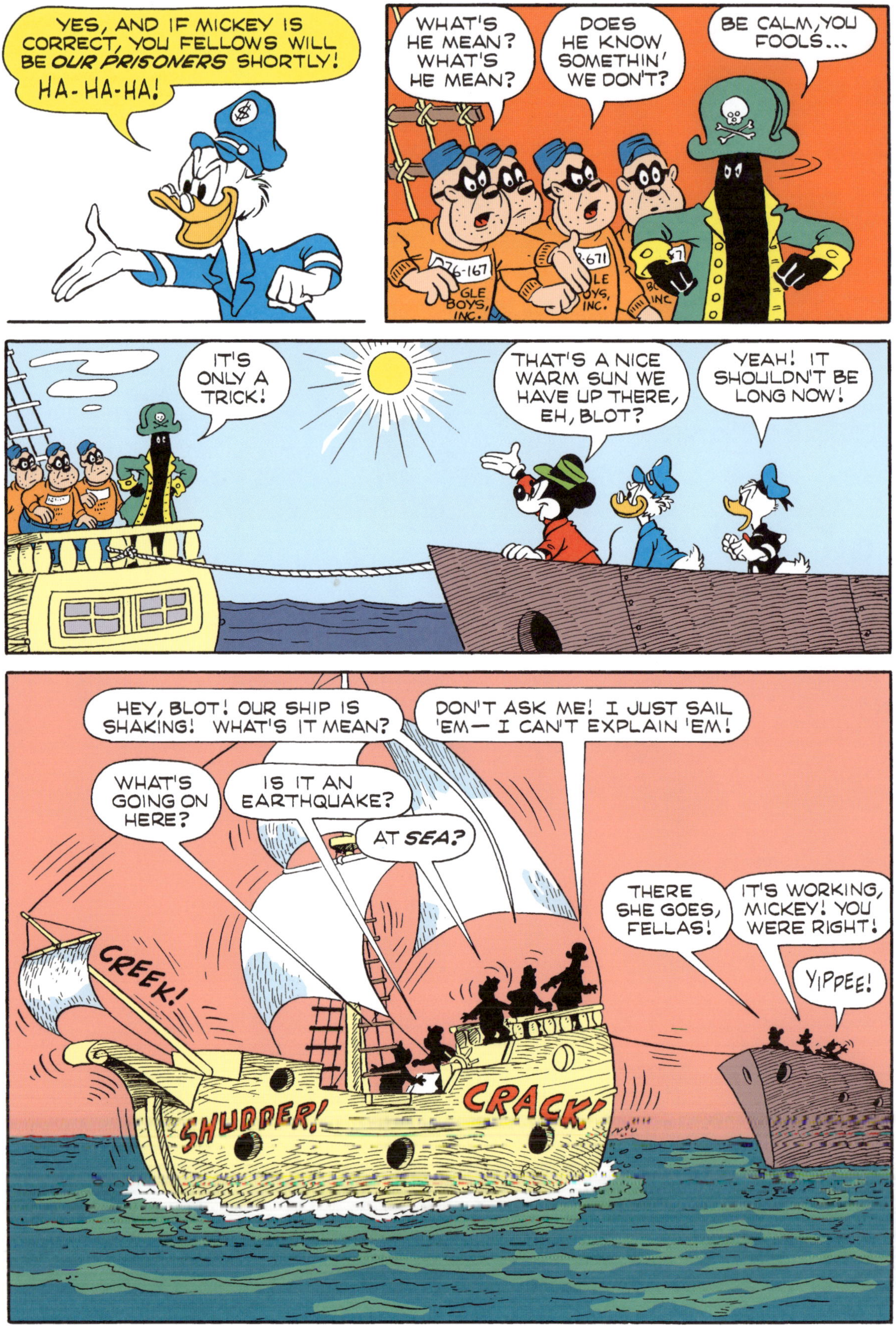

YES, AND IF MICKEY IS CORRECT, YOU FELLOWS WILL BE OUR PRISONERS SHORTLY!
HA-HA-HA!
WHAT'S HE MEAN? WHAT'S HE MEAN?
DOES HE KNOW SOMETHIN' WE DON'T?
BE CALM, YOU FOOLS...
IT'S ONLY A TRICK!
THAT'S A NICE WARM SUN WE HAVE UP THERE, EH, BLOT?
YEAH! IT SHOULDN'T BE LONG NOW!
HEY, BLOT! OUR SHIP IS SHAKING! WHAT'S IT MEAN?
DON'T ASK ME! I JUST SAIL 'EM— I CAN'T EXPLAIN 'EM!
WHAT'S GOING ON HERE?
IS IT AN EARTHQUAKE?
AT SEA?
CREEK!
SHUDDER!
CRACK!
THERE SHE GOES, FELLAS!
IT'S WORKING, MICKEY! YOU WERE RIGHT!
YIPPEE!

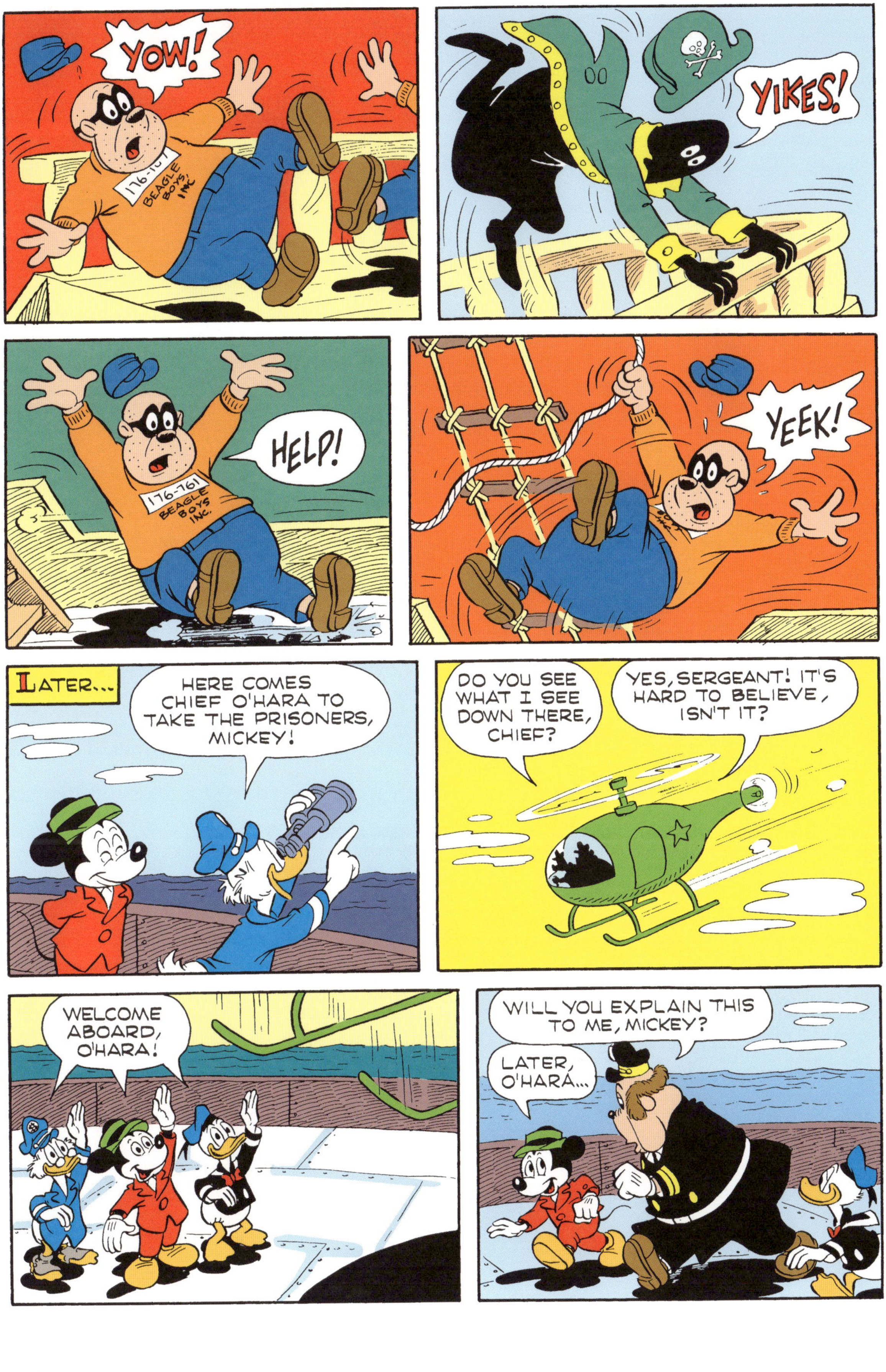
YOW!
YIKES!
176-167
BEAGLE BOYS INC.
HELP!
176-761
BEAGLE BOYS INC.
YEEK!
LATER...
HERE COMES CHIEF O'HARA TO TAKE THE PRISONERS, MICKEY!
DO YOU SEE WHAT I SEE DOWN THERE, CHIEF?
YES, SERGEANT! IT'S HARD TO BELIEVE, ISN'T IT?
WELCOME ABOARD, O'HARA!
WILL YOU EXPLAIN THIS TO ME, MICKEY?
LATER, O'HARA...

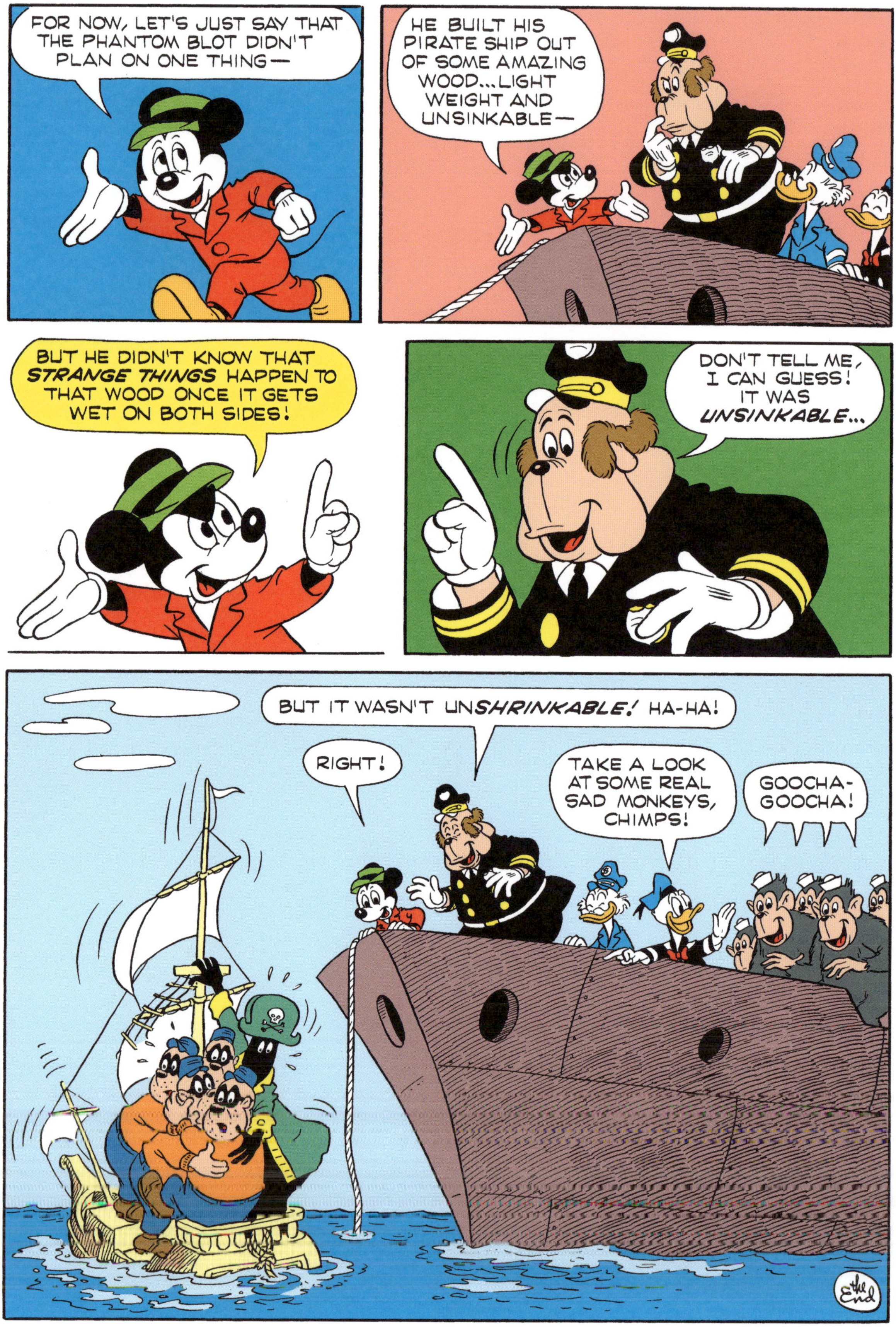

FOR NOW, LET'S JUST SAY THAT THE PHANTOM BLOT DIDN'T PLAN ON ONE THING—
HE BUILT HIS PIRATE SHIP OUT OF SOME AMAZING WOOD...LIGHT WEIGHT AND UNSINKABLE—
BUT HE DIDN'T KNOW THAT STRANGE THINGS HAPPEN TO THAT WOOD ONCE IT GETS WET ON BOTH SIDES!
DON'T TELL ME, I CAN GUESS! IT WAS UNSINKABLE...
BUT IT WASN'T UNSHRINKABLE! HA-HA!
RIGHT!
TAKE A LOOK AT SOME REAL SAD MONKEYS, CHIMPS!
GOOCHA-GOOCHA!
the End

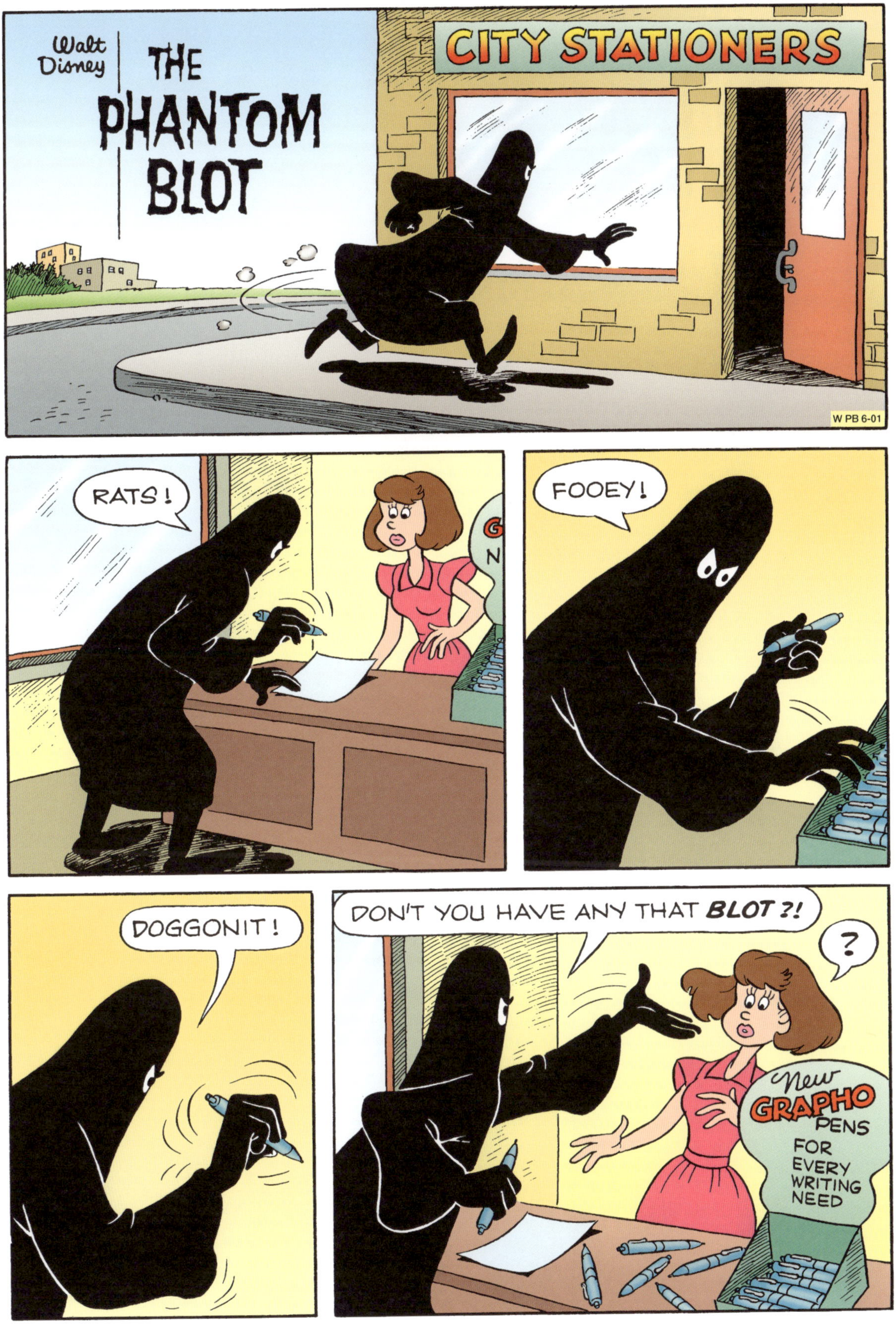
Walt Disney
THE PHANTOM BLOT
CITY STATIONERS
W PB 6-01
RATS!
FOOEY!
DOGGONIT!
DON'T YOU HAVE ANY THAT *BLOT* ?!
?
New GRAPHO PENS FOR EVERY WRITING NEED

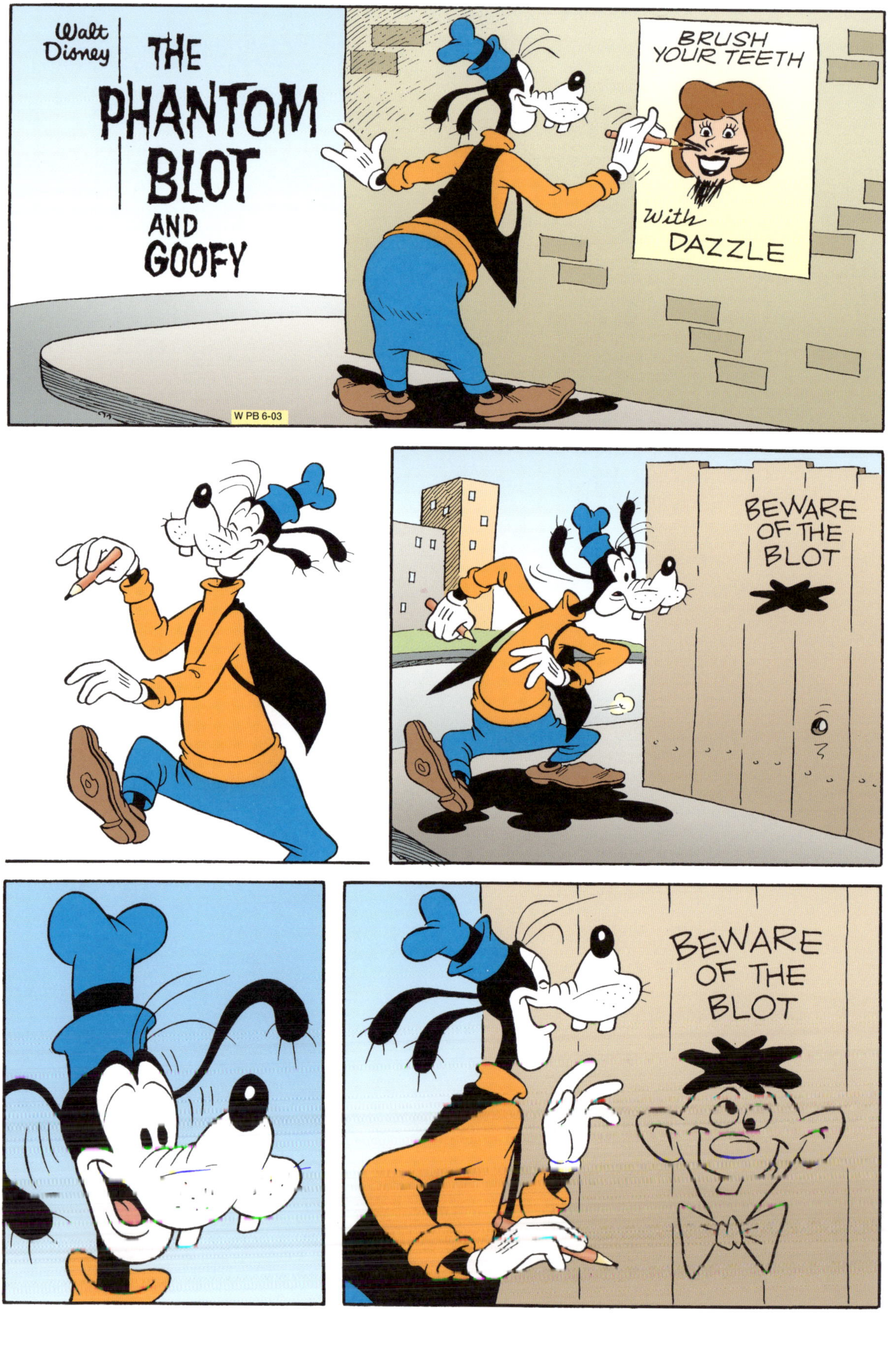
Walt Disney
THE PHANTOM BLOT AND GOOFY
BRUSH YOUR TEETH
with DAZZLE
W PB 6-03
BEWARE OF THE BLOT
BEWARE OF THE BLOT

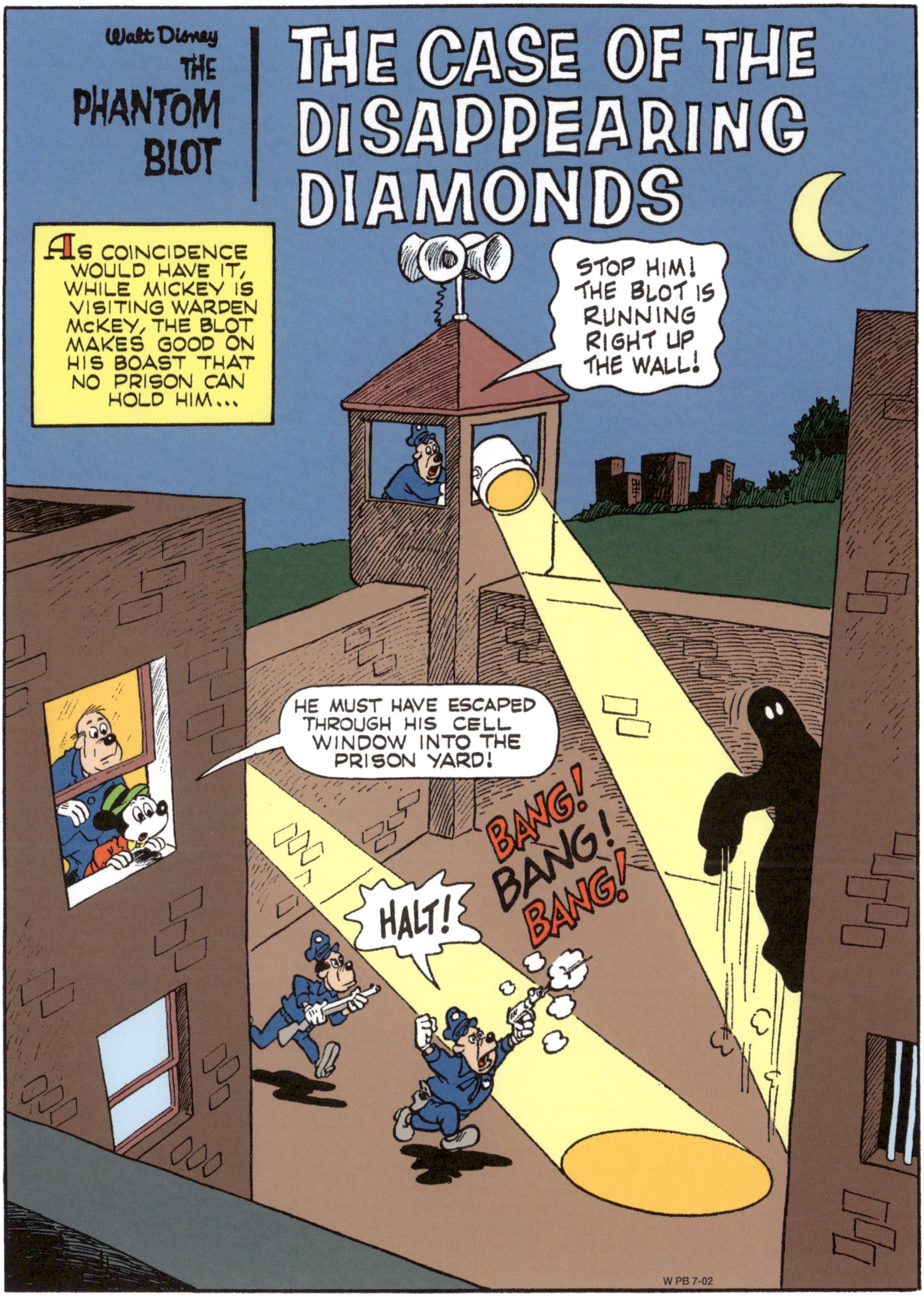
Walt Disney
THE PHANTOM BLOT
THE CASE OF THE DISAPPEARING DIAMONDS
AS COINCIDENCE WOULD HAVE IT, WHILE MICKEY IS VISITING WARDEN McKEY, THE BLOT MAKES GOOD ON HIS BOAST THAT NO PRISON CAN HOLD HIM...
STOP HIM! THE BLOT IS RUNNING RIGHT UP THE WALL!
HE MUST HAVE ESCAPED THROUGH HIS CELL WINDOW INTO THE PRISON YARD!
HALT!
BANG! BANG! BANG!
W PB 7-02

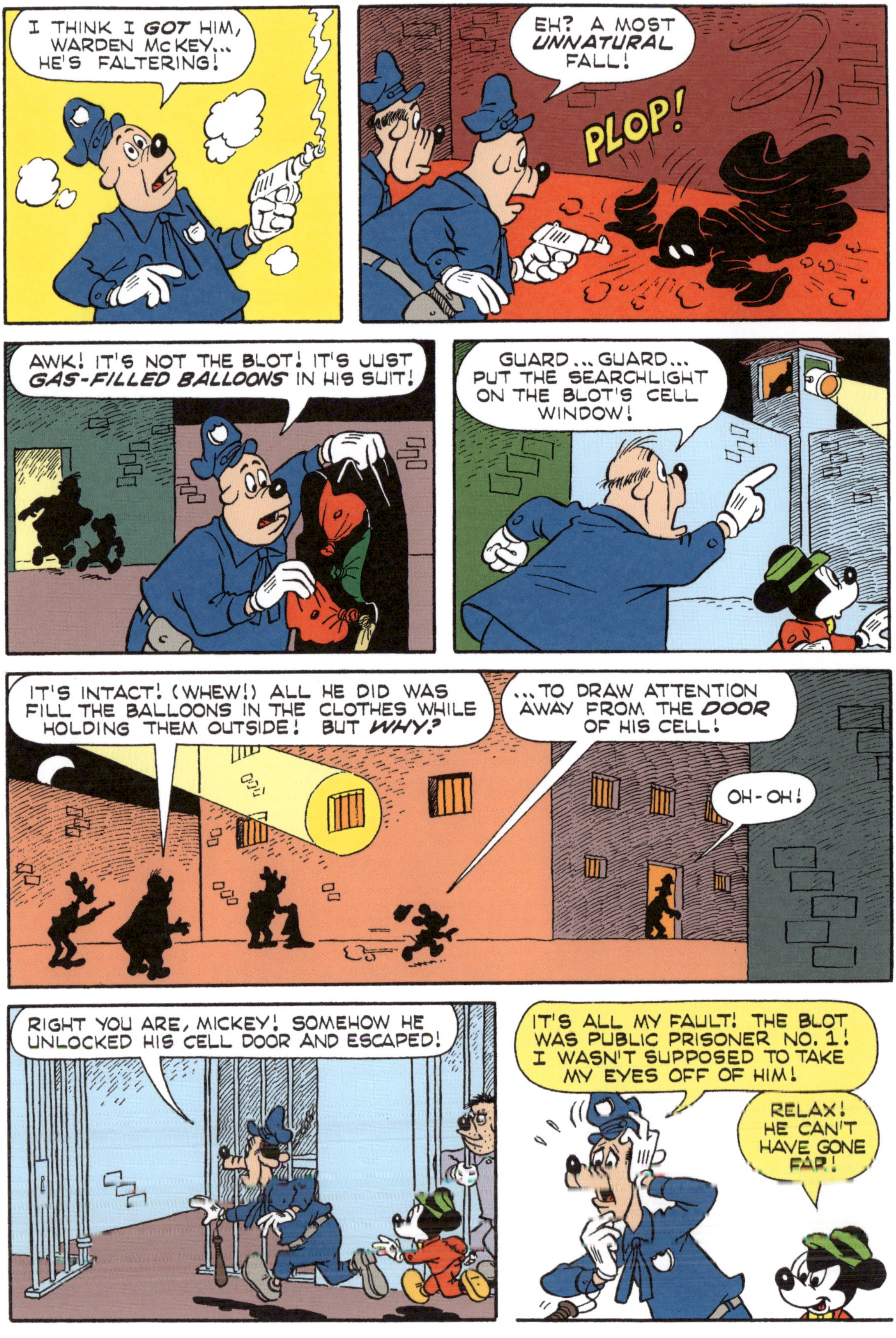
I THINK I GOT HIM, WARDEN McKEY... HE'S FALTERING!
EH? A MOST UNNATURAL FALL!
PLOP!
AWK! IT'S NOT THE BLOT! IT'S JUST GAS-FILLED BALLOONS IN HIS SUIT!
GUARD... GUARD... PUT THE SEARCHLIGHT ON THE BLOT'S CELL WINDOW!
IT'S INTACT! (WHEW!) ALL HE DID WAS FILL THE BALLOONS IN THE CLOTHES WHILE HOLDING THEM OUTSIDE! BUT WHY?
...TO DRAW ATTENTION AWAY FROM THE DOOR OF HIS CELL!
OH-OH!
RIGHT YOU ARE, MICKEY! SOMEHOW HE UNLOCKED HIS CELL DOOR AND ESCAPED!
IT'S ALL MY FAULT! THE BLOT WAS PUBLIC PRISONER NO. 1! I WASN'T SUPPOSED TO TAKE MY EYES OFF OF HIM!
RELAX! HE CAN'T HAVE GONE FAR!

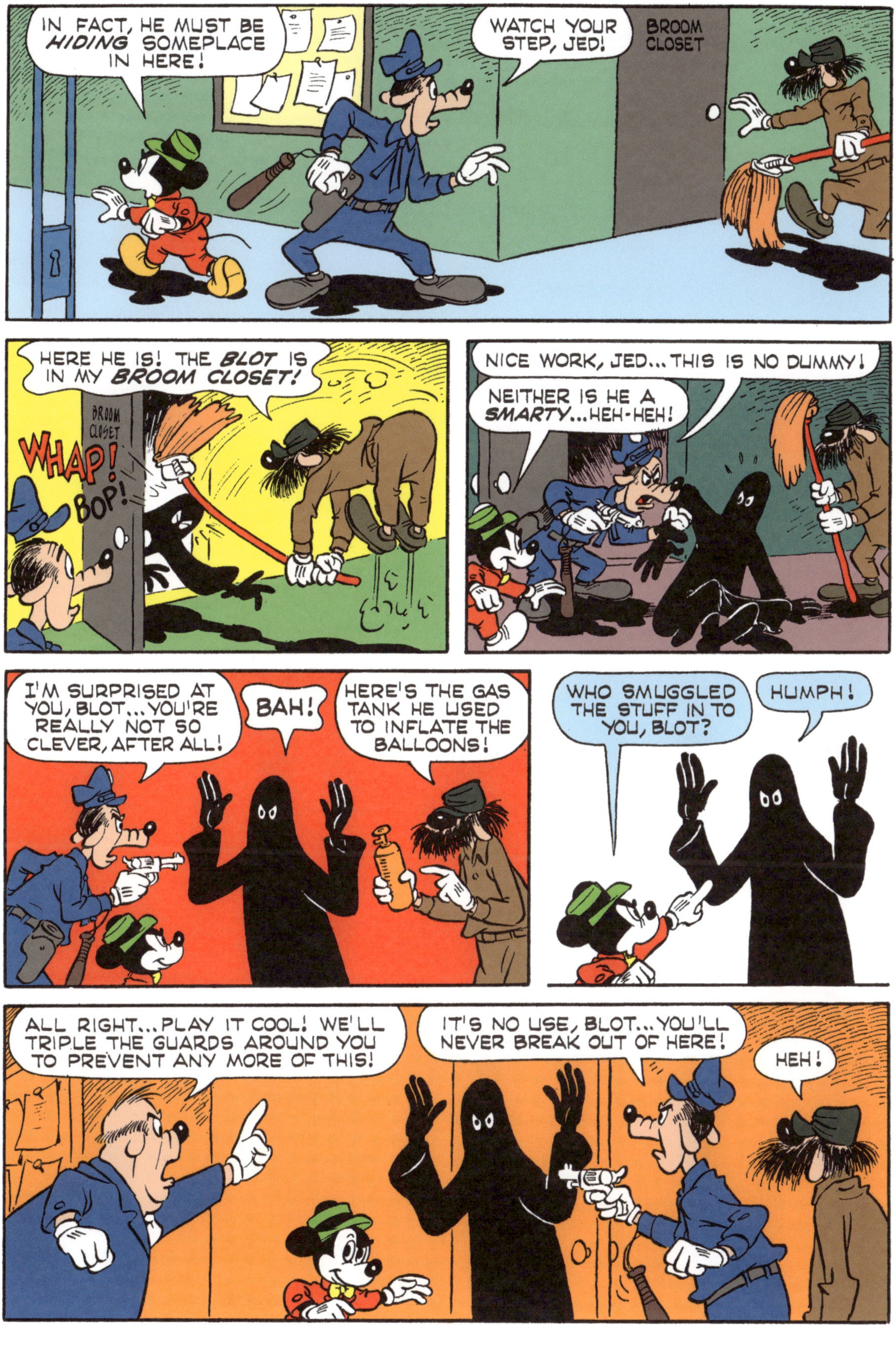
IN FACT, HE MUST BE HIDING SOMEPLACE IN HERE!
WATCH YOUR STEP, JED!
BROOM CLOSET
HERE HE IS! THE BLOT IS IN MY BROOM CLOSET!
BROOM CLOSET
WHAP!
BOP!
NICE WORK, JED... THIS IS NO DUMMY!
NEITHER IS HE A SMARTY...HEH-HEH!
I'M SURPRISED AT YOU, BLOT... YOU'RE REALLY NOT SO CLEVER, AFTER ALL!
BAH!
HERE'S THE GAS TANK HE USED TO INFLATE THE BALLOONS!
WHO SMUGGLED THE STUFF IN TO YOU, BLOT?
HUMPH!
ALL RIGHT... PLAY IT COOL! WE'LL TRIPLE THE GUARDS AROUND YOU TO PREVENT ANY MORE OF THIS!
IT'S NO USE, BLOT... YOU'LL NEVER BREAK OUT OF HERE!
HEH!

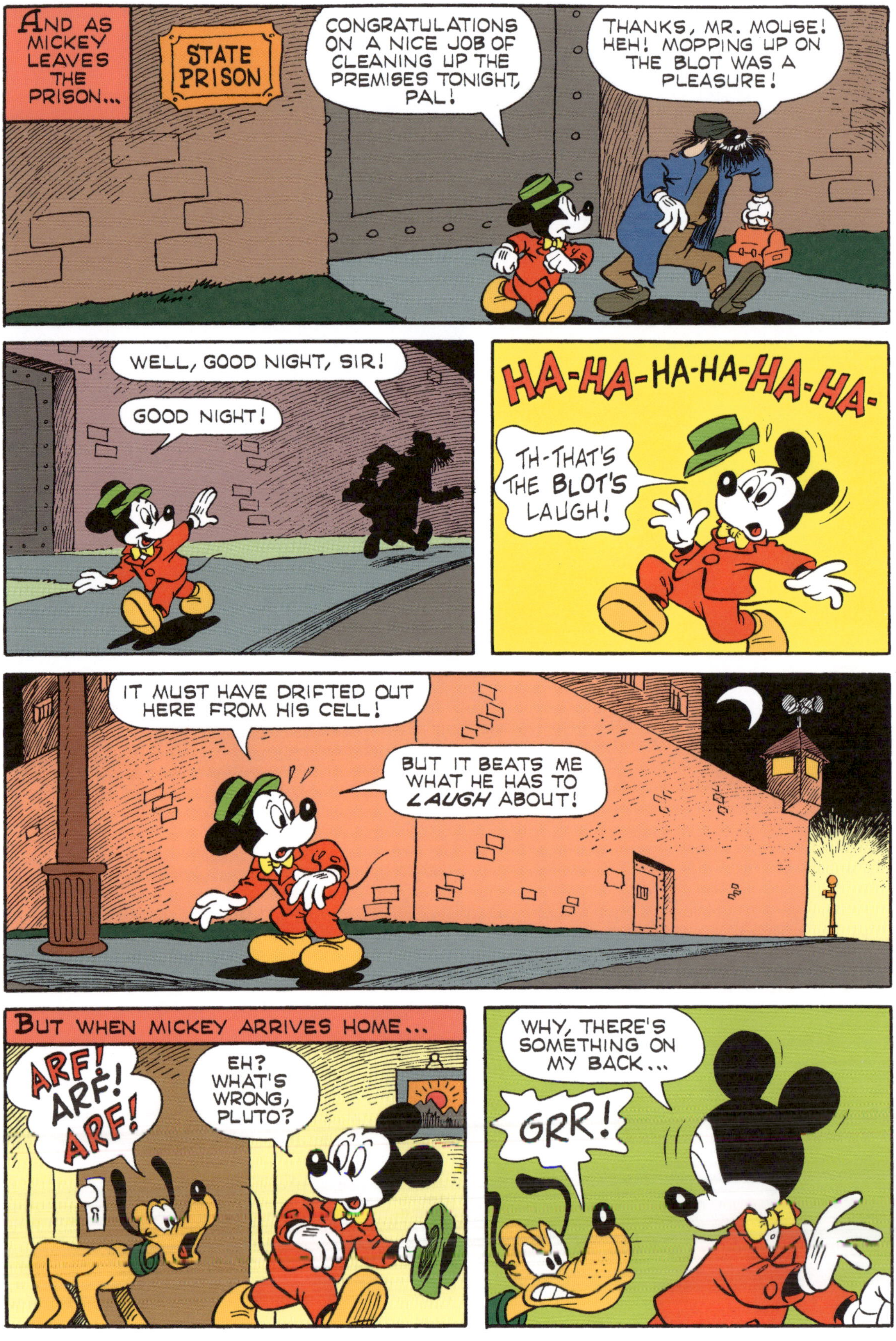
AND AS MICKEY LEAVES THE PRISON...
STATE PRISON
CONGRATULATIONS ON A NICE JOB OF CLEANING UP THE PREMISES TONIGHT, PAL!
THANKS, MR. MOUSE! HEH! MOPPING UP ON THE BLOT WAS A PLEASURE!
WELL, GOOD NIGHT, SIR!
GOOD NIGHT!
HA-HA-HA-HA-HA-HA-
TH-THAT'S THE BLOT'S LAUGH!
IT MUST HAVE DRIFTED OUT HERE FROM HIS CELL!
BUT IT BEATS ME WHAT HE HAS TO *LAUGH* ABOUT!
BUT WHEN MICKEY ARRIVES HOME...
ARF! ARF! ARF!
EH? WHAT'S WRONG, PLUTO?
WHY, THERE'S SOMETHING ON MY BACK...
GRR!

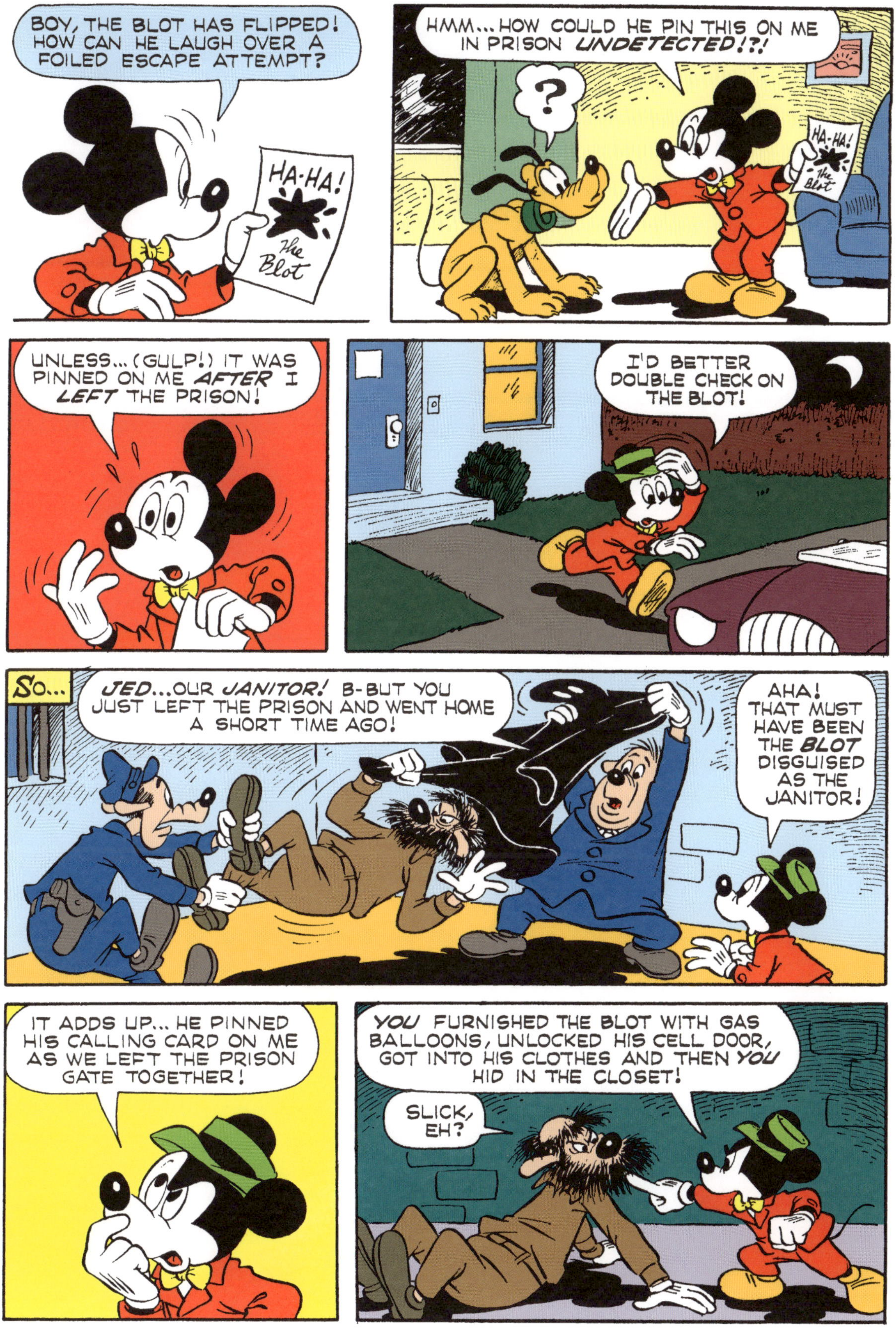
BOY, THE BLOT HAS FLIPPED! HOW CAN HE LAUGH OVER A FOILED ESCAPE ATTEMPT?
HA-HA! the Blot
HMM... HOW COULD HE PIN THIS ON ME IN PRISON UNDETECTED!?!
?
HA-HA! the Blot
UNLESS... (GULP!) IT WAS PINNED ON ME AFTER I LEFT THE PRISON!
I'D BETTER DOUBLE CHECK ON THE BLOT!
SO...
JED... OUR JANITOR! B-BUT YOU JUST LEFT THE PRISON AND WENT HOME A SHORT TIME AGO!
AHA! THAT MUST HAVE BEEN THE BLOT DISGUISED AS THE JANITOR!
IT ADDS UP... HE PINNED HIS CALLING CARD ON ME AS WE LEFT THE PRISON GATE TOGETHER!
YOU FURNISHED THE BLOT WITH GAS BALLOONS, UNLOCKED HIS CELL DOOR, GOT INTO HIS CLOTHES AND THEN YOU HID IN THE CLOSET!
SLICK, EH?

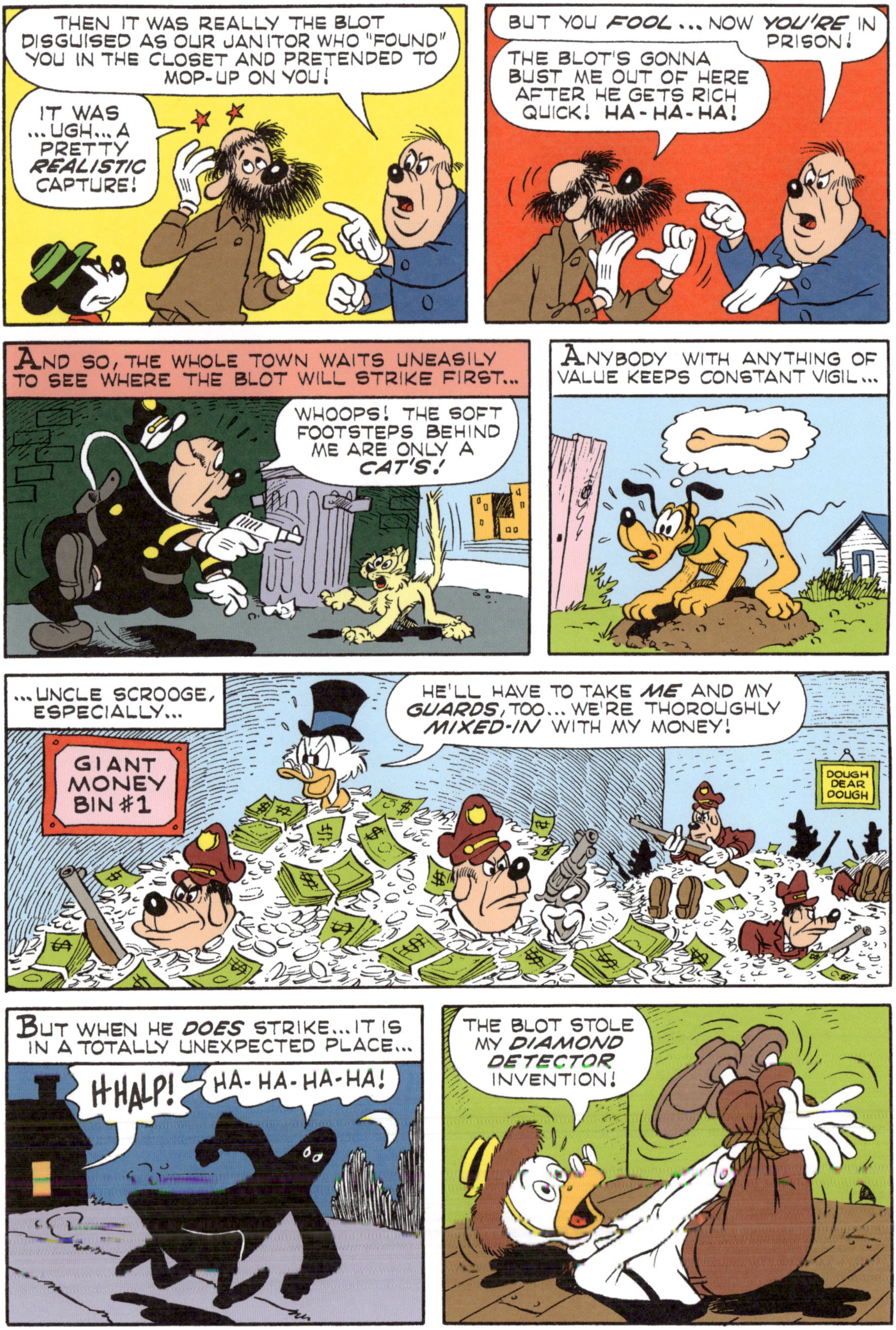
THEN IT WAS REALLY THE BLOT DISGUISED AS OUR JANITOR WHO "FOUND" YOU IN THE CLOSET AND PRETENDED TO MOP-UP ON YOU!
IT WAS ...UGH... A PRETTY *REALISTIC* CAPTURE!
BUT YOU *FOOL*... NOW *YOU'RE* IN PRISON!
THE BLOT'S GONNA BUST ME OUT OF HERE AFTER HE GETS RICH QUICK! HA-HA-HA!
AND SO, THE WHOLE TOWN WAITS UNEASILY TO SEE WHERE THE BLOT WILL STRIKE FIRST...
WHOOPS! THE SOFT FOOTSTEPS BEHIND ME ARE ONLY A *CAT'S!*
ANYBODY WITH ANYTHING OF VALUE KEEPS CONSTANT VIGIL...
...UNCLE SCROOGE, ESPECIALLY...
HE'LL HAVE TO TAKE *ME* AND MY *GUARDS*, TOO... WE'RE THOROUGHLY *MIXED-IN* WITH MY MONEY!
GIANT MONEY BIN #1
DOUGH DEAR DOUGH
BUT WHEN HE *DOES* STRIKE... IT IS IN A TOTALLY UNEXPECTED PLACE...
H-HALP!
HA-HA-HA-HA!
THE BLOT STOLE MY *DIAMOND DETECTOR* INVENTION!

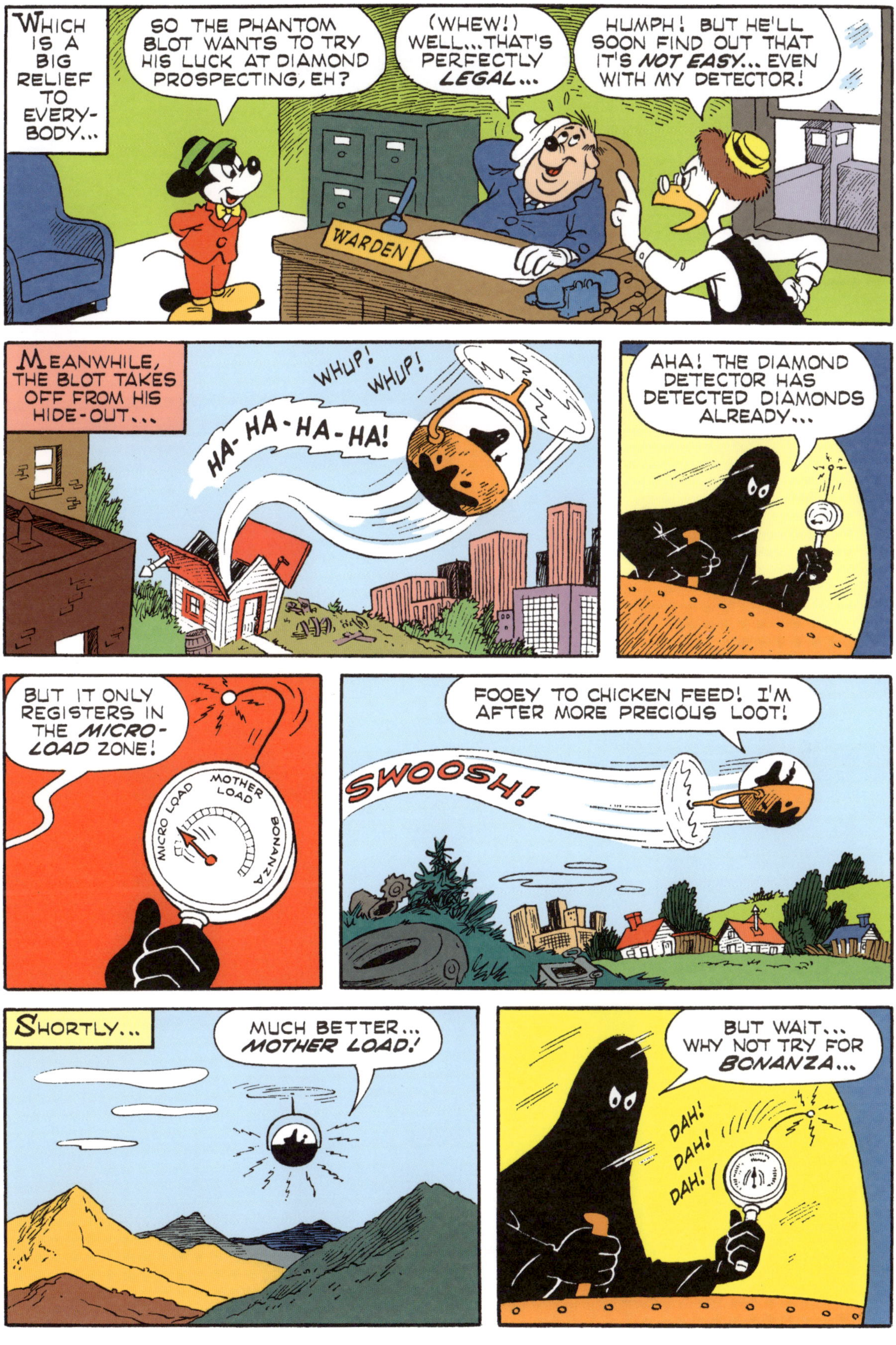
WHICH IS A BIG RELIEF TO EVERY-BODY...
SO THE PHANTOM BLOT WANTS TO TRY HIS LUCK AT DIAMOND PROSPECTING, EH?
(WHEW!) WELL...THAT'S PERFECTLY LEGAL...
HUMPH! BUT HE'LL SOON FIND OUT THAT IT'S NOT EASY... EVEN WITH MY DETECTOR!
WARDEN
MEANWHILE, THE BLOT TAKES OFF FROM HIS HIDE-OUT...
WHUP! WHUP!
HA-HA-HA-HA!
AHA! THE DIAMOND DETECTOR HAS DETECTED DIAMONDS ALREADY...
BUT IT ONLY REGISTERS IN THE MICRO-LOAD ZONE!
MICRO LOAD
MOTHER LOAD
BONANZA
FOOEY TO CHICKEN FEED! I'M AFTER MORE PRECIOUS LOOT!
SWOOSH!
SHORTLY...
MUCH BETTER... MOTHER LOAD!
BUT WAIT... WHY NOT TRY FOR BONANZA...
DAH! DAH! DAH!

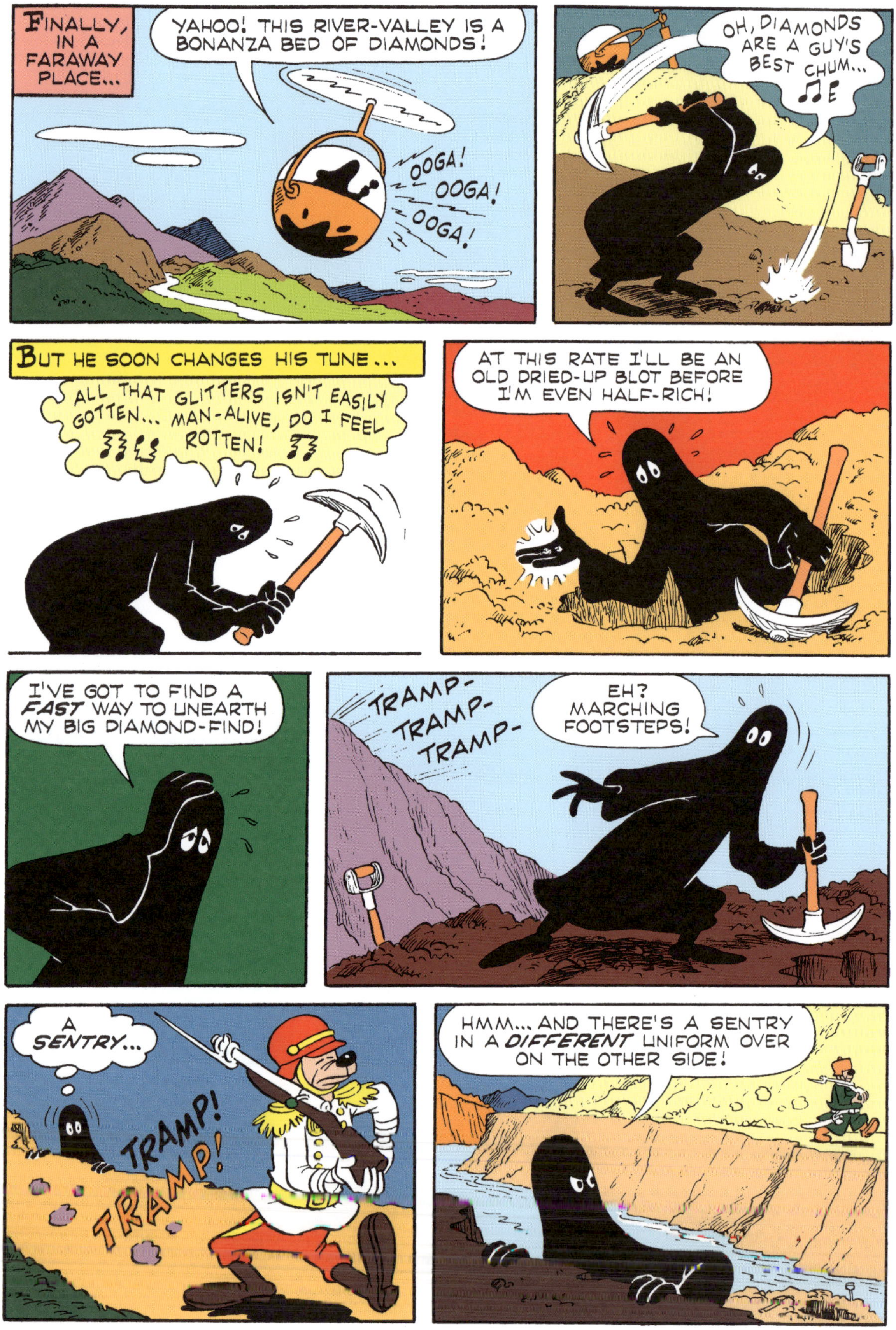

FINALLY, IN A FARAWAY PLACE...
YAHOO! THIS RIVER-VALLEY IS A BONANZA BED OF DIAMONDS!
OOGA! OOGA! OOGA!
OH, DIAMONDS ARE A GUY'S BEST CHUM...
BUT HE SOON CHANGES HIS TUNE...
ALL THAT GLITTERS ISN'T EASILY GOTTEN... MAN-ALIVE, DO I FEEL ROTTEN!
AT THIS RATE I'LL BE AN OLD DRIED-UP BLOT BEFORE I'M EVEN HALF-RICH!
I'VE GOT TO FIND A FAST WAY TO UNEARTH MY BIG DIAMOND-FIND!
TRAMP- TRAMP- TRAMP-
EH? MARCHING FOOTSTEPS!
A SENTRY...
TRAMP! TRAMP! TRAMP!
HMM... AND THERE'S A SENTRY IN A DIFFERENT UNIFORM OVER ON THE OTHER SIDE!

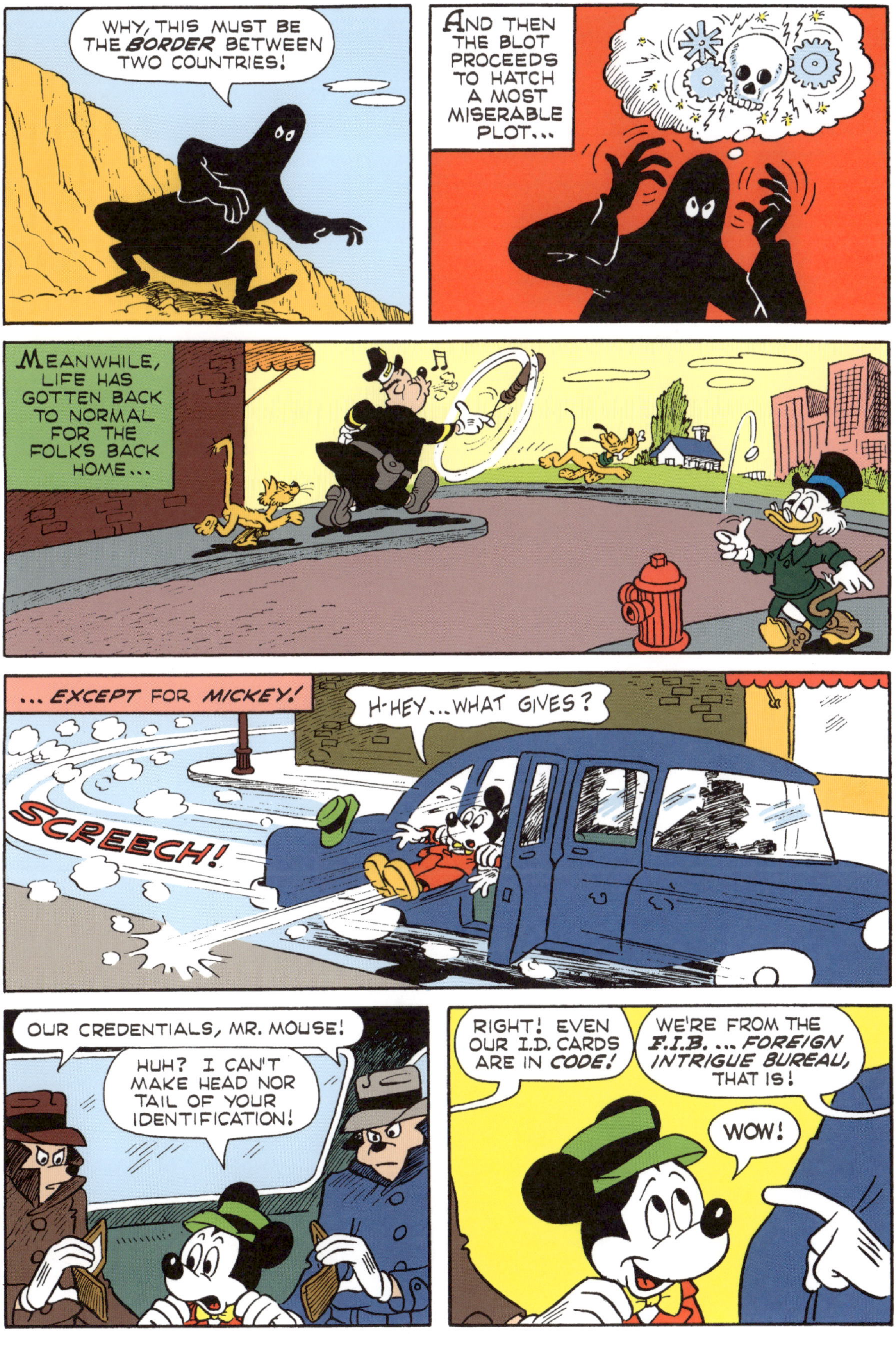
WHY, THIS MUST BE THE BORDER BETWEEN TWO COUNTRIES!
AND THEN THE BLOT PROCEEDS TO HATCH A MOST MISERABLE PLOT...
MEANWHILE, LIFE HAS GOTTEN BACK TO NORMAL FOR THE FOLKS BACK HOME...
...EXCEPT FOR MICKEY!
H-HEY...WHAT GIVES?
SCREECH!
OUR CREDENTIALS, MR. MOUSE!
HUH? I CAN'T MAKE HEAD NOR TAIL OF YOUR IDENTIFICATION!
RIGHT! EVEN OUR I.D. CARDS ARE IN CODE!
WE'RE FROM THE F.I.B. ... FOREIGN INTRIGUE BUREAU, THAT IS!
WOW!

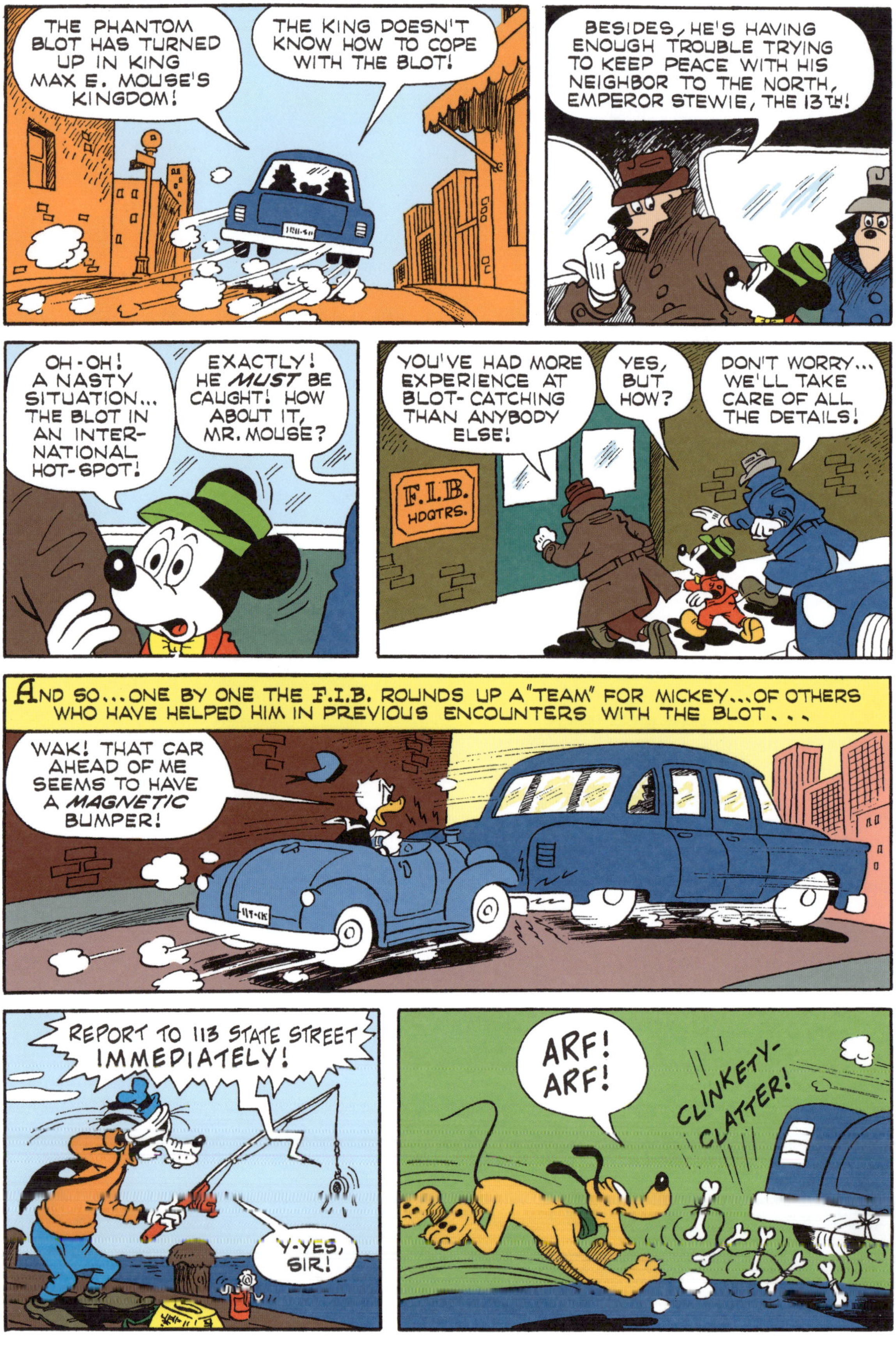
THE PHANTOM BLOT HAS TURNED UP IN KING MAX E. MOUSE'S KINGDOM!
THE KING DOESN'T KNOW HOW TO COPE WITH THE BLOT!
BESIDES, HE'S HAVING ENOUGH TROUBLE TRYING TO KEEP PEACE WITH HIS NEIGHBOR TO THE NORTH, EMPEROR STEWIE, THE 13TH!
OH-OH! A NASTY SITUATION... THE BLOT IN AN INTER-NATIONAL HOT-SPOT!
EXACTLY! HE MUST BE CAUGHT! HOW ABOUT IT, MR. MOUSE?
YOU'VE HAD MORE EXPERIENCE AT BLOT-CATCHING THAN ANYBODY ELSE!
YES, BUT HOW?
DON'T WORRY... WE'LL TAKE CARE OF ALL THE DETAILS!
F.I.B. HDQTRS.
AND SO...ONE BY ONE THE F.I.B. ROUNDS UP A "TEAM" FOR MICKEY...OF OTHERS WHO HAVE HELPED HIM IN PREVIOUS ENCOUNTERS WITH THE BLOT...
WAK! THAT CAR AHEAD OF ME SEEMS TO HAVE A MAGNETIC BUMPER!
REPORT TO 113 STATE STREET IMMEDIATELY!
Y-YES, SIR!
ARF! ARF!
CLINKETY-CLATTER!

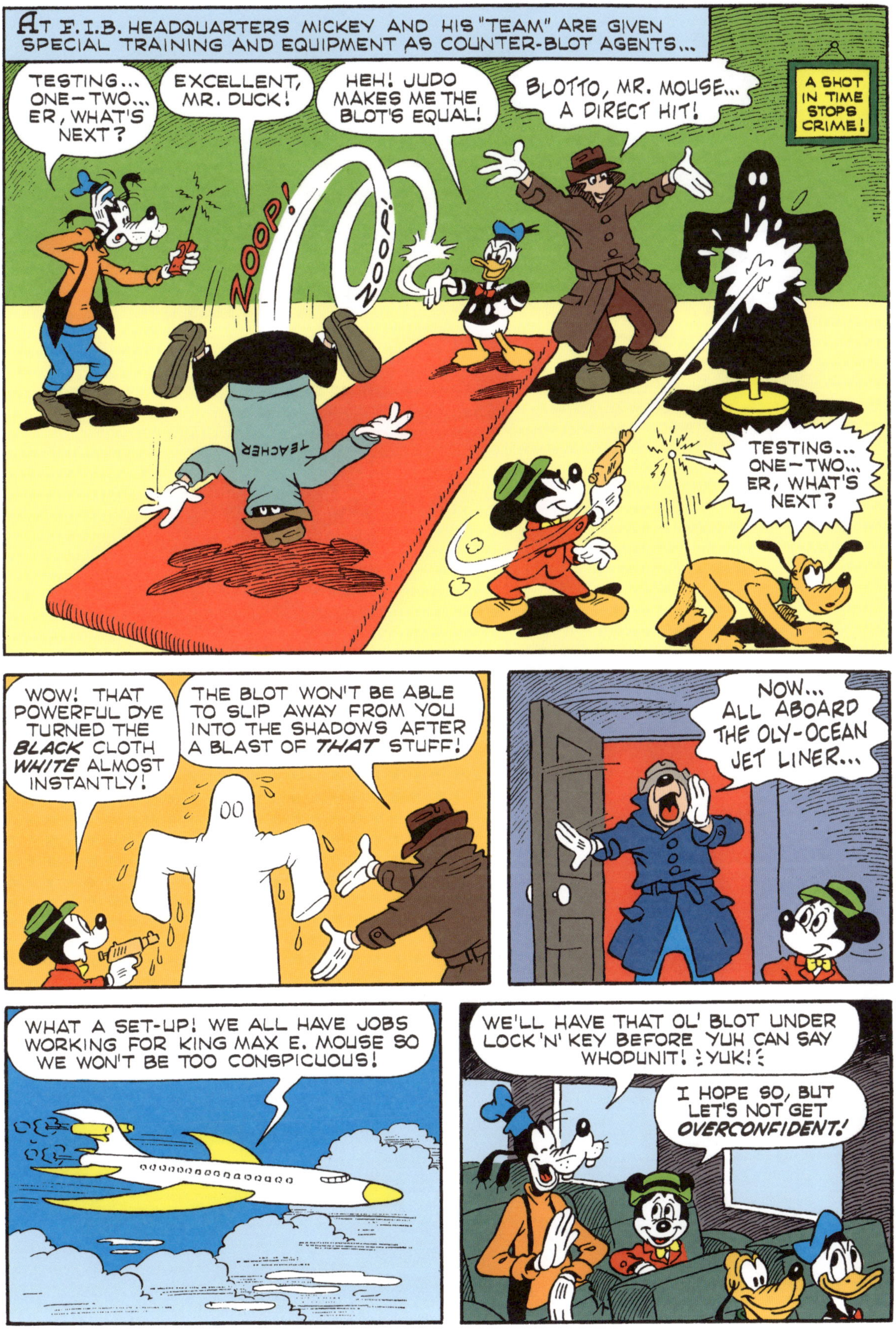
AT F.I.B. HEADQUARTERS MICKEY AND HIS "TEAM" ARE GIVEN SPECIAL TRAINING AND EQUIPMENT AS COUNTER-BLOT AGENTS...
TESTING... ONE—TWO... ER, WHAT'S NEXT?
EXCELLENT, MR. DUCK!
HEH! JUDO MAKES ME THE BLOT'S EQUAL!
BLOTTO, MR. MOUSE... A DIRECT HIT!
A SHOT IN TIME STOPS CRIME!
ZOOP!
ZOOP!
TEACHER
TESTING... ONE—TWO... ER, WHAT'S NEXT?
WOW! THAT POWERFUL DYE TURNED THE BLACK CLOTH WHITE ALMOST INSTANTLY!
THE BLOT WON'T BE ABLE TO SLIP AWAY FROM YOU INTO THE SHADOWS AFTER A BLAST OF THAT STUFF!
NOW... ALL ABOARD THE OLY-OCEAN JET LINER...
WHAT A SET-UP! WE ALL HAVE JOBS WORKING FOR KING MAX E. MOUSE SO WE WON'T BE TOO CONSPICUOUS!
WE'LL HAVE THAT OL' BLOT UNDER LOCK 'N' KEY BEFORE YUH CAN SAY WHODUNIT! YUK!
I HOPE SO, BUT LET'S NOT GET OVERCONFIDENT!

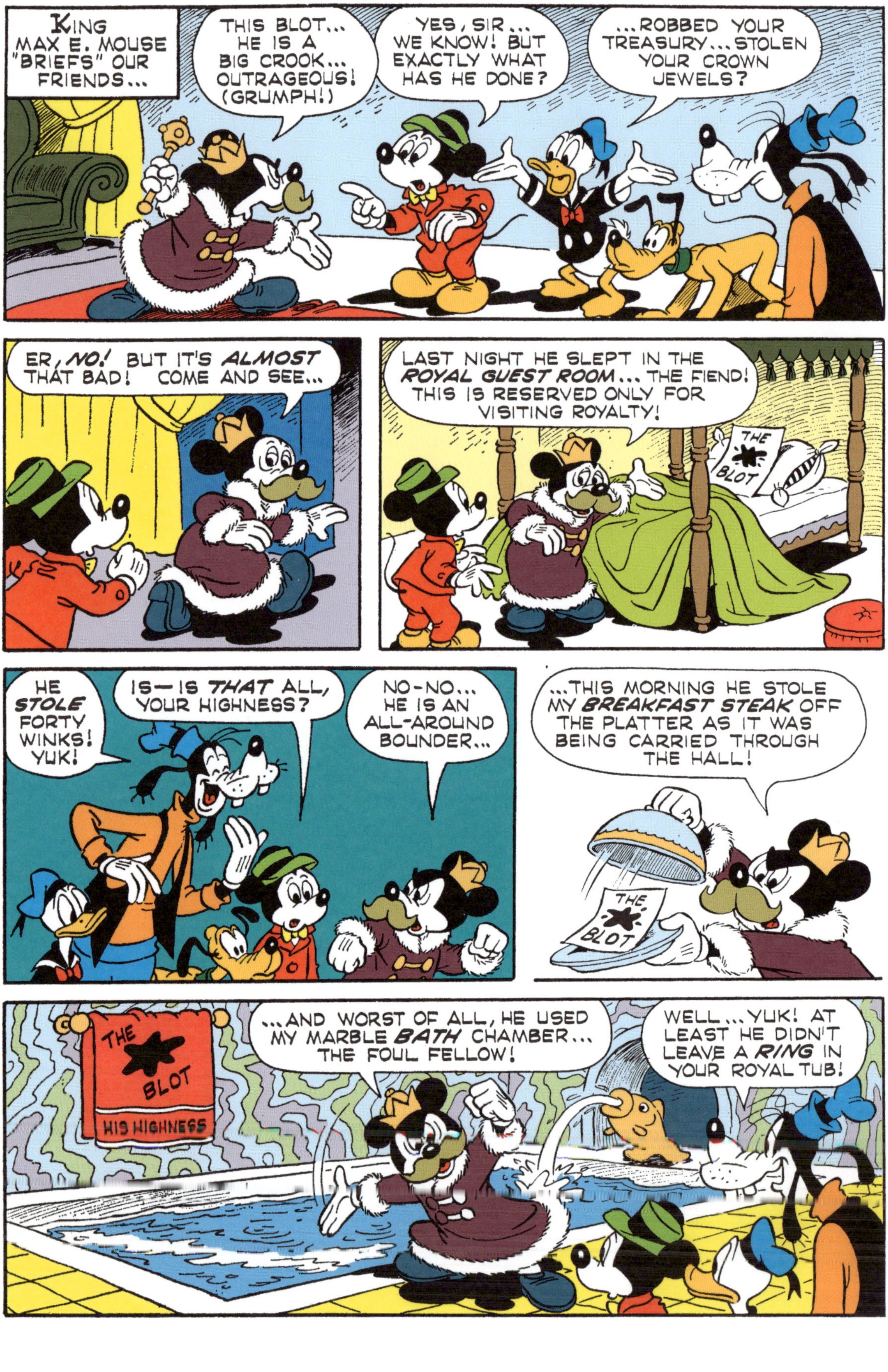
KING MAX E. MOUSE "BRIEFS" OUR FRIENDS...
THIS BLOT... HE IS A BIG CROOK... OUTRAGEOUS! (GRUMPH!)
YES, SIR... WE KNOW! BUT EXACTLY WHAT HAS HE DONE?
...ROBBED YOUR TREASURY... STOLEN YOUR CROWN JEWELS?
ER, NO! BUT IT'S ALMOST THAT BAD! COME AND SEE...
LAST NIGHT HE SLEPT IN THE ROYAL GUEST ROOM... THE FIEND! THIS IS RESERVED ONLY FOR VISITING ROYALTY!
THE BLOT
HE STOLE FORTY WINKS! YUK!
IS—IS THAT ALL, YOUR HIGHNESS?
NO-NO... HE IS AN ALL-AROUND BOUNDER...
...THIS MORNING HE STOLE MY BREAKFAST STEAK OFF THE PLATTER AS IT WAS BEING CARRIED THROUGH THE HALL!
THE BLOT
...AND WORST OF ALL, HE USED MY MARBLE BATH CHAMBER... THE FOUL FELLOW!
WELL... YUK! AT LEAST HE DIDN'T LEAVE A RING IN YOUR ROYAL TUB!
THE BLOT
HIS HIGHNESS

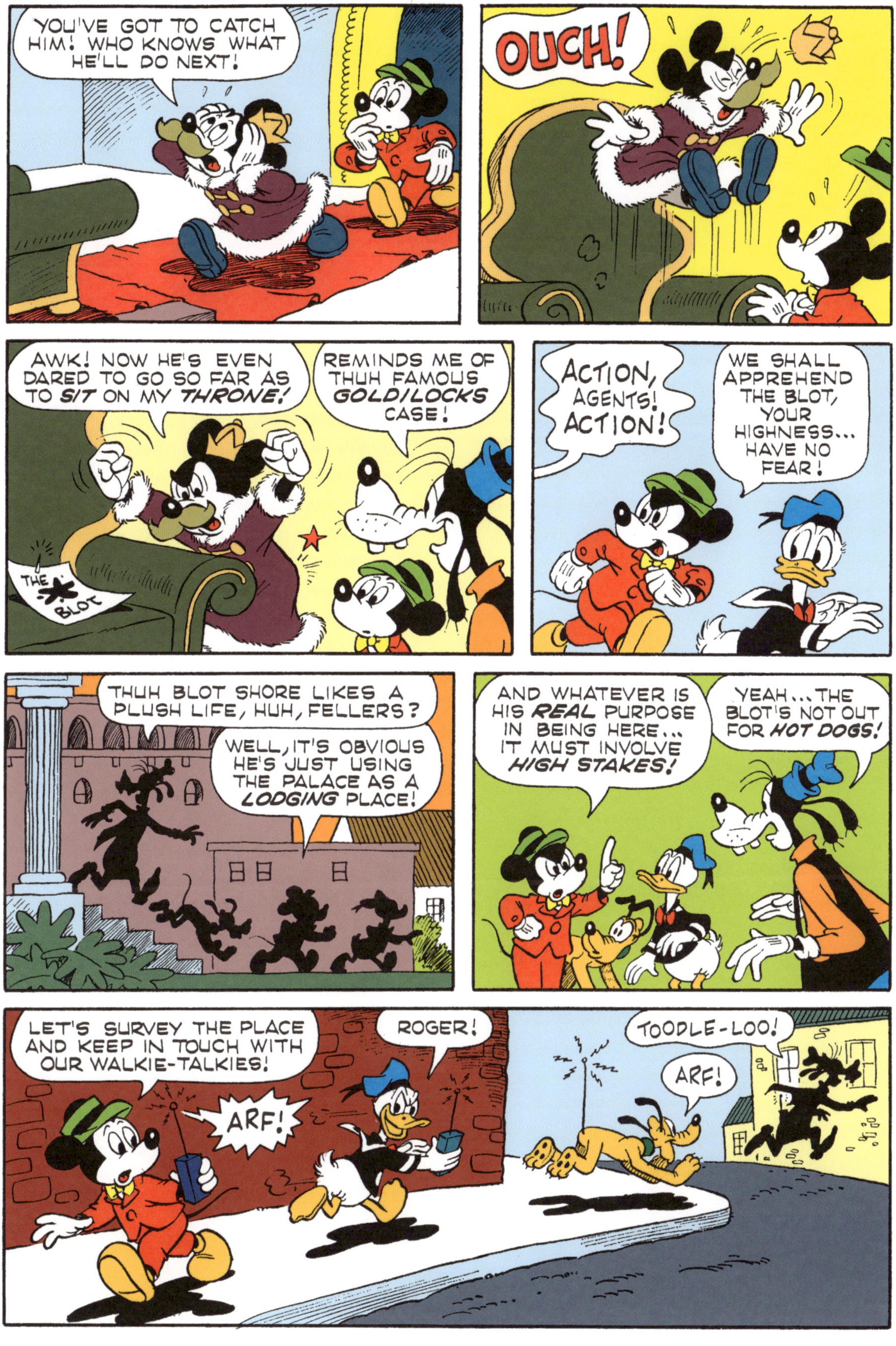
YOU'VE GOT TO CATCH HIM! WHO KNOWS WHAT HE'LL DO NEXT!
OUCH!
AWK! NOW HE'S EVEN DARED TO GO SO FAR AS TO SIT ON MY THRONE!
REMINDS ME OF THUH FAMOUS GOLDILOCKS CASE!
THE BLOT
ACTION, AGENTS! ACTION!
WE SHALL APPREHEND THE BLOT, YOUR HIGHNESS... HAVE NO FEAR!
THUH BLOT SHORE LIKES A PLUSH LIFE, HUH, FELLERS?
WELL, IT'S OBVIOUS HE'S JUST USING THE PALACE AS A LODGING PLACE!
AND WHATEVER IS HIS REAL PURPOSE IN BEING HERE... IT MUST INVOLVE HIGH STAKES!
YEAH... THE BLOT'S NOT OUT FOR HOT DOGS!
LET'S SURVEY THE PLACE AND KEEP IN TOUCH WITH OUR WALKIE-TALKIES!
ARF!
ROGER!
TOODLE-LOO!
ARF!

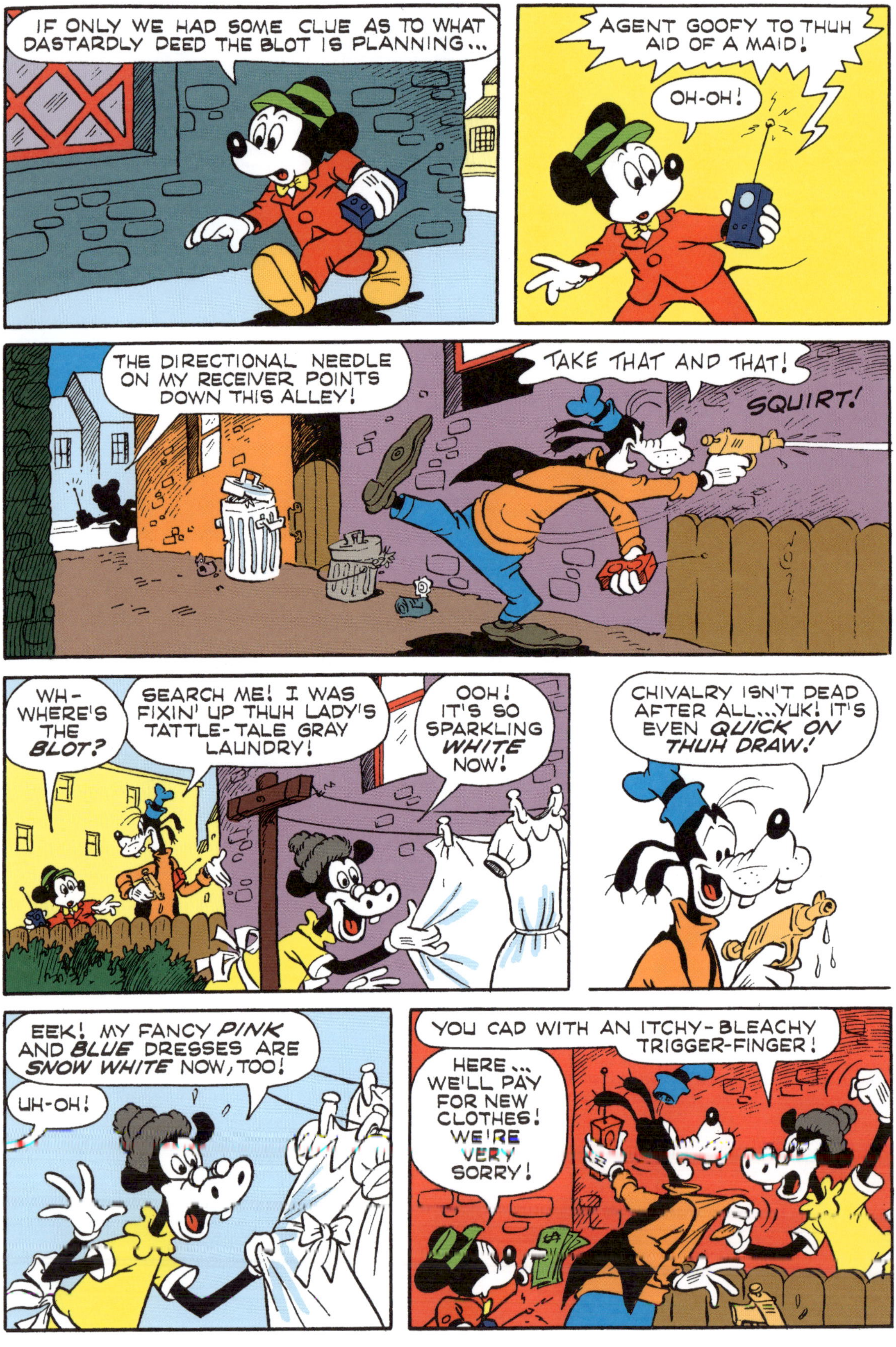
IF ONLY WE HAD SOME CLUE AS TO WHAT DASTARDLY DEED THE BLOT IS PLANNING...
AGENT GOOFY TO THUH AID OF A MAID!
OH-OH!
THE DIRECTIONAL NEEDLE ON MY RECEIVER POINTS DOWN THIS ALLEY!
TAKE THAT AND THAT!
SQUIRT!
WH-WHERE'S THE BLOT?
SEARCH ME! I WAS FIXIN' UP THUH LADY'S TATTLE-TALE GRAY LAUNDRY!
OOH! IT'S SO SPARKLING WHITE NOW!
CHIVALRY ISN'T DEAD AFTER ALL...YUK! IT'S EVEN QUICK ON THUH DRAW!
EEK! MY FANCY PINK AND BLUE DRESSES ARE SNOW WHITE NOW, TOO!
UH-OH!
YOU CAD WITH AN ITCHY-BLEACHY TRIGGER-FINGER!
HERE... WE'LL PAY FOR NEW CLOTHES! WE'RE VERY SORRY!

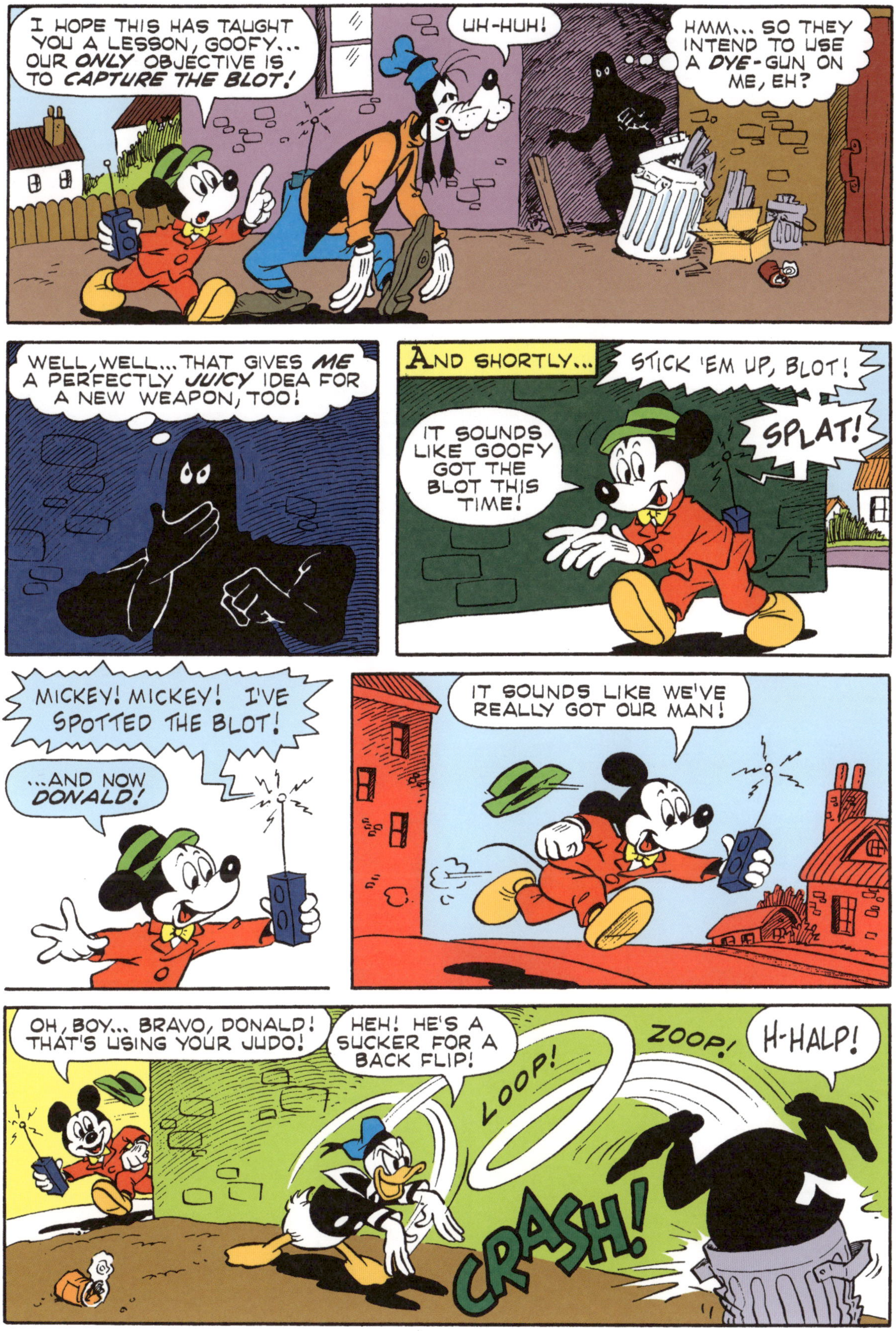
I HOPE THIS HAS TAUGHT YOU A LESSON, GOOFY... OUR ONLY OBJECTIVE IS TO CAPTURE THE BLOT!
UH-HUH!
HMM... SO THEY INTEND TO USE A DYE-GUN ON ME, EH?
WELL, WELL... THAT GIVES ME A PERFECTLY JUICY IDEA FOR A NEW WEAPON, TOO!
AND SHORTLY...
STICK 'EM UP, BLOT!
SPLAT!
IT SOUNDS LIKE GOOFY GOT THE BLOT THIS TIME!
MICKEY! MICKEY! I'VE SPOTTED THE BLOT!
...AND NOW DONALD!
IT SOUNDS LIKE WE'VE REALLY GOT OUR MAN!
OH, BOY... BRAVO, DONALD! THAT'S USING YOUR JUDO!
HEH! HE'S A SUCKER FOR A BACK FLIP!
LOOP!
ZOOP!
H-HALP!
CRASH!

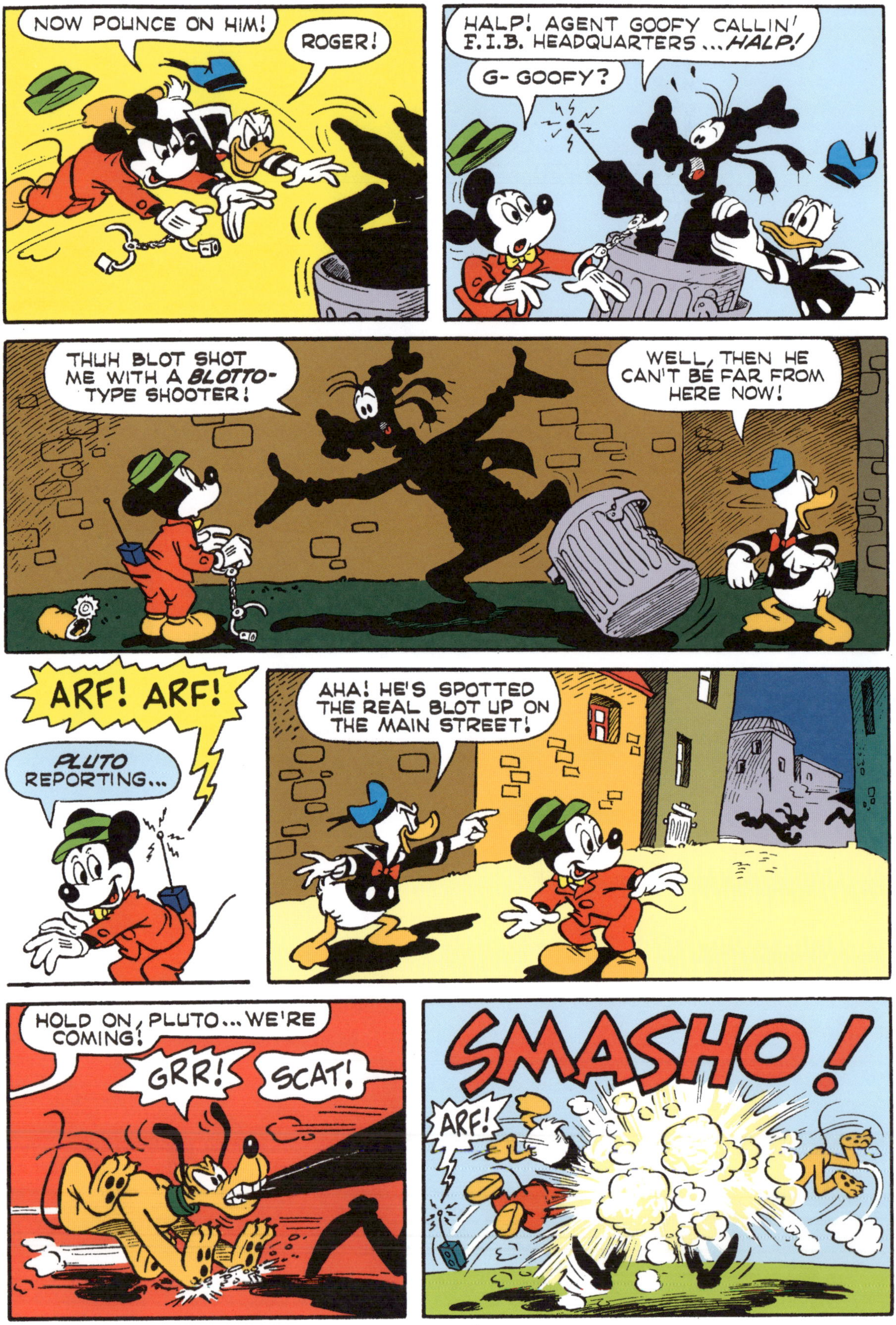
NOW POUNCE ON HIM!
ROGER!
HALP! AGENT GOOFY CALLIN' F.I.B. HEADQUARTERS ... HALP!
G- GOOFY?
THUH BLOT SHOT ME WITH A BLOTTO-TYPE SHOOTER!
WELL, THEN HE CAN'T BE FAR FROM HERE NOW!
ARF! ARF!
PLUTO REPORTING...
AHA! HE'S SPOTTED THE REAL BLOT UP ON THE MAIN STREET!
HOLD ON, PLUTO... WE'RE COMING!
GRR!
SCAT!
SMASHO!
ARF!

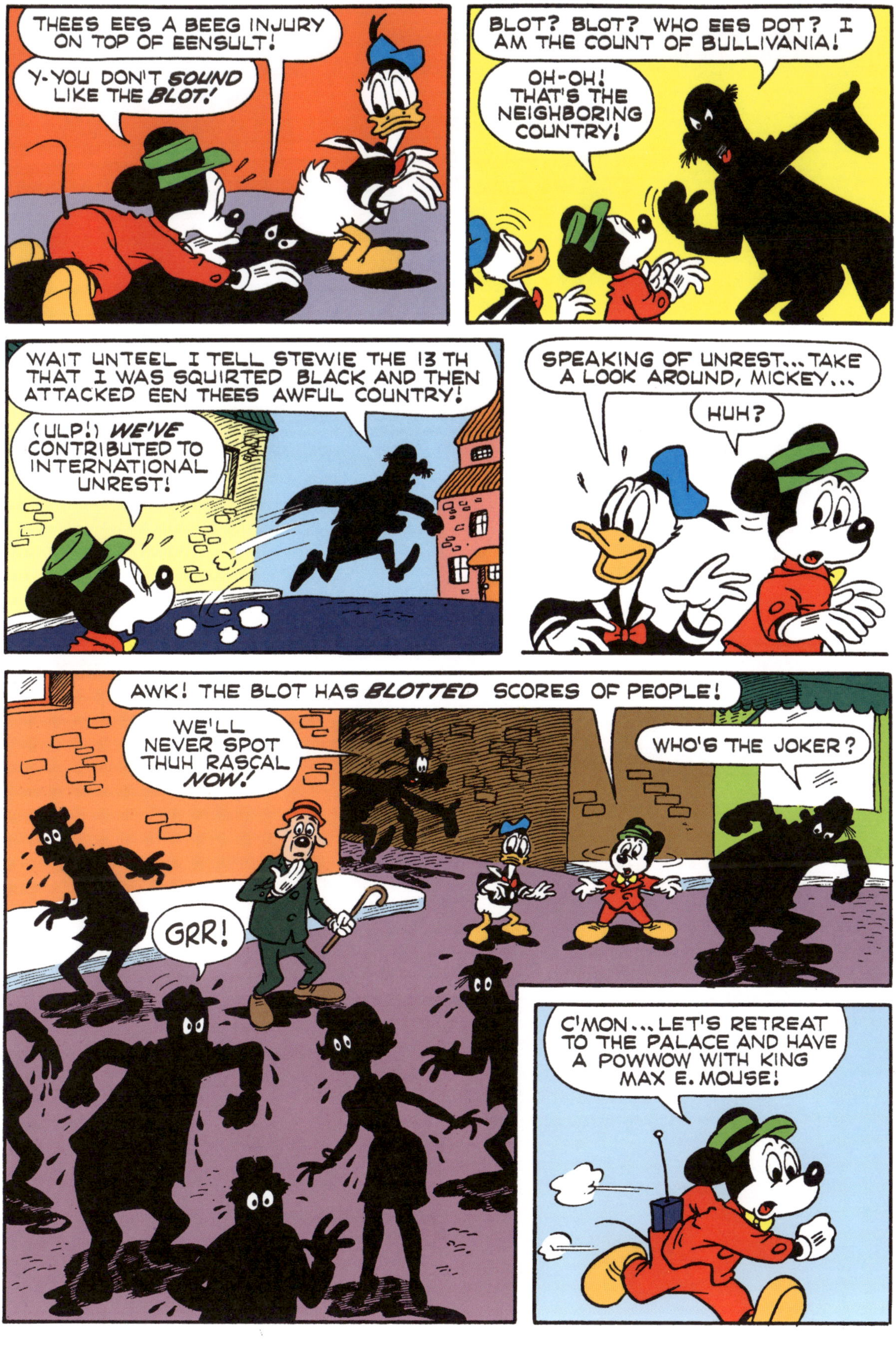
THEES EES A BEEG INJURY ON TOP OF EENSULT!
Y-YOU DON'T *SOUND* LIKE THE *BLOT!*
BLOT? BLOT? WHO EES DOT? I AM THE COUNT OF BULLIVANIA!
OH-OH! THAT'S THE NEIGHBORING COUNTRY!
WAIT UNTEEL I TELL STEWIE THE 13 TH THAT I WAS SQUIRTED BLACK AND THEN ATTACKED EEN THEES AWFUL COUNTRY!
(ULP!) *WE'VE* CONTRIBUTED TO INTERNATIONAL UNREST!
SPEAKING OF UNREST... TAKE A LOOK AROUND, MICKEY...
HUH?
AWK! THE BLOT HAS *BLOTTED* SCORES OF PEOPLE!
WE'LL NEVER SPOT THUH RASCAL *NOW!*
WHO'S THE JOKER?
GRR!
C'MON... LET'S RETREAT TO THE PALACE AND HAVE A POWWOW WITH KING MAX E. MOUSE!

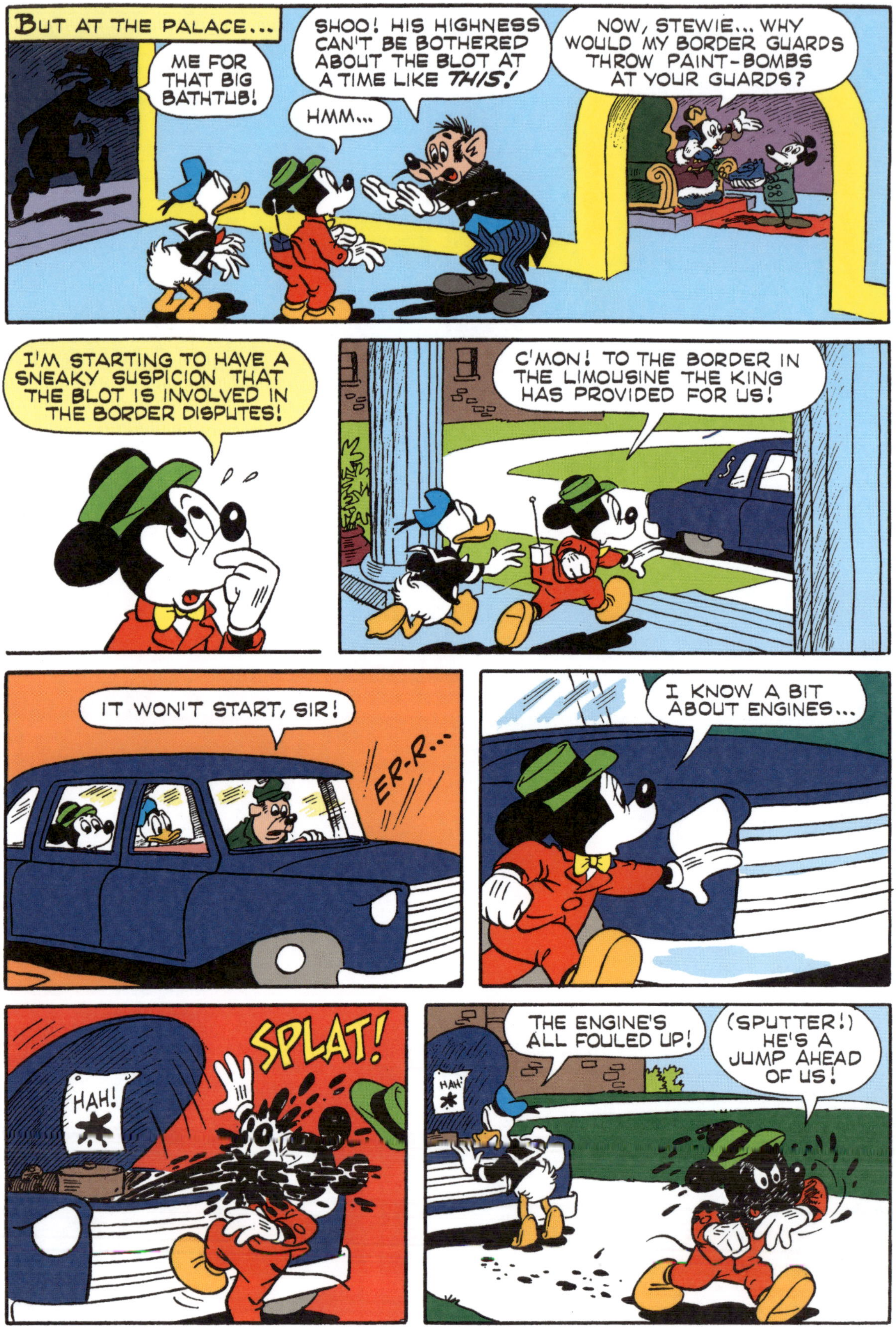
BUT AT THE PALACE...
ME FOR THAT BIG BATHTUB!
SHOO! HIS HIGHNESS CAN'T BE BOTHERED ABOUT THE BLOT AT A TIME LIKE THIS!
HMM...
NOW, STEWIE... WHY WOULD MY BORDER GUARDS THROW PAINT-BOMBS AT YOUR GUARDS?
I'M STARTING TO HAVE A SNEAKY SUSPICION THAT THE BLOT IS INVOLVED IN THE BORDER DISPUTES!
C'MON! TO THE BORDER IN THE LIMOUSINE THE KING HAS PROVIDED FOR US!
IT WON'T START, SIR!
ER-R...
I KNOW A BIT ABOUT ENGINES...
SPLAT!
HAH!
THE ENGINE'S ALL FOULED UP!
(SPUTTER!) HE'S A JUMP AHEAD OF US!

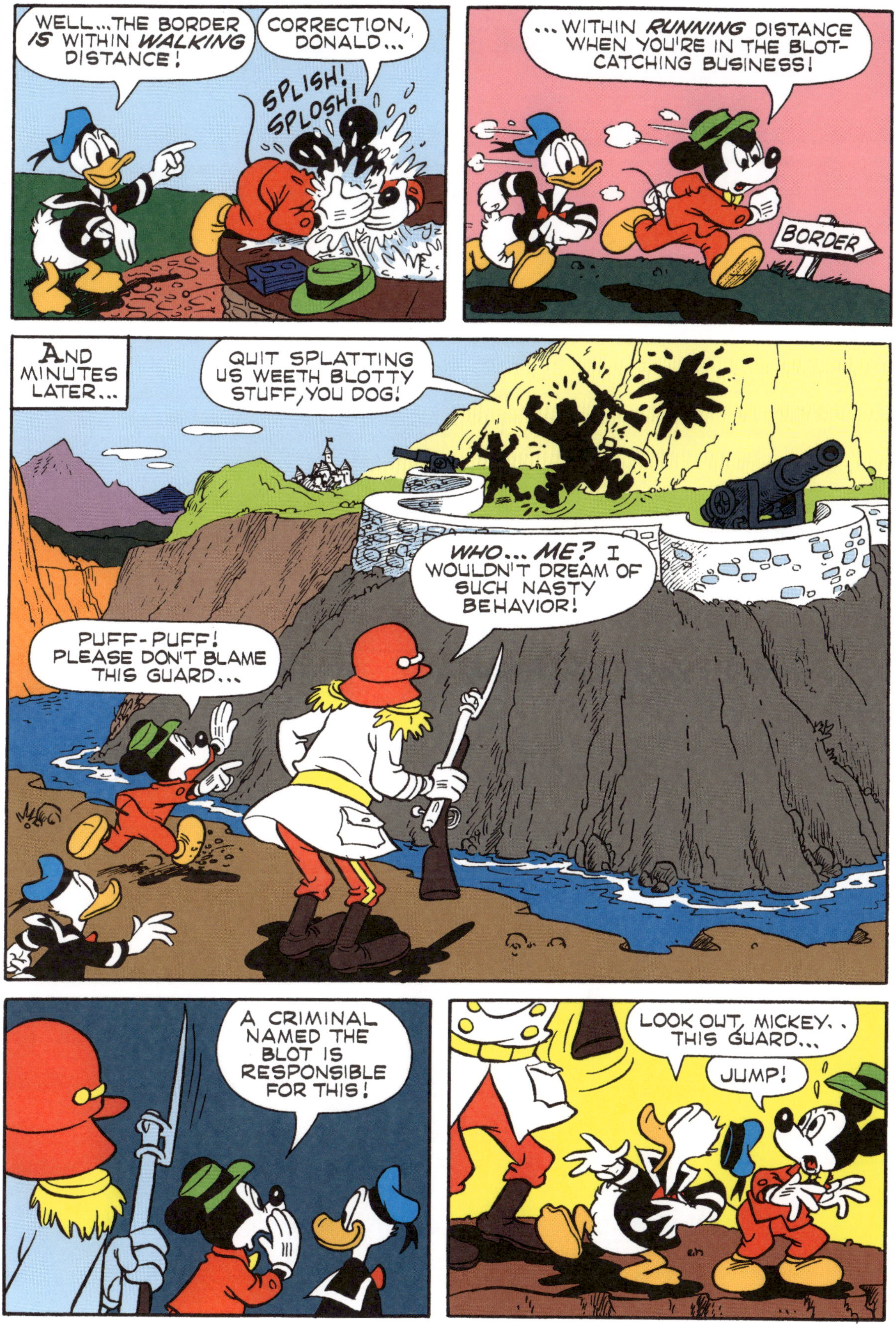
WELL... THE BORDER IS WITHIN WALKING DISTANCE!
CORRECTION, DONALD...
SPLISH! SPLOSH!
...WITHIN RUNNING DISTANCE WHEN YOU'RE IN THE BLOT-CATCHING BUSINESS!
BORDER
AND MINUTES LATER...
QUIT SPLATTING US WEETH BLOTTY STUFF, YOU DOG!
WHO... ME? I WOULDN'T DREAM OF SUCH NASTY BEHAVIOR!
PUFF-PUFF! PLEASE DON'T BLAME THIS GUARD...
A CRIMINAL NAMED THE BLOT IS RESPONSIBLE FOR THIS!
LOOK OUT, MICKEY.. THIS GUARD...
JUMP!

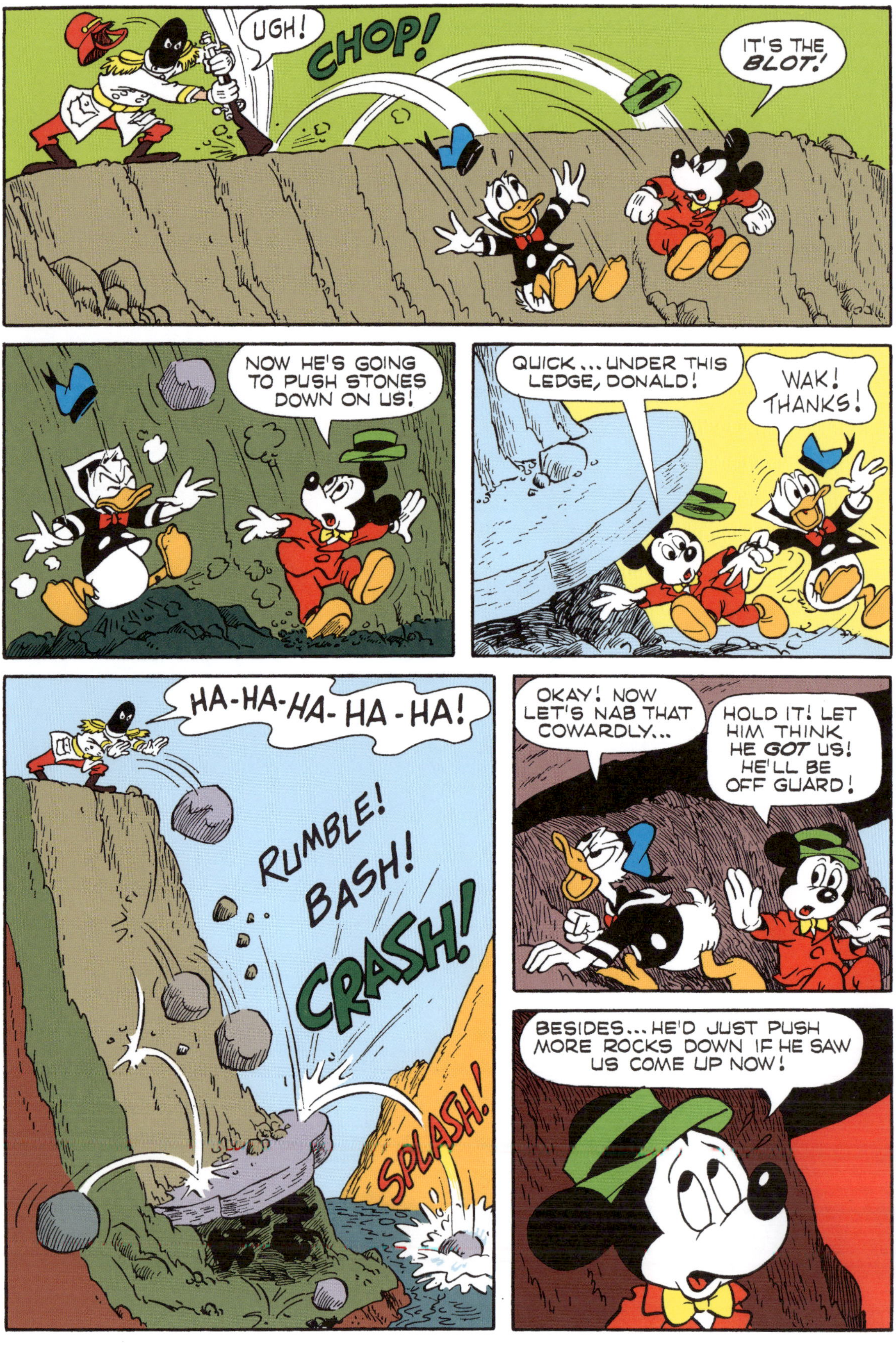
UGH!
CHOP!
IT'S THE BLOT!
NOW HE'S GOING TO PUSH STONES DOWN ON US!
QUICK ... UNDER THIS LEDGE, DONALD!
WAK! THANKS!
HA-HA-HA-HA-HA!
RUMBLE!
BASH!
CRASH!
SPLASH!
OKAY! NOW LET'S NAB THAT COWARDLY...
HOLD IT! LET HIM THINK HE GOT US! HE'LL BE OFF GUARD!
BESIDES... HE'D JUST PUSH MORE ROCKS DOWN IF HE SAW US COME UP NOW!

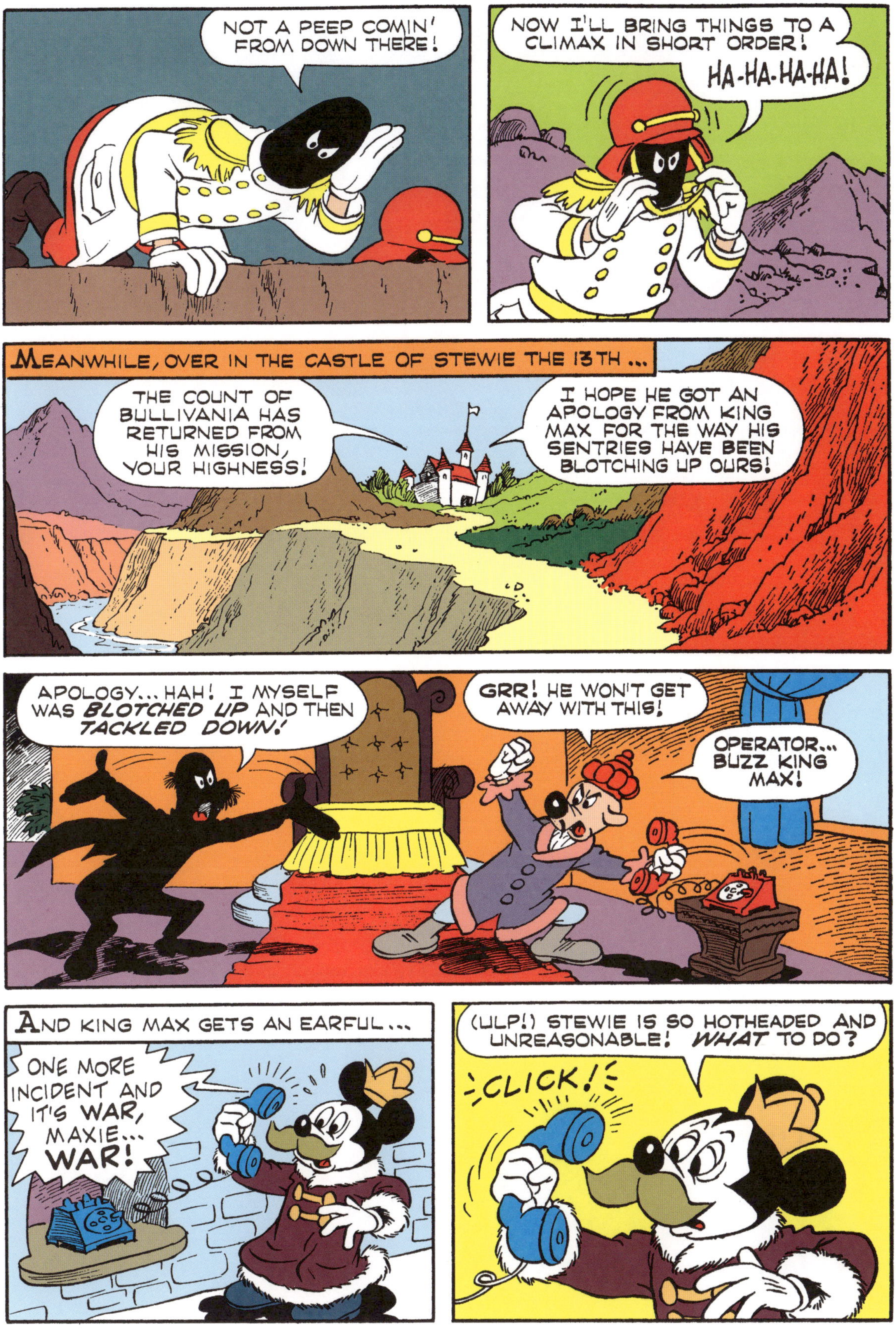

NOT A PEEP COMIN' FROM DOWN THERE!
NOW I'LL BRING THINGS TO A CLIMAX IN SHORT ORDER!
HA-HA-HA-HA!
MEANWHILE, OVER IN THE CASTLE OF STEWIE THE 13TH ...
THE COUNT OF BULLIVANIA HAS RETURNED FROM HIS MISSION, YOUR HIGHNESS!
I HOPE HE GOT AN APOLOGY FROM KING MAX FOR THE WAY HIS SENTRIES HAVE BEEN BLOTCHING UP OURS!
APOLOGY... HAH! I MYSELF WAS BLOTCHED UP AND THEN TACKLED DOWN!
GRR! HE WON'T GET AWAY WITH THIS!
OPERATOR... BUZZ KING MAX!
AND KING MAX GETS AN EARFUL...
ONE MORE INCIDENT AND IT'S WAR, MAXIE... WAR!
(ULP!) STEWIE IS SO HOTHEADED AND UNREASONABLE! WHAT TO DO?
CLICK!

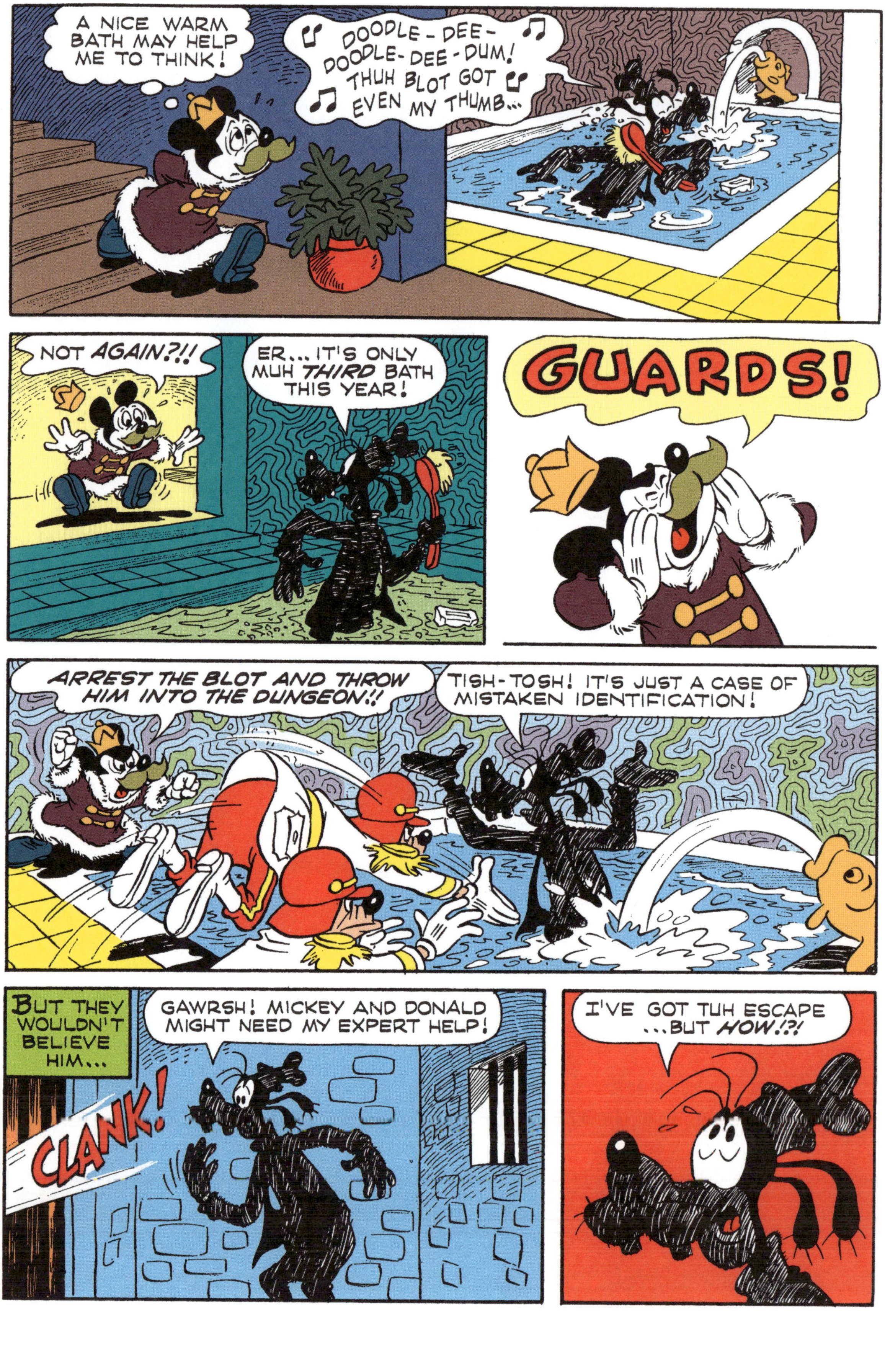
A NICE WARM BATH MAY HELP ME TO THINK!
DOODLE-DEE-DOODLE-DEE-DUM! THUH BLOT GOT EVEN MY THUMB...
NOT AGAIN?!!
ER... IT'S ONLY MUH THIRD BATH THIS YEAR!
GUARDS!
ARREST THE BLOT AND THROW HIM INTO THE DUNGEON!!
TISH-TOSH! IT'S JUST A CASE OF MISTAKEN IDENTIFICATION!
BUT THEY WOULDN'T BELIEVE HIM...
GAWRSH! MICKEY AND DONALD MIGHT NEED MY EXPERT HELP!
CLANK!
I'VE GOT TUH ESCAPE ...BUT HOW!?!

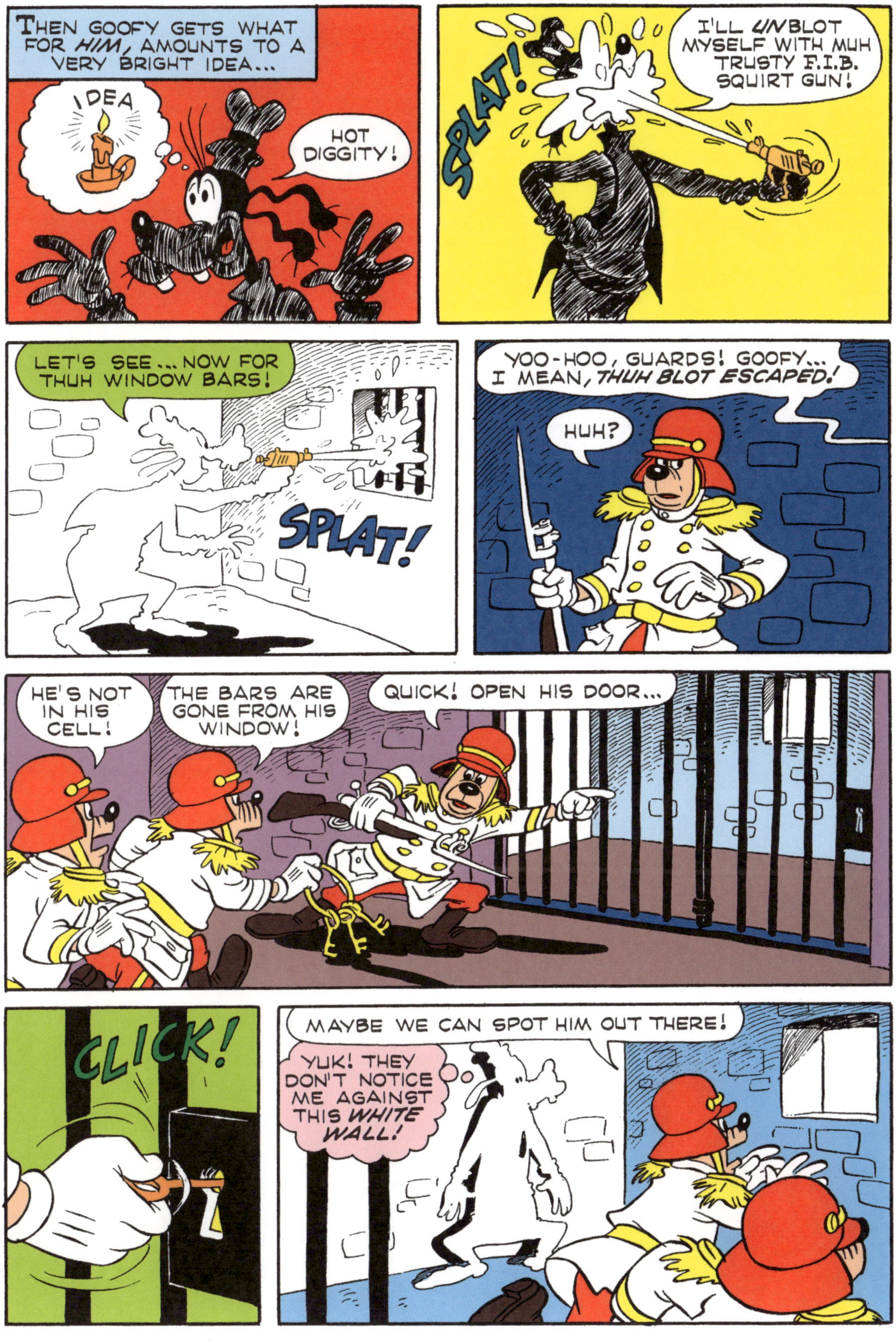
THEN GOOFY GETS WHAT FOR *HIM*, AMOUNTS TO A VERY BRIGHT IDEA...
IDEA
HOT DIGGITY!
SPLAT!
I'LL *UN*BLOT MYSELF WITH MUH TRUSTY F.I.B. SQUIRT GUN!
LET'S SEE... NOW FOR THUH WINDOW BARS!
SPLAT!
YOO-HOO, GUARDS! GOOFY... I MEAN, *THUH BLOT ESCAPED!*
HUH?
HE'S NOT IN HIS CELL!
THE BARS ARE GONE FROM HIS WINDOW!
QUICK! OPEN HIS DOOR...
CLICK!
MAYBE WE CAN SPOT HIM OUT THERE!
YUK! THEY DON'T NOTICE ME AGAINST THIS *WHITE WALL!*

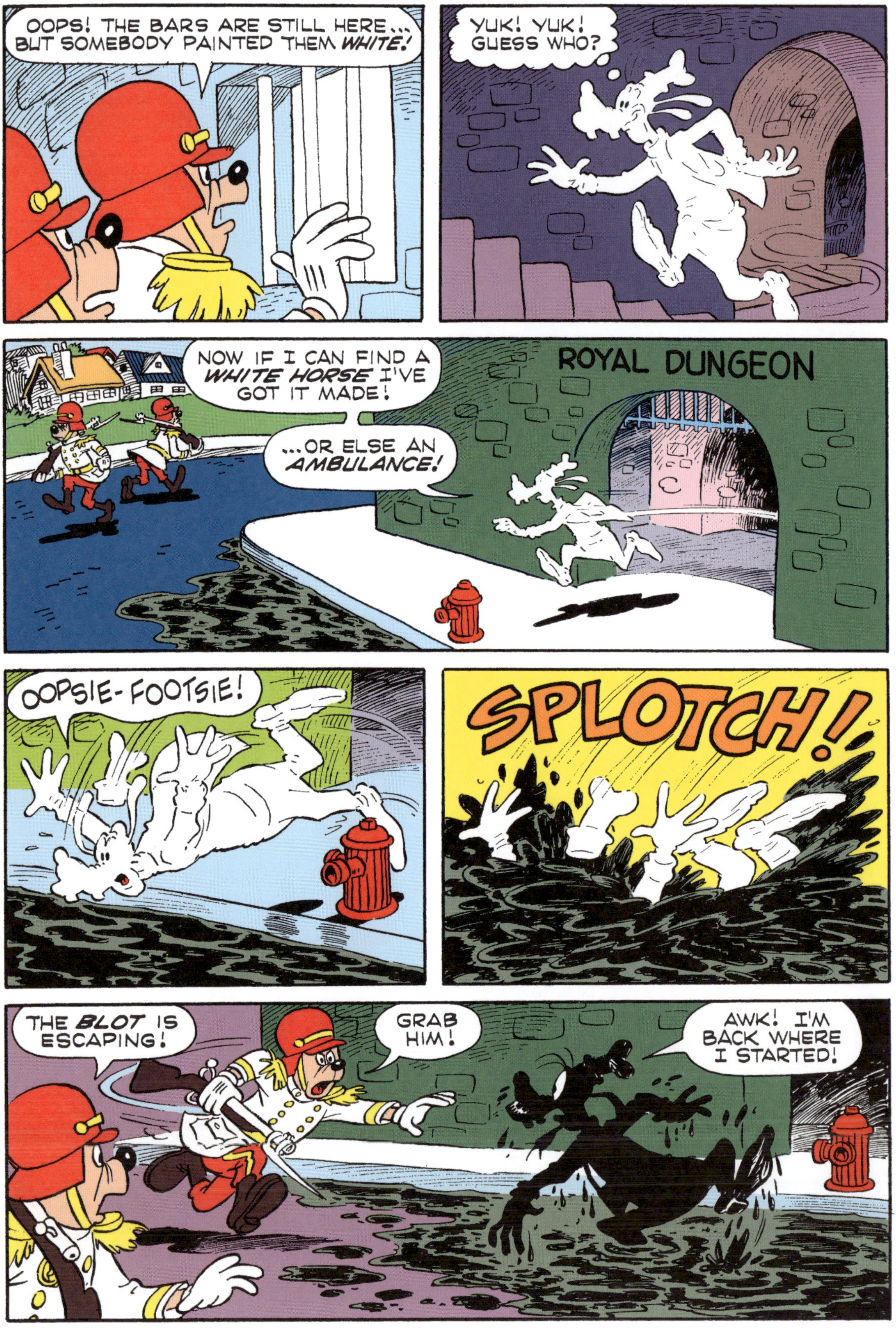
OOPS! THE BARS ARE STILL HERE... BUT SOMEBODY PAINTED THEM *WHITE!*
YUK! YUK! GUESS WHO?
NOW IF I CAN FIND A *WHITE HORSE* I'VE GOT IT MADE!
...OR ELSE AN *AMBULANCE!*
ROYAL DUNGEON
OOPSIE-FOOTSIE!
SPLOTCH!
THE *BLOT* IS ESCAPING!
GRAB HIM!
AWK! I'M BACK WHERE I STARTED!

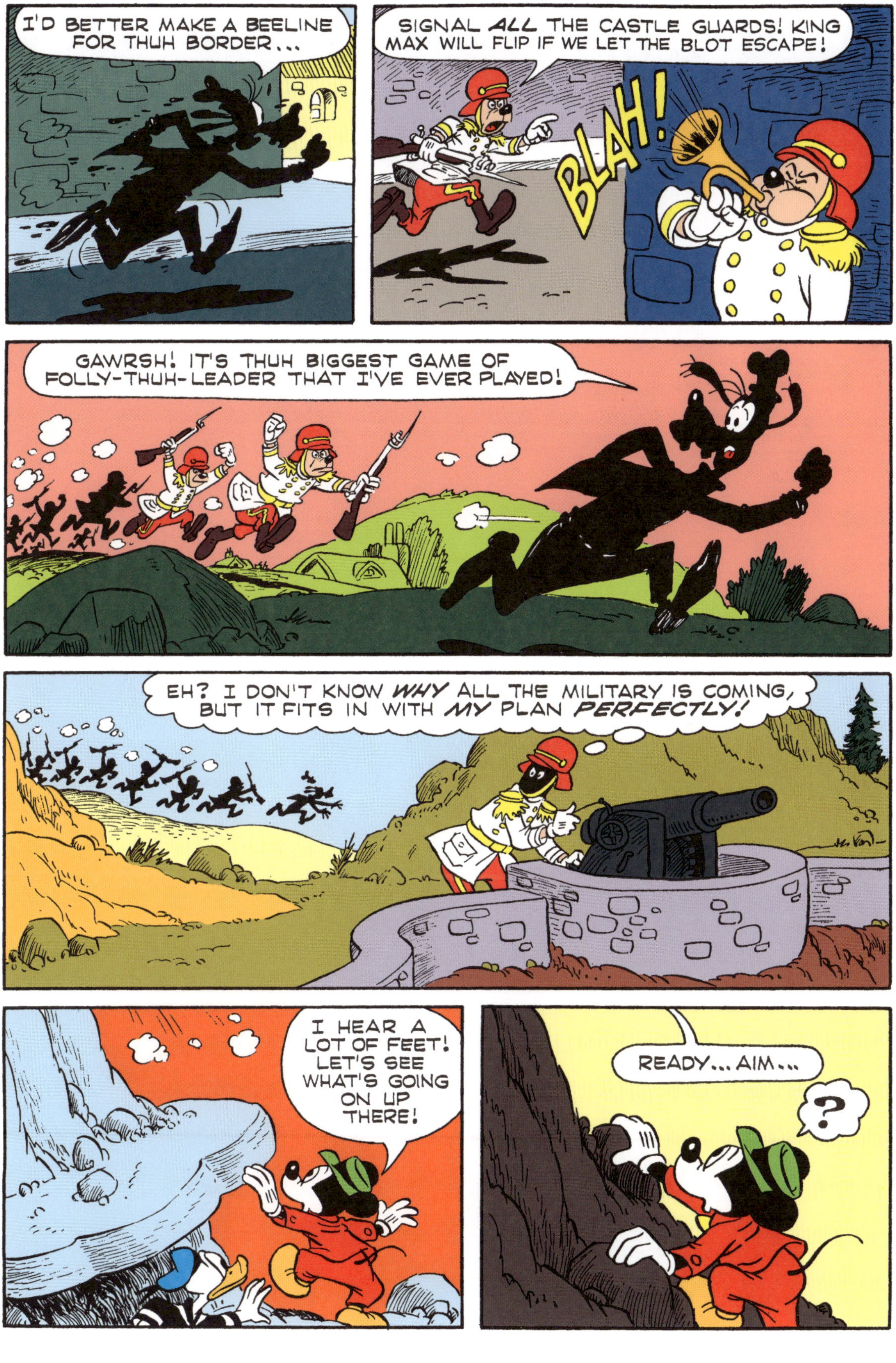
I'D BETTER MAKE A BEELINE FOR THUH BORDER...
SIGNAL ALL THE CASTLE GUARDS! KING MAX WILL FLIP IF WE LET THE BLOT ESCAPE!
BLAH!
GAWRSH! IT'S THUH BIGGEST GAME OF FOLLY-THUH-LEADER THAT I'VE EVER PLAYED!
EH? I DON'T KNOW WHY ALL THE MILITARY IS COMING, BUT IT FITS IN WITH MY PLAN PERFECTLY!
I HEAR A LOT OF FEET! LET'S SEE WHAT'S GOING ON UP THERE!
READY... AIM...
?

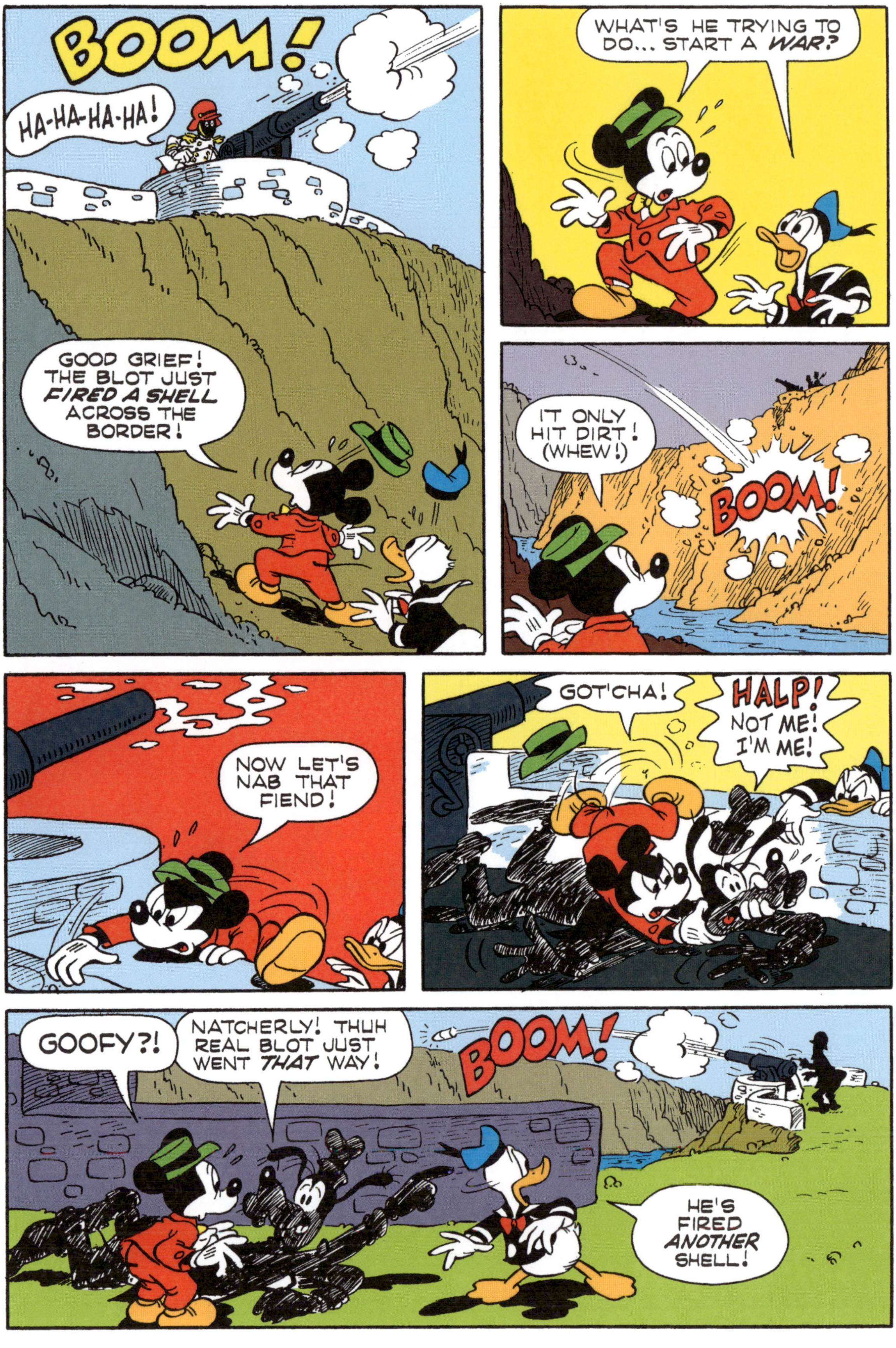
BOOM!
HA-HA-HA-HA!
WHAT'S HE TRYING TO DO... START A WAR?
GOOD GRIEF! THE BLOT JUST FIRED A SHELL ACROSS THE BORDER!
IT ONLY HIT DIRT! (WHEW!)
BOOM!
NOW LET'S NAB THAT FIEND!
GOT'CHA!
HALP! NOT ME! I'M ME!
GOOFY?!
NATCHERLY! THUH REAL BLOT JUST WENT THAT WAY!
BOOM!
HE'S FIRED ANOTHER SHELL!

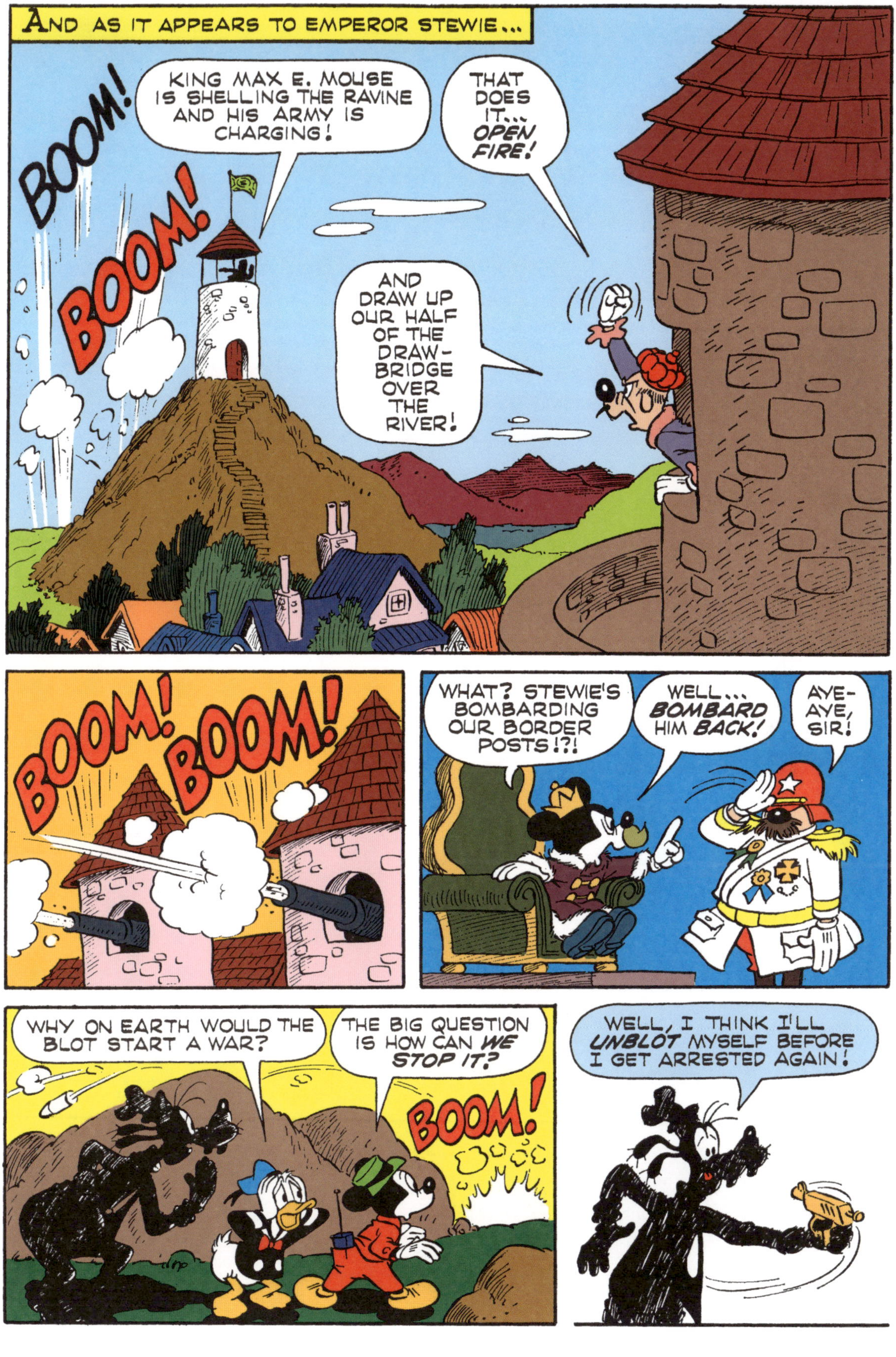
AND AS IT APPEARS TO EMPEROR STEWIE...
BOOM!
BOOM!
KING MAX E. MOUSE IS SHELLING THE RAVINE AND HIS ARMY IS CHARGING!
THAT DOES IT... OPEN FIRE!
AND DRAW UP OUR HALF OF THE DRAW-BRIDGE OVER THE RIVER!
BOOM! BOOM!
WHAT? STEWIE'S BOMBARDING OUR BORDER POSTS!?!
WELL... BOMBARD HIM BACK!
AYE-AYE, SIR!
WHY ON EARTH WOULD THE BLOT START A WAR?
THE BIG QUESTION IS HOW CAN WE STOP IT?
BOOM!
WELL, I THINK I'LL UNBLOT MYSELF BEFORE I GET ARRESTED AGAIN!

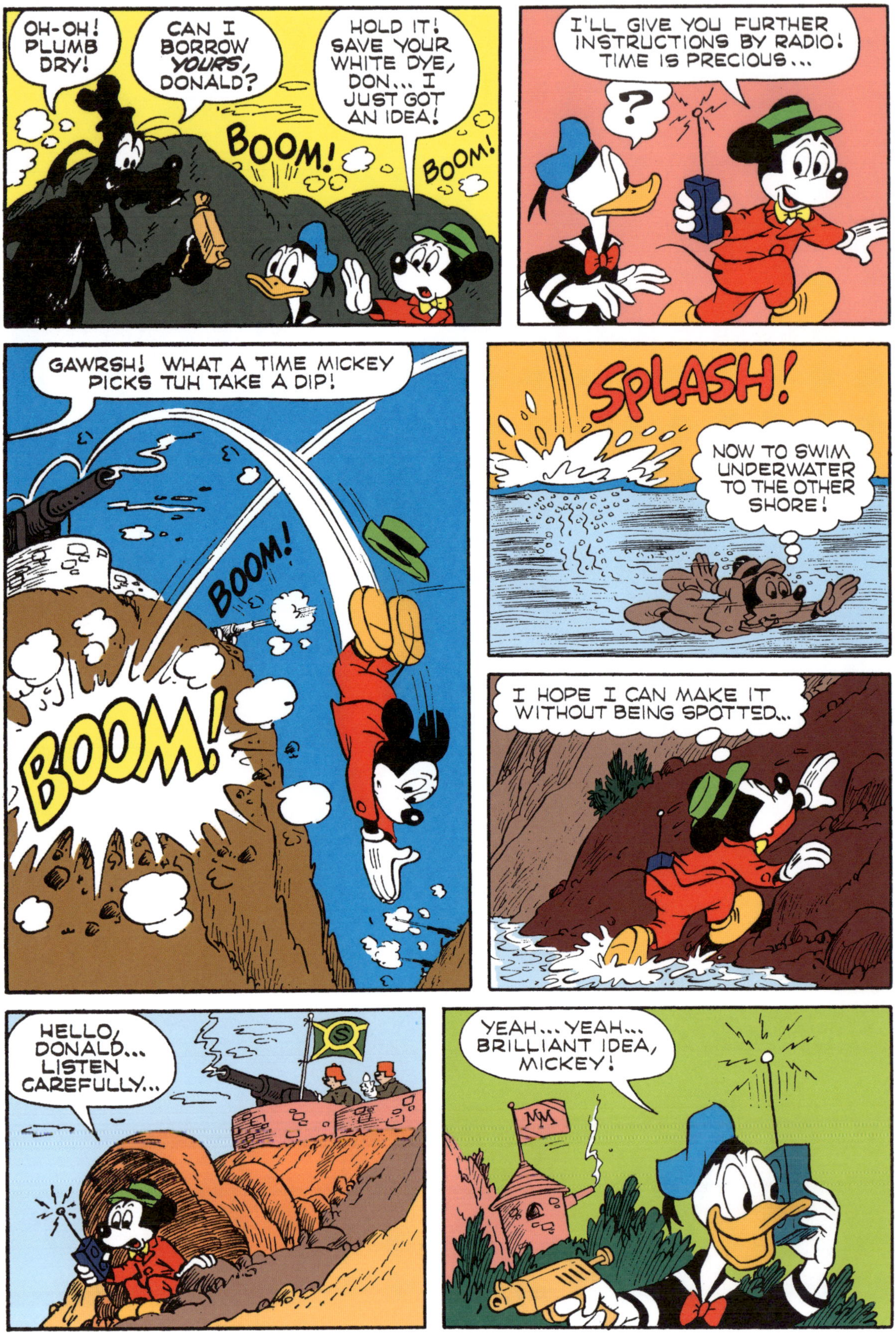
OH-OH! PLUMB DRY!
CAN I BORROW YOURS, DONALD?
HOLD IT! SAVE YOUR WHITE DYE, DON... I JUST GOT AN IDEA!
BOOM!
BOOM!
?
I'LL GIVE YOU FURTHER INSTRUCTIONS BY RADIO! TIME IS PRECIOUS...
GAWRSH! WHAT A TIME MICKEY PICKS TUH TAKE A DIP!
BOOM!
BOOM!
SPLASH!
NOW TO SWIM UNDERWATER TO THE OTHER SHORE!
I HOPE I CAN MAKE IT WITHOUT BEING SPOTTED...
HELLO, DONALD... LISTEN CAREFULLY...
YEAH... YEAH... BRILLIANT IDEA, MICKEY!

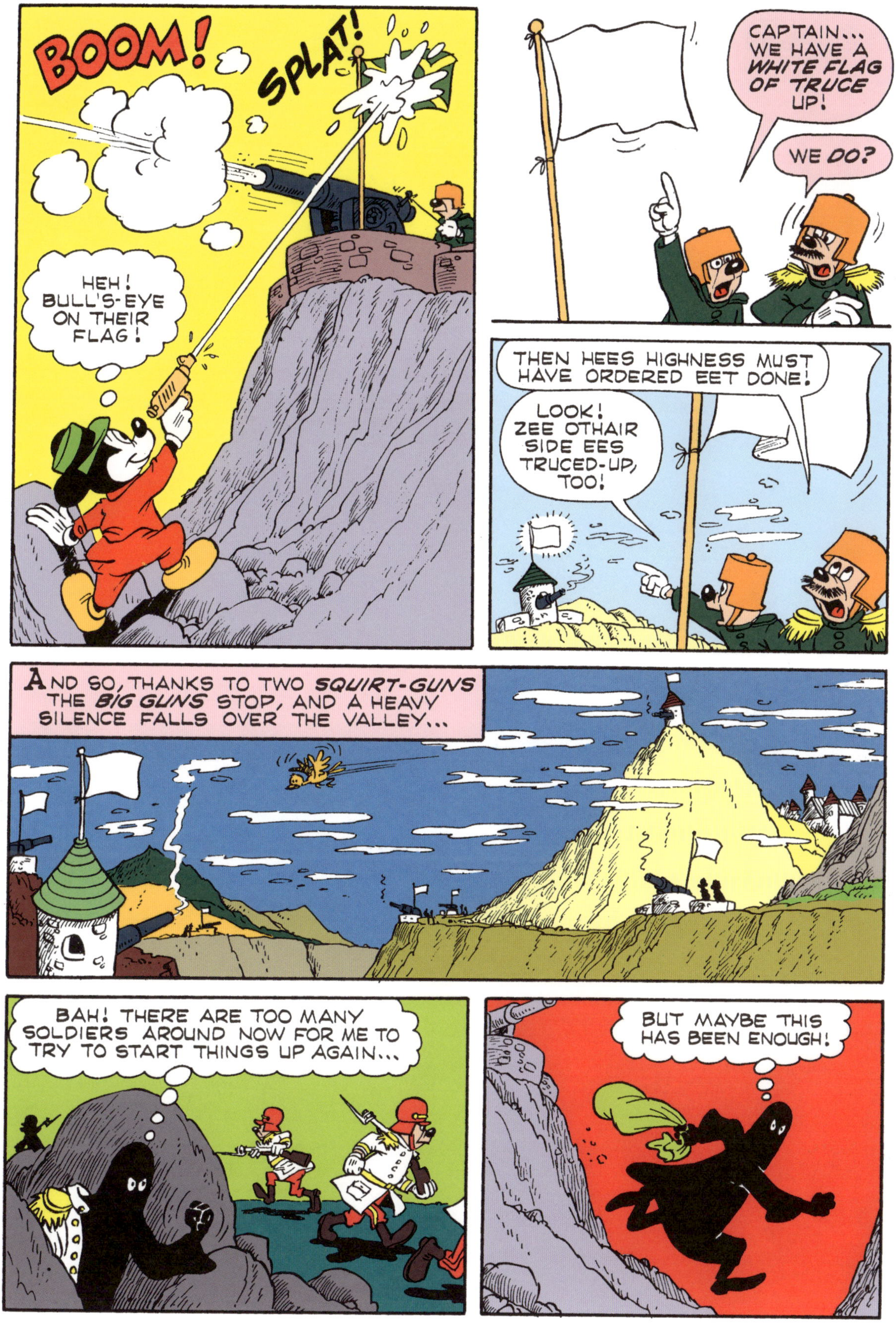
BOOM!
SPLAT!
HEH! BULL'S-EYE ON THEIR FLAG!
CAPTAIN... WE HAVE A WHITE FLAG OF TRUCE UP!
WE DO?
THEN HEES HIGHNESS MUST HAVE ORDERED EET DONE!
LOOK! ZEE OTHAIR SIDE EES TRUCED-UP, TOO!
AND SO, THANKS TO TWO SQUIRT-GUNS THE BIG GUNS STOP, AND A HEAVY SILENCE FALLS OVER THE VALLEY...
BAH! THERE ARE TOO MANY SOLDIERS AROUND NOW FOR ME TO TRY TO START THINGS UP AGAIN...
BUT MAYBE THIS HAS BEEN ENOUGH!

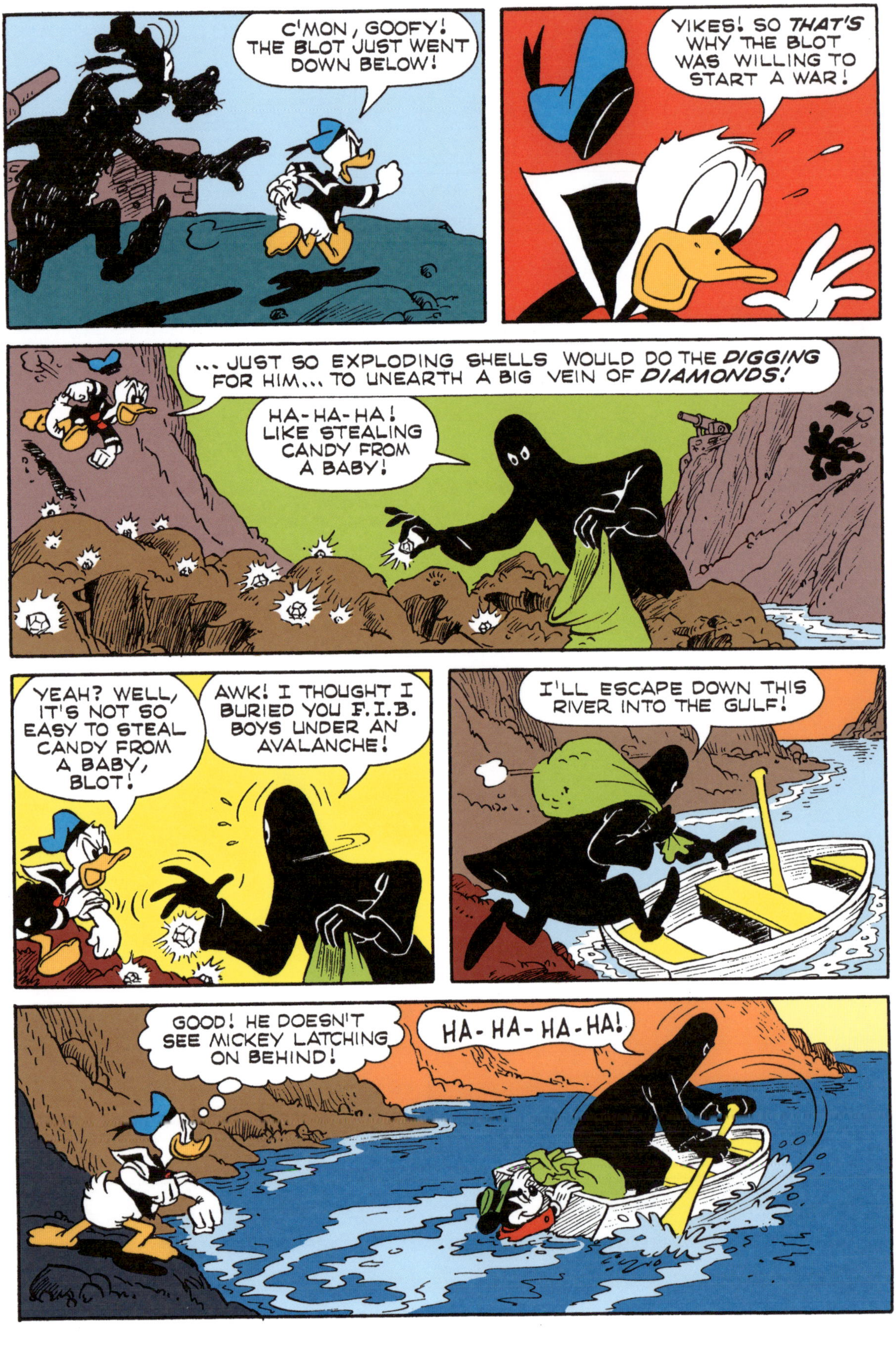
C'MON, GOOFY! THE BLOT JUST WENT DOWN BELOW!
YIKES! SO *THAT'S* WHY THE BLOT WAS WILLING TO START A WAR!
... JUST SO EXPLODING SHELLS WOULD DO THE *DIGGING* FOR HIM... TO UNEARTH A BIG VEIN OF *DIAMONDS!*
HA-HA-HA! LIKE STEALING CANDY FROM A BABY!
YEAH? WELL, IT'S NOT SO EASY TO STEAL CANDY FROM A BABY, BLOT!
AWK! I THOUGHT I BURIED YOU F.I.B. BOYS UNDER AN AVALANCHE!
I'LL ESCAPE DOWN THIS RIVER INTO THE GULF!
GOOD! HE DOESN'T SEE MICKEY LATCHING ON BEHIND!
HA-HA-HA-HA!

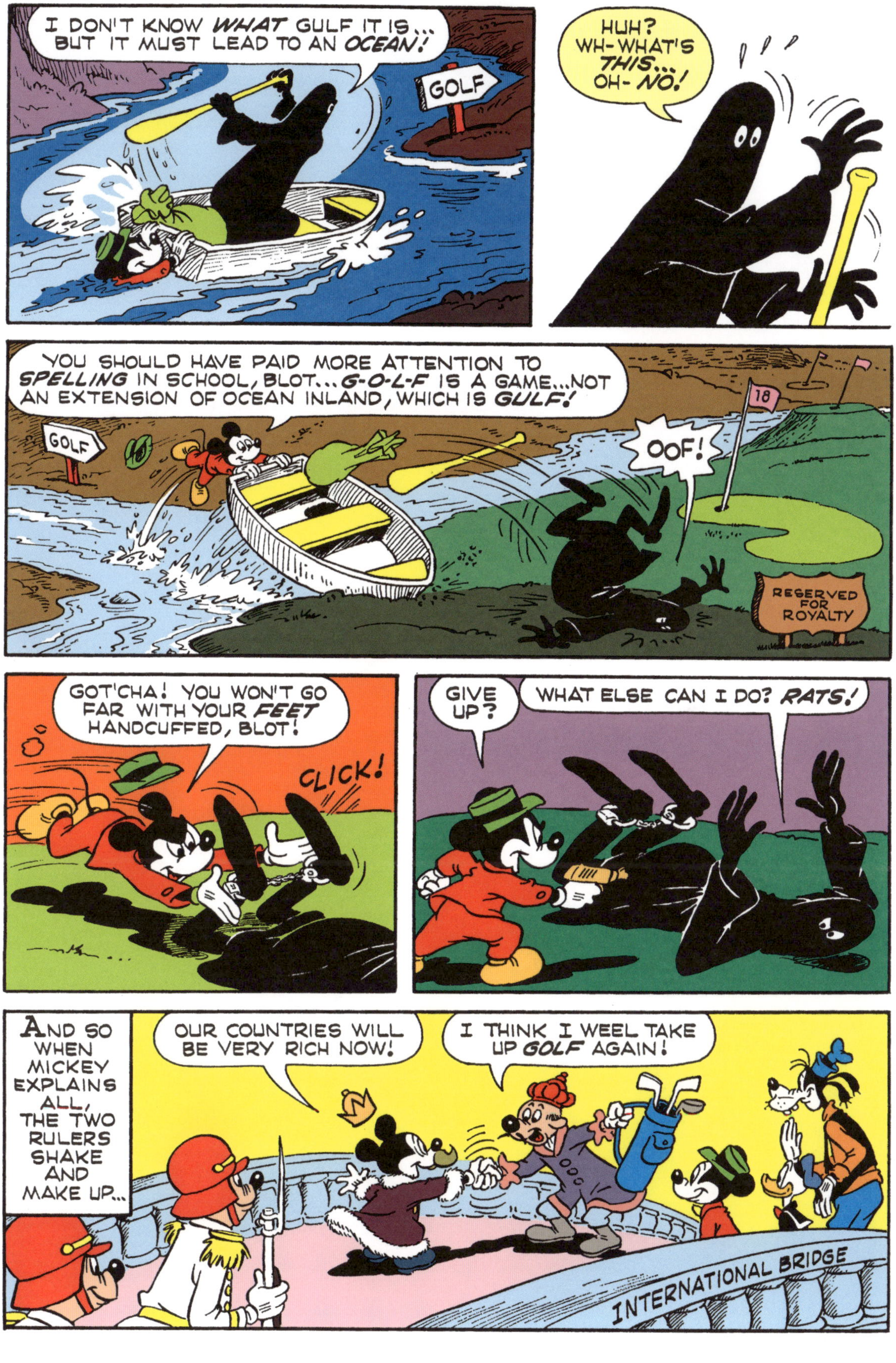

I DON'T KNOW WHAT GULF IT IS... BUT IT MUST LEAD TO AN OCEAN!
GOLF
HUH? WH-WHAT'S THIS... OH- NO!
YOU SHOULD HAVE PAID MORE ATTENTION TO SPELLING IN SCHOOL, BLOT... G-O-L-F IS A GAME...NOT AN EXTENSION OF OCEAN INLAND, WHICH IS GULF!
GOLF
18
OOF!
RESERVED FOR ROYALTY
GOT'CHA! YOU WON'T GO FAR WITH YOUR FEET HANDCUFFED, BLOT!
CLICK!
GIVE UP?
WHAT ELSE CAN I DO? RATS!
AND SO WHEN MICKEY EXPLAINS ALL, THE TWO RULERS SHAKE AND MAKE UP...
OUR COUNTRIES WILL BE VERY RICH NOW!
I THINK I WEEL TAKE UP GOLF AGAIN!
INTERNATIONAL BRIDGE

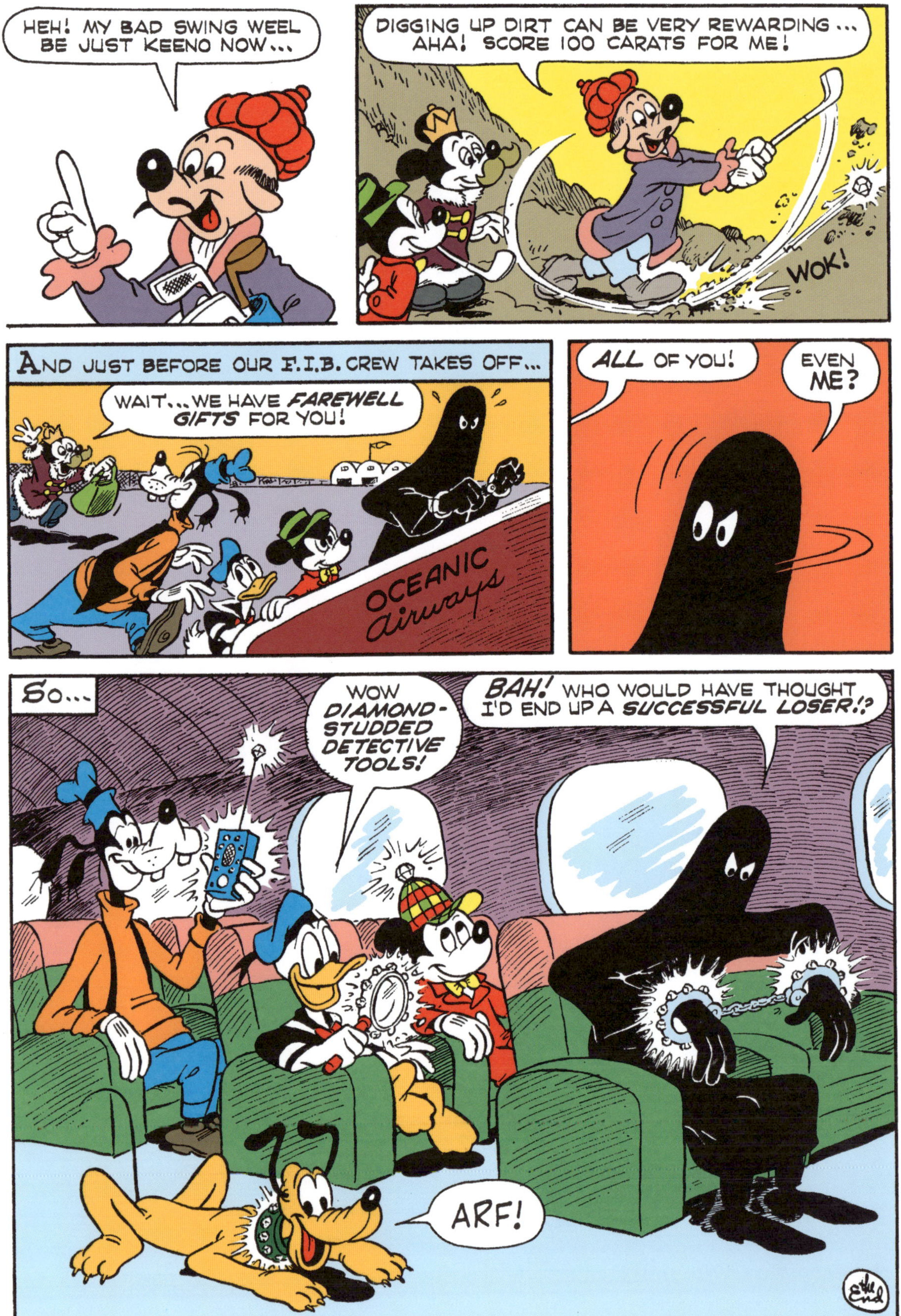
HEH! MY BAD SWING WEEL BE JUST KEENO NOW...
DIGGING UP DIRT CAN BE VERY REWARDING... AHA! SCORE 100 CARATS FOR ME!
WOK!
AND JUST BEFORE OUR F.I.B. CREW TAKES OFF...
WAIT... WE HAVE FAREWELL GIFTS FOR YOU!
OCEANIC Airways
ALL OF YOU!
EVEN ME?
SO...
WOW DIAMOND-STUDDED DETECTIVE TOOLS!
BAH! WHO WOULD HAVE THOUGHT I'D END UP A SUCCESSFUL LOSER!?
ARF!
The End

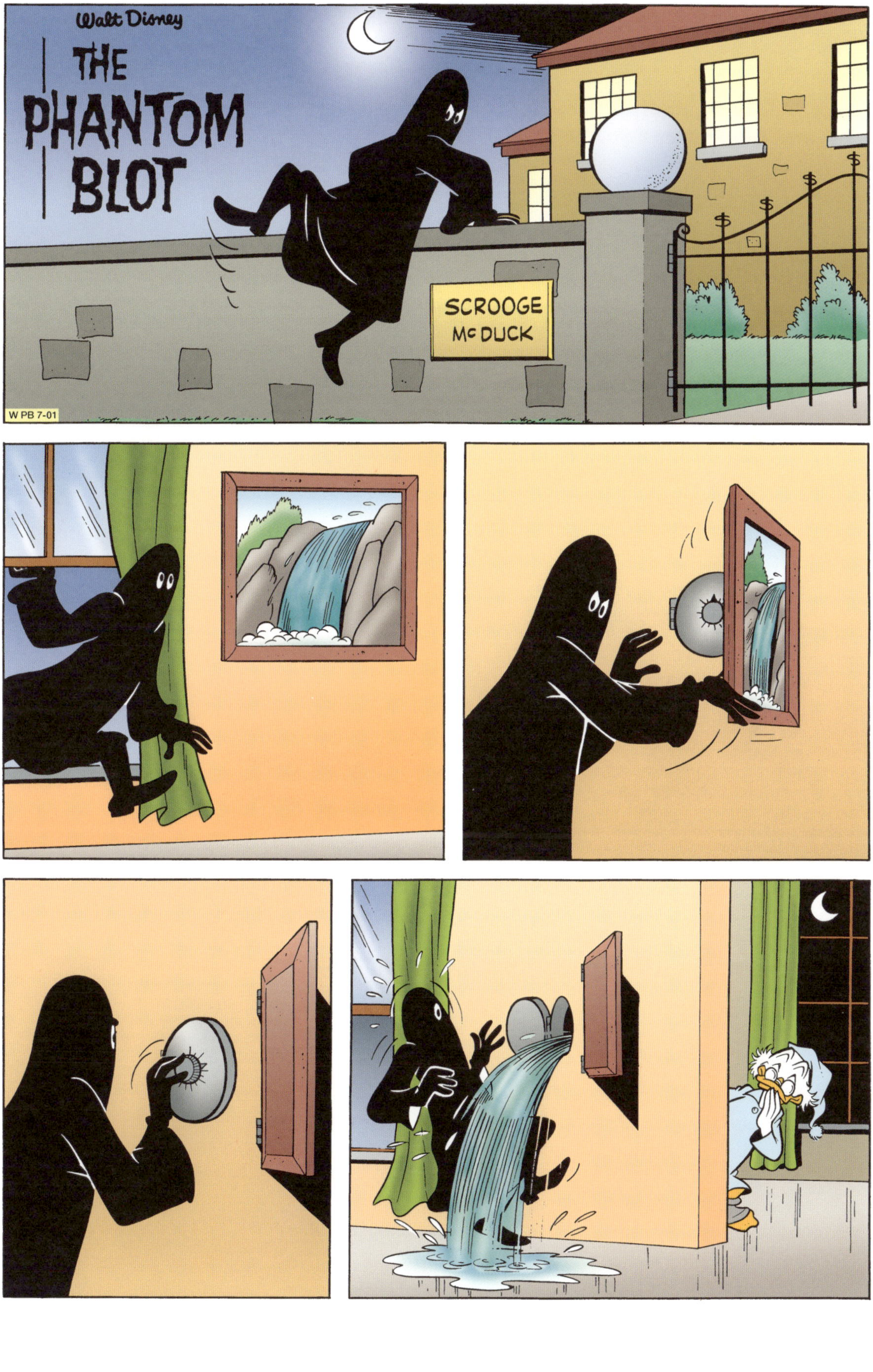
Walt Disney
THE PHANTOM BLOT
SCROOGE McDUCK
W PB 7-01

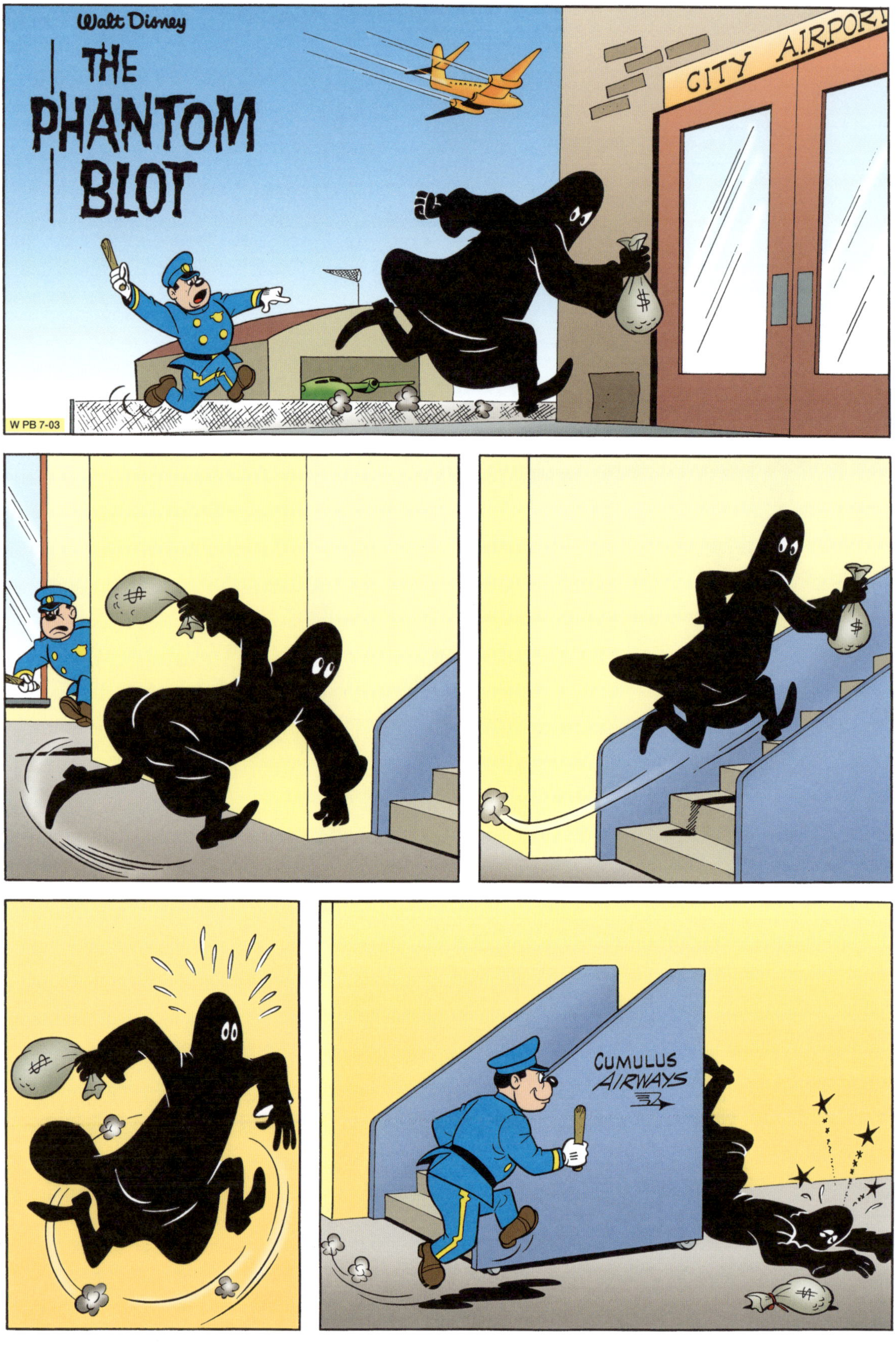
Walt Disney
THE PHANTOM BLOT
CITY AIRPORT
W PB 7-03
CUMULUS AIRWAYS

Paul Murry

by GERMUND VON WOWERN

IT WAS A cold winter's evening in the new year of 1938. Heavy snow covered northwest Missouri and the city of St. Joseph. Paul Murry, a 26-year-old artist and employee of the Artcrafts Engraving Co., suddenly found himself stranded in the city when his bus home was cancelled.

Unaware that he was making a life-changing decision, Murry walked over to the old Missouri Theater to see a new animated feature film, *Snow White and the Seven Dwarfs*. In an interview three decades later with comics scholar Donald Ault, Murry briefly recalled that long-ago evening: "I didn't realize when I was looking at [*Snow White and the Seven Dwarfs*], that five months later I would be in Hollywood."

At the time of Ault's interview, Murry could look back at thousands of penciled and inked comic book pages—his Mickey Mouse stories had been printed in hundreds of millions of newsstand comic books, and his Disney artwork had captivated children around the globe.

That snowy evening in 1938, little in Paul Murry's life foretold such a successful career. Born November 25, 1911, he was raised in Stanberry, 45 miles north of St. Joseph, and spent his young years on a farm, living with his grandparents and devoting himself to farm chores. His mother's fate is unknown; she disappears from records not long after his birth. His father remarried in 1917, just days after Paul's sixth birthday. Murry's unpretentious countryside childhood shaped him for life. The image of Murry that emerges from interviews, family members, and acquaintances is that of a highly pragmatic person. His granddaughter Shannon Murry captured his spirit perhaps better than anyone: "Paul liked things simple. He seemed to be a lonely man, yet preferred

Paul Murry in 1951. Photo © and courtesy Richard Huemer.

it that way. He always poked fun at everything, almost as if he saw life in a cartoon manner."

Yet he did not interact much with other professional artists, with whom he felt he had little in common. He loved the outdoors and playing the harmonica, and he often rose early to play before sitting down at his drawing table.

It was likely Murry's unyielding nature—combined with his interest in drawing—that landed him his employment at the engraving company, despite his lack of formal art education. According to Murry's own account, he entered a puzzle contest in 1937 and decorated his entry with drawings, which caught the eye of the organizers. Not only did he win first prize—a piano—but he was offered a position at the engraving company doing what he later described as "commercial advertising" art. With that work experience—and *Snow White* fresh in mind—he answered an ad from the Disney studio and was given a trainee position. His grandmother then sold the piano, which paid for his trip across the country.

Thus, on June 6, 1938, Murry walked through the doors of the Disney Studio for the first time. Less than four months later, on September 26, he was officially hired and placed in the training department. Murry's employment as in-betweener and assistant animator at the studio taught him a lot. He soon found himself assisting Fred Moore, the studio's principal Mickey man, whose animation work Murry admired immensely. Murry's years with Moore, which included work on *Fantasia* (1940), formed his view of what "Disney art" should look like. Moore's major lesson for Murry—which Murry carried with him to the comics—was that any Disney character drawn correctly had to lend itself to

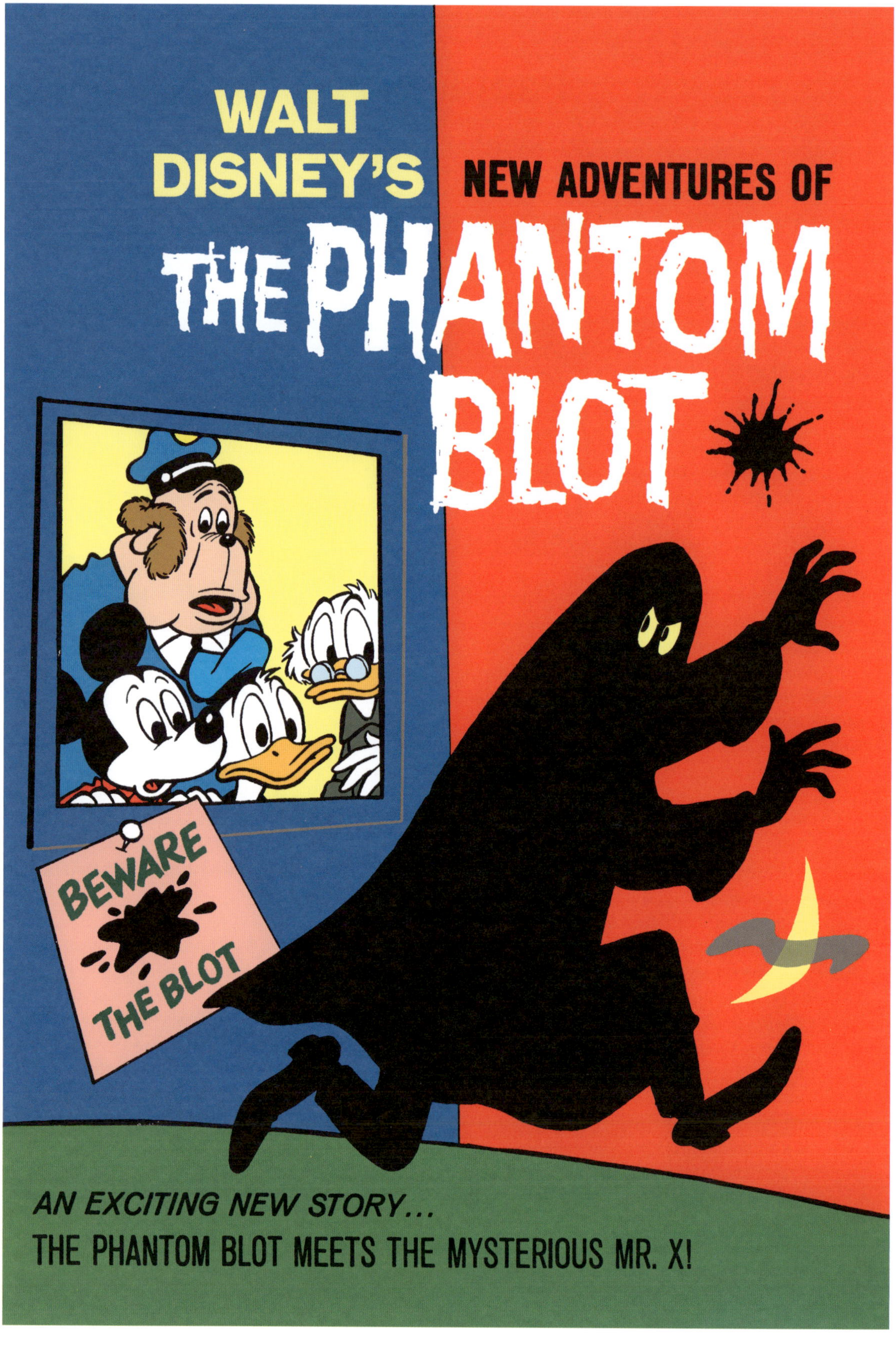
WALT DISNEY'S
NEW ADVENTURES OF
THE PHANTOM BLOT
BEWARE THE BLOT
AN EXCITING NEW STORY…
THE PHANTOM BLOT MEETS THE MYSTERIOUS MR. X!

animation. Murry never mimicked popular artists whose styles relied on improvising from panel to panel, imprecise ink lines, stiff poses, tweaking of perspectives, or breaking of the fourth wall. Instead, Murry's fairly thick ink lines, drawn with a seemingly determined and steady hand, gave his comics artwork a distinct and easily recognizable quality.

Murry was a fast learner in the Disney animation department. After *Fantasia*, he went on to work on *Dumbo* (1941), *Saludos Amigos* (1942), and *Song of the South* (1946). Gradually, however, he got more involved with the comic strip department—and with its manager, *Mickey Mouse* daily strip artist Floyd Gottfredson, who assigned Murry an increasing number of important jobs. His first comic art task was to pencil the José Carioca *Silly Symphonies* Sunday strips in early 1943, replacing artist Bob Grant, who had been drafted. The work suited Murry well. José was supplanted as the lead character in *Silly Symphonies* by Panchito, from the film *The Three Caballeros*, in 1944; then the *Symphonies* strip itself was replaced by *Uncle Remus and His Tales of Brer Rabbit* beginning October 14, 1945.

In a glimpse of what the future held for him, Murry also occasionally ghosted the *Mickey Mouse* daily strip between 1944 and 1946, when Gottfredson needed help to catch up on his deadlines. Seen from today's vantage point, these strips showcase Murry's eventual *Mickey Mouse* comic book style. But always the critic—not least of his own work—Murry did not hold his early *Mickey* newspaper strips in high regard when later asked about them.

Upon Murry's arrival in California, he had initially rented a studio apartment within walking distance of the Disney studio. But in 1939, he married and moved in with Gladys Bennett, already the mother of seven children. Their son together, John, was born in 1941, followed by their daughter Peggy in 1944. In 1946, with a total of nine children to support, they decided that Murry should leave his job with Disney and pursue a freelance career.

In the summer of 1946 they bought a piece of land in Wendling, Oregon, a lumber town in which the sawmill had closed a few months earlier and property was cheap. Murry got a job picking ferns, but he also produced a large number of gag cartoons. Murry had sold such gags to various magazines as early as 1943, while still working at Disney, but he seems to have ramped up to at least one inked cartoon per day from 1947 to 1949. Most of his cartoon work, though innocent by today's standards, was published in the risqué magazines of the time. For some, he teamed with gag writer George A. Posner, resulting in numerous cartoons signed "Posner Murry."

It was the Brer Rabbit characters that pulled Murry back to the Disney properties and the resumption of his comics career. His first stories for comic books were drawn for Western Publishing and appeared in Dell Publishing's *Four Color* #129, December 1946, a Brer Rabbit issue. (Western, which held the license to create Disney comic books, arranged financing and distribution through Dell, hired writers and artists, and then printed the comics on its own presses to Dell's order. Dell's logo appeared on the covers, so the comics Western produced and printed were referred to as "Dell Comics." In 1962, Western ended its deal with Dell and continued on its own as Gold Key Comics.)

In between work on gag cartoons, Murry also drew several Brer Rabbit and Li'l Bad Wolf stories in 1947 for Western's flagship title, *Walt Disney's Comics and Stories*, thus keeping his hand in the comic book business.

In 1949, the Murrys returned to California. After another brief stint as a Disney in-betweener, Murry partnered with former Disney and Max Fleischer talent Dick Huemer to draw a humorous cowboy newspaper comic strip called *Buck O'Rue*. Huemer had created the character as early as 1948, but two years later the project was still in a holding pattern. With Murry's bouncy graphic characterization added to the mix, however, the strip was picked up for syndication and debuted in January 1951. Set in Mesa Trubil—a Wild West town "so rotten it got booted out of the U.S. of A."—*Buck O'Rue* combined its Western landscapes with a wild and cartoony rogues' gallery, possessed of all the ingredients for soap opera and intrigue.

Unfortunately, while it is obvious from the artwork that Murry enjoyed *Buck O'Rue*, the strip ran for less than two years in a very limited number of newspapers. On the upside, the demise of *Buck O'Rue* coincided with an early 1950s sales boom in Western/Dell/Disney comics, and Murry was suddenly in the right place at the right time. Murry's first three Mickey Mouse stories were long ones: "The Monster Whale"

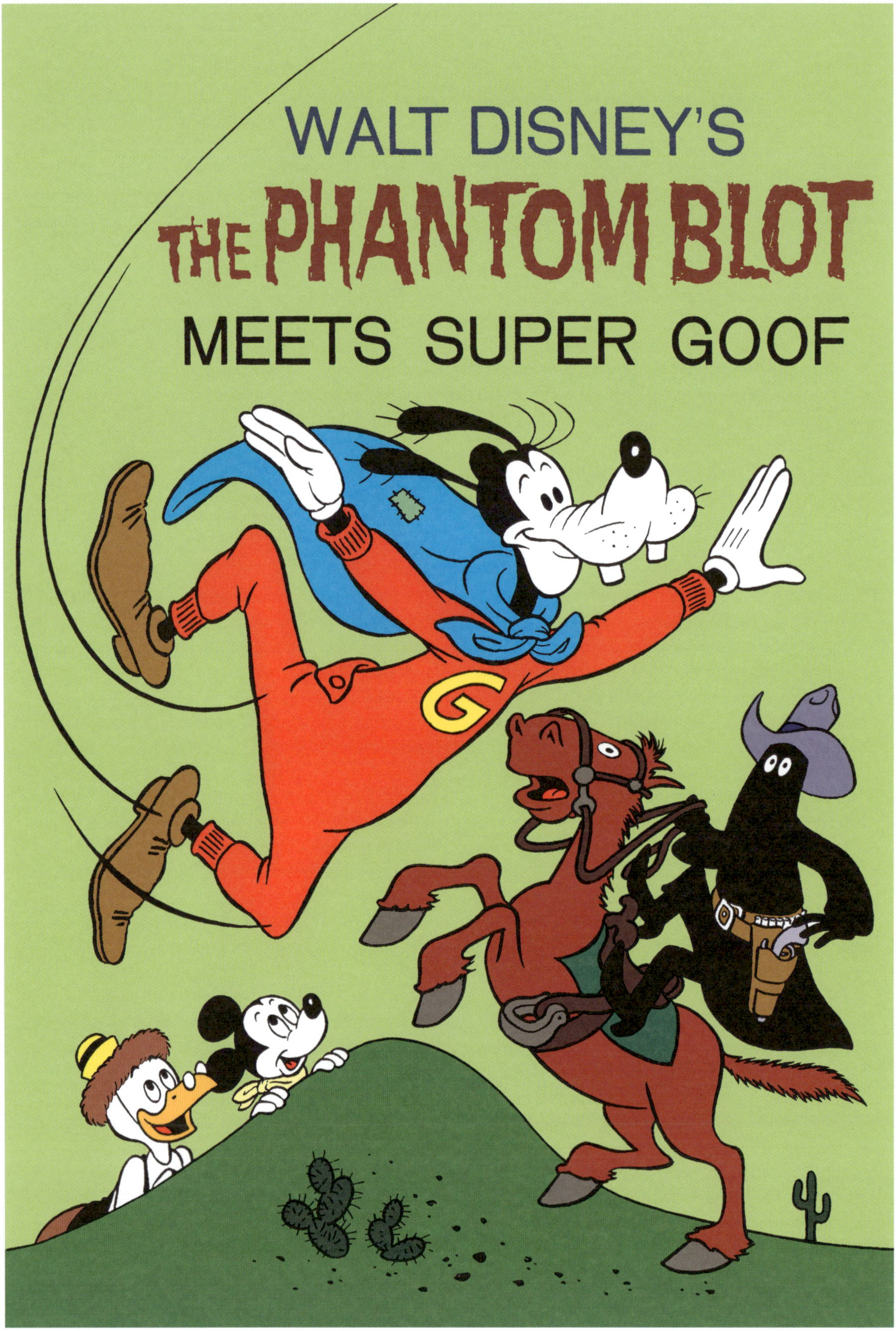
WALT DISNEY'S
THE PHANTOM BLOT
MEETS SUPER GOOF

CAST OF CHARACTERS
MICKEY MOUSE
PHANTOM BLOT
UNCLE SCROOGE
GOOFY
DONALD DUCK
CHIEF O'HARA
The MYSTERIOUS MR. X

GET READY... GET SET... HERE HE IS... GOOD OLD GOOFY IN AN EXCITING NEW ROLE AS THE AMAZING
SUPER GOOF!
SEE SUPER GOOF MATCH WITS AND DARING IN THE WILD WEST AGAINST THE DANGEROUS, DASTARDLY
PHANTOM BLOT!

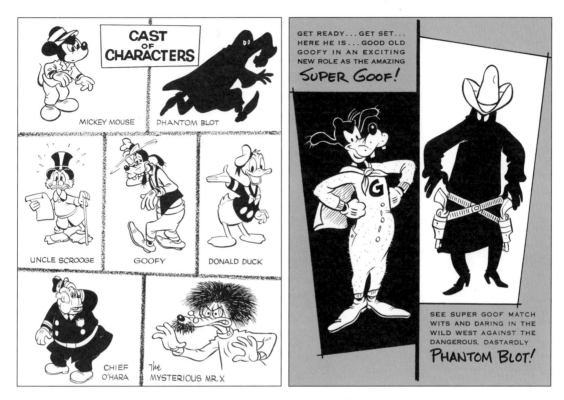

Paul Murry's uniquely animated Goofy seems to steal the show in the inside front cover compositions for *The Phantom Blot* #1 and 2, October 1964 and April 1965. The #1 collage includes reused Carl Barks drawings of Donald and Scrooge.

(24 pages, *Walt Disney's Vacation Parade* #1, July 1950), "The Mystery of the Double-Cross Ranch" (32 pages, *Four Color* #313, February 1951), and "The Ruby Eye of Homar Guy-Am" (16 pages, *Four Color* #343, August-September 1951). But it was only the start.

Mickey serials had been a regular feature in *Walt Disney's Comics and Stories* from the beginning, but they were just reformatted newspaper strip adventures, drawn primarily by Gottfredson. Now Western wanted to produce original Mickey comic book stories, so, in 1949, it began inviting artists to illustrate new adventures. Having already drawn the three *Four Color* stories, Murry fit the bill, and his chance came in 1953. Magic occurred instantly when Murry's artwork was paired with the skills of writer Carl Fallberg, who was also a cartoonist and a devoted railroad enthusiast. "The Last Resort," featured in Volume 3 of this series, was the first of their *Walt Disney's Comics and Stories* Mickey Mouse serials.

The comic book Mickey Mouse, as he had graphically evolved by that time, was a serious-minded and relatively inexpressive figure, so Murry instead relied on Goofy to bring graphic comedy and humor to the panels—sometimes he featured the Goof in action sequences that seem almost animated. It was Murry who introduced the classic comics pose of Goofy holding his hand in front of his mouth, all the better to make him look constantly dumbfounded.

Another integral part of the Fallberg/Murry stories' appeal was their settings: wild woods, rugged mountains, mysterious swamps, or deep underwater. Murry excelled in his intricate renderings of weather elements such as rain, fog, snow, wind, and storms, and Fallberg soon began supplying him with scripts designed specifically to capture that aspect of his imagination.

Thus, like his Disney comics contemporary, Carl Barks, Murry found a stable income—and began his work on the stories he is most associated with—shortly after turning 40 years old. Like Barks, Murry had already experienced years of hard work and struggle to support himself and his family. Like Barks, Murry used his life experience to create compelling stories well

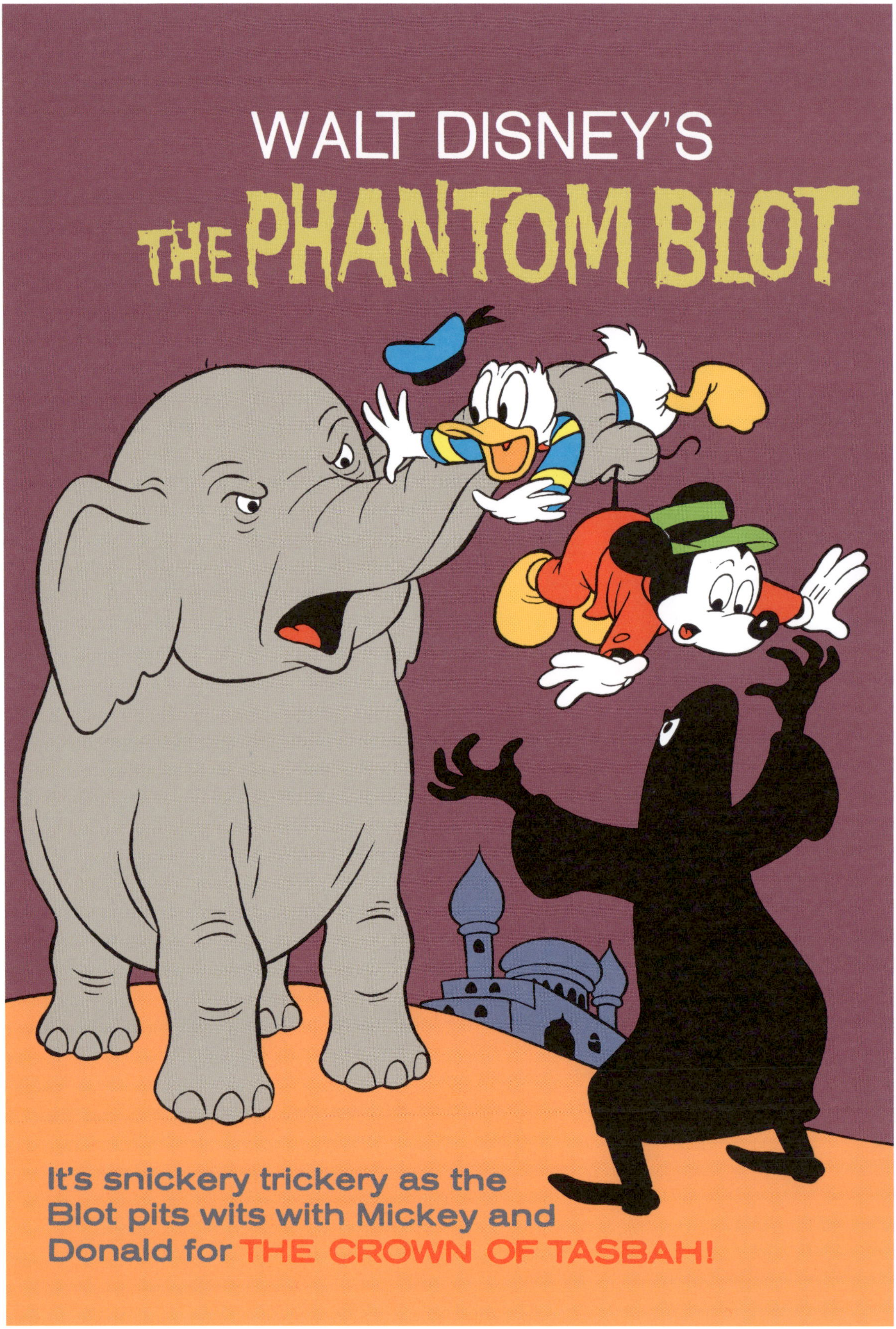
WALT DISNEY'S
THE PHANTOM BLOT
It's snickery trickery as the Blot pits wits with Mickey and Donald for THE CROWN OF TASBAH!

worth reading. The background elements of the Mickey Mouse stories inspired Murry to create graphically spectacular pages, while the use of the Disney characters allowed him to show off the storytelling skills he had first learned during his years in animation.

Carl Fallberg left the Mickey Mouse serials in 1962, and, with only a few exceptions, Murry continued to draw them until 1973. But they were not his sole output. With the exception of occasional gag pages, Murry never wrote his own stories—Western frequently called on him to draw scripts with a wide variety of other characters, including Donald Duck and Pluto, and he was even assigned a handful of non-Disney Woody Woodpecker stories.

That versatility made Murry a prominent artist in the mid-1960s transformation of American Disney comics. Declining sales and competition for readers drove the editors at Western to target the Disney stories at a younger audience. They also introduced new characters and combined heroes from previously separate universes within single stories: Goofy could team up with Mowgli, or Donald Duck with Captain Hook. The mix suited Murry well, and he became the main artist of novel comic book titles—such as *Super Goof* and this book's highlight, *The Phantom Blot*—which featured those crossover stories.

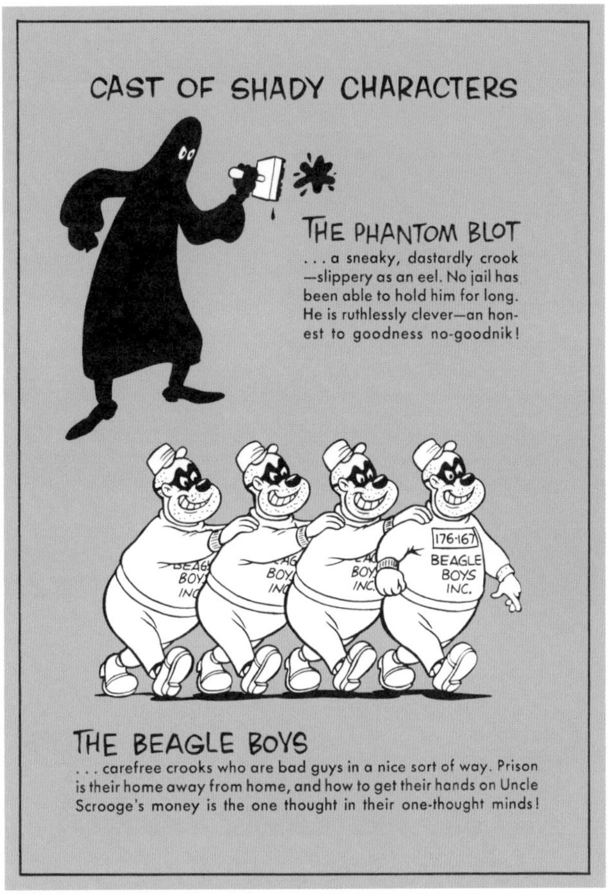
CAST OF SHADY CHARACTERS
THE PHANTOM BLOT
. . . a sneaky, dastardly crook —slippery as an eel. No jail has been able to hold him for long. He is ruthlessly clever—an honest to goodness no-goodnik!
176-167
BEAGLE BOYS INC.
THE BEAGLE BOYS
. . . carefree crooks who are bad guys in a nice sort of way. Prison is their home away from home, and how to get their hands on Uncle Scrooge's money is the one thought in their one-thought minds!

The inside front cover of *The Phantom Blot* #3, July 1965—drawn entirely by Paul Murry—provides an amusing introduction to the issue's crossover, contrasting the fiendish Blot with the frivolous Beagle Boys.

That peak in productivity was short-lived. In the 1970s, Murry's assignments turned him almost exclusively into a Mickey Mouse artist again, including, in 1971, a pivotal series of Mouse model sheets for Walt Disney Publications. As time wore on, Murry became less than enthusiastic about the comic books to which he contributed, gradually drawing fewer pages. His last regular Mickey Mouse story appeared in 1984 in *Walt Disney's Comics and Stories* #510, the final Western Publishing issue. Three more were later published posthumously. (Western had dropped its Gold Key brand in 1980 but continued publishing comics under its Whitman imprint until 1984, when it got out of the comics business altogether.)

Paul Murry spent his retirement years with his wife in their desert home just outside of Palmdale, California, taking wildlife and nature photographs, gardening their five acres, and playing his beloved harmonica. Comics became a very distant part of his life, and he likely preferred it that way. He died August 4, 1989, at age 77. But his delightful work lives on, and fans around the world continue to enjoy it.

Numerous scholars have generously shared information with me about Paul Murry's life and work. There is not room here to thank each one, but I would like to acknowledge three of them for their contributions: Donald Ault, for his devoted work preserving the history of many Disney comics artists, including taping a long interview with Paul Murry; Klaus Spillman, who interviewed Murry in letter form in the early 1980s; and last — but certainly not least — Murry's granddaughter Shannon Murry, who shared her insightful thoughts and knowledge about Murry's life and career.

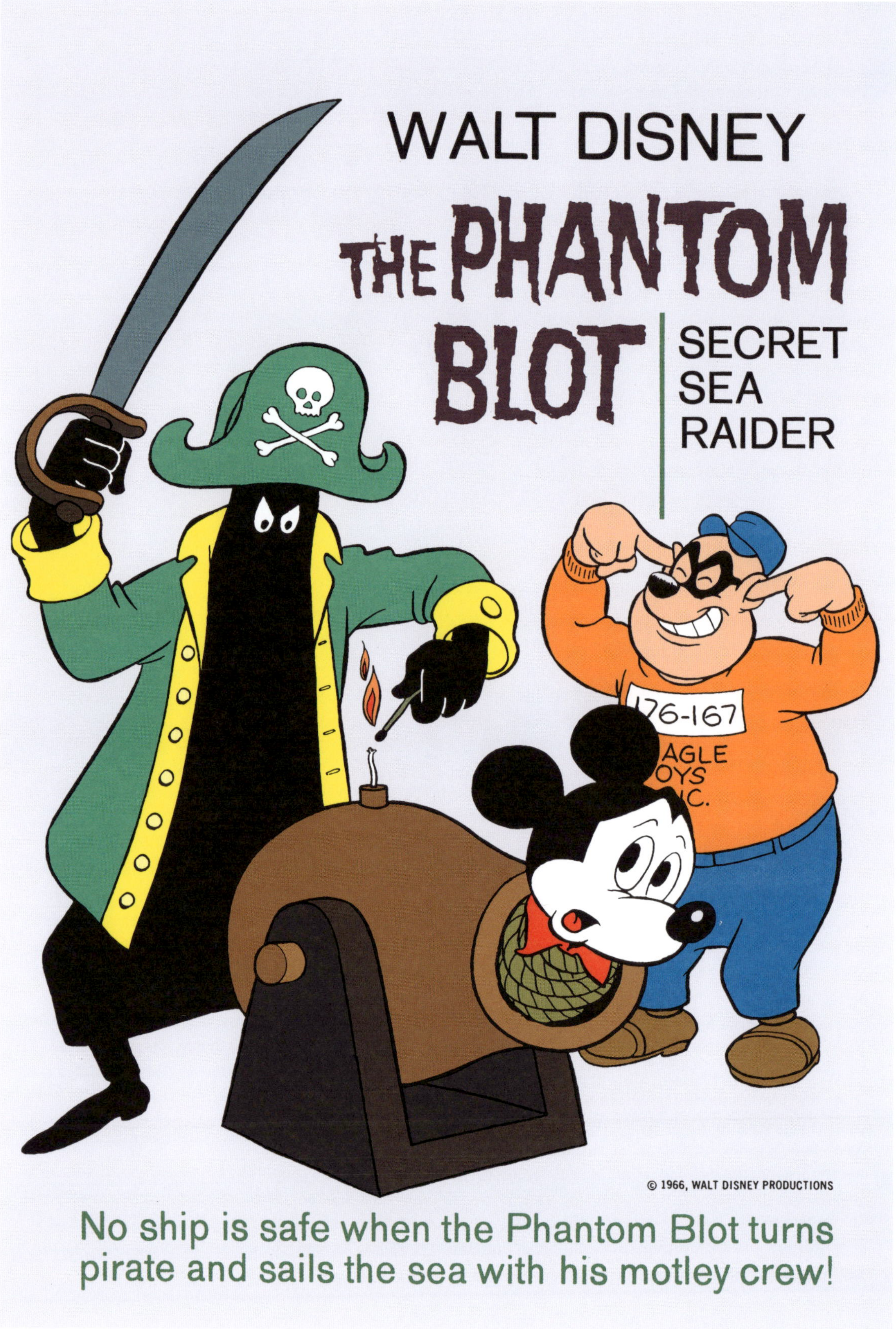
WALT DISNEY
THE PHANTOM BLOT
SECRET SEA RAIDER
176-167
© 1966, WALT DISNEY PRODUCTIONS
No ship is safe when the Phantom Blot turns pirate and sails the sea with his motley crew!

What the Blot Wrought

By JOE TORCIVIA

"[THE PHANTOM BLOT] WAS ABOUT the meanest criminal I ever faced," said Mickey. The year: 1964. The place: "The Return of the Phantom Blot" (*Walt Disney's Comics and Stories* #284-287), a story that would have implications far beyond the four issues in which it was originally serialized.

In the first issue of *Comics and Stories* since 1950 *not* to lead off with a Donald Duck story by Disney legend Carl Barks, comic book history would instead be made in the *back* of the magazine, where Mickey Mouse serials generally appeared. Up to this point in 1964—courtesy of artist Paul Murry—Mickey had often squared off against Pegleg Pete, as well as dog-faced felons of every size, shape, and temperament: thieves, pirates, rustlers, and smugglers. But no one quite like the Blot.

Bold, intriguing, even eerie, this "Phantom" was cloaked head-to-toe in black—perfect for blending into the darkness. With only emotionless white eyeholes to suggest a presence beneath, he seemed to be a foe for the ages. And that he was. The Blot was first created by Mouse master Floyd Gottfredson for a noteworthy 1939 newspaper strip serial, reprinted three times in comic books—once, in a redrawn version—between 1941 and 1955. Then came a long period of dormancy in the United States before his revival in 1964.[1]

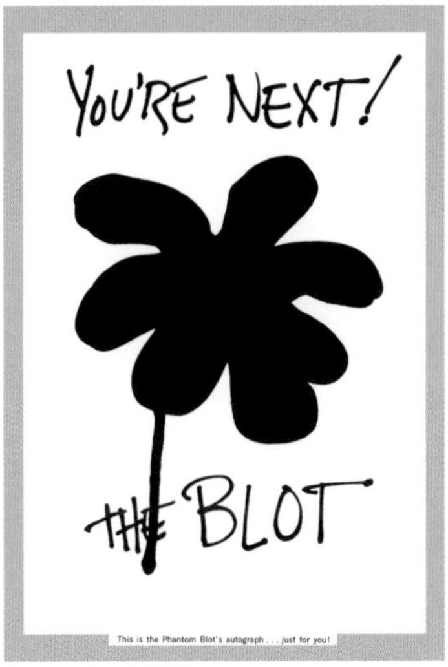
YOU'RE NEXT!
THE BLOT
"This is the Phantom Blot's autograph... just for you!" The inside back cover of *Phantom Blot* #1, initially a one-shot.

The editorial hands behind "The Return of the Phantom Blot" must have seen the great potential in this black-cloaked blackguard, as—immediately following the serial's four chapters—a one-shot titled *New Adventures of the Phantom Blot* was released. Given the long lead time that would have required to create this unprecedented spinoff, producer Western Publishing was evidently betting on the Blot to catch on while his revival was still underway.

Unprecedented it was, too. Just as the Blot was no ordinary Disney comic book bad guy, neither was the comic bearing his name an ordinary Disney comic book. In an age where the medium was still under the watchful eyes of the content-regulating Comics Code (or, in Disney comics' case, a program of self-enforcement), it seemed unimaginable for a *villain* to become the title character of a Silver Age comic book, even if he were brought to justice at the end of every issue. But Western took its chances. Perhaps the Blot's being a Disney character prevented the raising of eyebrows; doubtless it helped that, for his starring magazine, the Blot was rendered with eyeballs peering through his camouflaging black cloak, rather than the spookier blank circles through which he had previously peered with an unnerving absence of humanity.

In addition, *New Adventures of the Phantom Blot* offered a combination of characters unprecedented for the time, mixing the usually separate "Paul Murry Mickey Mouse comics universe" and "Carl Barks Duck comics universe" in one huge, event-level 32-page story. When the *Blot* one-shot proved a success, six more *Phantom Blot* issues were published, and these crossovers would be the hallmark of the series for its entire run! Besides combining Ducks and Mice, the title included Mad Madam Mim and introduced the concept of Goofy's secret identity of Super Goof.

Still, at the core of the *Phantom Blot* project lay a conflict that Disney fans will never forget: the stalwart Mickey Mouse pitted against *the meanest criminal he ever faced*, making for one of the most uncommonly memorable Disney comic book series of all!

1 Notably, the Blot's *European* revival came earlier, when Guido Martina and Romano Scarpa revived him for "The Phantom Blot's Double Mystery" (Italian *Topolino* #116-119, 1955; most recent American reprint in Fantagraphics' *Disney Masters* Vol. 5).

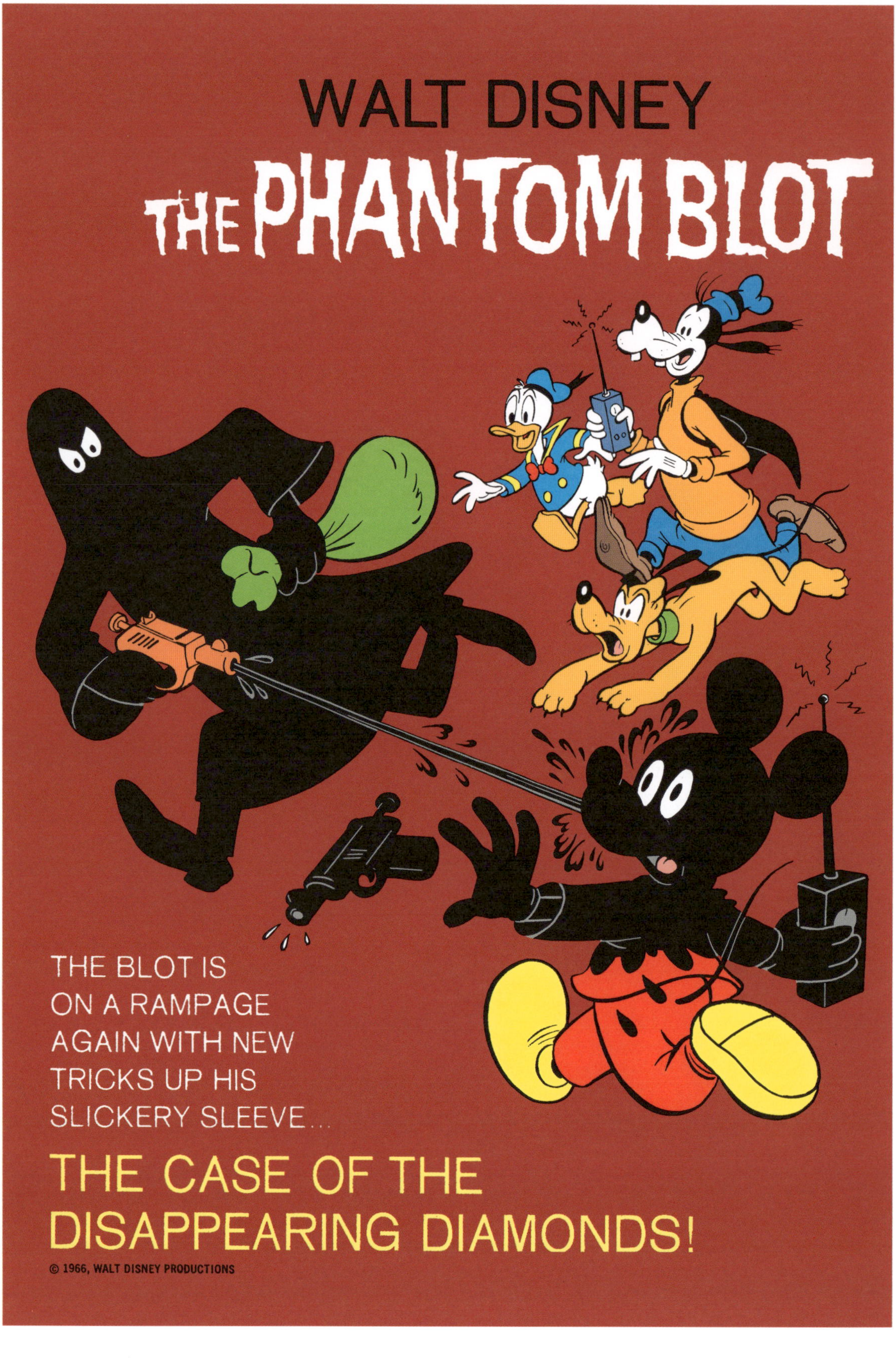
WALT DISNEY
THE PHANTOM BLOT
THE BLOT IS ON A RAMPAGE AGAIN WITH NEW TRICKS UP HIS SLICKERY SLEEVE...
THE CASE OF THE DISAPPEARING DIAMONDS!
© 1966, WALT DISNEY PRODUCTIONS